Publius Ovidius Naso

# METAMORPHOSES

Cover Photo: Correggio (1489-1534) Jupiter and Io. 1530. Kunsthistorisches Museum, Vienna, Austria. Photo credit: Erich Lessing/Art Resources NY.

Copyright 2004 Z. Philip Ambrose

ISBN 1-58510-103-6

10 9 8 7 6 5 4 3 2 1

# Publius Ovidius Naso

# METAMORPHOSES

## Translated with Introduction and Notes

by

Z. Philip Ambrose

*Carissimae uxori meae Margaritae*

*d. d. d.*

# TABLE OF CONTENTS

# PREFACE

Ovid's *Metamorphoses* has enjoyed unparalleled popularity as a sourcebook for painters, sculptors, writers, composers, and school teachers. That popularity stems from the high quality of its poetics, structure, versification, diction, and thought, as well as from its wealth of mythological information. As a result there have been many translations of this work into modern languages and English, and many excellent ones are available. I have rendered Ovid's dactylic hexameters with basically iambic lines of varied length and have kept the line numbering of the transmitted text. Almost as an experiment I have tried to maintain the inconsistency of Ovid's tenses in which the shifting back and forth between past and present tenses lends vividness to the narrative. Ultimately, the goal in these measures has been to encourage the reader's return to the original.

It has been the special purpose of this translation to enhance the effectiveness of the work as a mythological handbook by preserving virtually all of the proper names. Ovid's Alexandrian style deliberately challenged his reader's learning by using patronymics, place names, meaningful names (often of Greek origin), and obscure or rare names. The footnotes and the Index/Glossary are primarily intended to help the modern reader meet this challenge.

Some footnotes also refer to mythological material Ovid has derived from Greek epic or drama or, occasionally, from later sources. Specific authors referred to in these notes are briefly identified in the Index/Glossary. Only rarely do the footnotes refer to the rich secondary literature dealing with this work. The never-ending labor and delight of literary interpretation is left to the reader in the hope that the translation will be of help.

One of Ovid's most interesting achievements in this work is his success in weaving together a seemingly endless series of episodes, narrated by either himself or by his characters within embedded tales, without losing sight of the overarching direction and form of the epic. To help the reader contend with Ovid's frequent leaps, both ahead and back to the point of his original divagation, the principle episodes are listed at the beginning of each book and the subsections and digressions marked with indentations (or as needed with double indentations).

For those who wish to work with this translation while reading the *Metamorphoses* in Latin, there is a short list of available commentaries. In the Bibliography are also listed a few of the major books on the poet's life and works.

The illustrations are selected from editions of the *Metamorphoses* in the Bailey-Howe Library of the University of Vermont. Begun by Lester M. Prindle, Professor of Latin at the University of Vermont until his death in 1949, this fine collection was given by his widow, Olwen Prindle, to the University in 1963, where it has been faithfully tended and enlarged by the Curators of Special Collections, John L. Buechler from 1962 until his retirement in 1989 and, since then, Connell B. Gallagher.

This translation is based upon an eclectic use of modern editions, particularly those of Haupt-Ehwald, Anderson, and Tarrant. I am very grateful to Professor Tarrant for allowing me to see his new edition for the Oxford Classics Text series before its actual appearance in April 2004.

Ron Pullins and Linda Robertson of Focus Press deserve no end of thanks for their kind attention and help throughout this project, for example in producing it in two pre-publication versions, which allowed my students to help me improve the text. Special thanks in this regard I owe to Clayton Elliott and Rozenn Bailleul-LeSuer during their time as graduate students. I am also grateful to my colleagues, Professor Robert H. Rodgers, for thoughtful advice on textual problems, and Professor Barbara Saylor Rodgers, for help with the Index. I dedicate this book to my wife Gretchen Van Slyke in gratitude for her patient ear and heart.

Z. Philip Ambrose
Summer 2004

# INTRODUCTION

Posterity, learn, so that you realize that I, whom you read,
       am he who played lightly with love's tender dalliance.
My native land is Sulmo, richly abounding in chill waters,
       that lies nine times ten miles from the city.

*Ille ego qui fuerim, tenerorum lusor amorum,*
       *quem legis, ut noris, accipe posteritas.*
*Sulmo mihi patria est, gelidis uberrimus undis,*
       *milia qui novies distat ab urbe decem.*

                              *Tristia* 4. 10. 1-4


In Vergil Mantua rejoices, Verona in Catullus,
       the glory of the Paelignian folk will I be called.
*Mantua Vergilio, gaudet Verona Catullo;*
       *Paelignae dicar gloria gentis ego, ...*

                              *Amores* 3. 15. 7-10


    Sulmona today is a small city known throughout Italy for its colorful and tasty sugar-coated almonds. In the late Middle Ages Swabian entrepreneurs made it an important center for the working of gold and metals. Situated in a long valley beneath the brow of the towering Abruzzi, Sulmo, as it was known in antiquity, was the birthplace of Publius Ovidius Naso (20 March 43 B. C. - 17 A. D.). If Ovid had never left home, the dramatic landscape of this region, the homeland of a people called the Paeligni speaking a tongue close to Oscan, would have richly provided him with vivid images for the physical settings of his most important work, the *Metamorphoses*. This didactic epic in Latin dactylic hexameter is a complex tale, told with a disarmingly carefree air, that deliberately binds the destiny of gods and men to the world of animals and plants, to the plains, secluded vales and forbidding heights of earth, and to the birds of sky and sea. To watch for the sun after it first begins to cast its rays behind the jagged ridge of the Abruzzi is a wait of some two hours. It is to wait for Aurora to rise and for Phoebus to drive his chariot out of the East into the open sky.

But Ovid did not remain in Sulmo. His father sent him to Rome for an education that would prepare him for a life as a lawyer. Like many privileged students he toured Greece. Maturity soon brought the realization that it would be impossible for him not to write poetry (*Tristia* 4. 10. 23-25). This drive to live as a bard carried him through centuries of the Greek literary and mythological treasures: epic, tragedy and satyr play, elegiac and erotic poetry, and learned mythological handbooks. After some years of prominence and the production of a large number of poems in varied styles, Ovid was suddenly banished by the emperor Augustus in the year 8 A. D. to Tomis on the Black Sea, a world neither Roman nor Greek. Curiosity has produced much imaginative speculation about the cause of his exile, but only speculation. Ovid's own elegiacs, the *Epistles from Pontus (Epistulae ex Ponto)* and the *Sorrows (Tristia)*, tell us at least of his great desire to return and of his sadness in exile.

In the years just before his exile Ovid had woven, though according to him not finished (*Tristia* 1. 7), an epic in dactylic hexameter (shifting from the elegiac couplet consisting of a dactylic hexameter and a dactylic pentameter). He called his epic a *carmen perpetuum*, an everlasting, unbroken song, both Roman and Hellenic, that sets forth the creation of the cosmos and humanity as well as its fall from the paradise of the Golden Age in a chain of narratives (often narratives within narratives) of the interaction of persons human and divine; the scene moves from Greece to Egypt, from the Near East to North Africa, from Asia Minor westward to Sicily, Italy, and Rome and ultimately to the restoration of the Golden Age under the dominion of Augustus. *Changing Forms*, as we might call this amazing work, demonstrates at every step of the way that culture and nature, for better or worse, are one and the same, each employed by the poet to characterize or explain the other.

Ovid drew much of the mythical content of the *Metamorphoses* from the learned and fanciful poetry of the Alexandrians, the epics of Homer and Hesiod, the tragedies of Aeschylus, Sophocles and Euripides, and his Latin predecessors, especially Vergil. He also mined material he had already treated in works such as the *Fasti*, his poem on the festivals of the Roman calendar, the *Amores*, and the *Ars Amatoria*. Revealing hidden truth through change of form, *metamorphosis*, had already enjoyed a long tradition by Ovid's time. It is rather the call for a transfigured world that distinguishes the didactic purpose of Ovid's epic: to create a true Golden Age will require not just a *metamorphosis* but a *metanoia*, a change of heart and mind (the term is found in the *Gospels*). This change of heart is clearest at the close of Book 15: Readers will long disagree as to whether Ovid's tribute to Julius Caesar and his adoptive son, Augustus, is sincere or limned with flattery, but when (with whatever hyperbole) he notes

Augustus' attempt not to overshadow the works of his father and Julius Caesar's joy in the superior accomplishments of his son, Ovid is marking a fundamental change of heart: we are reminded that it was Jupiter who by banishing his father Saturn from power had been the first cause of decline of the Golden Age (Book 1. 113-12). Reconciliation of the fathers with the sons and the sons with the fathers; this is the example of Ovid's tribute to Augustus, who, Ovid says, had "by his own example set the rules of human conduct" (Book 15. 834). This reconciliation is in some sense a repudiation of the motivation running through much of this narrative. In a sense it is a repudiation of myth itself and a call for new myths modeled, for example, not on the loveless marriage of Jove and Juno, but on that of the noble Cadmus and Harmonia or the humble Baucis and Philemon.

Passing allusions and analogies to other myths left aside, there are over 150 episodes in the *Metamorphoses*. The very old and common practice of reading Ovid's episodes as distinct and separate narratives has had very productive results. The *Ganymede* and *Jupiter and Io* of Correggio (assumed name of Antonio Allegri, 1489-1534) or Ottavio Rinuccini's (1562-1621) *La Favola di Dafne*, used for operas by several composers of the Florentine *Camerata* like Marco da Gagliano (1575-1642) in 1608 and Jacopo Peri (1561-1633) in 1598, are characteristic masterpieces inspired by individual tales in the *Metamorphoses*. Ovid's own grouping of these episodes, however, produces other results and perhaps clearer indication of his own interpretation of the individual tales. The arrangement of these episodes lends to each book or group of books thematic unity or unities. Book 2, for example, with its emphasis upon the element of fire in the flight of Phaethon "Flame," is thematically bound by contrast to Book 1, whose narrative of the great Flood concentrates on the element of water. But the story of Phoebus' irrevocable promise to Phaethon, the story of the Raven and the Crow, Ocyrhoë's prophecy, the tattling Battus, and Aglauros' violation of Minerva's command form another theme: the power of words. The following summary of the work is offered as an introduction to its principal thematic structure.

Book 1 treats the change from chaos to creation, the proper ordering of the four elements, earth, air, fire, and water. Creation is in itself a form of metamorphosis and includes humanity, first by Prometheus, and then in recreated forms: the autochthonous re-birth effected by Deucalion and Pyrrha and the establishment of all the historical peoples of the world through the union of Jupiter and Io. The theme of strife between fathers and sons, important, as suggested above, in this epic as a whole, is introduced by Jupiter himself in expelling Saturn from power. The sources for sky-gods who displace their fathers go back to Hesiod's account in the *Theogony* of Ouranos, Cronos, and Zeus and to parallels in Hittite and Phoenician myth. Book 1 closes with "connective tissue" to Book 2 in a variant of the theme: Phaethon's anxiety about the true identity of his father.

The four harmoniously united elements of Book 1 re-appear in great conflict in Book 2. Contrary to nature, Phaethon enters the sky (air), in his reckless ride threatens to scorch Terra Mater (earth) with fire, is dashed himself by Jupiter's fire, and falls into the Po (water). The causality of Phaethon's fall is multiple, but central in it is the rashness of Apollo's initial promise to grant whatever favor Phaethon should ask. This harmful power of mere words is re-emphasized, as mentioned above, in the story of the Raven and the Crow, the death of Coronis, and Mercury's meeting with Battus. Mercury's deception in the theft of Apollo's cattle is paired with Jupiter's deception of Callisto and, with Mercury's help, of Europa. The rape of Europa that closes Book 2 not only balances the union of Jupiter and Io at the end of Book 1 but provides the transitional material to Book 3.

Books 3 and 4 might be called the Theban books. When Jupiter carried Europa away to Crete where she became the mother of Minos, her brother Cadmus is dispatched to find her by his father Agenor on penalty of exile should he fail to do so. He is led astray to the Greek mainland, where by slaying a great serpent and on Minerva's command sowing its teeth he becomes the founder of the Boeotians. The ensuing tragedies of his descendants, Actaeon, Semele, Pentheus, as well as that of Narcissus all involve a failure of recognition (the *anagnorisis* considered an essential element of tragedy in Aristotle's *Poetics*). Tiresias, blinded by Juno for knowing and telling the truth (a reprise of Ocyrhoë's behavior in Book 2), introduces the episodes of Narcissus and Pentheus. The embedded tale of Acoetes (probably Bacchus himself in disguise) and the ensuing death of Pentheus focus on Bacchus, the god of Greek drama and, as son of her husband Jupiter and Semele, the reason for Juno's hatred of Thebes.

The continued rejection of Bacchus by some in Boeotia motivates the opening of Book 4. Instead of worshiping the god, the daughters of Minyas, king of Boeotian Orchomenos, continue their weaving and take turns telling stories, all of which in some way involve weaving: Thisbe's veil, bloodied by the lioness; Vulcan's bronze net in which he catches Venus and Mars; Leucothoë, seduced by Apollo as she turns the spindle; Salmacis entangling Hermaphoditus. The metamorphosis of their looms into ivy and vines, symbols of Bacchus, precedes the daughters' transformation into bats. Despite Bacchus' vindication, Juno's opposition to the god continues unabated. She sends the snaky-clad Fury Tisiphone to madden Athamas and Ino by coiling about their breasts. Yet the theme takes a pleasant turn in the transformation of Cadmus and Harmonia into blissfully intertwined serpents (and no Tiresias to separate them!). While attention to Thebes ends with their metamorphosis, the theme of the opposition to Bacchus moves the scene to Juno's Argos, where Acrisius still bans the god's worship. From Acrisius the transition to his gorgon-slaying grandson Perseus is easy. Medusa's snaky gaze and Andromeda's unbinding (or binding in marriage) reveal the theme of serpent and weaving again in tandem. As Book 3 opened with Cadmus' slaying the serpent, so Book 4 ends with Perseus' brief account of how Minerva transformed the once beautiful tresses of Medusa into serpents.

Book 5 continues the *epyllion* or short epic of Perseus. After vanquishing Phineus, Perseus returns to Argos to restore Acrisius to the throne from which his twin brother had expelled him. Omitting the tradition that in games to celebrate his return Perseus accidentally slew Acrisius, Ovid treats the final punishment of Polydectes, his mother's oppressor, in only eight lines. The abrupt ending of the Perseus narrative leads to Minerva's visit to the Heliconian Muses, which accounts for more than half the book's length. An unidentified Muse tells Minerva how the nine daughters of Pierus challenged the nine Muses in a contest of song, judged by the Nymphs. The unidentified Muse reports briefly a Pierid's tale of Typhoeus and then at great length her sister Muse Calliope's tale of the Rape of Proserpina, a doubly embedded tale because much of it is in the form of direct narrative by Ceres or Arethusa.

The metamorphosis of the defeated Pierids into chattering magpies at the end of Book 5 provides the transition to Book 6 and the metamorphosis into a spider of Minerva's own challenger Arachne. Book 6 combines the themes of competition and weaving. Competition was an important feature of Greek culture on the field of battle, in games, and in drama. The dramatic festivals under the patronage of Dionysus at Athens were, in two senses of the word, contests (*agones*, cf. English "agony"). The poets competed with one another and the plays themselves always represent some kind of contest of words or action. Competition is the very subject matter chosen by Minerva for her tapestry. The first panel, illustrating her own contest with Neptune (Poseidon) for the patronage of Athens, is perhaps intended to suggest to Arachne that Minerva has no history of losing. Her next four examples are clearer: mortals who compete with gods are punished.

In Book 4 the daughters of Minyas told stories while they wove; in Book 6 Minerva and Arachne tell stories *by* weaving. Ovid knows that *textus* means not only "something woven" (compare English "textile" and "texture"), but "structure" and even "literary text." For the carefully structured poetry of Greek and Latin, and especially in the age of Augustus, to compose poetry was to practise the art of weaving. Consciousness of the intimate relationship of the arts, plastic, verbal, and musical, is reflected in a special literary technique called *ecphrasis*, the description of art or architecture in words (and since the words constitute a *carmen*, also in music). The description of the weaving of Minerva and Arachne is an example of this technique.

It is no wonder that Ovid's tales have inspired so many works of art: he himself took inspiration from art for his poetry. It is very probable that both Vergil and Ovid were influenced by sculpture, the one for his portrait of Laocoon in *Aeneid* 2, the other for his tale of Niobe's challenge of Latona in Book 6. The musical contest between Marsyas and Apollo anticipates the lyre's victory over Pan's pipe, narrated by Orpheus in Book 10, and is in contrast to the victory of Bacchus' instruments, the winds and drums, which prevents the sound of Orpheus' lyre from charming the Bacchants' missiles into obedience at the geninning of Book 11. In reflecting on Arachne's artistic contribution, we should not forget that however bold her revelations about the loves of Jupiter, Neptune, and Apollo, they are of a kind with Ovid's own tales about the gods; nor is Arachne alone in being punished for telling the truth. Though Arachne is punished for contending with a god, telling the truth *per se* in weaving is vindicated in the story of Philomela, who, bereft of tongue, is still able to reveal in weaving to Procne, her sister, how she had been raped by Tereus. Procne's vengeance against Tereus, her husband, is anticipated by the brief reference (401-11) to Pelops, who in weeping for the fate of Amphion and Niobe exposed his ivory shoulder, the prosthesis given him when the gods reassembled his body that had been mangled by his father Tantalus and served up to them as food. The final episode in Book 6 is the rape of Orithyia, another Athenian princess, by Boreas, the North Wind. That union produced Calais and Zetes, who would join the Minyans in the expedition for the Golden Fleece, the subject of the beginning of Book 7.

Book 7 makes use of an element borrowed from tragedy (and probably a part of Ovid's own lost Medea play): Medea's interior monologue in direct discourse (7. 11-71) had been anticipated briefly by Procne's agony at Book 6. 631-34 as she debates within herself whether to slaughter her son Itys. It anticipates similar ones by Scylla and Althaea in Book 8 and Byblis in Book 9. Book 7 introduces a series of heroes that continues for the remainder of the epic: Jason, Theseus, and Cephalus in Book 7, Nisus, Minos, and Meleager in Book 8, Hercules in Book 9, Orpheus in Books 10 and 11, Peleus, Ceyx in Book 11, Achilles in Book 12, Ajax, Ulysses, and Aeneas in Book 13, Aeneas and his Trojan followers, Romulus and Vertumnus in Book 14, Numa, Pythagoras, Cipus, Julius Caesar, and Augustus in Book 15. Just as the role of females in the first six books in no way cedes place to that of males, it is striking that a woman will play a major part in the narrative of most of these male heroes. A few examples include Medea (Jason, Theseus), Procris (Cephalus), Scylla (Nisus, Minos), Atalanta and Althaea (Meleager), Deianira and Alcmena (Hercules), Eurydice (Orpheus), Thetis and Psamathe (Peleus), Alcyone (Ceyx), Dido, Caeta, Sibyl, Lavinia (Aeneas), Pomona (Vertumnus), Hersilia (Romulus), Egeria (Numa), and Venus (Julius Caesar). The large place given to women in this epic by the author of the *Heroides* and *Amores* should not be surprising. Greek tragedy, one of his chief sources, assigns to female characters roles no less important than those of males. And beyond his tendency to involve women in his treatment of male characters, Ovid is concerned through the whole of this epic with the nature and condition *per se* of women. Just to list a few examples: their skills (Medea, the two Atalantas, Arachne), their sorrows (Hecuba, Iole, Dryope), their forbidden passions (Byblis, Myrrha, Iphis), their lustful behavior (Propoetides), their mistreatment (Medusa, Caenis, Lotis, Dryope), their loyalty as wives (Harmonia, Procris, Baucis, Alcyone, Egeria, Hersilia) and as mothers (Ceres, Latona, Telethusa, ), their destructive force (Furies, Harpies, Diana, Procne, Medea) and their creative powers (Nymphs, Muses, Venus, Ceres, Proserpina, Mother Earth).

Perhaps the most important unifying theme of Books 7 and 8 is the contrast between loyalty and disloyalty within the family. Jason's lineage from Aeolus, whose name means "changeful," is a determining factor in his career. Aeolid Jason is a wanderer, both geographically and in his loyalties. His adventures with the ship Argo are dedicated to the service of his father, Aeson, and in sharp contrast to Medea's disloyalty to her father in eloping with Jason after helping him gain the Golden Fleece. With Medea's aid Jason, whose name means "Healer," heals Aeson of his old age. But Jason, now the age-mate of his youthened father and without hope of inheriting the throne of Iolchus, moves to Corinth, where his disloyalty to Medea leads her to kill their own children. Medea flees to Athens, where she attempts to make Aegeus poison his own son. Minos' unsuccessful test of Aegina's loyalty to Athens and Cephalus' fatal test of his beloved wife Procris' faithfulness carry this theme to the end of the book.

The beginning of Book 8 recapitulates the pattern of a daughter's disloyalty to a father with which Book 7 began, but with one very important difference: Scylla betrays Nysus, the father, but fails to win Minos, the stranger. In the next tale, another stranger (Theseus) wins over a princess (Ariadne) to thwart her father (Minos) and then abandons her. Instead of reminding the reader that Theseus would return to Athens having forgotten to put up the white sails as the agreed-upon sign of victory over the Minotaur and thereby causing his father Aegeus to leap in grief into the sea, Ovid springs ahead to Daedalus' exile in Crete and the story of how a father's intelligence caused the death of a son. The fall of Icarus, in turn, returns attention to the reason for his father's exile from Athens: jealous of the inventive skills of his nephew Perdix, Daedalus had hurled him from the Athenian Acropolis. Minerva caught the boy and changed him into a partridge, ever to fly low and to rejoice in the death of his cousin who had flown too high.

The Calydonian Boar section of Book 8 brings the theme of family loyalty and disloyalty into greater and more problematic focus. When

Meleager kills his uncles for denying the claims of his bride Atalanta for special honors in having drawn the first blood from the boar, his mother Althaea must struggle between the moral claims upon her as sister and as mother. She decides for the sister and causes the death of her son. Balancing his mother's rejection, Meleager's sisters do him honor and in their lamentations are (except for Gorge and Deianira) transformed by Diana into guinea-hens. Oeneus ("Wine-man"), father of Meleager, must share responsibility for his son's death: because of his impiety towards Diana, she had dispatched the boar against his fields and vineyards.

The return home of Theseus and other heroes of the boar hunt is delayed by the flooding river Acheloüs. In the hospitality of the river-god's court the exchange of embedded tales continues the theme of family devotion. Acheloüs himself narrates the story of Perimele, cast by her father into the sea and changed into a small island. When Perithoüs doubts the power of the gods to effect such changes in shape, Lelex tells the story of Baucis and Philemon, which not only disproves Perithoüs' skepticism, but suits the context in three other ways: it is a story of hospitality told in well-hosted company; it is another flood story; and it is a story of perfect loyalty between husband and wife. Acceding to Theseus' request, Acheloüs tells another tale, the story of Erysichthon, who having violated the sacred tree of Ceres, goddess of agriculture (note the contrastive parallel with Oeneus who had violated the goddess of the hunt), is punished with an unquenchable hunger. When he discovers that his daughter has the power to change shapes (proving once again that miraculous metamorphosis is possible), Erysichthon in a vain attempt to satisfy his hunger abuses her by selling and re-selling her as a bride. We are not only reminded of the beginning of Book 7 with its implication that marriage *per se* involves abandonment of the father by the bride (Aeëtes by Medea), but introduced as it were to the opening of Book 9, a contest by two suitors for a bride.

Book 9 begins, accordingly, with another tale by Acheloüs: his failed contest with Hercules for the hand of Deianira, the daughter of Calydonian Oeneus. The thematic material of this book shifts from family loyalty and disloyalty to a varied array of stories having to do with the rules laid down by the Fates that govern life itself: fertility, sexuality, birth, aging, desire, and death. Fertility is suggested in the outcome of the wrestling match between Acheloüs and Hercules, the aetiological explanation of the origin of the Horn of Plenty, the *Cornu Copia*. Nessus' attempted rape of Deianira introduces a note of bestiality, Hercules' apotheosis suggests the possibility that the laws of nature can be broken, and Juno's failed attempt to prevent his birth implies the possibility that the will of the gods can be thwarted by mortals. The story of Dryope (with the embedded remembrance of Lotis' rape by Priapus) in which she is herself changed into a lotus is about birth and is told by Iole with the intent of comforting Alcmena, who had just recalled the difficult birth of her son Hercules. From birth and wayward sex, the narrative quickly moves to aging: Iolaus is made young again; Callirhoë's infant sons are brought to instant manhood. The story of Byblis and Caunus deals with incest, and the story of Iphis, born a girl, raised as a boy, and in love with and betrothed to Ianthe, suggests that sexual desire is a matter of nurture rather than nature (the very opposite conclusion is implied by Thetis' attempt in Book 13 to raise Achilles as a girl to keep him from going to Troy). On the appointed wedding day, Iphis is changed by Isis into a man and wed to Ianthe with "Venus and Juno and Hymen at the wedding fires."

Books 10 and 11 begin respectively with the deaths of Eurydice and Orpheus. Orpheus' summons to Hymen is in vain. On their wedding day Eurydice is bitten by a serpent as she strolls upon the green grass with her attendants. Vergil had explained in Book 4 of the *Georgics* that Eurydice was bitten while fleeing Aristaeus. Ovid saves that pattern for the end of Book 11 when Hesperia, fleeing Aesacus, is bitten by a serpent hiding in the grass. This framing device forms Books 10 and 11 into a single unit.

Orpheus' descent to the underworld to regain his bride gains for him one of the defining attributes of the Greek hero: the ability to descend to Hades and return. But the bard who had the power to move Pluto and Proserpina was unable to prevent himself from turning back his gaze at Eurydice and losing her again. The remainder of Book 10 consists of the embedded tales of the bereft Orpheus. The homosexual stories are attributed to Orpheus' devotion to Eurydice. But his aversion to women reaches a high pitch in the story of the Propoetides, whose lewd behavior, according to Orpheus, inspired Pygmalion to remain unwed and to attempt to create the ideal woman in sculpture. Venus fulfills Pygmalion's prayer that his "ivory maid" be brought to life and falls in love herself with Adonis, the child of Myrrha and her father Cinyras, who is the son of Paphos, the child of Pygmalion and his living statue. Just as Ovid frequently creates the fiction that not he but one or another of his characters has become the narrator, so in the story of Venus and Adonis Orpheus makes Venus become the narrator to Adonis of the story of Atalanta and Hippomenes.

Continuing the theme of music and song, the death of Orpheus leads to the aetiological myth for the foundation of Greek lyric poetry. In a kind of re-enactment of a *sparagmos* (rending of flesh) associated with the sacrificial victim in the worship of Bacchus (recall the fate of Pentheus at the end of Book 3), the Bacchant women, angered at their rejection by the bard, tear him apart. But Orpheus' head and his lyre, still sounding, float down the Hebrus river of Thrace out to sea and to the island of Lesbos, the home of the great poets Sappho and Alcaeus (7th century B.C.).

After punishing his Bacchants for killing Orpheus, Bacchus leaves Thrace in disgust for Asia Minor, the setting for the stories of Midas and Laomedon and eventually the Trojan War. In return for reuniting Bacchus with his foster father, Papa Silenus, Bacchus grants Midas' wish for the "golden touch," another example of the dangerous power of the imperfectly formulated word (we remember Phaethon, Semele, and have yet to hear the Sibyl's tale in Book 14). Lyre and reed compete again in the contest between Phoebus and Pan, similar, but with a comical outcome, to the contest of Phoebus and Marsyas in Book 6.

When Apollo and Neptune are defrauded by King Laomedon of their payment for rebuilding the walls of Troy, Neptune floods the land, and a sea monster claims Hesione, Laomedon's daughter. Hercules, in a repetition of the plot of Perseus and Andromeda, rescues her from the sea cliff to which she had been bound, but when he is denied the horses Laomedon had promised for the deed, he makes war on Troy and gives her as bride to his companion in the war, Telamon. Reference to Telamon shifts the narrative quickly to his brother Peleus.

After Peleus overcomes Thetis' resistance and makes her pregnant with Achilles, he is exiled for having earlier slain his half-brother Phocus. The exile brings him as a guest to the house of Ceyx, son of Lucifer and husband of Alcyone, daughter of Aeolus, god of the winds. Here, as in Book 8, the context of hospitality provides an occasion for an embedded tale: as Ceyx tells the fate of his brother Daedalion and his daughter Chione, Peleus is distracted by his herdsman who reports that a wolf has attacked the herd of cattle. Peleus recognizes this as the work of the Nereid Psamathe, still angry because of the death of her son Phocus. Thetis successfully intercedes with Psamathe on her husband's behalf, but the fates still require Peleus to move on to Thessaly where Acastus purifies him of his blood-guilt.

This brief interlude serves to break the narrative from Ceyx' embedded tale to Ovid's narrative of the romantic tale of Ceyx himself and his wife Alcyone. Structurally, Alcyone's loss of her husband balances the doomed love of Orpheus and Eurydice at the beginning of Book 10. The halcyon days that commemorate the love of Ceyx and Alcyone, transformed into birds that nest on becalmed seas, prepare thematically for the winds that are stilled by Diana at Aulis and the sacrifice of Iphigenia at the beginning of Book 12, for Alcyone is the daughter of Aeolus, king of the Winds, not the ancestor of Jason's family, but just as changeful. The final brief episode of Aesacus and Hesperia, in addition to framing the two books with the fatal bite of a serpent, has the effect of introducing the geographical shift from Troy in the East to the westward destiny of Trojan Aeneas and Rome: the name of Hesperia, nymph daughter of the Trojan river Cebren, means "Evening/West."

But first there are the Trojan War books themselves, Books 12 and 13. For the sacrifice of Iphigenia by the Greeks assembled at Aulis for the expedition against Troy at the beginning of Book 12 Ovid draws upon the tradition unreported by Homer but found in Euripides' *Iphigenia at Aulis* and *Iphigenia among the Taurians*. The book concludes with the death of Achilles. While at *Odyssey* 24. 35-97 the ghost of Agamemnon tells the ghost of Achilles of the latter's glorious funeral, the earliest source for how Achilles was killed by Paris and Apollo is the *Aithiopis*, one of the poems of the Epic Cycle. Ovid will wait until the debate between Ajax and Ulysses for the arms of Achilles in Book 13 to review some of the episodes in the *Iliad*, and turns in Book 12 to the Epic Cycle for the story of Achilles' battle with invulnerable Cycnus. The battle of the Lapiths and Centaurs, told in ten lines at *Odyssey* 21. 295-304, becomes the embedded tale of Nestor. Beginning with the story of Caeneus (once Caenis, but after her violation by Neptune, changed by the god into a male), Nestor's tale runs to 405 lines. After Pythagoras' 418 lines in Book 15, Nestor's is the second longest embedded tale and one of the longest monothematic narratives in the entire epic. We must smile with relief when after 251 lines he says, "Their wounds I don't recall, but I have noted the number and names." In maintaining its focus on Caeneus, however, the narrative is not without form, nor without charm, especially in its poignant memorial to a loving Centaur couple, Hylonome and Cyllarus. Book 12 ends with an encomium for Achilles echoed by the very end of Book 15: just as Ovid hopes to live forever by being read, so in death Achilles is metamorphosed into a few ashes (the great and noble tomb Agamemnon describes at *Odyssey* 24. 80-92 is not mentioned) and "glory that fills all the world" (very close to Agamemnon's words at *Odyssey* 24. 93-94).

With allusions not only to Homeric passages but also to Sophocles' *Ajax* and *Philoctetes*, Euripides' *Hecuba*, and Vergil's *Aeneid*, Book 13 treats the aftermath of the Trojan War from the perspective of both the Greeks and the Trojans. The debate between Ajax and Ulysses allows for a review of the war itself; the outcome of the debate is the suicide of Ajax, in contrast to Sophocles' versions, carried out in the presence of the Greek army with his blood inscribing itself on the petals of a flower as a cry of woe (recalling the death of Hyacinth); Hecuba laments the loss of her last two children, Polyxena and Polydorus; as in Euripides, Hecuba with the help of the other captive Trojan women deceives and blinds Polymestor and is changed into a bitch, moving even Juno to pity. Another mother's lament follows, that of Aurora for her son Memnon, slain by Achilles. In three lovely lines (620-22) Ovid associates the two sorrowing mothers and abruptly shifts to Aeneas and the survival of the household gods of Troy.

The account of Aeneas' journey fills the remainder of Book 13 and over half of Book 14, but there are many detours and interruptions in the narrative: when the Trojans reach the straits between Sicily and Italy, Scylla is there threatening the right, Charybdis the left (Book 13. 730). The Trojans, however, will not pass through the straits until 312 lines later at Book 14. 75. Ovid pauses for a breath of inspiration from the pastoral poet Theocritus for Polyphemus' pursuit of Galatea, narrated by Galatea herself to Scylla before the latter's disfigurement. Glaucus' failed attempt to woo the chaste Scylla with the tale of his transformation into a fish-bodied sea-god leads him to seek Circe's help, and the story continues into Book 14. Circe, enflamed with desire for but decisively rebuffed by Glaucus, indignantly turns her wrath against the innocent Scylla, transforming her into a dog-girdled monster whose hatred of Circe Ovid supplies as the reason for her attacking Odysseus' companions. Ovid adds another non-Homeric touch in giving her transformation a second stage and explaining that she would have killed more of Odysseus' men and sunk his ship had she not already become a cliff, an obstacle to sailors.

But at last Ovid returns to Aeneas and the Trojan ships, which after the long digression pass between Scylla and Charybdis in just one syllable more than one and a third hexameters. The diversion of their journey by Juno's storm and the sojourn in Dido's Carthage, treated by Vergil in *Aeneid* 1 and 4, is dispensed with in just under six lines and after a rapid course up the Italian coast Aeneas finds himself in the company of the Sibyl at Cumae. Though Vergilian elements remain, in particular the golden bough, the visit to father Anchises' shade in the Underworld, and the preview of his own "ancestors" (by which Ovid must mean the ancestors Aeneas gave to the Romans), what Vergil had related at length in *Aeneid* 6 in the descent (*katabasis*) to and passage through Elysium is told by Ovid with extreme brevity. Instead, during the journey up (*anabasis*) there is the Sibyl's embedded tale, not found in Vergil, of how Apollo courted her with a promise to give her anything she desired; because she asked for great age, foolishly forgetting to ask for eternal youth and still rejecting Apollo's suit, she has lived already seven centuries and must live for three more, and will eventually shrivel to nothing but voice. Does Ovid as would-be prophetic bard or *vates* feel an affinity with both Orpheus and the Sibyl?

In the following episode, Ovid pays tribute to a character invented by Vergil and invents one himself. In *Aeneid* 3 Achaemenides, a Greek mistakenly left behind by Odysseus, warns Aeneas away from the shores of the dangerous Cyclops. Just as Sinon in *Aeneid* 2, epitomizing Greek perfidy, had convinced the Trojans to open their walls for the Wooden Horse, so Achaemenides (the name perhaps drawn from the Achaemenid dynasty of the Persians, trained to ride horses, shoot straight, and tell the truth) not only saves the Trojans from the Cyclops but heralds an end to the enmity between Trojan and Greek. To ask the essential question, namely why a Greek is on board a Trojan ship, Ovid invents the figure of Macareus (the Greek name means "Happy" or "Fortunate") as a friend and companion of Ulysses. To Macareus, who had wearied of Ulysses' journey homeward and chosen to stay behind, Achaemenides recounts how, hiding in fear of death at the hands of the now blinded Cyclops, he revisited in his mind the awful sight of Polyphemus as he devoured many of his companions. But now, secure as a Greek on a Trojan ship, he asks his old companion to tell what happened to Ulysses and his men.

Macareus' response gives an Italic flavor to events known from the *Odyssey*. He situates the Laestrygonians on the coast of Italy at Formia, a city founded by Lamus, just south of Gaeta (named for Aeneas' nurse Caeta); after the account of Circe's transformation of himself and his companions into pigs and how Ulysses, protected by Mercury's gift of moly, forces her to restore their form, Macareus reports the embedded tale by a servant of Circe about Picus, the son of Saturn. Picus is king in Latium and in love with Canens, the daughter of Venilia and Janus, a nymph of beautiful voice. The story replicates much in the story of Glaucus: Circe falls in love with Picus at first sight when he had ventured into her woods for the hunt. When Circe's protestations of love are refused, she is enraged and changes him into a woodpecker. Canens searches in vain for her beloved Picus and vanishes into thin air at a place that retains her name, bestowed upon it by the Roman Muses, the Camenae.

Reconciliation between Greek and Trojan is further advanced by Diomedes' refusal (as in Vergil, but with different motivation) to send forces to assist Turnus against Aeneas. The narrative of war is rather quickly passed over and the Trojan settlement in Italy confirmed by the apotheosis of Aeneas as the god Indiges "Native." The reconciliation between his descendant Romans and rival Italian tribes is implied in the name of the deified Romulus, Quirinus, derived from the chief Sabine town of Cures. Between these two events is placed a story with a very propitious outcome for the new Roman people, the story of the nymph Pomona, devoted to her orchards and gardens, wooed successfully by Vertumnus, not by his many changes of form nor his cautionary tale of Iphis and Anaxarete, but by his own true and natural form.

It may be significant that Ovid omits any reference to one of the best known Roman myths, the strife between Romulus and his brother Remus. Its Greek parallel, the duel to the death of Oedipus' sons, Eteocles and Polyneices, which could have found a place in Books 3 and 4, the so-called Theban books, is only referred to briefly at Book 9. 405. Ovid, who stresses the theme of strife between fathers and sons, seems to avoid fraternal strife. By omitting this important Roman myth, the aetiological myth for the enduring civil strife in Roman history, did he hope to have a salutary effect upon history itself? Or do we have here again another example of Ovid's attempt to diverge from Vergil's *Aeneid*, in which Jupiter's account of Roman destiny culminates in the resolution of the enmity between Romulus and Remus.

> The savage centuries will then grow mild with cessation of wars;
> Pure good faith and Vesta and Quirinus with brother Remus
> will dispense law.

> *Aspera tum posits mitescent saecula bellis;*
> *cana Fides et Vesta, Remo cum fratre Quirinus*
> *iura dabunt*
>                                          *Aeneid* 1. 291-92

Ovid, instead, associates Romulus with the resolution of Roman competition with other Italic tribes for the hegemony of Italy in his shared rule with the Sabine king Titus Tatius. The book closes with the death and deification of Romulus as Quirinus and that of his devoted wife Hersilia as Hora, an Italic fertility goddess particularly associated with youth, like the Greek Hebe.

Rome, well established in Book 14, is now prepared for growth, refinement, healing, and learning. The themes of travel, transmigration, and transformation in Book 15 serve as a kind of meditation upon the value of metamorphosis itself. Numa, happy in his wife Egeria and with the Camenae as his guides, taught the Romans "sacrificial rites and converted a nation trained in cruel war to the arts of peace" (483-84). Ovid explains Numa's wisdom as the result of his quest of knowledge, his journey to Crotona, notable for its cult of Hercules and ties to Pythagoras. The wisdom of the historical Pythagoras (born ca. 570 at Samos, died in Metapontum in 496 B.C.) was itself partly attributed in antiquity to his wide travel, even to Egypt and Babylon. He settled in Crotona around 530 B.C. Even down to Ovid's time there had been various so-called Pythagorean sects and societies in southern Italy (Magna Graecia), many of whose practices for the purification of the soul were akin to those of Orphic religion. Among their beliefs were *metempsychosis* or transmigration of the soul at death of the body into another living body, the view that the body was the tomb of the soul from which the soul must seek liberation, and a taboo on the eating of flesh meat.

Perhaps the very length of Pythagoras' rambling sermon, the longest speech in the epic, is an indication of its importance. It contains ideas that probably did not belong to the historical Pythagoras of the 6th century B.C. "All things are in flux" (178), for example, is an expression found in Plato and in the pre-Socratic philosopher Heraclitus (late 6th century B.C.), and the four generative elements from which all things arise (239-250) would have been instantly recognized as the doctrine of Empedocles of Acragas (mid-5th century B.C.). There is no explicit reference to his notion of the cosmos and human soul as divine, consisting of a harmony of numbers, but perhaps the careful structure of Ovid's poetry as well as his tribute to Harmonia are a reflection of it. Certainly other themes of Pythagoras' speech—history and ever revolving time, transformations, and moral reformation reflected in vegetarianism—are central to Ovid's intention of composing a *carmen perpetuum* (Book 1. 4) with an account of all the transformations of the world down to the return to the Golden Age in his own day.

Ostensibly to comfort Egeria at the death of her husband Numa, but also as if to offer an additional example of Pythagoras' doctrine of regeneration, Ovid introduces the story of Hippolytus, restored to life by Aesculapius and Apollo and brought by Diana as Virbius to serve her cult at Aricia in Latium. Following Virbius' amazing tale are further miracles: Egeria's transformation into a cold spring, the birth of Tages, who first taught the Etruscans prophecy, from a clod of earth (another example of autochthonous birth), the greening of Romulus' spear, and the story of Cipus. Tages prophesies that the horns on Cipus' head portend that he will be king of Latium as soon as he is received into the city of Rome. Cipus, devoted to his people, contrives to have them send him into exile rather than fall under the sway of a king. The traditional republican aversion to monarchy after the expulsion in 509 B.C. of Tarquin the Proud, the last *rex* of Rome, is suggested by Ovid's nobles, who reward Cipus' self-sacrificial act. In the following episode the Senate continues to care for the welfare of the city by importing during a great plague the son of the god of healing. They bring Greek Asclepius, son of Apollo, from Epidauros and install him as Aesculapius in serpent's form on an island in the Tiber.

Health has been brought to Rome, or perhaps Greek *hygieia* in the form of Greek and Trojan reconciliation (Achaemenides, Diomedes), Greek myth and literature (Ovid's primary sources), Greek philosophy and religion (Pythagoras), seasoned by Roman Numa and Etruscan Tages. In the two remaining episodes Ovid turns to Julius Caesar and Augustus. Venus pleads for the life of her offspring Julius Caesar. Though unable to undo what the Fates have spun for the Ides of March, Venus is assured by Jove that the Fates have sealed that Caesar will become a god in the sky and that his son will be his heir and avenger, restoring peace to the land. As Jupiter controls sky, sea, and underworld, the earth is subject to Augustus. Both rule as fathers.

Ovid's epilogue recalls in its thought and wording Horace's "I have completed a monument more lasting than bronze (*Exegi monumentum aere perennius, Ode* 3. 30):

"And now I have finished my work, which neither Jove's wrath nor fire, nor sword nor devouring age will be able to destroy."
*Iamque opus exegi, quod nec Iovis ira nec ignis*
*nec poterit ferrum nec edax abolere vetustas.*

Book 15. 871-72

His final hope: that wherever Roman culture reigns supreme, he will survive in glory on the lips of his readers (877-89).

# BOOK 1

## 1-4 Prologue

My mind would tell of forms changed into
new bodies; gods, into my undertakings (for you changed even those[1])
breathe life[2] and from the first origin of the world
to my own times draw forth[3] a perpetual[4] song!

---

1 Translating either the *illas* of most MSS, referring to *formas* "forms," or the preferable *illa* of a medieval variant, accepted by Tarrant and Anderson. Ovid may mean that the gods, having changed his meter from elegiac couplets to the continuous dactylic hexameter of epic for the present work, should now breathe life into his *coeptis* "undertakings" (see E. J. Kenney, 1976). Another possibility would be to take *illa* as the "former," referring to and neatly balancing *corpora* "bodies" at the beginning of line 2. Corpora might be Ovid's "literary works," but at 15.252-53 Nature has the power to remake "new forms from other forms" *ex aliis alias reparat natura figuras* and Mother Earth acts in this way at 156-57, below. With this latter interpretation Ovid invokes the aid of the gods as the agents of the continuing changes he intends to write about.

2 Translating *adspirate,* as though the creation of a poem itself were a kind of metamorphosis. See note on 1. 405.

3 *Deducite*, a metaphor from spinning. See A. Keith (2002) on "thinning" the proposed epic with elegiac themes.

4 Translating *perpetuum*: Ovid's poem, while episodic, is to be an "unbroken" or "continuous" epic, and, as a classic, one that is "everlasting."

*1*

### 5-20  Chaos

Before the sea and dry land and the sky that covers all,                    5
of single guise was nature throughout the globe.
They called it Chaos,[5] a rough and unformed bulk,
of nought but sluggish weight, and together massed,
of matter, poorly joined, the discordant seeds.
No Titan[6] brought yet light to the world,                                 10
nor yet did waxing Phoebe[7] build her horns anew,
nor yet did Earth hang in the surrounding air,
supported by her own weight, nor had Amphitrite[8] stretched out
her arms over the dry lands' long shore.
While earth was there and sea and air,                                      15
yet was that earth unstable, that wave unswum,
that air lacking light; nothing kept its form,
one thing obstructed the other, since within that body joined in one
the cold fought with things warm, the wet with the dry,
the soft with the hard, with the weightless, those having weight.           20

### 21-88  Creation of the World

This strife did god, and better nature, dissolve.
For from the sky he cut apart the earth, and the waters from the earth,
and from the dense air divided the ethereal sky.
Once he had removed them from the dark and uncertain heap,
he bound each in its place, disjoined in concordant peace:                  25
the fiery force of the arched and weightless sky
shot up and in the heights above made its place;
the air is next to fire in lightness and place;
more dense than these, the earth attracted the heavier things,
pressed down by her own weight; the moisture flowing round                  30
possessed the remaining space and confined the solid orb.
When that god, whichever of the gods it was, cut off
the mass thus arranged and, thus cut off, into its parts compelled,
first, lest the earth not be equal in every part,
he rolled it into the shape of a huge globe.                                35
Then he commanded the waters to be poured forth and to swell
with rushing winds and to surround the shores of the encircled land;
he added springs and large still pools and lakes,
and down-sloping rivers he girded with slanting banks,

---

5 The word is cognate with English *gape* and *yawn*.
6 Though Ovid regularly equates Apollo with Sol, the Sun, the earlier Greeks distinguished Apollo from
    Helios, son of the Titan Hyperion and god of the sun. Here Ovid's name for Apollo seems to recall
    that earlier distinction.
7 The feminine form of Phoebus (Apollo), Phoebe means "The Bright One," and refers here to the
    Moon, often equated with Diana, the Greek Artemis.
8 A sea-goddess, by metonymy, the Sea.

which are, in varied regions, partly reabsorbed by the land itself,                    40
and partly pass through to the sea and, once received from the plain,
with freer water strike the shores instead of banks.
And he commanded the plains to spread, the valleys to subside
the woods with foliage to be covered, the rocky mountains to rise.
And as two zones on the right and the same number on the left          45
divide the sky, and a fifth more heated than they,
just so the care of the god distinguished in equal toll
the bounded mass, and stamped as many zones on earth.
Of these, the middle one the heat makes unfit to dwell;
deep snows hide two; the same number he placed between          50
and gave a temperate clime, mixed with heat and cold.
          Above these hung air; as much as water's weight
is lighter than earth's, by so much is air heavier than fire.
He ordered there the foggy mists, there the clouds to stand,
and thunder that would warn human minds,          55
the winds that with lightning produce the wintry cold.
Moreover, the framer of the world did not allow the winds
to own the air at random, for even now they are hard to restrain,
when each directs his blasts in different tracts,
from mangling the world; so great is the discord of brother winds.          60
So Eurus[9] retired to Aurora[10] and the Nabataean[11] realm
and to the Persian highlands set beneath morning's rays;
the West and where the shores are warmed by the falling sun
are nearest to Zephyrus[12]; Scythia[13] and the North
did bristling Boreas[14] invade; the opposing land          65
is moistened by frequent clouds and rain from Auster's[15] wind.
Above these he imposed, clear and lacking weight,
the aether,[16] containing nothing of earthly dross.
          No sooner had he enclosed all things within their given bounds,
when, long oppressed by the murky mist,          70
the stars began to shine in all the sky.
And lest any region of its proper creatures be deprived,
the stars and forms of the gods possess the celestial firmament,
the waters yielded themselves as home to the glistening fish,
the earth received the beasts, the mobile air the birds.          75

---

9 The East Wind.
10 The Greek Eos, the Dawn.
11 The Nabataeans were Arabs of the area around Petra, located in what is now Jordan.
12 The West Wind.
13 Region of a nomadic people above the Black Sea.
14 The North Wind.
15 The South Wind.
16 Or "ether," the upper, rarified, air, used frequently by Ovid for "heaven" or "sky."

*Creation of Man, Baur*

## 76-88   Humanity

A creature more sacred than these, and for lofty thought more fit
was lacking still, to rule over all the rest:
humanity was born, whether made from divine seed
by that creator of things, that origin of a better world,
or whether the earth, fresh and from the lofty aether lately drawn,          80
retained the seeds of its kindred sky.
The son of Iapetus[17] fashioned that earth, mingled with
the waters of rain, into the image of the gods that guide the world,
and, though all other animals look down upon the earth,
the face of humankind he made to behold the sky above,                       85
commanding it to raise aloft its gaze to the stars:
so thus it was that the earth, lately rude and without form,
was changed and dressed herself in humanity's unfamiliar forms.

## 89-150   The Four Ages

Begotten first was the golden age, which with master none,
nor law, did freely cultivate good faith and the right.                      90
Both punishment and fear were absent, nor were menacing words read,
inscribed on bronze, nor did the suppliant multitude fear
the face of its judge, but without a master was safe.
Not yet cut down, to visit foreign climes, had the pine
descended from its mountains to the flowing waves,                           95
and mortals knew no shores but their own;

---

17 Prometheus was the son of the Titan Iapetos, a name probably akin to the Hebrew Japheth, son of
   Noah, from whom the Javan, or Ionian Greeks, were descended.

not yet were towns girt with steep-banked moats;
no trumpet of straight, no horn of crescent bronze,
no helmets, no swords were there: soldiers unknown,
the peoples passed their easy life of leisure secure.                          100
The earth, too, duty free, but untouched by the rake
nor wounded by those plowshares, freely produced all;
content with food created at no one's command,
folks picked the fruit of the arbutus[18] and mountain rose[19]
and cornel-cherries and blackberries clinging to thorny vines,                 105
and acorns fallen from the spreading tree[20] of Jove.
The springtime was eternal, and, with breezes warmed,
the gentle zephyrs caressed the flowers born without seed;
the earth untilled soon brought forth fruit,
and, unrenewed, the field grew white with heavy ears of grain;                 110
there flowed now streams of nectar, now streams of milk,
and golden honey was distilled upon the greening oak.[21]
    When Saturn to gloomy Tartarus[22] had been dispatched
and the world was subject to Jove, the silver progeny arose,
to gold inferior, more precious than burnished bronze.                         115
Jove shortened the period of the former spring
and, over winters and summers and autumns of unequal length
and brief springtime, in four seasons he spread out the year.
Then first did air, burned by the arid heat,
grow white, and wind-compacted ice hung down;                                  120
then first did people enter houses; the houses were caves
and dense brush and branches bound with bark.
then first were Ceres'[23] seeds in long-drawn rows
concealed, and bullocks groaned, weighed down by the yoke.
    That age was followed by a third progeny, of bronze,                       125
more crude in spirit and more ready for bristling war,
yet not accursed; the final progeny was made of hard iron.
Straightway upon this age of baser metal did every wrong
break in, and sense of shame and truth and trust did flee,
in place of which there entered fraud and deceit                               130
and scheming and violence and a wicked love of gain.
The sailor put sails to the winds (nor did he know them well
till then), and what previously had stood upon the lofty hills
exulted[24] now as hulls upon the unfamiliar waves.
And what before was held in common like the light of the sun and the breeze    135

---

18 Wild strawberry.
19 *Fragum* 'strawberry or herb related to the rose.'
20 The oak.
21 The ilex, holm oak, Italian "*leccio*".
22 The Underworld.
23 The goddess of agriculture, the Greek Demeter.
24 Translating *exultavere*; with *insultavere*, "bobbed with insult as hulls upon the unfamiliar waves."

the wary surveyor with a long boundary marked.
Not only crops and necessary nourishment was the rich earth
required to give: the bowels of the earth were invaded as well;
the riches she had stowed away and removed to the Stygian shades
were dug out, an inducement to evil deeds.                                    140
Already, too, had harmful iron, and gold, more harmful than iron,
come forth, war comes forth, which fights with both,
and with its bloody hand strikes together the clashing arms.
They live by plunder: the host is not safe from the guest,
nor father-in-law from son-in-law, kindness among brothers is rare;          145
with murder the husband threatens his wife, the wife, her husband,
ferocious stepmothers ghastly poisons brew,
the son in advance of the day investigates his father's age;
defeated piety lies prostrate, and virgin Astraea[25] leaves,
as last of her heavenly beings, the earth now wet with gore.                 150

### 151-62   *The Gigantomachy*

And that the aether on high not be safer than the earth,
it's said that the giants thought to gain the heavenly realm
and heaped high the mountains to the stars.
The almighty father then battered Olympus with the launch
of his lightning and struck down Pelion from Ossa[26] beneath.               155

*Iron Age, Anonymous Venice ca. 1513*

25 The goddess of justice.
26 Pelion and Ossa are mountains of Thessaly. The Giants piled Pelion upon Ossa to reach Mt. Olympus,
   home of the Olympian gods, against whom they were revolting.

*Gigantomachy, Baur*

When these dire bodies lay buried beneath their own mass,
it's said Mother Earth, soaked through with her children's copious blood,
was sodden and enlivened that warm bloody gore
and, lest no memorial of her offspring remain,
transformed it into human shape; but this progeny                    160
was also disdainful of the gods above, most eager for savage slaughter
and violent: you could see that they were born of blood.[27]

### 163-252  *Lycaon*

When from his high citadel the Saturnian father[28] saw all this,
he groaned and, thinking of the foul banquets of Lycaon's[29] board,
a deed not yet known abroad because it was new,                      165
conceived a wrath huge in spirit and worthy of Jove
and summoned a council: those summoned were not delayed.
There is a celestial way, clear in the cloudless sky;
its name is "Milky," by its very whiteness distinct.
Through it the gods have access to the palace of the great Thunderer,[30]    170
his royal home: the courts of the noble gods on right
and left are thronged through their opened double doors.
The commons dwell apart in their place: on this side the mighty

---

27 This generation of earth-born mortals is in addition to that fashioned from earth by Prometheus (76-
    88). See Ovid, *Amores* 2. 1. 11-14.
28 Jupiter, son of Saturn, was known since the Homeric poems as the father of gods and men.
29 King of Arcadia, whose name is derived from Greek *lykos* 'wolf.'
30 Jupiter.

and famous sky-dwellers established their Penates;[31]
here is the place, which, if bold expression be allowed, 175
I should not hesitate to call the Palatine[32] homes of the sky.
    And so when the gods sat down in that marble retreat,
more lofty at his place and leaning upon his ivory staff,
Jove tossed three times and a fourth the awesome locks of his head
with which he moves the earth and sea and stars. 180
He then let loose his indignant tongue with words like these:
"More anxious for the terrestrial realm I was not
at that time when each of the snaky-footed ones[33] prepared
to cast his hundred arms over heaven made captive.
For though that foe was fierce, yet from but one 185
beginning and one body that conflict came;
but now must I, wherever Nereus[34] round the world resounds,
destroy the mortal race: by the infernal streams
I swear that glide beneath the earth through the Stygian grove!
All remedy should first be tried, but when the body cannot be cured, 190
it must be cut out by the sword, lest infected be the part that's pure.
I have the demigods, yes, rustic powers, nymphs
and fauns and satyrs and mountain-dwelling forest deities;
while these we've not yet deemed heaven's honor due,
we should allow them in the lands we've allotted to dwell secure. 195
Or think you, O gods, that *they* will be safe enough
while *I*, who wield the thunderbolt, who rule you for my own,
am by Lycaon, known for savagery, assailed with treachery?"
    They all then trembled and demanded with burning desire
the one who'd dared such things: as when the impious band raged 200
with Caesar's blood to extinguish the Roman name,
by such great terror of sudden ruin the human race
was thunderstruck and all the earth did shake.[35]
Not less agreeable to you, Augustus, was your people's respect
than that of his to Jove. When he with word and hand 205
had stilled their rumbling, all their silence kept.
When once clamor is checked, suppressed by the sternness of the king,
Jove broke again the silence with these words:
"That man in truth the penalty (of this have no fear) has paid;
his crime, however, and his punishment, I shall explain. 210
The infamy of the age had touched our ears;
desiring that it be false, from Olympus on high did I glide down

---

31 The Penates are the Roman household gods, particularly providing *penus* 'food' for the household. It
    never troubles Ovid to use the term as metonymy even for the household of the gods themselves.
32 The hill of Rome on which the emperor and prominent families lived
33 The Giants.
34 A god of the sea, here by metonymy the sea.
35 With the exception perhaps of 45-46, this is the first simile in the *Metamorphoses*, and like the first
    simile in Vergil's *Aeneid* 1. 148-52, it compares nature to politics.

and, as a god in human form, scour the earth.
To tell in full how much evil was found everywhere
requires much time: yet the evil reported was less than the truth.    215
I crossed the mountains of Maenala,[36] bristling with lairs of the wild,
and both Cyllene,[37] and cool Lycaeus'[38] piney woods:
from there the seat and inhospitable home of the Arcadian king
I enter as lingering dusk was drawing down the night.
I showed in signs that a god had come, and the people began    220
to pray. At first Lycaon laughs at the pious prayers,
but soon he says, "I'll prove with a clear test whether he's a god
or mortal: nor will the truth be open to doubt."
He plans to destroy me at night, heavy with sleep,
with sudden death; he chooses this as the test of truth;    225
and not content with that, of a hostage sent from the Molossian[39] folk
he opens the throat with the point of a sword
and then softens some of the half-dead limbs
in boiling water, some he roasts over fire.
As soon as he placed this on the table, did I with avenging flame    230
upon its lord and deserving Penates bring down the house;
The man flees in terror, and when he gained the stillness of the countryside
he howls and vainly tries to speak: on its own
his mouth gathers frothy madness, and, lusting for his wonted kill,
he turns against the flocks and now again in blood finds joy.    235
His finery disappears into fur, into legs his arms;
He's now a wolf and saves the traces of his earlier form.
The gray's the same, the same the violence of his face,
the same eyes gleam, of savagery the image remains.

*Lycaon, Solis*

---

36 In Arcadia.
37 Mountain in Arcadia, birthplace of Hermes (Mercury).
38 The name, meaning "Wolf-mountain," was sacred to Zeus (Jove) and Pan in Arcadia.
39 The Molossians lived in Epirus.

One house had fallen, but for one house to fall                                240
was not enough: throughout the earth's expanse the wild Erinys[40] reigns.
You might think there's a conspiracy of crime. Let all then pay at once
the punishment they've deserved; thus my sentence stands!"
        Some voice approval of Jove's ruling, applying to his rage
more goads, while others fulfill their part with applause.                     245
And yet the loss of human kind is cause for grief
to all, for what will be the future form of earth, bereft
of mortals, they ask, to altars who will bring frankincense,
does he intend to surrender the earth to be destroyed by wild beasts?
Despite such questions, for he would see to all himself,                       250
the king of the gods above forbids them to fear, and a breed
unlike the former folk he promises, of wondrous birth.

### 253-312   The Flood

        And near he was to showering his lightning against all the earth,
but feared lest the sacred aether by so many fires
catch flame and the long pole of heaven burn.                                  255
There was in the fates, he also recalls, to be a time
when sea, when earth, and heaven's royal home would catch fire
and burn,[41] and the world's elaborate mass collapse.
The missiles are laid aside, the Cyclopes[42] handiwork;
a different punishment finds his favor, to destroy the mortal race             260
beneath the waves and rain down cloudbursts from every part of the sky.
At once he shuts Aquilo[43] in Aeolus'[44] caves
and those breezes that put the gathered clouds to flight,
and sends Notus[45] out. Notus with soggy wings flies forth,
his terrible visage covered with the darkness of pitch;                        265
his beard heavy with storms, from his hoary hair the water flowed;
upon his brow sit the clouds, drenched with dew are his raiment and wings.
And when with his hand he presses the widely hanging clouds,
there is a thunderclap: then from the sky the storms pour thick.
The herald of Juno, Iris,[46] in various colors arrayed,                       270
absorbs water and brings nourishment to the clouds.
The crops are laid low and the farmer's hopes and prayers
lamented lie, and the long year's labor is brought to nil.
        And not content with his own sky is the wrath of Jove:
his sky-blue brother[47] aids him with auxiliary waves                         275

---

40 The Greek word for Fury, here in the sense of "criminal spirit."
41 The Stoic doctrine of *ekpyrosis*, or periodic world conflagrations.
42 Brontes, Steropes, and Arges; see Hes., *Theogony*, 140.
43 The god of the north or north-northeast wind.
44 God of the winds.
45 The Greek name for the god of the south or southwest wind, son of Eos (Aurora) and Astraeus.
46 The Rainbow, and herald of Juno.
47 Neptune.

*Flood, Anonymous Venice ca. 1513*

and calls together the rivers; after they've entered
the home of their king, "No need now," he says,
"for long exhortation. Your power pour forth,
your job is this: open wide your homes, unblock
your dams and to your currents give full rein."                     280
His order given, they go back and let loose the mouths of their springs
and with their courses unchecked run to the seas.
The god himself strikes the earth with his trident, and she
did quake, and from that impact opened wide her waters' ways.
The rivers spread out and run through the open fields,               285
and carry away trees and flocks and sown fields and men
and homes and, with their sacred objects, the inner shrines.
If any home remained and was able to hold firm, not cast down
by this great evil, yet its roof is by a higher wave
concealed, and its towers lie hidden beneath the flood.             290
     And now sea and land were indistinct;
the ocean was all, and the ocean lacked its shores.
One man holds to a hilltop, another sits in a curved bark
and pulls the oars there where lately he had plowed.
That man there over his crops and the roof beams of his sunken house  295
is sailing, this man has caught a fish at the top of an elm.
If chance allowed, anchor is dropped in a meadow's green,
or curved hulls graze the vineyards forced below;
and where of late graceful she-goats cropped the grass,
now odd-shaped seals their bodies lay.                               300

With wonder, beneath the water, on groves and cities and homes
the Nereids[48] gaze, and dolphins gain the woods and among
the lofty branches dart and strike the shaken oaks.
The wolf swims among the sheep, the wave the tawny lion lifts,
the wave lifts the tigers; no use to the boar is his lightning strikes,                305
nor swift legs to the stag, carried away by the waters;
and after searching long for land in which to light
the wandering bird with wearied wings falls into the sea.
The unlimited license of the ocean had covered the hills,
and strange floods were striking the mountain tops.                310
The greatest part was taken by the water: those the water spared
are by long fasting on meager fare subdued.

### 313-415   *Deucalion and Pyrrha*

Between the Aonian[49] and Oetaean[50] fields Phocis[51] lies,
a fruitful land while land it was, but at that time
a part of the sea and a broad plain of the sudden flood.                315
An arduous mountain there with twin peaks reaches towards the stars,
Parnassus by name, and its summit surmounts the clouds.
When here Deucalion—for the watery plain had covered all the rest—ran
aground, carried in a small raft with the consort of his bed,
they worshiped the Corycian[52] nymphs and mountain spirits and                320
prophetic Themis,[53] who held the oracle then.
No person was better than he, nor more a lover of the just
was any man, nor any woman more reverent than she towards the gods.
As Jupiter sees the world flooded with watery swamps
and just one man from so many thousands survive                325
and just one woman from so many thousands survive,
and innocent both, worshipers of deity both,
he scatters the clouds and, with stormy clouds by Aquilo's wind[54] dispelled,
he shows the sky to the earth, the firmament to the earth.
Nor does the wrath of the sea remain, and, his tricuspid spear laid down,                330
the ruler of the main soothes the waters, and, rising up over the deep,
his shoulders covered with inborn purple's shells,[55]
he calls the sky-blue Triton forth. Into the resounding conch
he orders him to breathe and the floods and streams,
with signal given, now recall. The hollow trumpet he takes,                335

---

48 Nymph daughters of the sea-god Nereus
49 Aonia is the part of Boeotia containing Mt. Helicon; by synecdoche (part for the whole) Aonia stands
    for Boeotia.
50 Mt. Oeta, forming the border of southern Thessaly, is where Hercules had himself burned alive.
51 Region between Locris and Boeotia in which Delphi is located.
52 Referring to the Corycian cave on Mt. Parnassus.
53 A goddess of justice, derived from the Greek verb meaning "to establish."
54 See 262.
55 The murex, the shellfish from which purple dye was extracted.

that twisting from its spiral below grows wide into a bell;
the trumpet that, when it takes in air upon the sea, makes full
with sound the shores that beneath either Phoebus[56] lie.
Then also when the god put it to his lips, made moist by his soggy beard,
and blew upon it, it sounded the bidden retreat, 340
and it was heard by all the waves of land and sea,
and all the waves that heard it were confined.
The sea now has a shore, the full rivers within their channels are contained,
the streams subside, the hills seem to come forth;
the soil rises, the ground swells with the decreasing waves: 345
and after the long day the woods their uncovered crests
reveal, and keep upon their foliage the abandoned mud.
The world had been restored. After he saw that it was void
and that deep silence oppressed the desolate lands,
Deucalion,[57] tears upwelling, speaks to Pyrrha[58] thus: 350
"O sister, O wife, O woman sole to survive,
whom common race and paternal cousin's state,
then marriage bed, now danger itself to me did join,
of all the lands that the settings and risings of the sun behold,
are we two the multitude; the rest the seas possess. 355
This title to our lives is even now not yet
quite sure. Even now the clouds bring terror to my mind.
If you without me had been spared by fate,
what would you think, my poor dear? How could you alone
endure the fear? With whom to console you would you grieve? 360
For, trust me, if you as well the sea had claimed, would I
have followed you, my wife, and the sea would own me as well!
O would that I might restore the peoples with my father's skills
and pour[59] souls into the molded shape of earth!
The mortal race resides in the two of us— 365
the gods have so decreed—we remain as models of humankind."
    When he had spoken, they continued to weep. They decided to beseech
the power of heaven and to seek aid through the sacred lots.
Without delay together they approach Cephisus'[60] stream,
as yet not clear, but already cutting its normal course. 370
From there, when they had bedewed with lustral waters
their clothes and heads, they wend unto the holy goddess' shrine
their steps; its pediments were green
with grimy moss, its altars stood unlit.
As soon as they touched the temple's steps, each fell prone 375

---

56 I.e., both at the rising and the setting of Phoebus, god of the sun.
57 Son of Prometheus.
58 Daughter of Epimetheus, the brother of Prometheus.
59 The image is from casting metals for statues.
60 The Cephisus river runs through Phocis and Boeotia.

upon the ground, and in fear gave kisses to the cold stone;
and said, "If the spirits divine by righteous prayers
are softened and yield, if the wrath of the gods is turned,
O Themis, tell by what means the fault of our race may be
repaired and bring help, O most merciful goddess, to its engulfed estate."    380
The goddess is moved and gave her prophetic response: "From the temple go
and cover your head and loosen the binding of your clothes
and toss behind your backs your great mother's bones."
They were for long struck dumb; the silence was broken by the voice
of Pyrrha first, and the commands of the goddess she refused to obey;    385
that she be forgiven she prays with trembling voice, and fears
to wound her mother's shade by tossing her bones.
And meanwhile they review the rendered prophecy's words,
obscure in their hidden tropes, turning them over between themselves.
And then Prometheus'[61] son with calming words Epimetheus'[62] child    390
did soothe, and "Either our good sense," he says, "deceives,
or the oracles are pious and counsel nothing ill.
The great mother is the earth. The stones in the body of the earth
I think are called bones. We are ordered to throw these behind our backs."
Although the Titan daughter[63] by the divination of her spouse is moved,    395
their hope is yet in doubt; to such extent do both distrust
divine advice. But what will it hurt to try?
Descending, they veil their heads and unbelted their clothes
and cast behind their footsteps the commanded stones.
The rocks—who would believe it without the witness of antiquity? —    400
begin to put off their hardness and their rigid state,
and soften gradually and, once softened, take on form.
Anon, when they grew and a softer nature came
upon them, one can see, yet not quite clear,
a form of man, but as though from marble only begun,[64]    405
much like rough images, not fully done.
The part of them, however, that was moist with a kind of sap,
and earthen, this was changed to serve as flesh;
the solid part that could not be bent was changed to bone;
what once was vein[65] remained under the same name:    410
and in a short time by the power of the gods the rocks
the man had cast with his hands took on the appearance of men,
and from the woman's cast was woman made anew.

---

61 Prometheus means "Forethought."
62 Epimetheus means "Afterthought."
63 More precisely, granddaughter of Iapetus, the Titan father of Epimetheus and Prometheus.
64 This passage is strong evidence that sculpture is not only important in particular myths such as
   Pygmalion and Niobe, but that Ovid conceives in sculptural terms his primary interest, the
   formation and re-formation of humanity.
65 I. e., pores or veins in the earth.

*Deucalion and Pyrrha, Solis*

From this we are a race both hard and acquainted with toil,
and give instructive proof of what origin we were born.                 415

### 416-51   *Python Slain by Apollo*

The earth gave birth to the other animals in diverse forms
of her free will, after the old moisture by the fire of the sun
had warmed, and the mud and watery swamps
had swollen with heat, and the fertile seeds of things,
when fed by the enlivening soil as in the mother's womb,                420
increased and in the interval took on a certain shape.
Thus when the seven-flowing Nile has left the soggy fields
and to its former channel returned its floods,
and when the ethereal star[66] has made the fresh slime hot,
the plowmen find many living things among the upturned clods;           425
among them some they see completed by
the time of birth itself, some they see only begun
and of their parts deprived and in the self-same body oft
one part alive, the other part only crude earth.
Because when moisture and heat are duly mixed,                          430
conception occurs, and from these two elements all things arise;
though fire is no friend of water, humid heat creates
all things, and this discordant concord is favorable for their birth.
And hence, the earth, all muddy from the recent flood,
grew warm again by the celestial suns and high heat;                    435
she put forth countless species, partly the ancient shapes
did she restore, partly new monsters did she create.
Indeed it was not her intent, but, vast Python, you as well,

66 The sun.

she bore then, and for the new peoples, O serpent unknown,
a terror you were; for so much of the mountain did you occupy.          440
The god who bears the bow[67] (never before having used
his deadly arms except for fugitive does and goats),
destroyed him, weighed down by a thousand darts,
the quiver nearly used, the venom through the dark wounds spent.
And lest the fame of the deed be destroyed by passing time,          445
he founded, sacred with their festive contests, games,
the so-called Pythian after the vanquished serpent's name.
Here any of the youths who with hand or feet or wheel
had won would receive the honor of an oaken branch.
No laurel was there yet, and, comely for their lengthy curls,          450
his temples Phoebus bound with leaves from any tree.

### 452-567   *Apollo and Daphne*

The first of Phoebus' loves was Daphne, Peneus'[68] child,
which no unwitting chance supplied, but rather Cupid's cruel wrath.
The Delian,[69] grown proud by the serpent's recent defeat,
had spied him trying to bend to the tight-stretched string the horns of the bow;  455
"What business have you, naughty boy, with the arms of the brave?"
he said; "Those ornaments you have for our shoulders are fit,
who to the wild can give and do give to the foe well-aimed wounds,
who recently laid with countless arrows the swollen Python low,

*Apollo and Python, Baur*

---

67 Apollo.
68 A river in Thessaly, a region of northern Greece.
69 Apollo, born on the island of Delos.

whose plague-bearing belly weighed down the fields.                                    460
You there, be content to inspire with your torch
one love or another, and do not to our praises assert a claim."
The son of Venus said to him, "Phoebus, let yours pierce all,
it's *you* my bow shall pierce; and as much as animals all
cede place to divinity, so much the less is your glory than mine."      465
He spoke and, with the air displaced by his shaken wings,
he promptly stood still on shady Parnassus' peak,
and from his arrow-bearing quiver drew out two darts
of different effect: this one chases off, that one causes love.
The one that causes, inlaid with gold, gleams with sharpened barb;     470
the one that chases is blunt and at the end of its shaft has lead.
The god plants this one in the Peneid nymph, but with that
he wounds the Apollonian marrow straight through the bone.
Straightway the one's in love, the other the very name of lover flees;
in woodland recesses and skins of captured wild beasts,                475
the rival of unwed Phoebe,[70] she takes delight.
A band confined her tresses unruly arranged;
her suitors were many, but averse to their suits,
intolerant and free of any man, she roams the trackless groves,
nor cares what Hymen is,[71] or marriage or love.                      480
Her father often said, "daughter, you owe to me a son-in-law;
her father often said, "grandchildren you owe to me, my child;"
but she, despising the marriage torches as a reproach,
had covered her lovely face with a bashful blush,
and clinging to her father's neck with her coaxing arms,               485
replied, "O father dearest, grant that I may enjoy
virginity forever. To Diana her father once granted this gift."
Her wish he granted, indeed; but your beauty denies what you
desire, and your lovely form is opposed to your prayer.
In love is Phoebus, and desires to marry Daphne, once she's seen,      490
and what he desires, he hopes for, and by his prophecies is deceived.
And as the lightweight stubble is burned once the grain's removed,
as hedges by campfires burn that the wayfarer by chance
too close did place or left when breaking camp at dawn,
just so the god went up in flames, just so with all his heart          495
he burns, and by hoping feeds his sterile love.
He looks at the tresses falling unadorned to her neck,
and "What if they were combed?," he says; he sees, shining with fire
like stars, her eyes; he sees her lips, which to have seen
is not enough; he praises her fingers and hands                        500
and arms and limbs, for the most part bare:

---

70 Phoebus' sister, Diana, here as goddess of the hunt and chastity.
71 Processional marriage song and god of marriage.

if any are hidden, he deems them better. Faster than the gentle breeze
she flees, nor does she stop at the words of him who calls her back:
"O nymph, daughter of Peneus, I pray, please wait; I pursue not as a foe:
O nymph, please wait! So the lamb flees the wolf, the stag the lion,                505
the doves the eagle with trembling wing,
each one its enemies. But the cause of my pursuit is love.
Ah wretched me! I fear you may fall down or, unworthy to wound,
your legs be marked by the briars and I be cause of pain to you.
The places where you rush are rough. With more restraint, I pray              510
do run, and check your flight: with more restraint will I pursue!
Inquire who likes you. Not some man of the hills,
no shepherd I, not here over my herds and flocks
do I as rustic watch. You know not, you know not, O thoughtless one,
from whom you flee, and, hence, you flee. Me the Delphic land              515
and Claros[72] and Tenedos[73] and Patara's[74] royal household serve.
My father is Jupiter. Through me what will be and was
and is is shown; through me do songs and the strings agree.
Though ours is sure, than ours is one arrow yet
more sure, that made within this empty breast its wound.                  520
The find of medicine is mine, and throughout the world I'm called
the Helper, and subject to us is the power of herbs.
Alas for me, that herb there's none to cure my love,
that arts are useless to their master that are useful to all."
As he was about to say more, Peneus' daughter ran in fright              525
and fled, both him and his unfinished words,
and even then she seemed fair: her body was bared by the winds,
the countering gusts made the opposing garments shake,
and gentle breezes left the driven locks in a trail,
and beauty's form was increased by flight. But since no more              530
the youthful god endures to waste his blandishments, and as Amor himself
kept urging, he follows her tracks with quickened pace.
As when the hound of Gallic breed[75] espies the hare upon
the open field, and this one seeks with feet his prey, that one his escape:
The one, it seems, near the catch, and now, now more,                    535
expects he has it and presses his pace with snout outstretched,
the other is unsure if it's been caught and from the very jaws
escapes and leaves behind the molesting mouth:
just so were the god and maid, he quick with hope, she with fear.
Abetted with Amor's wings, the pursuer, though,                          540
is faster and denies all rest and to the back of her who flees

---

72 Town of Ionia with an oracle of Apollo.
73 Island off the coast near the site of Troy, with a temple of Apollo.
74 Coastal city of Lycia, region of Anatolia (Asia Minor), with an oracle of Apollo.
75 Probably the greyhound.

bends near and breathes upon the locks spreading over her neck.
Her strength consumed, she paled, and, vanquished by                                    543
[the toil of flight, she says, "Earth, open wide, or spoil
by change this shape, which caused me to be harmed.][76]                               545
the toil of swift flight, looked to Peneus' stream.                                    544a
"O father," she says," bring help, if you rivers have divine strength.                  546
Destroy by changing the shape with which I too much pleased."                           547
Her prayer scarcely ended, a heavy torpor seized her limbs;
her soft bosom is girdled with slender bark;
her hair into leaves, her arms into branches grow;                                     550
her feet of late so swift in lazy roots are fixed;
a treetop is her head; but her shining beauty remains.
Yet Phoebus even loves the tree, and, right hand placed upon the trunk,
he feels her breast still beating in fear beneath the bark
and, grasping the branches with his arms like limbs,                                   555
puts kisses to the wood: but the wood refused those kisses still.
To which the god replied, "But since my wife you cannot be,
you shall be mine even as a tree. You my hair will hold
forever, you my quiver, O laurel,[77] you my lyre.
And Latin generals you will join when joyful voice                                     560
the Triumph sings and the Capitoline[78] views the long parades.
At the Augustan doors,[79] as well, shall you stand
most faithful guard before the house and there protect the oak between.[80]
And as my head is youthful with locks unshorn,
so you as well with perpetual honors of leaf be clad."                                 565
The words of Paean[81] were done. Now the laurel with her leaves
gave nod and seemed to have moved her top like a head.

### 568-746   Io, Argus

Haemonia[82] has a vale by woody cliffs
enclosed; they call it Tempe: through it Peneus[83], erupting from                      570
the foot of Pindus,[84] with foaming waters runs.
And by his heavy falls he gathers fogs stirring with fine mists,

---

76 Tarrant's *OCT* brackets 544-45:
   [victa labore fugae 'Tellus' ait 'hisce, vel istam544
   quae facit ut laedar mutando perde figuram.']545
77 Daphne in Greek means "Laurel" or "Bay-tree."
78 Hill of Rome, site of the Temple of Jupiter.
79 Two laurel trees grew on the Palatine Hill before the palace of the emperor Augustus (63 B.C. - 14 A.D.).
80 Augustus, as savior of his people, had received the wreath of oak, the *corona civica,* the "civic crown" awarded for saving the life of another in battle. The wreath was hung over the door of his palace. Perhaps this Roman conclusion to the story hearkens back to the point that before the laurel an oaken wreath was the victor's award at Delphi (see 449).
81 Apollo as god of healing.
82 By metonymy, Thessaly, named after its eponymous hero Haemon, the father of Thessalus.
83 Major river of Thessaly, flowing into the Aegean Sea through the vale of Tempe.
84 A mountain range separating Epirus and Thessaly.

*Apollo and Python, Apollo and Daphne, Anonymous Venice ca. 1513*

and rains down upon the tops of the forest with dew
and wearies more than neighboring parts with sound.
This was the home, this the seat, this the inner recess
of the great stream; residing here in his rocky cave                    575
to his waves he gives laws, and to the nymphs that worship his waves.
The native rivers gather there first,
unsure whether to congratulate the father or console—
the poplar-bearing Sperchios[85] and the Enipeus[86] that takes no rest
and old Apidanos[87] and Aeas[88] and Amphrysos[89] soft;                580
And soon other rivers who, wherever their current drove,
made weary with wandering, led down their waters to the sea.

### 583-600   *Io and Jupiter*

   The only river not there is Inachus, who, in a deep cavern hid,
increases with tears his waters and most wretchedly bemoans
the loss of his daughter Io. Whether she lives he doesn't know,         585
or if she's among the shades, but whom he never finds
he thinks to be nowhere and in his mind fears things worse.
When Jupiter had seen her returning from her father's stream,
he said, "O maiden, worthy of Jove, and by your couch

---

85 This river flows into the Aegean Sea by way of the Gulf of Malia.
86 Flowing north, a tributary of the Peneus.
87 Flowing north, a tributary of the Enipeus.
88 River of Epirus, flowing into the Adriatic Sea. Also spelled Aous, according to Pliny, *Nat. Hist.* 3.
    145, called by the Greeks the Aoos.
89 River of Thessaly, flowing into the Aegean Sea by way of the Gulf of Pagasa.

about to make some man or other happy, seek the shadows of                           590
deep groves," and he beckoned towards the shady glens,
"while it is hot and the sun is highest in mid-course.
But if you're afraid to enter the lairs of the wild alone,
a god will be your guardian as you enter the safe recesses of the glens,
and not a common god, but I who wield with my great hand                             595
the scepter of heaven, but I who hurl the wide-ranging thunderbolt.
Do not flee from me," for fleeing she was. Already had she left
the pastures of Lerna[90] and Mt. Lyrceum's[91] fields, planted thick
with trees, when the god induced a dark fog and hid far and wide
the lands, and checked her flight and stole her shame.                               600

### 601-723  *Argus and Mercury*

As Juno, meanwhile, looked down into Argos' midst,
amazed that the swifts clouds had wrought the face of night
upon the shining day, and having sensed that those clouds
were neither from the river nor released from the humid earth,
she looks about for the whereabouts of her spouse, as one                            605
who knows the tricks of her mate and so often caught him in the act!
Not finding him in heaven, she says, "mistaken or misused
am I," and, gliding down from the ethereal heights,
she landed on the earth and bade the clouds recede.
His spouse's arrival he had sensed in advance and changed                            610

*Io and Jupiter, Baur*

---

90 The spring inhabited by the Hydra, near Argos.
91 A spring on Mt. Lyrceum, on the border of Arcadia, the source of the Inachus river that runs through
  the Argolid.

into a shining heifer the appearance of Inachus' child
(the cow, too, was lovely). Saturnia[92] applauds the beauty of the cow,
although unwilling, and whose it is and from where, she fails not to ask,
and to what flock it belongs, as if she didn't know the truth.
That she was born of earth is Jupiter's lie, that the author of the deed          615
be left unsought. Saturnia requests her as a gift.
What should he do? To sign over his love is a cruel thing,
but to refuse, suspicious. From that side, a sense of shame persuades,
from this side, love protests. Shame would have been conquered by love,
except that, were so slight a gift as a cow denied                                620
to partner of kinship and couch, it could not have seemed a cow.
With concubine surrendered, the goddess did not at once shed all alarm,
both fearing Jove and anxiously[93] suspecting a trick,
until she handed her over to Argus, Arestor's[94] son, to guard.
    Now Argus' head was girt with a hundred eyes;                               625
By turns would pairs of these take their repose,
while all the others kept watch and at their post remained.
Wherever he stood, within his view was Io held;
whichever way he turned, he kept Io before his eyes.
He lets her graze during the day; when the sun is below the deep earth,          630
he shuts her up and puts a bridle about her undeserving neck.
She feeds on the leaves of trees and bitter herbs,
and for a bed, on the earth, not always laid with grass,
she sleeps distraught and drinks from muddy streams.
When even as a suppliant to Argus she sought to stretch                          635
her arms, to Argus she had no arms to stretch;
with mouth that sought to complain she mooed,
and at the sounds was scared and terrified by her own voice.
She came as well to the banks where she oft was wont to play,
the banks of Inachus, and when in the water she saw                              640
the strange horns, she was frightened and in panic fled.
The Naiads[95] are ignorant, ignorant is Inachus himself
of who she is. Yet behind her father she trails, and trails her sisters, too,
and lets herself be touched and to her admirers presents herself.
Old Inachus stretched forth the grass that he had plucked;                       645
she licks his hand and kisses her father's palms,
nor holds back her tears and, if only words were to come,
for help she would beg and tell her name and fate.
The letter in place of words that her hoof had drawn in the dust
produced the sorrowful sign that her body had been changed.                      650

---

92 The epithet Saturnia signifies that Juno is the daughter of Saturn.
93 "Alarm", "feared," and " anxiously" translate *metum... timuit... fuit anxia*, a good example of Ovid's
    use of *variatio*, the rhetorical figure of variety.
94 Unknown.
95 River nymphs.

"O wretched me," exclaims father Inachus, and (as she moaned)
embracing the horns and the heifer's snowy neck,
"O wretched me," is his refrain. "Are you the child I sought
through every land? Unfound were you a lighter source
of grief than found. You're silent and to ours no mutual words     655
return, but draw only sighs from your deep breast,
and all you can do is respond with mooing to my words.
Yet I in my ignorance made ready for you the torches and marriage bed;
my foremost hope was for a son-in-law, for progeny, the next;
your husband now from the herd must come, from the herd a son as well.     660
Nor may I end such terrible pain by death;
but being a god is harmful and the door of death,
closed shut, extends our grief for all eternity."
Then star-eyed Argus drives him[96] away lamenting so,
and takes the daughter stolen from her father to another field,     665
while he himself a far-off lofty mountain peak
secures, from where in all directions to sit and watch.
Nor can the ruler of the gods the Phoronid's[97] vast misfortune more
abide, and calls his son, the one the shining Pleiad[98] bore,
and gives him the orders for Argus' death.     670
It takes little time to fit the wings to his feet, and to his mighty hand
the sleep-bringing staff, and to his tresses a cap.
When these he had arranged, from his father's citadel the son of Jove
sprang down to earth. The cap he then removed
and set aside the wings; the staff alone was kept,     675
with which like a shepherd he drives his stolen goats as he roams
about the countryside, and sings upon his ordered reeds.
With this new sound Juno's guard was taken. "But you,
whoever you are, could sit down with me on this rock,"
says Argus, "since there's no place for the flock     680
with richer grass, and you see the shade that shepherds like."
And Atlas' grandson[99] sat down, and, chatting long about this and that,
in converse held the passing day, and in singing to the fitted reeds,
attempts with song to overcome those watchful lights.[100]
The other strives, just the same, to conquer gentle sleep,     685
and though upon his eyes in part a slumbers falls,
another part no less keeps watch. He inquires as well (for the pipe
was recently invented) how it was it came to be.

---

96 Translating *maerentem*; with *maerentes*, "them."

97 Io, expressed by the patronymic formed from Phoroneus, the son of Inachus. Such imprecision in the
use of patronymics is common.

98 Maia, mother of Mercury (Hermes), was one of the Pleiades, the seven daughters of Pleione and
Atlas.

99 Ovid calls Mercury here *Atlantiades*, the patronymic of Atlas, since Mercury's mother was Maia, the
daughter of Atlas and Pleione.

100 Ovid repeatedly refers to the hundred eyes of Argus as "lights."

### 689-712   Mercury's Tale of Syrinx and Pan

The god then said, "In Arcadia's mountains chill,
among the Hamadryads[101] of Nonacris[102] a Naiad there was,                           690
most famous; Syrinx she was called by the Nymphs.
Not only once had she escaped the Satyrs' pursuit
and whatever gods the shady wood and fertile land
contained. She worshiped the Ortygian[103] goddess in her
pursuits, especially in virginity, and, dressed in Diana's way,                          695
she would have deceived and been thought Latona's child, had not
her bow been made of ivory, Diana's made of gold.
But even so she did deceive. As she returns from Lycaeus'[104] hill,
Pan sees her, and, his head encircled with sharp pine,
addresses to her words like these,"[105] —those words were left unsaid:                 700
already, his prayers refused, the nymph through the wild
had fled until to sandy Ladon's[106] peaceful stream
she came. Now there, as the waters blocked her course,
she begged her watery sisters to modify her form.
And Pan, when thinking he had Syrinx within his grasp,                                   705
instead of the nymph's body had embraced marshy reeds;
and when he sighed to himself, the wind that moved in the reeds
had made the merest sound, like someone's complaint.
By this new skill and pleasant sound the god was charmed
and said, "This conversation with you I'll keep even yet."                               710
and thus, with reeds unequal, held fast by wax,
among themselves conjoined, he kept the name[107] of the girl.

### 713-23   Argus Beheaded

As he was about to tell all this, the Cyllenian[108] saw
that all the eyes had sunk, those lights closed shut by sleep.
At once he stops his speech and makes the slumber firm                                   715
by stroking those languid lights with his magic wand.
Without delay, he strikes him as he nods, with his crescent sword,
just where the head is next the neck, and casts him from the rock,
all gory, and stains the jagged cliff with blood.
You're fallen, Argus, and, for all those lights, whatever light                          720

---

101 Nymphs whose lives are co-terminous (Greek *hama* 'together') with the oaks (Greek *drys*) in which
    they dwell.
102 Nonacris, a mountain, city, and region, is here used by synecdoche (part for the whole) or metonymy
    for Arcadia.
103 Referring to "Quail Island," the old name of Delos, where Diana was born.
104 Mt. Lycaeus, meaning "Wolf-Mountain," was sacred to Zeus and Pan.
105 At this point Ovid breaks into Mercury's embedded tale and quickly finishes the story himself.
106 River in Arcadia.
107 Syrinx means "Pipe."
108 Mercury, born on Mt. Cyllene in Arcadia.

*Pan and Syrinx, Baur*

you had is put out, and those hundred eyes are held by one long night.
Saturnia[109] picks them up and in the wings of her bird
inlays, and fills with brilliant gems the tail.

### 724-46   *Io Restored to Human Form*

At once is she inflamed, nor delayed was the time for her wrath:
she hurled a frightening Erinys[110] against the eyes and mind                725
of her Argive rival, and planted hidden goads within her breast,
and drove her out as a fugitive through all the world.
You waited, O Nile, as the last of her boundless toils;
as soon as she had touched you, she fell to her knees
upon the bank of your stream and, with her neck thrown back            730
to raise her face (it was all she could raise) towards the stars above,
with moaning and tears and a mooing that made doleful sounds
she seemed to voice her complaint to Jove and to pray for an end of woe.
Embracing the neck of his wife[111] with his arms,
he begs that she end the punishment at last and says, "In time       735
to come put off your fear; she[112] will never be a cause of pain
to you," and bids the Stygian marshes heed what he said.
The goddess appeased, the other receives her former face
becoming what she was before. The bristles from her body flee,
the horns decrease, smaller becomes the orb of her eye,               740

---

109 Juno; see on 1. 612.
110 Here the Greek for "Avenging Fury." Contrast the note on 1. 241.
111 Juno.
112 Io.

*Argus and Mercury, Baur*

her gaping mouth contracts, both shoulders and hands return,
the hooves dissolve, each disappearing into five nails.
Of ox no form remains, except her radiance;
the nymph, content in the use of two feet,
stands up, and fears to speak lest in the manner of a cow          745
she moo, and shyly tries again her interrupted speech.
Now worshiped is she as a most honored goddess by the linen-wearing[113] throng.

### 747-79  *Epaphus and Phaethon*

Believed is it now that Epaphus[114] was born of the seed
of Jove at last, and, throughout the cities, he possesses shrines
nearby his mother.[115] To him the equal in mind and years          750
was Phaethon, born of Sol,[116] who once was talking big,
not ceding rank to him and haughty in having Phoebus as his sire.
The grandson of Inachus couldn't stand it; "You're crazy to believe,"
he says, "all your mother says, and you're puffed up with the idea of a sire
who's not." Though Phaethon blushed, his shame repressed his wrath;          755
he took to Clymene, his mother, Epaphus' reproach;
"And what will make you grieve yet more," he said, "O mother, free as I am,

---

113 Referring to the Egyptians, whose Isis the Greeks identified with their Io.
114 The name is derived by folk-etymology from the Greek verb meaning "to touch," recalling how Zeus "touched" Io at the mouth of the Nile and made her pregnant with Epaphus, whose name is perhaps tied to Apis, the Egyptian bull-god.
115 The temples of Isis, identified with Io.
116 The Sun, a common name for Apollo and Phoebus in Ovid.

and fierce as I am, I was silent. That such insults could be said
against us and could not be refuted is a shame!
But if in fact I was created from celestial seed,                                    760
give forth a sign of kinship so great and assert my heavenly birth!
He spoke and wrapped his arms around his mother's neck,
and by his own and Merops'[117] head and his sisters' wedding brands
he prayed that of his true father he be granted signs.
It was not clear if Clymene was stirred more by Phaethon's prayers                   765
or more by pique at the alleged charge; and to the sky she stretched
both arms and, gazing at the light of the sun,
replied, "By this light, glorious with glistening rays,
which hears and sees us, my son, to you I swear
that you were sprung from him you see, from him who controls                         770
the world, the Sun. If I speak false, may he deny
his sight to me, and let yon light to our eyes be the very last.
And no long task is it for you to know your father's Penates;[118]
the home from where he rises is adjacent to our land.
In fact, if you wish, go and seek the truth from him."                              775
He leaps at once with joy at what his mother says,
and Phaethon conceives of highest heaven with his mind,
and through his Ethiopians and Indians, set beneath the sunlit fires,
he passes, and eagerly approaches his father's rising-place.

---

117 Merops, King of the Ethiopians and, as husband of Clymene, the assumed mortal father of
     Phaethon.
118 Household-gods, metonymy for "house."

# BOOK 2

### 1-400   Phaethon continued

The palace of the Sun with its lofty columns rose high,
illumined with glittering gold and pyrope,[1] imitating flames;
bright ivory covered its ridge poles,
its folding double doors gleamed with argent light.
Its substance was outdone by craftsmanship: for Mulciber[2] there          5
had carved the seas girding the lands in the midst,
the orb of earth and the sky that hangs above the orb.
The wave contains the sky-blue gods, Triton[3] of song
and changeful Proteus[4] and Aegaeon,[5] weighing down
the huge backs of whales with his limbs,                                    10
and Doris[6] and her daughters, of whom some seem to swim,
while others sit on a rock and dry their green hair,

---

1 Red bronze, or alloy of gold and bronze, or any red gems like garnets. The word, meaning "fire-faced,"
  is as rare in Latin as in English.
2 A title of Vulcan, god of the forge and fire, from the Latin verb for 'stroke, graze lightly.'
3 Son of Neptune, Triton is a sea-god, half man, half fish in form. He blows on a conch to stir or quell
  the waves.
4 A sea-god who herded Neptune's (Poseidon's) seals.
5 This giant, also called Briareus, had a hundred hands.
6 A sea-goddess, mother of the Nereids and other sea-nymphs.

while others ride on fishes: their faces are not all alike,
and yet not quite different, as among sisters is right.
The land has men and cities and woods and wild                              15
and rivers and nymphs and all the other spirits of the countryside.
Above these is set the image of the shining sky,
with six signs on the doors on the right and as many on the left.
  As soon as Clymene's child had made the steep climb,
arrived and entered his doubted parent's home,                              20
straightway to his father's face he bore his steps
and stopped at some distance, for he could not endure
close up the light: in purple robe arrayed, Phoebus sat
upon his throne that with emeralds shone bright.
To right and left were Day and Month and Year                               25
and Centuries and Hours, in equal intervals placed,
and Spring stood there, newly bound with flowering crown,
and naked Summer stood there and wore garlands made from ears of grain,
and, stained by trampled grapes, Autumn stood there
and icy Winter, shaggy with his hoary locks.                                30
  The Sun, as he sat in the midst with his all-seeing eyes,
observed the youth's terror at the novelty of things
and says, "Why do you come? What do you seek in this citadel,
O Phaethon, offspring a father could scarce deny?"
And he replies, "O universal light of the boundless world,                  35
O father Phoebus,[7] if you grant me the use of this name
and Clymene conceals no guilt beneath a false claim,
give tokens, sire, that I be thought your son in truth
and take away this error from our minds!"[8]
The father, after he had spoken, removed those sparkling rays               40
encircling all his head and commanded him to draw near.
Embracing him, he says, "You don't deserve
to be denied as mine, and Clymene's report of your origin is true;
and that you be less in doubt, ask whatever favor you please, that you
may have it directly from me! As witness of this promise let that marsh[9]  45
the gods swear by be present, though to my eyes unknown!"
No sooner had he finished, than the other demands for a day
his father's chariot and the right to guide his swift-footed steeds.
  The father regretted that he had sworn: three times and a fourth
he struck his illustrious head, saying, "How rash                           50
my words were made by yours; O would that I might refuse
that promise! This one thing, my son, would I deny you, I confess.
But warn against this action I can: your intention is unsafe!

---

7 Phoebus as "Bright One" is the appropriate appellation for Apollo in this sentence.
8 The "royal we" here is a nice touch for a youth seeking to prove his royal status.
9 The Styx.

You seek great favors, Phaethon, which neither suit
your strength nor your youthful years:                                55
your fate is mortal, not mortal is what you desire.
Indeed, to more than the gods above are allowed to achieve
do you in ignorance aspire: they all do as they like,
yet none of them is able to stand in the fire-bringing car
but me; even he who vast Olympus rules,                               60
who hurls the savage lightning with his terrible right hand,
will not drive this chariot: and what have we greater than Jove?
So arduous is the beginning of the path that even fresh with the morn
the horses struggle: the highest path is in the middle of the sky,
from where to behold the sea and lands often causes even me          65
to fear and makes my heart tremble with terror and awe;
the final path is straight down and requires sure control:
then even she who receives me in her waves below,
even Tethys[10] herself often fears that I'll be dashed headlong.
What's more, the sky is by a constant spinning seized                70
and draws and turns with a rapid whirlwind the lofty stars.
I strive against it, and the force doesn't conquer me,
although it does all else, and against the rapid orbit I am borne.
Suppose you have the chariot. What will you do? Will you be able to advance
against the spinning poles so that the swift axis not carry you away?  75
You think, perhaps, that the groves and cities of the gods
are there and the shrines rich with gifts: in fact
the journey is through the treacherous lairs and forms of wild beasts!
Although you hold to the course and are not diverted by mistake,
you still will pass through the horns of the opposing bull,          80
the Haemonian[11] archer and the violent Lion's maw
and, as he bends his arms in a long bow,
the Scorpion and the Crab, bowing in the opposite direction his arms.
The spirited four-footed ones with the fires
contained in their breasts, exhaled through nostrils and mouths,     85
you have no power to control; even me they hardly obey
when their keen spirits have warmed and their necks oppose the reins.
But you, lest I be the author to you of a fatal gift,
my son, take heed, and, while you can, correct your wish!
Indeed, that you may believe yourself born of our blood,             90
you're seeking sure tokens: in fearing, sure tokens I give
and prove myself a father with a father's dread. Regard my face,
behold my eyes, and would that you could plant them
within your heart and there within perceive a father's care!
Upon all the wealth the world contains cast your gaze at last        95

---

10 Goddess of the sea, by metonymy, the sea.
11 Thessalian (see on 1. 569). The archer is Orion.

and from the good things of sky and earth and sea, so many and so great,
demand what you will; no rebuff will you endure.
From this one thing I seek release, whose real name is punishment,
not honor. Punishment as a favor, Phaethon, is your demand!
O foolish one, why do you cling to my neck with your coaxing arms?          100
O do not doubt! It will be granted (by the waters of the Styx we swore),
whatever you choose; but do more wisely choose!"
       He ended his warning; yet the other rejected his words,
both pressing for his request and burning with desire for the car.
And so, the father having delayed as long as he could,          105
led forth the youth to the lofty chariot, Vulcan's gift.
Its axle was golden, golden the tongue, golden the wheel's
rimmed curve, silver the order of the spokes;
and over the yoke chrysolites and well placed gems
returned to Phoebus his reflected bright light.          110
       As great-hearted Phaethon admired those things
and examined the work, lo, awake, from her golden-red source,
Aurora made open the purple doors and rose-
filled courts: the stars disperse, their ranks
by Lucifer[12] driven, the last to leave his post in the sky.          115
As Titan sees Lucifer seek the earth and the world grow red,
the horns, as well, fading away, as it were, of the last of the moon,
he orders the swift Horae[13] to yoke the steeds.
The goddesses swiftly fulfill the commands
and lead, breathing fire and filled with ambrosia, from the lofty stalls          120
the four-footed ones and apply the clashing reins.
The father then touched the face of his son
with holy liniment to tolerate the violent flame
and placed the rays upon his hair and spoke from his anxious heart,
repeating the sighs that foretold his grief.          125
"At least if these admonitions of a father you can obey,
then spare the whip, my boy, and more firmly use the reins!
Because they race at will, to restrain their spirit is your task.
And do not choose the path through the five zones straight ahead!
The track is cut on a slant with a wide curve,          130
and, bound within the limit of the three zones and poles,
avoids the south and Arctos[14] joined to Aquilo's[15] winds:
Let your course be there, the wheel-tracks you will plainly see;
and so the sky and earth may have equal heat,

---

12 Lucifer, the "Light-bringer," the Morning Star, was the son of Aurora and Cephalus. He is also the
    father of Ceyx (see 11. 271 with note).
13 The Hours, as at 25.
14 Ursa Major, the Bear.
15 The god of the north or northeast wind.

do not press low nor drive the chariot[16] sky high.                                      135
Go higher and you will cremate the celestial homes,
go lower, the earth; your safest route is by the middle course.
Don't let the wheel[17] turn you towards the twisted Serpent too much to the right,
nor too much to the left towards the Altar pressed low:
between the two hold your course. To Fortune I entrust all else.                           140
I hope that she helps and looks after you better than you look after yourself.
While I am speaking, moist night has touched the turning posts
implanted on the Hesperian[18] shore. We're not free to delay!
We're summoned: Aurora shines forth with shadows dispelled.
Take up the reins with your hand, or, if your heart is moveable,                           145
our counsel, not our chariot, employ!
And while you can and even yet on firm ground stand
and not yet drive untrained the axles[19] wrongly sought,
let *me* give to the earth that light that you unharmed behold!"
He mounts the light chariot with his youthful form                                         150
and standing tall, with his hands at the touch of the offered reins
takes joy, and from there to his reluctant father gives thanks.
Swift Pyrois, meanwhile, and Eous and Aethon, the steeds
of Sol, and Phlegon[20] as fourth fill the air
with flame-bearing snorting and beat at the gates with their hooves.                       155
When Tethys,[21] ignorant of her grandson's fate,
had opened them, and access was granted to the boundless sky,
they seize the course and with feet running through the air
divide the resisting clouds and, raised aloft upon their wings,
excel the winds of Eurus,[22] that from the same direction rise.                           160
But light was the weight that not one of the horses of Sol
could recognize, and their yoke lacked its wonted gravity.
As curved ships falter without a proper load
and by excessive lightness are born unstable upon the sea,
just so the chariot, lacking its usual burden, gives a leap into the air,                  165
and from below is jolted to the heights like an unmanned car.
As soon as they felt it, the yoked four horses rush forth
and leave the worn path behind nor in their earlier order run.
He's frightened, himself, knowing not how to control the imparted reins,
nor where the path, nor how to command them, if he knows.                                  170
For then the cool Triones[23] first grew warm from the rays,

---

16 Translating *currum*; with *cursum*, "your course."
17 Metonymy for "chariot."
18 "Western" or "Evening."
19 Another use of metonymy for "chariot."
20 The names of the Sun's four horses are meaningful and of Greek origin: "Fiery," "Dawn," "Flash," and "Flame."
21 Wife of Oceanus and mother of Clymene.
22 The god of the east winds.

attempting in vain to be dipped into the forbidden sea;
the Serpent, that was set beside the icy pole,
before always sluggish from the cold and dangerous to none,
grew hot and from the heat assumed unusual wrath:                          175
Boötes,[24] you as well, they say, were disturbed and fled,
although you were slow and held back by your cart.
    But as unhappy Phaethon from the ethereal heights
perceived the earth spreading out farther and farther below,
he paled, and his knees shook with sudden fear,                            180
and over his eyes the shadows spread despite such light.
And now he would prefer never to have touched his father's steeds,
displeased to know his kin and to have prevailed with his request;
desiring now to be called the son of Merops,[25] he is born along,
just like a ship of pine, by Boreas dashed, whose helmsman has let         185
the vanquished rudder go and left it to the gods and his oaths.
What should he do? Much of heaven lies abandoned at his back,
before his eyes lies more: in his mind he measures both,
and now—where he's not fated to arrive —
he looks to the west, at times looks back to the east,                     190
and, knowing not what to do, stands amazed, neither releasing the reins
nor able to hold them, and does not know the horses' names.
He trembles as he also beholds wondrous things scattered across
the varied sky and images of huge wild beasts.
In that place Scorpio curves his arms into twin bows                       195
and extends, with his tail and arms bent round either side,
his limbs into the space of two other signs:
the boy, seeing him, soaked in the black venom's sweat
with curved barb threatening to strike,
was witless with chill terror and let go of the reins.                     200
As soon as they felt the reins lying upon the surface of their backs,
the horses go astray and, with no one to hold them back,
they pass through the air of unknown territory, and whither the urge impelled
they headlong dash unchecked and charge amongst the stars
implanted in the lofty aether and carry away the chariot over trackless ways.   205
One moment they seek the heights, the next over headlong paths
and downwards to a position nearer the earth are they born,
and Luna[26] is amazed to see her brother's horses running below
her own, and the clouds are scorched and pour forth smoke.

---

23 Literally, the "Plowers," referring to the Oxen in the constellation frequently called the Charles' Wain
or Wagon, more commonly known as Ursa Major or the Big Dipper.
24 Also known as Arcturus or Arctophylax, the "Guardian of the Bear," Boötes, is a northern con-
stellation, represented here as the "Herdsman" who tends the plow drawn by the Seven Oxen, the
Septentriones (the Big Dipper or Big Bear).
25 See on 1. 763.
26 The Moon, Diana.

The earth, where she is highest, is caught up in flames,                                210
and, being split, is rife with cracks and dries out, of moisture bereft.
The pastures grow white, the trees burn with their leaves,
and fuel for their own ruin the dry crops provide.
But these are my small complaints: Great cities are being ruined, walls and all,
and by the fires whole nations with their peoples are being turned              215
to ash; the forests with their mountains are on fire;
aflame is Athos[27] and Cilician[28] Taurus[29] and Tmolus,[30] and Oeta[31] too,
and Ida[32] now, once very rich in springs, is dry
and also maiden Helicon,[33] and Haemus[34] (Oeagrian[35] not yet):
with twin fires is Aetna[36] aflame over a vast expanse,                              220
and twin-capped Parnassus and Eyrx[37] and Cynthus[38] and Othrys[39]
and finally Rhodope[40] and Mimas,[41] too, will lose their snows
and Dindyma[42] and Mycale[43] and Cithaeron[44] for mysteries born.
Her cold is no use to Scythia: the Caucasus burns,
and Ossa with Pindus, and Olympus greater than both,                           225
and the airy Alps and cloud-bringing Apennines.
      In truth does Phaethon then see the earth everywhere
in flames and cannot bear such heat as this;
as though from the depths of a furnace he draws in with his mouth
the overheated air and feels his chariot glow hot,                               230
can no longer bear the cinders and the discharge
of ash, and on all sides is involved in hot smoke;
and where he goes or where he is, covered in the pitchy gloom,
he knows not, and is swept away at the whim of the racing steeds.
They think it was then that, the blood to their bodies' surface drawn,          235
the Ethiopian peoples assumed the color black;
then Libya, her moisture robbed by the heat,

---

27 A mountain on Acte, the westernmost of the three peninsulas that make up Chalcidice, projecting south into the Aegean Sea from Macedonia.
28 Area of southeastern Asia Minor.
29 Mountain range in southern Asia Minor.
30 Mountain of Lydia in Asia Minor.
31 Mountain on the border of southern Thessaly, also spelled Oete.
32 Also spelled Ide, either the mountain range near Troy in Phrygia, site of the Judgment of Paris and the Rape of Ganymede, or the mountain in Crete where Zeus was born.
33 Mountain of Boeotia sacred to Apollo and the Muses, hence *virgineus Helicon.*
34 Mountain range in northern Thrace.
35 Oeagrus, King of Thrace, is sometimes the father of Orpheus, hence *nondum Oeagrius* means "before the time of Orpheus." Orpheus is also said to be the son of Apollo.
36 Or Aetne or Etna, volcanic mountain in northeastern Sicily.
37 Mountain in northwestern Sicily.
38 Hill of Delos where Diana and Apollo were born.
39 Mountain range in southern Thessaly.
40 Mountain range of western Thrace.
41 Mountain range of Ionia near Erythrae, opposite the island of Chios.
42 Mountain in Phrygia sacred to Cybele.
43 Mountainous area on the coast of Asia Minor opposite Samos.
44 Mountain in southern Boeotia sacred to the Muses and, as here, to the worship of Bacchus, hence "for mysteries born."

dried up; then the nymphs wept for their fountains and lakes,
their hair in disarray; Boeotia her Dirce[45] seeks
and Argos her Amymone,[46] Ephyre[47] her Pirenian[48] spring.                    240
Nor did the rivers, allotted space between divided banks,
abide in safety: Tanais[49] steamed in his waters' midst,
and old man Peneus[50] and Caicus,[51] sprung from Teuthras'[52] line,
and swift Ismenos[53] and Phegian[54] Erymanthus[55] as well
and yellow Lycormas[56] and Xanthus,[57] about to burn again,[58]                 245
Maeander,[59] too, that upon its winding waters plays,
Mygdonian[60] Melas,[61] as well, and the Eurotas[62] Taenarus[63] owns.
Euphrates of Babylon also caught fire, Orontes[64] caught fire,
and swift Thermodon[65] and Ganges, and Phasis[66] and Hister,[67] too;
aboil is Alpheos,[68] the Spercheian[69] banks are ablaze,                        250
the gold that Tagus[70] carries with his stream now flows in flames,
and, having before thronged the Maeonian[71] banks with song,
the river fowl have grown hot in Cayster's[72] midst;
and Nile fled in terror to the extremes of the earth
and hid his head, which to this day lies hidden: the seven mouths                255
lie empty with dust, seven vales without a stream.
The same fate dries the Ismarian[73] rivers, Hebrus and Strymon[74] both,
and those of the west, Rhine, Rhone and Po,
and Tiber, who had been promised control of the world.

45 Wife of King Lycus of Thebes. She was slain by Amphion and Zethus and changed into a spring.
46 A spring in Argos, named after a daughter of Danaus.
47 An old name for Corinth.
48 The spring of Pirene on the citadel of Corinth was created by the stamp of Pegasus' hoof and was
   sacred to the Muses.
49 The Don.
50 Thessalian river, father of Daphne; Cf. 1. 452 ff.
51 River of Mysia, in Asia Minor.
52 Teuthras was King of Mysia.
53 A river of Boeotia near Thebes.
54 Pertaining to Phegeus, King of Arcadian Psophis, father of Arsinoë or Alphesiboea, who became the
   bride of Alcmaeon.
55 Here not the mountain, but the river of Arcadia.
56 Old name for the river Evenus in Aetolia (west central Greece, north of the Gulf of Corinth).
57 Here, a river of the Troad.
58 As it did in Homer, *Il.* 21. 328-82.
59 River of Phrygia, source of English *meander*. See 9. 450-53.
60 Pertaining to the Mygdones, a people of Macedonia.
61 River of Thrace.
62 A river of Laconia, on which Sparta is situated.
63 Taenarus is the southernmost promontory of the Peloponnesus in Laconia.
64 A river of Syria, upon which Antioch is situated.
65 A river of Pontus, a region bordering on the Black Sea (Pontus), where the Amazons lived.
66 The principal river of Colchis, Kingdom of Aeëtes, father of Medea.
67 The Lower Danube.
68 River of Elis in the Peloponnesus.
69 The Spercheios is a river of Thessaly.
70 River flowing from Spain into the Atlantic through Portugal.
71 Another name for Lydia.
72 The Cayster is a river of Lydia noted for its swans, here probably the "river fowl."
73 Referring to Mt. Ismaros of Thrace, hence by metonymy, "Thracian."
74 The Strymon is on the border of Thrace and Macedonia.

And all the ground splits apart, and into Tartarus through cracks          260
the light bores and frightens the infernal king and his wife;[75]
the sea shrinks, and now there's a field of dry sand
that once was ocean, and, once covered by the deep watery plain,
the mountains rise up and swell the Cyclades'[76] scattered sum.
The fish seek the depths, nor do the curved dolphins dare                  265
to raise themselves above the water's surface into the familiar breeze;
the upturned bodies of seals on the water's top
float lifeless: the story is that even Nereus[77] himself
and Doris and their daughters hid deep down in tepid caves.
From the waters had Neptune thrice dared to extend                         270
his angry face and arms, thrice unable to bear the heat of the air.
     Yet nurturing Tellus,[78] surrounded by the sea,
amid the ocean's waters and fountains contracted on every side,
that buried themselves in their dark mother's bowels,
heaved up, dry to the neck, her downcast face                              275
and put her hand to her brow, and with a great shake
that caused everything to tremble, settled down a bit
below her usual place, and said with her holy voice:
"If this is your pleasure and I deserve it, O greatest of gods,
why do your thunderbolts hold back? If I must die by the force of fire,    280
allow me to die by *your* fire and lighten my ruin, knowing you as the cause!
I scarce can loosen my throat for these very words"
(the heat had forced shut her mouth); "just look how my hair is singed,
and at the soot, so much in my eyes, so much upon my face!
Is this the fruit, this, for fertility and duty fulfilled, the reward      285
you pay me for enduring the wounds of the curved plow
and the harrows and for being worked throughout the year,
for granting fodder and sweet nurture for the flock, and grain
for human kind, and incense as well for you?
Suppose I do deserve destruction: why have the waves,                      290
why has your brother deserved it? Why does, his portion betrayed,
the level of his waters sink and stand farther from the sky?
Yet if you are touched neither by your brother's goodwill nor mine,
have pity at least on your sky! Look about to either side:
both poles are burning! If *they* are ruined by fire,                      295
your courts will collapse! Look how Atlas himself toils
and on his shoulders barely holds up the heavenly vault!
If ocean, if the dry lands, if the palace of the sky, should fall,
we'll be confounded[79] into the ancient chaos! Snatch from the flames

---

75 Pluto and Proserpina.
76 The "circling" islands of the Aegean sea.
77 A sea-god, husband of Doris, and by her father of fifty daughters, the Nereids.
78 *Alma Tellus*, the Earth Goddess. See on 1. 15.

whatever remains, and take thought for the sum of things!"                                    300
When Tellus had finished speaking, for she could bear the heat
no longer nor say more, she withdrew her face
into herself and into the caves nearer the shades.
The all-powerful father in turn, having testified to the gods above
and to him who had given the chariot, that without his aid                                    305
all things would perish in a dreadful doom, in steep ascent seeks his citadel,
from where he is wont to fill the broad earth with clouds,
from where he moves his thunder and hurls his lightning flash.
But neither had he clouds any longer with which to fill
the earth, nor rains to let down from the sky:                                                310
he thunders and, balanced from his right ear, sent the lightning bolt
against the charioteer and from life and wheels at once
expelled him and with savage fires subdued the fires.
In panic the horses leap the other way
and pull their necks from the yoke and leave the broken reins behind:                         315
the harnesses lie there, there, torn from the wagon tongue,
the axle lies, here the spokes of the shattered wheels,
and scattered far and wide are the remains of the mangled car.
       But Phaethon, his golden hair disfigured by flame,
is flung headlong and in a long trajectory through the air                                    320
is borne, as sometimes from the serene sky a star,
although not truly fallen, might have seemed to fall.
Far from his native land in another part of the world
the river Eridanus[80] picks him up and bathes his smoking face.
The Naiads of Hesperia[81] place the body, smoking with jagged flame,                         325
within a tomb, and also mark with a poem the stone:
HERE· LIES· PHAETHON· DRIVER· OF· HIS· FATHER'S· TEAM·
WHICH·IF· HE· HELD· IT· NOT· YET· FAILED· IN· A· GREAT· ATTEMPT.[82]
       The father, wretched then with painful grief,
had hidden his darkened face, and, if we are to believe it, one                               330
day passed, they say, without the sun: the destructive fires
provided the light and were of some use in that distress.

### 333-66   *Clymene and the Heliades*

But Clymene, after saying what there was to say
in great disasters like this, maddened with grief
and having torn her breast, inspected the whole earth                                         335
in search first of the lifeless limbs, and then the bones;

---

79 *Confundimur,* literally "poured/mixed together."
80 The usual Greek name for the Po.
81 The West.
82 The epitaph reads as follows:
    HIC· SITVS· EST· PHAETHON· CVRRVS· AVRIGA· PATERNI·
    QVEM· SI· NON· TENVIT· MAGNI· TAMEN· EXCIDIT· AVSIS·

*Phaethon, Anonymous Venice ca. 1513*

discovering the bones, however, buried upon a foreign shore,
she lay down at the sight and drenched with tears
the name written in marble as she held it to her naked breast.
No less do the Heliades[83] offer weeping and death's                340
vain gifts, their tears, and, beating their breasts with their palms,
to Phaethon, never to hear their sad complaints,
call night and day, and prostrate lie upon the tomb.
The moon had four times filled her orb with horns conjoined;
those girls after their fashion (for fashion is by usage made)        345
had issued their lament: Phaethusa,[84] oldest sister of the group,
desiring to lie prostrate upon the ground, complained
her feet had grown stiff; attempting to draw near to her,
fair Lampetie[85] was held by a sudden root;
a third, as she made ready to tear her hair with her hands,           350
tore leaves away instead; this one complains that her limbs are held by a trunk,
another, that her arms have become spreading limbs,
and while they wonder at this, bark enfolds their groins
and gradually over their wombs and breasts and shoulders and hands
advances, and only voices that called for their mother remained.      355
The mother, what is she to do, but, where impulse leads,
to go here and there and plant kisses while she can?
That's not enough: she tries to tear the bodies from the trunks

---

83 Daughters of Helios, the Greek god of the sun.
84 The Heliades have appropriately meaningful names: Phaethusa "Shining Brightly."
85 "The Bright One."

*Heliades, Solis*

and with her hands breaks the tender branches, but from there
the bloody drops flow as though from a wound.                                    360
"I pray, mother, spare me," a wounded one exclaims,
"I pray, do spare me: our body is being mangled in the tree.
and now, farewell," but bark enveloped her final words.
From there flow tears and, distilled, grow hard in the sun,
and amber[86] from the fresh branches is received                               365
by that clear stream and sent to be worn[87] by Latin brides.

### 367-80  Cycnus

Attending this wonder was Cycnus,[88] the son of Sthenelus:[89]
though joined by blood to you on your mother's side,
yet closer still was he to you in spirit, Phaethon. His kingdom left behind
(for over the tribes of the Ligurians and their great cities he had reigned),    370
that man had filled the green banks and stream
of Eridanus with protests, and the woods your sisters had increased,
and then his voice became thin, and hoary plumes imitate
his hair, and his neck extends from his chest
at length, and a linkage ties his ruddy toes, his side                           375
is covered with plumage, his mouth has a beak without a point.
A strange new bird now, Cycnus entrusts himself
to neither sky nor Jove, for mindful of the fire unjustly sent,[90]
he haunts the ponds and open lakes, for, despising fire,

---

86 Translating *electra*.
87 Translating *gestanda*; with *spectanda*, "admired."
88 The name means "Swan." Other characters in Ovid have the same name.
89 This Sthenelus is otherwise unknown.
90 The thunderbolt of Jove.

he chose to inhabit the rivers as the opponents of flames.                    380

### 381-400   *Phoebus' Grief*

Now Phaethon's father, squalid and without
his normal beauty, as he's wont to be when his orb
is dimmed in eclipse, hates the light and himself and the day
and gives his mind over to mourning and to mourning adds wrath,
refusing his service to the world. "From the beginning of my life,"      385
he says, "my lot has been without repose, and I am sick and tired
of endless deeds, of labors without respect!
Let someone else drive the chariot that brings the light!
If no one will and all the gods admit they can't,
let Jupiter drive it himself, so that at least, while he's trying our reins,   390
the lightning designed to orphan fathers he lay aside at last!
He'll know, having felt the fiery-footed horses' strength,
that he who has not controlled them well has not deserved to die."
As Sol says this, all the divinities stand around,
and, that he not desire to fill the universe with shade,              395
with suppliant voice appeal. For the fires he hurled, even Jupiter makes
excuses and to his pleas adds in regal fashion his threats.
Then Phoebus recovers, maddened and still trembling with fright,
his horses and rages in pain at them with spur and lash;
(for angry he was) and charges and blames them for the fate of his son.   400

### 401-530   *Jupiter in Arcadia*

The all-powerful father then circles the great walls of the sky
and ascertains whether anything was weakened by the force of the fire
and near collapse. When he sees that everything is firm
and has its proper strength, he examines the earth
and human works. Yet dearer to him is the care                       405
of his Arcadia: the springs and rivers, not yet daring to glide,
he freshens, grass to the earth and leaves to the trees
he gives and orders the damaged forests to grow green again.
And during his frequent comings and goings, from Nonacrina[91] a maid
caught his eye, and, once kindled, the fires grew hot within his bones.   410
Her task was not to soften wool for clothes
nor vary the style of her hair, once she had bound with a brooch
her dress and with white fillet her neglected locks;
she took with her hand now the light javelin, now the bow,
a soldier of Phoebe:[92] nor in the region of Maenalos[93] was any other girl   415
more pleasing than she to Trivia.[94] But no power is long.

---

91 Mountain and city in Arcadia.
92 Diana.
93 Arcadian mountain range.

The sun was high, beyond the middle of his course,
when entering a woody grove that no age had felled,
she took from her shoulder her quiver and unbent
her pliant bow and lay upon the grass-covered ground                               420
and rested upon the painted quiver her neck.
As Jupiter saw her weary and without a guard,
"This surely is a stolen pleasure my wife will not learn of," he says,
"or if she does, the strife will be worth the reward, will be indeed!"
At once he puts on Diana's appearance and dress                                    425
and says, "O maiden, member of my company,
upon what hills have you been hunting?" From the grass the maid
rose up and said, "Greetings, divinity, greater than Jove,
were I to judge, though he may hear me say it." He smiles and hears,
delighted to be preferred to himself; his kisses are                               430
not modest enough nor to be granted this way by a maid.
As she was about to say in what forest had been her hunt,
he stops her with his embrace and not blameless betrays himself.
Indeed, she resists, as much as a woman could
(Saturnia,[95] you would be kinder, if only you had seen);                         435
indeed, she fights, but whom could a girl overcome,
or who overcome Jove? Jupiter seeks the aether of the gods above,
victorious: but she hates the grove and the knowing woods.
Withdrawing from there, she almost forgot to take
the arrow-filled quiver and her suspended bow.                                     440
        And lo, attended by her chorus, Dictynna,[96] afoot
through lofty Maenalos and proud with the kill of the wild,
espies her and once she's seen calls her: when called, she fled
and feared at first, lest Jupiter be disguised in her.
But after she sees nymphs keeping pace with her,                                   445
she realized that there was no deceit and approached their band.
Alas! how difficult it is not to betray her guilt with her face!
She scarcely lifts her eyes from the ground, nor at
her usual place beside the goddess nor at the front of the line,
but keeps her silence and gives signs of her wounded shame with a blush.   450
And were she not a virgin, Diana could have perceived
her guilt from a thousand tokens: the *nymphs*, it's said, *did* perceive.
The lunar horns were rising again in their ninth orb when
the goddess, languid from the hunt beneath her brother's flames,
arrived at the cool grove from which a murmuring stream                            455
flowed smoothly and stirred the well-worn sands.

---

94 *Trivia,* the goddess of the Three-Ways, is a name of Diana, Luna, and Hecate, worshiped in statues
   with three heads at the meeting of three roads. Cf. English *trivial.*
95 The usual epithet of Juno.
96 The Cretan Artemis, identified with Diana.

While praising the spot, she touched the surface of the water with her foot,
and praised the waters, too. "Every observer," she says, "is out of sight.
Within the brimming waters let us dip our bodies stripped!"
The Parrhasian girl[97] grew red; all the others take off their gowns;    460
one only seeks delay: as she hesitated, her dress was removed by force,
and once it was off, her naked body revealed her guilt.
And to the stunned girl, who sought to cover her belly with her hands,
she said, "Get you far from here and do not pollute the sacred springs!"
And Cynthia[98] ordered her to withdraw from the band.    465
The wife of the mighty Thunderer had found this out before,
postponing the grave penalty for the proper time.
No cause for delay remains as now the boy Arcas (by this, too,
was Juno distressed) had been born of the concubine.
As soon as to this purpose she turned her cruel mind and eye,    470
she said, "Adulteress, I suppose this yet remained,
that you should be fertile, and this insult be by a birth
revealed, and to Jove's disgrace confirmed by a birth.
By no means will you go unpunished: that beauty of yours will I take away
in which, misguided one, you delight yourself and our husband as well."    475
She spoke and as the girl turned towards her, she grabbed her hair from the front
and laid her out flat upon the ground. As a suppliant, the girl stretched forth her arms:
the arms begin to bristle with black fur,
the hands to bend and to grow into curved claws
that do the work of feet, and the mouth, once praised    480
by Jove, to become deformed with gaping jaws.
And lest prayers and pleading words move sympathy,
her faculty of speech is taken away: an angry voice, full of threats
and stirring terror, comes from her raspy throat;
her former mind remains (and remained in the resulting bear),    485
and, with incessant growling having testified to her pains,
she raises whatever sort of hands she has to the sky and stars
and feels the thanklessness of Jove she cannot tell.
Alas, how often, not daring to rest in the deserted woods,
she wandered before her house and sometimes in her own fields!    490
Alas, how often she was driven over the rocks by the barking dogs
and, out of fear of hunters, as a huntress in terror fled!
She often hid when beasts appeared, forgetting what she was,
and though a bear, trembled at the bears she saw in the hills,
and, though her father[99] was among them, she was terrified by wolves.    495

---

97 Parrhasia is a town in Arcadia. Ovid calls her Callisto in *Fasti* 2. 156, but never names her in the *Metamorphoses*, preferring instead epithets like "the Parrhasian girl." She is the daughter of Lycaon (see 495).
98 Diana.
99 Lycaon.

### 496-530   *Arcas and His Mother Changed to Constellations*

Behold, the Lycaonian[100] mother's unwitting child
is present, Arcas, about three times five years of age.
And as he hunts the wild, as he chooses the proper glens,
and with his netted traps ranges through the Erymanthian woods,
he chances upon his mother. At the sight of Arcas she held still                    500
and seemed to recognize him: but the other recoiled
and at the constant stare of her eyes, upon him fixed,
in ignorance was alarmed and, as she yearned for him to draw near,
prepared to thrust in her breast a wounding spear:
all-powerful Jove intervened and in one stroke removed both them          505
and sacrilege by seizing and carrying them through the void upon the wind.
He placed them in the sky and made them neighboring stars.
    When Juno saw the concubine shining forth among the stars,
she swelled with rage and went down to white-capped Tethys[101] in the sea,
to old man Oceanus,[102] whom the gods often revere,                              510
and (though they already know) begins to tell her journey's cause:
"You wonder why from my ethereal home as queen of the gods
I've come to you? A rival holds my place in the sky!
Consider me a liar unless, when night has made the world grow dim,
you've seen those newly honored stars, my wounds,                              515
assigned a place in the sky out there, where, orbiting the farthest pole,
the final and shortest circle goes round!
Indeed, will anyone hesitate to insult
or fear to offend Juno, since I alone, when meaning to harm, only help?
Ah me, how much I've wrought! Our power, how vast!                          520
When I forbade her to be human, lo, she became a goddess! Thus do I
impose my punishment upon the guilty, thus the greatness of my might!
Let him reclaim her former appearance and put off
her savage face, as he did with Argive Phoronis[103] before!
With Juno expelled, why doesn't he marry her                                   525
and place her in my bed and take Lycaon for a father-in-law?
But if you are touched by contempt for the wrong done your foster-child,
prohibit the Septentriones[104] from your sky-blue flood,
and those stars received in heaven as the price of shame
drive off, lest into sea's pure waters the concubine be dipped!"              530

---

100 As daughter of Lycaon.
101 The sea-goddess and Titan sister and wife of Oceanus.
102 Son of Uranus and Ge (Sky and Earth), Oceanus' sea was thought to encircle the earth.
103 Io, as sister of Phoroneus, son of Inachus.
104 The Seven-Oxen. See 171 and 176, with notes.

*Callisto, Diana, Juno, Anonymous Venice ca. 1513*

### 531-632   *The Raven and the Crow*

The gods of the sea nodded their assent: her graceful chariot drawn
by painted peacocks, Saturnia proceeds through the clear upper air,
those peacocks so lately painted after Argus was slain,
as once, though shining white before, were you yourself,
loquacious raven, suddenly changed into blackened wings.                535
This bird in fact was once like silver with snowy plumes,
a bird to equal all the spotless doves,
as white as the geese[105] whose watchful voice
would save the Capitoline, and as the swan who loves the stream.
The tongue caused the harm: for the loquacious one with active tongue        540
whose color was white is now the opposite of white.

### 542-95   *Coronis and the Crow's Story*

More lovely than Larissaean[106] Coronis[107] was none
in all Haemonia:[108] You liked her, Delphic one, indeed,
while she was either chaste or undetected, but Phoebus' bird[109]

---

105 Livy, 5. 47, recounts the story of how the cackling geese warned the Romans of the invading Gauls
   in the early 4th century B.C.E.
106 Larissa was a city of Thessaly.
107 Daughter of Phlegyas of Larissa. Ovid chooses the name from Greek *korone* "crow," and for its
   apparent connection to Latin *cornix* "crow," in contrast to *corvus* "raven." It is somewhat confusing
   that the father of the crow is named Coroneus, 569, but this similarity of names forms a special
   bond of empathy between the crow and the plight of Coronis, whom the raven will betray and
   Apollo will kill.
108 Thessaly.
109 The raven of 535, considered a prophetic bird, and sacred to Apollo of Delphi.

found out her adultery and, to expose 545
her hidden guilt, the inexorable tattle-tale
was making his way to his master. The garrulous crow
with wings aflutter follows along to learn all,
and once she heard the cause, "Useless is the path
you take," she says, "do not spurn the forewarnings of my tongue! 550
Consider what I was and am and ask whether it was right:
you'll find that honesty does harm. For there was a time
when Pallas[110] had shut Erichthonius,[111] a child without a mother born,
into a chest woven from Actaean[112] wicker-work
and given it to the three daughters of Cecrops[113] of double-bodied form 555
and set the rule that they not look upon what she had hidden away.
Concealed in dense foliage, I was looking from a slender elm
at what they did: two guard without deceit their charge,
Pandrosos and Herse; the third calls her sisters timorous:
Aglauros with her hand unties the knots, and within 560
they see the infant and, stretched out beside him, a snake.
I tell the goddess of the deed, in return for which
the thanks is this: I'm declared Minerva's exiled guardian
and set behind the bird of night![114] My punishment
can warn the birds not to seek trouble with their voice. 565
As though she didn't seek me out of her own accord—
I never asked for such an honor! You can ask Pallas herself about this:
though angry, even in her anger this she'll not deny.
For famous Coroneus[115] gave me birth on Phocaean soil
(I tell you what you know), and I had been a royal girl 570
and by wealthy suitors (scorn me not!) was I pursued.
My beauty harmed me. For when at a leisurely pace
along the shore I was strolling on a sandy dune, as I often do,
the god of the sea caught sight of me and grew hot; and when
by pleading with coaxing words he'd spent his time in vain, 575
he offers force and pursuit. I flee and leave the shore's
packed sand and in the soft sand weary myself in vain.
And then I call on gods and humankind; nor does my voice
touch any mortal: for a virgin's sake the Virgin[116] is moved

110 Athena, the Roman Minerva, patron of Athens.
111 Sprung from the seed of Hephaestus (Vulcan) as he pursued Athena. When his seed fell on her leg, she wiped it off in disgust and cast it onto the ground, out of which Erichthonius was born. The Athenians are often called Erechtheids.
112 I.e., "Attic" or "Athenian" from Greek *akte* "headland, peninsula," the shape of Attica, the land mass in which Athens is situated.
113 Cecrops was an early king of Athens who settled the dispute between Athena and Poseidon over the patronage of the city. The Athenians are frequently called Cecropidae. As a sign of the autochthonous origin of the Athenians their early kings, including Cecrops, had serpent legs, hence "double-bodied."
114 The owl, Nyctimene. See 590.
115 See on 542.
116 Minerva.

and offered help. I was stretching my arms to the sky:                                      580
my arms begin to grow black with light plumes;
I struggled to throw my dress from my shoulders, but it
was plumage and had driven its roots into my skin;
I tried to beat my bare breast with my palms,
but now I had neither palms nor bare breast;                                                 585
I kept on running, but the sand no longer held back my feet;
instead, I was born along the surface of ground; and next through the air
I'm carried aloft and given to Minerva as a companion without blame.
What good is this, however, if changed into a bird
for monstrous crime[117] Nyctimene has taken over my rank?                                   590
Or have you not heard that story, throughout all Lesbos known
so widely, that Nyctimene violated her father's couch?
She may be a bird, but conscious of her guilt
she shuns being seen, and the light, and conceals her shame
in shadows and is driven by all the rest[118] from all the sky."                            595

### 596-632   The Raven's Reply and the Death of Coronis

The raven replied, "May this be a summons of woe
upon your own head, I pray: this vain omen we reject!"
Not quitting the journey he had begun, he tells his lord
he saw Coronis lying with an Haemonian youth.
The charge once heard, the lover's laurel slipped off,                                      600
the countenance of the god, his color and the pick of his lyre
together fell, and as his mind swelled to a boiling wrath,
he seizes his wonted arms and bends from its horns the pliant bow,
and pierced that breast, to his own breast so oft
conjoined, with an inescapable dart. She groaned                                            605
when struck, and, once from her body the iron barb
was drawn, she bathed her fair limbs in crimson[119] blood
and said, "Phoebus, it was right for me to suffer your punishment,
but first I should have given birth; now two of us will die as one."
She said just this and then poured out her life with her blood;                             610
the chill of death took hold of a body devoid of life.
Oh, his regrets! the lover of cruel punishment too late
detests himself for having listened, for having been so inflamed with rage,
detests the bird through whom he was forced to learn
the accusation and cause of his grief, and detests his bow                                  615
no less than his hand and with his hand the shafts and reckless darts;

---

117 Nyctimene was the unwitting victim of incest with her father, here probably Epopeus, king of
     Lesbos. Other sources make her the daughter of Nyctaeus, a Boeotian king, or of Proteus.
118 I. e., of the birds. Owls are particularly hated by crows.
119 *Puniceo*: the Phoenicians (Latin *Poeni*) got their name from their trade in purple or copper or from
     their copper skin.

he fondles the fallen girl and struggles to conquer fate
with tardy aid and plies his healing arts in vain.
On seeing these efforts useless and on the ready pyre
her limbs about to burn in those final fires,                                        620
then truly did he pour forth moaning (for celestial faces must not
be stained by tears), drawn from the bottom of his heart,
not different than when, as the heifer looks on,
a hammer, leveled at the right ear of a suckling calf,
has smashed the hollow temples with a ringing blow.                                  625
When he had poured unwelcome perfumes upon that breast
and offered his embraces and justly performed what was unjustly due,
yet Phoebus could not bear that into the same ashes his seed
should fall, and from the flames and his mother's womb
tore free his son and brought him to double-bodied Chiron's cave,                    630
and, though the raven expected rewards for his truthful tongue,
among the white birds Apollo forbade him to live.

### 633-75   Chiron and Ocyrhoë

The half-wild one[120] was in the meantime happy in his foster-son
of stock divine and in that honor mixed with toil was finding joy,
when, lo, her shoulders protected by her locks,                                      635
the Centaur's daughter arrives, whom the nymph Chariclo
had born one day on the banks of a rapid stream and called
Ocyrhoë:[121] who, not content to have learned
her father's arts, used to sing the secrets of the fates.
So when she received the prophetic madness in her mind                               640
and warmed with the god that she held within her heart,
she looked at the infant and said, "As bringer-of-health to all the world
wax strong, my child. Mortal bodies will often owe to you
their lives. The souls of the dead will you restore to life
and justly so. And once you've dared to do this against the will of the gods,[122]  645
your grandfather's[123] flames will prevent you from doing it a second time,
and from a god you'll become a bloodless corpse and then a god
from the corpse you were, and twice renew your fates.
You also, dear father, now immortal and born
according to the rule of birth that you abide for eternity,                          650
will want the power to die when you are tortured by
the cursed serpent's blood received within thy wounded limbs,
and from your eternal state the gods will make

---

120 *Semifer*, referring to the Centaur Chiron, half human, half horse.
121 The name, from the Greek, means "Swift-running."
122 See 15. 531-46 for the story of Aesculapius' restoration of Hippolytus to life.
123 Jupiter.

you suffer death and the triple goddesses[124] untie your threads."
For him fate held something more, but from the depths of her breast         655
she heaves a sigh, and welling tears roll down her cheeks.
"The fates prevent me," she says, "and more than this
I may not say, and the use of my voice is barred.
Not worth so great a price were those arts that brought the wrath
of god against me: I wish I hadn't known the things to come!         660
My human appearance seems now subdued,
now grass is what I like for food, now running on the open plains
is my desire: I'm being turned into a mare and my kindred shape.
Why then completely? My father, indeed, is double in form."
In saying this the final part of her complaint         665
was barely grasped, and her words were slurred;
and soon they seemed neither words nor the proper sound of a mare,
but like the imitation of a mare, and in a short time
she brought forth definite neighing and moved her arms upon the grass.
Her fingers then come together and the five nails         670
are bound by a light hoof with unbroken horn, her mouth
and neck increase in size, the largest part of her cloak
becomes a tail, the wandering tresses lying upon her neck
extended in a mane on the right, and at the same time both voice
and face were changed; these wonders also supplied a name.[125]         675

### 676-707   Mercury, Battus and the Cattle of Apollo

The hero born of Philyra[126] wept and implored your help
in vain, O Delphic one.[127] But you could not rescind great Jove's
commands, and, if you could rescind them, you were
not there: you were tending Elis[128] and the Messenian[129] fields,
that time when you were wearing the herdsman's cloak         680
of hide, and the burden of your left hand was a staff from the woods,
and of the other the pipe of seven unequal reeds.
While love[130] is your concern, while you are soothed by your pipe,
untended, they say, off to Pylian[131] fields
your oxen wandered: these the son of Atlas' daughter[132] sees         685

---

124 The triple Fates, the Greek *Moirae*, the Roman *Parcae*. Their Greek names, known from Hes., *Theogony*, 903-906, were Clotho "Spinner," Lachesis "Allotter," and Atropos, "Inflexible."
125 Hippe "Mare" or Melanippe "Black Mare." Her original name, Ocyrhoë "Swift-running," is a suitable epithet for a mare. Euripides produced a *Melanippe the Wise*, now lost but for fragments.
126 Philyra "Lyre-lover" was the nymph mother of Chiron by Cronos (Saturn). The *philyra* is the linden (the Latin *tilia*), one of the trees in the audience for Orpheus' tales (see 11. 92). Philyra's "heroic" child Chiron was the lyre teacher of such heroes as Achilles and Jason.
127 With this address to Apollo, Ovid begins his version of the ancient tale of Hermes' (Mercury's) theft of Apollo's cattle, found in the *Homeric Hymn to Hermes*, 4. 67 ff.
128 Region in the northwest of the Peloponnesus.
129 Messenia is the region south of Elis and west of Laconia.
130 Probably for Hymenaeus, son of Magnes and Perimele.
131 Pylos was the city of Nestor.
132 Maia, mother of Mercury.

and hides them, driven away by his craft, in the woods.
The theft had no one noticed but one old man,
well known in that countryside; all the locals called him Battus.[133]
This man kept wealthy Neleus'[134] grassy pastures and glens,
the shepherd of his herd of nobles mares.                                    690
Because Mercury feared[135] this man, he drew him aside:
"Whoever you are, my friend," he says, "in case someone asks
about this herd, deny you've seen it, and lest your help
go unrepaid, take this sleek cow as your reward!"
and gave it. The stranger accepted it and returned these words:               695
"Go safely on your way! For sooner will that stone tell your theft than I,"
and pointed to the stone. The son of Jove pretends to depart;
but soon, returning with voice and form alike transformed,
he said, "Sir rustic, if in these parts you've seen
some oxen passing, lend your aid and be not silent about the theft!          700
And as a reward you'll receive a cow together with her bull."
The old man, his profit doubled, replies, "At the foot
of yonder hills they'll be." And they were at the foot of those hills.
The offspring[136] of Atlas laughed, replying, "O treacherous man,
do you betray me to myself?" and turned that perjured breast                 705
to solid flint; the touchstone it is called, and even now
the old infamy remains upon that undeserving stone.

### 708-832    *Mercury in Athens, Aglauros and Envy*

From here the bearer of the caduceus[137] raised himself on balanced wings,
and as he flew over the Munychian[138] fields, looked down upon
the plain Minerva loved and learnèd Lyceum's[139] trees.                     710
By chance that day, virgin girls, as custom required,
upon their heads to Pallas' festive citadel
were bringing in festooned baskets their pure and holy gifts.[140]
The wingèd god sees them returning from there
and flies not straight ahead, but circles again and again:                   715
and as the kite, that swiftest of birds, the entrails espied,
but timid yet because the priests stand close about the sacrifice,

---

133 The name means "Chatterbox."
134 Son of Neptune and the nymph Tyro, and father of Nestor. See 11. 550 ff.
135 Translating *timuit*; with *tenuit* "When Mercury stopped this man, ..."
136 As grandson.
137 The staff of Mercury, wrapped with two serpents and tipped with wings. The word is related to the Greek word for the herald's staff.
138 Munychia was the hill fortress of the Piraeus, the port of Athens.
139 The Lyceum at Athens was a gymnasium in a grove dedicated to Apollo Lykeios "Defender against Wolves." Built in the late 5th century, it would become the school of Aristotle and the Peripatetic philosophers in the 4th.
140 At the Greater Panathenaic Festival, held every four years in the month of Hekatombaion, first month of the Athenian year, the girls of Athens processed with a new embroidered robe, the *peplos*, for Athena.

*Battus and Mercury, Solis*

deflects his flight in a circle and does not venture farther off
and circles eagerly with flapping wings about his hoped-for prize,
just so does Cyllenius[141] nimbly over the Attic citadel                           720
incline his course and wheel about through the same airy path.
As much more brightly than all the other stars
shines Lucifer, and as much as golden Phoebe shines more
than Lucifer, so much did Herse surpass all the other girls
as she processed and was the glory of her companions' parade.                       725
The son of Jove was astonished at her beauty and, hovering in the air,
inflamed no less than when a Balearic[142] sling shoots forth
a leaden bullet: it flies and in flying grows hot and finds
within the clouds the fires it did not have before.
He changes course and, sky left behind, seeks the ground                            730
and takes no disguise, so great in his appearance his trust.
Although this trust was justified, he carefully enhanced his looks no less
and smoothes his hair, and adjusts his cloak, so that it hang
just right, so that the hem and all its gold be seen;
so that his right hand's staff with which he brings and wards off sleep             735
be polished; so that upon his elegant feet the winged sandals gleam.

    A part of the house, set aside, contained three rooms
ornate with ivory and tortoise shell. You, Pandrosos, had the one on the right,
Aglauros the one on the left, Herse the middle one.
The girl who possessed the left one saw Mercury coming first                        740
and dared to inquire of the god his name
and reason for his coming; this was the response to her
of Atlas' and Pleione's grandson: "It is I who carry through the air

---

141 Mercury, born on Mt. Cyllene in Arcadia.
142 The people of the Balearic Islands were noted slingers.

my father's expressed commands; my father is Jupiter himself.
Nor shall I falsify my purpose: but to your sister to be true                                    745
should be your desire and to be called the maternal aunt of my child.
The purpose of my coming is Herse; that you help a lover is our request."
Aglauros looks at him with the same eyes she recently gazed
upon the secrets of fair-haired Minerva unobserved,
and for her services demands a great weight                                                      750
of gold: in the meantime she makes him leave the house.
       The warrior goddess turned an angry eye towards her
and drew a sigh with such emotion from deep within
that equally shook both her breast and the aegis, placed upon
that stalwart breast: this was the girl, she recalls, who with impious hand       755
revealed her secrets at that time when, against her rules,
she gazed upon the Lemnian's[143] child, without a mother born,
and wanted to find favor with a god and favor with her sister now,
and also to be rich when she had gained the gold of her greedy demands.
At once she heads to Envy's dwelling, sordid with black                                     760
decay: her house is concealed in a deep recess
deprived of sun, closed to any breeze,
austere and completely full of sluggish cold
and always lacking fire, always abundant with gloom.
The warrior-maid, she who was to be feared in war, as she arrived,                     765
stopped still before the house (for it was not right for her
to enter the dwelling) and pounds the doorposts with the butt of her spear.
When struck, the doors spread wide. She sees Envy feeding within
on serpent flesh, her vices' nourishment,
and once she sees her, averts her eyes; but Envy gets                                        770
up slowly from the ground and leaves
the bodies of half-eaten serpents and moves with sluggish pace.
And when she saw the goddess, lovely in weapons and form,
she groaned and made a face that caused the goddess to sigh.
A pallor settles on her face, in all her body decay.                                              775
Her eyes are never direct, livid with tartar are her teeth.
Her heart is green with gall, suffused with venom, her tongue.
No smile is there, unless someone appears to be moved by pain.
Excited by waking cares, she enjoys no sleep,
but sees as unwelcome, indeed in seeing them wastes away,                                 780
the successes of people, and consumes and is consumed at once,
her own tormentor. Even though she hated her,
Tritonia[144] addresses her briefly with words like these:

---

143 Vulcan's favorite dwelling place was the island of Lemnos, noted for its volcanic fires. For the child
    Erichthonius, see 553, with note.
144 An epithet of Minerva, who is said to have first revealed herself at Lake Triton on the border of
    Numidia in Northwest Africa.

*Pallas and Envy, Picart*

"Infect one of Cecrops' daughters with rot:
This is your task. Aglauros is the one." Scarcely saying more,    785
she fled and, pressing against it with her spear, pushed off from the earth.
    But Envy, looking askance at the goddess in flight,
emitted a slight murmur and felt pain because Minerva would have
success, and takes her staff, which spiny chains
encircled, and, veiled by black clouds,    790
wherever she walks, tramples down the flowering fields
and parches the grass and eats away the tops of the trees,
and with her breath pollutes the peoples and towns
and homes, and finally spies Tritonia's citadel
in flower with inborn grace and wealth and joyful peace,    795
and scarcely keeps from crying since she sees nothing to cry about.
But after she came into Cecrops' daughter's room,
she carries out her orders and with a hand dipped in ferrous rust
anoints her breast and fills her heart with prickly thorns
and breathes in a harmful and pitch-like poison and spreads    800
it through her bones and sprinkles venom within her lungs,
and, lest the causes of her woe stray too far afield,
she plants her sister before her eyes and her sister's bliss
in marriage and, in a beautiful image, the god,
and magnifies all. By all this provoked,    805
the Cecropid daughter is bitten by hidden grief and, anxious by night
and anxious by day, she groans and most wretchedly melts

with slow decay, as ice is impaired by an uncertain sun;
and by the happiness of Herse is she no less consumed
than when a fire is set beneath the thorny undergrowth,                    810
emitting no flames but burning with a smoldering heat.[145]
At times she wanted to die to keep from seeing such a thing,
at times to tell it to her rigid father as a reproach.
At last she sits athwart upon the threshold to exclude[146]
the god as he comes. As he expressed his blandishments                    815
and prayers and sweetest of words, she said "Desist!
I'm not going to budge from here until you're driven away!"
In quick reply Cyllenius says, "Let's abide by your decree!"
With his celestial wand he opened wide the doors: but when
she tries to raise those limbs, folded where she sat,                    820
benumbed with weight, they can't be moved:
she struggles indeed to lift herself with body erect,
but the joints of her knees are rigid, and a chill
glides over her nails, and her veins grow pale with loss of blood;
and as the incurable evil of cancer is wont                    825
to spread widely and infect the healthy with corrupted parts,
just so this lethal winter crept gradually into her heart
and closed her vital passages and means of breath.
She didn't try to speak, and had she tried, she would
have had no vocal passage; rock possessed her neck,                    830
her mouth became hard, and she sat there like a statue without blood.
Nor was the stone white: her mind had made it dark.[147]

*Aglauros Foiled, Solis*

---

145 Perhaps as in peat bogs.
146 Mercury is here the *exclusus amator*, the "excluded lover," found often in Latin elegiac poetry.
147 The story of Aglauros appears to have something to do with the origin of the herm, a pillar holding
    a bust of Hermes at the entrance of a house. See Pausanias 1. 24. 3.

### 833-75   *Jupiter and Europa*

When for her words and blasphemous mind
the offspring of Atlas had taken vengeance, he left behind
the land under Pallas' sway and entered the aether with wings unfurled.   835
His father called him aside and without telling the object of his love,
"My son," he says, "as faithful servant of my commands,
"dispel delay and glide down quickly in your usual way,
and where the earth observes your mother from the left
(the natives call the place Sidon by name),   840
go there, and when you see from afar the king's herd
upon a hillside pasture grazing, turn in towards the shore!"
He spoke, and already driven from the hill,
the cattle approach the bidden shores, where, accompanied
by Tyrian maids, the daughter of the great king was wont to play.   845
Not suited nor in one home well-placed
are love and high position; the weighty authority of his scepter left behind,
that father and ruler of the gods, whose right hand is armed
with three-pronged fires, who with his nod shakes the world,
puts on the shape of a bull and, mixed among the cows,   850
he lows and handsomely makes encounter[148] upon the tender grass.
He has, indeed, the color of snow that neither tracks of the heavy foot
have trampled nor rainy Auster's[149] wind destroyed.
His neck swells with muscles, from his shoulders the dewlaps hang,
his horns in fact were small, but you might contend   855
that they were made by hand, more pellucid than a perfect gem.[150]
His forehead posed no threats, his eye no fear:
his face is peaceful. The daughter[151] of Agenor[152] is amazed
that he is so handsome, that he makes no show of fight.
At first she feared to touch him, however mild,   860
but soon goes near and stretches forth flowers to the shining white face.
The lover is glad and, in anticipation of his hoped-for desire,
put kisses to her hands; now just barely, barely, can he wait for the rest.
At one moment he's playful and leaps about upon the fresh grass,
the next he's laying his snowy side upon the yellow sand;   865
and little by little, having dispelled her fear, he offers his breast
to be stroked by the maiden hand, then his horns
to wreathe with fresh garlands; the royal maiden also dared,

---

148 Ovid's *obambulat* suggests that the bull not only wanders among the herd, but pauses to "meet"
each one, thus anticipating his meeting with Europa.
149 The South Wind.
150 Perhaps Ovid means alabaster, translucent gypsum.
151 Europa.
152 Ovid makes Agenor, son of Neptune and Libya, the father of Cadmus and Europa. By some accounts
(Apollodorus, 3. 1. 1), Agenor was the father of Europa and three sons, Cadmus, Phoenix, and
Cilix, but Homer and others make Phoenix the father of Europa. Apollonius of Rhodes, 3. 1186,
makes Phoenix also the father of Cadmus.

*Europa, Anonymous Venice ca. 1513*

not knowing whom she mounted, to sit upon the back of the bull,
as gradually the god from the land and dry shore                                    870
begins to place the perjured tracks of his feet into the waves.
From there he moves further and through the plains of the open sea
transports his prize: she fears and, stolen away, looks back
to the shore left behind and clings to his horn with her right hand, the left
placed on his back; her tremulous veils billow in the breeze.                       875

# BOOK 3

## *1-137 Cadmus*

By now the god had put off the deceiving image of the bull,
confessed who he was, and reached the Dictaean[1] fields.
Not knowing this, her father orders Cadmus to go
in search of the stolen girl, imposing banishment, if he failed,
a punishment, both pious and criminal in the same act.                    5
Having roamed the earth as an exile (for who can detect
the tricks of Jove?), Agenor's son avoids his land
and father's wrath and as a suppliant consults
the oracles of Phoebus and seeks a land in which to dwell.
"A cow will meet you," says Phoebus, "in a lonely field,                  10
unused to the yoke and exempt from the curvèd plow.
With her as your guide make your way and, where she rests upon the grass,
see to the raising of walls and call that place Boeotia.[2]
Not quite has Cadmus descended from the Castalian cave[3]
before he sees an untended heifer, moving slow                           15
and bearing no sign of service on her neck.
He follows and tracks her, his pace restrained,
and silently worships Phoebus as the author of his path.
Already had he left the shallows of Cephisus[4] and Panope's[5] fields:

---

1 Mt. Dicte is in Crete.
2 Boeotia means something like "Cow-country," from Greek *bous*, cognate with Latin *bos* "cow."
3 The "Castalian cave," referring to the source of the Castalian spring at Delphi, and thus metonymy
    for Delphi.
4 A river of Phocis, near Delphi.
5 A city of Phocis.

the cow stopped and, raising her lovely forehead with its lofty horns     20
up towards the sky, with lowing stirred the air
and then, looking back at her companion following at her back,
lay down and lowered her flank to the tender grass.
     In gratitude Cadmus presses to the foreign ground
his lips and greets the unknown mountains and fields.     25
To Jove he readies sacrifice: he orders servants to go
and seek waters for libations from living springs.
     An ancient forest was there, never violated by the axe
and in its midst a cave, dense with branches and vines
and making a humble bower with fittings of stones     30
and rich in abundant waters: inside the cave
a serpent lay hidden, sired by Mars, unmatched in crests and gold:
his eyes gleam with fire, with venom all his body swells,
his three tongues quiver, in triple order stand his teeth.
As soon as those who had set out from the people of Tyre[6] had touched     35
this grove with ill-starred feet, and a vessel sent down into the spring
had made a noise, out of the long cave the dark blue serpent thrust
his head, emitting awful hissing sounds.
The vessels fell from their hands and the blood left
their bodies and a sudden trembling seized their astonished limbs.     40
He twists his scaly orbs in rolling coils
and slithers with a leap into an gigantic arch;
with more than half his form raised erect into the air
he gazes down upon the whole grove and has a body as large,
if you could see it all, as the space that divides the twin Bears.     45
Without delay he attacks the Phoenicians either preparing to fight
or flee or prevented by fright from either choice:
he kills some with his jaws, others with his long coils,
still others with the foul and fatal venom he exhales.
     The sun at its highest had already made the shadows small:     50
Agenor's son wonders why his companions are delayed
and sets out to track down his men. His shield was
a lion's stolen skin, his weapons a spear splendid with iron,
a javelin, and, surpassing every weapon, his mind and heart.
On entering the grove and seeing the bodies of the slain     55
and, with his vast body towering above, the victorious foe,
whose bloody tongue was licking the pitiful wounds,
he said, "Either the avenger, most faithful bodies, of your death
or the companion will I be." He spoke, and lifted with his right hand
a millstone-boulder and with a mighty heave hurled its weight.     60
Its impact would have moved high walls

---

6 A city of Phoenicia.

*Cadmus and Serpent, Baur*

with lofty towers: unwounded remained the snake,
and, only defended by scales for a cuirass and his hide's
black hardness, he repelled the blows from his skin.
That hardness, though, did not defeat as well the javelin          65
that, fixed into the fold of his stubborn spine,
stood fast and with all its iron reached into his bowels deep within.
In pain he twisted his ferocious head toward his back
and looked at his wounds and bit at the implanted spear,
and when he loosened it with great effort, he barely tore          70
it from his back; the iron part, however, stuck in his bones.
But after new cause was added to his usual wrath,
his throat swelled with all its veins in flood,
and whitish foam flowed throughout his plague-bearing jaws,
and earth resounds, scraped smooth by his scales, and black breath leaves   75
his Stygian mouth and putrefies the air.
At times, with his spirals making a huge orb
he coils himself up, at times he stands up straighter than the trunk of a tree,[7]
and now with enormous force like a river driven by storms
he moves and disturbs with his breast the woods that stand in his way.    80
Agenor's son withdraws a bit and with the lion's spoils[8]
fends off the attack and slows the threatening mouth
with outstretched spear; the other rages and upon the spear's iron
lays harmless wounds and plants his teeth in its point.

7 Or "than the beam of a roof."
8 His shield. See 2. 52.

And now from the poison-bearing palate the blood                                    85
began to ooze and with drops had dyed the verdant grass;
yet slight was the wound, because he had pulled back from the blow
and held back his stricken neck and prevented by retreat
the blow from settling and didn't allow it to go very far,
until Agenor's son, pressed the spear already cast into the throat                  90
by driving ever on until at his back an oak tree blocked
the other's movement and neck and oak alike were pierced.
The weight of the serpent bent the tree, which groaned
because its wood was being thrashed by the lower part of that tail.
As victor contemplated the size of the vanquished foe,                              95
a voice was suddenly heard (and it was not possible to say
from where, but it was heard): "O you of Agenor born, why do
you wonder at the conquered snake? You will also cause wonder as snake."
     His color and composure had long been lost
because of his fright, and cold terror made his hair stand on end:                  100
behold, the patroness of the hero, gliding down from the airy sky,
is present, Pallas, and orders him to plant in tilled earth
the viper's teeth for the growth of a people to come.
Obeying, he laid open the furrows with the weight of a plow
and scattered upon the ground as seeds of mortals the bidden teeth.                 105
And then (past all believing) the clods began to move,
and from the furrows the point of a spear appeared,
soon, with their painted cones,[9] nodding helmets of heads,
soon shoulders and chests and weapon-laden arms
stand out, and up rises a shield-bearing crop of men.                               110
As, when in the festival theaters the curtains are raised,
the pictures are wont to rise and show the faces first,
the rest gradually, and then, raised in one smooth swoop
and lying completely open, place the feet at the bottom edge.
Alarmed by this strange new foe, Cadmus prepared to seize his arms;                 115
but one of the people that earth had created exclaims,
"Do not seize arms nor involve yourself in civil strife."
And then he strikes one of his earthborn brothers with a rigid sword
in close combat, and is felled himself by a javelin from afar.
The one who had given the other to death not longer lives                           120
than he and breathes out the air he had just received;
in equal manner the whole mob rages, and all
the sudden brothers in their own work of Mars[10] fall with mutual wounds.
And now the youths, allotted a brief space of life,
were beating their bloody mother with their warmed breasts,                         125
except for five survivors, of whom one was Echion.

---

9 For holding the crests.
10 Metonymy for "war."

*The Spartoi, Solis*

He threw upon the ground his arms as Tritonis[11] warned
and sought and gave a pledge of fraternal peace.
The Sidonian visitor had these as the comrades of his work
when he established a city, as ordered by Phoebus' prophecies.                130
    Now Thebes was standing; now, Cadmus, you could appear
content in exile: as parents-in-law had Venus and Mars[12]
become your kin; to this add a family from such a great wife,
so many daughters and sons and grandsons, dearest of hopes,
and these young men already. But surely man's final day                      135
must one await, and no one should be called blest
before death and final rites.

### 138-252  Actaeon

    Your grandson, Cadmus, amid so many fortunate things,
was first cause of grief, and those alien horns added to
his forehead, and you, O dogs, glutted with your master's blood.             140
But if you well inquire, you will find a charge of misfortune upon
him, not one of crime; for what crime did mere wandering contain?[13]
    The mountain was stained with the slaughter of various wild beasts,
and mid-day had shrunk the shadows of things,
and equidistant was the sun from either goal,                                145
when with calm voice a Hyantean[14] young man compels
his labors' companions as they roamed the trackless haunts:
"The nets and the sword are soaked, my comrades, with the gore of the wild:

---

11 Minerva.
12 Parents of Harmonia.
13 Translating *quod enim scelus error habebat?* *Error* refers here to Actaeon's wandering but produces
    a paradox: "What fault did error contain?" See 175 *errans* "wandering."
14 I. e., "Boeotian." The Hyantes were an ancient tribe of Boeotia.

the day has been lucky enough. Aurora again,
transported on saffron wheels, will return the light,                    150
and we will renew our intended work; now Phoebus stands
apart alike from either goal and cracks the fields with heat;
so halt your present work and remove the knotty nets."
The men fulfill the orders and interrupt their work.
        There was a vale, thick with pointed cypress and spruce,        155
named Gargaphie, to high-belted Diana sacrosanct.
Within its furthest recess there is a forest cave
worked out without art; nature had imitated art
through her own genius, for with living pumice-stone
and porous tufa she had drawn out a natural arch.                       160
A little fountain of clear water gurgles on the right,
its widening pool surrounded by a grassy bank.
The goddess of the forests when weary of the hunt
would here relax her virgin limbs within the dewy spring.
When she arrived, she handed off to one of her nymphs,                  165
her arms-bearer, her javelin and quiver and bow to keep;
a second held out her arms for the cloak she removed;
two others removed the bindings from her feet; more skilled than these,
Ismenian[15] Crocale gathered the locks that spread over her neck
into a bun, although her own were let down.                             170
Hyale[16] and Rhanis[17] and Psecas[18] and Phiale[19] and Nephele[20]
draw water and pour it from capacious urns.
And while Titania[21] there in her familiar waters is bathed,
behold, the grandson of Cadmus, a part of his labors adjourned,
is wandering through the unfamiliar woods with wary steps              175
and comes into the grove: the fates were bringing him here.
As soon as he entered the cave all dewy with springs,
the nymphs, nude as they were, at the sight of a man
did beat their breasts and filled with sudden howls
the whole grove and, having thronged around                            180
Diana, covered her with their bodies. But taller than these
the goddess was and towered above them all by a head.
The color created by the blow of the opposing sun
upon the clouds or of the purple Dawn,[22]
this color lay upon the face of Diana seen nude.                       185
Although the band of her companions was closely packed,

---

15 Ismenus was a river-god of Boeotia.
16 The names of these nymphs have associations with water in Greek. *Hyale* means "Rainy."
17 "Droplet."
18 "Rain-drop."
19 "Libation bowl."
20 "Cloud."
21 See with note 1. 10.
22 Translating *Aurorae.*

she stood there with her side turned away and bent back
her face and, as though she wished she had her arrows at hand,
drew forth the water that she did have and drenched
the manly face, and, as she sprinkles with vengeful waters his hair,                     190
she adds these words that foretold the doom to come:
"You may tell now that I was seen disrobed,
if tell you could." With no more threats than these
she gives to his sprinkled head the horns of a lively stag,
she gives breadth to his neck and points to the tops of his ears;                        195
she changes his hands to hooves, to long legs
his arms and veils his body with a spotted hide;
and fear as well is added. The hero-son of Autonoë flees
and marvels that in his running he is so swift.
But as he sees his face in the water and the horns,                                      200
he meant to say, "Alas poor me!" but no voice came forth.
He moaned (that was his speech), and tears over a face not his own
poured forth: his mind alone remained untouched.
What should he do? Return to his home and royal house,
or hide in the woods? The former, shame, the latter fear forestalls.                     205
And as he ponders, the dogs see him and Melampus[23] first
and wise Ichnobates[24] gave the signal with their howls,
the Cnossian[25] Ichnobates, and Melampus of Spartan breed.
At that the others dash forward faster than the rapid wind,
Oribasos[26] and Pamphaos[27] and Dorceus[28], Arcadians all,                            210
with Laelaps[29] fierce Theron[30] and stalwart Nebrophonos[31]
and Pterelas,[32] useful of foot, and Agre,[33] for her nose,
and Hylaeus,[34] lately hit by a boar,
and wolf-born Nape[35] and Poemenis,[36] who tends the flocks,
Harpyia,[37] too, along with two pups,                                                   215
and Ladon[38] with his narrow flanks

---

23 The dogs all have meaningful Greek names: *Melampus* "Black-paw."
24 "Tracker."
25 From Cnossos on Crete.
26 "Mountain-ranger."
27 "Omnivorous."
28 "Gazelle-like."
29 "Whirlwind."
30 "Hunter."
31 "Fawn-killer."
32 "Winged-one."
33 "The Chaser."
34 "Woody."
35 "Vale."
36 "Shepherd."
37 "Snatcher."
38 "Grabber."

and Dromas[39] and Canache[40] and Sticte[41] and Tigris[42] and Alce,[43] too,
and Leucon[44] with snowy fur and Asbolos[45] with black
and powerful Lacon[46] and Aello,[47] in running strong,
and Thoos[48] and swift Lycisce[49] with her brother Cyprius,[50]                    220
and marked on his black forehead with a middle of white,
Harpalos[51] and Melaneus[52] and, with shaggy body, Lachne[53]
and, sired by Dictaeos[54] onto a Laconian[55] bitch,
Labros[56] and Agriodus[57] and Hylactor[58] with his sharp voice
and those whom to name would only delay; that pack, lusty for loot,              225
pursued through cliffs and crags and inaccessible rocks,
wherever it is hard, wherever there was no trail.
Actaeon flees over the paths he had often pursued;
alas, he flees his own servants. He wanted to cry
"Actaeon[59] I am, acknowledge your lord!"                                        230
His mind lacked the words; with barking resounds the air.
The first wounds Melanchaetes[60] made in his back,
the next, Therodamas;[61] Oresitrophos[62] to his shoulder clung
(arriving later than the others, but with the mountain shortcut
now at the front of the trail); as they held back their lord,                     235
the rest of the pack arrives and in his body set their teeth.
No longer is there room for wounds, he groans with a sound,
though not that of a man, nor yet one that a stag
could give, and fills the familiar ridges with sad complaints
and, fallen to his knees as a suppliant and like one who pleads,                  240
he casts about his silent glances as though they were his arms.
His comrades, though, urge on the pack with their usual commands,

---

39 "Racer."
40 "Splash."
41 "Spot."
42 "Tiger."
43 "Strength."
44 "Whitey."
45 "Sooty."
46 "Laconian," i.e., "Spartan."
47 "Tornado."
48 "Swifty."
49 "Wolf-like bitch."
50 "From Cyprus."
51 "Seizer."
52 "Blackie."
53 "Furry."
54 "From Mt. Dicte," after a mountain in Crete, or simply "Cretan."
55 I. e., Spartan.
56 "Furious" or "Boisterous" or "Greedy."
57 "Wild-fang."
58 "Barker."
59 The literal meaning of *Actaeon* "Dwelling on the headlands or coast" seems not to be significant to
   the story.
60 "Black-haired."
61 "Subduer of Wild Beasts."
62 "Mountain-reared."

*Actaeon and Diana and Hounds, Anonymous Venice ca. 1513*

not knowing the truth, and look for Actaeon with their eyes,
as though competing to cry out for the absent Actaeon
(who turns his head at his name) and of his absence complain,                    245
and of his being slow to catch sight of the proffered prey.
He wished indeed to be absent, but he is present, he wished to see,
and not also feel, the fierce deeds of his hounds.
They gather round on every side and, plunging into that body their snouts,
tear limb from limb their lord under the deceiving image of a stag;              250
nor till his life was ended by the copious wounds,
was quivered[63] Diana's anger stilled, they say.

### 253-315  *Semele*

Opinion is divided: to some the goddess seems
more violent than just, others are approving and call
her worthy for her stern virginity; each side finds its arguments.               255
Jove's wife alone does not so much say whether she approves
or blames as rejoice at destruction within the house
derived from Agenor, and from the Tyrian concubine[64]
transfers her accumulated wrath against those allied to her by blood.
For lo!, to her earlier reason a fresh one is added, her grief that from the seed   260
of mighty Jupiter Semele is pregnant. She lets her tongue give way to abuse,
and said, "What have I gained by my frequent complaints?
I must attack the woman herself; I'll destroy that woman herself

---

63 Many illustrations and paintings of this scene show that Diana had indeed taken up her discarded
   quiver and added her shots to the kill.
64 Europa.

if rightly I'm called Juno the Greatest, if my right hand justly wields
the gem-studded staff, if I am queen and of Jove                            265
the sister and wife, at any rate, the sister. But even though in the deceit,
she's satisfied, I suppose, and brief though this insult be to our marriage bed,
she's pregnant now (that was lacking) and bears with the fullness of her womb
the obvious reproach and wants to be a mother (a privilege scarcely mine)
to one who's born of Jove: so proud she is in the beauty of her form.       270
I'll make that pride betray her, and I'm not Saturnia if she by Jove
is not plunged in ruin and does not cross the waters of the Styx!"
With this she rises from her throne and, hidden in a yellow cloud,
approaches the threshold of Semele, nor did she take away the cloud
before disguising herself as a old woman and on her temples putting grey    275
and creasing her skin with wrinkles and bearing her bent limbs
with trembling steps, assuming as well an old woman's voice:
she looked like Beroë herself, the Epidaurian[65] nurse of Semele.
So when the opportunity arose for a good long chat,
they came to the name of Jove; that Beroë sighed and said,
"I hope he's Jupiter, but yet I fear all this: under the name                280
of gods have many invaded the rooms of the chaste.
And being Jove is not enough; let him give a proof of his love,
if truly he's who he says he is; and as big and as he is
when lofty Juno receives him, request that, just as big and just so,         285
he give to you his embrace and dress himself in advance with his usual signs."
With words like these had Juno primed
the ignorant daughter of Cadmus: she asks Jove for an unnamed boon.
The god replies to her, "Just choose, nothing will be denied.
And that you trust me more, let the spirit of the Stygian torrent be         290
our witness, that god who's feared by gods."
Delighted in her woe and too persuasive and about to die
because of her lover's obedience, Semele spoke:
"The way Saturnia embraces you when you engage in Venus' bond,
in that way give yourself to me." As she spoke, the god wanted to shut       295
her mouth, but her hasty words had already come forth into the air.
He groaned; but neither unchoose can she nor he
unswear, and therefore with great sadness climbed
the lofty aether and with his face drew the clouds in his train
and to them added storms and lightning mixed in the winds                   300
and thunder and the ineluctable lightning bolt.
As far as he can, he tries to shed his strength
and is not armed with the fire with which he had dashed
down hundred-handed Typhon: there's too much ferocity in that.
There is another, a lighter lightning, to which the Cyclopes' right hand     305

---

65 Ovid seems to have invented Beroë's origin from Epidaurus, the sanctuary of Asclepius on the east
   coast of the Peloponnesus.

*Jupiter and Semele, Solis*

instilled less savage flame, less wrath: the gods above
call these the weapons of the second rank; he seizes these
and enters the home of Agenor's line. The mortal body cannot bear
the heavenly din, and burns with these conjugal gifts.
Not yet completely formed, the infant from the mother's womb                310
is snatched and delicately sewn (if one is supposed to believe it)[66] into
the father's thigh and completes the maternal term.
In secret his mother's sister Ino raised him in his cradle years.
Thereafter he was given up, and the Nysaean nymphs[67] in their caves
concealed him and gave him nourishment from their milk.                     315

### 316-38  *Tiresias*

And while this is happening on earth by the law
of fate and the cradle of twice-born Bacchus is secure,
they say that by chance Jove, relaxed by nectar, set aside
his heavy cares and at leisure exchanged some light-hearted jests
with Juno and said, "Surely yours is without doubt                          320
a pleasure greater than that which touches males."
She disagrees. They decided to seek the opinion of wise
Tiresias: Venus was known to him in both kinds.
For he had violated the copulating bodies of two great snakes
amid the lush forest with the blow of his stick,                            325
and, changed from a man (miraculously), when as a woman he
had spent seven autumns, in the eighth he saw those very snakes
again and said, "If the power of a blow upon you is so great

---

66 Skepticism about this story is expressed at length by Cadmus and Tiresias in Euripides' *Bacchae*,
   especially 286-297. It is curious that Tiresias becomes the subject of Ovid's next tale.
67 Referring to Mt. Nysa, located in the East, usually India and sometimes used to explain the name
   Dionysus, i.e. the "Zeus of Mt. Nysa."

that it changes the one who made it into the opposite form,
I'll strike you once again." And when the serpents were struck,                330
his earlier form returned and his original appearance came back.
Therefore, the chosen arbiter for this playful dispute
confirmed the judgment of Jove. Saturnia, said to have been aggrieved
more gravely than justice or the matter allowed,
condemned their judge's eyes to eternal night.                                 335
But yet the omnipotent father (for no god may undo
the deeds of another god), in compensation for that stolen light,
bestowed the knowledge of the future and lightened with honor that punishment.

### 339-510  *Narcissus and Echo*

Throughout the Aonian cities that man, most celebrated by fame,
returned blameless responses to the people who asked.                          340
First trials of his credibility and voice were made
by sea-blue Liriope,[68] whom once in his winding stream
Cephisus[69] caught and, captured within his waves,
did violence to. That loveliest nymph from her swollen womb
gave birth to a child, who even then could be loved and whom                   345
she called Narcissus. When the prophetic seer was asked
if he would see a long span of ripe old age,
the answer was, "If he doesn't know himself."
For long the words of the augur[70] seemed pointless: the story's end
confirmed the words, the novelty of his madness, and the nature of his death. 350
For when Cephisus' son had added one year to three times five
and could appear as either a boy or a youth,
there were many youths, many girls who desired him;
but (so unbending was his pride in his youthful form)
no youths, no girls have moved him.                                            355
And as he drives into his nets the fearful stags,
a nymph of notable voice, who had learned neither to be silent to one
who speaks nor to speak first, caught sight of him, Echo, repeater of sounds.
Till now was Echo a body, not a voice; and nevertheless
the prattler still has no other use of her mouth but this:                     360
she has the ability to repeat the very last of many words.
(The work of Juno this was because, when she might have caught
the nymphs on the mountain lying beneath her Jove,
that girl deliberately detained the goddess with lengthy talk
until the nymphs had fled. When Saturnia realized this,                        365
she says, "The power of this tongue by which I've been tricked

---

68 The Greek name of the mother of Narcissus seems to mean "Lily-faced," appropriate to the lily that
   Narcissus will become.
69 A river in Phocis and Boeotia.
70 Strictly, one who prophesies by observation of birds. The term here is probably chosen partly for
   sake of variety, partly for metrical reasons as the equivalent of *vates*, "seer."

shall be made small for you and the usage of your voice extremely brief."
And she confirmed her threats: the nymph only twins the final words
of one who speaks and repeats the words she has heard.)
When seeing, therefore, Narcissus roaming through the trackless countryside    370
she warmed and follows in secret his trail;
the more she follows, the warmer the flame becomes,
not otherwise than when, smeared upon the top of a torch,
tenacious sulfur catches quickly the tendered flames.
Alas, how often she wished to approach with flattering words    375
and ply her languid prayers! Her nature forbids
nor lets her begin: but what it does allow, she's prepared for that:
to wait for sounds to which she might send back her words.
By chance the boy, enticed away from his companions' loyal band,
had said, "Someone's here?" and Echo had replied "Someone's here."    380
Amazed, he casts in all directions his gaze
and shouts with a loud voice "Come!" She calls the one who calls.
He turns around and, when no one comes, calls again, "So why
do you avoid me?" and got back as many words as he spoke.
Persisting and deceived by the image of the other voice,    385
he says, "Let's come together here," and never more willing to respond
to any sound, Echo returned "let's come together here!"
and favors her own words herself and having emerged from the woods
was coming to throw her arms about the neck she desired.
He flees and in fleeing says, "Take away your hands with their embrace,    390
for may I die before you have access to us."
She answers nothing but "you have access to us."
Rejected, she hides in the woods and covers her blushing face
with leafy boughs and from then on lives in lonely caves.
But yet her love stands fixed and grows with the pain of defeat:    395
her wakeful cares make her wretched body thin,
decay contracts her skin and into the air all
her body's sap departs; only voice and bones remain:
the voice remains; they say the bones took on the shape of stone.
Henceforth, concealed in the woods and on no mountain seen,    400
by all is she heard: what lives within her is sound.

      He thus made sport of her and, thus, other nymphs,
from mountain waters sprung, and, thus, earlier, the company of men:
of those, one he had scorned raised his hands toward the sky and said
"May he thus love, and thus not gain the one he loves!"    405
The goddess of Rhamnus[71] paid heed to his just requests.
There was a fountain, free of slime, whose silver waters gleamed,
which neither shepherds nor mountain-grazing goats

---

71 Nemesis "Destruction," who had her sanctuary at Rhamnus in Attica.

had touched nor any flock, which no bird
nor beast had troubled, nor even a branch fallen from a tree.          410
Around about there was grass, which the near-by water fed,
nor would the forest allow the sun to heat the place.
Here lay the boy one day, wearied by the heat and pursuit of the hunt,
attracted by the appearance of the place and by the spring.
And when he sought to quench his thirst, another thirst arose,          415
and when he drank, overcome by the image of the form he saw,
he loves a hope without a body, and what is water he takes for flesh.
Struck dumb is he at himself, and with unchanging gaze
he stands, like a statue formed from Parian marble, transfixed.
And when he lies on the ground, he looks at twin stars, his eyes,          420
and at his locks, worthy of Bacchus, worthy of Apollo, too,
and beardless cheeks and ivory neck and the beauty of
his face and a ruddiness mixed with the fairness of snow,
admiring all the things for which he himself is admired.
Not knowing it, he desires himself, and he who approves is approved,          425
and while he seeks, he is sought, and at once is warmed and warms.
How often did he give his empty kisses to that deceiving spring!
How often, reaching for the neck he saw, did he dip his arms
into the midst of those waters and in them fail to find himself!
He knows not what he sees, but burns for what he sees:          430
the same error that deceives incites as well his eyes.
O credulous one, why do you clutch at the fleeting images in vain?
For what you seek is nowhere; what you love you will destroy.
Oh, turn away, for what you see is a reflected image, an empty form,
containing nothing in itself; it comes and stays with you,          435
with you it departs, if you could depart.
Concern for Ceres,[72] concern for sleep cannot
pull him away from there, but, stretched out upon the shady grass,
he gazes with insatiable eye at the deceptive form
and through his own eyes destroys himself; rising up somewhat          440
and lifting his arms towards the surrounding woods,
he says, "Did anyone, O you forests, more cruelly love?
You know, after all, since for many were you convenient for trysts.
Do you remember, through all the centuries of your life,
that anyone in all that time wasted away like this?          445
I like what I see and what I see and like
I still cannot find: so great is the error that holds a man in love.
And that I grieve the more, we are separated by no great sea
nor distance nor mountains nor walls with gates that are shut:
we're kept apart by a little water! He wants to be held:          450
but yet as often as we extend to the clear waters our lips,

---

72 I. e., food, since Ceres is the goddess of agriculture.

he struggles to reach me with his upturned mouth.
You'd think he could be touched: we lovers are hindered by something so small.
Whoever you are, come out to me! Why are you, singular boy, deceiving me?
And when I seek you, where do you retreat? Surely it's not my beauty or age   455
you're fleeing, since even nymphs have been in love with me.
Your friendly face promises some kind of hope,
and when I extend my arms to you, you extend yours of your own accord;
whenever I've smiled, you smile back; and often I've seen your tears
as I myself am weeping; at my nod you return the same sign,                    460
and though I see from the motion of your lovely mouth
that you are sending back words, they do not reach our ears.
That fellow, it's me! I've got it now, by my own image I'm not deceived.
I burn with love for myself. I both create and endure the flames.
What should I do? Be sought or seek? What indeed shall I seek?                 465
The thing I love is within me. Availability has made me powerless!
O would that I could withdraw from this body of ours!
A strange vow is this in a lover, that I should desire the absence of what we[73] love.
Already grief is robbing me of my strength, and of the span of my life
not much remains, and I'm being destroyed in the prime of life.               470
And death is not a burden for me since death will quell my pain;
I wish that he in whom I delight might be longer-lived.
United now in spirit the two of us will die in one breath."
He spoke and, scarcely sane, returned to that same face
and with his tears disturbed the waters and obscured                          475
the form by the movement of the surface. When he saw it leave,
he shouted, "Where are you going, cruel one? Stay and leave me not,
your lover. Although we cannot touch, allow yourself to be seen
and to my wretched madness give yourself as nourishment."
And as he grieved, he pulled off his cloak from its upper hem                 480
and beat his breast with his marble-like palms.
His beaten breast took on the hue of rosy red,
not other than that of apples that are partly white,
but partly red, or as in the changing clusters the grapes
take on their purple color when not yet ripe.                                 485
As soon as he saw this within the water, again grown clear,
no longer could he bear it, but as in the gentle heat
the yellow wax is wont to melt and like the morning dew
beneath the warming sun, thus enfeebled by love,
he melts and little by little is eaten away by the hidden fire;               490
and now there is no color of whiteness mixed with red,
nor vigor nor strength nor all the things that pleased before,
nor did the body remain that Echo once had loved.

---

73 Scattered through Narcissus' words is the "royal we," here and in the previous line perhaps for
   metrical reasons.

Yet as she saw this, remembering and vexed,
she grieved, and as often as the pitiable boy said, "Alas,"                    495
with echoing sounds she repeated, "Alas!"
Whenever he struck his shoulders with his hands,
she, too, returned the same sound of those blows.
His final words as he gazed into the familiar waters were these:
"Alas, boy, beloved in vain!" And every time                                  500
the place returned the words and with every "Farewell!" Echo replied
"Farewell." He laid his weary head upon the verdant grass;
death closed his eyes as they admired their master's form.
But even then, received into that infernal home,
he looked at himself in the Stygian water. The sister Naiads wept            505
and offered to their brother their severed locks,
and Dryads wept; to their weeping Echo resounds.
And now they ready the pyre, the brandished torches, and the bier:
the body was not to be found; a yellow flower in the body's stead
they find girt round with petals of white.                                    510

### 511-733  Pentheus

        Discovery of the matter had won for the prophet deservèd fame
throughout the Achaean cities, and great was the seer's repute.[74]
But Echion's son, Pentheus, the only one of them all,
the scorner of the gods, despises the old man and mocks
his prophecies and chides him for his darkness[75] and                        515
the loss of his stolen light. The other, shaking his temples, hoary with white,
replies, "How happy you would be," he says, "if you of this light
yourself were deprived so that you not behold the Bacchic rites.
The day will come, which I foresee as not far away,
when Liber,[76] Semele's new child, will come to this place.                  520
Unless you deign to honor him with shrines, you'll be
dismembered and scattered in a thousand places, and stain with blood
the forests and your mother and your mother's sisters as well.
It will be so, for you will not deign to honor the spirit of the god,
and you will regret that I in my darkness saw too well."                      525
For saying this the son of Echion drove him away.
        His words prove true and the prophet's responses come to pass.
At Liber's presence the fields resound with festive howls;
a rushing mob of women, mixed with men, and daughters-in-law
and common folk and nobles is drawn to the unknown rites.                     530
"What madness, O serpent-born people, children of Mars,
has dashed your wits?" says Pentheus. "Is merest bronze

---

74 Here the story returns to Tiresias, who had predicted Narcissus' future (see 3. 348).
75 *Tenebras* here implies "obscurity," "ignorance," and "blindness."
76 A Latin name for Bacchus.

*Narcissus and Echo, Anonymous Venice ca. 1513*

when struck by bronze so strong, and the pipe with its curvèd bell,
and cheating magic, that you, whom neither the sword nor trump
of war nor the battle lines of brandished arms could fill with fear,          535
are overcome by women's voices and wine-driven rage
and foul-mouthed throngs and hollow drums?
Should I not be amazed, old men, at you, having traveled the ocean wide
and set in this home your exiled Penates[77] and here your Tyre,
who let yourselves be taken without a fight, [78] and at you, young men,          540
of livelier age and nearer my own, who should be bearing arms,
not thyrsuses,[79] and be covered by helmets, not wreaths?
Be mindful, I pray, of what stock your were born;
assume the spirit of him who ruined many, though one,
that serpent. For his fountains and lake the serpent died:          545
but you must be victorious for your fame!
Just as the serpent sent the strong to their death, so repel now the weak
and save your ancestral honor. If the fates forbade
that Thebes should long remain, would that engines of war and men
should overthrow her walls, and iron and fire should ring:          550
for blameless would we be in our misery, our fate would be bewailed
and not concealed, and our tears would bear no shame.
But now will Thebes be taken by an unarmed boy,
whom neither wars assist nor arms nor cavalry,
but hair drenched in myrrh and supple crowns          555

---

77 Household gods. See 1. 174 and note.
78 Translating *sine Marte* " without Mars."
79 The thyrsus is the technical name in Greek for the Maenads' spear-like wand capped by a pine-cone.

and purple and gold woven into his painted gowns.
Indeed, I'll make him by force without delay (just stand aside)
admit he's feigned a father and fabricated his sacred rites.
Or is it to be that, though Acrisius[80] had sense enough to despise
him as an empty deity and to close the Argive gates to him when he came,    560
this immigrant will terrify Pentheus and all of Thebes?
Go quickly," he commands his servants, "go bring
their leader in chains and let my command find no delay."
His grandfather[81] and Athamas[82] and his thronging people chide
him with their words and strive to hold him back.    565
The warnings make him even harsher and, when restrained,
his madness is stirred and grows, and the very attempts to restrain did harm:
thus I[83] myself have seen unhindered a rushing stream
quite gently and with measured murmur fall,
but where obstructing rocks and logs held it back,    570
it foamed and boiled and ran more savage opposed.

### 572-700  *Acoetes and the Tyrrhenian Sailors*

Behold, all bloodied they return and when their master asks
where Bacchus is, they say they've not seen Bacchus. They say
"This fellow, however, the companion and servant of his rites,
we took," and hand him over with hands tied behind his back,    575
a person of Tyrrhenian[84] origin who observed the rites of the god.
As Pentheus inspects him with eyes made huge by rage,
—although by no means delaying the hour of his punishment—
he says, "You are about to die and soon will give precedent
to others by your death: reveal your name and your parents' name    580
and country and why these people are celebrating these unaccustomed rites."
Without the slightest fear, he replied, "Acoetes is my name,
my land, Maeonia, my parents of humble plebeian stock.[85]
No fields did my father leave me for sturdy oxen to till
or wooly flocks or any herds of kine.    585
A poor man he was, who with hook and line
and reedy rod would catch the leaping fish.
His art was his estate. When he handed down his art,
he said, 'Receive all the wealth I have, successor and heir
to my pursuit.' And when he died, he left nothing more to me    590

---

80 This king of Argos, father of Danaë, opposed the worship of Dionysus.
81 Cadmus.
82 This son of Thessalian Aeolus moved to Boeotia, became king of Orchomenus, and married Ino, a
daughter of Cadmus.
83 Ovid.
84 The Tyrrhenians were a people of Lydia (Maeonia) from which the Etruscans were thought to have
originated. The Tyrrhenian pirates here are Etruscans.
85 Translating *humili de plebe*, an expression adding a Roman flavor to the story. The Bacchanalia were
suppressed by the Roman Senate in 186 B.C. (see Livy 39. 8-18).

than waters: this is the only patrimony I claim.
So not forever to cleave to the same old crags, I soon
learned how to bend the rudder of a boat with my guiding hand
and noted with my eyes the rainy star of the Olenian[86] goat,
Taygete[87] and the Hyades and the Bear,[88]                          595
the homes of the winds and ports that were apt for ships.
In route for Delos by chance, towards the shores of the Chian[89] land
I ply my course and gain the beach with my skillful oars
and give a light-footed leap and set myself upon the soggy sand.
As soon as night was past (Aurora had just begun                      600
to blush), I rise, for fresh water give the command,
and show the way that leads to the springs
while I myself from a high rise seek out a breeze
and summon my companions and return to my ship.
'Look here, we're back,' says Opheltes, the first of my troop,        605
and thinking that he's acquired some booty in the deserted field,
he's leading a boy with the beauty of a maiden down the beach,
who seems to stagger, heavy with sleep and unmixed wine
and scarcely able to follow; as I gaze at his style and face and pace,
I saw nothing there that could be deemed of mortal kind.              610
I sensed it and told my comrades, 'What divinity in him
there is I hesitate to name, but in that body is a god.
Whoever you are, Oh may you favor our labors here.
Forgive these men, I also pray.' 'Do not pray for us,'
says Dictys,[90] than whom none was quicker to climb                  615
the lofty yard-arms and grasping a rope to slide back down again.
With this did Libys, with this the ruddy Melanthus[91] agree,
with this Alcimedon as well and he who with his voice
supplied the measured cadence of the oars, the driver of their spirits, Epopeus;
with this all the others agreed: their desire for plunder is so blind.  620
'No matter, I will not allow this ship of pine to be stained
by such a weight of sacrilege,' I said. 'I have the greatest authority here,'
and on the gangplank I block the way. Raging most recklessly of all
that band was Lycabas, expelled from a Tuscan town
and paying the price of an awful murder with banishment.             625
As I resist, he pounded my throat with his youthful fist
and would have hurled me overboard into the sea
had I not madly clung to the rope.
The impious mob approves the deed; then Bacchus at length
(for Bacchus he was), as though the shouts had dissolved             630

86 Referring to Aege, the daughter of Olenus, identified with the star Capella.
87 One of the Pleiades.
88 Translating *Arcton* "Arctos," the Big and Little Dipper.
89 Chios is an island in the Aegean.
90 The name means "Net-fisher" in Greek.
91 The name means "Black-flower/Swarthy" in Greek.

his sleep and sense had returned to his breast,
says, 'What are you doing? What uproar is this? Sailors, tell me how
I came to be here? Where are you planning to carry me?'
'Belay your fear,' said Proreus,[92] 'and name the ports
you wish us to touch to set you in the land of your choice.'                    635
Replying, Liber says, 'toward Naxos turn your course.
My home is there, the land will be hospitable to you.'
The liars swear by the sea and all the gods
to do just this and order me to raise the sails of the painted ship.
Though Naxos lay on the right, when I set the sails to the right,           640
Opheltes says, 'You fool, what *are* you doing? Acoetes, are
you mad?' With each man out for himself,[93] most signal with a nod,
while others express their desire with a whisper to my ear, 'Turn left!'
Dumbfounded I was. 'Someone else must take the helm,' I said,
removing myself from service to their crime and craft.                       645
Upbraided by all am I, and a murmur runs through all the crew,
from whom Aethalion[94] avers, 'As though in you alone
depended the safety of us all!' and takes my place,
assumes my tasks and, with Naxos abandoned, seeks a different course.
The god then playfully, as if only now aware of their deceit,               650
looked out from the crescent ship upon the sea,
and seeming to weep, says, 'These are not the shores
you promised me, nor this the land that I desired.
For what wrong have I deserved to be punished? What is
your glory if you young men, being many, deceive one boy?'               655
Already had I begun to weep: that impious band
just laugh at my tears and with quickening oars beat the waves.
I swear to you by him (for no god is more powerful than he),
I'm telling you things that are as true
as hard to believe: the ship stood still in the sea,                             660
no less than if a dry dock were holding it fast.
In wonder they persist in flailing the oars,
unfurl the sails and with this twofold means try to run.
But ivy impedes the oars and in tangling bonds
and heavily clustered flowers creep over and adorn the sails.              665
With brow wreathed in clusters of grapes, he himself
bestirs a spear[95] enveloped in leafy curls;
around him tigers lie and lynxes' phantom shapes
and fierce bodies of painted panthers as well.
The men jumped ship, whether the cause of this                              670

92 The name means "Man at the Prow" in Greek.
93 Translating the manuscript's *pro se quisque timet.*
94 The name means "Swarthy" in Greek. Perhaps the colorful names of Aethalion and Melanthus
  foreshadow their metamorphosis into the dark-skinned dolphins. See 671.
95 The thyrsus.

was madness or fright, and Medon first grew black
throughout his body and begins to be bent,
his spine distinctly curved: 'What marvel are you becoming,'
said Lycabas to him, and his mouth gaped wide as he spoke,
his nose was bowed, and his hardened skin wore scales.                           675
But Libys, in seeking to ply the resisting oars
beheld his hands as they sprang back, reduced in size:
no longer hands, but now able to be called fins.
Another, desiring to reach out his arms to the twisted ropes,
possessed no arms and, bent backwards with body maimed,                          680
he leapt into the waves. The tip of his tail is forked
just like the horns of the half-moon, extending into a curve.
They're leaping all about and dewy with spray,
and rise again and return again beneath sea,
and play like a troop of dancers and toss their jolly forms                      685
and from their broad nostrils blow out the inhaled sea.
Out of the twenty there were (this the number carried by
that ship), I alone remained, with trembling body, cold with fear,
and hardly myself. The god comforts me and says,
'Cast fear from your heart and make for Dia.'[96] When I arrived,               690
I joined the sacred rites and often celebrate the Bacchic rites."
      "To your long digressions," said Pentheus, "we have lent our ears,
that anger delayed might lose its force.
Be off with this man, attendants, and send
his body, crucified with dreadful torments, to the Stygian night."               695
At once Tyrrhenian Acoetes is dragged away
and shut within a sturdy house; and while the cruel instruments
are readied for the sentence of death, the iron and fire,
the doors of themselves opened wide, and from his limbs,
the story goes, the chains with none to loosen them fall away.                   700

### 701-33   *The Death of Pentheus*

      The son of Echion persists, nor issues orders now for others to go,
but goes himself, where Cithaeron, chosen for performing the sacred rites,
was echoing with the Bacchants' shrill voices and songs.
Just as an eager horse, when with tuneful bronze
the trumpeter of war has given the signal, acquires a love for the fray,         705
just so the air, smitten by the long howling, stirred Pentheus,
and once again the clamor he heard made his anger grow hot.
About midway up a mountain, there is a plain quite free of trees,
with woods encircling its edge and visible from every side.[97]

---

96 Another name for Naxos.
97 The translator is reminded by these lines of the serene high Piano della Cinquemiglia, some twelve
    miles SSE of Ovid's native Sulmo (modern Sulmona).

*Death of Pentheus, Baur*

As he observed the sacred rites with eyes profane,                                        710
the first to see him, the first to be impelled in a mad rush,
the first to violate her Pentheus with thyrsus flung
was his own mother, who shouted, "Come here, my sisters two!
That boar which wanders huge within our fields,
that boar is mine to strike." The whole crowd is enraged                         715
and rushes madly against one man; they all converge and chase
the frightened man, now indeed afraid, now uttering less violent words,
now blaming himself, confessing now that he was wrong.
        Though wounded, he said, "Dear aunt, by Actaeon's[98] shades,
please help! Let the heart of Autonoë be moved!                                      720
She knew not who Actaeon was and tore away
the right arm of the suppliant; the other was torn by Ino's wrenching force.
No arm to stretch out to his mother did the unfortunate one have,
but showing the mutilations of those wounds made by the sundered limbs,
he says, "O mother, behold." At the sight Agave howled                         725
and tossed her head and shook her hair in the breeze
and grasped with bloodied fingers the head she had wrenched away
and shouts, "Io! My comrades, this labor is our victory!"
When touched by autumn's chill, no more quickly are leaves,
already clinging weakly to the lofty tree, torn away by the wind              730
than are the limbs of the man torn away by these impious hands.
        Once warned by examples like these, the Ismenides[99] celebrate the new rites
and offer incense and give the sacred altars their care.

---

98 Actaeon was the son of Autonoë.
99 The Theban women.

# BOOK 4

| 1-415 | The Daughters of Minyas |
|---|---|
| 36-166 | One sister Tells the Tale of Pyramus and Thisbe |
| 167-273 | Leuconoë's Tale of Leucothoë (and of Venus and Mars). |
| 274-388 | Alcithoë's Tale of Salmacis and Hermaphroditus. |
| 416-562 | Athamas and Ino |
| 563-603 | The End of Cadmus and Harmonia |
| 604-803 | Perseus and Andromeda |

## 1-415  The Daughters of Minyas

Alcithoë, the daughter of Minyas,[1] does not propose
acceptance of the god's rites, but rashly even now
denies that Bacchus is the offspring of Jove, and as allies of her impiety
she has her sisters. The priest has given the order to celebrate
the feast, that servants be immune from their labors, and their mistresses          5
should cover their breasts with hides, untie the bindings of their locks,
set garlands upon their hair, and take the leafy thyrsus in their hands,
and warned that the wrath of the god would be savage if he
were scorned. Both matrons and young women obey
and leave the looms and baskets and unfinished work          10
and offer incense and call him Bacchus and Bromius[2] and Lyaeus,[3] too,
and born of fire and twice-sired, twice-mothered, him alone;[4]
and add to these the names Nysaeus[5] and unshorn Thyoneus,[6]
Lenaeus,[7] the sower of the genial grape,
Nyctelius,[8] and father Eleleus and Euhan and Iacchus[9]          15

---

1 King of Orchomenos in Boeotia.
2 "The Thunderer."
3 "The One Who Sets Free" from the Greek *lyein*. Cf. Latin *Liber*.
4 Rescued from the flames which consumed his mother Semele, Bacchus is sewn into the thigh of his father and born again from Zeus/Jupiter as his second mother (see 3. 310-13).
5 Nysa was a legendary mountain in the vicinity of India where Dionysus was alleged to have been born, the name perhaps having been invented to explain the god's name, the "Zeus of Nysa." The stem of the Greek *Zeus* is *Di-*. Or, according to Cicero, *De Natura Deorum*, 3.58, from Nisus, as the father of Bacchus, by Thyone.
6 From Thyone, another name for Semele, the mother of Bacchus. The name evokes the Greek *thyias* "Bacchant" and the verb *thyein* "rage."
7 The *lenos* was the Greek wine-press. The *Lenai* were the Bacchanals. The *Lenaea* was one of the dramatic festivals of Athens in honor of Dionysus.
8 "The Night-time One," because the rites of Bacchus were sometimes performed at night.
9 These three names are derived from the cries of the worshippers of Bacchus.

and what many other names among the peoples of Greece
you have, O Liber.[10] For youth unending is yours,
as an eternal boy are you, you, the most handsome in heaven above
admired. When you stand forth without your horns[11]
your head is maiden-like; the Orient is conquered by you                    20
as far as dusky India that the distant Ganges stains.
O venerable one, you slaughter Pentheus and Lycurgus of the double axe,
profaners both, and cast the Tyrrhenian bodies into the sea;
you press the necks of double-yoked lynxes adorned
with painted reins; the Bacchants and Satyrs are in your train,             25
and that old man,[12] filled with wine, who supports with his staff
his tottering limbs and clings unsteadily to his ass's sagging back.
Wherever you process, together the clamor of youths
and women's voices and hand-beaten drums
and concave brasses[13] resound and the long stop[14] of the boxwood pipe.   30
    "Be present, appeased and gentle," the Ismenides[15] implore
and tend with care the rites he commands; indoors Minyas' daughters alone
disturb the festive days with Minerva's untimely work
and spin the wool or turn the strings with their thumbs
or cleave to the loom or urge on their handmaids to their tasks.            35

### 36-166   *One Sister Tells the Tale of Pyramus and Thisbe.*

    Of these one said, as she drew out a thread with her thumb,
"While others shirk and celebrate those fictitious rites,
let us as well, detained by Pallas, a better deity,
with varied conversation lighten the useful work of our hands
and take turns in offering our company's ready ears                         40
some means of keeping the time from seeming so long."
Approving her words, the sisters command the first to tell a tale.
Because she knows so many stories, she wonders which to tell
and hesitates whether to tell of you, Dercetis[16] of Babylon, transformed
with scales covering your limbs, who, the people of Palestine               45
believe, made the stagnant waters move with your form,
or rather how her daughter, by sprouting wings,
in shining towers spent her final years,
or how a Naiad by incantation and exceedingly powerful herbs

---

10 From the Latin, "Free."
11 Bacchus is often represented with horns.
12 Papa-Silenus. See on 11. 90.
13 Cymbals and/or trumpets.
14 Translating *longo foramine* "with its long hole," perhaps the bottom hole that produces the deepest
    pitch of the pipe.
15 The women of Thebes, named after the river Ismenos flowing through Thebes.
16 The Syrian goddess, who threw herself into the sea in shame for her love of a youth by whom she
    gave birth to Semiramis, the legendary queen supposed to have built Babylon and associated with
    the historical 9th-century queen Sammuramat.

transformed the silent fish into the bodies of youths 50
until she suffered the same herself, or how the tree
that bore white fruit now by the touch of blood produces black.
She chooses this one, since the tale is not well known,
beginning this way as the wool obeyed her threads:
"Once Pyramus and Thisbe, the former the handsomest of youths, 55
the latter, the finest girl of all the East possessed,
resided in houses that touched, where Semiramis, they say,
had girt her city with walls of brick.
Proximity made them acquainted and brought their paths together first.
In time their love increased; by the law of the marriage torch 60
they would have been joined had their parents not refused.
But even they could not forbid that both captive minds should burn alike.
With no one in whom to confide, they speak by nods and signs.
The more it is hidden, the hotter seethes the hidden fire.
The wall common to both houses was split with a slender crack 65
as it was being built, and the crack had grown in time.
That fault, through all the years perceived by none
(but what does love not perceive?), you lovers were first to see
and made yourselves a path and through that path
would safely pass with the merest whisper your blandishments. 70
When often, Thisbe on this side and Pyramus on that,
the breath of each mouth in turn had been caught,
they used to say, 'O hateful wall, why do you stand in the lovers' way?
How much would it cost for you to allow our bodies to be joined
or, if this is too much, to open wide that we might kiss? 75
And we are not ungrateful and confess we owe to you
that passage to loving ears has been granted our words.'
     Conversing in vain like this from either post
at night, they said, 'Farewell,' and to their own side
imparted kisses that would not reach the other side. 80
Aurora's next approach had removed the fires of night,
and Sol had dried with his rays the frost on the grass:
they came together at their usual place. In soft whispers then,
complaining much at first, they plan in silence of night
to try to deceive their guards and to get out through the doors 85
and, after leaving the house and even the homes of the city behind,
so that they not go astray in making their way over the field,
to meet at the burial mound of Ninus[17] and under the cover of a tree
to hide: a tree was there, very full of snow-white fruit,
a lofty mulberry adjacent to an icy spring. 90
The plans are approved; the light of day, seeming slow to descend,

---

17 Husband of Semiramis, the legendary Assyrian king, founder of Nineveh.

into the waters sinks, and from those waters comes forth the night.
The hinges turned, the clever Thisbe emerges through the dark,
deceives her guards by veiling her face
and reaches the tomb and sits beneath the stated tree. 95
Her love was making her bold: but lo, there comes
from recent slaughter a lioness, her jaws smeared with foam,
who seeks to slake her thirst in the water of the nearby spring.
From far away Babylonian Thisbe saw her through the rays of the moon
and fled with fearful foot into the darkness of a cave, 100
and as she fled, she left behind the veil that had slipped from her back.
The savage lioness had slaked with abundant water her thirst
and, while returning to the forest, found by chance the flimsy veil,
without the girl herself, and mauled it with her bloody jaws.
When Pyramus, having departed later, beheld in the deep dust 105
the certain track of the beast, a pallor come over all his face.
And when in fact he also found her garment stained with blood,
he says, 'One night two lovers will destroy,
of whom she most deserved a long life;
the guilty soul was ours.[18] Poor dear, the one who destroyed you was I, 110
who ordered you to come by night to this fearful place
and came not hither first. Tear this body of ours
and with your savage teeth devour these cursèd bowels,
whatever lions you are that dwell beneath this rock!
But praying for death is the part of a timid man.' He picks up Thisbe's veil 115
and takes it to the shade of the designated tree,
and, as he gave his tears, gave his lips to the cloth he knew,
he said, 'Receive a draught of our blood as well,'
and thrust into his loins the sword with which he was girt,
and with no delay withdrew it, dying from the surging wound. 120
And as he lay on his back upon the ground, the gory blood leapt high,
not other than if from a fault in its lead a pipe
were broken and through the hissing crack should spurt
the gentle waters far and part the air with their pulse.
The fruit of the tree by the spray of the gore 125
is turned in appearance to black, and the blood-soaked root
embellishes the pendant mulberry with purple hue.
        "Behold, her fear not yet allayed, she returns,
her lover not to confuse, and with eyes and mind looks for the youth,
so eager to tell all the perils she had escaped. 130
And when she recognizes the place and the form of the tree she had seen,
the color of the berry confuses her, uncertain if this is the one.
And as she hesitates, she sees the quivering members that pulse
against the bloody ground and withdraws her step

---

18 Poetic plural for "mine."

*Pyramus and Thisbe, Solis*

and, wearing a face paler than boxwood, shuddered like the sea    135
that ripples when its surface is graced by the slightest breeze.
But after pausing, she recognized her love,
and beat her undeserving limbs with resounding blows
and tore her hair and, embracing the body she loved,
made full its wounds with weeping and with the blood    140
combined her tears and planted kisses upon the frigid face:
'O Pyramus,' she cried, 'what misfortune has taken you from me?
O Pyramus, answer me! Your Thisbe, dearest, is calling you.
Give ear and lift your fallen face!'
At Thisbe's name, Pyramus lifted up his eyes,    145
now heavy with death, and closed them at the sight of her.
And after she recognizes her garment and sees without its sword
the ivory scabbard, she says, 'It was your hand and love
that ruined you, unhappy man. Yet for this one thing my hand
is brave, and love have I as well: this will give the strength to wound.    150
Allow me to follow the dead and of your death be called
the saddest cause and companion; and you whom death alone
could tear from me will not by death be torn.
For this, however, by the words of us both be implored,
O parents, most unfortunate, mine and his,    155
that, just as we by determined loved, by our final hour were joined,
you not begrudge us to be laid to rest in a common tomb.
but thou, O tree that now gives cover to the wretched corpse
of one and soon will cover those of two,
retain the symbols of this death and keep somber and dusky your fruit,    160
forever suited to grief, the proof of our common blood.'

She spoke and with the point placed at the base of her breast,
she fell upon it, still warm from death.
The gods, however, had been touched by her prayers, her parents were touched:
for black is the color of the fruit when it is ripe,                    165
and what survives on the pyre remains at rest within one urn."

### 167-273   Leuconoë's Tale of Leucothoë (and of Venus and Mars)

Her story ended, and after a brief pause Leuconoë[19]
began to speak: her sisters ceased their talk.
"This very Sun as well, who governs all with his starry light,
was captured by Love: we shall tell the loves of Sol.                   170
They say that the adultery of Venus and Mars
this god was first to have seen. This god sees everything first.
Annoyed at the deed, he revealed to her husband,[20] of Juno born,
the theft of the marriage bed and the place of the theft. But Vulcan forgot
his thoughts and dropped the work of his skillful right hand.           175
At once he perfected graceful chains of bronze
and nets and snares to deceive the eyes
(the slenderest threads would not outdo that work,
not even the spider web that from the highest rafter hangs)
and made them yield to gentle motions and the slightest touch           180
and lays them all around the bed just right.
And when his wife and the adulterer came together to the same bed,
within those chains prepared by the husband's skill and new device
they both were caught and in the midst of their embrace held fast.
The Lemnian[21] at once laid open the double ivory doors                185
and ushered in the gods: that pair lay bound
disgracefully, and one[22] of the not unhappy gods would like, he says,
to be disgraced that way. The gods above laughed and for long
in all of heaven this was the most widely told story of all.

"Cythera's[23] goddess exacted unforgetting penalty for the informer's tale 190
and wounds in turn the one who had wounded their hidden love
by means of an equal love. O son of Hyperion,[24] what use to you now
your beauty, your color and your radiated light?
In fact, you, who burn every land with your fires,
are burning yourself with a new fire. You, who must perceive all things, 195
observe Leucothoë[25] and on this maid alone keep fixed

---

19 Leuconoë whose name means "Bright Mind" will tell the story of Leucothoë "Brightly Rushing."
20 Vulcan, the Greek Hephaestus. For the story see Homer, *Odyssey* 8. 266-366.
21 Vulcan is associated with the volcanic island of Lemnos in the Aegean Sea.
22 According to Hom., *Od.* 8. 348-342, it was Hermes' remark that moved the gods to laughter at the scene. For the union of Mercury with Venus, see 288.
23 Venus (Aphrodite) was born near this island according to Hes., *Theog.* 192.
24 Here Hyperion is the father of the Sun, not as at 15. 406-407 the Sun-god himself.
25 Daughter of Orchamus, King of Babylon. This tale, like that of Pyramus and Thisbe, seems to come from the Near East.

*Venus and Mars, Anonymous Venice ca. 1513*

the eyes you owe to the world. Sometimes you're late to rise from the East
and sometimes tardy to fall into the waves
and in the dalliance of your gaze extend the hours of the winter days.
At times you fail and the fault of your mind affects your light,                        200
and in your darkened state you put fear into mortal hearts.
Nor is it the image of the moon standing closer to the earth
that makes you pale: that color of yours is caused by love.
Your love is for one alone, and neither Rhodos[26] nor Clymene[27]
detains you, nor Aeaean Circe's mother[28] most fair,                                  205
nor Clytie,[29] who, though rejected, pursued
your bed and at that very time felt a grievous wound:
Leucothoë made you forget many girls, the one
whom Eurynome, loveliest of the sweet-scented race,[30]
had born; but after the daughter grew, by as much did she                             210
surpass her mother, as her mother all others surpassed.
Her father, Orchamus, ruled the cities of Achaemenia[31]
and from the first beginnings is numbered seventh in Belus'[32] line.
Beneath the Hesperian pole is the pasture of the horses of the Sun:

---

26 Pindar, *Olympian* 7. 100-140, recounts how because Helios was forgotten when the gods divided up
   the earth, Zeus made the island of Rhodes rise up from the sea for the Sun-god, who sired seven
   sons by the nymph Rhodos.
27 Daughter of Oceanus and Tethys and mother by Apollo of Phaethon.
28 Perse, mother by Apollo of Circe, who lived on the island of Aeaea.
29 Another daughter of Oceanus, enamored of Apollo.
30 I. e., Persian.
31 According to Herodotus 1. 125 and 7. 11, Achaemenes founded Persia.
32 *Belus*, derived from Phoenician *Baal* "Owner, Lord," is the name of many Near-Eastern rulers, inclu-
   ding the ancestor of the Belides (= Danaids), the father of Dido, and this founder of the Assyrian
   kingdom.

ambrosia is the fodder that nourishes their limbs, 215
made weary by their diurnal service, and restores them for toil.
And while the four-footed ones there graze upon the heavenly grass
and night completes her turn, the god enters the chamber of his love,
disguised with the face of Eurynome, the mother, and among
the twice six handmaidens beholds Leucothoë 220
who draws the slender thread from the spindle she turns.
When, therefore, just like a mother to her daughter, he gave a kiss,
he says, 'Depart, you servants girls, there's a secret matter here.
Do not deprive a mother of the opportunity of speaking privately.'
When they had obeyed and the god was left without a witness in the room, 225
he said, 'It is I who measure out the lengthy years,
who see all things, and through whom the earth sees all,
the eye of the world: be sure, you please me.' She's frightened and in her fear
both spindle and distaff from her slackened fingers fell.
Her fear itself was lovely, and he without further delay 230
returned to his true form and usual sheen.
The maid, though frightened by this unexpected sight, was conquered by
the splendor of the god, laid aside her complaints and yielded to his force.
        "Since Clytie is jealous (for unrestrained had been
her love of Sol) and goaded with wrath at the concubine, 235
she tells abroad the adultery and to the father maligns
the girl. Ferocious and unrestrained is he as his daughter prays
and stretches her hands to the light of the Sun; and as she says,
'He forced me against my will!' he cruelly buries her deep
within the earth and sets above her a mound of heavy sand. 240
Hyperion's son demolishes it with his rays
and gives you a path by which you might reveal your buried face;
but you no longer could raise your head, wearied by the weight of earth,
O nymph, and you lay there, a bloodless corpse.
The ruler of the flying steeds is said to have seen 245
no sight more painful since the fires of Phaethon.
He tries, indeed, to summon back the living warmth
into the frigid limbs with the force of his rays,
but since to his efforts, however great, destiny stands opposed,
he sprinkled with sweet-smelling nectar both the body and the place 250
and, first complaining greatly, said, 'You will yet touch the sky!'
At once her body, with heavenly nectar imbued,
dissolved and moistened the earth with its scent,
and bit by bit as the roots were moved, rising through the clods
a stalk of incense broke through the burial mound with its crest. 255
        "But Clytie, though love might have excused her pain
and pain her informing, the author of light no more
attends and ends his bond of Venus with her.

From that time on she wasted away, having plied an insane love;
unable to bear the nymphs and beneath Jove's open sky both night and day,   260
she sits upon the ground, naked, her naked hair unkempt.
For nine days without touching water or food,
she fed her fast on merest dew and tears,
nor did she move from the ground: she only watched
the face of the god as he passed and towards him bent her gaze.                    265
They say her limbs grew fixed in the soil, and in part
her face's complexion was changed by a sickly pallor into bloodless grass.
In part, there is redness, and a flower covers her face,
much like the violet. No matter how restrained by her roots,
she turns towards Sol and, transformed, retains her love."                          270
    Her tale was over and the amazing deed had caught their ears;
while some deny it could have happened, some declare
that real gods can do everything, but Bacchus is not one of those.

### 274-388   *Alcithoë's Tale of Salmacis and Hermaphroditus.*

    The sisters grew still and called for Alcithoë.[33]
While running the shuttle through the threads of the upright warp,              275
she said, "I'll leave untold the shepherd's well-known love
of Daphnis[34] of Ida, whom a nymph, enraged at his concubine,
converted into a rock: so great is the grief that makes lovers burn!
And I'll not tell how once, with the law of nature revised,
there was the ambiguous Sithon,[35] now a woman, now a man.                    280
And you as well, Celmis,[36] now adamant, most faithful once
to little Jove, and the Curetes, sown in an abundant rain, [37]
and Crocus with Smilax[38] into tiny flowers turned,
I'll leave unsung and hold your minds with something new and sweet.
Her ill-repute, its source, how through her evil waters' strength              285
Salmacis weakens and softens limbs by her touch,
now learn. The cause is hidden, but the force of the spring quite infamous.
The son that to Mercury Cythera's goddess[39] bore
the Naiads of Ida nourished to manhood in their caves.
Upon his face the mother and father could both                                 290
be seen; he took from them as well his name.[40]
As soon as he completed thrice five years, he left

---

33 The leader of the opposition to Bacchus: see 4. 1.
34 The Sicilian shepherd of the pastoral poetry of Theocritus and Vergil. Blinded for his infidelity, he
    became the inventor of pastoral music. His connection to Mt. Ida of Phrygia is unclear.
35 An eponymous hero of the Sithonians, an ancient name for Thracians. See 6. 588 and 13. 571.
36 This servant of the Phrygian goddess Cybele invented working in bronze.
37 A unique reference to the birth of the Curetes, the young Cretan males who protected the infant Zeus
    from his father Cronos.
38 Bindweed.
39 Venus.
40 Hermaphroditus.

his father's mountains and, with Ida, his nurse, left behind,
found pleasure in roaming through places unknown
and seeing streams unknown. His curiosity reduced the toil.                    295
He even went to the cities of Lycia and those, to Lycia near,
of Caria: here he finds a pool with water shining clear
down to the very bottom. In it no marshy reeds,
nor sterile sedge nor cat-tails sharp at the tip:
the water is completely clear, but the bank of the pool                        300
is girt with flourishing turf and ever verdant grass.
A nymph dwelt there, but not one suited to the hunt
or wont to bend the bow or to compete in the chase,
to swift Diana the only one of the Naiads unknown.
The story goes that her sisters had often said to her,                         305
'Salmacis, either take up the painted quiver or the javelin
and mix your leisure with the harshness of the hunt.'
But she takes up neither the painted quiver nor javelin
nor mixes her leisure with the harshness of the hunt,
but only washes her lovely limbs in her spring,                                310
and often combs out her hair with a Cytorian[41] comb,
and looks into the waters to determine how she should look.
And now, her body covered by a transparent robe,
she lies down on the tender leaves or on the tender grass,
or often picks the flowers. And picking flowers also then                      315
by chance, she sees the boy and chose to have the boy she saw.
However, she didn't go near, although she yearned to go near,
before she composed herself, before she examined her robes
and fixed her face and deserved to be considered fair.
That done, she began to speak: 'O boy, to be thought a god,                    320
indeed, most worthy, or Cupid, if you are a god,
or if a mortal, blessed are those who gave you birth
and happy your brother and fortunate in truth
your sister, if you have one, and the nurse who gave you her breast.
Yet far, far more blest than all of these is your bride                        325
if one you have, one, if you've deemed one worthy of the wedding torch.
But if there is someone, let my pleasure remain concealed,
or if there's none, let me be the one, let's enter the same bridal-bed.'
With this the naiad grew still; a redness stained the face of the boy
(what love was he didn't know), but it became him to have blushed.             330
The apples have this color when they hang from a sunny tree,
or ivory when stained or when in her bright phase the moon
grows red, for whom brass, summoned to help, resounds in vain.[42]

---

41 Mt. Cytorus in Paphlagonia, a region of Asia Minor, rich in the boxwood used for combs.
42 Clashing symbols were used to restore the moon in eclipse, thought to be the work of enchantresses.

He says to the nymph, endlessly demanding sisterly kisses at least
and throwing her arms around his ivory neck,      335
'Please stop, or shall I leave you and this place?'
Salmacis was frightened and says, 'Of this place I give you free use,
O guest,' and, reversing her steps, she pretends to depart,
even then looking back, and, concealed in the scrubby wood,
removed from sight and crouching down on her knees. But he,      340
supposing himself unobserved upon the deserted grass,
goes here and from here to there and puts the tips
of his feet in the playful waters and wets his soles as far as the heels.
And soon, taken with the waters' seductive chill,
he lays aside from his tender body the concealments of his soft attire.      345
And then in truth he pleased, and with desire for the naked form
Salmacis burned; the eyes of the nymph were hot,
not other than, shining at his height in a cloudless sky,
when Phoebus is reflected in the image of an opposing glass,
and barely enduring the delay, barely postponing her joy,      350
now seeks to embrace him, now, insane, scarcely contains herself.
He slaps his body with his open palms and quickly leapt
into the waters and, drawing back each arm in turn,
gleams brightly within the clear-flowing waters, as if one were to enclose
unblemished lilies or ivory statues within translucent glass.      355
'The victory is ours, and he is mine,' the naiad exclaims,
and, every garment cast away, she lets herself into the waves
and holds him as he fights and seizes his struggling lips
and lays her hands on him below and touches his unwilling breast
and folds herself around the youth, on this side and that.      360
While he resists and seeks to slip away,
she finally entangles him, like the serpent, caught by the royal bird
and raised aloft, that binds the hanging head and feet
and encircles with its tail the spreading wings,
or like the ivy that conceals the lofty trunk,      365
and like the octopus that holds its captive foe
beneath the waters, having extended on every side its whip-like arms.
The grandson of Atlas[43] stands firm and to the nymph her hoped-for joys
denies: she presses on and, with all her body joined to his,
in clinging to him declared, 'Fight though you may, you foolish one,      370
you'll not escape. May you gods command it so,
and let no day take him from me nor me from him.'
Her prayers found their gods: for the bodies of both
are melded and joined, and upon them one face is set,
as when someone inserts branches within one bark,      375

---

43 Atlas was the father of Mercury (Hermes) by Maia. Perhaps the patronymic *Atlantiades* is chosen
   here to compare the endurance of Atlas to the firm resistance of Hermaphroditus.

*Hermaphroditus and Salmacis, Solis*

and sees them joined as they grow and equally mature,
just so, as their members came together in that stubborn embrace,
they are not two, but a double form, nor so as to be called
a boy or girl, and seem neither and both.
And so, when he sees that the clear water into which he had entered as a man   380
had made him half a man and that in them his limbs had grown soft,
Hermaphroditus stretches out his hands and says,
but now not with the voice of a man, 'Bring help to your son,
O father and mother, to him who has his name from both of you:
let any man who comes into these waters go hence                               385
but half a man and by the waters' touch let him be softened at once.'
Each parent was moved, and the words of their biform son
confirmed and stained the spring with an impure drug."

      Her words had come to an end, and the Minyan offspring still
pressed on with their work and spurned the god and profaned his feast,         390
when suddenly unseen drums with raucous sounds
grew noisy and to the pipe with the curved horn
and tingling cymbals of brass resound amid the scent of crocus and myrrh,
and—quite beyond belief—the looms begin to grow green
and into the appearance of ivy the hanging cloth took leaf.                    395
A part becomes vine, and that which had just been thread
is changing into tendril; from the warp comes forth the leaf of the vine.
Upon the painted grapes purple applies its gleaming hue.
And now the day was spent, and the time was drawing nigh
that you might call neither darkness nor light,                                400
but with its light the edge of ambiguous night.
The houses suddenly seem to shake, and the lamps, rich with oil,
to burn, and the altars to glow red with fires,

and empty images of savage beasts to howl.
The sisters already are hiding throughout the smoke-filled house                405
and scattered in various places to avoid the fires and lights,
and as they seek the shadows, over their tender limbs
a thin layer of skin spreads and hides their arms in slender wings.
Precisely how they lost their former shape
the shadows refuse to reveal. No feathers lift them up,                          410
but even so they lift themselves upon translucent wings.
Attempting to speak, they emit a sound like their bodies, very slight,
and with their squeaking carry on their light complaints,
and, shunning the light, fill not forests but fly through homes
at night and from late evening take their name.[44]                              415

### 416-562   *Athamas and Ino*

In truth was Bacchus' name then memorable in all
of Thebes, and his maternal aunt[45] tells everywhere
the new god's mighty powers, and of so many sisters[46] she alone
was free of sorrow, except for that her sisters caused.
Observing her, in her children and marriage with Athamas[47]                     420
so proud in spirit, and in her foster child,[48] Juno could
not bear it and thought to herself, "Could the son of that concubine
transform Maeonian[49] sailors and sink them in the sea,
permit a mother to mangle the bowels of a son
and cover three daughters of Minyas with strange new wings,                      425
while Juno can do no more than bewail her unrequited pains?
Is this enough for me? Is this the only power we have?
He teaches me himself what I should do (for it's right to learn from one's foes)
and through the slaughter of Pentheus, he shows well enough and more
what rage can do. Why not let Ino be goaded and go                               430
into a rage according to the examples of her kin?"
There is a sloping path, gloomy with sinister yew;
it leads through the muted silence to the homes of the dead below.
The sluggish Styx[50] exhales its clouds, and recent shades
descend that way and the specters who have found a tomb.                         435
Both pallor and winter control that broad and rugged place, and where
the path is that leads to the Stygian city the new shades know not,
nor where to find the forbidding palace of murky Dis.[51]

---

44 Latin *vespertiliones* "bats" is derived from *vesper* "evening." Cf. Danish *aften-bakke* "evening-flutterers."
45 Ino.
46 Autonoë, Semele, and Agave, the mother of Pentheus.
47 See note on 3. 564.
48 Bacchus, whom Ino raised after he was born from Zeus' thigh.
49 Lydian or Tyrrhenian (see on 3. 576).
50 River of the Underworld.
51 Ruler of the Underworld.

The city controls a thousand doors and open gates
on every side, and as from all the dry land the sea receives its streams,    440
just so that place receives all souls and is not too small
for any people nor feels invaded by a mob.
They wander bloodless without body and bones, these shades,
and some frequent the forum, some the palace of the tyrant below,
while some ply certain arts, imitations of their former life,    445
another part are pressed by their punishments.
Her heavenly home abandoned, she endures to take that path
(Saturnian[52] Juno applied to her hatred such great wrath).
As soon as she entered the place and by her body's weight
the threshold had groaned, Cerberus raised up his three mouths    450
and barked three times at once. She summoned the sisters[53] born
of Night, that stern and implacable god.
Before the doors of that prison, closed shut by adamant, they sat
and combed out terrible serpents from their hair.
As soon as they recognized her among the shadows of the dark,    455
the goddesses arose. The place is called the Home of the Damned.
There, offering his bowels to be torn, was Tityos,[54] stretched out
over a field of nine acres; for you Tantalus,[55]
no water is caught, and the tree hanging above you flees your grasp;
and, Sisyphus, you're either seeking or pushing the rock that will return;    460
Ixion[56] is being turned, both following and fleeing himself;
having dared to contrive their father's nephews' death,
the Belides[57] unceasingly seek again the waters they lose.
    Saturnia, after gazing fiercely at all of these,
especially at Ixion, from whom she turned away,    465
then looks at Sisyphus and says, "Of the brothers[58] why does he
endure perpetual punishment, while Athamas the Proud
enjoys a sumptuous palace and with his wife holds me in contempt
forever?" And she explains the reasons for her journey and her hate
and what she desires: what she desires is that Cadmus' royal home    470
not stand and madness drive Athamas into crime.
Her promises, commands and prayers she combines into one

---

52 Because she is the daughter of Saturn.
53 The Avenging Deities or Furies called in Greek the Erinyes, in Latin the Dirae.
54 For attempting to rape Latona, this giant is punished by having his liver eaten daily by a vulture in the Underworld.
55 For violating the banquet of the gods, Tantalus is unable to reach the waters in which he stands to quench his thirst, nor reach the fruit of the tree above him.
56 Ixion, king of Thessaly, attempted to rape Hera (Juno), but Zeus (Jupiter) substituted a cloud-image for his wife, upon whom Ixion fathered Centaurus "Wind-goader," who became the father of the Centaurs.
57 Following their father's orders, all but one of the fifty daughters of Danaus, son of Belus, slew their cousins, the sons of Aegyptus, on their wedding night. Their punishment in the Underworld is to draw water with sieves.
58 The sons of Aeolus.

and stirs up the goddesses. Tisiphone[59] was roused
by Juno's words and made her grey locks shake
and thrust back one of the snakes that covered her mouth                    475
and speaks this way: "No need for a long and roundabout speech.
Consider done your every command. This loveless realm
desert and betake yourself to the breezes of a better sky."
Delighted, Juno returns. As she prepares to enter the sky
Thaumantian[60] Iris with showered waters makes her pure.                   480
Without delay hostile Tisiphone takes the torch soaked
in blood and puts on a cloak, red with runny gore,
and girds herself with a twisted snake
and leaves her home; Grief is her companion as she goes
and Fear and Terror and Madness with frightened mien.                       485
She stopped at the threshold; the doors-posts of Aeolus shook,
they say, and pallor infected the maple doors,
and Sol shuns the place. The wife is completely terrified by the signs,
and terrified is Athamas, and they start to leave the house:
the wretched Erinys[61] sat in the entrance and blocked their way,          490
and, reaching out her arms fettered in snaky coils,
she shook her curly locks; the snakes are stirred with sound,
and some lie upon her shoulders, others, sliding down around her breast,
make hissing sounds and vomit gore with their flickering tongues.
And then she seized two snakes and tore them from her hair                  495
and hurled them with her plague-bearing hand;
they wander over the bosoms of Ino and Athamas
and breathe into them their obnoxious breath: they set no wounds
upon their limbs, their *minds* feel the awful blows.
Of liquid poisons she had brought with her monstrous draughts,              500
Echidna's[62] venom and the foam from Cerberus' mouths,
forgetfulness and rambling wandering of the blinded mind
and crime and tears and madness and lust for the kill.
All this she had ground together and cooked, mixed with recent blood
and stirred with green hemlock, in hollow bronze.                           505
And as they stood in terror, the maddening venom sank
into the breasts of both and moved into the inmost recesses of their hearts.
She then whirled again and again in the same orb
her flaming torch and pursued fire with moving fire.
Victorious thus and her mission fulfilled, she returns to the empty realm   510

---

59 One of the Furies. Her name means "Avenger of Murder."
60 Iris, goddess of the rainbow, was the daughter of Thaumas and Electra, the daughter of Ocean. See
    Hes., *Theog.* 265.
61 Greek for "Fury," i. e., Tisiphone.
62 According to Hes, *Theog.* 306-315, Echidna, half woman, half serpent, was the mother by Typhon of
    Orthus, Cerberus, and the Lernan Hydra. Hesiod gives Cerberus fifty mouths but later sources and
    art give him three or even two.

*Tisiphone Maddens Ino and Athamas, Picart*

of mighty Dis and loosens from her waist the serpents she had worn.

At once the son of Aeolus, raging in the midst of his hall,
exclaims, "Io! Comrades, extend your nets over these woods!
I've just now seen here a lioness with her twin cubs,"
and madly pursues the tracks of his wild wife                               515
and from her bosom tears Learchus, laughing and stretching out
his little arms, and whirls him twice and thrice through the air
just like a sling and cruelly dashes the infant face
upon the unyielding stone. Then at last the mother is moved,
and, whether grief did this, or the sprinkled venom was the cause,          520
she howls and, quite insane and hair disheveled, flees
and, carrying you, little Melicertes, in her naked arms,
she shouts, "Evoe, Bacchus!" At the name of Bacchus Juno laughed
and said, "May your foster-child[63] ever bring you such rewards."
A crag hangs high over the sea, whose lower part is hollowed by             525
the waves and from the waters it overhangs fends off the rains;
its top is steep and stretches forth its brow into the open sea.
Since madness had made her strong, Ino gains this peak
and slowed by no fear casts herself upon the deep,
her burden with her; when struck, the waves grew white.                     530
But Venus, taking pity upon her undeserving granddaughter's[64] woes,

---

63 See 3. 313.
64 The mother of Ino is Harmonia, daughter of Venus and Mars, and wife of Cadmus.

with coaxing words addressed her uncle thus: "O god of the waves,
whose power, Neptune, has yielded place only to the sky,
I'm asking for something great, indeed, but take you pity upon my kin
whom you behold now being cast into the vast Ionian sea[65]          535
and add them to the number of your gods. I have some favor with the sea,
provided that once in the midst of the deep I was congealed
from foam and my name in Greek survives from that."[66]
Assenting to her prayers, Neptune took from them
their mortal part and imposed an awesome majesty                     540
and changed both their name and form,
declaring Palaemon a god along with his mother Leucothoë.
    As best they could, her Sidonian[67] companions, followed her,
and found final footprints at the edge of the cliff,
and, thinking there to be no doubt about her death, with their palms  545
bewailed the House of Cadmus, having torn their garments and their hair;
and since there was little justice and too much cruelty towards the concubine,[68]
they bore a grudge against the goddess. Juno could not bear
reproof and said, "I shall make you yourselves the greatest proof
that I am cruel." Her words were followed by deeds.                   550
For she who had been especially reverent said, "I shall follow the queen
into the sea," and, as she was about to take her leap,
could move no more at all and remained fixed to the crag;
a second, when she tried to strike her breast with the usual sign
of grief, felt the arms she sought grow stiff;                       555
and that one, stretching by chance her hands towards the waves of the sea,
was turned to stone and extended her hands into the same waves;
of this one, as she seized and tore the hair from the top of her head,
immediately you could see the fingers grown hard within her hair;
in whatever gesture each was caught, she was held fast;              560
a few were changed to birds, and even now in that swirling flood
the Ismenides skim the waves with the tips of their wings.

### 563-603   *The End of Cadmus and Harmonia*

    Not knowing that his daughter and little grandson were gods of the sea,
Agenor's son was overwhelmed by grief and a series of woes;
because of the many portents he had seen, the founder left           565
his city, though the fortune of the place,
not his own oppressed him; forced to wander long,
he reached the region of Illyria as an exile with his wife.

---

65 Although the traditional place for Ino's leap into the sea is the cliff of Moluris on the Saronic Gulf,
    Ovid only refers to the Ionian Sea, which forms the southern part of the Adriatic.
66 Aphrodite, because she was born from *aphros* "foam" or the "sperm" of the genitals of Uranus.
67 I.e., Theban, because the Thebans were descendants of Cadmus, the Phoenician.
68 Semele.

And now, burdened with troubles and years, they call to mind
the early fortunes of their house and review in conversation their toils.     570
"You don't suppose that serpent was sacred that I pierced with my spear
back then when after leaving Sidon I strew
the viperous teeth as strange seeds over the ground?"
says Cadmus. "If the gods are avenging him with such determined wrath,
may I myself, I pray, be stretched into a long belly as a snake."     575
He spoke and into a long belly is stretched out.
He sees the scales grow upon his hardened skin,
the black of his body varied with dots of blue;
he falls down prone upon this chest, and his legs, formed into one,
grow gradually narrow to a smooth point.     580
His arms yet remain; he stretches forth the arms that remain,
and, with the tears streaming down what is still a human face,
he said, "Come, O wife, come, poor dear,
and while there yet survives a part of me, touch me and take
my hand, while it is a hand, while the serpent has not all of me."     585
        Indeed, he wants to say more, but suddenly his tongue
is split into two parts, and, as he speaks, he has
no words to use, and whenever he tries to express any complaints
he hisses; nature left to him this voice.
His wife, striking her naked breast with her hand, exclaims,     590
"Wait, Cadmus, unhappy man, and shed this monstrous garb.
What is this, Cadmus? Where is your foot? Where are your shoulders and hands
and color and face and, as I speak, all the rest? Why not, O heavenly gods,
turn me as well into the same kind of snake?"
She finished speaking; he was licking the face of his wife     595
and moving into the beloved bosom, as though he knew it well,
imparting his embraces and seeking the familiar neck.
Whoever is present (there were attendants) is terrified; but she
caresses the crested dragon's sinuous neck,
and suddenly there are two, and they creep in conjoined coils,     600
until they enter the hidden recesses of the nearby grove.
And even now they flee no one nor wound nor harm,
and what they were before these dragons remember in peace.
        But nevertheless to both for their altered forms
their grandson[69] had brought great comfort, whom     605
defeated India worshiped, and Achaea in established temples revered.

---

69 Bacchus.

*Cadmus and Harmonia Become Snakes, Solis*

### 604-803    *Perseus and Andromeda*

The son of Abas alone, born from the same stock,
Acrisius,[70] remains to keep the god from the city walls
of Argos and to raise arms against him and to disclaim
his origin from Jove; indeed he denied that Perseus was Jove's,          610
whom Danaë had conceived in a shower of gold.
Acrisius, however, soon (for so great is the power of truth)
regrets as much having profaned the god as having not recognized
his grandson; the one was now installed in heaven, but
the other, bringing back the famous spoils[71] of the snaky monster, plied       615
the gentle breeze with whistling wings.
And when the victor hovered above the Libyan sands,
some bloody drops of the Gorgon's head fell,
received by the ground and brought to life as various snakes;
henceforth that land is teeming and infested with asps.          620

From there, driven by discordant winds through the great immensity,
in the manner of a watery cloud he is carried now here, now there

---

70 The following table demonstrates that Acrisius, king of Argos, and Bacchus were of the same stock:

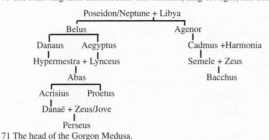

71 The head of the Gorgon Medusa.

and from the lofty sky looks down far and wide
upon the distant lands and flies about over all the globe.
Three times he saw the frigid Bears, three times the arms of the Crab,      625
again and again carried off to the setting and the rising of the Sun.
And now at the fall of day, fearing to entrust himself to the night,
he stopped in the Hesperian clime,[72] Atlas' realm,
and sought a little rest, until Lucifer[73] might evoke
Aurora's fires, and Aurora the chariot of the day.      630
    Excelling all mankind with his enormous body, here
was Atlas, the son of Iapetus; this ultimate region of earth
was under this king, and the sea which sets beneath Sol's panting steeds
its waters and receives the weary axles of his car.
He had a thousand flocks and as many herds of cattle, that ranged      635
upon the grassy fields, and no adjoining lands confined his own.
The leaves of the trees, shining with radiant gold,
concealed the branches of gold and fruit of gold.
"O host," says Perseus to him, "If you are touched
by pride of great birth, the author of my birth is Jove;      640
or if you're an admirer of deeds, you will admire what I've done.
I'm seeking hospitality and rest." But he was mindful of
an ancient prophecy (Themis of Parnassus had foretold this lot):
"A time will come, O Atlas, when your tree will be of its gold
despoiled, and a son of Jove will have title to this theft."      645
    In fear of this, Atlas had enclosed his orchards with solid walls
and given them to a vast dragon's care and guard
and held at bay all foreigners from his lands.
To this one as well he says, "Go away lest neither the pride
in what you falsely claim nor Jupiter be of help to you!"      650
To threats he adds force and with his hands tries
to drive him away, as he hesitates and mixes brave with peaceful words.
Inferior in strength (for who would be a match for the strength
of Atlas?), he says, "But since our goodwill to you is of little worth,
receive this gift," and from his left side, turning himself      655
the other way, he thrust forth Medusa's repulsive face.
As big as he was, Atlas becomes a mountain: for his beard and hair
become forests, the ridges are his shoulders and hands,
what was his head before is now the peak of the mountain top,
his bones become stone. Then in every direction raised aloft,      660
he grew immense in size (so did you gods decree) and all
the sky with its many stars upon him found support.
    Hippotades[74] had shut in their eternal prison the winds,

---

72 Hesperia is the West, from the Greek for "evening."
73 See on 11. 295.
74 The god of the winds, Aeolus, son or descendant of Hippotes.

*Atlas and Perseus, Baur*

and, as the brightest in the lofty sky and admonisher of toil,
had Lucifer risen: Perseus takes again his wings                                665
and ties them to either side of his feet and with the sickle girds
himself, and, stirring his winged sandals, splits the liquid air.
With countless peoples left behind around and below,
he spies the tribes of the Ethiopians and the Cephean[75] fields.
And there, to pay for her mother's tongue, Andromeda,                           670
though guiltless herself, had by Ammon[76] been unjustly sent.
As soon as Abas' descendant saw her with her arms bound
upon the rugged cliff (except for the slight breeze that had moved
her hair and her eyes that flowed with tepid tears,
he would have thought her a work of marble), unawares he caught fire          675
and stood amazed and, swept away by the beauty of the form he saw,
almost forgot to beat his wings in the air.
When he stopped, he said, "O lady undeserving such chains,
but rather those by which passionate lovers are joined,
reveal, I pray, your name and that of your land                                680
and why you wear these bonds." The maiden is silent at first
and dares not address the man, and with her hands,
were they not bound, she would have covered her face;
her eyes (this much she could do), she filled with welling tears.
And as he pressed again and again for a response, lest she appear             685

---

75 Belonging to Cepheus, king of the Ethiopians.
76 The Egyptian ram-headed god identified with Jupiter, who had an oracle at Ammonium in Libya.

to wish to conceal wrongs of her own, she tells her name
and that of her land and how great her mother's[77] pride
had been in her beauty; and with all not yet revealed, a wave
resounds, and emerging from the vast sea a menacing monster looms
which filled the water's wide plain beneath his breast.                          690
The maiden is crying aloud; the father in mourning with
the mother is present, both in despair, but more justly she.
They offer no aid, only the weeping that suits the time
and lamentation, and as to that fettered body they cling,
the stranger says, "Long is the time you can expect                              695
for tears, brief is the hour for bringing help.
If I were her suitor, Perseus, son of Jove and of her
whom Jupiter filled with fecund gold when she had been confined,
the Perseus who vanquished the snaky-haired Gorgon and
with beating wings made bold to venture upon the breezes of the ethereal air,   700
it's sure that to all others I would be preferred as a son-in-law.
To such a great dowry I mean to add merit, if only the gods allow.
That she be mine if rescued by my virtue is what I seek."
Accepting the terms (for who would hesitate?),
the parents plead, and promise a kingdom for dowry as well.                      705
Behold, as a ship with attached prow headlong plows
the waters, driven by the sweating arms of youths,
just so was the beast as it parted the waters by the force of its breast;
as far away from the rocks he was as a Balearic[78] sling
can cast through the midst of the sky a bullet of lead,                          710
when suddenly the youth pushed off from the earth with his feet
and rose aloft into the clouds; when upon the surface of the sea
the shadow of the man was seen, the beast raged at the shadow he saw.
And as the bird of Jove, when he spies in the empty field
a serpent offering his blue-black back to Phoebus' light                         715
attacks it from behind, lest it twist back its savage mouth,
implanting his eager claws into the scaly neck,
just so, hurled headlong through space by his swift flight,
the Inachid[79] bore down upon the back of the beast, and, as it roared,
into its right shoulder sank his sword up to its curving hook.                   720
Offended by the grievous wound, one moment it lifts itself aloft into the air,
the next, dives into the water, and again, like a ferocious boar,
in terror at the raucous sound of the dogs, it turns around;
the eager jaws the other escapes upon his rapid wings, and, where
he finds an opening, strikes with the sickle-shaped sword first the back,        725

---

77 Cassiopea (see 738), who had boasted that she was more beautiful than the Nereids. For her pride
   Ammon required that Cepheus bind his daughter to a crag as an offering to a sea-monster. See
   Apollodorus 2. 4. 3.
78 The Balearic Islands were noted for their slingers.
79 Perseus is a descendant of the Argive river, Inachus, father of Io.

*Perseus and Andromeda, Solis*

encrusted with hollow shells, and then the ribs of his sides,
and next where the tail grew very thin into the form of a fish.
A flood mixed with punic-red blood the beast
discharges from its mouth; the pinions grow wet and heavy from the spray;
and Perseus, no longer daring to trust in his sodden sandal-wings,                    730
espies a crag whose very top stands out above
the waters when still, but is hidden when the sea is stirred.
Supporting himself on it, his left hand grasping the top of the rock,
he aimed and drove his sword into the bowels thrice and a fourth time again.

　　　Applause and shouting filled the shores and the celestial homes              735
of the gods; Cassiopea and father Cepheus rejoice and greet
their son-in-law and call him the defense
and savior of their house; released from her chains
the maiden comes forth, of the labor both prize and cause;
the hero washes his triumphant hands with water he had drawn;                     740
and lest the rough sand mar the serpent-bearing head,
he makes the ground soft with leaves and spreads out strands
born of the sea and lays upon them Phorcynid[80] Medusa's face.
The core of the fresh and absorbent strands were even yet alive
and grasped the force of the monster and by its touch grew hard                    745
and took on new stiffness in their branches and leaves.
The sea-nymphs, too, attempt this amazing deed
with many strands and delight to find the same result
and tossing the seeds from them over the waters repeat the deed;
and even to this day the nature of coral has remained the same,                    750

---

80 The patronymic of Phorcys, father of Medusa and the other Gorgons, and later changed into
　a sea-god.

becoming hard in contact with air, and what
had been in the sea a pliant twig, above the sea becomes a rock.
    To three divinities[81] he set up three altars of turf,
to Mercury the one on the left, to you, warrior maiden, the one on the right;
the altar of Jove was in the middle. To Minerva is sacrificed a cow,         755
a calf to the wing-footed one, a bull to you, O greatest of gods.
Straightway he took Andromeda and therewith for so great a deed
the prize. The wedding torches by Hymenaeus[82] and Love
were brandished, the fires drenched with copious scents
and festoons of flowers hanging from the roof, and everywhere lyres     760
and tuneful reeds and singing, the joyful signs
of happy minds, resound. When the double doors are opened, the courts
of gold are all revealed, and to the king's banquet, laid
with sumptuous fare, the Cephenian[83] nobles come.
    When once they had finished the meal, they relaxed their minds     765
with noble Bacchus' gift and the descendant of Lynceus[84] inquired about
the culture and nature of the place, and the ways and mind of the men.    767
The one who explained it all then said, "Now, O bravest of men,    769
I pray you, Perseus, explain with what valor and with what    770
great skills you removed the head with its hair of snakes."[85]
The kinsman of Agenor[86] tells of a place that lay
below cold Atlas,[87] made safe by the fortification of that solid mass;
and that at its entrance twin sisters dwelt,
the daughters of Phorcys, who shared the use of a single eye.    775
With cunning and furtive guile, as the eye was being passed back and forth,
he reached out his hand and grabbed it,[88] and, passing through far off, obscure,
and out of the way places and beetling crags and rugged woods,
he touched down upon the Gorgon dwellings, and scattered through the fields

---

81 To Mercury and Minerva, who had helped him slay the Gorgon, and to Jove, his father.
82 Or Hymen, god of marriage.
83 The Cephenes were a people of Ethiopia.
84 Lyncides, i.e., Perseus. See note to 608.
85 With Haupt and Ehwald most conclude that line 768, containing the name of the one responding
    to Perseus' question, has fallen out. See the critical note in Haupt and Ehwald. Marzolla (1979)
    proposes:
        *quaerit Lyncides: quaerenti protinus unus*
        *narrat Cephenum moresque animumque virorum.*
        *Quae simul edocuit,....*
            The scion of Lynceus inquired: and to his question straightway did one
            explain the customs and mind of the Cephenian men.
            As soon as he had told of these things, he said, "Now, O bravest of men..."
    Tarrant also excludes 768, but also reads *quae* for the mss *qui* in 769.
86 See again note to 608: Although Agenor is the brother of Belus from whom Perseus is descended, he
    is not the ancestor of Perseus.
87 It is an inconsistency in the narrative that the Graeae (Grey Hags) are here made to dwell under
    Mt. Atlas, before the gaze of the beheaded Medusa had turned the Titan Atlas to into a mountain
    of stone.
88 By stealing the one eye of the Graeae, Perseus forced them to divulge the way to nymphs who had
    winged sandals, the wallet, and the cap of invisibility (Apollodorus 2. 4. 2. 5). With the winged
    sandals Perseus flew to the Ocean where the Gorgons, the sisters of the Graeae, were.

and ways he saw the images of men and beasts                                    780
transformed from their true nature at the sight of Medusa to stone.
But he in the bronze shield carried by his left hand
had gazed at the horrible Medusa's reflected form,[89]
and while heavy sleep held her and her snakes,
had snatched her head from her neck, and Pegasus, swift                          785
of wing, and his brother[90] had been born from their mother's blood.
He added as well his long journey's perils, not feigned,
the seas, the lands he had seen beneath him from on high,
the stars he had touched with his beating wings.
    Before they expected, however, he fell silent; of the crowd                 790
of nobles one speaks up, inquiring why of the sisters she alone
wore serpents woven into the braids of her hair.
    Their guest replies, "Because what you seek is worthy to be told,
hear now the cause of what you've asked about. That woman, most noted for
her beauty, was of many suitors the envied goal,                                795
in all of whose features none was more remarkable than
her hair. I met a man who said he had seen it himself.
The ruler of the sea had violated her in Minerva's shrine,
it's said: the daughter of Jove had turned away
and covered her chaste eyes with the aegis,[91] and, lest this go               800
unpunished, she changed the Gorgonian tresses into filthy snakes.
And even now, to frighten her foes with stunning fear
she wears the serpents she created upon her opposing breast."

---

89 Lest he himself be turned to stone.
90 Chrysaor "Golden Sword," to become by the Oceanid Callirhoë the father of three-headed Geryones
    and the Echidna (Hes., *Theog.* 287-288 and 981-982).
91 The goatskin shield lent to Minerva by Jupiter.

# BOOK 5

## 1-235  Perseus and Phineus

As Danaë's heroic son relates these things
among the Cephenians,[1] the royal courts are filled
with noisy confusion, and the clamor of the songs
proclaims not the marriage feast but rather savage war.
That banquet transformed into a sudden brawl                                    5
you might compare to the sea whose calm
the winds' wild fury makes rough with rolling waves.
And Phineus is first among them, the bold advocate of war,
who brandishes his ashen spear with its point of bronze
and says, "See here, here I am, the avenger of my stolen bride;                  10
no wings nor a Jupiter allegedly changed to gold
will steal you from me!" Phineus prepares to hurl the spear,
but Cepheus cries out, "My brother, what insanity drives
you towards this furious act? Is this proper thanks
for such great deeds? Is this the wedding gift you pay for the saving of her life? 15
For, if you want the truth, Perseus was not the one
who took her from you, but the power of the Nereids
and horn-wearing Ammon and the monster from the sea
that sought to glut itself on my own flesh; she was stolen from you
when she was about to die; unless, cruel one, you demand                         20

---

1 The Ethiopians, named for Cepheus, their king.

her death and consolation for yourself by causing grief to me.
It wasn't enough, I suppose, that she was chained while you stood by
and offered no help, either as uncle or promised spouse;
and, just because someone rescued her, will you take it ill
and steal the reward? If that reward seems great to you,                              25
you ought to have sought it from the crag to which it was fixed.
Let him receive it now who sought it, through whom my old age
was not left childless, who bargained for it by word and deed,
and realize that he was not preferred over you but over certain death."
Without replying, Phineus stared first at Cepheus and then                            30
at Perseus, unsure at which of the two he should aim.
But after the brief delay he aimed and hurled the spear in vain
at Perseus with all the strength his anger could supply.
It was then, at last, as the spear stuck in the couch,
that Perseus leapt up from the coverlets, and, casting back                           35
the missile, would have split that hostile breast, had Phineus not gone
behind an altar: and, unjustly, the altar defended the ill-starred man.
The point, however, failed not to be fixed in Rhoetus' face,
who, after falling and wrenching the iron from his bones,
convulses and spews the laden tables with blood.                                      40
Indeed the crowd is then enflamed with irrepressible wrath;
they hurl their spears, some claiming that both Cepheus and
his son-in-law should die; but Cepheus had left
the threshold of the palace, calling to witness law and trust
and gods of hospitality that all this was being done against his will.                45
The warrior Pallas is there protecting her brother with her aegis-shield
and giving him courage. Athis of India was there, whom they think
Limnaee, daughter of the Ganges river, bore beneath the glassy waves.
His beauty was rare and with costly grooming greater still,
his body was firmed now with twice eight years,                                       50
his raiment was a cloak of Tyrian purple hemmed in gold:
a golden necklace adorned his neck,
a curved band held his tresses damp with myrrh.
Though skilled indeed in hitting targets however far away
by hurling the javelin, even more skilled was he in the use of the bow,               55
whose pliant horns his hand was bending when Perseus took
a log that was burning on the altar and struck
and smashed his face into a mass of broken bones.
        The one closest to him saw him there,
those much admired features bathed in blood,                                          60
Assyrian Lycabas, a comrade and no concealer of his true love,
and after weeping for Athis, breathing out his life
because of the wound, he snatched up the bow
that Athis had strung and said, "Let the contest be

with me! Not long will you rejoice in the death of a boy!     65
For this you gain more disgrace than praise." Before all this
was fully said, the penetrating dart flashed from the string,
but hung, eluded, within the garment's many folds.
Acrisius' offspring turns the sickle famed by Medusa's death
and drives it through his breast; yet even as he died,     70
his eyes swimming beneath the black of night,
he turned around to look at Athis, lay down at his side,
and took to the shades the comfort of a common death.
    Behold there, Phorbas of Syene,[2] born of Metion,
and Amphimedon the Libyan, eager to join the fray,     75
had slipped and fallen in the blood which warmed
and moistened the ground all about; the sword stopped them as they tried
to rise, driven through the ribs of the one and Phorbas' throat.
    But Actor's son, Eurytus, whose weapon was a broad double-axe,
is sought by Perseus, not with the sickle, but instead, raising high     80
in both his hands a mixing bowl, conspicuously embossed,
of very great weight, and enormous in size,
he dashes it against the man, who vomits red gore
and, falling backwards, beats the ground with his dying head.
He next lays low Polydegmon, born of Semiramis' blood,     85
Caucasian Abaris, Lycetus, descendant of Sperchios,[3]
and Helices, with unshorn locks, and Phlegyas and Clytus, too,
and heaps up piles of dying men beneath his heel.
    And Phineus lacks the courage to fight hand to hand with his foe,
and hurls a javelin that goes astray and hits Idas, who in vain     90
has stayed out of the fight and followed the arms of neither side.
Observing the merciless Phineus with angry eyes,
he says, "Because I am forced to take sides, accept the foe
that you have made and pay for this wound with a wound!"
And having drawn the spear from his body and ready to hurl it back,     95
he faints and falls upon limbs made weak by loss of blood.
Hodites, then, first of the Cephenians after the king,
is slain by the sword of Clymenus, Prothoënor by Hypseus is struck,
and Lyncides[4] strikes Hypseus. Among them was also Emathion,
now grand in years, devoted to justice and reverent towards the gods;     100
although his years keep him from going to war, he fights with speech,
and now has come forth and curses their wicked arms.
As he embraced the altar with his trembling palms,
his head was cut off by Chromis and on the altar fell headlong,
and even there the tongue of the man, still half-alive, uttered words     105

---

2 A town of the Upper Nile, now Aswan.
3 A river in Thessaly.
4 Perseus, as descendant of Lynceus, the father of Abas. Cf. 185. See on 4. 608

of execration as he breathed out his soul into the midst of the flames.
    The twin brothers Ammon and Broteas,
invincible at boxing, if boxing gloves could conquer swords,
fell next by Phineus' hand, and Ampycus, Ceres' priest,
his temples veiled in a band of white,                                    110
and you, as well, Lampetides, not summoned for this work
but rather to move the lyre, a work of peace,
commanded to honor the festive meal with song.
He stood quite apart, holding his plectrum, unsuited to war,
as Pettalus mocked him and said, "Sing the rest to the shades            115
of Styx!" and then into his left temple planted the point of his sword.
The other fell and with his dying fingers tried again
the strings of his lyre, and at his fall there was a pitiful song.
But fierce Lycormas does not allow him to die unavenged
and from the right door-post tore loose a sturdy bar                     120
and smashed it right through the bones of his neck
and left him stretched out upon the ground like a slaughtered bull.
Cinyphian[5] Pelates was also trying to remove the bar of the jamb,
but in the attempt, his right hand was caught by the spear
of Corythus of Marmarica[6] and pinned to the wood.                      125
And Abas dug into the side of Pelates, now fastened there,
who did not fall, but dying, hung by his hand from the door.
Melaneus is also laid low, in Perseus' camp,
and Dorylas, the richest man of the Nasamonian[7] land,
the wealthy Dorylas, than whom none possessed                            130
more land or amassed so many piles of spice.
A spear was cast from the side that stood fixed in his groin,
a death-bringing hit. After the author of the wound beheld
him gasping out his life and rolling his eyes,
the Bactrian[8] Halcyoneus exclaimed, "Of all the lands of the earth,    135
possess alone the one upon which you lie!" And life leaves the bloodless corpse.
But vengeful Abantiades[9] snatches the spear from the warm wound
and hurls it against Halcyoneus; it struck him right in the nose
and drove through his neck and stuck out on either side.
While Fortune abetted his hand, he felled both Clytius                   140
and Clanis, from the same mother born, but now with different wounds:
his sturdy arm drove the ashen spear through both thighs
of Clytius, but Clanis bit the spear with his mouth.
And Celadon of Mendes[10] fell and Astreus fell,

---

5 Referring to the Cinyps River in Africa.
6 Region of North Africa between Egypt and Cyrenaica.
7 Nasamonia was a region of Libya.
8 From the city of Bactra in Persia.
9 Perseus, as a descendant of Abas (not the Abas of 126). See note on 4. 608.
10 A city in Egypt.

created by an uncertain father and a mother of Palestine,                                    145
and Aethion, in foreseeing the future once skilled,
but this time misled by a deceptive bird, and Thoactes who bore
the king's arms, and Agyrtes, notorious for having slain his sire.
  But more remains for wearied Perseus, for the mind of all
were set to oppose him, and all around him the battle lines conspire     150
in favor of a cause that assailed deserving deeds and trust.
On his side was his father-in-law, honest in vain, and his new bride,
along with her mother. While their howling fills the courts,
the sound of arms and the groans of the fallen drown it out;
Bellona[11] drenches all the while the polluted household-gods          155
with copious blood and renews the battle again and again.
  One man is surrounded by Phineus and a thousand[12] in his train:
more densely than the hail of winter the missiles fly
on either side of him and past his eyes and ears.
He leans his shoulders against a great column's stone                     160
to keep his back secure, and, turning to face
attacking lines, he holds them off as they come. On the left
comes Molpeus of Chaonia,[13] Nabataean[14] Ethemon on the right.
And as a tigress, hearing in two different vales
the lowing of cattle and, goaded by her belly's need,                     165
knows not upon which to rush and yearns to rush upon both,
just so does Perseus, uncertain whether to head for the left or the right,
deter Molpeus with a leg-piercing wound
and lets him flee; but Ethemon gives him no time
and furiously attempts to wound his lofty neck,                           170
but thrusting the sword with careless force
has broken it by striking the column's outer edge:
the blade has split apart and is lodged within its owner's throat.
The blow, however, has not been strong enough to cause
his death, so Perseus sinks the Cyllenian[15] sickle deep into            175
the man, frightened and extending his unarmed hands in vain.
  But Perseus, seeing his strength yielding before the crowd,
exclaimed, "Since you yourselves force me to seek help
from my own foe: turn your faces away if any friend
be present!" and then held out the Gorgon's face.                         180
But Thescelus said, "Seek someone else to frighten with
your miracles!" And as he prepared to cast
the deadly spear, he stood fixed as a marble statue in the very act.
Next after him, Ampyx aimed his sword at the breast

---

11 Goddess of War.
12 Hyperbole? Compare 208-209.
13 A country in Epirus.
14 A people of northern Arabia.
15 Mercury (Hermes), born on Mt. Cyllene in Arcadia, gave Perseus the *harpe* , the "sickle."

of Lyncides so filled with courage: and as he aimed,                          185
his right hand grew rigid and moved neither forward or back.
But Nileus, who falsely claimed to have sprung
from sevenfold Nile, and who upon his shield had embossed
the seven streams, partly in silver and partly in gold,
says, "Perseus, behold the origin of our race:                                190
great consolation for your death will you carry to the shades
to have died at the hand of so great a man." The final part of his words
were lost in the midst of being heard, and you might think his mouth
desired to speak, but there is no passage there for his words.
And Eryx upbraided them, saying, "Your torpor comes                           195
from want of courage, not from the Gorgon's might. Attack with me
and bring to the ground this youth who wields his magic arms!"
He was indeed about to attack: the earth held fast his steps,
and there he remained like a motionless rock, a statue in arms.
        While all of these got their just deserts, there was also one,        200
Aconteus, a soldier fighting for Perseus, who as he fought,
was hardened into a sudden rock at the sight of the Gorgon's head;
Astyages, thinking him still alive, strikes him with
his long sword: with high-pitched ringing resounded the sword.
Amazed, Astyages drew the same nature upon himself,                           205
an image of wonder abiding upon his marble face.
To tell the names of the men in that crowd would cause
delay: two hundred bodies remained after the fight,
two hundred bodies had grown rigid when the Gorgon was seen.
Then finally Phineus regretted his unjust war.                                210
But what was he to do? He sees images differing in stance
and recognizes his men and, calling upon each by name,
he pleads for help and touches in disbelief the bodies next
to him: they're marble! He turns around and thus as a suppliant,
extending his hands and arms aslant[16] to admit defeat,                      215
he says, "You win, Perseus! Take away your monster and the stonifying gaze
of your Medusa, and whatever she is take her away, I pray!
For we were driven to war by neither hatred nor desire
to rule as king, but stirred our weapons for the sake of a bride!
Your claim was stronger in merits, mine in time:[17]                          220
I'm not ashamed to yield. Grant me nothing, O most valiant one,
except this life of mine, all the rest shall be yours!"
To him, who spoke without daring to look at the one
to whom he was pleading, Perseus replies, "Because,
O Phineus, you greatest of cowards, I shall grant both what I can             225
and for a coward a great favor, lay aside your fear: iron shall do

16 I. e., in order to avoid the Gorgon's gaze, he does not look directly at Perseus.
17 Because Andromeda has been promised first to Phineus.

*Perseus' Wedding Battle with Phineus, Baur*

no harm to you, for I shall let you become a monument to last
forever, and you shall always be seen in the home of my father-in-law,
so that my wife may be consoled by the image of her promised groom."
He spoke and carried Phorcys'[18] daughter where                                     230
the frightened face of Phineus had turned away.
As even then he tried to avert his eyes, his neck
grew rigid, and the liquid in his eyes hardened to rock,
but still his fearful mouth and suppliant gaze were fixed
in marble with his submissive hands and servile face.                                235

### 236-49  *Proetus and Polydectes*

Abantiades[19] with his bride enters his ancestral walls[20]
and, as his undeserving grandfather's avenging champion,
makes war against Proetus, who had by force of arms expelled
Acrisius and taken possession of his brother's citadel.
But neither with the aid of arms nor ill-gotten citadel                              240
did he survive the snake-bearing monster's angry eyes.
But you, Polydectes, ruler of little Seriphus,
were softened neither by the young man's bravery, observed
in so many feats, nor by his troubles, but implacably harsh, you ply
your hatred and set no end to your wicked wrath.                                     245
You even detract from his praise and claim that Medusa's death

18 Medusa. Phorcys was the father of the Gorgons and the Graeae.
19 Perseus.
20 Argos.

was feigned. "We will give you proof of the truth.
Protect your eyes!" says Perseus and with Medusa's face
transformed the face of the king to bloodless stone.

### 250-678  *Pallas as Guest of the Heliconian Muses*

Through all of this Tritonia[21] to her brother born of gold                  250
had made herself the companion, but now, hidden in hollow cloud,
she leaves Seriphus with Cythnus and Gyarus[22] left behind on her right,
and, using what seemed the shortest path over the sea,
makes straight for Thebes and the Maidens'[23] Helicon. Having gained
the mountain, she stopped and to her learned sisters said this:                 255
"Report of a new fountain has reached our ears,
created by the hard hoof of the Medusan flying horse.[24]
The reason for my journey is this. I wanted to behold
the marvelous deed, for I saw him born from his mother's blood."
Urania[25] replied, "Whatever the reason for your wanting to see               260
our home, O goddess, most welcome are you to our heart;
however, the story is true: Pegasus *is* the origin of this spring,"[26]
and to the sacred waters she drew Pallas apart.
Admiring at length the waves created by the blows of the hoof,
Minerva looks about the groves of the ancient woods                            265
and caves and the grasses set off by countless flowers
and calls the Mnemonides[27] blessed in their pursuit and home.
Then one of the sisters addressed her thus:

### 269-93  *Pyreneus*

"If virtue had not led you to greater deeds,
you would have become a part of our chorus, O Tritonia.                        270
Your words are true and rightly do you praise our interests and home,
and pleasing is our lot, if only we be secure.
But everything (for nothing is forbidden in crime)
makes virgin minds afraid, and harsh Pyreneus[28] ranges before
our faces, and I have not regained full command of my mind.                    275
With Thracian soldiers he had seized by force
both Daulis[29] and the fields of Phocis and kept them under an unjust rule.
When we were seeking the temple of Parnassus, he saw us as we came,

---

21 Minerva, half-sister to Perseus, sired by the Jove's shower of gold.
22 Aegean islands.
23 I. e., the Muses of Mt. Helicon.
24 Pegasus, born from the neck of Medusa, pregnant by Neptune (Poseidon), Hes., *Theog.* 278-86. See
   4. 785-86.
25 Muse of astronomy.
26 Often called Hippocrene, "the Fountain of the Horse."
27 The Muses, daughters of Mnemosyne "Memory" and Zeus.
28 A king of Thrace.
29 A city of Phocis, close to Delphi and Mt. Parnassus.

and, respecting our divinity with dishonest mien,
declared, 'Mnemonides' (for he recognized us), 'please stop          280
and do not hesitate to take refuge in my house against the heavy sky
and storm' (for there was a storm). 'The lesser gods
have often entered my house.' Moved by the weather and his words,
we nodded assent to the man and entered the first part of the house.
The rain had abated and, with Auster overcome by Aquilo's winds,      285
the somber clouds were fleeing, and the sky had cleared.
We had the urge to leave, but Pyreneus locked shut his house
and threatened force, which we eluded by using our wings.
Appearing to intend pursuit, he stood high upon his citadel
and said, 'The path you have will be mine as well,'                   290
and hurls himself insanely from the highest tower's peak
and falls headlong, smashing the bones of his face as he hits
the ground, and, dying, stains it with his wicked blood."

### 294-678   *The Daughters of Pierus*

The muse was still speaking when wings were heard through the air
and words of greeting, coming from the lofty branches of the trees.    295
The daughter of Jove looks up and searches for the source of the sound
of tongues that speak so clearly she thinks it human speech.
A bird it was instead. Lamenting their fate,
nine magpies had perched on the branches, copying everything.
The goddess spoke to the wondering goddess, "Just lately these girls   300
were vanquished in a contest and increased the number of the birds.
Rich Pierus was their father in Pella's land;[30]
Euhippe, daughter of Paeon, was their mother, who invoked
nine times Lucina's[31] might nine times to give birth.
The foolish sisters, swollen with pride in the number of their band,   305
come through so many Haemonian, so many Achaean towns
to us and issue their challenge with words like these:
'Deceive no longer the untutored masses with your vacuous charm.
Contend with us, if you have the confidence,
O Thespian maidens.[32] In neither voice nor art                       310
will we be conquered, and we are equal in number to you. Either you
depart Hyantean[33] Aganippe[34] and Medusa's fountain[35] in defeat,
or we will concede the Emathian[36] plain all the way

---

30 Macedonia.
31 Goddess of Light or the Moon, identified with Juno and Diana.
32 Thespiae was a town on Mt. Helicon.
33 Boeotian.
34 The Muses' fountain in Boeotia.
35 See 256-59.
36 A part of Macedonia.

to snowy Paeonia.[37] This contest let the nymphs decide!'
Disgraceful it was to compete, more disgraceful yet to concede.                    315
The nymphs were chosen as judges and swear by their streams
and settle down upon the seats of living rock.

### 318-33   Typhoeus

"The one who first demanded the competition, before the lots were drawn,
recounts in song the wars of the gods, granting the giants honor undeserved
while making light of the deeds of the greater gods;                    320
and how Typhoeus, let loose from his home beneath the earth,
caused fear among the heavenly gods and how they turned
their backs in flight until, all wearied, the Egyptian land
received them, and Nile, divided into his seven mouths.
She tells how even there the earthborn Typhoeus came                    325
and how the gods assumed false shapes to hide themselves;
'And Jupiter became the leader of the flock: and even now,
therefore, is Libyan Ammon[38] fashioned with crescent horns;
the Delian god[39] hid in a raven, Semele's offspring[40] in a goat,
the sister of Phoebus in a cat, Saturnia in a snow-white cow,                    330
and Venus[41] in a fish, Cyllenius[42] in the ibis' wings.'
"Thus far she had moved her voice tunefully to the lyre:
We maidens of Aonia[43] are challenged, —but you are not
at leisure perhaps and have no time to offer your ears to our songs."
"O have no doubts and relay to me in order your song!"                    335
says Pallas and has taken her seat in the refreshing shade of the grove.
The muse replies: "We placed our trust in one to oversee the strife;
and, with her ivy-wreathed tresses unbound, Calliope
stands forth and tests the mournful strings with her thumb
and as she strikes the strings composes this song:                    340

### 341-661   Ceres

"The first to turn the soil was Ceres with crescent plow,
the first she was to give grain and merciful nourishment from
the fields, and first to give laws; all of these are Ceres' gift;
of her must I sing! if only I might recite
a song worthy of a goddess! Surely she is a goddess worthy of song.                    345
"The vast Trinacrian[44] island upon the giant's limbs

---

37 Northern Macedonia.
38 The Egyptian Ammon, represented by the ram, had a sanctuary in Libya.
39 Apollo, associated with the Egyptian falcon-shaped Horus.
40 Bacchus, identified with Osiris.
41 Perhaps the Syrian goddess Dercetis. In *Fasti* 2. 249 ff. Venus flees to the Euphrates and is rescued
    by fish.
42 Hermes (Mercury), identified with Thoth.
43 The district of Boeotia containing Mt. Helicon.
44 "Triangular," referring to Sicily.

was heaped and weighed down Typhoeus beneath its great mass
because he dared to hope for an ethereal home.[45]
He often strains, of course, and struggles to rise again,
but by Ausonian Pelorus[46] his right hand is held down,                     350
his left by you, Pachynus,[47] and by Lilybaeum[48] his legs;
as Aetna weighs down his head, Typhoeus, on his back below,
discharges sand and vomits flame from his savage mouth.
He often struggles to remove the weight of the earth
and roll from his body both the great mountains and the towns:               355
from that the earth quakes, and the king of the silent dead himself
grows pale lest the ground open up, unroofed with a gaping hole,
and day invade and terrify the trembling shades.

### 359-571   *Pluto and Proserpina*

   " 'The tyrant, fearing this destruction, had left
his gloomy home and, carried upon a chariot of black steeds,                 360
was visiting warily the foundations of the Sicilian land.
When he determined clearly that no place had collapsed
and put aside his fears, Erycina[49] sees him roaming about
and, sitting down upon her mountain and embracing her winged son,
then said, "My son, my arms and hands, source of my might,                   365
take up those darts, O Cupid, with which you overcome all
and send those arrows flying into the breast of the god
to whom the final portion of the three-fold[50] kingdom fell by lot.
Of Jove himself you, you of the sea's vanquished might
are master and of him who rules the powers of the sea:                       370
so why is Tartarus neglected? Why not extend your mother's and
your own authority? This has to do with one third of the world
and yet in heaven, where our forbearance is long,
we're spurned, and with me is Amor's[51] power being reduced.
You see, don't you, that Pallas and Diana, the wielder of the javelin,       375
have nothing to do with me. The virgin daughter of Ceres, too,
if we allow her; for she is laying claim to similar hopes.
But you, to help our allied realm, if you find that pleasing at all,
unite the goddess to her uncle." Venus spoke; he unloosed
his quiver and, guided by his mother, of the thousand darts                  380
selected one, than which sharper was none
nor less unsure, nor more obedient to the bow;

---

45 Typhoeus or Typhon challenged the reign of Zeus.
46 Promontory on the northeast coast of Sicily.
47 Southeastern promontory of Sicily.
48 Promontory of southern Sicily.
49 Venus, worshipped on Mt. Eryx in northwest Sicily.
50 Heaven was allotted to Jupiter, the Sea to Neptune, the Underworld to Pluto.
51 Cupid.

he bent the pliant horn against his knee
and struck Dis[52] to the heart with the barb-fitted reed.
    "There is a lake of deep water not far from Henna's[53] walls,     385
named Pergus. Not even Cayster[54] hears more songs
of swans upon its gliding waves than this lake.
A forest crowns the waters, encircling it on all sides
and with its foliage like a tent deflects Phoebus' heated blows;
the branches offer coolness, the moist earth Tyrian flowers of varied hue:[55]   390
perpetual springtime is there. While Proserpina plays
within the grove and gathers violets or lilies of shining white,
and while with girlhood's delight she fills her lap
and basket and in gathering competes with her comrades in age,
almost as soon as she was seen, she was loved and seized by Dis:      395
so headstrong was his love. The frightened goddess cries out
with sorrowful voice for her mother and companions repeatedly,
and since she had ripped the top of her gown,
the flowers she had gathered fell out of her slackened cloak.
So great was the innocence of her girlhood's years      400
that this loss as well caused virgin grief.
The ravisher drives his chariot and, calling each by name,
exhorts his horses, over whose necks and manes
he lashes the reins, dyed with dark rust.
He rides through deep lakes and sulphurous pools      405
that boil where the land of the Palici[56] is cracked
and where the Bacchiadae,[57] a people born of Corinth that lies
beside two seas, established their walls between two ports of unlike size.
    "Between Cyane[58] and Pisaean Arethusa[59] there is a place
that forms a bay enclosed by its narrow horns of land:      410
Cyane was here after whom the pool was named,
of Sicily's nymphs the most renowned.
She rose from the midst of the pool as far as the top of her waist
and recognized the goddess. "You will go no farther," she says;
"You cannot be the son-in-law of Ceres against her will: the lady was    415
for wooing, not ravishing. But if to compare great things
with small I be allowed, Anapis loved me, too;
yet courted and not, like this one, in fright did I wed."

---

52 Pluto.
53 A town of central Sicily (the modern Enna), associated with Ceres and Proserpina.
54 A river of Lydia noted for its swans. See 2. 253.
55 The translation seeks to incorporate divergent readings of the manuscripts: *Tyrios* "Tyrian, i.e.,
   crimson" and *varios* "varied," since she picks both purple and white flowers (line 392).
56 Sons of Jupiter and the nymph Thalia. At Palica, southeast of Henna, they had a cult and two sacred
   lakes bubbling with hot springs.
57 These descendants of the Heraclid Bacchis were a leading family of Corinth and had founded
   Syracuse in Sicily. Syracuse had a larger and smaller harbor.
58 A spring flowing into the Anapis river near Syracuse, named after the nymph.
59 A pool near Syracuse, named after a nymph of Elis, near Pisa in the Peloponnesus.

*Rape of Proserpina, Anonymous, Amsterdam, 1703*

She spoke, extending her arms to both sides,
and blocked the way. The Saturnian[60] contained no more his wrath          420
and, urging on his ferocious steeds into the pool,
and thrusting his royal scepter with his mighty arm
he drove it into the depths; the stricken earth, having made a way to Tartarus,
received the plunging chariot within the crater's midst.

  "Cyane, though, lamenting the stolen goddess and her fountain's rights  425
thus scorned, and bearing an inconsolable wound
within her silent mind, is all dissolved in tears
and melts away into those waters where she only now
had been the great divinity: you could have seen her limbs grow soft,
the bones forced to bend, her nails hard no more;          430
and first of all her softest parts are liquefied,
her sky-blue tresses and fingers and legs and feet;
for brief is the change to icy waters for smaller limbs;
and then the shoulders and back and flank
and breasts fade away and vanish into narrow streams;          435
and finally in place of living blood into her corrupted veins
flows water, and nothing remains that you might grasp.

  "The frightened mother, meanwhile, sought in vain
her daughter in every land, on every ocean deep.
Aurora, approaching with her moistened tresses, saw          440
her nowhere tarrying, nor did Hesperus.[61] In each hand

---

60 Pluto, as son of Saturn.
61 The evening star.

she lit flame-bearing torches of pine with Aetna's fires
and carried them restlessly through the icy shade of night;
as once again the nourishing day had dulled the stars,
she looked for her child from the rising to the setting of the sun.          445
When weary from her labors, she had gained a thirst, and no spring
had moistened her mouth, she spied a thatch covered hut
by chance and knocked upon its humble doors; and out
there came an old woman, who looked at the goddess and gave
her when she asked sweet water sprinkled with toasted barley-meal.          450
As she was drinking what she had been given, an impudent
and rude-mouthed boy stood before the goddess, who laughed
at her and called her greedy. Offended, the goddess drenched him while
he spoke with the undrunk portion of the liquid mixed with barley-meal:
his face was imbued with spots and what before he moved as arms,          455
he moved as legs; a tail is added to his altered limbs
and, lest he have great power to harm, he is shrunk into
a meager form, less than a tiny lizard in length.
He fled the startled old woman as she wept, afraid to touch
the marvelous creature, and seeks a place to hide, and gains          460
a name[62] that suits his shame and a body spangled with varied spots.
    "To tell what lands and what seas the goddess roamed
would take too long; when there remained no place in the world
to look, she returns to Sicily, and continuing to search as she goes,
she went to Cyane as well. If she had not been changed,          465
she would have told her all; but though she wanted to,
she had no mouth or tongue or means by which to speak;
she did, however, make obvious signs and on the surface of her waves
displayed the belt, well-known to the mother, that had slipped
by chance from Persephone within that sacred pool.          470
As soon as she saw it, as if she had recognized at last
that she had been raped, the goddess tore at her disheveled locks,
repeatedly pounding her breast with her palms.
She still knew not where she was; but all the lands she blames
as ingrates and unworthy of the gift of grain,          475
Trinacria[63] above all others, in which she had found
the clues of her loss. For this she dashed with savage hand
the plow that turned the clods and in equal fashion, enraged,
she gave to death the farmers and oxen that till the fields and bid
the fields default on their deposit and vitiated the seeds.          480
The earth's fertility established through the whole wide world
lay ruined; the crops died in their very first leaf,

---

62 Latin *stellio* "gecko," hence the play with *stellatus* "starred" or *stillatus* "spangled."
63 Sicily.

one day excessive sun destroys, the next, excessive rain.
Both stars and winds work their harm, and greedy birds
gather the scattered seeds while thistles and weeds                     485
and grass, ever invincible, assail the harvests of grain.
    "Alphean Arethusa[64] then raised her head from the Elean[65] waves
and pushed towards her ears the dewy tresses from her brow
and says, "O mother of the virgin sought throughout the world
and of the grain, cease now your measureless toil                      490
and vent not your violent wrath upon the earth, for she is loyal to you.
The earth did no wrong and was opened against her will for the theft;
nor am I a suppliant for my country: I came here as a guest.
My country is Pisa,[66] and from Elis I claim my origin;
I dwell in Sicania[67] as a foreigner, but I prefer this land          495
to every other soil: these household gods do I, Arethusa, call
my home. O most gentle one, keep it safe.
The reason I left my land and was carried over the waves
of such a great sea to Ortygia[68] the proper time will come
for me to tell, when you are relieved of care                          500
and have a happier countenance. The porous earth
affords me the way, and as I am carried off through the caverns below
I raise my head up here and behold unfamiliar stars.
So while I'm gliding along the Stygian stream beneath
the earth, our eyes beheld your Proserpina there:                      505
her face was sad, indeed, and even then not free of fear,
but yet, she was a queen, the greatest woman, no less, in the unseen world,
in fact, the powerful wife of the tyrant of the underworld."
The mother stood amazed like a stone at the words she heard
and was a long time like one struck dumb, and as by grievous pain      510
her grievous madness was overcome, into the ethereal realm
she rides away upon her chariot: there, gloom upon all her face,
her hair unbound, she stood indignant before the presence of Jove
and says, "For your blood and mine, I've come as a suppliant,
O Jupiter: if a mother's favor has no power, may at least              515
a daughter move her father and may your care, we pray,
be not the less for the reason that she was born of me.
Behold, the daughter I long have sought has at last
been found, if you call finding losing more surely or
call finding knowing where she is. That she was ravished, we will bear, 520

---

64 Arethusa was a nymph pursued by Alpheus, a river running from Arcadia through Elis in the
    northwest Peloponnesus and then under the sea to Syracuse in Sicily. See 572-641.
65 Pertaining to Elis.
66 The district in Elis around Olympia.
67 An old name for Sicily.
68 "Quail Island," not referring to the old name of Delos or to Ephesus, but to an island at the entrance
    to the port of Syracuse.

provided he return her! Your daughter does not deserve
a pirate as a spouse, even if she is my daughter no more."
Replying, Jupiter says, "Our daughter is to us both a concern
and pledge; but if to this matter we may apply
true words, it was done not for the sake of harm but of love,                   525
nor will this son-in-law be cause for shame to us,
if only you, dear goddess, allow it. Not to mention the rest, how great
it is to be the brother of Jove! And what about all the rest, and that
he's second to me only by lot?[69] But if you have such a great desire
to break them up, Proserpina will return to the sky,                            530
but only under this strict rule, that she not have touched food
down there with her mouth; for the pact of the Parcae[70] so prescribes."
        "Although he had spoken, Ceres was fixed upon regaining her child.
But this the fates do not allow, since the maiden had broken her fast
and, wandering in the well-tended gardens alone,                                535
had plucked a Punic apple[71] from a bending tree
and seven seeds, extracted from its pallid skin,
had pressed with her mouth; Ascalaphus was the only one
who saw this, whom, it's said, Orphne once,
by no means the least famous among the Avernal[72] nymphs,                      540
had born to her Acheron within the dark woods.
He sees and, by his telling, cruelly blocks her return.
The queen of Erebos[73] moaned and made into an ill-omened bird
that witness and spraying its head with the water of Phlegethon
converted it into beak and feathers and enormous eyes.                          545
Deprived of himself, he is cloaked in tawny wings,
his head gains size, into long talons his nails are bent;
he scarcely moves the feathers that have sprung up on his sluggish arms;
he turns into a shameful bird, prophet of coming grief,
the lazy horned-owl, for mortals an omen dire.                                  550
        "Although it may seem because of his tattling tongue
that he deserved his punishment, why is it that you, the Acheloides,[74]
have faces of a maiden but the plumage and feet of birds?
Or is it because, while Proserpina was picking spring flowers, you,
O skillful Sirens, were among the number of her friends?                        555
You sought her throughout the world in vain and then,
so that the seas should feel your care, straightway
you prayed that you might stand with oarage of wings

---

69 At *Iliad* 15. 189-93 Poseidon explains that by lot he had been awarded the sea, Hades the underworld,
    and Zeus the sky, but that all three shared equally Olympus and the earth.
70 The Roman Fates.
71 The pomegranate.
72 Pertaining to Avernus, i. e., the lake near the Bay of Naples beside an entrance to the Underworld.
73 Greek for "Darkness," i. e., the Underworld.
74 Daughters of Acheloüs, a river in northwest Greece.

above the waves, and won over the gods and saw
your limbs grow tawny with sudden plumes.    560
But lest that tunefulness born for soothing the ears
and such a great endowment of voice and tongue be lost,
your virgin visage and human voice remained.
  "But fair to both his brother and grieving sister, Jove
divides the revolving year into equal parts:    565
the goddess, a deity common now to either realm,
is with her mother as many months as with her spouse.
Immediately are the mind and mien of her face transformed;
for she who might have seemed sad even to Dis
has now the brow of a joyful goddess, like the sun, which before was veiled    570
with watery clouds and then emerges from the vanquished clouds.

### 572-641  *Arethusa*

  "Content with the return of her daughter, nourishing Ceres asks
the cause of your flight, Arethusa, and why you're now a sacred spring.
The waves grew silent as their goddess raised her head
above the deep spring and, after drying her mossy tresses with her hands,    575
related the former love of the Elean stream.
She said, "Of Achaia's nymphs I was one,
and none more eagerly roamed the glades
and none more eagerly laid the traps.
Though fame for my beauty I had never sought,    580
and though I was strong, I had won a name for my form.
My face, too much praised, was no help to me,
and as a country girl I blushed in the gift of bodily form
that other girls like to have and thought giving pleasure a fault.
As I was returning weary from the Stymphalian forest (I recall),    585
the weather was hot and labor had made the heat twice as great:
I come upon waters that moved without an eddy, without a sound,
pellucid to the bottom, through which every deep-lying stone
was countable, waters you might think were hardly moving at all.
White willows and poplars fed by the waters produced    590
a natural shade upon the sloping banks.
Approaching, I first dipped in the sole of my foot,
then went up to my thigh and not content with that I undo clothes
and lay the soft garments on a bending willow branch
and sink into the waters nude. And gliding in a thousand ways    595
while striking and stroking the waters and tossing my flailing arms,
I hear some kind of murmur from deep within the pool
and, frightened, step out upon the edge of the nearer bank.
'To where do you rush, Arethusa?' had Alpheus said from his waves,
'to where do you rush?' said he with raucous voice to me.    600

I'm fleeing just as I was, unclad (the other bank possessed
my clothes): he presses on all the more and burns
and, since I was nude, I seemed more ready for him.
As much as I ran, so much did that wild fellow press after me,
as doves are wont with trembling wing to flee the hawk,                    605
the hawk to follow hard upon the frightened doves.
Beneath Orchomenus and Psophis and Cyllene, too,
the vales of Maenalus, icy Erymanthus, and Elis I
continued to run, nor was he swifter than I.
Unequal to his strength, I could not keep the pace                         610
for long, and he had the endurance for the lengthy task.
But just the same, through fields, through tree-covered hills,
and rocks and crags and where there was no path, I ran.
The sun was at my back: I saw advancing before my feet
his lengthy shadow, unless fear it was that saw all that;                  615
but certainly the sound of his feet caused terror, and the huge
expulsions of breath from his mouth were blowing the bands of my hair.
Exhausted by the toil of flight, I say, 'We are caught. Give aid,
Diana, to your arms-bearer, whom you have often allowed
to bear your bow and the arrows your quiver holds!'                        620
The goddess is moved and, having split the clouds, threw one
around me: the river searches for me concealed in mist
and at a loss looks about the hollow clouds and twice
unwittingly circles the place in which the goddess had hidden me
and twice called out, 'Halloo, Arethusa, Arethusa, Halloo!'               625
What hope for a wretch like me was there? Like that of the lamb
that hears the wolves howling about the lofty folds
or of the hare lying concealed in the brush that beholds
the threatening mouths of dogs and dares not let its body move?
But still he does not leave, for he does not see any prints                630
on further of my feet: he guards both the cloud and the place.
My limbs are seized by cold sweat,
my whole body is dripping with blue green drops,
wherever I move my foot a pool oozes, and from my hair
there falls a dew, and quicker than I now retell the deed,                 635
I'm changing into water. But yet the river knows the waters he loved
and set aside the appearance he had assumed of a man,
he changes into his own waters in order to be mingled with me.
Then Delia[75] breaks open the ground, and I, plunged into hidden caves,
am carried to Ortygia,[76] which, named for my goddess, was dear          640
to me and first returned me to the air above."

---

75 Diana, because she was born on the island of Delos.
76 See 1. 694 and note. Here Ortygia refers to the island in the port of Syracuse. See 499.

*Ceres, Triptolemus and King Lyncus, Baur*

### 642-66  *Triptolemus and Lyncus*

"This much from Arethusa. The fertile goddess hitched
twin snakes to her chariot and curbed their mouths with the reins
and rode between the sky and earth through the air
and sent her chariot to Tritonia's town for Triptolemus                      645
and ordered him to scatter some of the seeds she had given him
on ground never tilled and some on ground not tilled for many years.
Already above Europe and Asia's land had the youth, raised on high
been carried: he approaches now the Scythian shores.
The king there is Lyncus; Triptolemus enters the household gods of the king.  650
When asked how he came, the reason for the journey, and his name
and country, he said, "Bright Athens is my fatherland,
Triptolemus my name; I have come neither by ship over sea
nor foot over land: the air of the sky opened a path for me.
I bring the gifts of Ceres, which when sown upon the broad fields           655
return the grain-bearing harvests and kindly nourishment."
The foreigner was jealous and, wanting himself to be
the author of so great a gift, gave him hospitality and, when deep
in sleep, attacks him with his sword: as he tries to pierce his breast,
the goddess Ceres changes him to a lynx and orders again                    660
the Mopsopian[77] youth to drive her sacred team through the air.'

---

77 I.e., Athenian, referring to Mopsus an earlier king of Athens.

### 662-78    The End of the Daughters of Pierus

"Our oldest sister had finished her learned song.[78]
The nymphs with one accord decreed that the goddesses who dwell
on Helicon had won. When the vanquished girls hurled abuse,
I[79] said, 'Since punishment for competing with us is not enough,                    665
and now you add curses to your wrong, and we are not free
to practise longer our patience, we shall proceed
to punishments and follow where our anger bids.'
Rejecting the words of warning the Emathides[80] laugh.
They try to speak and to shake in our faces their reckless fists                    670
and saw feathers growing from their fingernails
and plumage covering their arms.
They see one another's faces grow hard into rigid beaks
and different birds being added to the woods.
And as they seek to beat their breasts, raised aloft by their moving arms,          675
they hung in the air as magpies, that source of scorn in the woods.
Still now the birds retain their original facility for speech,
their raucous garrulity and inordinate desire to talk."

---

78 Translating *doctos*. With *dictos*, "song that I have reported."
79 The Muse who begins speaking at 337.
80 Daughters of Pierus, King of Emathia. See 313.

# BOOK 6

1-145      Arachne and Minerva
146-312    Niobe
313-81     Latona in Lycia
382-400    The Contest between Marsyas and Phoebus
401-11     Pelops Made Whole
412-674    Tereus, Procne and Philomela
675-721    Boreas and Orithyia; Calais and Zetes

## 1-145  *Arachne and Minerva*

Tritonia[1] had offered her ears to such tales as these
approving both the Aonids[2] songs and the justice of their wrath.
And then to herself: "To praise is not enough, let us be praised ourselves
and not allow without penalty our divine power to be scorned."
With this she turned her attention to Maeonian[3] Arachne's fate,          5
who in the art of working wool, she had heard, would not
cede pride of praise to her. In neither status nor family origin lay
her fame but in her art: her father was Idmon of Colophon,[4]
who dyed with Phocaean[5] purple the spongy wool;
her mother had died, a woman herself of humble folk                        10
just like her husband; but the girl had through the Lydian towns
acquired a memorable name for her pursuit, even though
she lived in little Hypaepa and came from a simple home.
In order to see her admirable work,
Timolus'[6] nymphs often left their olive groves,                          15
the nymphs of Pactolus[7] often left their stream.
The joy was not only in looking at the cloth she wove,
but also at how she made it: so great was the grace of her art,
in rolling the raw wool first into balls,
or shaping the mass with her fingers and, softening the wool               20

1 Minerva.
2 The Muses, so called because Mt. Helicon was in Aonia, a part of Boeotia.
3 Maeonia is another name for Lydia in Asia Minor.
4 A city of Ionia.
5 Phocaea was the most northern of the cities of Ionia.
6 A mountain in Lydia.
7 The Pactolus was a river in Lydia.

*125*

by adding more and repeatedly stretching it to look like clouds,
or turning the rounded spindle with her lightly moving thumb,
or adding designs with her needle; taught by Pallas, you might suppose.
But she herself denied it and, offended at the claim of a teacher so great,
declares, "Let her compete with me. If defeated, there is nothing I'd refuse!"  25
      Pretending to be an old woman, Pallas decks with false gray
her temples and also supports her feeble limbs with a cane.
She began this way: "Greater age is not entirely a thing
we would avoid: for with the later years comes skill.
Do not refuse my advice: seek for yourself repute  30
as greatest among mortals for working wool,
give place to the goddess, bold girl, and for your words
with suppliant voice seek her pardon. She will pardon if you ask."
Arachne looked at her fiercely, leaving the threads she had begun
and scarcely keeping her hands off her. Confessing anger on her face,  35
she answered Pallas in disguise with words like these:
"You come here witless and worn with long age.
Too long a life is harmful. If you have a daughter-in-law
or if you have a daughter, let her hear those words of yours;
I'm fully capable of counseling myself, and lest you think  40
you've helped by your warning, our opinion remains unchanged.
Why doesn't she come herself? Why does she refuse to vie with me?"
"She *has* come!" the goddess then replies, removing her old woman's guise,
and Pallas was revealed: the goddess is venerated by the nymphs
and married daughters of Mygdonia:[8] this maiden alone is unafraid,  45
but nonetheless she blushed and a sudden flush of redness marked
her face despite herself, then faded as when the air takes on
a purple hue when Aurora begins to move,
but soon grows bright with the rising of the sun.
Persisting in her intention and desire for the foolish prize,  50
she rushes to her doom; nor does the daughter of Jove refuse
or warn her further or the contest any longer delay.
At once both set up matching looms on opposite sides
and stretch upon them the slender warp.[9]
Upon the warp beam the upright threads are bound, held apart by the reed,  55
between them sharp shuttles insert the woof,
and once the fingers have finished drawing it through the warp,
the woof is tamped down by the teeth cut into the pounded comb.
They both are swift, and, with their robes girt up to their breasts,
they move their skillful arms, deceiving their toil with zeal.  60
On one side the purple that had known the Tyrian vat of bronze

8 Originally, an area of Macedonia, but emigrants of this tribe also settled in Phrygia, next to Lydia, in
   Asia Minor.
9 The vertical threads.

is woven in and subtle shades of slight difference;
just as the rainbows when the sun has been stricken by rain
imbue the big sky with an enormous arch,
in which albeit a thousand colors brightly shine, nonetheless 65
the change from one to the other deceives the observing eyes:
so much alike they are where they touch, yet so different at the extremes.
On that side soft gold is added to the threads
and in the texture is woven an ancient myth.
    Cecropian[10] Pallas depicts the rock on the Hill of Mars[11] 70
as well as the ancient dispute about the name of the land.[12]
With Jove in the middle twice six celestial beings with solemn mien
are seated on their lofty thrones; each face is inscribed
to show which god it is: royalty is seen in the image of Jove;
she makes the god of the sea stand and with his long trident strike 75
the rugged rocks and out of the midst of the blow to the rock
a spring has sprung forth, a pledge with which he would claim the town.
But to herself she gives the shield, gives the sharp-cusped spear,
the helmet for her head, defends with the aegis her breast,
and shows the earth, smitten by the cusp of her spear, 80
bring forth the shoot of the olive tree, graying with fruit,
and marveling gods and Victory at the end of her work.
To make her rival for praise by examples understand
what price to expect for such insane audacity,
she adds four contests, one on each of the four sides, 85
each bright with color and clear in its brief designs:
one corner contains Thracian Rhodope and Haemus,[13] too,
chill mountains now, mortal bodies once,
who took to themselves the names of the highest gods.
Another has the Pygmy mother's[14] pitiful doom, 90
the one whom Juno defeated in strife and ordered to be
a crane and upon her own people to declare war;
she also worked Antigone[15] into the design, who once dared
compete with mighty Jove's wife and by royal Juno was turned
into a bird: neither Ilium[16] availed her, shining white, 95
nor having Laomedon[17] as father, from praising herself
with her new wings and the chattering beak of a stork.

---

10 Referring to Athens, one of whose early kings was Cecrops.
11 The Areopagus, where Athena had established a court to hear the trial of Orestes in Aeschylus' *Eumenides.*
12 The dispute, settled by Cecrops, between Athena and Poseidon for patronage over the city.
13 Brother and sister who named themselves Zeus and Hera.
14 The Pygmy queen was irreverent to Hera and Artemis and had herself worshiped by her own people. One of her names was Gerana (= "Crane" in Greek). The story is derived from Boeus' *Ornithogonia* according to Athenaeus 9. 392 and Antoninus Liberalis 16.
15 Daughter of Laomedon, not the daughter of Oedipus.
16 Troy.
17 A Trojan king.

The last remaining corner contained Cinyras[18] of daughters bereft;
and he, embracing the temple steps, his daughters' limbs,
and prostrate upon the stone, appears to weep.                                                    100
She girded the outer edge with peaceful olive-trees,
and thus with her own tree she finished her work.
      The girl from Maeonia depicts Europa deceived
by the image of the bull: you'd think the bull were real, real the sea;
the maiden herself seemed to gaze at the land left behind,                                         105
to call for her comrades and to fear the touch
of the dancing waves and to draw back the soles of her feet.
She showed Asteria[19] in a struggling eagle's grasp,
and Leda she showed lying beneath the wings of the swan;
She showed as well how Jupiter, hidden beneath the satyr's form,                                   110
had filled the lovely daughter of Nyctaeus[20] with twin young,
and how he was Amphitryon when he took you, Tirynthian maid,[21]
and how he deceived Danaë as gold, Asopus'[22] daughter as fire,
Mnemosyne[23] as a shepherd, Deo's[24] daughter as a spotted snake.
And you as well, O Neptune, changed into an savage bull,                                           115
she mounted on the Aeolian maid;[25] in the guise of Enipeus[26] you
begot the Aloidae,[27] deceived Bisaltis[28] as a ram,
and with her yellow hair that most gentle mother of grain
knew you as a horse, the snaky-haired mother of the winged horse
knew you as a bird, Melantho[29] knew you in the dolphin's guise:                                  120
to all of them she gave the fitting appearance of their place and face.
On that side is Phoebus with a rustic's form,[30]
and how he bore now the wings of a hawk and now the lion's hide,
how as a shepherd he took in Isse, the daughter of Macareus,[31]
how Liber[32] deceived Erigone in the guise of grapes,                                             125

---

18 Unknown and not the Cinyras of 10. 299 ff.
19 The sister of Leto (Latona), changed into a quail at Delos.
20 Antiope, mother of Amphion and Zethus, was the daughter of Nyctaeus, son of the Theban Sown
   Man Chthonius. Another daughter of Nyctaeus is Nyctimene (see 2. 589-95).
21 Amphitryon, king of Tiryns, had taken refuge in Thebes with his wife Alcmene. Zeus took the form
   of Amphitryon and became the father of Heracles.
22 Asopus, a river of Boeotia, was the father of Aegina.
23 Greek for "Memory," the mother of the Muses.
24 Another name for the Greek Demeter and Latin Ceres. By Persephone, his own daughter, Zeus sired
   Zagreus, the underworld Dionyus.
25 Canace or Arne, the daughter of Aeolus.
26 River god of Thessaly.
27 By Poseidon, Iphimedeia, wife of Aloeus, bore the giants Otus and Ephialtes.
28 Neptune changed Theophane, daughter of Thessalian Bisaltes, into a ewe.
29 Daughter of Deucalion.
30 When he served Admetus as a cowherd.
31 King of Lesbos.
32 The god of license, Bacchus, or Dionysus, who in return for his hospitality, gave the gift of wine to
   Icarus or Icarius of Attica, the father of Erigone. When Icarius shared the wine with some country-
   folk, they became intoxicated and killed him. When Erigone, searching with her dog Maera, found
   Icarius' body, she hanged herself in grief. She became the star Virgo; Icarius became Boötes.
   Maera became the Dog-Star. See 10. 451.

*Arachne and Minerva, Baur*

how Saturn as a horse created Chiron in double form.
The last part of her work, in the border all around,
contains, among the clinging ivy, flowers intertwined.
  That work could neither Pallas nor Malice endure:
the fair-haired Maiden was angry at the other's success          130
and ripped up the web with its pictures and heaven's faults
and, holding a shuttle from the Cytorian mount,[33]
struck thrice and a fourth time Idmonian Arachne's brow.
The unhappy girl did not bear it and bound in a noose
her saucy neck: taking pity, Pallas raised her as she hung       135
and said in turn, "Live indeed, but hang, you foolish girl,
and let this same form of penalty, lest in future you have no fear,
be set upon your kind and descendants yet to come!"
Departing, she sprinkled her with juices of Hecate's herbs:
and suddenly her hair, when touched by the awful drug,           140
receded, and with it her nostrils and ears, and her head
became very small; and her body as a whole was small:
the merest fingers cling to her side as legs,
her stomach comprised all the rest, but from it still she sends
a thread and, as a spider, plies her former loom.                145

---

33 Mt. Cytorus, in Paphlagonia, was noted for boxwood, from which the shuttle was made.

## 146-312  Niobe

All Lydia is abuzz, and through all the Phrygian towns
report of the deed proceeds, filling the wide world with talk.
Before her marriage[34] Niobe had met that girl,
when as a young girl she lived in Maeonia and Sipylus.[35]
But by the punishment of Arachne, her compatriot, she heeded not          150
the warning to yield to heavenly beings and to employ modest speech.
Her pride was supported by many things, but her husband's art,[36]
the family status of both of them, nor yet their kingdom's might
pleased her so much, though all these did please,
as her own offspring; Niobe would have been called                        155
the happiest of mothers, if she had not seemed so to herself.
For Manto, born of Tiresias and a seer of things to come,
compelled by the divine, had gone out into the streets
inspired with prophecy: "O Ismenides,[37] go in throngs
and offer to Latona and to both of those to Latona born                   160
your faithful prayers and incense, binding with laurel your hair:
Latona so orders through my mouth." In obeying her commands,
the Theban women adorn their brows with wreaths
and offer incense and words of prayer to the holy flames.

Behold, Niobe arrives, attended by a great throng of followers,           165
outstanding in her Phrygian robes woven with gold.
As much as anger allows her to be, she is lovely and moves
her decorous head and the tresses that over either shoulder spilled.
She stopped and, as she moved her proud gaze all about,
exclaims, "What madness is this, to prefer to those seen                  170
divinities ones you've only heard about? Why do altars Latona revere
when my divinity lacks incense yet? Of Tantalus I was born,
the only one who had permission to touch the tables of the gods;
the sister[38] of the Pleiades is my mother and Atlas, greatest in size,
my grandfather, who bears upon his neck the pole of the sky;              175
my other grandfather is Jupiter in whom as my father-in-law[39]
I glory as well. The Phrygian peoples fear me, and under my sway
is Cadmus' kingdom, and the walls committed to the lyre of my spouse,
as well as their people, are ruled by my husband and me.
No matter to what part of the house I turn my eyes,                       180
are riches seen beyond measure; to this is added the fact
that I have a face worthy of a goddess; and to this seven daughters add,
and just as many sons, and soon both sons- and daughters-in-law!

---

34 To Amphion, ruling Thebes jointly with his brother Zethus.
35 A mountain in Lydia.
36 By playing the lyre, her husband Amphion had once built the walls of Thebes.
37 The daughters of Ismenus, a river near Thebes, i.e. "Theban women."
38 Dione, daughter of Atlas.
39 By Antiope, daughter of Nyctaeus, Zeus was the father of Zethus and Amphion, Niobe's husband.

Now ask yourselves whether our pride is justified
and dare to prefer to me the Titan girl, born of some Coeus[40] I                    185
don't know, Latona, that one to whom all the world one time
refused the slightest space for her to give birth!
Your goddess was received by neither sky nor water nor land,
an exile from the world, until Delos pitied the wanderer
and said, 'You wander as a guest upon the land, I upon the sea,'                     190
and granted her unstable[41] space. She became
the mother of two: only a seventh of what my womb has produced.
Would any deny that I am happy? And who would also deny
that happy I shall remain? Plenty has made me secure.
Too great am I for Fortune to do me harm,                                           195
and should she take away much, much will I retain.
My wealth has dispelled all worry. Imagine that I could be
deprived of just a part of this tribe of children I have:
even then I would not be reduced to the level of only two,
Latona's crowd, of which how far is she from being bereft?                          200
Abandon the rites at once, you've done enough, and remove
the laurel from your hair!" They take it off and leave the rites undone,
but, as they can, venerate with silent murmurs the goddess' might.

 The goddess was indignant and upon Cynthus' highest peak
she spoke with her twin offspring in words like these:                              205
"Just look at me your mother, proud in your birth,
to none of the goddesses but Juno willing to cede place,
yet doubting whether I am a goddess and for all time
excluded from sacred rites, unless, my children, my altar has your help.
And this is not my only grief; insult is added to the awful deed                    210
by Tantalus' daughter, who has dared to honor her offspring more than you
and said that I was childless—may it happen to her!—
and wickedly displayed her father's tongue!"[42]
Latona was about to add a request to what she had said
when Phoebus says, "Enough! Punishment is delayed by long complaint!"   215
Then Phoebe[43] said the same and with a quick descent through the air,
concealed in clouds, they landed upon the Cadmeian citadel.

 A broad and level field lay open before the walls
that horses had constantly beaten down, where many wheels
and rigid hooves had softened the clods beneath.                                    220
Of Amphion's seven sons some are mounting there
strong steeds and pressing those backs made red
with Tyrian dye and holding the reins, heavy with gold.

---

40 One of the twelve Titans, father of Latona.
41 Because Delos was thought to be a floating island.
42 Tantalus was known for his insolent speech, whether in revealing the secrets of the gods or claiming
 status equal to theirs.
43 Diana.

Of these Ismenus, who was the first to burden his mother's womb,
while bending the course of his steed into a fixed curve                    225
and checking its foaming mouth, exclaims,
"Ah me!" and there, implanted in the middle of his chest,
he bears a dart and with the reins falling from his dying grasp
he sinks down gradually from the horse's right shoulder to his side.
Having heard the sound of the quiver through the empty air, Sipylus next    230
was giving his horse full rein, as when the captain, suspecting a storm
from the appearance of clouds, extends the sails
that hang on every side lest the slightest breeze escape.
The unavoidable arrow finds him even giving full rein:
the quivering shaft is fixed at the top of his neck,                        235
the naked iron protrudes from his throat.
Bent forward, as he was, he topples over the mane
and unchecked limbs and stains the soil with steamy blood.
Unfortunate Phaedimus and Tantalus, of his grandfather's name
the heir, having finished their usual tasks,                                240
had gone on to gleaming wrestling, that work of youths;
already in tight embrace had they pressed struggling chest
to struggling chest; when, sped by taut-stretched bow,
the arrow pierced them both, joined just as they were.
No sooner had they groaned than they laid upon the ground                   245
their limbs, doubled over in pain, and prostrate turned aloft
their final gaze and breathed out their last.
Alphenor looks on and, beating his grief-torn breast,
runs forward and, as he lifts the chill limbs in his embrace,
collapses in his act of piety; for the Delian god broke                     250
the inner bonds of his heart with his prophetic shaft of steel.
As soon as it was removed, the point tore away
a part of his lung, and his soul and blood spewed forth into the air.
But unshorn Damasichthon was dealt not just one wound:
precisely where the leg begins and ligaments of                             255
the knee form a spongy connection was he struck.
And as he tries with his hand to extract the lethal shaft,
another arrow is driven up to its feathers into his throat.
His blood pushed it on through and, welling up,
springs forth with a leap, drilling a stream through the air.               260
The last, Ilioneus, had raised his arms in prayer to no avail
and said, "O gods, one and all," (not knowing that he need
not pray to all) "have mercy!" The Wielder of the Bow was moved
but only after the arrow could no longer be recalled.
He fell, just the same, to his death despite the minor wound,               265
his heart not deeply pierced by the shaft.

*Niobe, Clouwet*

Report of the awful deed and her people's grief
and tears for her children informed the mother of her sudden calamity,
amazed that it could happen and angry that the gods
had dared to do it and had so much authority; 270
because[44] Amphion, the father, had driven a sword through his breast
and by his death made an end of his grief and his life.
Alas, how different this Niobe from the Niobe that was,
who lately had driven her people from Latona's altar-shrine
and, head held high in haughty pride, had strode through the city's midst, 275
the envy of her people, but now to be pitied by even the foe!
She falls upon the cold members and frantically
implants her final kisses upon all her sons,
from whom she raises to heaven the arms she has bruised
and says, "Cruel Latona, feed upon our grief, 280
yes feed!," and added, "upon my sorrow glut your breast
and glut your savage heart! Through seven deaths have I
been carried to my tomb: exult and triumph as my victorious foe!
But why victorious? Wretched though I am, I still have more
than you in your happiness; even after so many deaths I win!" 285
    She spoke, and the string of the tensed bow was heard.
It frightened everyone except for Niobe alone:
in woe she is bold. The sisters were standing, robed in black,
their hair disheveled, in front of their brothers' biers.
In drawing a shaft from a brother's vital parts one of these 290

---

44 Explaining why Niobe's reaction could not be tempered by her husband.

collapsed, with her lips placed upon him, in a mortal swoon.
A second, attempting to console her mother's woe
fell suddenly silent and doubled over from an unseen wound.
[She closed her mouth, except for the passing of her dying breath.][45]
In frustrated flight this one falls, while there one falls                          295
in death upon her sister. Here one hides, there you could see
one tremble. When six had been sent to death and suffered wounds,
the last one remained, whom her mother with all her form,
with all her robes concealed, "Leave one, the smallest of all!
Of all the many I demand the smallest, " she cried, "and only one."         300
And as she pleads, the one she pleads for falls: Niobe sits down bereft
amongst her lifeless sons and daughters and spouse
and stiffens in her woes. Her tresses are not moved by the breeze,
a bloodless color lies upon her face, within her sad cheeks
her eyes stare motionless, upon her form there is nothing alive.            305
Her tongue itself within her hardened mouth
is frozen, and her veins are no longer able to be moved.
Her neck cannot be bent, her arms cannot be moved,
her foot cannot advance; her innards are also stone.
And yet she weeps and, enveloped within a whorl of strong wind,            310
she's carried off to her homeland;[46] there, fixed upon a mountain peak,
she wastes away and, turned to marble, flows even now with tears.

### 313-81   *Latona in Lycia*

        In truth then every man and woman fears
the manifest wrath of the goddess, and with even less reserve
do all attend her cult and venerate the great power of                       315
the twin-bearing goddess. And as usual, because of recent events
they tell again those of yore. One says, "Of Lycia's fertile fields
the farmers also spurned the goddess and not without penalty.
Indeed the story is little known because of the low birth of these men,
but even so, it is strange: I saw in person both the pool and the place       320
made famous by this wonder, for my father, rather old and unfit
to travel, had ordered me to drive down from there a herd
of chosen oxen and had himself given me from that tribe
a guide. As I walked with him through the fields,
behold, there in the middle of the lake, an altar black                       325
with ashes stood surrounded by trembling reeds.
My guide then paused with a reverent murmur said,
'Be kind to me,' and with similar murmur I said, 'Be kind!'
I asked then whether the altar belonged to the naiads or
to Faunus or a native god, to which my host replied:                         330

---

45 A line condemned and bracketed in most editions.
46 Phrygia.

*Latona, Twins, and Frogmen, Solis*

'Young man, in this altar there is no mountain god.
The goddess whom once the royal consort denied access to the world
lays claim to it, she whom wandering Delos scarcely received
despite her prayers when the island was floating lightly about.
Reclining there next to a palm and Pallas' tree,[47]                        335
against the will of their stepmother, she gave birth to the twins.
From here[48] as well the new mother is said to have fled
from Juno and carried in her bosom her children, divinities both.
And now in Lycia, the land of the Chimaera, as the sun
burned hard upon the fields, the goddess, wearied by long toil,            340
and parched by the solar heat, conceived a thirst,
and her hungry babes had drained her breasts of milk.
She spied by chance at the bottom of a vale a modest lake
of water; the farmers there were gathering the canes,
the bushy osiers, and marsh-loving sedge.                                  345
Titania[49] approached and pressed her knee to the ground,
preparing to drink the water, cool and clear.
The rustic mob forbids. The goddess addressed those who forbid this way:
"What makes you keep me from the water? The use of water is open to all,
for nature established neither the sun nor the air as private property,    350
nor simple waves: I have come for a public right.
But that you grant it I beg you as your suppliant. My intent
was not to wash my body here or bathe my wearied limbs
within these waters, but just to slake my thirst. My mouth as I speak

---

47 The olive.
48 Delos.
49 Latona (Leto), daughter of the Titans Coeus and Phoebe.

lacks moisture and my throat is dry and scarcely offers my voice a path.      355
A draught of water would seem like nectar to me and, I confess,
quite like the gift of life itself. With this water you will have given me life.
May these move you as well, who stretch their tender arms
up to my breast," (by chance the babes were stretching forth their arms).
    "Whom could the goddess' charming words not have moved?      360
Yet they continue to deny her prayers and add
their threats, if she should refuse to go away, and insults, too.
And this is not enough. With their hands and feet they roiled
the water itself and from the very bottom of the lake
dislodged the mud, leaping about spitefully everywhere.      365
Her wrath postponed her thirst, for Coeus' daughter no more
was suppliant to the unworthy, nor longer content to speak
in words weaker than a goddess should. She raised her palms to the stars
and said, "May you live forever in this pond of yours!"
The wishes of the goddess come true: They like to live beneath      370
the waters, now submerging their whole bodies within the deep pool,
now popping up their heads, and swimming along the surface of the lake,
or often sitting on the bank of the pond and often jumping back
into the cooling waters, but even now exercising their ugly tongues
with quarreling and, with every sense of shame dispelled      375
(to be under water makes no difference), under water they try to taunt.
Their voices are also hoarse, and their inflated necks swell,
and railing their insults makes their gaping jaws grow wide.
Their ugly heads are extended, their necks seem to disappear,
their backs are green, the bellies, the largest part of their bodies, are white,      380
and from the muddy lake leap forth new frogs.'"

### 382-400   *The Contest between Marsyas and Phoebus*

    When someone or other had recounted the death of the men
of Lycia's folk, another calls the satyr to mind
whom, vanquished on the Tritonian[50] reed, Latous[51] forced
to pay the penalty. "Why are you taking me from myself?" he asks.      385
"Alas, I repent, alas," he cried, "No reed is worth so much."
And as he cried, his skin was peeled from the surface of his limbs,
and all that was left was a wound; the blood is flowing from all his parts,
and tendons are bared and exposed, and without his skin
his quivering veins are vivid; you could see his innards throb      390
and count the lobes of his lungs gleaming within his chest.
The country folk, the woodland divinities, the fauns,

---

50 Referring to Minerva, who had rejected the double-reed *aulos* because playing it disfigured her
    cheeks. Marsyas, the satyr, discovered the instrument and, delighted with its sound, dared to
    challenge Apollo to a contest between *aulos* and lyre. See Apollodorus, *Library* 1. 4. 2.
51 Latona's son, Apollo.

*Marsyas, Anonymous, Venice ca. 1513*

his brother satyrs and Olympus,[52] even then dear to him
did weep, and nymphs and anyone who upon those hills
looked after the wooly flocks and horned herds. 395
The fertile earth was soaked and having been soaked drew in
the falling tears and drank them into her deepest veins:
and when she turned them to water, she let them run into the empty air
and, as upon the steep-sloping banks they sought the running sea,
they take the name of Marsyas, Phrygia's clearest stream. 400

### 401-11 *Pelops Made Whole*

From stories like these the gathering[53] suddenly returns
to current times and mourns for Amphion and his offspring's demise.
The mother is blamed, but one is said even then to have wept
for her, Pelops, who, removing his robe from his breast,
revealed the ivory that in his left shoulder had been set. 405
This shoulder was the same color as the right one at the time of his birth,
and made of flesh, but the gods had joined together, they say,
his body mangled by his father's hands. All parts had been found,
except the place between the neck and upper arm.
In place of the missing part was set a piece 410
of ivory, and by that deed was Pelops made whole.

---

52 His father (so Apollodorus) or his pupil on the *aulos* (so Hyginus).
53 Referring to the group of men and women who were inspired by the tragedy of Niobe to narrate
   similar tales at 313 ff.

### 412-674   *Tereus, Procne and Philomela*

The neighboring princes gather, and cities nearby
besought their kings to come with sympathy,
both Argos and Sparta and from Mycenae Pelops' sons
and Calydon, which pitiless Diana did not yet hate,                    415
and fertile Orchomenos and Corinth, famous for bronze,
and fierce Messene, Patrae and Cleonae, lying low,
and Nelean Pylos and Troezen, still under Pittheus' rule,
and all the other cities that the Isthmus on two seas contains
and those the Isthmus on two seas beholds beyond;                     420
but who could believe it? Athens, you alone refused.
Your duty was prevented by war, and, transported by sea,
invading foreign forces were harrowing the Mopsopian[54] walls.
With allied forces Thracian Tereus had put these
to flight and enjoyed in victory a brilliant name.                    425
This man, powerful in wealth and men and claiming descent
by chance from Gradivus,[55] had Pandion allied to himself
by marriage with Procne; neither Juno, goddess of brides,
nor Hymenaeus nor the Graces attended that marriage bed:
the Eumenides held forth torches stolen from funereal rites,          430
the Eumenides spread out the couch, and, ill-omened for the house,
the horned-owl alit and sat upon the marriage chamber roof.
Conjoined beneath this omen were Procne and Tereus, became
beneath this omen parents; delighted with them indeed
was Thrace, and the parents themselves thanked the gods; both the day  435
on which Pandion's daughter was married to their famous king
and that on which Itys was born did the Thracians order to be called festivals:
so hidden does profit lie!
                    The Titan had already brought
through five autumns the year's recurring times
when Procne, working her charm upon her husband, said                 440
to him, "If you love me at all, either to visit my sister let me go
or let my sister come here: you will promise your father-in-law
that she will return in a short time; in allowing me to see
my sister, you'll have given me the equivalent of a great gift."
The ships are launched at his command upon the deep, and with sail     445
and oar he enters the Cecropian[56] harbor and touches the Piraean[57] shore.
As soon as opportunity allowed, right hand to father-in-law's
right hand is joined, and, with that favorable sign, they talk.
When he began to tell the cause of his arrival, his wife's

---

54 Mopsopia was an ancient name of Athens, from an early King Mopsopus.
55 Epithet of Mars.
56 Cecrops was an early King of Athens.
57 The Piraeus is one of the harbors of Athens.

commands, and to promise of the one sent a the swift return,                    450
behold, Philomela approaches in great finery arrayed,
in form yet finer, as we usually hear
the naiads and dryads are who walk within the woods
if only you allowed them similar finery and dress.
On seeing the maiden, Tereus was inflamed no less                               455
than if someone were setting fire to ripened yellow grain
or burning leaves and grass stored within a barn.
Indeed, her face is worthy, but innate lust pricked
him, too, and the people in that region are prone
to Venus: he burns with his own and his people's vice.                          460
He felt the urge to corrupt her companions' care,
her nurse's trust and even to stir the girl herself
with sumptuous gifts and waste his whole realm
or even to rape her and preserve by cruel war what he had raped;
there is no end to what he would dare to do, made captive by his                465
unbridled lust, nor does his heart conceal the flames within.
Impatient now, he returns with eager voice
to Procne's commands and in them expresses his own desires.
His lust was making him eloquent and every time he pled
beyond what was right, he claimed that Procne wished it so.                     470
He added tears as well, as though she had commanded even these.
O gods above, how vast the dark night concealed
in human hearts! By his very striving for wickedness is Tereus
considered faithful and by his guilt gains praise.
For since Philomela seeks the same thing, and with her arms                     475
hugs fawningly her father's shoulders to gain her wish
to visit her sister, and for her sake and, against it too, asks the boon.
Observing her, Tereus imagines himself already caressing her,
and, seeing the kisses and arms thrown round that neck,
acquires all the goads and torches and food his madness needs,                  480
and, every time she embraces her father, he
would want to be that father. (For not even then would he less impious be!)
The parent is won over by the prayers of both: she rejoices and thanks
her father and thinks that both sisters have won
in what will bring great sorrow to both.                                        485
        A little labor yet remained for Phoebus, and his steeds
were pounding Olympus'[58] downward slope with their hooves:
the royal banquet is laid upon the tables and Bacchus in cups
of gold; then their bodies are given over to peaceful sleep.
But though the Odrysian[59] king had retired, he burns for her,                 490
and, as he recalls her face and carriage and hands,

---

58 Here "Olympus" stands for "heaven."
59 I. e., Thracian. The Odrysae were a tribe of Thracians.

he conjures up what he desires but has not yet seen
and feeds himself those fires as emotion dispels his sleep.
    At dawn's light, taking hold of his son-in-law's hand as he left,
Pandion entrusted to him his journey's companion, his tears welling up:   495
"This girl, dear son, because a pious reason compels
and both girls desire it, (you, Tereus, desired it, too)
I give to you and by our mutual trust and kindred hearts I beseech
you as a suppliant by the gods above that you guard her with paternal love
and, as a sweet solace for my old age, return her to me   500
as soon as possible (the slightest delay will seem too long to us);
and you as well, (for having your sister far off is enough),
return as soon as possible to me, Philomela, if you have any piety at all!
He kissed his daughter and gave his commands
and midst the commands were falling gentle tears;   505
and for a pledge of faith he asked for the right hand of each,
and as he joined the proffered hands, he asked them to greet
with words of remembrance his daughter and grandson, absent now;
his final farewell scarcely said, his throat was filled
with sobbing, and truly did he fear the forebodings of his mind.   510
    At last when Philomela is placed aboard the pious ship
and oars have stirred the deep and land is left behind,
"We've won," he exclaims, "my prayers are carried with me now!"
In triumph scarcely postponing the pleasures on his mind,
the barbarous man never takes his eyes from her,   515
no different than when with hooked-shaped claws that predator,
the bird of Jove, deposits a hare within his lofty nest;
the captive cannot flee, the captor beholds his reward.
    The journey now was done, and now onto their shores
they landed from the weary ships, when the king drags   520
Pandion's daughter into a lofty stable hidden within the ancient woods,
and there shuts her up, pale, frightened, both afraid of everything
and asking, now tearfully, where her sister is;
admitting his crime, he ravishes the maiden all alone
by force as she cries out often to her father in vain,   525
and often to her sister, and most of all to the mighty gods.
She trembles as a timorous and wounded lamb, which from the grey
wolf's mouth is shaken free but thinks itself not yet secure,
and as the dove, its pinions now soaked with its own blood,
still cowers and fears the greedy claws in which it was clasped.   530
As soon as she recovered her senses, her mangled hair a mess,
like one having lacerated her arms in lamentation and grief,
she stretches forth her palms and says, "O barbarous man of dreadful deeds,
O cruel man, do the commands of a father given with pious tears
not move you nor a sister's care nor my   535

*Rape of Philomela, Solis*

virginity nor marriage vows? You have perverted all:
the concubine rival of my sister have I become,
a double husband you, and I am due the punishment of a foe!
Lest any crime remain untried, O faithless man, why not take
this life of mine? Would that you had done so before                                              540
that wicked act with me: for then my shade were free of blame.
But if the gods above behold this, if the power of the gods
amount to something, if with me the world has not passed away,
a day will come when you will pay me for this! I myself, all shame
abandoned, will tell your deeds: if I get the chance,                                                545
I'll go to the people; if I'm held in confinement in the woods,
I'll fill the woods and move the very rocks with my tale;
the sky will hear of this, and a god, if there is one therein!"
        The cruel king was stirred to wrath by such words,
to fear no less, and goaded by both wrath and fear,                                                550
he frees of its sheath the sword he wore
and, grabbing her by the hair and pinning her hands behind
her back, he forces her to suffer shackles; Philomela offered her throat
and conceived a hope for her death when she saw the sword:
but as she complained, calling again and again upon her father's name           555
and struggling to speak, he caught her tongue with a set of tongs
and cut it out with his sword. The end of the root of the tongue darts forth,
the tongue itself lies trembling and murmuring upon the dark earth,
and as the tail of the mutilated serpent is wont to thrash about,
it throbs and seeks in dying to find its mistress's tracks.                                         560
And even after this crime (I hardly dare to believe it), they say
that man sought again and again the wounded body with his lust.
        He dares to return to Procne when these deeds are done;

she asks for her sister when she sees her husband, but he
responds with forced moaning and tells a false story of her death.                565
His tears make it believable. Procne tears away the robe
that gleams upon her shoulders with a broad band of gold
and puts on a dark mantle and constructs
an empty tomb and brings offerings to the fictive shade
and mourns the fate of a sister not thus to be mourned.                570
    The god had circled round the twice six signs of the completed year.
What is Philomela to do? The guards prevent escape,
the stable walls are built firmly with solid rock,
her muted mouth cannot report the crime. But the wit
of grief is great, and contrivance comes to wretched estate:                575
with skill she hangs the web upon the barbarous loom
and weaves purple signs into the threads of white,
as evidence of crime; she gives to a servant the finished work
and with her gesture asks her to bring it to her mistress; upon the request
she bore it to Procne and does not know what she brings with it.                580
The wife of the savage king unrolls the cloth
and reads the wretched song of her fate
and (that she could is amazing!) keeps her silence: grief contains
her mouth, and words failed her tongue as it searched in vain
for adequate protest, nor was there time to weep. Instead, she rushes to mix  585
all right and wrong together, intent upon the thought of revenge.
    The time had come for the Sithonian[60] women to celebrate
the usual third-year[61] rites of Bacchus: (the night was privy to the rites,
at night Rhodope[62] resounds with the ringing of high-pitched bronze)
at night the queen emerges from her home and equips                590
herself for the rites of the god and puts on the maenadic arms;
her head is covered with tendrils, deerskins hang
upon her left side, upon her shoulder lies a light-weight spear.
A throng of her companions is with her as, driven through
the woods, Procne, inspiring terror and goaded by the rage of grief,                595
pretends to celebrate your rites, O Bacchus: she comes to the stable at length
and howls and shouts "Evoe" and smashes the gates
and seizes her sister and puts the signs of Bacchus upon
the stolen one and conceals with vines of ivy her face
and takes away the astonished girl and brings her within her walls.                600
    When Philomela saw that she had set foot within the wicked house,
the unhappy woman shuddered, and her whole face grew pale;
when Procne found the right place, she removed the emblems of the rites
and takes the veil from her wretched sister's dishonored face

---

60 The Sithonians were a tribe of Thrace; i. e., "Thracian."
61 *Trieterica sacra*, rites celebrated every other year, i. e., biennially.
62 A mountain range of western Thrace.

and seeks her embrace; but in response she cannot bear                                605
to lift her eyes, considering herself her sister's rival concubine.
With gaze lowered towards the ground and longing to swear
and call the gods to witness that that shame was brought upon
herself by force, her hands took the place of her voice. But Procne burns
and cannot contain her wrath and blaming her sister's tears,                           610
declares, "This is not the time to act with tears but with the sword,
or if you have it, something that can overcome the sword;
for every unspeakable deed, my sister, am I prepared:
for I shall either set with torches the royal house aflame
and cast the author of the deed, Tereus, into the midst of the flames                  615
or tear out his tongue with the sword, and eyes and the members that deprived
you of your honor or drive out with a thousand wounds
his guilty soul! Whatever I devise, it will be great,
but what it will be, I'm still unsure. While Procne was relating this,
along came Itys to his mother; by him is she advised                                   620
what she could do, and gazing at him with merciless eyes, she said,
"Aha, how like your father you are," and saying no more
prepares a tragic deed and boils with silent wrath.
But as her son drew near and to his mother brought
his greetings and drew to himself her neck with his little arms                        625
and joined his lips to hers mixed with boyish charms,
the mother indeed is moved, and her wrath is broken and checked,
and tears well up and moisten her eyes against her will;
but even as she felt her resolve wavering with excess of piety,
she turned again from him towards her sister's face                                    630
and, looking at each in turn, she says, "Why does one advance
his charms, the other remain silent with tongue torn out?
If he calls me mother, why shouldn't she call me sister as well?
Consider, O daughter of Pandion, to what husband you are wed!
Degenerate are you! Piety towards a husband like Tereus is a crime!"                   635
Unhesitating, she dragged Itys away, just like the doe's suckling fawn
a Ganges tigress in the dense forest has stolen away,
and when they gained a remote section of the lofty house,
the boy stretches forth his hands and already foreseeing his fate
cries out, "Mother, Mother!" and tries to embrace her neck                             640
when Procne strikes with the sword where his breast joins his side,
nor does she avert her eyes. To cause his death one blow were enough
but Philomela laid open his throat with a sword as well,
and both tear apart the limbs while they yet retained
some life. Some parts seethe within the cauldron's hollow bronze,                      645
while others sizzle upon spits; the secluded chamber flows with gore.
      The wife brought to this banquet Tereus unawares
and, feigning that this rite was a family tradition which

a husband alone might attend, she sent companions and servants away.
While Tereus himself sits exalted upon the ancestral banquet chair,                     650
he eats and fills his belly with his own flesh.
So great is the darkness of his mind that he says, "Have Itys brought to me!"
Unable to conceal her cruel delight and now eager to come forth as
the messenger of her slaughter, Procne replies,
"You hold within the one you demand." He looks about                                   655
and asks where he is. And as he looks about and repeats his command,
just as she was, with hair spattered with frenzy's gore,
forth sprang Philomela and cast Itys' bloody head
into his father's face nor would she have at any time
more wanted the power to speak and profess her joy with fitting words.                 660
The Thracian thrust back the table with a great shout
and summons the serpent sisters from the valley of the Styx
and now, had he the power, he longs to open his breast
to drive out the dire meal and make the flesh come forth,
and now he weeps and calls himself the wretched tomb of his son,                       665
and now he pursues Pandion's daughters with naked sword.
The bodies of the Cecropides you would think were suspended with wings:
they *were* suspended with wings! The one seeks the woods,
the other the house, nor even then had from their breasts
the signs of slaughter vanished, and their plumage is marked with blood.               670
The husband in his grief and eager with desire for revenge
is changed into a bird upon whose head stands a crest.
In place of his long spear an immense beak juts forth:
the name of the bird is the hoopoe,[63] whose face appears to be armed.

### 675-721   *Boreas and Orithyia; Calais and Zetes*

Before his time and the final days of long old age                                     675
this grief sent Pandion to Tartarus' shades.
Erechtheus assumes the scepter of the place and the helm of state,
more powerful in justice or strength of arms one cannot be sure.
Four youths indeed had he created and as many of
the female lot, of which equal in beauty were two.                                     680
Of these Aeolid[64] Cephalus was happy with you,
O Procris, as his spouse; Tereus and the Thracians damaged Boreas'[65] suit,
and long did the god do without the Orithyia he loved,
while courting her and preferring to use persuasion instead of force;
but when with wooing nothing happened, he bristled with                                685

---

63 Translating *epops*, borrowed from the Greek, presumably the *upupa epops*, a large thrush with curved
  bill and crest.
64 According to Apollodorus, Cephalus was son of Deion (son of Aeolus, king of Thessaly) or Deineus
  or Hermes.
65 The North Wind.

*Feast of Itys, Baur*

the wrath more usual and natural to that wind,
and said, "It serves me right, for why did I abandon those weapons of mine,
ferocity and might and wrath and menacing moods,
and proffer prayers, the use of which puts me to shame?
For force is suited to me: with force I put to flight the gloomy clouds,        690
with force I lash the deep and overturn the knotty oaks
and stiffen the snows and beat the earth with hail;
I also, when I join my brothers in the open sky
(for that is my field of battle), struggle with such great intensity
that at our meeting the ether in our midst resounds        695
and fires leap apart crashing from the hollow clouds;
I also, when entering the arched hollows of the earth
and fiercely pressing the weight of my back against the lowest caves,
disturb with quaking the shades and all the globe.
I should have sought her chamber with these resources, and not asked        700
Erechtheus to be a father-in-law but made him one."
When Boreas had uttered these words or words not weaker than these,
he shook his wings, whose beatings buffet all
the earth and rough up the breadth of the sea,
and dragging his dusty cloak over the tops of the heights,        705
he sweeps the ground and, hidden in darkness, with love
embraces within his dusky wings Orithyia grown pale with fear.
And as he flies, his fires were stirred and burned more violently,
nor did he relax the reins of his airy course until

the predator gained the people and walls of the Ciconians.[66]                      710
The Actaean[67] maiden there became the cool king's wife
and also a mother, giving birth to twins,
in all else like their mother, but having their father's wings.
They say that wings and bodies were not born at the same time,
but rather so long as the beard was absent beneath their ruddy locks,       715
both Calais and Zetes as boys remained without wings;
but soon for both the wings, in the manner of birds, began
to gird their sides, and the cheeks of both were gilt with gold.
When therefore the age of boyhood yielded to youth,
they sought with the Minyans the fleece radiant with shining wool           720
upon the first ship to pass through an unfamiliar sea.

---

66 Thracians, i. e., loosely Boreas' homeland.
67 I. e., Athenian.

# BOOK 7

## 1-158　Jason and Medea

Already the Minyans were cutting the deep in their Pagasaean[1] ship,
and Phineus,[2] dragging out in endless night his helpless old age,
appeared, and the sons of Aquilo[3] born had chased
away the bird-maidens[4] from the wretched old man's mouth,
and having endured many things under brilliant Jason, at last　　　　5
had reached the muddy Phasis'[5] swift running waves.
And as they approach the king and demand Phrixus'[6] fleece
and to the Minyans the terrible terms of great toils are told,
the daughter of Aeëtes conceives in the meantime mighty fires
and having struggled long with herself could not by reason defeat　　10
her passion. "Medea, you resist in vain: some god
opposes you," she says, "I wonder if this is not the thing,
or something like it, that is called being in love.
For why do my father's demands seem so harsh to me?
In fact they are too harsh! Why is it that I fear for the life　　　　15
of him I just saw? What is the cause for so great a fear?

---

1 From Pagasa, a sea-coast town of Thessaly.
2 Not the Phineus of Book 5, but rather a Thracian king and blind prophet of Apollo; for mistreating his
　　sons the Harpies befouled his food until they were driven away by Calais and Zetes in return for
　　Phineus' showing them the way to Colchis.
3 The North-northeast Wind, here identical to Boreas.
4 The Harpies.
5 The river of Colchis on the eastern shore of the Black Sea (Euxine).
6 Phrixus, son of Athamas and Nephele, has given Aeëtes the golden fleece of the ram upon which he
　　had flown to Colchis.

Dash out the flames kindled within your virgin breast,
unhappy one, if you can! If I could, better off were I!
But some strange force weighs upon me against my will, and desire
persuades me to do one thing, the mind another: I see the better course,      20
approve it, pursue the worse. Why for this guest, O royal maiden, do
you burn and conceive a desire for marriage in a foreign world?
This land can supply something for you to love as well. Whether he
shall live or die depends upon the gods. But let him live! To pray for this
is right, even without love: for what wrong has Jason done?      25
By Jason's youth who, unless cruel, is not touched,
and by his birth and virtue? Who, to omit all the rest,
cannot by his speech be moved? For surely he has moved my heart!
But if I do not help him, he will be blasted by the breath
of bulls and either confront his crop as a foe, the earth-born enemy,      30
or to the greedy dragon be offered like a prey of the wild.
If I shall let this happen, I shall declare myself
of tigress born and to have a heart of iron and stone!
Why do I not behold him dying and in looking pollute
my eyes? Why do I not urge against him the bulls,      35
and fierce men born of earth and the dragon that never sleeps?
O may the gods wish for better things! Things not invoked
by prayers but by my deeds! Shall I betray my father's realm,
and by our aid shall some stranger be saved,
so that, once saved, he leave me and give his sails to the winds      40
and be another's husband, while I, Medea, be abandoned to punishment?
If he can do this and prefer another to us,
then let the ingrate die! But in him is not the kind of face,
the kind of nobility of mind, the kind of graceful form,
to cause me to fear deceit and forgetfulness of our deserts.      45
And in advance he will pledge his loyalty, and I shall compel the gods
to witness our alliance. Why do you fear what is safe? Gird yourself,
dispel delay: Jason will forever be in your debt,
unite you to himself with the solemn marriage torch, and throughout
Pelasgian cities throngs of women will celebrate you as savior!      50
Shall I, then, quit my sister and brother and father and gods
and native soil, carried away by the winds?
My father, yes, is cruel; barbaric, yes, my land.
My brother is yet a little child; my sister's vows are with me,
the greatest[7] of gods is within me! I shall not leave great things behind,      55
great things shall I pursue: a name for having saved Achaea's youth,
and knowledge of a better land, and towns, whose renown
is strong even here, and the culture and arts of those lands,

---

7 Presumably, *Amor* "Love."

and him for whom I would gladly exchange all the wealth the orb contains,
the son of Aeson, with whom as my spouse I shall be held content          60
and dear to the gods and shall touch the stars with my head.
But what about certain mountains that clash together in the waves,
they say, and Charybdis, hostile to ships,
now sucking down the sea, now spewing it back, and, girt
with savage dogs, rapacious Scylla, barking in the Sicilian deep?          65
But holding what I love, and cleaving to Jason's breast,
shall I be carried over the ocean far: in his embrace I'll have nothing to fear,
or, if I fear, my fears shall be for my husband alone.
You call this marriage, and set a specious name
upon your guilt, Medea? Consider how great                                  70
the wrong is you're undertaking, and, while you can, flee from crime!"
She spoke, and before her eyes Justice and Piety and Shame
stood gathered, and Desire was turning her back in defeat.
      Medea was going to the ancient altar of Perseid[8] Hecate
that lay concealed by a shady grove in a woody recess;                     75
and now her resolve was firm, and her passion repressed and cooled;
but when she sees Aeson's son, the stifled flame flared up again.
Her cheeks reddened and her whole face was aglow,
just as a tiny spark that has lain concealed beneath
the layer of ash when fed by the winds is wont                             80
to grow and, thus stirred, to regain its former strength,
so now her feeble love, which you would have thought already inert,
when seeing the youth, burst forth at the sight of his presence in flame.
As chance would have it, the son of Aeson was handsomer
that day: the lover you could forgive.                                     85
She stares and upon his face for the first time then
she holds her eyes fixed and in her madness thinks
she sees a face not mortal and does she turn her gaze from him;
but as the stranger began to speak and took her hand
and sought her help with lowered voice                                     90
and promised his couch, she replies with copious tears:
"I see what I am doing: no ignorance of the truth,
but love itself, will lead me astray. You will be saved with my help,
but having been saved, you must fulfill your promises! He swears
upon the rites of the triform goddess[9] and the divine spirit in that grove  95
and by the father[10] of his future father-in-law beholding everything,
the outcome of his ventures and his perils so great:
she trusted him, and he received at once the enchanted herbs

---

8 According to Hes., *Theog.* 409, Hecate was the daughter of Asteria and Perses, son of the Titan Crius.
   See also Apollod. 1. 2. 4.
9 The statues of Hecate often had three heads or three bodies.
10 The Sun (Helios or Sol), father of Aeëtes.

and learned their use and to his lodgings returned content.
      Aurora had already driven away the shining stars:          100
the tribes assemble in the sacred field of Mars
and take their places upon the high ground; the king himself, arrayed
in purple and distinguished by his ivory scepter, was seated in the midst of the host.
Behold, from their nostrils of adamant the brazen-footed bulls
blow out the breath of Vulcan, and touched by the steam        105
the grasses blaze, and, just as well-stoked furnaces are wont to ring,
or stones released from the earthen kiln
catch fire by the liquid water's spray,
just so are the bulls' chests, teeming with pent-up flames,
and parched-dry throats aroar; but against them Aeson's son      110
advances. They turn their grim and terrible faces toward
the face of their opponent, their horns fixed with iron as well,
and paw the dusty ground with their furrowed feet
and fill the place with smoke-producing bellowing.
The Minyans stiffened with fear; Jason draws near and does not feel     115
the fires they exhale,—so great is the power of the drugs,
and strokes their hanging dewlaps with his daring right hand
and forces them, once set beneath the yoke, to bear
the plow's heavy weight and split the plain unused to iron:
the Colchians are amazed, the Minyans' cries increase      120
and bolster his courage. Then from the helmet of bronze
he takes the serpent teeth and scatters them upon the plowed fields.
The earth softens the seeds that with powerful poison had been imbued;
the sown teeth are growing and taking on new shapes;
and just as within the mother's womb the infant assumes human form    125
and inwardly is composed throughout its parts
and not until the proper time comes forth into the air,
just so, when from the bowels of pregnant earth the image of man
is formed, it emerges from the fruitful field,
and what is more amazing, it emerges brandishing arms.      130
On seeing them preparing to hurl the sharp-pointed spears
against the head of the Haemonian[11] youth,
the spirits and faces of the Pelasgians were downcast in fear;
Medea, too, who had made him safe, was afraid,
and as she saw so many foes attacking this one young man,      135
she paled and sat there in a sudden bloodless chill,
and lest the herbals she gave him be too weak, she intones
an intercessory charm and invokes her secret skills.
He hurls a heavy boulder into his enemies' midst,
repels the work of Mars and directs it against his foes themselves:    140

---

11 I.e., Thessalian.

*Jason and the Dragon, Baur*

the earthborn brothers perish with mutual wounds
and fall in the field of civil war. The Achaeans congratulate
and hold the victor and cling to him with eager embrace.
Barbarian woman, you, too, would have liked to embrace
the victor: shame blocked your attempt, but you would have embraced     145
the man, had your fear of disrepute not held you back.[12]
You are allowed to rejoice with silent affections and express
your thanks to your chants and to the gods, the authors of these events.
    The task remains of using herbs to put the ever-watchful dragon to sleep.
Conspicuous for its crest and triple tongues and curvèd fangs,     150
the dragon was the terrible guardian of a golden tree.
When Jason sprinkled it with the herb's Lethean juice
and spoke three times the words that bring placid sleep
and settle the swollen sea and turbulent streams,
upon those eyes came unfamiliar sleep. Aeson's heroic son     155
acquires the gold and, proud in his spoils,
transporting the author of his reward, his second spoils,
the victor reached the port of Iolchos with his bride.

### 159-293   *Aeson Rejuvenated*

    As matrons of Haemonia, in return for their rescued sons,
and aged fathers are bringing gifts and melting upon the flames     160
oblations of incense and bringing in, its horns gilt with gold,
the promised victim, among the thankful Aeson is not found,
already nearing death and weary with his ancient years.
The son of Aeson then says: "O wife, to whom, I admit,

---

12 Lines 144-46 appear to confuse two manuscript traditions. Some MSS transpose 145 and 146; some
    editors omit 145 (Heinsius). Anderson keeps the order, Tarrant transposes and brackets 145-46.

I owe my rescue, even though you have given all to me                165
and past all believing is the sum of your worthy deeds,
yet, if they have the power (and what power do charms not have?),
remove from me my years and give to my father those that are removed!"
Nor could he restrain his tears: moved is she by the loyalty of him who asked,
and to her different mind comes the Aeëtes she had left behind.        170
But not confessing such emotions, she replies,
"What evil has issued from your mouth, my husband? Do I,
indeed, appear to be able to transfer to anyone part of your life?
Unjust is what you ask, nor allowed by Hecate. But try
I shall to give a greater gift, Jason, than what you ask.              175
By means of my skills, not by your years, we shall try to call back
the ancient life of my father-in-law, if only the goddess of triple form
shall help and with her power assent to my egregiously bold attempt."
    Three nights were lacking before the horns would completely meet
and make an orb; but when the moon shone at its most full             180
and looked down with solid image upon the lands,
Medea, arrayed in unbelted gowns, leaves the house,
her feet left bare, upon her shoulders her tresses lying unbound,
and wanders through the mute silence of midnight,
alone: mortals and birds and beasts were relaxed                     185
in deep repose, from the hedgerow, no murmur is heard,[13]            186
[as though asleep, from the serpent no murmur is heard,][14]          186a
and silent are the motionless leaves, silent the humid air,
the stars alone are moving with light: extending her arms to them,
she spins around three times, three times with waters drawn from a stream
bedews her hair and with triple howling loosens her mouth            190
and, having kneeled upon the hard earth, declares,
"O Night, to secrets most loyal, and whatever golden stars
succeed with the Moon the fires of day,
and you, triple-headed Hecate, who know the plans I've begun
and come as the attendant of magicians' songs and skills,            195
and Earth, who equip magicians with powerful herbs,
and breezes and winds and mountains and rivers and lakes,
and all the gods of the groves and all the gods of night, draw near,
by whose assistance, when I wanted it, the rivers, as their banks stood amazed,
returned to their sources, and I make the driven seas stand still,    200
and dash the calm seas with song, drive the clouds away
and bring forth the clouds, and drive away and summon the winds,
and break the serpents' jaws with words and charms,

---

13 Translating Heinsius' *solverat alta quies, nullo cum murmure saepes*; Anderson: 186 ... *serpit* and
    186a ... *serpens*; Ehwald: 186 ... *serpit* and 186a ... *saepes*; Tarrant: 186 ... *saepes* and brackets
    186a ... *serpens*.
14 Translating Anderson's and Tarrant's 186a (see preceding note).

and living rocks and oaks torn from their ground
and move the forests and order the mountains to shake                               205
and earth to moan and ghosts come forth from the tombs!
And you, O Moon,[15] I draw down as well, although Temesean[16] bronze
should threaten your labors.[17] The chariot of my grandfather[18] as well
grows pale by my charms, by our poisons Aurora grows pale!
For me you dulled the flames of the bulls and pressed                               210
their necks, unused to burdens, into the crooked plow,
and caused the serpent-born men to turn fierce war against themselves
and put to sleep the custodian who knew not sleep, and,
deceiving its defender, you sent the gold to the cities of Greece.
I now need juices with which to rejuvenate old age                                  215
and make it flower again and regain its former years,
and you will supply them. For neither have the stars shone in vain
nor is my car here present in vain, drawn by the dragons' necks.[19]
The car was present, sent down from the sky.
As soon as she mounted it and stroked the dragons' bridled necks                    220
and tossed the light reins with her hands,
she soars aloft and looks down upon Thessalian Tempe below
and bends her serpents to the regions she wants:
she spies the grasses Ossa has raised, those of lofty Pelion
and Othrys and Pindus, and those of Olympus greater than Pindus, too;              225
of those she liked, some she pulled out by the roots,
but some she cut with the curved blade of the brazen scythe.
Upon the banks of the Apidanus were many other herbs she liked,
upon the banks of the Amphrysus, too, nor immune were you, Enipeus;
nor did the waters of Peneus nor Spercheus fail                                     230
to offer something, and Boebe's[20] rush-filled shore;
she plucked as well from Euboean Anthedon[21] life-giving grass,
which Glaucus'[22] transformed body had not yet given renown.
     Already the ninth day and ninth night had watched
as she surveyed all the fields from the chariot of dragons' wings                   235
and then returned; the dragons had not been touched except by the scent,
but, even then, they shed the skin of their ancient years.
Approaching, she stopped outside the threshold and gate.
With sky alone for shelter, she shuns her husband's touch

---

15 *Luna.*
16 Temesa, wherever located (Cyprus or South Italy) was a proverbial source of bronze. Cf. *Odyssey,*
    1. 182.
17 The eclipses of the Moon were called *labores* "labors."
18 The Sun.
19 In earlier times the chariot of Helios was thought to be driven by dragons, not horses.
20 Boebe is a lake in Thessaly; Apidanus, Amphrysus, Enipeus, Peneus, and Spercheus are rivers in
    Thessaly.
21 Boeotian town on the coast facing the island of Euboea.
22 The story of this fisherman from Anthedon is told in 13. 904 ff.

and raised two altars made of mossy turf,                                      240
to Hecate one on the right, but on the left the other to Youth
and swathed them in vervain and woodland leaves.
This done, nearby she digs out two pits in the earth,
and makes her sacrifices, and into a black fleece's throat
she thrusts the knife and drenches the gaping pits with blood.                 245
Then tipping over it cups of flowing wine[23]
and tipping also other cups of fresh warm milk,
while pouring a libation of words, she conjures up the chthonic powers
and calls upon the king of the shades and his stolen wife
to be not quick to defraud the aged soul of its limbs.                         250
        As soon as her prayers, murmured and long, had placated these,
she ordered the body of Aeson to be ushered forth into the open air
and, casting him into a deep sleep by her spells,
she stretched him as though lifeless upon the grass.
She orders Aeson's son to stand apart, the ministers as well apart,            255
and warns all profane eyes away from her secret rites.
As ordered, they scatter; Medea, with streaming hair
in bacchant ritual circles the altar flames,
and, having dipped forked torches in the black pit of blood,
she lit them thus imbued with the twin altars' flames and thrice              260
with flame, thrice with water, thrice with sulphur sprinkles the ancient man.
        But meanwhile in the readied pot the powerful drug
is boiling and seething and white with swelling foam.
Therein she boils together roots cut from the Haemonian vale
and seeds and flowers and bitter sap;                                          265
she adds to these stones sought from the farthest Orient
and sands washed by Ocean's tidal stream;
she adds as well white frost collected under the all-night moon
and eerie wings of the owl along with its flesh
and innards cut from the ambiguous wolf, wont to change                        270
its bestial appearance into a man; the concoction did not lack
the scaly membrane of the slender Cinyphian[24] water-snake
and liver of long-lived stag; on top of all these she adds
the eggs and head of a crow that had endured nine generations of man.
With these and a thousand things without name                                  275
the foreign woman had prepared her greater than mortal plan,
when, taking a branch of sweet olive, now long dried,
she stirred all together and mixed the bottom with the top.
Behold the ancient branch when turned within the hot bronze vat
at first becomes green and then soon puts on leaves                            280

---

23 Some MSS have *mellis*, "honey," rather than *vini*, "wine." Tarrant chooses *mellis*, Anderson and
   Ehwald *vini*.
24 The river Cinyps was in Libya, notorious for its serpents. See 4. 617-620.

*Aeson Rejuvenated, Baur*

and suddenly with heavy olives is weighed down:
wherever the fire splashed foam from the hollow bronze
and heated drops fell upon the earth,
the ground is clad in springtime and flowers and soft meadows rise.
As soon as Medea saw this, she drew her sword                                    285
and opened the old man's throat and, after letting the blood
run out, refills it with her concoctions; after Aeson drank them in,
received either by mouth or wound, his beard and hair
put off their whiteness and assumed the color black,
his thinness vanishes, his pallor and signs of age depart,                       290
his hollow wrinkles with new flesh are filled,
and all his limbs prosper with strength: Aeson is amazed,
remembering himself as he was four times ten years ago.

### 294-349   *Pelias Punished*

On high had Liber[25] observed this wondrous work
and, thus advised that the youthful years might to his nurses be restored,        295
received from the woman of Colchis this boon.
Lest guile should cease, the Phasian[26] woman feigned
a quarrel with her husband and as a suppliant to the threshold of Pelias
takes flight; his daughters, because the man himself was heavy with age,
received her well; the cunning Colchian in no time at all                         300
deceived them with the false appearance of amity,

---

25 The God of License, one of the Latin names for Bacchus.
26 Pertaining to the river Phasis that passes through Colchis.

and as she related the greatest of her deeds, how Aeson's years
had been removed, and dwells at length on this theme,
the maiden daughters of Pelias are made to hope
that similar skill might make their own father grow young again,                    305
and ask this favor and promise her an unlimited reward.
A brief while she says nothing and seems to be in doubt
and holds their avid minds in suspense with feigned sincerity.
But soon, after giving her consent, she says, "That trust in this gift
be stronger, the eldest member of your flock                                        310
of sheep will through my drugs become a lamb."
Straightway a wooly ram, worn with countless years,
is introduced, its horns curved round to his hollow brows;
when with an Haemonian blade she pierced its listless throat
and stained the knife with only a little blood,                                     315
the poisoner plunged the members of the sheep and powerful drugs
into the hollow bronze: it shrinks the body's limbs
and burns away the horns and with the horns the years no less,
and from the midst of the bronze caldron a bleating is heard:
without delay, before those marveling at the bleating, a lamb springs out           320
and runs away in play and seeks an udder filled with milk.
The daughters of Pelias were stunned and, once
the promises produced belief, were eager all the more.
        Three times had Phoebus removed the yokes from the horses that
had plunged into the Ebro river, and on the fourth night the radiant stars          325
were shining when the treacherous daughter of Aeëtes pours
upon the swirling flame pure water and feckless herbs.
Already a death-like sleep held the king, his body relaxed,
and with the king his guards as well, a sleep
produced by incantations and the potency of a magical tongue.                       330
The daughters, as bidden, had with the Colchian entered the room
and gathered round the couch: "Why do you hesitate, you sluggards?"
she says, "Draw your swords and extract the ancient blood,
that I may fill the empty veins with the blood of youth.
In your hands is your father's life and youth.                                      335
If you have any piety and ply not empty hopes,
bestow this favor upon your father and with your weapons drive out
old age and with the thrust of your sword release the gory blood."
By this encouragement, as each was pious, the more was she first in impiety
and, lest she be wicked, does wickedness: nevertheless scarcely one                 340
can bear to behold her blows; they avert their eyes
and, looking away, administer their unseen wounds with cruel hands.
Though bleeding profusely, upon his elbow he yet lifts his limbs
and, half-mutilated, attempts to rise from the couch, and amidst
so many swords stretches out his pallid arms and says,                              345

*Death of Pelias, Solis*

"O daughters, what are you doing? Who has armed you for
your father's doom?" Their minds and hands recoil:
and as he is about to say more, the Colchian excised his throat and words
and plunged his mangled body into the boiling waves.

## 350-403   *Medea's Flight*

Had she not fled upon her winged serpents into the air,                    350
from punishment she would not have been spared. She escaped
aloft, above shady Pelion, Philyra's home,[27] and above
Mount Othrys and, from what happened to old Cerambus, a region well-known:
with help from the nymphs Cerambus[28] was lifted into the air on wings
and, when the heavy earth was buried beneath the invading sea,             355
avoided unsubmerged Deucalion's waves.
She passed Aeolian Pitane[29] on her left,
the image of the long serpent, made of stone,[30]
and Ida's[31] grove, where Liber hid the theft by his son,
a bullock, beneath the false guise of a stag,[32]                          360
and where Corythus' father[33] was buried beneath a bit of sand,
and fields which Maera with strange howling terrified,
and Eurypylus' city, where the matrons of Cos
wore horns when Hercules' army withdrew,[34]

27 I.e. the haunts of the Centaur Chiron, son of Philyra and Cronus (Saturn).
28 According to Nicander Cerambus was changed into a beetle (the meaning of his name) by the
   nymphs.
29 City on the coast of Asia Minor.
30 Probably the serpent that had attacked the head of Orpheus on Lesbos and was turned to stone by
   Apollo.
31 The mountain in the Troad.
32 This story is elsewhere unattested.
33 Corythus was the son of Paris and Oenone or Helen.
34 See Apollodorus 2. 7. 1. for Hercules' attack upon King Eurypylus of Cos.

and Phoebus' Rhodes and the Telchines[35] of Ialysus,          365
with eyes that vitiated everything by their very glance,
(whom Jupiter hated and plunged into his brother's[36] waves);
she also crossed ancient Cea's[37] Cartheian[38] walls,
where father Alcidamas would marvel that from
his daughter's body a peaceful dove would be born.[39]          370
And next she sees the lake of Hyrie[40] and Cycneian[41] Tempe, too,
made famous by the sudden swan: for Phylius there
because of a boy's command[42] had rendered tame
both birds and a ferocious lion, and, ordered to defeat
a bull, had defeated it and, enraged that he had so often been refused     375
in love, withheld the final reward to the boy who demanded the bull;
the boy indignantly said, "You will wish that you had given it,"
and from a high rock leapt down; all thought that he had fallen in the abyss:
in fact as a swan he was soaring with wings in the air;
his mother Hyrie, however, not knowing that he was safe,         380
had melted away and created a pool that bore her name.
Nearby lies Pleuron,[43] where with trembling wings
the daughter of Ophius,[44] Combe,[45] escaped the wounds of her sons;
she next beholds on the island of Celaurea[46] Leto's fields
which saw their king transformed with his wife into a bird.         385
Cyllene[47] is on her right, where Menephron[48] would take
his mother to bed in the manner of savage beasts;
she sees from afar Cephisus,[49] bewailing his grandson's[50] fate,
the one transformed by Apollo into a swollen seal,
and Eumelus' home, the one mourning his son in the air.[51]         390
    At length she reached Pirenian Ephyre[52] upon her snaky wings:

---

35 Wonder-working smiths in iron and bronze of Ialysus, a city of Rhodes.
36 Neptune's.
37 Cea is the Latin form of the Greek island Ceos, near the eastern shore of the Peloponnesus.
38 Carthaea is a town on the island of Ceos.
39 According to Nicander *Heteroeumena* 3 (see Antonin. Lib. 1), when Alcidamas reneged on his
    promise to marry his daughter Ctesylla to Hermochares, the gods helped the latter seduce her and
    then killed her and transformed her body into a dove.
40 Mother of Cycnus, whose tears were changed into the lake that bears her name.
41 Pertaining to Cycnus, who was changed into a swan.
42 According to Nicander *Heteroeumena*. 3 (see Antonin. Lib. 12), Cycnus ordered his lover Phylius
    to kill man-eating vultures and a lion and to lead a wild bull to the altar of Zeus. Heracles helped
    Phylius accomplish the tasks.
43 A city in Aetolia.
44 Ancestor of the Ophieis, a people of Aetolia.
45 Mother of the Curetes of Aetolia, confused with those of Crete. See 4. 282. This story is elsewhere
    unattested.
46 An island sacred to Leto (Latona), off the coast of the Argolid.
47 Mountain in Arcadia, where Mercury was born.
48 According to Hyginus *Fab.* 253 Menephron committed incest with his daughter Cyllene and his
    mother Blias.
49 A river of Phocis and Boeotia.
50 One of the sons of Praxithea, granddaughter of the river god Cephisus.
51 According to Antoninus Liberalis 18, the Theban priest Eumelus struck his son Botres for eating part
    of a sacrificial animal being offered to Apollo, who transformed him into a bird.
52 The spring of Pirene was at Ephyre, the ancient name of Corinth.

*Medea Kills Her Children, Picart*

the ancients say that in the early days it was here
that mortal bodies from rainy mushrooms sprang.
But after the new bride by Colchian poisons was burned
and both seas saw the home of the king afire, 395
her impious sword is drenched in the blood of her sons,
and, having avenged herself foully, from Jason's weapons the mother escapes.
Transported from here upon Titan's[53] serpents she goes
into the citadel of Pallas, which beheld you, Phene most just
and you, old Periphas,[54] as you together flew, 400
and Polypemon's[55] granddaughter lifted aloft on her new wings.
When Aegeus, in this deed alone to be condemned, took her in,
this hospitality was not enough: he also took her to his marriage bed.

### 404-52 *Theseus and Aegeus*

By this time Theseus was there, the father's unknown progeny,
who by his virtue had pacified the Isthmus between two seas: 405
To cause his ruin Medea mixes the aconite she long ago
had brought with her from the Scythian shores.

---

53 As in Euripides' play, Medea escapes upon the serpent-drawn chariot of the Titan Helios, the Sun-god, her grandfather.

54 According to Antoninus Liberalis 6, Zeus prepared to strike the just king Periphas and his wife Phene with his thunderbolt because the Athenians honored the king in divine terms, but at Apollo's request transformed Periphas into an eagle and Phene (= "Sea-eagle" in Greek) into an osprey.

55 Another name for Procrustes, the father of Sciron, who cast his daughter Alcyone into the sea for her unchastity.

That poison, they say, had come from the teeth of Echidna's dog:[56]
there is a hidden cave with a glooming yawning maw;
upon its path the hero of Tiryns dragged Cerberus                                   410
in woven chains of adamant; resisting and turning his flashing eyes
away from the brightness of day and stirred
by furious wrath, the dog made full the air
with barking from triple mouths of equal force
and spewed white foam upon the verdant fields;                                      415
that foam, they think, congealed and acquiring the soil's rich
and fecund nourishment acquired the power to harm;
because it grows and flourishes upon hard peaks of stone,
the country folk are wont to call it aconite.[57] Through the cunning of
his wife the father himself, Aegeus, offered it to his son as if to his foe.        420
The cup offered by that unwitting right hand
had Theseus taken when the father upon the sword's ivory hilt
discerned the family's emblems and dashed the crime from his mouth.
That wife escapes death in a murky mist summoned by her charms.

　　　The father, however, though glad that his son was unharmed,          425
is stunned that a monstrous crime could have been so narrowly
averted: he graces the altars with fires
and heaps the gods with gifts, and axes strike
the brawny necks of bulls, their foreheads with garlands bound.
No day, they say, had dawned more celebrated by                                     430
Erechtheus' descendants: the elders lay on feasts
together with the commons and, their minds inspired
by wine, are singing hymns of praise:[58] "Thee, mighty Theseus,
does Marathon admire for the blood of the Cretan bull,
and that the farmer at Cromyon[59] unfearing plows his fields                       435
is thy work and service; the land of Epidaurus because of thee
beheld the club-wielding son[60] of Vulcan bite the dust;
the shore of Cephisus beheld harsh Procrustes'[61] death,
Eleusis, dear to Ceres, beheld Cercyon's death.
That Sinis[62] fell, who evilly employed his might,                                 440
who had the strength to bend a trunk and pulled down
the pines from their height to earth that would scatter bodies far and wide.

---

56 Cerberus.
57 Ovid's etymologizing is untranslatable: *cautis* "crag" and *cos* "whetstone" are suggested as the origin
　　of *aconite*, more commonly called wolf's-bane.
58 Hill compares Ovid's catalogue of Theseus' heroic feats to that of the Greek lyric poet Bacchylides
　　(ca. 520-450 B.C.), *Hymn to Theseus*, 18. 16-30..
59 A village near Corinth, whose fields were ravaged by an enormous sow.
60 Periphetes.
61 Procrustes "Stretcher" was another name for Polypemon "Causing much pain" and Damastes
　　"Destroyer." This bandit forced his guests to fit his bed, either by stretching them or paring them
　　down.
62 "The Harmer," also called Pityokamptes, "Pine-Bender." After tying strangers to two pines that he
　　had bent down to the ground, Sinis tore asunder their bodies by releasing the trees.

*Near Death of Theseus, Baur*

The way to Alcathoë[63] and the Lelegeian[64] walls are open and safe
since Sciron's[65] end was settled, and to the brigand's scattered bones
the earth denies a resting place, a resting place the waves;                    445
the length of time, they say, changed the long-tossed bones
to stony cliffs: of Sciron the cliffs retain the name.
If we should hope to recount thy honors and years,
thy deeds would outweigh thy years. For thee, O hero most brave,
we raise the people's prayers, to thee the draught of Bacchus consume."          450
The palace rings with the people's approval and the prayers
of devotees, and in all the city no place is sad.

### 453-500  *Minos, Aeacus*

But yet (there is no joy that comes unmixed,
and those who rejoice will never be free of care)
his son's recovery Aegeus received not without concern:                          455
for Minos was ready for war; in manpower however strong,
in ships as well, he is strongest in his paternal wrath,
avenging the death of Androgeos[66] with justifiable arms.
Acquiring allied forces before beginning the war,
he wanders about the seas with his swift fleet, the mainstay of his might:       460

---

63 Poetic name for Megara, a city on the Isthmus, whose destroyed walls were rebuilt by Alcathoüs,
   the son of Pelops
64 The Leleges were the ancient population of Megara.
65 The robber Sciron cast travelers from the cliffs of Megara to feed a turtle. Theseus killed him in the
   same way. His bones became the Scironian rocks.
66 Who died either having been sent by Aegeus to face the bull of Marathon, or having been ambushed
   by competitors after he had been victorious in the Panathenaic Games.

he gains Anaphe[67] here and Astypaleia's[68] kingdom there,
Anaphe with promises, Astypaleia's kingdom through war;
next, low-lying Myconos and Cimolus'[69] chalky fields
and thyme-flowered Syros and Seriphos' plains
and marble-rich Paros and that place Sithonian[70] Arne's[71] impiety          465
betrayed: she demanded and took the gold
and then was changed into that bird that even now delights
in gold, the jackdaw, black of foot and covered in wings of black.
        But neither Oliaros[72] nor Tenos nor Andros nor Didyme
nor Gyaros and Peparethos, in gleaming olives rich,                          470
gave aid to the barks of Cnossos; turning to the left
from there Minos seeks Oenopia, the Aeacids' realm:
the ancients called it Oenopia, but Aeacus himself
referred to it as Aegina from his mother's name.
A throng rushes out and wants to meet a man of such                          475
great fame; Telamon and Peleus, younger than Telamon,
go forth to meet him, and Phocus, in that brood, the third;
and even Aeacus, slowed by weight of years, comes out
and seeks to know the purpose of his coming here.
Reminded of his paternal grief and heaving a sigh,                          480
the ruler of a hundred tribes[73] replies to him this way:
"I pray you, help me with arms, taken up on behalf of my son
and be a part of a righteous war; I seek reparations for a tomb."
Asopus' offspring[74] replied, "Invalid is what you seek,
and not to be done by my city, for there is no land                         485
so closely bound as ours to that of Cecrops: so strong is our pact."
Annoyed, he said in departing, "Your pact will cost you much,"
and thought it more useful to threaten war
than wage it and consume the strength of his forces in advance.
The Lyctian[75] fleet was still visible from the Oenopian walls             490
when, driven by a steady wind, an Attic hull
arrives and enters the friendly port with Cephalus on board
and carrying at the same time the petitions of the fatherland.
The young men of Aeacus' line, despite not having seen him for a long time,
still recognized Cephalus and gave him their hands                          495
and led him to their father's house: the hero, a wonder to behold,
retaining still the proof of the beauty of his former years

---

67 An island in the Cyclades.
68 An island in the Sporades.
69 An island in the Cyclades.
70 I.e., Thracian.
71 The story of Arne is unknown.
72 Here begins a list of Aegean islands that did not join Minos.
73 Hom., *Il.* 2. 649, refers to Crete "of a hundred cities."
74 Aeacus was the grandson of the river-god Asopus.
75 Lyctus is a city of Crete.

advances, bearing the olive branch of his native land,
and with him, the elder, on the right and left
were two lesser in age, Clytos and Butes, Pallas'[76] sons.                    500

### 501-613   *The Plague on the Island of Aegina*

The meeting's opening formalities had been exchanged,
when Cephalus delivers the petitions of the Cecropidae[77] and asks
for aid and cites the ancestral pact and oaths,
and adds the further point that the sovereignty of all Achaea[78] was at stake.
When eloquence had thus abetted the petition's cause,                         505
supporting himself with his left hand upon the scepter's hilt, Aeacus
replied, "Ask not for aid, just take it, Athens, and consider yours
without a doubt the forces this island has
and everything that forms this realm of mine.
We do not lack for strength; my army is large enough for me and the foe;     510
thanks be to the gods, the time is opportune and affords no excuse."
"Indeed, let it be so!" says Cephalus, "I hope your city grows
in citizens. When I arrived just now, I was delighted in fact
that young men so fine, so equal in age
came out to meet us; among them, though, there are many I miss,              515
whom formerly I met when I was received into your town."
Emitting a groan, Aeacus with a sad voice declared:
"Lamentable was the beginning followed by a happier fate;
I wish that I could tell you the second without the first!
I'll tell you each in turn, nor keep you with a long-winded tale.            520
The bones and ashes lie buried of those your good memory has missed,
and what a large part of my kingdom passed away with them!
A dreadful plague sent by unfair Juno's anger at my people befell
our land, that was named for the rival concubine[79] she despised.
As long as the illness seemed mortal and the pernicious cause               525
of such a great calamity lay hidden, we fought it with the healing art:
destruction exceeded the ability to help, which lay in defeat.
At first the sky, covered in thick darkness, oppressed
the lands and imprisoned the sluggish heat in clouds;
and after the moon four times had joined her horns to fill her orb          530
and four times, grown thin, had refilled her orb,
the hot south winds blew with death-bringing heat.
It's also known that infection invaded the fountains and lakes
and many thousands of serpents ranged over the barren fields
and with their poisons defiled the streams.                                 535

---

76 Pallas was a son of Pandion and brother of Aegeus.
77 The Athenians as descendants of Cecrops.
78 Synecdoche for "Greece."
79 Aegina, daughter of Asopus.

At first the destruction of dogs and birds and oxen and sheep
and animals of the wild revealed the power of the sudden disease.
The unhappy plowman is amazed at the sturdy bulls
that fall while working and in the middle of the furrow collapse;
the bleating of the wool-bearing flocks is weak,                                            540
their wool falls off of its own accord, their bodies waste away;
the horse, once eager and of great renown in the dusty race,
has lost its winning spirit, unmindful of the triumphs of old
and moans in the stable, consigned to die an indolent death.
The boar remembers not how to grow angry, nor the deer to trust          545
its running flight, nor bears how to attack the sturdy flocks.
All nature is listless: in the woods and fields and ways
repulsive bodies lie, the air defiled by the stench.
Amazing though my tale, those bodies neither greedy vultures nor dogs
nor hoary wolves have touched; they fall in decay and liquefy,              550
spread harm and contagion with their exhalations far and wide.
        "The plague overtakes the wretched farmers with greater harm
and has full sway within the great city's walls.
The inner organs first grow hot, and of the hidden flame
the sign is a red flush and a gasping for breath;                                          555
the tongue is rough and swollen from the fever; the gaping mouth
is parched by tepid winds and tries to suck in the heavy air.
They cannot bear to lie in bed or endure to be covered,
but lay their breasts upon the hard ground, yet by
the soil their bodies are not cooled, their bodies make hot the soil.         560
There is no one to rein in the disease, the healers themselves
break out with the violent scourge, their skills bring only harm.
The closer each one is and more faithfully serves the sick,
the quicker one is to die, and once they lose all hope
and see that the end of the sickness is death,                                            565
they yield to their desires and for what is useful have no concern:
for nothing is useful. Shame is set aside and, strewn about,
they cleave to fountains and streams and copious wells,
yet thirst is not sooner extinguished by drinking than life.
Made heavy by drinking, many cannot rise and perish with                     570
the waters themselves, yet from those same waters another will drink.
The miserable sick despise their beds so much
they leap from them or, if lacking strength to stand,
they roll themselves out upon the ground, and each one flees
his household gods and thinks his home a place of death,                        575
and, since the cause lies hidden, that place is held to blame.
You could have seen people half alive roaming the streets,
as long as they could stand, and others weeping as they lie upon the ground
and, in their final motion, casting about their eyes,

they stretch their arms to the overhanging sky,                              580
exhaling their last wherever death takes them, now here, now there.
　　　"What then was I to think? The proper thing,
perhaps, to hate my life and seek to share my people's fate?
Wherever one turned one's eyes, the people were there
laid low, just as, when the branches are moved,                              585
the rotten apples fall and acorns from the shaken oaks.
You see before you a temple raised high with many steps,
possessed by Jupiter. Who did not upon the altars there
place incense in vain? How often did spouse for spouse,
a father for son, in uttering words of prayer                                590
not end his life upon the altars he invoked,
and in his hand was incense discovered still unconsumed!
How often bulls were brought to the temples, and, as the priest
conceived his prayers and poured pure wine between the horns,
fell down without even waiting for the deadly blow!                          595
When I myself made offerings to Jove for myself, my native land,
and my three sons, the victim bellowed ominously
and suddenly collapsed without being struck
and stained the knife with only the slightest blood.
Its sickened innards had also lost the signs of truth                        600
and warnings of the gods: the baneful sickness reaches the very bowels.
I saw cadavers cast out in front of the sacred doors,
in front of the very altars, to make death even more despised.
Some close their lives with the noose and put to flight the fear
of death through death and by their own will summon the approaching doom. 605
The bodies dispatched to death are carried away without
the usual rites (the funerals would have overburdened the gates):
they either weigh down the earth unburied or are heaped without
due honors upon high pyres; reverence is long gone,
and for the pyres they fight and burn to gain another's fires.               610
To mourn, there are none, as the souls wander unwept
of mothers and brides and elders and youths,
nor is there space for the tombs nor trees enough for the fires.

### 614-60   *The Myrmidons*

　　　"Astounded by this whirlwind of woe,
I said, 'O Jupiter, if what they say is not false,                           615
that you took Asopus' daughter's Aegina into your embrace,
and you, great father, are not ashamed to have fathered me,
give back to me my people or send me also to the grave!'
Jove gave a sign with approving thunder and lightning bolt.
I said in reply, 'I accept these signs. I pray that these signs             620
of your intent be happy ones! The omen you give I consider a pledge.'

By chance there stood nearby, with branches spreading unusually wide,
an oak sacred to Jove, that came from Dodona's[80] seed;
we saw there in a long file prosperous ants
transporting great burdens in their tiny mouths,                                     625
maintaining their path along the wrinkled bark;
while noting with wonder their number, I remarked,
'O father, grant me this many citizens and make full my empty walls!'
The lofty oak trembled and, as its branches moved without a breath of wind,
it gave a sound: in trembling fear my members quaked,                                630
my hair stood on end; however, I kissed both the earth
and oak, but still did not confess my hope;
yet hope I did and held fondly my hopes in my heart.
Night falls and sleep overtakes our bodies occupied
by cares: before my eyes that oak seemed to appear,                                  635
with just as many branches and just as many creatures upon
the branches, and with similar motion seems to begin to shake
and scatter that grain-bearing army upon the fields below;
they suddenly seem to grow and more and more
to lift themselves from the ground and stand tall with trunks made straight,  640
and, shedding their thinness and the number of their feet and swarthy hue,
to take upon their members human form.
My sleep departs: in waking I blame my eyes and complain
that help there is none from the gods; yet in the palace arose
a great disturbance, and I seemed to hear the voices of men,                         645
a sound now unfamiliar; I am thinking that these, too, are just
a dream, when Telamon comes rushing up and through the open doors
said, 'Father, beyond all hope and belief are the things you will see:
come out!' I do come out, and there I seemed to behold
the kind of men I saw in the image of the dream and see                              650
and know them each in turn: approaching they hail their king.
I pay my vows to Jove and among the fresh population divide
the city and the fields, of their former tillers bereft,
and call them Myrmidons, nor falsify the origin of their name.[81]
Their bodies you have seen; the character they had before,                           655
they keep even now: a frugal race, enduring toil,
steadfast in pursuit of gain, and to its gains holding fast.
These men, your equals in age and spirit will follow you to war
as soon as favoring Eurus[82] that brought you here"
(for Eurus had brought him there) "has been changed to Auster's[83] wind."    660

---

80 The oak at Dodona in Epirus, the oracle of Zeus, whose leaves supplied the responses.
81 Myrmidons, here derived from the Greek word for "ant," *myrmex*.
82 The east wind.
83 The south wind.

*Myrmidons, Solis*

### 661-865   Cephalus and Procris

    With this and similar conversation they filled
the lengthy day; to dining the final part of the day
is given, to sleep, the night. The golden Sun had raised his radiant face,
and Eurus kept blowing and holding back the sails that wanted to return:
the sons of Pallas come to Cephalus, older than they,            665
and Cephalus with the sons of Pallas come to the king;
the king, however, was still deep in sleep.
The son of Aeacus, Phocus,[84] at the threshold took them in,
for Telamon and his brother[85] were drafting men for the war.
Into the inner chambers and lovely rooms Phocus leads        670
the sons of Cecrops and sits down together with them.
He notices that Aeolides[86] carried in his right hand
a spear made of unknown wood, whose point was made of gold.
When just a few words had been exchanged, Phocus broke in to say,
"I'm much a man of the woods and hunting wild prey;        675
for long now I have been wondering from what wood that spear
was cut: for surely, had it been made of ash,
its color would be blond; if from cornel-cherry, it would be full of knots.
I'm at a loss as to what it's from, but a finer hurling spear
than this our eyes have never seen."        680
The second of the two Attic brothers replied,
"You'll like its use more than its shape:
it hits whatever it seeks and is not guided by luck;

---

84 Son of Aeacus and Psamathe, later murdered by his half-brothers Peleus and Telamon (see on
    11. 267).
85 Peleus, the future father of Achilles (see 11. 221-65).
86 Cephalus, as grandson of Aeolus.

it also flies back by itself when smeared with blood."
In truth the Nereian youth[87] wants to know all,                                   685
the reason why it was given, its source, and who the author was
of such a great gift. Then Cephalus tells what he wants to know,
but telling what it cost him causes shame. Touched with grief,
he holds his silence, and then, with tears welling up for the wife
he lost, he tells this story: "This spear, goddess-born, makes me weep      690
and long will do so (who would believe it?) if the fates permit long life
to me. This spear has ruined me along with my wife.
I wish I had always been without this boon!
    "My wife was Procris, the sister of Orithyia, the stolen bride,
(if Orithyia's name perhaps is more familiar to your ears),                     695
and if you were to compare the beauty and manner of the two,
of ravishment she was the more worthy! Her father Erechtheus joined her to me,
and love joined her to me. I was called fortunate, and I was indeed;
the gods decided otherwise, or else, perhaps, I should be so even now.
A second month was passing since the sacred marriage rites:                    700
as I was spreading my nets for the horn-bearing stags
upon the summit of ever-flowering Hymettus' ridge,
the rosy goddess Aurora dispels the morning shade
and steals me away, against my will. I'll tell the truth, if I may
without offending the goddess: for all that she's remarkable for her rosy face, 705
that she controls the confines of the day and night,
that she is nourished by the waters of nectar,—it was Procris I loved;
my heart belonged to Procris, Procris was always on my lips.
I talked about the rites of the couch, our love-making, our fresh
new marriage and the first embraces of my now deserted bed:                    710
the goddess was moved and said, 'Enough of your complaints,
you ingrate! Keep your Procris, but if my mind foretells the truth,
you'll wish you hadn't!' and, stirred to wrath, she let me go back to her.
As I return and review in mind what the goddess warned,
anxiety sets in that perhaps my wife had not upheld                            715
our marriage vows: her beauty and age compelled
suspicion of adultery, although her character denied belief;
but I had long been away, and she from whom I returned
was just such an example of blame, and we lovers fear all.
To seek a reason to complain, I decide to test with gifts                      720
her faith and chastity; Aurora assists my fear
and changes my appearance (I think I felt the change).
I enter Palladian Athens in disguise
and enter the home; the very house is free from blame
and gives signs of purity and was anxious for its stolen lord:                 725
by using a thousand tricks I just barely gained access to the Erechtheid.

---

87 Phocus, son of Psamathe, one of the daughters of Nereus, god of the sea.

On seeing her, I stood amazed and almost abandoned the tests
I'd planned of her faithfulness; I barely kept from confessing the truth,
or, as I should have, barely kept from kissing her.
Downcast and sad was she (but in that sadness no woman could          730
have been more lovely than she) and grieved with longing for
her stolen husband: imagine, Phocus, how lovely she was
and how becoming to her was grief itself!
Why tell how many times her modest ways repelled
our efforts to test her, how many times she said,          735
'For only one I save myself; wherever he is, for only one
I save my pleasure.' Who would not have found this great proof
of faith sufficient? But I'm not satisfied and fight to wound
myself! By telling her that I'll give her a fortune for one night
and ever increasing the size of the gifts, I forced her at last          740
to hesitate and proclaim myself the unhappy victor: 'O wicked one,
a feigning adulterer is here. As your husband I was true. By me
as witness have you been caught, deceitful woman!' No reply from her.
In silent shame the conquered woman merely fled the deceitful house
and wicked husband. Because of my offense she loathed the whole race          745
of men and roamed the mountains, of Diana's pursuits a devotee.
In my abandoned state, a fiery passion more furious yet
invades my bones: I begged her forgiveness and admitted I
was wrong and at the offer of gifts would also have yielded to
a similar error, if so many gifts had been given in fact.          750
When I had thus confessed, she first avenged her wounded pride
and then returns to me and passes in harmony pleasant years;
she even gives me, as though she had given the merest gift,
the gift of a dog that her own very Cynthia had given her:
'In running,' she had said, 'it will outshine all the rest.'          755
She gives at the same time the javelin you see in my hands.
Does the fortune of both interest you? Hear now
a wondrous thing: by its novelty you will be moved!
   "The son of Laius[88] had solved the riddles the wit of those
before him had not understood, and having hurled herself down,          760
the vague seer[89] lay prostrate, unmindful of her enigmatic words:
[of course, nurturing Themis[90] leaves such things not unavenged!]
straightway a second plague[91] is let loose upon Aonian Thebes,
and many country folk feared the beast would bring ruin to both
themselves and their flocks; we young men from nearby          765
arrive and surround the wide fields with hunting nets.

---

88 A rare reference to Oedipus in the *Metamorphoses* (see 15. 429).
89 The riddling Sphinx.
90 Themis is the Greek goddess of justice. This line, of obscure origin and meaning, is bracketed by
   most editors.
91 The vixen of Tecmessa, a mountain near Thebes.

With little effort the creature leaped over the nets
and got past the tops of the lines of the traps we had set:
we set loose the dogs, but she flees them as they pursue
and mocks, no slower than a bird, those hundred hounds.                        770
With wide assent they ask me for Laelaps, my hound
(for this was the name of my gift), already struggling to flee
his chain and pulling at the restraints upon his neck.
No sooner was he let free than we failed to see where he was;
the dust, still warm, retained the tracks of his feet,                         775
but he was stolen from our sight: no spear is swifter than he,
nor bullets hurled by the twisted lash of the catapult,
nor any light arrow, made of reed, dispatched from a Gortynian[92] bow.
The top of the hill in the mist hung over the fields below:
I climb the hill and catch sight of a strange race,                            780
in which one moment the beast seems to be caught,
the next, to elude the wounding jaws; the sly critter does not
take flight in one direction, but deceives the pursuer's mouth
by going in a circle, to weaken the charge of the foe:
the other comes close, pursuing with equal pace and though                     785
he seems to have him, he doesn't, and snaps his jaws at the empty air.
I turned to the javelin for help. In balancing it with my right hand
and trying to fit my fingers into the strap, I turned my eyes
away. But when I returned them to the same position again,
I saw in the midst of the plain two marble forms:                             790
you'd think that one were in flight, the other in pursuit.
A god, I suppose, wanted them both to remain unbeaten in
their course, if any god was concerned for them."
So far his tale, and then he fell silent. "What is alleged against the javelin?"
asked Phocus. So then Cephalus related the charge against the javelin.        795
     "Contentment, Phocus, is the beginning of our grief:
I'll tell of the former first. A delight it is to remember the happy time,
O son of Aeacus, when in those early years I was rightly
content in my wife, she in her husband content.
Concern for each other and conjugal love possessed us both;                   800
she wouldn't have preferred the bed of Jove to my love,
nor would another have attracted me, not even if Venus herself
had come; our hearts were burning with equal flames.
My custom was, when the sun was barely striking the ridges with
its rays, to go to the woods with youthful eagerness for the hunt,            805
but with me neither attendants or horses or keen-scented hounds
were wont to come or follow along the knotted nets:
my javelin made me safe; but when with slaughter of the wild

---

92 I.e., Cretan.

*Death of Procris, Baur*

my hand had had its fill, I used to return to the cool and shade
and breeze that came out from the chill of the vale:                          810
I liked to court a gentle breeze in the midday heat,
I liked to wait for the breeze, that respite from my toil.
'Come, Aura,'[93] (for I remember it well), I used to sing,
'My dearest, help me and come into our embrace,
and please reduce, as you do, this heat in which we burn!'                    815
Perhaps I may have added (for so my fate was leading me) much
sweet talk and used to say, 'You are my great desire,'
and, 'You refresh me and comfort me,
you make me love the woods and solitary retreats:
your breath is always caught by my lips.'                                     820
I don't know who it was who lent his ear to be deceived by my
ambiguous words and thought the name 'Aura,' so often invoked,
belonged to a nymph: he thought I was in love with a nymph.
The thoughtless informer of this quickly fashioned charge goes straight
to Procris and repeats with whispering tongue what he had heard.             825
A credulous thing is love: immediately she collapsed and fell
in grief (as I was told); after a long time she comes to,
declares herself the wretched victim of fate,
complains of my lack of faith and, moved by the empty charge,
she feared something that was not, feared a name without                     830
a body and ached as unhappy as if there were in fact a concubine.
The wretched woman, however, often hesitated and hoped she was wrong,

93 *Aura* "Breeze," perhaps recalling the name of Aurora and her warning at 711-13.

denying the truth of the report and, unless she saw it herself,
would not condemn her husband's misdeed.
Aurora's lights had dispelled the night when I                                    835
go out and seek the woods and, lying victorious on the grass,
said, 'Come, Aura, and refresh us from our toil!'
And of a sudden I seem to hear moaning amidst my words,
I know not what they are; I said again, however, 'Come, dearest and best!'
A fallen leaf makes again a gentle, rustling sound.                               840
I think it's a beast and hurled my javelin:
and Procris it was, and, holding the wound in her breast,
she cries, 'Alas!' As soon as I knew the voice of my faithful wife,
I quickly ran distraught towards her voice.
I find her half alive and disfigured in her blood-spattered robes               845
and drawing out (wretched me!) her gift from the wound;
within my gentle arms I lift her up, more dear to me than myself
and, tearing her robe from her breast, I bind
the savage wound and try to stem the blood
and beg her not to leave me cursed by her death.                                 850
Her strength failing, she forces herself at the point of death
to say these few words: 'By the vows of our bed
and by the gods above and my own I beg you as a suppliant,
and by whatever I have done for you and by the love
abiding even now as I die, the cause of my death,                                855
do not allow Aura to take my place in our marriage bed!'
She spoke, and then I saw at last that the error was in the name
and told her so. But what good was it to tell her the truth?
She's failing, and the little strength yet left is fleeing with her blood,
and while she's able to look at all, she looks at me                             860
and breathes her unhappy soul upon me and within our mouth.[94]
But from her happier face she seems to die relieved of care."

  The weeping hero was telling this to us as we wept,
and lo, Aeacus walks in with both his sons and new
recruits, whom Cephalus received with their valiant arms.                        865

---

94 He receives with a kiss her dying breath.

# BOOK 8

## 1-151 Nisus and Scylla

As Lucifer was discovering the shining day and putting to flight
the hours of night, the winds of Eurus fall, and the moist clouds rise up:
the peaceful breezes of Auster give to Aeacus' returning sons
and Cephalus good sailing; rejoicing to be driven so,
they entered ahead of time the ports they sought.                               5
But meanwhile Minos is wreaking havoc on the Lelegeian[1] shores
and making a test of his Martian strength
against the city of Alcathoüs, which Nisus rules, upon whose head,
amidst its honored grey and at the very crown, a splendid lock
of purple was fixed to guarantee the safety of his great reign.                 10
        The rising moon had six times raised again her horns,
and still the outcome of the war was unsettled, and long
between the two cities has Victory been flying with doubtful wings.
The royal turret stood upon the tuneful walls
on which the son of Leto is said to have laid                                   15
his golden lyre: its sound was embedded in the stone.
The daughter of Nisus often used to climb its height
and try with a little pebble to make the rocks resound,
in peacetime; but even in war she often looked down
from it upon the contests of stubborn Mars,                                     20
and, since the war was long, she now knew the chieftains by name,

---

1 The Megarians were called Leleges after Lelex, who came from Egypt and ruled over Megara
  (Pausanias 1. 39.6).

their arms and horses and the Cydonaean[2] quivers and dress.
She knew, above the others, the face of the leader, Europa's son,
she knew it better than she should have: Minos, in this judge's view,
if hiding his head in a plume-crested casque,                                    25
was handsome in a helmet; or, having taken up a shield
agleam with bronze, had taken up his shield with grace,
or, when he hurled a sturdy spear with the force of his arms,
the maiden extolled the union of skill and strength;
or, when he bent the expansive bow to the inserted shaft,                        30
she swore that Phoebus, armed with his arrows, stood there.
But when in truth he removed the bronze armor and bared that face
and, clad in purple, pressed his white steed's back adorned
with painted caparison, and reined in its foaming mouth,
the maiden daughter of Nisus was scarcely herself, scarcely sound               35
of mind: happy she called the javelin he touched,
and happy the reins guided by that hand.
She felt impelled, if only she could, to carry through
the enemy line her virgin paces, she felt impelled
to cast her body from the turret's height into                                   40
the Cnossian[3] camp or open wide the brazen gates to the foe
or do whatever else, if Minos wished it. As she sat
observing the gleaming tents of the Dictaean[4] king,
she says, "I do not know whether to rejoice or grieve at this
lamentable war; I grieve because Minos is his lover's foe.                      45
But if there had been no war, he never would have been known to me.
Yet if he had taken me as a hostage, he could have avoided war:
with me as his companion he would have held me as a pledge of peace.
If she who bore you, most beautiful of kings, was herself
like you, the god[5] deservedly burned for her.                                  50
Thrice happy would I be, alas, if I could glide through the air
on wings and stand within the camp of the Cnossian king,
confess myself and my flames and ask with what dowry he would
be bought, but let him wish to buy me, not demand my country's citadel!
Away with my hopes for marriage before I be capable                             55
of treason! Yet often, for many, the clemency of
a gentle victor makes defeat a useful thing.
He surely wages a justified war for the son that was slain:
he has a strong case and defends that case with arms,
and I am sure we shall be beaten. If this is the result the city awaits,         60

---

2 Cydonia was a town of Crete. The Megarians were called Leleges after Lelex, who came from Egypt
    and ruled over Megara (Pausanias 1. 39. 6).
3 Referring to Knossos on Crete.
4 Referring to Mt. Dicte on Crete.
5 Jupiter.

why ought his Mars open up for him these walls of mine
and not our love? It would be better without death and delay
for him to have been able to win, and without the cost of his blood.
Of course, I should not fear that anyone, Minos, would unwittingly wound
your breast: for who is so harsh as to dare,                                          65
and not unwittingly, to aim a savage spear at you?"
Her plan convinces, and her decision stands to trade
her native land as a dowry for herself and impose an end to war;
but willingness is not enough! "Watchmen tend the doors,
and father has the keys to the gates: him alone do I fear,                           70
unhappy me, for he alone delays my plans.
If only the gods would make me fatherless! We are all,
of course, gods to ourselves: Fortune opposes listless prayers.
Another woman, kindled with such great desire, by now
would happily have destroyed anything that opposed her love.                         75
And why should any woman be braver than I? I would dare
to walk through fires and swords: but in this case no need
for fires and swords, my father's lock is what I need!
More precious to me than gold is that lock.
That purple will make me happy and win me my desire."                                80
          Such words as these she spoke as night sets in,
that greatest nurse of cares, and in the darkness her boldness grew.
The first repose was there, when sleep holds the breasts
made weary by the cares of the day: in silence she enters her father's room
and (oh, the crime!) the daughter deprives her father of his fateful lock,           85
and, having gained her abominable spoils,
she quickly brought them with her and went forth from the gate
into the midst of the enemy (such confidence she had in her deed)
and comes before the king. This is what she said to the frightened man:
"This crime was inspired by love: the royal child of Nisus, Scylla my name,   90
I give to you my country's household gods and mine.
I ask for no reward but you: take this pledge of love,
this purple lock and do not think that I give you a lock
but rather my father's head!" Her wicked hand
then offered the gift. But Minos refused the proffered gift,                         95
confounded by the sight of this strange deed, and said:
"May all the gods remove you from their world,
you insult to our age, and may both earth and sea be denied to you!
Most surely I shall not suffer Crete, the cradle of Jove,
my world, to come in contact with a monster so vile!"                               100
He spoke; and when upon his captured foe this authority
imposed his laws, he ordered the lines that held the fleet
to be released and rowers to board[6] the bronze-tipped ships.

---

6 Translating loosely *impleri*; with *impelli*, translate "to drive."

When Scylla saw that the ships were launched and at sea
and that the commander did not reward her crime,                                    105
now finished with prayers, she shifted to violent wrath
and, stretching forth her hands, her hair flowing loose in her rage,
exclaims, "With the author of your triumph left behind, whither do you flee,
preferred as you were to my country, to my father preferred?
O cruel one, whither do you flee, whose victory is our crime                         110
and service? Did our gifts not move you, our love
not move you, nor that all my hope was heaped on you
alone? So where shall I turn now, deserted as I am?
To country? It lies in defeat! But suppose it yet survived?
By my betrayal it is closed to me! Face my father, you say?                          115
Whom I handed over to you! I have earned my people's hate,
their neighbors fear my example: shut out are we from all
the world so that Crete might welcome us.
But if you deny me this as well and, ingrate, abandon us,
your mother is not Europa, but rather Syrtis,[7] unkind to guests,                   120
Armenian tigresses and Charybdis, driven by Auster's winds.
Nor were you born of Jove, nor your mother by the guise of the bull
seduced: a lie, that story of your birth! But real
and wild and for no heifer captured by love was that bull
that gave you birth. Exact your punishment,                                          125
O Nisus, father! Rejoice in our ills, O walls that I
betrayed! For I confess, I earned them and deserve to die.
But just the same, let one of those whom I did impiously harm
destroy me! For why should you, who triumphed by my crime
reproach my crime? This evil deed against father and fatherland,                     130
regard it as in your service! A worthy mate for you was she
who with that wood adulterously deceived the savage bull
and from her womb brought forth discordant offspring.[8] Does what I say
at all reach your ears, or do the winds carry empty away
my words, you ungrateful man, as well as your ships?                                 135
At last I cease to wonder that Pasiphaë preferred the bull
to you: you were even more of a beast than he.
Alas, poor me! He orders his men to hurry! The sea resounds,
thrown back by the oars, and my land and I together recede from view.
You act in vain and in vain have you forgotten what I have done for you:   140
pursue you I shall, like it or not, and holding on to the curve of your stern,
be dragged along over the wide sea." No sooner had she spoken than she jumped
into the waves and follows after the barks, desire furnishing the strength,

---

7 Dangerous sandbanks off the coast of Libya.
8 Pasiphaë, wife of Minos, conceived a passion for the bull that Minos had promised to sacrifice to
   Poseidon. Daedalus made of wood a hollow image of a cow, in which she consorted with the bull
   and gave birth to the hybrid Minotaur, with the body of a man and head of a bull. See 155-56.

*Scylla with Lock of Nisus, Solis*

and as an unwelcome fellow traveler clings to the Cnossian keel.
Her father, observing this (for he was already soaring in the air, 145
transformed into an eagle of the sea[9] with tawny wings),
came down to tear her clinging there with his curvèd beak.
In fear she let go the stern and, as she fell, a gentle breeze
appeared to hold her up and keep her from touching the water's plain.
A feather she was: transformed into a feathered bird; 150
they call her Ciris the Cutter, a name she got from cutting hair.[10]

### 152-82 *The Minotaur and Ariadne*

As soon as Minos reached the land of the Curetes[11] with his ships,
he paid his vows to Jove with the carcasses of a hundred bulls
and richly hung the palace with the spoils of war.
The scandal of his family had grown, and everyone knew the vile 155
adultery of the mother through the strangeness of the monster's double form,
so Minos determines to remove this shame from his marriage bed
and hide it within a house of many parts and hidden rooms.[12]
The man whose genius was most acclaimed in the builder's art
was Daedalus. Designing the work, he mixes up the marks 160
and with the winding ambiguity of various ways leads the eyes astray.
Not otherwise does the flowing Maeander[13] play upon the Phrygian fields
and flow this way and that in its confusing course,
colliding with itself and seeing its own waves approach,

---

9 Of the genus *Haliaeetus*.
10 Ciris, a sea-bird flying just above the water's surface, means the "Trimmer", from the Greek *keiro* "cut hair."
11 Priests of Cybele in Crete.
12 The Labyrinth at Knossos.
13 A winding river of Asia Minor.

*Labyrinth, Solis*

now forcing its uncertain stream towards its source, 165
now heading for the open sea. With similar confusion Daedalus fills
the countless wandering passages. The house has such power to deceive
that Daedalus himself could barely return to the entrance way.
    When Minos had shut that twin shape of bull and youth
within this place, and when, the monster having twice fed on Attic blood, 170
the third allotment[14] was demanded after each nine years,
and when through a maiden's[15] help that difficult path, retraced by none
before, was discovered by rewinding the thread,
straightway did Aegeus' son make off with Minos' daughter and sail
for Dia[16] and cruelly abandon his traveling mate upon 175
that shore; deserted thus and much aggrieved she was
as Liber took her into his helpful embrace and, to make
her bright with an everlasting star, he took the crown from her brow
and placed it within the sky: it flies through the thin air
and as it flies, its jewels become bright fires 180
and, keeping the appearance of a crown, find a place
between the Kneeler[17] and the Holder of the Snake.[18]

### 183-235 Daedalus and Icarus

    At this same time, Daedalus, despising Crete
and his long exile and moved with love for the place of his birth,
was closed in by the sea. "Both land and sea are closed to me," 185

14 The children of Athens were selected by lot as tribute to the Minotaur, in recompense for the death
    of Androgeos, the son of Minos. See 7. 453-58.
15 Ariadne, daughter of Minos and Pasiphaë.
16 Another name for the island of Naxos.
17 Constellation of the Kneeling Hercules.
18 Ophiuchus.

he says, "but the sky at least lies open; we shall take that route:
though Minos may own all, he does not own the air."
He spoke and turns his mind to unknown skills
and remakes nature, for he lays feathers down in a row,
beginning with the smallest and setting a longer one after each.    190
They rose in a slope, or so you might think: just as the rustic pipe
of old grows larger little by little with its unequal reeds.
And then he ties them at the middle and bottom with wax and twine
and, thus composed, bends them with a gentle curve
to imitate true birds. The boy Icarus stands nearby    195
and, unaware that he was touching his doom
and smiling now as the variable breeze had moved
the feathers he touched, he used his thumb
to soften the yellow wax and with his playing delayed
his father's amazing work. When once to the project the final touch    200
was given, the artisan balanced his own body upon
the twofold wings and hung within the air he had stirred.
He teaches his son and says, "I warn you, Icarus,
to run the middle course lest by flying too low
the wave should weigh the feathers down, or if too high, the fire    205
should burn them: fly midway between them. And do not look
upon Boötes[19] or Helice[20] and the sword Orion has drawn:
with me as your guide take your course!" And as he teaches how
to fly, he fits to his shoulders the unfamiliar wings.
Between the work and warnings the old man's cheeks grew moist;    210
the fatherly hands were shaking; he gave kisses to his son,
to be repeated never again, and, lifted up upon his wings,
he flies in front and fears for his companion, just like the bird
that from the high nest has drawn its tender young into the air,
and orders him to follow and teaches him the dangerous skills    215
and moves his own wings and looks back at the wings of his son.
A fisherman, while fishing with a limber cane,
or shepherd leaning on his staff or farmer on the handle of his plough
observed them and stood struck dumb and thought they were gods
with power to fly through the air. And now on the left    220
was Juno's Samos (both Delos and Paros had already been passed),
Lebinthus[21] was on the right and Calymne[22] rich in honey when
the boy begins to delight in his daring flight
and left his leader and, moved with yearning for the sky,
assumed a higher course. The nearness of the searing sun    225

---

19 The Herdsman (see 2. 176).
20 Another name for the Ursa Major.
21 One of the islands in the Sporades.
22 Another island in the Aegean.

*Icarus' Death, Baur*

makes soft the sweet-smelling wax that held together the wings;
the wax had melted: the boy flaps his naked limbs,
bereft of their oarage, and caught no air,
and then the mouth that called out his father's name in the sky
was taking in the water that took its name from him.[23]                    230
The unhappy father, however, no longer a father, said, "Icarus,
where are you, Icarus?" and said it again, "Where should I look for you?"
and kept saying, "Icarus." He caught sight of the wings in the waves
and cursed his art and placed the body within a tomb,
and from the boy within the tomb the land was named.                     235

### 236-59  *Perdix*

As he was laying the body of his unfortunate son within the tomb,
a chatty partridge looked out from a muddy ditch
and beat an applause with its wings and testified to its joy in song,
at that time a singular bird and one not seen in earlier years,
just recently changed to a bird, but, Daedalus, long a source of blame for you.  240
For ignorant of the fates, his sister had entrusted her son to him
to be instructed, when twice six birthdays of the boy had passed,
because his mind was capable of learning; that boy,
when noticing the spines in the middle of the fish,
drew from it a model and cut a continuous row of teeth                    245
into sharp iron and discovered therewith the use of the saw.
The very first was he to bind two arms of iron from a single knot

---

23 The Icarian Sea.

so that, with the distance between them remaining the same,
one arm stood fixed while the other described an orb.
In envy Daedalus cast the lad from Minerva's sacred citadel     250
headlong and claimed that he had fallen; but since
she favors intelligent minds, Pallas caught him
and changed him into a bird and in mid-air vested him with wings.
His former intelligence, however, entered into the swift moving wings
and feet, and the name he had before remained.     255
This bird, nevertheless, does not raise its body high
or make its nest in branches and lofty peaks:
it flits about upon the ground and in the hedges lays its eggs
and, ever mindful of its former fall, fears the heights.

### 260-546   Meleager and the Calydonian Boar

By now the land of Etna held Daedalus, worn with fatigue,     260
and Cocalus,[24] having taken up arms for the suppliant,
was found to be kind; by now the Athenians had ceased
to pay the lamentable tribute, through Theseus' laudable work.
Their temples were crowned with garlands as they invoke
and honor Minerva, the warrior, along with Jove and the other gods,     265
with sacrifice of blood and tubs of incense and giving of gifts.
Wide-roaming fame had spread throughout the Argive towns
the name of Theseus, and the tribes which rich Achaea held
implored in their great peril his aid,
and Calydon, although it did have Meleager, sought his aid,     270
and came as a suppliant with anxious appeals. The cause
of their request: the avenging servant of hostile Diana was there,
a boar. They say that Oeneus for the bounty of the prosperous year
had offered to Ceres the first fruits of the harvest, to Lyaeus[25] his wine,
and poured to yellow-haired Minerva offerings of Pallas' oil.     275
The highly prized respect began with the rural gods and reached
the gods above: they say the only altars that received
no incense were those of Leto's neglected child.
The gods are also touched by anger. "But we'll not let this pass
unpunished, and though dishonored, we'll not be called unavenged as well,"     280
she says, and through the fields of Oeneus the scorned goddess sent
a boar as her avenger, not smaller than grassy Epirus' bulls
and bigger than those of Sicily's fields:
its eyes flash with blood and fire, its lofty neck is stiff,
its stiff hairs bristle like rigid shafts of spears     285

---

24 King Cocalus of Camicus defended Daedalus from Minos, who pursued him to Sicily and by some
    accounts was killed there. See, Herodotus, 7. 169, Diodorus 4. 79, and Apollodorus, *Epitome* 1.
    13-15.
25 Another of the many names of Bacchus, this one meaning "Liberator." Cf. *Liber.*

and stand like a line of palisades, like lofty spears, those hairs.[26]
With raucous squealing over its shoulders flowed steamy froth,
its tusks are the equal of Indian elephant tusks,
its mouth sends forth lightning, its breath sets the foliage afire.
It tramples now the crops still growing in the blade,                                    290
and harvests now the ripened hope of the farmer doomed to weep
and cuts down the burgeoning heads of Ceres' grain: the threshing floor
awaits in vain, the granary in vain, the promised crops.
The heavy grapes upon the trailing vine are strewn about
and both the berry and branch of the olive, ever in green.                              295
Its fury rages against the flocks as well: neither shepherd nor dog
is able to defend them, nor truculent bulls their herds.
The people are in flight and think themselves unsafe
unless within the city's walls, until Meleager and along
with him a chosen band of youths came together in pursuit of praise:            300
the twin Tyndarids, in boxing distinguished the one,[27]
the other[28] in horsemanship, and Jason, builder of the very first ship,
and Theseus with Pirithoüs, in happy accord,
and two sons of Thestias[29] and Aphareus' sons,
both Lynceus and Idas, swift-footed, Caeneus,[30] not a woman now,           305
and fierce Leucippus and Acastus, noted for the spear,
Hippothoüs and Dryas and Phoenix, Amyntor's son,
and two sons of Actor[31] and Phyleus, whom Elis sent.
And Telamon was not absent, and great Achilles' sire,
and with the son of Pheres[32] and Hantaean[33] Iolaus, too,                        310
were brave Eurytion and Echion, in speed unexcelled.
Narycian[34] Lelex and Panopeus and Hyleus and fierce
Hippasus and Nestor, now in his early years,
and those Hippocoön from ancient Amyclae sent,
the father-in-law[35] of Penelope with Parrhasian[36] Ancaeus,[37] too,          315
and Ampyx' sagacious son[38] and, still safe from his wife,
the son[39] of Oecleus, and the Tegean girl,[40] the glory of the Lycaean[41] woods:

---

26 Line 286 omitted in many MSS and editions.
27 Castor.
28 Pollux (Greek, Polydeuces).
29 Plexippus and Toxeus, the brothers of Althaea, mother of Meleager.
30 See 12. 169 ff.
31 Eurytus and Cleatus.
32 Admetus.
33 I.e., Boeotian. See 3. 146-47.
34 Naryx was a city of Locris.
35 Laërtes.
36 Town and mountain in Arcadia.
37 Son of Lycurgus of Arcadia.
38 Mopsus, the prophet.
39 Amphiaräus, husband of Eriphyle.
40 Atalanta, daughter of Iasion or Iasus of Tegea in Arcadia.
41 Mt. Lycaeus is in Arcadia.

a fine brooch was pinned to the top of her robe,
her hair was plain, done up in a single bun;
suspended from her left shoulder an ivory case      320
that guarded her arrows clattered, her left hand also held
her bow; her face in all its manner was such that truly you
would say that it were girlish in a boy and boyish in a girl.
As soon as he sees her, the Calydonian hero longed for her
and (god forefend!) drank in hidden flames and says,      325
"O happy the man whom she will deign to marry!" Neither time
nor sense of shame allows him to say more:
the greater work of a great challenge urges him on.
     A forest dense with branches, that no earlier age had cut,
arises from the plain and looks down upon the sloping fields.      330
Arriving there, some of the men proceed to spread their nets
while some release the dogs from their chains, and some pursue
the footprints, all eager to discover their dangerous foe.
A hollow glen was there, into which the rain water's streams
would run; pliant willows grew in the bottom of the draw      335
and slender sedge and swamp rushes
and osiers and short swamp plants beneath tall cane:
from here the boar is flushed and drives headlong against
his enemies, like the fires forced from the beaten clouds.
The grove is wrecked by his attack, and the broken trees      340
resound as they crash; the youths give a shout and hold
their spears, tipped with broad iron points, outstretched
in their brave hands. The beast rushes on, scatters the barking dogs
that stand in his furious path, and with his swiping blows drives them off.
The first spear, aimed by Echion's arm, was all in vain      345
and left only a mark on the trunk of a maple tree;
the next, if only it had not been cast with excessive force,
appeared as if it were going to pierce the back at which it was aimed:
it overshoots; Pagasaean[42] Jason was the author of the throw.
"O Phoebus," says Ampyx' son,[43] "if I've worshiped you      350
and worship you now, grant my petition and let my spear find its goal!"
As much as he could, the god assented to his prayers: the boar is struck by him
but left without a wound: Diana had taken from the spear
in flight its iron: the wooden shaft came without its point.
The wrath of the beast was stirred, not weaker than lightning it burned:      355
the fire darts forth from its eyes and bursts forth from his chest,
and as a rock flies when shot from the taut rope of a catapult
and aimed at either the walls or a tower full of fighting men,
the wound-dealing boar is borne with determined attack

---

42 Jason was from the town of Pagasa in Thessaly.
43 Mopsus.

against the youths and lays both Eupalamus and Pelagon flat,                    360
defending the right flank: their comrades quickly carried them from where
they lay, but Enaesimus, the son of Hippocoön did not escape
the death-bearing blows: in terror and about to turn and run,
he lost the use of the muscles in his severed knee.
Perhaps the hero of Pylos[44] would have perished before                        365
the Trojan era, but making a huge effort after positioning his spear,
he vaulted into the branches of a tree that stood nearby
and from this place of safety looked down upon the foe he had escaped.
Upon the oaken trunk the savage beast was whetting his tusks
and threatening destruction; trusting in his resharpened arms,                  370
he gashed with his hook-shaped snout the thigh of great Eurytus' son.[45]
The twins,[46] those brothers not yet heavenly stars,
distinguished both, both brighter than snow,
were mounted on horses and both were brandishing in the air
with tremulant motion the well-launched tips of spears.                         375
They would have hit the mark, if the bristling beast had not
gone into a dark and wooded place inaccessible to horse and spear.
In hot pursuit and in his eagerness not taking care as he advanced,
tripped up by the root of a tree, Telamon fell flat on his face.
As Peleus was lifting him up, the Tegean heroine[47] fitted to the string       380
a speedy arrow and drives it from the well-bent bow.
The shaft, implanted beneath the ear of the beast, just grazed
the surface of the body and reddened the bristles with a bit of blood.
However, no happier than she in the success of her blow
was Meleager: he was first, it is thought, to have seen                         385
and first to have shown to comrades the blood he had seen
and to have said, "You will gain the prize for valor that you have earned."
The men were flushed and urge themselves on and raise
their courage with clamor and hurl without order their spears:
their number does harm to their effect and impedes the intended blows.          390
Behold, Arcadian Ancaeus, wielder of a double-axe, raged against his fate,
and said, "Learn how superior to womanish arms stand the arms
of men, O youths, and let me do my work!
Although Latona's daughter protects this beast with her arms,
my own right hand will destroy it despite Diana's will."                        395
Puffed up with his pompous speech he had spoken these words,
and, lifting his double-edged axe in both his hands,
had risen on his toes and hanging there was ready to strike:
amid this daring act the beast caught him where the way to death
is quickest and aimed his tusks into the top of his groin.                      400

44 Nestor's city on the west coast of the Peloponnesus.
45 Hippasus.
46 Castor and Pollux.
47 Atalanta.

*Calydonian Boar, Anonymous, Venice ca. 1513*

Ancaeus falls and his innards, balled together with copious blood,
spill out in a stream: the earth is soaked with his gore.
Against his foe Ixion's son Pirithoüs advanced
and in his sturdy right hand brandished the hunting-spear.
To him the son of Aegeus says, "Stand apart! You are dearer to me        405
than life itself and part of my soul! It is right for brave men
to fight from afar! To Ancaeus rash valor brought harm."
He spoke and hurled the cornel spear heavy with its cusp of bronze.
Well launched though it was and able to reach its goal,
a leafy branch of an oak tree stood in the way.                          410
The son of Aeson hurled another spear, which chance diverted from
the beast into a barker's unmerited doom and, hurled clear through
the abdomen, implanted it through the abdomen into the ground.
The hand of Oeneus' son had different results: after casting two spears,
the first stood in the earth, the second in the middle of the back.      415
Without delay, as the beast raged and twisted its body round
and round and spewed forth squealing foam and blood,
the author of the wound is there and rouses his enemy's wrath
and buries his shining hunting-spear into the shoulders of the foe.
His comrades show their joy with approving shouts                        420
and seek out the victor to give him their right hands,
admiring in wonder the enormous beast
outstretched upon a deal of ground, nor even now consider it safe
to touch it, but even now each bloodies within it his spear.
        ·   The hero pressed his foot against that fatal head,           425
and then he said, "Take my rightful part of the spoils,

Nonacrian lass, and let my glory be shared with you."
At once he gives to her the spoils, the head, distinguished with
its mighty tusks, and the back, bristling with hairy spikes.
The author of the gift and the gift itself bring joy to her;                    430
the others are envious, and through the host of men a murmur was heard.
Among them, stretching out their arms and exclaiming in a loud voice,
"Come, woman, put them down, don't usurp the honors that are ours,
and don't trust too much in your beauty, lest though captivated now by love,
your benefactor abandon your cause," the sons of Thestias deprive           435
her of the reward and him of the right to give the reward.
The scion of Mars,[48] swollen with wrath and gnashing his teeth, did not
endure it and said, "Learn now, usurpers of another's due praise,
how different threats are from deeds!" and with impious iron opened up
Plexippus' breast, who was not at all fearing such a thing.                   440
As Toxeus wondered what he should do, desiring both to avenge
his brother and fearing he might suffer his brother's fate,
the other gives him little time to hesitate and with fraternal blood
re-warmed the spear from the earlier slaughter still warm.

While bringing gifts to the shrine of the gods for her victorious son,       445
Althaea sees her murdered brothers being brought back.
She beats her breast and fills the city with cries of woe
and changed her robes of gold for robes of black:
but when she learned the author of the killing, all her grief
subsided and from tears was turned to a love for revenge.                     450

There was a log that the triple sisters had set afire
as Thestius' daughter[49] yet lay in the toils of giving birth
and, spinning their fatal threads with the press of their thumbs,
had then exclaimed, "We give to this log and to you, born just now,
an equal measure of time." As soon as the goddesses, their chant now done,   455
had left, the mother tore the burning branch from the fire
and sprinkled it with running water. It long
had lain concealed within the palace, in an inner recess,
and, thus preserved, had saved your years, O youth.
His mother brought it out and ordered kindling and pine brands               460
set up, and, when the pile was ready, she set to it the hostile fire.
Four times she tried to lay the log upon the flames,
four times she stopped herself: mother and sister are at war,
and two divergent names are tearing one breast apart.
In fear of the coming crime her face often grew pale,                        465
and boiling anger often brought to her eyes its flush,
and sometimes her countenance seemed bent on something fierce,
and sometimes, you would think it filled with tenderness;

---

48 Meleager is the great-grandson of Mars.
49 Althaea.

and when savage passion had dried the tears of her mind,
the tears were found again no less, and as a ship,                              470
seized by the wind and by the tide that opposed the wind,
feels twin forces and yields uncertainly to both,
no differently does Thestius' daughter wander in uncertain moods
and one moment cools and the next rekindles her wrath.
The sister begins to be better than the parent, nevertheless,                   475
and that she appease her consanguine shades with blood,
is pious through impiety. For after the death-bearing fire
grew strong, she said, "Let this pyre consume the flesh of my womb"
and as she held in her dreadful hand the fatal wood,
she stood before the sepulchral altar distraught                                480
and said, "O triple goddesses of vengeance, Eumenides,
your faces turn now to these our dreadful rites!
I punish and do wrong; death must be avenged by death,
to crime must crime be added, for funerals another funeral supplied:
let perish this impious house under a mountain of grief!                         485
Will Oeneus be content to enjoy his son as conqueror
while Thestius is bereft of sons? Better that both of you shall mourn.
But you, fraternal shades and fresh new souls,
discern my service and receive these gifts for the dead,
provided at great cost, the pernicious pledge of our womb!                      490
Ah me! What am I doing? Brothers, this mother forgive!
My hands are too weak to fulfill my plan: we admit he deserves
to die; it is of the author of the death that I disapprove.
Shall he therefore go unpunished and as victor and alive
and swollen with his own success possess the kingdom of Calydon,                495
while you lie defeated, paltry ashes and frigid shades?
By no means will I endure it: let that wicked man die
and let him bring his father's hope and the kingdom and fatherland
to ruin! Where is my mother's mind? Where of mothers the pious laws
and where the toils I endured for twice five months?                            500
O would that you had been consumed as an infant in those first fires,
and I had been able to bear it! Because of our gift you lived!
Now shall you die by your own merit! Receive your reward for the deed
and give back your soul given twice, first at birth and next when the log
was stolen, or add me to my brothers' tombs!                                    505
I both desire it and cannot. What should I do? While my brothers' wounds
appear before my eyes and the image of a slaughter so great,
both piety and the name of mother break my heart.
Alas poor me! The victory you win will be evil, brothers, but you will win,
if only I myself may follow you and the consolation I shall have given you!  510
She spoke and, turning her face away, with trembling right hand
she threw the deadly firebrand into the midst of the fire:

*Meleager's Death, Solis*

the log itself either did in fact or seemed to emit
a groan as it was caught up and burned in the unwilling flames.
    Not knowing why and far from those flames, Meleager burns        515
and feels his insides being consumed by those hidden fires
and with his courageous strength suppresses enormous pains.
That he should fall victim to a bloodless and unheroic death,
however, he regrets and calls happy Ancaeus' wounds.
He calls upon his aged father and brothers and pious sisters with a moan,   520
and also the companion of his bed with his final words,
and even perhaps his mother. The fire and pain increase
and then grow easier; as soon as both are extinct,
his spirit gradually departs into the gentle air,
and gradually hoary ashes envelop the burning coals.        525
    High Calydon is brought low: men, young and old, lament,
the people and their leaders mourn, and, rending their hair,
the mothers of Calydon, daughters of Evenus,[50] beat their breasts;
the father befouls his white hair and aged face with dust,
collapsed upon the ground, and rebukes the length of his life,      530
for from the mother that hand, now conscious of its awful deed,
exacted punishment by driving a sword through her flesh.
If god had given me a hundred mouths
resounding with tongues, capacious wit and all of Helicon,
I still could not convey the sadness of his wretched sisters'[51] words.   535
Unmindful of their appearance, they beat their breasts black and blue,
and while that body still remains they embrace that body again and again,

---

50 I.e., the women descended from Calydon's river Evenus.
51 The sisters of Meleager, and daughters of Oeneus, will be turned into guinea-hens. Other authors call
  them *Meleagrides,* because *Meleagris* in Greek means "guinea-hen."

give kisses to it and give kisses to the erected bier.
And when it is turned to ashes, they gather the ashes and press them to their breasts
and, fallen prostrate upon the tomb and embracing the name                    540
engraved upon the stone, pour tears upon the name.
Latona's daughter, sated at last with the slaughter of Parthaon's[52] house,
puts feathers upon the bodies of all the daughters and lifts them up,
except for Gorge and noble Alcmena's daughter-in-law,[53]
and spreads over their arms long wings and turns                              545
their mouths to horn and sends them transformed into the air.

### 547-884   In the house of Acheloüs

### 547-610   Acheloüs and Perimele

While this was happening, Theseus, his part in the common task
complete, was on his way to Tritonis'[54] Erechthean citadel.
The stream of Acheloüs, swollen with rain, blocked his path
and caused delay. "Come into my house, O famous Cecropid,"                    550
he says, "and do not entrust yourself to the rapacious waves
that like to sweep away whole beams and with a mighty roar
make boulders churn sidelong. I've seen lofty stables near the bank,
along with their animals, being swept away; for the bulls to be brave
and for the horses to be swift brought no advantage then.                     555
This river, swollen from the melting mountain snow, has overwhelmed
within its swirling stream many bodies of young men, too.
Repose is safer until the stream flows again within
its usual course and its own channel regains its tranquil waves."
The son of Aegeus agrees and replies, "I'll use both your home                560
and your advice, Acheloüs;" and he used them both.
He enters the courtyard carved from porous pumice and tufa, light
in weight: the floor was moist with tender moss,
the ceiling paneled with alternating murex and conch.
Hyperion[55] by now had completed two-thirds of the day                       565
as Theseus and the companions of his toils reclined upon
their couches, here Ixion's son, there Lelex, the hero of
Troezen, whose brow was already sprinkled with grey,
and others whom with equal respect the Acarnanian[56] river-god
had deigned to welcome, most delighted to have such company.                  570
At once the nymphs, their feet unsandaled, piled high
the tables with sumptuous food, and when the feast was removed,
poured unmixed wine into jeweled vessels. The mighty hero then,
his gaze upon sea below, says, "Tell me, what is that place?

---

52 Father of Oeneus.
53 Deianira.
54 Minerva (Athena).
55 The Sun.
56 Acarnania was a region of northwest Greece through which the Acheloüs flows.

That island there, what is its name,                                              575
although it appears not to be just one?"
The river-god says, "What you see comprises in fact not one,
but five separate islands. The distance conceals that they are distinct.
That you may wonder less at Diana's deed when she was scorned,
these islands had been naiads. After they had sacrificed                          580
ten bulls and summoned all the country deities to their rites,
neglecting me, they performed their festal choruses of song and dance.
I swelled with rage, as much as I have ever been in full flood.
In such a state, equally furious in mind and in wave,
I tore the forests from the forests, the fields from the fields                   585
and with the land I rolled those nymphs, at last now mindful of me,
into the sea. Our flood and that of the sea
divided the connected land and separated it into
as many Echinades as you see in the midst of the waves.
But as you yourself observe, far away, —see there, far away,                      590
one island is pleasing to me; sailors call it Perimele:
the right to be called a virgin I took away from her.
Enraged by this, her father Hippodamas cast her body from a cliff
into the deep, intending his daughter's death.
I rescued her and held her up as she swam, and 'O Trident-bearer,' I said,        595
'allotted the realm of the wandering waves, the nearest to the firmament,[57]    596
bring help, I pray, to the daughter immersed by a father's cruelty;               601
allow her a place, O Neptune, or let her be that place herself!'
And as I spoke, new earth embraced her swimming limbs                             609
and from her transformed members a heavy island grew."                            610

### 611-724   Baucis and Philemon

With this, the river-god was silent. The miracle had moved
them all; for believing it, that scorner of the gods,
the fierce-minded son[58] of Ixion, scoffs at them.
"Your stories are false, Acheloüs, and you deem the gods

---

57 Lines 597-600 and 603-608 are bracketed in most editions:
    [to which all we sacred rivers run and have our end,                          597
    be present now and calmly hearken, O Neptune, to my prayer.
    I harmed her whom I carry now. If Hippodamas,
    her father were kind or just, or if less impious as well,                     600
    he should have taken pity upon her and forgiven us.                           600a
    But since the dry-land is now closed to her by a father's cruelty,]           600b
    bring help, I pray, to the daughter immersed by a father's cruelty,          601
    allow her a place, O Neptune, or let her be that place herself!
    [and let me embrace her myself].' [The ocean king moved his head             603
    and, giving his full consent, he smote the waves.
    The nymph was frightened, yet swam, and, as she swam, I myself                605
    was touching her breasts heaving with trembling fear.
    And as I fondled them, I perceived that her whole body was growing hard,
    her midriff being hidden by the enveloping earth.]
58 Pirithoüs.

too powerful, if they give and take away figures," he said.                    615
They all were struck dumb and did not approve of such words.
Before all the others Lelex, mature in mind and age,
replies this way: "The power of heaven is immense and has
no limit, and whatever the gods above desire is fulfilled.
That you may have no doubt of this, next to a linden there is an oak     620
upon the hills of Phrygia, surrounded by a modest wall:
I've seen the place myself; for Pittheus sent me into
the fields of Pelops, over which his father[59] once had ruled.
Not far from there is a swampy area, habitable land in earlier times,
but now its waters are full of divers and marsh-dwelling coots;           625
to this place came Jupiter in human form, and with his father came
the wielder of the caduceus, the grandson[60] of Atlas, having doffed his wings.
A thousand homes had they approached in search of lodgings and repose,
a thousand homes closed and barred; one, however, took them in,
a little one indeed, covered with marshy reeds and thatch,                  630
but pious Baucis and old Philemon, her equal in age,
within that cottage were joined in the years of their youth,
within that cottage had grown old together. By confessing it,
they made their poverty light, and by enduring it with patient hearts.
It makes no sense for you to ask for the masters and servants there:      635
the whole house consists of two, the same give orders and obey.
When therefore the residents of heaven to these Penates[61] came down
and lowered their heads to enter those humble doors,
the old man urged them to rest their limbs upon the bench he had set up,
on which Baucis had taken pains to lay a rudely woven spread.            640
She also had removed the tepid ashes from the hearth
and stirred yesterday's coals to life and fed them with dry bark
and leaves and produced flames with her old-woman's lungs
and then brought down from the roof well-split firewood and
dry sticks, and broke them up and put them under a small copper pot;    645
and from the greens her husband had gathered from the well-watered plot
she trimmed the outer leaves. Her husband takes a two-pronged fork
and lifted a smoky slab of bacon off a blackened beam
and cut from the well-aged slab a slice or two
and softened the part he had cut in the boiling waves.                       650
And meanwhile they deceive the intervening hours with talk
and keep them from feeling any delay. There was a beech-wood tub
that hung there from its sturdy handle on a nail;
when filled with lukewarm water, it receives and soothes
their limbs. A cushion filled with soft swamp-grass is laid upon          655a

---

59 Pelops was the father of Pittheus.
60 Mercury, son of Jupiter and Maia, the daughter of the Titan Atlas.
61 The household gods, standing for the house itself.

| | |
|---|---|
| the middle of a couch with willow frame and feet; | 656a |
| [they fluff up a cushion filled with soft river grass | 655 |
| that lay upon a couch of willow frame and feet;] | 656 |
| they cover it with coverlets used for festive days, | |
| but even these spreads were ordinary and old, | |
| by no means unsuited to a willow bed. | |
| The gods recline. The old woman, girt up and trembling, sets down | 660 |
| a table, but the third leg of the table was different in length; | |
| a potsherd made it even, and after the shim had removed | |
| the slope, green mint wiped the leveled table clean. | |
| Placed here were berries of pure Minerva, twofold in hue,[62] | |
| and autumn's cornel cherries, preserved in pure lees of wine, | 665 |
| and endives and radishes and lumps of clotted milk | |
| and eggs turned gently in the cooler ash, | |
| all this in earthenware; afterwards arrive a mixing bowl, | |
| engraved in similar 'silver,' and cups made of beech, | |
| their hollow parts coated with tawny wax. | 670 |
| There is a short wait, and then the hearth released the steaming food; | |
| again wines, not long in age, are offered and removed, | |
| allowing a short pause for the second course. | |
| On this side were nuts, on that, Carian figs mixed with wrinkled dates, | |
| and plums and perfumed apples on trays of reeds | 675 |
| and grapes plucked from the purple vines; | |
| and in the middle a bright honeycomb. To top it all off | |
| good faces were there, and goodwill, neither sluggish nor poor. | |
| "And during the meal every time the mixing bowl is drained, | |
| they see it filled again of its own accord and of itself the wine supplied; | 680 |
| Astonished and frightened by the strangeness of this thing, | |
| both Baucis and timid Philemon lift their hands and turn to prayer | |
| and ask forgiveness for the feast and for having nothing prepared. | |
| There was a single goose, the sentinel of the simple house, | |
| which now its masters were preparing to sacrifice for the visiting gods; | 685 |
| the goose was fast of wing and wearies those who are slow of limb, | |
| eluding them long and finally seeming to have fled to the gods | |
| themselves. The divinities forbid it to be killed | |
| and said, 'We are gods; your impious neighborhood will pay | |
| the punishment it deserves, but you will be granted immunity from | 690 |
| this woe. Just abandon now your home | |
| and follow our steps and go to the mountain heights | |
| with us.' They both obey and, supported on canes, | 693 |
| [with us. They both obey and, with the gods walking ahead, | 693a |
| they ease their limbs with canes and, slow because of their aged years,][63] | 693b |

---

62 I.e., from the tree sacred to Minerva some of the olives are black, some still green.
63 693a-693b repeat the sense of 693.

*Baucis and Philemon, Amsterdam, 1703*

work hard to set their steps upon the long ascent.
When they were still an arrow's flight from the top,     695
they turn their gaze around and see below that all
has been flooded by a swamp and that their house alone remains.
And as they wonder and weep for their people's fate,
that former house, for even two masters small,
is changed into a temple; columns replaced the split wooden props,     700
the straw grows yellow and looks like a gilded house,
reliefs are on the doors and the ground with marble paved.
Saturnius then uttered this from his placid mouth:
'Say now, just old man and woman worthy for a man who is just,
what you desire.' After speaking with Baucis a short while,     705
Philemon reveals their common decision to the gods:
'To be the priests and caretakers of your shrines
is our request and, since we have passed our years in harmony,
that one and the same hour take us away, and that I never see
the pyre of my wife, and that I should never be laid by her within the tomb.' 710
Fulfillment follows their prayers; over the temple they kept their watch
as long as they were granted life. And enfeebled by years and age,
it chanced that as they stood before the hallowed steps and told again
the story of the place, Baucis saw Philemon sprouting leaves,
Philemon, an old man, saw Baucis sprouting leaves.     715
And, with the top of the tree now rising over the faces of both,
while still they could, they exchanged their mutual words

and at the same time said 'Farewell, my spouse!' and at the same time the bark
concealed their faces: even now the Thyneian[64] inhabitant there
will show adjoining trunks arising from a double stock.                      720
The old-timers were not lying when they told me this
(they had no reason to lie); indeed I saw wreaths hanging upon
the branches and, putting on fresh garlands myself, I said,
'May those the gods protect be gods, and worshipers be worshiped in turn.'"

### 725-884   *Erysichthon and his Daughter*

The story was over and both the author and subject had moved them all,  725
especially Theseus, who desired to hear more of the gods' miraculous deeds.
The Calydonian river-god, supported upon one elbow, addresses him
with words like these: "O bravest of men, there are some whose form
has once been changed and in its transformation has remained.
For others it is lawful to change into many shapes, as with you,           730
O Proteus, you that dwell within the sea that embraces the land.
For people have seen you once as a youth, as a lion once,
one day you were a violent boar, one day a serpent on whom
folks feared to tread, and then horns used to turn you into a bull;
you often were able to appear as a stone and also often as a tree,         735
and sometimes, imitating the flowing water's face,
a river you were, and sometimes the fire that opposes the waves.
"Autolycus'[65] wife, the daughter of Erysichthon, possessed
this right no less: her father was the one who scorned the power of
the gods and on their altars made no sweet incense burn;                   740
he's even said to have desecrated a grove of Ceres with an axe,
and outraged its ancient trees with iron.
There stood therein an oak with the strength of many years,
a grove in itself; fillets and memorial tablets and wreaths
hung round it, proofs of effective prayer.                                 745
Beneath this oak dryads often performed their dances and songs,
and often joined their hands in a line and made a circle around
the mass of the trunk, and the circumference of the oak
completed thrice five ells, and the height of the forest lay
as far below it as beneath all the forest lay the grass.                   750
The son of Triopas,[66] despite all this, did not from it hold back
his iron and orders his servants to cut down the sacred oak,
and, as he sees them hesitate to follow his orders, from one
of them the cursèd man grabbed an axe and uttered these words:
'Suppose this tree be not only beloved by a goddess, but in fact           755

---

64 I.e., Bithynian. The Thyni were a people of Thrace that emigrated to Bithynia.
65 Father of Anticleia, the mother of Odysseus, and noted as a trickster. In post-Homeric sources
    (followed by Ovid at 11. 313-15) he is the son of Mercury and Chione, in Homer Hermes is his
    patron and endowed him with his thievery (*Od.* 19. 396-97).
66 A king of Thessaly, father of Erysichthon.

*Erysichthon and Tree, Solis*

a goddess itself, just the same its leafy top will touch the ground!'
He spoke, and as he aimed his weapon to make slanting blows,
the Deoian[67] oak trembled and gave a groan
and all together the leaves and acorns began
to fade and the long branches grew pale as well.                          760
And when the impious hand made a wound in its trunk,
no less did blood flow from that shattered bark
than when a huge bull falls before the altar as a sacrifice
and gore pours forth from the severed neck.
They all were stunned to silence, and someone in the crowd             765
makes bold to prevent the wicked deed and hinder the cruel axe:
the man of Thessaly looks at him and says, 'For your pious mind
receive a reward!' and turns his weapon away from the oak
against the man and cuts off his head and returns to slashing the oak,
and from the midst of the oak this sound is heard:                      770
'Within this wood I dwell, a nymph of Ceres most beloved,
and as I die I prophesy that punishment awaits
you for your deeds, a consolation for my death.'
He carries out his crime and the tree totters at last
beneath the countless blows and, drawn down by ropes,                  775
collapsed and flattened a great swath of forest with its weight.
　　　"The dryads were stunned by the damage done to them
and to the grove. These sisters, in mourning and clad in black,
go forth to Ceres and plead for Erysichthon's punishment.
She nodded to them her consent, and with a motion of her lovely head   780
she shook the fields laden with burgeoning grain

---

67 Deo is another name for Ceres.

and undertakes a pitiable kind of punishment
(although that man was to be pitied by none for his deeds):
to harass him with plague-bringing Famine. Because
the goddess cannot approach her (for the fates do not allow                    785
that Ceres and Famine come together), she compels a rustic oread,
a mountain divinity, with the following words:
'There is a place in icy Scythia's far off shores
with sad and sterile soil, a land with neither grain nor tree;
benumbing Cold and Pallor and Fear dwell there                                 790
and hungry Famine: order her to hide herself within
the wretched heart of that impious man; let Plenty not
defeat her nor, challenging my strength, prevail,
and lest the lengthy journey daunt you, take my chariot
and take my serpents and guide them on high with the reins!'                   795
and gave her the reins. Borne through the air in the chariot she had received,
the oread came to Scythia: upon a rocky mountain peak
(they call it Caucasus) she lightened the serpents' necks
and looks for Famine and finds her in a stony field,
there picking at the sparse grass with her nails and teeth.                     800
Her hair was shaggy, her eyes were hollow, pallor filled her face,
her lips were ashen, her jaws were scabrous with blight,
her skin was hard and through it her innards could be seen;
the dry bones protruded from her hollow loins,
in place of a belly there was just a belly's place; you'd think her breasts     805
were hanging loose and only held by the joints of her spine.
Privation had enlarged her joints, and the knobs of her knees
were swollen, and with ungainly swelling her ankles bulged.
    "On seeing her from afar (for she did not dare draw near),
the oread gave the commands of the goddess and, tarrying awhile,               810
despite the fact that she was at a distance and had only just arrived,
she thought she felt the sensation of hunger and, reversing the reins,
directed on high her serpents back to Haemonia[68] again.
    "Though Famine is always opposed to the other's work,
she carried out the commands of Ceres and, borne by the wind                   815
through the air to the house she was assigned, she enters at once
the chamber of the impious man, now deeply dissolved in sleep
(for it is night), and enfolds him in her arms' embrace
and plants herself within the man and blows upon his throat and breast
and face and sprinkles hunger throughout his empty veins.                      820
Her orders fulfilled, she deserts the world of fertility
and turns again to those impoverished homes, her wonted caves.[69]
    "Sweet Sleep was yet caressing Erysichthon with gentle wings:

---

68 Thessaly.
69 Some MSS have *arva* "fields."

*Erysichthon Sells His Daughter, Baur*

he searches for food even within the images of sleep
and moves his empty mouth and wearies teeth against teeth                    825
and exercises his deluded throat with imagined food,
devouring vainly nothing but air instead of a feast;
but when his rest is banished, a passion to eat
holds sway over his greedy jaws and heated bowels.
Without delay he calls for what the sea, the earth, the air                    830
produce and complains of the meagerness of the tables set
before him and seeks feast upon feast; and what would be enough
for cities and a nation is not enough for one,
and he desires to sink yet more within his gut.
And as the ocean receives the streams of all the earth                         835
and is not sated with water and drinks down the rivers from afar,
and as voracious fire never refuses nourishment
and burns up countless logs and the more there is
the more it seeks, made all the greedier by the mass itself,
just so does profane Erysichthon's mouth receive every feast                   840
and order another at once. All food in him
is cause for food and by eating constantly[70] turns to empty space.
     "By now the hunger and pit of his stomach had thinned
his patrimony, but even still the awful hunger remained
quite unreduced, and the ardor of his gullet flourished, still                 845
unsated. At last when all his wealth lay cast into his bowels,
his daughter was left, who deserved no such father as he.
In vain he sells her, too: the noble girl refuses a lord

---

70 Construing *semper* "constantly" with both *fit* "turns to" and *edendo* "by [his] eating."

and stretching her hands towards the sea nearby, she says,
'Deliver me from a master, you who of our ravished virginity          850
possess the prize!' Neptune possessed it indeed
and did not scorn her prayer. A would-be master has just
now seen her, but Neptune changes her form and puts upon her
the face of a man and the garb suited to those who catch fish.
The master says when seeing her thus, 'O you who conceal             855
the dangling bronze hook with a little food, wielder of the cane,
I hope the sea is calm and the fish in the wave
is credulous and feels not the barb until he is hooked:
the girl who with tousled hair and shabby dress
stood on this shore (for I saw her standing here),                   860
please tell me where she is: for her footprints stop here.'
She sensed that the gift of the god was granted and, rejoicing
that she was being sought out, answered the inquirer thus:
'Forgive me, whoever you are, but I have never turned my eyes
away from the deep waters here and have been intent upon my work,    865
and lest you doubt, so may the god of the sea assist my skill,
no man has ever stood upon this shore,
nor any woman, except for me.'
The master trusted her and with foot reversed pressed the sand
and went away deceived; her former shape was returned to her.        870
But when he realized that his daughter had bodies of many shapes,
the father traded the Triopeid[71] to many masters, but she
as mare, as bird, as ox, or now a stag escaped
and furnished her greedy father with ill-gotten food.
But when the power of that evil condition had eaten away all         875
his substance and fed the grievous sickness anew,
the man began to tear at his own limbs with his rending jaws
and wretchedly nourished his body by making it small.
      "Why should I tarry with stories of others? Even I of late possessed,
young man, the power of changing my body, though limited in extent.  880
For sometimes I'm as you see me now, while sometimes I'm bent into a snake,
and sometimes as leader of the herd I put on horns, —
so long as I could, horns. But now one side of my brow
is lacking its weapon, as you see." Groans followed his words.

---

71 So-called because her father Erysichthon was the son of Triopas. Others call her Mestra (Hes.,
   *Catalogue of Women*, Fr. 43a. 2. 3. and Scholiast to Lycophron 1393).

# BOOK 9

### 1-97 Acheloüs and Hercules

The hero son[1] of Neptune asks the cause of the groans
and the god's disfigured brow; the Calydonian river began
this way, his disheveled locks bound up by reeds:
"A sad favor you seek. For who when conquered likes to recall
his battles? But I shall tell all in order, nor was it so bad          5
to be defeated as it is glorious to have fought,
and great is my comfort in having a victor so great.
If to your ears in conversation the name
of Deianira has come, this very beautiful maiden
was once of many suitors the long-sought hope.          10
Among them, when entrance to the house of the father-in-law[2]
I sought was gained, I said, 'Accept me as your son-in-law,
O son of Parthaon.' And Alcides[3] said the same. The others conceded
to only two. He claimed to offer Jove as an in-law and his labors' fame,
the commands of his step-mother's[4] that he had sustained.          15
In countering I said, 'For a god to concede to a mortal is base—
he wasn't yet a god—you see that I am the master of
the waters that flow in winding courses through your realm.
Nor am I sent as a stranger from foreign shores to be a son-in-law;
a native son I'll be and a part of what is yours.          20

---

1 Theseus, of whom both Aegeus and Neptune were considered the father.
2 Oeneus.
3 Hercules, grandson of Alceus.
4 Juno.

But let it not be held against me either that royal Juno does not
despise me or for commanded labors there is no debt to pay.
And as for your claim, O son of Alcmena, to have been born
of Jupiter, either he is not your father, or if he is, your father through an offense.
You seek a father through your mother's adultery. So choose:                25
do you want Jove as a fictitious father or to have been born in shame?'
As I am saying this, he is glaring at me with an angry eye
and lacking the strength to control any longer his burning wrath
replies in just these words: 'I think the hand is better than the tongue.
So long as I prevail in battle, go ahead and win in debate.'                30
And then he comes at me in a fury. I was ashamed, having talked so big,
to yield: I threw off from my body my cloak of green
and put up my arms and held out from my chest my clenched hands
in proper position and readied my limbs for the fight.
He picks up dust in the hollow of his palms and sprinkles me                35
and then by the touch of the tawny sand grew yellow in turn.
And then he grabs my neck and then my legs and next my groin,
or so you would think, and harries me from every side.
My weight defends me and I was being attacked in vain;
not different than a massive cliff, that with a mighty roar                  40
the waves oppose, it stands there, made safe by its very weight.
We stand apart a little and then come together in battle again
and hold our footing, determined not to yield, and foot was locked
with foot, and, leaning against him with all my chest,
I pressed fingers with fingers and brow with brow.                          45
Brave bulls I have seen contend not differently
in vying for a mate, the reward of the strife, the finest in all
the pasture: the herd looks on in fear, not knowing who
awaits the victory over so great a realm.
Three times without success Alcides tried to thrust away                    50
my chest that pressed against him; at the fourth attempt
he broke my hold and loosened my encircling arms
and all at once turned aside my attack with his hand—I've chosen to admit
the truth—and planted himself heavily upon my back.
If you can believe it—for I seek no glory with a fictitious tale,           55
I thought a mountain was weighing me down.
With difficulty I inserted my sweat-streaming arms
between us, with difficulty I broke from my body his hard embrace.
By pressing the attack as I pant for breath, he keeps me from regaining strength
and gets a hold around my neck. The earth is then at last                   60
pressed down by our knee, and I bit the sand with my mouth.
Outdone in strength, I have recourse to my stratagems,
and in the form of a long serpent, I slip away from the man.
But after I had rolled my body into winding coils

*Hercules and Acheloüs, Solis*

and darted with savage hissing my furrowed tongue,                    65
he laughed, and the man of Tiryns[5] mocked our arts
and said, 'The labor of my cradle was to conquer snakes,
and even though you, Acheloüs, were to outdo all
the other serpents, what part of the Lernaean hydra will you,
one serpent, be? She was renewed by her wounds                       70
and not one of her heads, a hundred in number, was safely cut
without its neck made stronger by an identical heir.
I vanquished her, branching out with vipers born from the kill
and growing from harm, and, once she was vanquished, I laid her bare.
Now what do you think you're going to do, feigning a serpent's shape,    75
and wielding borrowed weapons, and hidden in precarious form?'
And having spoken, he fastened his fingers in a chain about
the top of my neck: I was being choked as though my throat were pinched
by tongs, and I struggled to tear loose my jaws from the grip of his thumbs.
Defeated in this form, too, I had left only a third,                 80
the form of a fearsome bull. My members changed into a bull, I fight again.
He wraps his arms about the muscles on my left
and as I speed away he follows, pulling me back, and, gripping my hard horns,
he presses them into the ground and upon the deep sand lays me out flat.
And this was not enough: while his fierce right hand held              85

---

5 Hercules' mortal parents were from Tiryns, a city in the Argolid.

my rigid horn, he broke it off and tore it from my mangled brow.
The naiads made it sacred, filling it with fruit and sweet-smelling flowers;
and Good Abundance is now rich because of my horn."
    The river-god had spoken: and a nymph, girt like
Diana, a servant of his, her tresses falling down on both sides,                90
came in and brought all of autumn in the abundant horn
and, as a second course, apples full and ripe.
The light of dawn arrives; and as the sun begins to strike the peaks,
the young men depart, nor did they wait for the river's streams
to settle and glide in peace and for all his waters to subside.                 95
And Acheloüs concealed his rustic face, and his head
deprived of its horn, in the midst of his waves.

### 98-133   Nessus

    The sacrifice of his stolen beauty caused him grief,
but he was otherwise unharmed. The damage to his head
he hides in willow branches or with reeds superimposed.                        100
But you, wild Nessus, were destroyed by passion for
the very same maid, your body pierced by a swift-flying barb.
For as he sought his ancestral walls again with his new bride,
the son of Jove had come to Evenus'[6] rapid waves.
More ample than usual, increased by the winter storms,                         105
the stream was teeming with whirlpools and unable to be crossed.
He has no fear for himself but is worried about his bride
as Nessus approaches, full of strength in his limbs and familiar with
the fording places, and says, "Alcides, use my service to set
her on that bank. Use your own strength and swim!"                             110
Quite pale with fear and fearing both the river and Nessus himself,
the frightened maid of Calydon was handed over by the Aonian[7] man
to Nessus. At once, just as he was, weighed down by the quiver and lion skin—
for both his club and well-curved bow he had thrown to the other bank—
he said, "Since I have undertaken this, let this flood be overcome,"           115
and does not hesitate or seek the place where the stream is most
accessible and spurns to be carried across where the waters would obey.
And just as he has the far bank in his grasp and is picking up the bow
already there, he perceives the voice of his wife, and to Nessus, about to betray
his burden, he cries aloud, "Where has trust in your hooves carried you      120
astray, you violent creature? We mean you, Nessus of double form!
Give heed and do not usurp what is ours!
If you are not moved by fear of me, at least your father's[8] wheel

---

6 A river near Calydon.
7 Hercules is called Aonian, because Aonia is a region of Boeotia, the land of his native Thebes.
8 Ixion, the father of Nessus, had attempted to rape Juno, for which he was punished in Hades by being
    tied to a whirling wheel.

*Hercules, Nessus and Deianira, Baur*

should have the power to prevent you from forbidden lusts.
You'll not escape, though you trust in the help of your equine half;          125
with wounding arrows, not with feet shall I pursue." His final words
proved true, and a shooting arrow pierces the fleeing form.
The barbed iron was protruding from his chest.
As soon as it was pulled out, blood shot forth
from both of the passages, mixed with the poison of Lernaean slime.          130
When Nessus caught it, he says to himself, "Let us not die unavenged,"
and, smearing a shirt with his heated gore, he gives
it as a gift to the ravished maid as a stimulus for love.

### 134-272   *Hercules' Death*

A long period of time intervened, and the deeds
of mighty Hercules had filled the world and his stepmother's hate.          135
The victor from Oechalia[9] was preparing at Cenaeum[10] sacrifices owed
to Jove, when loquacious Rumor reached your ears ahead of him,
O Deianira, who delights in adding falsehood to truth
and, starting as a little thing, grows large through her lies,
reporting that for Iole Amphitryon's[11] son was burning with love.          140
The lover believes, and terrified by the story of the new love,
indulges tears at first and, poor creature, in weeping pours out
her grief. But soon thereafter, she says to herself, "Why weep?

9 Hercules had defeated Eurytus, King of Oechalia, a city of Euboea, and captured Iole, the daughter of
    Eurytus. See Sophocles' *Trachiniae.*
10 In northwest Euboea.
11 Alcmena's husband and mortal "father" of Hercules.

The concubine will take pleasure in these tears of ours.
But since she is coming, I must hurry and hit upon a plan,                    145
while time allows and the other woman does not yet possess our bed.
Shall I complain or keep still? Return to Calydon or stay?
Get out of the house? Or, if for no other reason, stay in the way?
Or what if, remembering that I am your sister, Meleager, I prepare
a daring deed and to show how much insult can do,                            150
how strong a woman's grief can be, I strangle the whore!"
Her mind turns to various courses. To all of them
she preferred to send the cloak imbued with Nessus' blood,
that it should restore the strength of enfeebled love.
And ignorant herself, she gives to Lichas, not knowing what he bears,        155
the cause of her own grief and commands, most pitiful woman, that he
convey that gift to her husband. The hero accepts it unawares,
and draws upon his shoulders the Lernaean hydra's venomous juice.
     While he was offering incense and intercessory prayers to the first flames
and pouring upon the marble altar wine from a flat bowl,                      160
the force of that evil grew warm and, released by the flames,
came out and flowed deeply into the body of Hercules.
As long as he could, with his usual courage he repressed his groans.
But after his endurance was surpassed by the pains, he overturned
the altar and filled the woods of Oeta[12] with his cries.                   165
He tries without delay to tear away the death-bearing cloak:
but where it is pulled, it pulls away his skin, a disgusting thing to tell,
and either sticks to his limbs when he tries in vain to tear it away
or else exposes his lacerated limbs and enormous bones.
The gore itself hisses like a plate glowing with heat when dipped into       170
a frigid lake and boils with the poison's heat.
The greedy flames consume his vital parts without restraint
and from his body flows dark blue sweat;
his roasting sinews sizzle and as the invisible plague liquefies
his marrow, he raises his open hands to the stars                            175
and cries aloud, "Saturnia,[13] glut yourself upon our ruin, glut yourself,
and look at this pestilence, O cruel one, from above
and sate your savage heart. Or if I may be pitied by a foe,
that is, by you, remove my soul, detested and sick
from awful torments and born for toils.                                      180
To me will death be a gift; a gift suitable for a stepmother to give!
For this did I overthrow Busiris who stained his shrines
with strangers' blood? And from ferocious Antaeus stole
his mother's nourishment? And that the Iberian[14] shepherd's triple form

---

12 A mountain range in northern Greece.
13 Juno, daughter of Saturn.
14 Geryon.

did not deter me, or your triple form, either, Cerberus?                                       185
That you, my hands, oppressed the strong bull's horns?
That Elis knows your work, the Stymphalian waters, and the
Parthenian grove? Through your strength
the belt adorned with Thermodontic gold was brought back,
and apples kept under the sleepless dragon's constant guard?                                   190
That Centaurs could not defend themselves against me, nor the boar
that devastated Arcady? Or that the hydra found no defense
in growing larger from her wounds and gaining redoubled strength?
And what about the Thracian horses I saw made fat
with human blood and their stables filled with mangled flesh,                                  195
and, having seen, struck down both the horses and their lord?
The massive creature of Nemea lies vanquished by these arms:
I bore the sky upon this neck.[15] The cruel wife of Jove
is wearied by giving orders: I remain unworn by deeds!
But here is now a new kind of plague that neither strength                                     200
nor spears nor weapons can resist. There wanders deep within
my lungs a consuming fire that feeds upon all my limbs.
Yet still Eurystheus thrives! And are there those who believe
that gods exist?" he said, and over lofty Oeta he wanders ill
and not unlike a bull that bears a hunter's shaft                                              205
implanted in its body when the author of the deed has fled.
If you were there, you would see him often uttering groans,
and often bellowing and often attempting to tear off the whole cloak
and laying low great trunks of trees and full of wrath upon
the mountains or stretching forth his arms to his father's sky.                                210
         And lo, he catches sight of Lichas there hiding in fear
beneath a hollow rock, and when his pain had gathered all
its fury, he said, "Did you, O Lichas, give me this deadly gift?
Will you become the author of my death?" The other quakes
and pales with fear and timidly offers words of excuse.                                        215
Alcides snatches him up as he speaks on bended knees
and whirling him around thrice and four times hurls the man
with greater force than a catapult into the Euboean waves.
The man still hanging in the airy breezes grew hard:
as rains are held to congeal within the frigid winds                                           220
and turn to snow, and from the churning snows a soft mass
to be compressed and rolled together, compacted into hail,
just so was he hurled by those strong arms out upon the void
and bloodless with fear and possessing not a drop
of moisture he was turned, so earlier ages say, to a rigid mass of flint.                      225
A crag stands out even now just above the plain of the Euboean deep,
preserving the vestiges of its human form, and sailors fear,

---

15 Hercules held the sky on his neck while Atlas fetched the golden apples of the Hesperides.

as if it had sensation, to tread upon it and name
it Lichas. But you, O famous offspring of Jove,
felled trees that upon steep Oeta had grown                                    230
and built them into a pyre and order Poeas' son,[16] who tended the fire
he set beneath, to bear the bow and ample quiver and
the arrows that once again would behold the kingdom of Troy.
And while the pile is consumed by the greedy fires,
you spread the Nemean pelt upon the top of the heap of wood                     235
and with your neck placed in repose upon your club lie back,
your face no different than if you were reclining as a banqueter,
in garlands crowned, amidst the vessels filled with unmixed wine.
The flames, now sturdy and spreading on every side,
were heading for those fearless limbs and their                                240
despiser. The gods were fearful for the savior of the earth.
Saturnius,[17] because he knew this, addresses them
with happy mien, "Your concern is our joy
O gods of heaven, and I am pleased and grateful with all my heart
that I am called the ruler and father of a thankful tribe                       245
and that my offspring is safe through your favor as well.
For though this favor results from his extraordinary deeds,
I'm in your debt no less. However, let not your faithful hearts
grow faint with groundless fear. Pay no heed to Oeta's flames!
The one who vanquished all will vanquish the fires you see,                     250
and only his maternal part will perceive the might
of Vulcan. The eternal part he derives from me is immune
and free of death and invincible by any flame.
This part, its role on earth now done, I shall welcome within
the shores of heaven and trust that my deed will make                          255
the gods all rejoice. Nevertheless, if anyone, anyone
by chance shall take it ill that Hercules is a god, that person will
object to the prize, but recognize its merits and, even unwillingly, approve."
The gods agree. The royal consort also appeared to accept
the words of Jove without a stern face, all at least except                     260
his final words, and was annoyed that she had been rebuked.
Whatever was destructible by flame had Mulciber[18] by now
removed, and the figure of Hercules did not remain
in recognizable form. He has nothing derived from
his mother's form and keeps only the marks of Jove.                            265
And as a serpent, when old age is sloughed off with its skin,
rejoices renewed and gleams within its fresh new scales,
just so, when the Tirynthian shed his mortal limbs,

---

16 Philoctetes. See Sophocles' *Philoctetes.*
17 Jupiter.
18 An epithet of Vulcan, the "Smelter."

*Death and Deification of Hercules, Baur*

he waxes in his better part and assumes a greater size,
becoming august with the increased weight of his rank.                          270
The all-powerful father caught him up into the hollow clouds
and in his four-horse chariot[19] introduced him to the shining stars.

### 273-323  *Alcmena, Juno, and Galathis*

The weight was felt by Atlas. And even then Eurystheus,
the son of Sthenelus, had not ended his anger and furiously plied the hate
he had for the father against his offspring. Yet, troubled by her life's long cares, 275
Alcmena of Argos[20] has in Iole now a place to lay her ancient complaints,
and someone to whom to recount the well-attested labors of her son,
or those of her own. Obeying Hercules' commands, Hyllus[21] had
received Iole into his marriage chamber and into his heart,
and filled her womb with well-born seed; to her did thus                         280
Alcmena begin: "May the gods be kind to you at least
and take away all delay that day when your time arrives
and you invoke Ilithyia[22] the guardian of those in fearful travail,
the one who for Juno's sake was so hard on me.
For when the natal day of labor-bearing Hercules                                 285
arrived and the tenth sign was being pressed by the sun,
the heaviness was stretching my womb and the burden was
so great that you could say that the author of the hidden weight

---

19 Compare the apotheosis of Romulus, 14. 818-28.
20 Originally of Tiryns in the Argolid, Alcmena went with Amphitryon, her husband, into exile to
   Thebes after he accidentally killed Electryon, her father.
21 Hercules' son.
22 Greek goddess of childbirth.

was Jove. Already the travail was greater than I
could bear. In fact, even now as I speak, cold fear                    290
possesses my limbs, and memory is a part of the pain.
For seven nights and as many days, in agony and weary with woe,
I stretched my hands to heaven and with a great cry
invoked Lucina[23] and the Nixi,[24] her peers.
Lucina came indeed, but, bribed in advance,                    295
desired to hand over to unfair Juno my head.
And as she hears my groans, she sits down upon
that altar before the door and, with her right leg pressed
against her left knee and with her fingers interlocked,
held back my delivery. She also uttered noiseless charms.             300
The charms restrained the birthing I had begun.
I struggle and, out of my mind, place blame in vain
on ingrate Jove and want to die and complain in words
that could have moved hard granite. The Cadmeian matrons are there
and add their prayers and urge me on amid my pain.                    305
Galanthis, one of my attendants and from the common folk,
with flaxen hair, was there, diligent in fulfilling commands
and loved for her assistance. She sensed that something was awry
because of unfair Juno, and, as she often went in and out
the door, she saw the goddess sitting there upon                    310
the altar, holding her hands joined upon her knees,
and says, 'Whoever you are, congratulate our mistress. She's been released!
The prayer of Argive Alcmena in childbirth has been fulfilled.'
The goddess of birth jumped up and in her fear released
the hands she had joined: with these bonds relaxed I am also released.   315
The story goes that Galanthis laughed when she saw the goddess deceived.
The cruel goddess grabbed her by the hair as she laughed
and dragged her and restrained her as she tried to lift her body from
the ground and changed into forelegs her arms.
Her former liveliness remains: nor did her body lose                 320
its color: but her shape is not the same as before.
Because she had helped the one in labor with her lying mouth,
she still gives birth with her mouth and as before frequents our house."[25]

## 324-93  Dryope

     Alcmena spoke and, feeling the warning in her former servant's fate,
she groaned. Her daughter-in-law addressed the grieving woman thus:      325
"O mother, you are moved by the stolen form of one not of our blood,

---

23 Goddess associated with light and the Moon, often identified with Juno or Diana.
24 Or Nixae or Nixūs, a group of three Roman goddesses (or gods?) of childbirth. The name means
   "Pains" and is related to the verb *nitor* "struggle, strain (particularly in childbirth)."
25 Although it was commonly held in antiquity that weasels give birth through their mouths, it is true
   that they often live among the tiles of Italian country roofs.

*Alcmena's Labor, Solis*

when all is said and done. What if I should relate to you
my sister's amazing fate? But tears and grief hold me back
and keep me from speaking. She was her mother's only child
—my father sired me by another woman—and the most famous of all          330
the maids of Oechalia for her beauty, Dryope. After losing her maidenhood
and suffering the force of that god who rules Delphi and Delos both,
Andraemon welcomes her and is considered happy in his wife.
There is a lake that creates with its gradual banks
the form of a sloping seashore; a grove of myrtle crowns its top.          335
Dryope had come here not knowing the fates, and, what
will more offend you, to offer garlands to the nymphs.
Within her bosom she carried the boy, his first year not yet complete,
a gentle burden, and was feeding it with the boon of her tepid milk.
Not far from the pond, imitating the colors of Tyre,          340
in hope of berries, the aquatic lotus bloomed.
Dryope had plucked from it as amusements for her child
some flowers, and I was thinking to do the same, for I
was also there—when I saw that from the flower drops of blood
were dripping and that, quaking with horror, the branches moved.          345
You probably know that, as the rustics were slow to relate,
in fleeing the vile assaults of Priapus, the nymph Lotis was transformed
and, having fixed her visage within this plant, preserved her name.
        "My sister had no knowledge of this. When in fright
she sought to retreat and, with prayers to the nymphs, to depart,          350

her feet were rooted to the ground. She fights to break loose
but nothing moved except her upper body. From below, tough bark
creeps up and little by little confines her groin.
Observing this, she tried to tear her hair with her hands,
but leaves filled her hands: her whole head was bound by leaves.                355
The boy Amphissos, however (for his grandfather Eurytus had bestowed
this name upon him), feels his mother's breast grow hard;
nor when he tugs does the flow of milk ensue.
Observing this cruel fate, I was there and could
not come to your aid, my sister, and, as much as I could,                       360
restrained the growing trunk and branches with my embrace,
and, I confess, I wanted to hide myself within that bark.
        "Behold, her husband Andraemon and pitiful father arrive
and look for Dryope: and, as they look for Dryope, I
point to the lotus. They apply their kisses to the tepid wood,                  365
and embrace and cling to the roots of their tree.
My dear sister had nothing but her face that was
not tree: her tears bedew the leaves that had been
her sorrowful body and, while her mouth could still provide
a path for speech, she filled the air with complaints like these:              370
'If for the wretched they have any care, I swear by the gods
that I did not deserve this evil. I suffer punishment without a crime.
In innocence have we lived. If I lie, may I become dry
and lose the leaves I have and be felled by axes and burned.
But take this infant from his mother's limbs,                                   375
and give him to a nurse and let him often receive
his milk beneath our tree, and play beneath our tree.
And when he learns to talk, teach him to greet
his mother and sadly say, "My mother hides within this trunk."
But give him a fear of pools and keep him from plucking flowers from           380
the trees and let him consider bodies of goddesses all the shrubs.
Farewell dear husband, and you, my sister, and father, too!
If you are still devoted to me, protect our branches from
the sharp sickle's wound and from the browsing flocks.
And since I cannot bend down to you,                                            385
raise up your arms to me and come to our lips
while yet I have touch and lift up my little one to me!
No more can I speak, for over my fair white neck
soft bark is creeping. The top of the tree is covering me.
Remove your hands from my eyes. Without your pious act                          390
the spreading bark itself is closing my dying eyes!'
Together her lips had ceased to speak and to be. And long
the branches, freshly created from her transformed body, stayed warm."

### 394-417    *Iolaus, Callirhoë's Sons*

And while Iole was telling her amazing tale and while
Alcmena, though crying herself, used her thumbs to dry                    395
the tears of Eurytus's daughter, a strange thing occurred
that checked all grief. For on the lofty threshold stood
not quite a boy, concealing his cheeks in uncertain down:
behold, Iolaus is there, his face restored to its early years.
This gift had Junonian Hebe given to him,                                 400
persuaded by the prayers of the man. And when she prepared to swear
that after this man never to another would she give such a gift,
she met the opposition of Themis:[26] "For even now is Thebes
astir with civil war," she said, " and by no means will Capaneus[27]
be vanquished except by Jove, and brothers[28] will be equal in wounds,  405
and earth will open up and the prophet,[29] still living, will see
her shades; and a son[30] will take vengeance upon a parent to avenge
a parent and be pious and accursed by one and the same deed,
confounded by woe and driven in exile from mind and home
and harried by the avenging Eumenides[31] of his mother and her shades,  410
until the time his wife[32] shall demand of him the fatal gold[33]
and when the Phegeian[34] sword shall have tapped a kinsman's side.
Callirhoë, Acheloüs' daughter, will then at last as a suppliant beg
of mighty Jove that he add years to her infant sons
and not leave the murder of the avenger[35] unavenged.                   415
Persuaded by her words, Jupiter will use in advance his stepdaughter's gifts[36]
(she was his daughter-in-law,[37] too,) to make grown men of those in beardless years."

---

26 Greek goddess of Justice.
27 One of the seven against Thebes, whom Zeus struck by lightning. See Aeschylus' *Seven vs. Thebes,*
   and Euripides' *Suppliants.*
28 Eteocles and Polyneices, the sons of Oedipus, who slay each other.
29 Amphiaräus.
30 To avenge his father's death, Alcmaeon will slay his mother Eriphyle, who had required her husband
   Amphiaräus to support the Argive expedition against Thebes. Eriphyle had a "marriage contract"
   that allowed her to prevail in all disputes with her husband. Knowing this, Polyneices bribed her
   with the golden necklace of his mother Harmonia to lend her support for the war against Thebes.
31 The more correct term would have been *Erinyes* "Furies."
32 Callirhoë, daughter of Acheloüs, second wife of Alcmaeon.
33 Since Alcmaeon had already given Eriphyle's necklace to his first wife, the daughter of Phegeus, he
   had to return to Psophis to try to retrieve it through false pretenses. Phegeus discovers the truth and
   has his sons murder Alcmaeon.
34 Belonging to Phegeus, king of Psophis, and father of Alphesiboea, the first wife of Alcmaeon. See
   on 411.
35 Translating *ultoris* (of Ms F), referring to Alcmaeon, who had avenged his father Amphiaräus. Ms M
   has *victoris,* "of the victor," accepted by Ehwald, Anderson, and Tarrant, who brackets the line.
36 I. e., the power of Hebe, goddess of youth, to make boys into young men.
37 Hebe was the daughter of Juno, born without a father, and the wife of Jupiter's deified son Hercules.
   The boys grow immediately to manhood and avenge their father Alcmaeon. Hes., *Theog.* 922-23,
   represents a different tradition, that Zeus and Hera were the parents of Hebe.

### 418-53   *Miletus*

As soon as the prophetic mouth of Themis, who knows
the future, told all this, the gods above in varied speeches did protest,
and raised a murmur, wanting to know why others had not                                    420
this gift as well. Pallantias[38] complains of her husband's aged years,
and gentle Ceres complains that Iasion[39] has grown gray,
while Mulciber[40] demands that life be restored
to Erichthonius,[41] and care for the future touches Venus, too,
who bargains to renew Anchises' years.                                                     425
Each god has a special concern: sedition is growing, stirred
by partiality, until Jupiter opened his mouth
and said, "Oh, if you have any sense of respect for me,
where are you headed with this? Does anyone think
he has the power to overcome the fates? By the fates did Iolaus turn                        430
again to his former years. To the fates the sons Callirhoë owe
their growth to manhood, not to ambition or arms.
And that you may bear this with better spirit, you as well
as I are ruled by the fates. If to change them I had the strength,
advancing years would not bend low our Aeacus now,                                         435
and Rhadamanthus would have the eternal flower of youth
along with my own Minos, who for the bitter weight of age
is held in contempt and reigns no more with the status he had before."
        Jove's words moved the gods and none continued to complain
when seeing Rhadamanthus and Aeacus weary with age,                                        440
and also Minos, who while he was in the fullness of life
had overawed great nations merely with his name;
yet now he was feeble and feared Miletus, Deione's son
and proud in his father Phoebus and in the strength of youth,
and, though Minos thought he was rising against his realm,                                 445
he nonetheless dared not bar him from his ancestral home.
Miletus, you flee of your own volition and with a swift bark
pass through the Aegean waters and on Asia's shores
build walls that bear their founder's name.[42]
In this place, as she follows the curves of her father's banks,                            450
the daughter of Meander, so often flowing back upon himself,
is known by you, Cyanee, with exceptional beauty endowed,
who brought forth children, Byblis and Caunus, twins.

---

38 Aurora, daughter of the Titan Pallas and wife of Tithonus.
39 Son of Jupiter and the Pleiad Electra, brother of Dardanus, and lover of Ceres.
40 Vulcan.
41 The son of Vulcan (Hephaestus), "a child without a mother born," See 2. 553 with note.
42 The Ionian city of Miletus.

### 454-665   Byblis and Caunus

The case of Byblis shows that girls should love what they should,
since Byblis was swept away by desire for her brother, of Apollo's line,       455
and not as a sister did she love her brother nor as she should.
At first in fact she does not recognize any fires
or think she does anything wrong when she often joins
her kisses to his and wraps her arms about her brother's neck;
by piety's deceitful guise is she long misled.                                 460
And little by little her love is bent, and she decks herself out
when planning to visit her brother and tries too hard
to look lovely and, if any other girl looks lovelier to him,
she envies her. But she does not yet see herself and, subject to this flame,
expresses no hope, even though it rages within her heart.                      465
She sometimes calls him master, sometimes she hates the names
that blood-kin use, preferring him to call her Byblis instead of sister now.
    But in her waking hours she dared not let lewd hopes
invade her mind; when once dissolved in peaceful repose,
she often sees what she desires: she also saw her body in                      470
her brother's embrace and blushed even as she lay in sleep.
Sleep goes away; she long lies silent and seeks the vision of herself
again that she had seen in repose and with hesitating mind declares:
"O wretched me! what does the still night's vision mean?
How much would I avoid what it suggests! Why did I see these dreams?           475
He is indeed a handsome man, even to hostile eyes,
and pleasing, and I could love him were he not
my brother and were he suitable for me. But being his sister offends.
So long as waking I never attempt to commit such a thing,
may sleep return to me often with a similar dream!                             480
In sleep there is no witness, nor absent is simulated desire.
By Venus and winged Cupid with his tender mother, how great
the joys I felt! How clearly was I touched by desire!
How fully did I yield in the depths of my heart!
How pleasing it is to recall it! Even though the pleasure was brief,           485
and night ran swift in envy of our schemes.
    "Alas, if only I could be united by changing my name,
how fine a daughter-in-law, Caunus, to your father would I be!
How fine a son-in-law, Caunus, to my father would you be!
All things in common would we own, if the gods made it so,                     490
except our grandparents: I'd want you to be more nobly born than I!
You will, therefore, make somebody a mother, you most beautiful man;
to wretched me, however, allotted the same parents as you,
will you be nothing but a brother. We shall share only what offends.
What do those visions mean therefore to me? What sort of weight               495
do dreams have anyway? Or do dreams even have any weight?

Gods help me! But gods did possess their sisters after all.
Thus Saturn married Ops,[43] related to him by blood,
Oceanus, Tethys[44], and Juno, Olympus' king.
The gods have their own laws! Why do I try to judge the ways          500
of men by those of heaven and by those different bonds?
Forbidden passion will either be dispelled from our heart,
or if I cannot do that, I pray that I may die instead,
and on my couch in death be laid, and lying there receive
my brother's kisses. But such a thing requires the will of two!       505
Suppose it pleases me: he will think it a crime.
But Aeolus' sons shunned not their sisters' beds![45]
Yet where did I learn of them? Why do I cite such examples as these?
What madness is this? Vile flames, get you far away from here,
and only as is meet for a sister let my brother be loved!             510
If, though, he first were taken himself with love for me,
perhaps to his passion I might accede.
Since I would not have refused his courtship, I myself
shall court him! Will you be able to speak? Able to confess?
I shall be able, for love will compel! Or if shame seals my lips,     515
a private letter will confess my hidden fires!"
　　　This pleases her, this opinion conquers her faltering mind.
She lifts herself upon her side, with her left elbow's support,
and says, "He'll see: let us confess our unsound love!
Alas for me, where am I falling? What fire does my mind conceive?"    520
Reflecting thus, she set down the words with trembling hand.
Her right hand holds the stylus, the other holds the tablet's empty wax.
She starts and stops, she writes, and what she writes she faults,
she makes a note and erases it, changes, blames, and approves
and lays aside in turn the tablet and takes it up again.              525
She knows not what she wants; whatever she seems about to do
displeases her. Upon her face there is boldness mixed with shame.
Although she had written "sister," she decided to delete that word
and in the place of "sister" incised these words upon the corrected wax:
"Good health to you, not to be had by the lover who sends it to you   530
unless you return it: it causes shame, shame, to disclose the name,
and if you ask what I desire, I should wish that without my name
my cause might be pled, and that I as Byblis remain unknown
until the hope of my prayers' fulfillment has been made sure.
You could have seen the signs of a wounded breast:                    535
my wasting color and complexion and often teary eyes
and sighs provoked for no apparent cause,

---

43 Roman goddess of Plenty.
44 The Titan sea-goddess.
45 The six sons of Aeolus, god of the winds, married their sisters. See Hom. *Od.* 10. 7-12.

my frequent embraces, and, if perhaps you had noticed them,
the kisses that did not feel like those a sister would give.
Although I bore a grievous wound within my soul,                                        540
and though the fiery madness raged within me, I did everything
(the gods are my witness) to return at last to health,
and fought at length to flee the violent arms
of Cupid, unhappy me, and bore much harsher things
than you might think a girl could endure. I'm forced to confess,                        545
now vanquished, and to beg your help with my fearful pleas.
To save, to destroy a lover you have the power alone:
choose which to do. No enemy begs this of you,
but she who already very closely joined to you seeks closer still
to be and with a tighter bond to be bound to you.                                        550
Old graybeards will know the laws, and what is allowed and wrong
and right, let them inquire of that and continue their scrutiny of the laws.
To those in our years is Venus compliant and bold.
We do not know yet what is allowed, and think that anything
is fair, and follow the examples of the mighty gods.                                     555
By neither a harsh father nor reverence for repute
nor fear will we be restrained: but if there be a cause for fear,
beneath the name of brother we shall cover our stolen joys.
I am at liberty to tell you my hidden thoughts:
we hug each other and publicly join our lips.                                            560
How much is lacking yet? Have pity on one confessing her love,
refusing to confess, had the ultimate passion not compelled;
earn not the fame, inscribed upon my tomb, of having caused my death."
        Her hand plowed full the wax with such vain words,
and, when she stopped, the final line clung to the tablet's very edge.                   565
She signed at once the crimes impressed therein with her jeweled seal
and stained the letter with her tears (all moisture had left her tongue).
She summoned one of her servants, as she blushed with shame,
and, flattering him nervously, said, "Most faithful servant, take
this letter,"—and after a long pause—"to our brother, please."                          570
The tablet slipped, as she handed it over, and fell from her hands.
Disturbed by the omen, she dispatched it just the same. The servant found
a suitable moment and went and delivered the words lying hidden within.
The scion of Maeander[46] was thunderstruck with instant rage
and, after reading only a part, cast down the tablet he had received,                    575
and, scarcely restraining his hands from the frightened servant's throat,
exclaims, "O wicked author of forbidden love, flee while you can,
for if your doom didn't bring with it our own disgrace,
you surely would have paid me with your death!"
The servant flees in terror and to his mistress reports the fierce                       580

46 Caunus, son of Miletus, and grandson of Maeander.

response of Caunus. You hear your rejection, Byblis, and pale.
Your body, beset by an icy chill, is overcome with fright.
Yet as your senses return, your passions return in like degree,
and, gasping for air, your tongue utters words like these:
"Just what I deserve! For why was I so bold as to give proof                 585
of this my wound? Why, when such things were to be concealed,
was I so quick to entrust my words to a tablet written in haste?
I should have tried to express in ambiguous terms
the feelings of my mind. To assure a favorable wind
I should have tested with part of the sail the nature of the breeze         590
and run my course over the sea in safety, but now
I've filled the sails with uncertain winds.
And so I'm being thrust upon the rocks and overwhelmed
and dashed by the ocean, and my sails have no means of retreat.
      "Consider also that by obvious omens I was being restrained          595
from giving in to my love when, as I was bidding my servant to bear
the message, the waxen tablet fell from my hand and caused my hopes to fall.
Was not that day, or even all my desire, or rather at least
the day to be postponed? For god himself had warned
and given certain signs, if only I had not lost my wits.                    600
I should have spoken directly myself and not relied upon
the wax and opened up my passions face to face.
He would have seen the tears, seen a lover's face;
I could have said more than the tablet could contain.
I could have placed my arms about his unwilling neck,                       605
and, if rejected, I could have appeared about to die,
embraced his feet, and, lying prostrate, begged him for my life.
I could have done all manner of things, and if each single deed
did not succeed, then all together might have bent his will.
Perhaps the messenger was partly at fault: he didn't make                   610
the right approach, didn't choose the right moment, I think,
and didn't wait for an hour when his mind was free of other things.
      "These reasons weakened my case, for he was not of tigress born,
nor does he have a heart of solid iron or rigid flint
or adamantine steel, nor is that man suckled by a lioness.                  615
He shall be vanquished! He must be sought out again, and I
shall never weary in my attempts so long as I draw breath.
For in the first place, if it were possible to undo what I have done,
I shouldn't have done it; second best is for my plan to prevail!
Indeed, though I were to abandon my desires, he cannot but                  620
retain forever the memory of my reckless deeds.
And I shall seem inconstant in my desires, were I to desist,
or even to have tempted him and to have trapped him by deceit,
for surely he will think that I was not overwhelmed by him

whose burning urgings are most powerful, a god, but merely by lust!　625
And finally, I cannot undo the wrong that I have done!
I wrote, and I pursued: my intentions have been disclosed;
I cannot be thought without guilt simply by doing nothing more.
So much remains to fulfill my desires, so little to complete my crime."
She spoke and, (so great was the strife within her uncertain mind)　630
although she regrets having tried, she wants to try again. She shuns
restraint and commits herself to be rejected again and again.
When soon there is no end to this, the man flees both country and crime
and lays down new walls[47] in a foreign land.
They say in truth that then Miletus' wretched child　635
completely lost her senses; in truth she then tore from her breast
her robe and beat her arms as she raged;
and now she is plainly mad and confesses her hope
for unpermitted love by leaving her detested household gods
and fatherland and follows her fugitive brother's tracks.　640
And just as the Ismarian[48] bacchants, O son of Semele,
are moved by your thyrsus[49] and celebrate your triennial rites,
no differently did the women of Bubassus[50] see Byblis raise
a howl through the fields. When these were left behind,
she roams through Caria and warlike Leleges[51] and Lycia.　645
Already had she left Cragos[52] behind and Limyre[53] and Xanthus' waves
and even the ridge where the Chimaera[54] displays her fire,
the breast and face of a lion, and a serpent's tail.
Beyond the forested ridge, wearied by pursuit, you collapse
and, with your tresses strewn upon the bare ground,　650
there prostrate you press your face, Byblis, against the fallen leaves.
The Lelegeian nymphs try often to lift her in
their gentle arms, often instruct her how to cure her love
and offer comfort to her unhearing mind.
As Byblis lies in silence, her nails clutching the verdant grass,　655
she moistens the grass with a stream of tears.
They say the Naiads had supplied a vein for them
that could not ever dry. What greater gift had they to give?
At once, as drops of pitch ooze from the hewn bark of pine,
or sticky asphalt flowing from the heavy earth,　660
or as, at the arrival of Favonius'[55] gentle breeze,

---

47 The city of Caunus in Caria, a region of Asia Minor.
48 Theban.
49 A spear-like wand, tipped by a pine cone.
50 Town of Caria.
51 Carian tribe noted for piracy.
52 Mountain of Lycia.
53 Town in southwest Lycia on the Limyre river.
54 See 6. 339.
55 The West Wind.

the waves frozen by the cold are softened by the sun,
just so, consumed by her tears, is Phoebean[56] Byblis changed
into a fountain, which now within those vales preserves
the name of its mistress and flows beneath a dusky oak.                      665

### 666-797    Iphis and Ianthe

The hundred cities of Crete would have been filled
with talk about this strange prodigy, had Crete not brought to light
a marvel closer to home when the girl Iphis was transformed.
For once, near the kingdom of Cnossos, the Phaestian land[57]
gave birth to Ligdus, a man of free-born plebeian stock                      670
of unknown family name; his wealth was not greater than
his humble birth, yet the honesty of his life
was free from fault. The ears of his pregnant wife heard
the warning of his words as her labor approached:
"Two things have I prayed for: that you be relieved with minimal pain        675
and that you bear a male. The other lot[58] is too burdensome
and fortune denies it strength. Therefore, although I loath this thing,
if chance would have it that of your labor a girl is born,
unwillingly I give this command (may piety forgive me!), let her be killed."
When he had spoken, they bathed their faces with copious tears,             680
the giver of the order no less than she to whom the order was given.
But Telethusa continues to badger her husband in vain
with prayers that he not restrict so narrowly her hopes.
Unmoved is Ligdus' mind. She scarcely could longer bear
her belly now heavy with its fully ripened weight                            685
when in the middle of the night within the form of a dream
before her couch stood or seemed to stand the daughter of Inachus,[59]
accompanied by a procession of holy ones. Upon her brow was set
the crescent horns with a wreath of grain, yellow with shining gold,
and all her royal ornaments; Anubis[60] the barker was there with her        690
and holy Bubastis,[61] and Apis[62] of varied hue,
and he who represses his voice and with his finger urges the silence of all,[63]
and rattles were there, and Osiris[64] for whom the search is never at an end,

---

56 Byblis as daughter of Miletus is the granddaughter of Apollo.
57 Circumlocution for "Crete," referring to the city of Phaestus.
58 Being female.
59 Io, whom Greeks and Romans associated with the Egyptian Isis.
60 The jackal-headed god.
61 The cat-goddess, to whom cats were both sacred and regularly sacrificed.
62 The sacred bull of Memphis, black with a white diamond on his forehead, the image of an eagle
    on its back, a tail of two colors, and a scarab under its tongue according to Herodotus 3. 28, who
    equates it with Epaphus.
63 Horus, son of Isis and Osiris, in his infant form as Harpocrates, who enjoins silence by pressing his
    finger to his mouth.
64 Husband of Isis and god of fertility.

*Isis and Telthusa, Picart*

and also the foreign[65] serpent filled with poisons producing sleep.
The goddess addressed her as though she had been shaken awake                 695
and seeing clearly: "O Telethusa, one of my own, dismiss
your heavy cares, confound your husband's commands.
And do not hesitate, when Lucina[66] has lightened you in birth,
to raise whatever the child will be. I am a goddess of help;
invoke my aid and I shall bring it; you will not complain                     700
that you have worshiped my power in vain." She warned and left
the room. The Cretan woman rejoiced as she rose from her bed
and lifted her innocent hands as a suppliant to the stars
and prayed that her vision would be fulfilled.

   And when the pains of labor increased and her burden thrust
itself into the air and to the unsuspecting father a female child was born,   705
the mother lied and ordered it to be nurtured as a boy. The deed
gained credence, for the only one aware of the deception was the nurse.
The father gave his prayers of thanks and imposed an ancestral name:
the grandfather had been Iphis. The mother rejoiced in the name
because its gender was common, and she would deceive no one with it.          710
From then on, the lie, a deception born of love, remained concealed.
The dress of the child was a boy's; the face, whether you assign

---

65 Since serpents were not native, it was thought, to Crete; this serpent is an attribute of Isis as goddess
    of healing.
66 See 294.

it to a girl or to a boy, would have been finely formed for either one.
        A third year had already been added to ten, meanwhile,
when, Iphis, your father betrothed fair-haired Ianthe to you,                    715
among the girls of Phaestus most admired for the dowry of
her beauty, Dictaean[67] Telestes' child.
In age they were equal, equal in beauty, and had gained
their first skills from the same teachers in the basics of life.
From this did love touch the tender hearts of both,                             720
imparting an equal wound in both, but not with equal hope:
Ianthe awaits her marriage and the appointed day for the wedding torch
and thinks that the girl she believes will be her husband is a man.
And loving a girl she despairs of having, which itself
increases the flames of her passion, Iphis burns as a maiden for a maid         725
and, hardly holding back her tears, exclaims, "What end remains for me,
whom feelings of a strange love, unnatural and known to none,
have captured? If the gods desired to spare me this,
they should have spared me; if not, and they desired to ruin me,
they should at least have given me a natural and normal woe.                    730
For love does not warm the cow for a cow nor mares for mares:
the ram burns for the ewes, and the stag is pursed by his doe.
The birds mate this way, and among all the creatures that live
no female is for a female seized with desire.
I wish that I were not a female! But yet, lest Crete not spawn every kind        735
of monster, the daughter of the Sun[68] loved the bull,—
a woman at least, desiring a male. More insane is my love than hers,
to tell the truth. But she pursued the object of her lust;
employing deception and the image[69] of a cow, she submitted to
the bull, and it was the adulterer[70] who was deceived.                        740
Though skill should flow my way from all the world,
though Daedalus fly back with his waxen wings,
what could he do for me? Surely not with learned skills
turn me, a girl, into a boy! Nor surely, Ianthe, transform you!
        "So, Iphis, take courage and steel yourself                            745
and banish these foolish fires that cannot be fulfilled!
Admit to yourself that you were born a woman, unless you want to deceive
yourself, and seek what is right and, as a woman, love what you should!
For hope it is that creates, hope it is that nourishes love.
This hope has been denied you by nature. No chaperone                          750
prevents you from a fond embrace, no wary husband's care,
no father's severity, nor does the girl herself refuse your suit,
but nevertheless she cannot be yours, nor, were all things possible,

---

67 Pertaining to Mt. Dicte, hence "Cretan."
68 Pasiphaë, mother of the Minotaur.
69 Constructed for her by Daedalus, 8. 132.
70 The bull.

*Isis, Iphis and Ianthe, Baur*

could you be happy, not even if men and gods should toil to make it so.
Not one of my prayers even now has been left unfulfilled;                    755
the gods have readily given me all they could;
and what I have desired, my father desires, and the girl herself desires,
and future father-in-law, but nature will not have it, more powerful
than all of these, nature who alone works me ill. Lo, the longed-for time
arrives and the wedding day is at hand, and soon my Ianthe will not         760
be mine: in the midst of the waves we will thirst!
For why should Juno who sponsors brides, why should Hymen attend
these rites, where he who receives is absent and both of us must lift the veil?"[71]
She checked her tongue after these words. The other girl yearns
no less and prays, O Hymen, that you quickly come.                          765
Afraid of what Ianthe desires, Telethusa seeks delay,
postponing now by feigning illness, often giving in excuse
ill-omened visions. By now she had used up every resource
of pretense, and the long deferred date for the wedding had
arrived, and one day only remained. But she removed                         770
the fillets from both her own and her daughter's head.
With hair flowing freely she embraced the altar and said,
"O Isis, thou who dost dwell in Paraetonium[72] and the Mareotic fields[73]
and Pharos[74] and the Nile divided into seven horns,
assist us, I pray, and bring healing to our fear!                           775

---

71 "Receives," translating *qui ducat*. The Roman groom "leads/receives" the bride (accusative) into his
    household, the bride "lifts the veil for her husband" *nubet* (with dative).
72 Town on the coast of North Africa.
73 Territory around Mareota, a lake and city in Lower Egypt.
74 A little island lying opposite Alexandria that was famous for its lighthouse.

For thee, O goddess, thee and thine emblems did I see of old
and recognized them all and the accompanying brass
and sound of the sistrum,[75] and marked within my mindful heart
what you decreed. Because my daughter lives and I was not condemned,
behold, all this is thy plan and gift. Have pity on the both of us          780
and lend thine aid!" Her tears followed her words.
The goddess appeared to have made her altar move (and it had in fact),
the temple doors trembled and her horns that imitated the moon
gleamed bright and the sound of the rattling sistrum was heard.
Not yet quite free from fear, but happy with this favorable sign,          785
the mother left the temple. Iphis attended her as she went,
the daughter's pace now faster than usual, no pallor remaining in her face,
her strength increased, her countenance more severe,
her unkempt tresses reduced in length,
possessing more vigor than she had as a girl. For you who were          790
but lately a girl are now a boy! Give the temples their due!
Be glad with unfearing confidence! They do give the temples their gifts
and add an inscription. The inscription contained a brief ode:
A ·Boy· Paid· Dues· That· Iphis· A· Girl· Had· Vowed.
The light of the following day had spread its rays over the whole world          795
when Venus and Juno and Hymen at the wedding fires
assembled and as a boy did Iphis his Ianthe gain.

---

75 A kind of rattle consisting of a metal frame holding metal rods, used in the worship of Isis.

# BOOK 10

## 1-85  Orpheus and Eurydice

From there Hymen, garbed in his saffron robe, departs
and through the vast sky makes for the Ciconians'[1] shores,
invoked by Orpheus' voice, but all in vain.
Though he was present, he brought neither ceremonial words
nor joyful countenances nor omen of good luck.                                    5
The very torch he carried was ever hissing smoke that filled
the eyes with tears and found no flame even when waved about.
The outcome was worse than the omen: for as the brand-new bride,
attended by a host of naiads, wanders about the grassy green,
a serpent bites her on the ankle, and she succumbs.                               10
As soon as the Rhodopeian[2] bard had filled the upper air
with his complaint, he would not leave even the shades below
untried and dared to make the descent to the Styx through the gate
of Taenarus,[3] and through the unsubstantial folk and phantoms that had
obtained a tomb he made his way to Persephone and to the one who reigned   15
as lord of the shades, and as he plied the strings to his songs,
declares, "Ye powers divine of the world set beneath the earth,
to which all we who were mortal born relapse,
if it is lawful and ye allow me, with all false obscurity laid aside,
to tell the truth, not here to see dim Tartarus ·                                20

---

1 Thracians, like Orpheus.
2 A Thracian mountain, named for Rhodope. See 6. 87-89 and note. Orpheus was from Thrace.
3 Southernmost promontory of the Peloponnesus, thought to be an entrance to the underworld.

*Eurydice Bitten by Serpent, Anonymous, Venice ca. 1513*

did I descend nor to curb the triple necks,
all shaggy with serpents, of Medusa's monstrous child:
the cause of my journey is a wife, in whom a trodden viper poured
its venom and stole away the waxing years of her youth.
I wanted to endure it and shall not deny that I have tried:                    25
but Love has conquered. The god is well known in the realm above,
if here, I do not know, yet I divine that even here is he well known,
if not untrue that tale of ancient plunder be,
and Love did join the two of you as well. Through this frightful place,
through this vast Chaos and the silence of this enormous realm,              30
reweave, I pray you, Eurydice's too hurried fate.
We, who tarry but a little while above, owe our all to you,
and later—or sooner—hasten to a single resting place.
Our paths are all directed here, our final home, and ye
possess the longest dominion over human kind.                               35
This woman, when ripe with age she has duly spent her years,
will also be within your power. We ask to enjoy her as a boon;
but if the fates refuse this respite for a wife, my desire
is not to go back: rejoice in the death of two."

    The bloodless spirits wept for him as he sang           40
and moved the strings to his words; and Tantalus sought not
to catch the retreating wave, and Ixion's wheel, amazed, stood still,
the vultures tore not at the liver and the Belides tended not
their urns, and, Sisyphus, you sat down upon your rock.
The story goes that then for the first time tears made wet                  45
the cheeks of the Eumenides, overcome by the song,

*Orpheus Charms Pluto and Proserpina, Solis*

nor could the royal consort nor he who rules below refuse his prayer;
they summon Eurydice: she was among the recent shades
and entered with a step made slow by her wound.
The hero of Rhodope received her together with the decree                    50
that he not turn back his eyes toward her until he had left
the vale of Avernus,[4] or what they granted would be undone.
In mutual silence they seize the rising path,
obscure, steep, dense with murky fog,
and were not far from the verge of upper earth:                              55
here, lest she falter, in fear and eager to see,
he bent in love his eyes, and straightway she slipped back
and stretching out arms and seeking to catch and be caught,
the unhappy one[5] clasped nothing but the retreating air.
And dying again, of her husband she made no complaint                        60
(what could she blame except that she had been loved?)
and said her final "farewell," which now his ears could scarcely hear,
and wended her way again to where she had been.
        Struck dumb was Orpheus by his wife's double death, just like
the one[6] who saw with fright the dog's triple necks, the middle one        65

---

4 Lake Avernus on the bay of Naples was considered an entrance to the Underworld. Vergil, *Aeneid* 6.
   237-240, says that the Greeks derived the word from *aornon* "birdless" because the lake's fetid
   odor prevented birds from flying over it.
5 Whether Orpheus or Eurydice Ovid leaves ambiguous, perhaps deliberately since the actions are
   appropriate for both.
6 A unidentified man was turned to stone at the sight of Cerberus, led in chains to the upper world by
   Hercules.

*Orpheus Looks Back at Eurydice, Baur*

in chains, whose fear did not abate until by nature herself
his previous body was dressed in stone;
and he who drew blame upon himself, Olenos, and wished
to seem guilty, and you, so confident in your beauty's form,
unhappy Lethaea,[7] formerly two hearts completely joined,      70
now stones, which rainy Ida[8] supports.
He prayed in vain and wanted to cross over again:
the ferry man blocked his way. For seven days, nevertheless,
without the gift of Ceres he sat in squalor upon the bank;
his nourishment was sorrow, grief of mind and tears.      75
Complaining that the gods of Erebos[9] were cruel, he withdrew
to lofty Rhodope and Haemus,[10] buffeted by Aquilo's[11] winds.
    A third time had Titan bound and finished the year
in watery Pisces while Orpheus shunned all love
of women, either because it had brought him woe      80
or he had given his pledge; yet many women burned
to hold the bard in their embrace, many, rejected, felt grief.
The author was he of the custom among the tribes of Thrace
of shifting their love to tender youths and those at the verge of youth
and plucking that brief spring of life and those first buds.      85

---

7 The wife of Olenus, who had offended some goddess by boasting of her beauty. Olenus gained his
    wish of sharing, though innocent himself, the fate of his wife.
8 The mountain in Crete.
9 Greek for "Darkness," i. e., the Underworld.
10 Another mountain in Thrace.
11 The North Wind.

## 86-142  *Cyparissus*

There was a hill and on the hill a field
of very great expanse that blades of grass made green.
There was no shade, but after the god-sprung bard
had there sat down and moved his strings to sound,
the shade arrived: not absent was the Chaonian tree,[12]                90
and not the Heliades' grove,[13] nor the oak's lofty boughs,
nor supple lindens, nor beech and laurel unwed;[14]
and fragile hazels came and the ash, so useful for spears,
and firs, free of knots, and holm-oak, with acorns bowed,
the genial plane-tree and maple of varied hue,                          95
and river-dwelling willows and the lotus, that in water thrives,
and box, ever green, and slender tamarisks
and double-colored myrtle and viburnum, with berries blue.
And you came too, ivy of winding foot, and in your train
the grape-bearing vines and, wrapped in vines, the elms                100
and mountain ash and spruces and arbutus, weighed down
with ruddy fruit, and pliant palms, the victor's prize,
and pine, with high-girt foliage and leafy peak,
held dear by the mother of the gods, if Cybele's Attis[15] shed
in truth his human form for it and hardened within that trunk.         105
       The cypress, resembling a cone, was among this crowd,
a tree now, earlier a boy beloved by that god
who rules his lyre with strings and with strings his bow.
For by the nymphs that dwelt in Carthaea's[16] fields
a stag was held sacred, whose expansive rack                           110
supplied its head with lofty shade.
The antlers shone with gold, and from its sleek neck
a jeweled collar hung and over its shoulders fell.
A silver amulet, bound with slender rawhide, played
upon his forehead; and from both ears similar beads                    115
of bronze about its hollow temples beamed.
Quite free of fear, all natural caution laid aside,
it used to frequent human homes and offer its neck
for stroking to hands however unknown.
But more than to anyone was it dear to you,                            120
O Cyparissus, you the most handsome of Ceos' folk:

---

12 The oak of Chaonia in Epirus, sacred to Jupiter at Dodona.
13 The daughters of Helios were transformed into poplars: Ovid, *Ep. ex Ponto* 1. 2. 33. See *Met.* 2. 340-66.
14 Alluding to Daphne.
15 The beautiful Phrygian shepherd loved by Cybele. Here alone is there allusion to his having been changed into a fir tree, beneath which he had emasculated himself after Cybele had maddened him.
16 Carthaea was a town on the island of Ceos. See on 7. 368.

*Apollo and Cyparissus, Baur*

you led the stag to fresh pastures, you led it to springs
of flowing water, you used to weave varied flowers for
its antlers, now sitting as a rider upon its back,
now curbing its mouth with purple reins.                                  125
     It was the heat of noon, and in the sultry sun
the curving arms of the shore-dwelling Crab grew warm:
the weary stag lay its limbs upon the grassy earth
and drew forth the cool from the woody shade.
The boy Cyparissus unwittingly pierced it with                            130
his well-honed javelin and, when he saw it dying from the painful wound,
decided he wanted to die as well. What comforting words
did Phoebus not speak and what admonitions that he mourn
in moderation and in proportion to the cause! The other moans
no less and begs of the gods a final favor: to let him forever grieve.    135
His vital fluids now exhausted by the endless flood of tears,
his members began to turn to the color of green,
and now those locks which lately hung upon his snowy brow,
began to take the shape of bristling foliage and, now stiff
with graceful top, to gaze upon the starry sky.                           140
The god groaned with sorrow and said, "You will be mourned
by us, and you will mourn for others and attend those who grieve."

*Orpheus Charms the Beasts, Anonymous, Venice ca. 1513*

### 143-739   *The Songs of Orpheus*

The bard had attracted such a grove and sat within
the gathering of wild beasts and birds, in the middle of the crowd.
When he had sufficiently moved and tested the strings with his thumb          145
and heard the varied modes in concord ring, no matter how diverse
the melody, he moved his voice with the following song:
"O mother Muse,[17] from Jove, for all things obey the rule of Jove,
inspire our song! Jove's power I've often told
before: of Giants have I with sterner plectrum sung                           150
and thunderbolts victoriously strewn upon Phlegraean[18] fields.
A slenderer lyre is needed now. Let us sing of boys
beloved of gods, and girls smitten by forbidden fires
who earned the punishment they deserved for lust.

### 155-219   *Ganymede, Hyacinth*

"The king of the gods burned once for Phrygian Ganymede                       155
and something was found that Jupiter preferred to be than what
he was. He deigns, however, not to be changed to any bird
except the one that had the strength to bear his thunderbolts.
Without delay he beat the air with his deceitful wings
and stole away the Iliad[19] boy, who even now mixes the cups                 160
and serves, against the will of Juno, nectar for Jove.

---

17 Orpheus was son of Apollo and the Muse Calliope.
18 Phlegra 'Flaming' was a region of Macedonia, scene of the battle between the Giants and
   Olympians.
19 I. e., Trojan.

*Rape of Ganymede, Picart*

"Amyclus' son,[20] you also would Phoebus have set within the sky
if only the gloomy fates had granted a place to put you there.
Where possible, though, you are immortal, and when the spring
repels the winter and Aries[21] takes watery Pisces'[22] place,                          165
you always rise and flower upon the greening turf.
Before all others did my father delight in you, and Delphi, whose place
was in the center of the globe, lacked its presiding deity
whenever the god visited Eurotas[23] and Sparta that has no walls;
at that time the god holds in honor neither his arrows nor lyre:                          170
unmindful of his nature, he refuses not to bear the hunting nets,
or to restrain the hounds or to venture as a companion upon
the mountain's rugged ridge, feeding with long association his flames.
As Titan[24] was nearly now midway between the coming and banishment
of night, and was standing at equal distance from both,                                  175
they lightened their bodies of raiment and from the rich olive's oil
gleamed bright and with the broad discus begin to compete.
Into the airy breezes Phoebus balanced and cast it first
and with its weight dispersed the opposing clouds.
The heavy discus fell after a long time upon the solid ground                            180

20 Hyacinthus, son of King Amyclus of Sparta.
21 The Ram.
22 The constellation of the two Fishes.
23 The river that runs through Sparta.
24 Here Titan, the Sun-god, and Apollo are distinguished. See note on 1.10.

*Apollo and Hyacinthus, Baur*

and demonstrated both the skill and strength of the god.
Unthinking and impelled by desire for the game, the Taenarid[25] youth
ran headlong to pick up the discus, but the hardened earth
cast back the orb with a glancing blow[26] into your face,
O Hyacinth. The god himself paled at the same time as                                 185
the youth and gathered up the limbs as they collapsed,
now warms you, now dries the awful wound,
now checks your fleeing spirit by applying his healing herbs.
His arts are without avail: the wound could not be healed.
Just as, if someone crushes violets and poppies in a well-watered plot          190
and lilies, bristling with their yellow tongues,
they let down enfeebled their shriveled heads,
unable to hold themselves erect, and lie face-down upon the ground:
so prostrate lies that dying face, and, its vigor gone,
his neck is a burden to itself as upon his shoulder it falls.                          195
'O scion of Oebalus,[27] you are fallen, cheated of the prime of youth,'
says Phoebus, 'and I am witness to your wound and my fault.
You are my grief and my guilt: my hand in your death
must be inscribed. The author of your death am I.
But what is my fault, unless to have played can be called                          200
a fault, unless to have loved can be called a fault?
Ah, would that it were possible to die with you and give up
my life! But since we are constrained by the law of fate,

---

25 I. e., "Spartan," after Cape Taenarus in southern Laconia.
26 Translating Merkel's emendation *verbere*.
27 A Spartan king, father of Tyndareus, and ancestor of Hyacinth.

forever will you be with me and remain fixed upon my mindful lips.
Our lyre, struck by our hand, our songs will sing of you, of you,     205
and as a flower with its inscription will you imitate our lament.
The time will come when the bravest hero[28] will add himself
into the flower and upon this same petal be read.'
Indeed, as such things were uttered by Apollo's mouth,
behold, the blood which had spilled upon the ground and marked     210
the grass, is grass no more, and, more brilliant than the purple of Tyre,
a flower arises and takes the form of a lily, although
its color is purple and the latter has a silvery hue.
For Phoebus this is not enough (for he was the author of
this honor): he writes his lament upon the petals, and AI AI[29]     215
is written upon the flower, and letters of death are drawn.
It shames not Sparta to have given birth to Hyacinth: for to
this day his honor endures, and, celebrated in the manner of
their forebears, the annual Hyacinthia returns with festive display.

## 220-43   *The Cerastae and the Propoetides*

"But if perchance you should ask Amathus,[30] rich in metal ores,     220
if she is happy to have given birth to the Propoetides, she would reject
both them and those whose brows were once by twin horns embossed,
from which they even bore the name of Cerastae.[31]
Before their doors stood the altar of Jove, the Protector of Guests,
replete with doleful crime.[32] If someone saw it stained with blood,     225
he would believe that suckling calves had been slaughtered there
and Amathusian sheep with their first two teeth:
the victim was a guest! Offended by the unholy rites
the kindly goddess Venus herself was ready to leave
her cities and the Ophiusian[33] land. 'But how have these pleasant climes     230
done wrong, how have my cities sinned? What is their fault?' she said.
'With exile let this impious clan give recompense instead,
or death or whatever there is between exile and death.
And what can this be but a punishment through change of form?'
In hesitating how to change them, she turned her gaze to the horns     235
and is reminded that these could be left to them,
and their copious bodies she transforms into savage bulls.
"The lewd Propoetides, however, made bold to deny
that Venus was a goddess. For this they were first, it's said,

---

28 Ajax. See 13. 395.
29 These letters pronounced as one word form the vocative of the name "Ajax."
30 City of Cyprus, sacred to Venus.
31 From the Greek word for "horn."
32 Translating *lugubris sceleris,* but the text is corrupt. With Madvig's *ignarus sceleris,* followed by
    Tarrant, translate "untouched by crime/ with crime unacquainted."
33 Ophiusa "Infested by Snakes" is an old name for Cyprus.

to sell their bodies and their honor, because of the goddess' wrath,                240
and as their shame gave way and upon their faces the blood grew hard,
with little change required, they were turned to rigid flint.[34]

### 243-97    *Pygmalion and Paphos*

    "Because Pygmalion had seen them passing their lives in shame,
repelled by the many faults that nature had given to
the feminine mind, he lived as a bachelor without a wife                245
and long had lacked a partner for his marriage bed.
But meanwhile he had happily sculpted snow-white ivory
with marvelous skill and given it the shape in which
no woman could be born and conceived a love for his work.
The face was that of a true maiden, which you would have thought                250
alive and wanting to be moved, if modesty did not stand in the way:
concealed so much is art by its own art. Pygmalion is amazed
and fills his heart with flames for the simulated form.
He often applies his hands to the work to test whether the body is real
or ivory and does not yet admit that it is ivory.                255
He gives it kisses and thinks them returned and holds and talks to it
and thinks that his fingers sink within the parts he has touched,
then fears a bruise might appear upon the body that he has embraced,
and sometimes offers flattery, sometimes brings to her those gifts
that girls so like, the shells and smooth little stones                260
and little birds and flowers of countless hue
and lilies and painted balls and, fallen from a tree,
the tears of the Heliades.[35] With garments he decks her limbs,
puts jeweled rings upon her fingers, puts dangling necklaces about her neck;
light pearls hang from her ears and garlands over her breast:                265
they all become her; and no less fair does she appear when nude.
He places her upon quilts dyed with the Sidonian conch
and calls her the companion of his couch and lays her neck
upon the softness of feathers as though she would feel their touch.
    "The festal day of Venus had come, and all of Cyprus was thronged                270
with worshipers, and when, their wide-curving horns now dressed in gold,
the heifers had fallen, stricken at their snow-white necks,
and clouds of incense rose, Pygmalion, bringing to the altar his gift,
stood still and timidly prayed, 'If ye gods can do all things,
my wish is for,' he dared not say, 'the ivory maid,'                275
but said instead 'a wife like the ivory maid.'
Since Venus was present at her festival, she sensed the meaning of

---

34 Since they were so shamelessly hard-hearted as to be unable to blush, it required only a little change
   to turn them into stone.
35 When the daughters of Helios wept for fallen Phaethon, their brother, they were changed to trees
   and their tears to amber.

his prayers and, as an omen of her friendly intent,
three times the flame grew bright and shot its peak across the sky.
When he returned, he sought the image of his girl, 280
and, lying upon the couch, he plied his kisses: she seemed to warm;
again he puts his mouth to hers and tried her breast with his hands:
thus tried, the ivory grows soft and with its hardness laid aside
it sinks and yields to the fingers, just as the beeswax of Mount
Hymettus[36] softens in the sun and, molded by the thumb, 285
is fashioned into many shapes and becomes useful through use itself.
Though dazed, he feels both hesitant joy and fear of being deceived,
and in his love again and again his hands retest his hopes.
It was a body! The veins pulse when touched by his thumb!
In truth this hero of Paphos then found a host of words with which 290
to render thanks to Venus, and pressed those lips so real
with his own lips, and the maiden felt the kisses he gave
and blushed and, raising her timid gaze to the light,
beheld together both her lover and the sky.
The goddess attends the marriage she had made, and when nine times 295
the horns of the moon had filled their orb,
the girl gave birth to Paphos, from whom the island[37] has its name.

### 298-502    *Myrrha and Cinyras*

"Of her is born that man, who, if childless, could
have been considered among the blest, Cinyras by name.
A cursèd tale I shall sing; away, all daughters, all fathers, away! 300
Or, if my songs shall soothe your minds,
on this occasion put no faith in me, do not believe this deed,
or, if you do believe it, believe as well the punishment for the deed.
If, nevertheless, nature seems to allow this crime,
I thank the Ismarian[38] tribes and our part of the world, 305
I thank this land, that it is far from those climes
that spawned a sacrilege so great: let Panchaia's[39] earth
be rich in balsam and cinnamon, and let it bear its costus-root[40]
and incense exuded from wood and flowers of other kinds,
but only if it bear myrrh as well: a new tree was not worth so great a price. 310
The love god Cupid denies that his darts brought you this harm,
O Myrrha, and claims his torches are not the cause of this crime.
With Stygian torch and swollen vipers were you inspired
by one of those three sisters:[41] to hate a father is a crime,

---

36 Mt. Hymettus in Attica was known for its honey.
37 Paphos is a city of Cyprus. The island of Cyprus is sometimes called "Paphian."
38 Thracian, referring to the region of Orpheus' origin.
39 An imaginary island off Arabia in the Indian Ocean.
40 An aromatic plant, *Saussurea lappa*, yielding an oil for perfume.
41 The three Erinyes or Furies, Allecto, Tisiphone, and Megaera.

*Pygmalion, Solis*

this love, however, is a greater crime than hate. From everywhere          315
distinguished rulers desired you, and from all the Orient young men
attend the contest for the marriage bed: Myrrha, of all of these
select one, so long as a certain one be not among them all.
Indeed, she feels her passion and fights against that unclean love
and says to herself, 'Have I lost my mind? What am I about?          320
O gods, I pray, and Piety, and of parents the Holy Laws,
ward off this sacrilege and oppose our crime,
if crime, indeed, it is. For Piety is said not to condemn
this form of Venus: all other animals have intercourse
without distinction, nor for an heifer is it held base          325
to bear her father on her back, the stallion's daughter becomes
his bride, and the goat consorts with the flocks he has made,
and even the bird conceives from him by whose seed she was conceived.
O happy they to whom this is granted! Human anxiety
has given spiteful laws, and what nature permits,          330
these envious laws forbid. Yet tribes are said to exist
in which the father to the daughter, and mother to the son,
is joined, and piety increases when love is twinned.
Alas for me that to have been born there was not my lot
and I must suffer by the chance of place!—Why do I dwell on that?          335
Forbidden hopes, be gone! Worthy of love is he,
but as a father.—Therefore, if of great Cinyras I
were not the daughter, with Cinyras I could lie:

but now, since he is mine, he is not mine, and proximity itself
is cause for my loss: more power were mine as an alien.                               340
I'd like to go far away and leave my country's bounds,
if only I could escape wrongdoing, but even as I go I am restrained
by evil flames, desiring to see Cinyras face to face and touch and speak
and kiss him, if nothing more is left to me.
O impious maiden, can you expect to have more than this?                              345
Do you perceive how many laws and names you confound?
Do you intend to be your mother's rival and your father's paramour?
Do you intend to be called your brother's mother and the sister of your son?
And will you not fear the sisters coiffured with black snakes
whom guilty hearts see threatening them before their eyes                             350
and faces with cruel torches? No, so long as you have not allowed
disgrace to stain your body, do not conceive it in your mind,
nor with forbidden lust pollute mighty nature's bonds!
You want it, admittedly. Reality forbids; that man is pious and
of duty mindful—O would that mad desire like mine were his as well!'                  355
      "Her words were spoken, but Cinyras, by the worthy supply
of suitors made hesitant as to what he should do, inquires of her,
upon reciting the names, to which husband she wishes to belong.
At first she says nothing, and then, gazing upon her father's face,
she burns and her eyes are suffused with tepid dew.                                   360
Cinyras, thinking this sprang from a maiden's fears,
forbids her to cry and dries her cheeks and kisses her lips;
rejoicing too much at these gifts, Myrrha, when asked what sort
of man she would choose, responded, 'One like you.'
But he approves the words he failed to understand                                     365
and says, 'May you always be so pious.' At the name of piety,
the maiden, conscious of her crime, lowered her eyes.
      "The middle of the night had come and sleep had relaxed
both bodies and cares; but the Cinyreian maid lies awake,
beset by indomitable fires, and reviews her raving hopes,                             370
despairing one moment, then wanting to make the attempt,
and feeling both shame and desire, without discovering what
to do, and just as a large tree struck by an axe, when just
the final blow remains, is unclear where it will fall and thus
is feared on every side, so her mind, faltering from diverse blows,                   375
flits hither and thither, impelled in both directions at once;
no limit to love, no respite from love is found but death.
Death pleases. She rises, determined to bind in a noose
her neck. With her girdle tied to the highest beam, she said,
'Cinyras dear, farewell, and understand the cause of my death!'                       380
and then began to fasten the cord around her pallid neck.
      "The murmur of her words reached her nurse's faithful ears,

they say, as she guarded the threshold of her foster child.
The aged woman rises up and flings back the doors. When she sees
the instruments of the intended death, she cries out at once                    385
and beats her bosom and rends her clothes and, snatching from her neck
the cord, she rips it apart; then at last she takes time to weep
and then to take her in her arms and ask the reason for the noose.
The maiden is speechless and still and gazes motionless at the floor,
and vexed that her attempts at death, too slow, had been surprised.             390
The aged woman presses on and, baring her hoary head
and empty breasts, beseeches her by her cradle and first nourishment
to tell her the cause of her grief. At her appeal the girl turns away
and groans; the nurse is determined to discover the cause,
to promise, indeed, not only her trust. 'Say,' she says, 'what you need         395
and let me help you: my old age is not sluggish to act.
In case of madness, I know a woman with charms and herbs that cure;
in case someone's hurt you, you'll be protected by a magic spell;
but if the gods are angry, their anger will be stilled by sacrifice.
What more should I imagine? Surely fortune and home                             400
are safe and running smooth: your mother and father are alive.'
On hearing 'father,' Myrrha drew from her breast a deep breath;
but even now the mind of the nurse imagined no sacrilege
and yet perceived that some love was involved;
persistent in her purpose, she begs her to reveal to her                        405
whatever it is, and raises to her ancient bosom the weeping girl,
and, thus enfolding her body within her feeble arms,
she says, 'We know, you're in love! In this (put away your fear!)
my diligence will serve you well, and never will
your father find out.' Distraught, the girl leapt from her lap                  410
and pressing her face into the couch, she says, 'Be gone, I pray,
and pity my sad disgrace.' And when the other continued, she said,
'Be gone, or stop asking why I grieve. What you strive to learn is a crime!'
The old woman shudders and stretches forth her hands that tremble with years
and fear, and as a suppliant falls prostrate before her nursling's feet,        415
now coaxing her, now,—if she is not informed,
alarming her, with threats to reveal the noose and her attempt
to die, and promises her help if she reveals her love.
The girl lifts up her head and fills her nurse's breast
with up-welling tears and, as often as she tries to confess,                    420
she checks her words and covers her face in her gown
and said, 'O mother, happy in your spouse!'
Just this much, and then she groaned. Into the nurse's limbs
a cold tremor penetrated all the way to the bones, and on all
her head the shaggy gray tresses stood rigid on end.                            425
To drive away this dreadful love, if she could, she went on

to say many things. The maiden knows that she is not falsely advised,
but is determined to die, if she cannot consummate her love.
The nurse says, 'Live, win your—,' 'father' she dare not say,
and then was silent and confirmed her promises by the gods.                    430
        "The pious matrons were celebrating Ceres' annual festival,
the one in which, veiling their bodies in snowy attire,
they offer as first fruits of their harvest wheaten wreaths
and for nine nights counted the love and touch of males
forbidden: Cenchreis is in that throng,                                         435
the wife of the king, and attends the secret rites.
So long as the couch was unfilled by its lawful wife,
the diligent nurse, having made Cinyras heavy with wine,
made reference to a sincere lover, while concealing the name,
and praises her beauty; when he inquired about her age,                         440
she says, 'The same as Myrrha's.' When she had received the command
to bring her forth and returned to her quarters, she said, 'Rejoice,
my daughter, we have won!' The unhappy maiden felt
no joy in all her heart, and with foreboding her bosom grieves,
but nevertheless she does rejoice: so great is the discord within her mind.     445
        "It was the hour when all things are quiet, and Boötes
among the plowmen had bent the Wagon with its slanting pole.[42]
The girl approaches her evil deed; the gilded moon flees from the sky,
the murky clouds cover the hiding stars;
night lacks its fires; Icarus, you were first to hide your face,                450
and you, Erigone,[43] because of a pious love of a sire.
Three times was she called back by the sign of the stumbling foot,
three times the funereal owl gave as an omen its song of death:
she goes, just the same, and the shadows of black night diminish her shame;
her left hand grasps the hand of the nurse, the other moves about               455
attempting to find the way through the darkness. She reaches now
the threshold of the bedroom, and opens now the door, now is led within:
her knees tremble, her legs give way, her complexion and blood
take flight, and her mind abandons her as she goes.
The closer she is to her wicked deed, the more she shrinks from it,             460
regretting her boldness and wanting to turn back without being recognized.
The ancient hand leads her on as she hesitates and, when she had brought
her to the lofty couch and handed her over, she said, 'Receive
her, she is your, Cinyras,' and brought the cursed bodies into one embrace.
The father receives into his sullied bed his very flesh,                        465
dispelling her girlish fears and admonishing her in her fright.
Perhaps he even used the word 'daughter' with reference to her age,

---

42 The reference is to the Charles' Wain, also called Ursa Major and the Big Dipper, which reaches it
    height in the sky at midnight.
43 See on 6. 125.

*Myrrha and Cinyras, Solis*

and she, 'father,' lest the crime not lack its appropriate names.
    "She left the bedroom, full of her father, and within her baleful womb
she bears the incestuous seed and carries the crime conceived therein.    470
The following night repeats the sin, and that is not the end of it,
for finally Cinyras, after lying with her so often, is eager to know
his lover, and brings in a lamp and beholds both
his crime and his daughter. His words restrained by grief,
he draws his gleaming sword from the sheath where it hangs;    475
but Myrrha runs away, through the gloom and gift of dark night
escaping death; having wandered through the broad fields,
she leaves behind Arabia with its palms and Panchaia's[44] lands
and roamed for nine horns of the returning moon,
when finally, exhausted, in the land of Saba she found her rest;    480
she scarce could bear the burden of her womb. Uncertain how to pray
and wavering between fear of death and disgust with life,
she formulated her prayers this way: 'Oh gods, if any of you
are open to my confession, harsh punishment is what I deserve,
I do not deny it, but lest by surviving I violate those who live    485
or those who are dead by dying, ban me from the realms of both:
transform me and deny me both life and death!'
Some deity was open to her plea: her final wishes at least
had found their gods. For as she spoke earth overwhelmed

---

44 An island east of Arabia.

her legs, and jagged roots spread out, bursting through                 490
the nails of her toes, supports for a tall trunk of a tree;
her bones gained strength, and from the marrow that remained
her blood turns into sap, into great branches her arms are turned,
her fingers into little ones, and her skin hardens with bark.
The growing tree had girded tightly her heavy womb                 495
and hardened her breasts and was encroaching upon her neck:
she did not bear the wait and, meeting the advancing wood,
she hid her body within it and buried her face within the bark.
Although she had lost her old sensations along with her form,
she weeps even yet, and tepid drops ooze from the tree.                 500
But even in tears there is honor, and the myrrh distilled from the bark
retains the name of its mistress, which no generation will leave unsaid.

### 503-739   Venus and Adonis

"The infant had grown within the womb, however wrongly conceived,
and sought now the path by which to leave its mother and
reveal itself; within the tree the heavy belly swells.                 505
The burden strains the mother; these labor pains have no words,
nor can Lucina[45] be summoned by the voice of her giving birth.
The tree, however, is like the struggling woman, and, bending low,
is full of groaning and moist with falling tears.
Beside its suffering branches kindly Lucina took her stand                 510
and stretched forth her hands and spoke the word that hasten birth:
the tree produces cracks and from its broken bark puts forth
a living burden, and a boy cries out in distress. Upon soft grass
the naiads laid it and anointed it with his mother's tears.
His face even Envy would praise; for just as the forms                 515
of naked Gods of Love within a painting are shown,
just so was he, but, lest the costume set them apart,
a quiver, light in weight, add to him or remove from both.
        "Deceptively, fleeting time glides along unseen,
and nothing is swifter than the years: the offspring of                 520
his sister and grandfather, lately concealed within the tree,
just lately brought to birth, just lately a most comely babe,
is soon a youth, soon a man, soon more handsome than before,
soon pleasing even Venus and avenging his mother's fires.
For as her quivered boy was giving his mother a kiss,                 525
unwittingly he grazed her breast with a protruding barb;
the wounded goddess thrust back the boy: at first the wound,
more deeply driven than it seemed, had deceived the goddess herself.
Entranced by male beauty, she no longer tends Cythera's[46] shores

---

45 "She who brings to light," Goddess of childbirth, equated with Juno or Diana.
46 Venus was said to have been born out of the sea near this island in the Aegean.

*Birth of Adonis, Picart*

nor seeks out Paphos,[47] surrounded by the deep sea,　　　　530
nor fishy Cnidos[48] and Amathus,[49] heavy with metal-ores;
she even abandons heaven: to heaven is Adonis preferred.
She cleaves to him, is his companion and, though in the past,
accustomed to enjoy the shade and cultivate it to increase
her beauty, she wanders now over the hills and woods and thorny rocks,　　535
just like Diana, with her robe gathered up to her knees,
encouraging the dogs and chasing after animals safe to take,
the fleet-footed hares or stags with their lofty horns
or does; she stays away from the powerful boars,
avoids the ravishing wolves and claw-armed bears,　　　　540
and lions, drenched and sated by the slaughter of the herd.
And you as well she warns to fear these, if in warning she could be
of any help to you, Adonis, and says, 'Be brave against those
that flee, against the bold no boldness is safe.
Do not be reckless, young man, mindful of the risk to me,　　545
and do not harry wild beasts whom nature has armed,
so that your glory not come at great cost to me. Neither youth,
nor beauty, nor all that has moved Venus moves bristled boars
and lions and the eyes and minds of wild beasts.
Keen boars have the stroke of lightning in their curving tusks,　　550

47 City of Cyprus, sacred to Venus.
48 City of Caria in Asia Minor, sacred to Venus.
49 Another city of Cyprus, sacred to Venus.

in tawny lions there is striking force and enormous wrath,
and all that kind is odious to me.' When he asks why,
she says, 'I shall tell, and you will be amazed at the monstrous
result of an ancient crime. But today's unaccustomed work has left
me tired, and, look there, a poplar beckons with its timely shade,          555
the turf provides a couch: I want to rest here awhile with you
upon the ground,' and she reclined and lay upon the grass
and placing her neck on the bosom of the reclining youth,
she speaks and interposes her kisses among her words:

### 560-707   Venus' Tale of Atalanta and Hippomenes

   " 'Perhaps you have heard of a certain girl who surpassed          560
swift men in contests of running: that story was no mere tale;
she did surpass them. You could not possibly say whether she
excelled more because of the reputation of her feet or fineness of her form.
When asking a god whom she should marry, he said, "No need,
have you, Atalanta, of a husband. Avoid taking a spouse.          565
But you will not escape and, though alive, you will lose yourself."
Alarmed by the oracle of the god, she lives unmarried in the dense woods
and forcefully puts to flight the pressing throng of suitors with this
condition: "I cannot be had," she said, "unless I first
be vanquished in running. In a footrace contend with me:          570
the reward to the swift will be the marriage chamber and a bride;
the penalty for the slow will be death: of this contest let this be the rule."
She was indeed unkind, but (for the power of beauty is so great)
there came a reckless throng of suitors even despite this rule.
Hippomenes had sat as a spectator of this unfair race.          575
"Is anyone going to seek a bride with such peril as this?"
had been his words along with condemnation of excessive love;
but as he saw her face and her body when her robe has been laid aside,
like mine, or, like yours if you were to become a girl, he was stunned
to silence and, lifting his hands, he said, "Forgive me all          580
whom I have blamed! Not yet had I known the prize
that you were seeking." Even as he praised her, his passion caught fire,
and hopes that none of the youths will run faster than she,
and out of jealousy fears that one might. "But why
should I leave untried the outcome of this race?" he said,          585
"For god himself helps the bold!" While Hippomenes
is turning this over in his mind, the maid flies by with winged pace.
Though to the Aonian[50] youth she seemed to move not slower than
a Scythian arrow, he wondered at her loveliness even more:
and running itself contributed also to that loveliness.          590
The breeze sweeps back the wings of her swiftly moving feet,

---

50 Theban or Boeotian.

and over her ivory back her tresses are tossed, and about
the back of her knees the bordered bindings shine bright;
her body had spread over her maiden whiteness a ruddy blush,
no different than when gleaming courts are stained                    595
with simulated shade by a purple veil.
The guest is marking all this as the goal is passed,
and conquering Atalanta receives the festal crown.
The conquered groan and pay the contracted penalty.
    " 'Undaunted by their doom, the youth took                        600
his stand in the midst and with his gaze fixed upon the maid
exclaims, "Why in the defeat of sluggards do you seek easy fame?
Compete with me! If fortune will have given me the strength,
you will not disdain to have been vanquished by one so great:
my father, you see, is Megareus of Onchestus,[51] of whom            605
the grandfather is Neptune, which makes me great-grandson of the king
of waters, nor is my valor beneath my family's; but if I lose,
Hippomenes' defeat will bring you a great and memorable name."
The daughter of Schoeneus looks at him with softened gaze as he speaks,
not sure whether she prefers to be defeated or to win,               610
and says: "What god, unjust to the fair, wants this man
to lose and bids him risk his own dear life to seek
this marriage? In my judgment I am not worth so great a price.
I am not touched by his beauty (although I could have been)
but by the fact that he is yet a boy; I am moved not by him, but by his age.  615
And what about his valor and his mind, unafraid of death?
And what about his being fourth in a watery origin?
And what about his being in love and thinking that marrying me
is worth his death, should pitiless fortune deny me to him?
O stranger, away with you and abandon this marriage while you can!   620
A marriage with me is cruel; no girl would refuse to marry you,
and you might be chosen by a sensible girl.
But why this care of mine for you, when so many have already died?
He'll have to take care of himself! Let him perish, since by the death
of all these suitors he's not been warned and cares so little for life!  625
Then will he die because he longed to live with me,
and suffer an undeserved death as the price of love?
Our victory will bring unbearable hostility.
The fault, however, is not mine! Would that you would desist,
or, since you have lost your mind, would that you were swifter than I!  630
How virginal those looks upon his boyish face!
Oh, wretched Hippomenes, I wish I'd never been seen by you,
for you deserved to live! But if I had been happier,
and the opposing Fates had not denied marriage to me,

---

51 City of Boeotia.

you were the one with whom I should have wished to share the marriage bed." 635
Her words were done, and, inexperienced and touched by first desire,
not knowing what she is doing, she is in love and does not sense it as love.
    " 'Now father and people are demanding the usual race
as Neptune's descendant, Hippomenes, calls to me
with anxious voice and says, "I pray that Cytherea be with me                    640
in what I dare to do and assist the fires that she has inspired."
The not unfriendly breeze conveyed his winning prayers to me:
and I am moved, I confess, nor was there much time allowed to help.
There is a field that the natives after Tamasus[52] have named,
the best part of the Cyprian land, which the elders of old                       645
established as sacred to me and ordered my temples to receive
this gift; in the middle of the field there gleams a tree,
its foliage tawny, its branches crackling with tawny gold:
I came from there carrying three golden apples that I had plucked
with my own hand by chance, beheld by no one but Hippomenes,                      650
whom I approached and taught what use they might serve.
The tuba gives the signal, and each darts headlong from
the starting gate and grazes with nimble foot the top of the sand:
you might even think they could skim with dry foot the surface of
the sea and scurry over the ripe harvest's standing stalks of grain.             655
Increasing the eagerness of the youth are the clamor, support
and words of those who say, "Now, now's the time to press on!
Make haste, Hippomenes! Employ now all your strength!
No dawdling: you're going to win!" It is unclear who rejoiced the more,
Megareus' heroic son or the maiden of Schoeneus in what they said.               660
How many times, when she could have passed him, did she delay
and leave behind unwillingly that face upon which she long had gazed!
Dry gasps for air were coming from his weary mouth,
and still the finish line was far away: then at last
did Neptune's progeny let fall one of the three arboreal fruits.[53]             665
The maiden was stunned and, desiring the shining fruit, she turned
aside from her course and picked up the golden object as it rolled;
Hippomenes passed her by: the spectators roared with applause.
But with a burst of speed she made up lost time
and put the youth behind her again:                                              670
and once again, with the toss of the second apple, is she
delayed and catches up and passes the man. The homestretch of
the race remained; "Now," he says," be with me, goddess, author of
my gift!" And, to make her return more slowly, he cast
with youthful strength the shining gold obliquely off to the side of the field.  675
The maiden seemed to hesitate. Should she go after it? I made

---

52 A city of Cyprus.
53 Circumlocution for the three golden apples.

her pick it up and added to the apple she lifted extra weight
and held her back both by the weight of the load and the delay.
To make my story no slower than the race itself,
the maiden was overtaken: the victor married his reward.                    680
      " 'Adonis, did I deserve some thanks, some offering
of incense? He was thoughtless and neither offered me thanks
nor gave me incense. I am suddenly moved to wrath,
and, angry at the insult, take care not to be insulted ever again,
inciting myself to make an example of the both of them.                     685
A temple, which long ago famous Echion had built to fulfill
a vow to the Mother of the gods, was hidden within a woody grove:
in passing by, they were persuaded by the journey's length to rest;
Hippomenes was seized in that place by an untimely desire
to lie with her, a desire inspired by our divinity.                         690
Near by the temple there was a secluded recess, dimly lit,[54]
much like a cave, roofed with native volcanic rock,
made holy by ancient veneration, where the priest
had brought together many wooden images of old;
he entered this place and defiled its holiness with forbidden lust.         695
The sacred images avert their eyes, and the Mother with turreted crown[55]
was on the verge of plunging the guilty pair into the waters of the Styx:
the punishment seemed too slight; and therefore tawny manes
conceal their necks, once smooth, their fingers curl into claws,
their shoulders become forequarters, all their weight is thrust            700
into their chests, their tails sweep across the top of the sand,
their faces are filled with wrath, they utter growls in place of words,
they make the forests their marriage chamber, whom others must fear,
yet press Cybele's bit, their teeth subdued, as lions. These must you,
so dear to me, and with them all the race of beasts that offer not         705
their backs to flight, but their breast to the fray,
avoid so that your bravery be not ruinous to both of us.'

### 708-39   The Death of Adonis

      "She gave her warning and with her span of swans
sets on her way through the air, but to warnings his bravery stands opposed.
By chance his dogs, having followed a clear trail, had roused              710
a boar from its lair, and as it made ready to emerge from the woods,
the scion of Cinyras had pierced it with a slanting blow:
at once, the savage boar with its spreading snout expelled the spear,
now stained with its blood, pursuing the youth, who was now afraid
and seeking safety, and buried his tusks to the hilt into                  715
his groin and laid him prostrate and dying upon the yellow sand.

---

54 Explaining why Hippomenes does not see the sacred images in 694.
55 Cybele wore a wall-like crown.

*Death of Adonis, Solis*

The goddess of Cythera, born upon her light chariot through the air
on olorine wings, to Cyprus had not yet arrived:
she recognized from afar the groans of the dying boy
and bent her white birds in that direction and, when from heaven above       720
she saw him lifeless and his body lying in his own blood,
she sprang down and tore both her breast and her hair
and beat upon her bosom with indignant hands
and made complaint with the Fates: 'But not everything
will stay within your power,' she said. 'My grief will abide       725
forever as a memorial to my Adonis, and the image of his death
will carry out an annual reenactment of our grief;
his blood, however, will be changed into a flower. Persephone,[56]
were you allowed to change the limbs of a girl into fragrant mint,
while it is begrudged to me that I should transform       730
the hero of Cinyras' line?' Having said this, she sprinkled the gore
with fragrant nectar: when it was thus imbued,
it swelled, as when from yellow mud clear bubbles are wont
to rise, and with no more than an hour's delay
a flower arose that shared the color of blood,       735
like that the pomegranates are wont to conceal
beneath their rugged skin. Their bloom is brief,
for since it clings but poorly and easily falls for lack of weight,
the very winds that give it its name[57] shake it off."

---

56 Ovid uses here the Greek form of the name of Proserpina.
57 Adonis is transformed into the anemone "wind-flower."

# BOOK 11

## *1-84  The Death of Orpheus*

While with such song the Thracian bard leads the woods
and minds of the beasts and rocks to follow him,
behold, the Ciconian daughters, their frenzied breasts
concealed in skins of the wild, from the top of a hill
catch sight of Orpheus as he set his songs to the sounding strings.        5
Her hair tossed through the gentle breezes, one of these says,
"There, there, he is, the one who holds us in contempt!" and slings
a spear towards the singing mouth of the Apollonian bard,
but, fitted out with leaves, it makes a mark without a wound.
The missile of another is a stone, which when cast is vanquished in      10
mid-air by the lovely song of the voice and the lyre
and like a suppliant repentant for such a mad deed
lay prostrate before his feet. Yet the outrageous strife
increases, all restraint is gone, and the wild Erinys[1] reigns;
and all the missiles would have been softened by the song, had not      15
great clamor and the Berecyntian pipes with curving horns
and drums and clapping of hands and Bacchic howls
drowned out the lyre with their sound, until at last the rocks
grew red from the blood of the bard no longer heard.
The ones astonished even yet by the singer's voice,                      20
the countless birds and serpents and line of beasts,
the proof of Orpheus' triumph, those the maenads seized at first;

---

1 Greek for Fury.

*Orpheus Killed by Maenads, Baur*

and then with bloodied hands against Orpheus they turn
and gather round him like the birds whenever they spy
the bird of night[2] astray in the light of day, and, forming all around        25
a theater, as when in the morning arena[3] the stag is about to fall
as prey to the dogs, they aim for the bard and throw
their wands[4] still green with foliage, not made for this use.
Some hurl clods of earth, others branches ripped from trees,
still others sharp stones; and lest their fury lack for arms,        30
by chance some oxen pulling the plow were working the earth,
and not far from there, producing the fruit of great sweat,
were brawny farmers, digging the hard fields.
As soon as they saw that troop, they flee and leave behind
the tools of their toil so that strewn over the empty fields        35
lie hoes and long-handled mattocks and heavy rakes.
The women seized these and tore apart the bulls despite
their menacing horns and run back to fulfill the doom of the bard,
and as he stretches forth his hands and then for the first time
speaks words without effect and moves nothing with his voice,        40
the impious women destroy him, and through that mouth
(by Jupiter!), which stones had heeded and minds of beasts
had understood, his soul expired and was dispersed to the winds.
        The sorrowful birds wept for you, Orpheus, for you that host
of beasts, for you the rigid stones, for you the woods, that often had sought        45

---

2 The owl.
3 The Roman amphitheater with its hunting spectacles.
4 The Greek *thyrsus*, the technical term for the pine-cone-tipped wand, carried by the maenads or
   bacchants, the frenzied worshipers of Bacchus.

*Muses Mourn Orpheus, Solis*

your songs, did weep, the trees dropped their leaves and mourned
for you as if their hair were shorn. It is said that by their own tears
the very rivers swelled, and naiads[5] and dryads,[6] trimmed
their clothes in somber colors and let their tresses flow in disarray.
The limbs lie in diverse parts; but you, Hebrus,[7] received the head          50
and lyre: and (a marvel it was!) as it glides in the midst of the stream,
the lyre makes some tearful complaint, some tearful word is murmured by
the lifeless tongue, the banks with some tearful echo respond.
Already carried out to sea, the head, tongue and lyre leave
their native stream and reach Methymna[8] on Lesbos' shore:          55
upon these foreign sands a ferocious serpent attacks
your unprotected head and curls, bespattered with dripping foam.
But finally Phoebus is there and fends off the serpent when it
prepares to bite and congeals into stone its open jaws
and hardens, in just that pose, its gaping maw.          60
   Beneath the earth goes his shade, and all the places he had seen
before, he recognizes and, scanning the fields of pious folk,
he finds Eurydice and enfolds her within his yearning arms.
They both stroll now with a common stride,

5 Water nymphs.
6 Wood nymphs.
7 The Hebrus was a river of Thrace, the homeland of Orpheus.
8 A city of Lesbos.

and now he follows in her train, now takes the lead,     65
now Orpheus looks back safely upon his Eurydice.
Lyaeus[9] does not leave this crime unavenged,
and, grieving at the loss of the singing priest of his sacred rites,
at once bound fast with twisted roots in the forest all
the women of the Edoni[10] who had beheld the wicked deed;     70
he drew out as far as possible the toes of each
and sank their tips into the solid earth,
and as a bird that has placed its foot into the trap
laid by the clever fowler and felt itself caught
and beats its wings and through its frightened motion draws tight     75
the bonds, just so, as each of the women was bound fast to the ground,
and sought in vain panic to escape, the toughness of the root
confines her still and in her frenzy holds her back,
and while she wonders where her finger are, where her foot, where her nails,
she watches as the wood encroaches upon the smoothness of her calves     80
and, trying to strike her thigh with her grieving right hand,
she struck the sturdy oak, and her bosom becomes oak,
her shoulders oak as well; her extended arms you might think
were truly branches, and not be deceived in thinking so.

### 85-193 Midas

    And this is not enough for Bacchus. He quits these very fields     85
and with a better chorus seeks the vineyards of his own
Timolus[11] and Pactolus,[12] though it was not golden yet
nor envied at that time for its precious sands.
Both satyrs and bacchants attend him, his usual troop;
Silenus,[13] however, was missing: staggering with age and unmixed wine,     90
he had been caught by Phrygian rustics, who bound him with a crown
of flowers and led him to Midas, the king, to whom Thracian Orpheus and
Cecropian[14] Eumolpus[15] had imparted Bacchus' sacred rites.
As soon as Midas recognized his friend, the companion of these rites,
he raised a feast in gracious honor of the coming of his guest,     95
which lasted twice five days and consecutive nights.
Already had the eleventh Lucifer confined the heavenly host
of stars, when with joy the king comes to the fields

---

9 Bacchus as deliverer (through wine), from the Greek *lyein* "loosen."
10 A tribe of Thrace.
11 Or Tmolus, the mountain in Lydia, also the god of the mountain. Bacchus is sometimes thought to
    have come from Lydia.
12 A river of Lydia, famed for its gold.
13 The Papa-Silenus, foster father of Dionysus and a troop of satyrs, is a principal character in Euripides'
    satyr-play, *Cyclops* .
14 Cecrops was an early king of Athens.
15 Another Thracian bard, priest of Ceres, who founded the Eleusinian mysteries. The Eumolpidae,
    descendants of Eumolpus, were the hereditary priests of these mysteries at Eleusis, near Athens.

*Silenus and Midas, Solis*

of Lydia and restores Silenus to his youthful foster-child.[16]

The god granted him the pleasing but useless gift                    100
of choosing a favor, delighted to have his foster-father back.
But Midas, proceeding to misuse the boon, says, "Bring to pass
that all I touch with my body be turned to tawny gold."
Then Liber nodded assent to the choice, bestowed the dangerous gift,
and grieved that Midas had not made a better request.               105
The Berecyntian hero[17] departs content and happy in the evil thing
and tests the veracity of the promise by touching things in turn,
and, scarcely believing his eyes, from the lofty oak did not
draw down a branch of green: the branch had turned to gold!
He picks up a rock from the ground: the rock also paled with gold;  110
he also touches a clod: at his powerful touch the clod
became a heavy mass; he broke off heads of Ceres' ripening grain:
the harvest was golden; he holds an apple plucked from a tree:
you'd think the Hesperides[18] had given it; if he applied his fingers to
the lofty door-posts, the door-posts seemed to radiate with light.  115
When even in clear water he had washed his hands,
the water flowing from his hands could have deceived Danaë.
His mind scarcely comprehends its hopes, imagining all

---

16 Bacchus.
17 Midas, so called because of the Lydian mountain Berecyntus.
18 Three Hesperides (the name means "Daughters of Evening") in a garden in the western Ocean
   guarded a tree of golden apples given to Hera by Earth as a wedding gift. To retrieve them was one
   of the labors of Heracles.

converted to gold. His servants set a table before him as he rejoiced,
piled high with food and not lacking for roasted grain:[19]                    120
but then in truth, when his right hand had touched
the gifts of Ceres, the gifts of Ceres grew hard,
or when his hungry teeth attempted to bite
into the food, the teeth only pressed yellow plates;
when he had mixed with pure water the author of the gift,[20]                  125
you might have thought that liquid gold were flowing through his jaws.
      The novelty of this evil left him thunderstruck;
both rich and wretched, he chooses to flee from wealth and hates
what he had prayed for. No abundance relieves his appetite; his throat
is dry and burns; deservedly tortured by the hated gold, he lifts            130
his shining arms and hands towards heaven and says,
"Forgive me, father Lenaeus![21] We have sinned! But grant
me mercy, I pray, and save me from this shining punishment!"
The spirit of the gods is kind: the penitent sinner is restored
by Bacchus, who frees the granted favor of its promised force.              135
"But lest," he says, "you remain imbued with ill-chosen gold,
go forth to the stream that next to mighty Sardis[22] lies
and over Tmolus'[23] ridge make your way upstream
until you come to the river's source;
and where most abundantly the foaming fountain wells up                     140
submerge your head and body and at the same time wash away
your stain." The king approached the ordered water: the golden touch
imbued the river and receded from the human body into the stream.
But even now from the seeds received from the ancient vein
the fields are hard and pale with clods made wet by gold.                   145
      Despising now all wealth, Midas favored the woods and fields
and Pan, a constant denizen of those mountain caves,
but just as before his intellect remained sluggish with fat,[24]
and once again his foolish wits would bring their master harm.
For towering Tmolus, gazing far and wide from its heights upon              150
the deep, extending far upon both its arduous slopes,
was bound by Sardis on this side and little Hypaepa on that.
While Pan was flaunting there his sibilant sounds among the gentle nymphs
and playing upon the wax-bound reeds a carefree song,
he dared to scorn Apollo's singing in comparison with his own,             155
and entered an uneven contest with Tmolus as judge.

---

19 I.e., bread.
20 I.e., Bacchus, standing here for wine.
21 The god of the wine-press, Bacchus.
22 Chief city of Lydia.
23 The epithet modifying *iugum* "ridge" is unclear in the manuscript. I translate Heinsius' *Tmoli*, the
    Lydian mountain near the river Pactolus and the city Sardis.
24 Though Midas had rid his body of gold, his mind was still sluggish with its former greed. *Pingue
    ingenuum*, literally "rich mind," figuratively "sluggish mind." Compare "fat head."

*Contest of Apollo and Pan (Midas with Asses' Ears), Baur*

Upon his mountain the aged judge took his seat and frees
his ears from the trees: his dark-blue locks were only wrapped
with oak, and round his hollow temples acorns hang.
On seeing the god of the flocks, he said, "This judge                    160
will act without delay." First Pan plays upon his rustic reeds
and with his barbarous song drove Midas (who was there
by chance to hear him sing) quite wild; next sacred Tmolus turned
his face to Phoebus' mouth: Tmolus' forest followed his countenance.
The fair-haired head of Phoebus was bound with Parnassian laurel leaves,   165
his cloak, imbued with Tyrian purple, swept the ground;
his left hand held the lyre, embossed with gems
and Indic ivory, while the other hand held the pick.
The very picture of the artist he was. Then with learned thumb
he stirred the strings, and Tmolus, taken with their charm,               170
commands Pan to lower his reeds in submission to the lyre.
        The judgment and opinion of the holy mountain please all;
the sentence is blamed and called unjust by the words
of Midas alone; and the Delian god does not
permit those stolid ears to retain their shape,                          175
but draws out their length and fills them with bristles of gray
and makes them floppy and gives them the power to be moved:
the rest of him is human, in this feature alone he is marked
and wears the ears of a slow-moving ass.
He seeks to hide this and attempts to free his temples of their          180
repulsive disgrace by means of a turban of purple hue;
however, the servant assigned to cut his long locks
had seen it, who, though daring not reveal the disgrace

he saw, but desiring to air it abroad
and unable to keep silent, went away and dug a hole                           185
and with a low whispering voice relays to the hole
the nature of his master's ears that he had seen
and buried the testimony of his voice by covering the hole
with earth and silently went away from the covered pit.
A grove begins to rise there, thick with quavering reeds;                     190
when they had ripened after the passage of one full year, the reeds
betrayed the turner of the soil: for by the motion of the soft south wind
that grove repeats the buried words and exposed the master's ears.

### 194-220  Laomedon

Latona's son, now avenged, left Tmolus and, born through the clear air
beyond the narrow sea of Helle, the daughter of Nephele,[25]                  195
alit in the region belonging to Laomedon.[26]
Sigeum's deep was on the right, Rhoeteum's[27] on the left,
where once an ancient altar was consecrated to
the Panomphaean Thunderer.[28] From there he sees Laomedon
beginning to build the walls of new Troy and the great aim                    200
advancing with no uneasy toil and requiring no modest means;
along with the trident-wielding father of the swollen deep
he puts on human form and with the tyrant of Phrygia
constructs the walls, agreeing to fortifications in return for gold.
The work was done: the king denied the payment and, as                        205
a capstone to perfidy, adds breach of oath to his lying words.
The ruler of the sea declares, "Not unpunished will you be,"
and turns all the waters towards the shores of greedy Troy
and filled the land with the form of the sea and took away
the livelihood of the farmers and covered the fields with the flood.         210
This punishment is not enough; the daughter[29] of the king
is claimed by a monster of the sea. When she is bound to a hard crag,
Alcides[30] frees her and claims as his promised reward the horses agreed
upon,[31] and when payment for this mighty act was denied,
he captures conquered Troy's twice-perjured walls.                           215
And Telamon,[32] his partner in war, did not leave without reward

---

25 Nephele "Cloud" was the first wife of Athamas. She rescued her children, Helle and Phrixus, by
   placing them on a flying ram having a golden fleece. Helle fell off in to the sea that was named for
   her, the Hellespont "Sea of Helle."
26 King of Troy.
27 Sigeum and Rhoeteum were promontories on the Hellespont.
28 Zeus Panomphaeus, Zeus (Jupiter) author of divination (from Greek *pan* "all" + *omphe* "voice").
29 Hesione.
30 Hercules.
31 According to Ehwald, the horses promised to Tros for the stolen Ganymede (see Hom. *Il.*
   5. 265-67).
32 Telamon and Peleus were sons of Aeacus, son of Jupiter and Aegina.

*Neptune and Apollo Build the Walls of Troy, Solis*

and takes possession of Hesione as a gift. For Peleus
was already famous for his goddess spouse and no more proud of his grandsire's name
than that of his father-in-law;[33] for, though to be the grandson of Jove
had fallen not to one, to him alone had it fallen to have a goddess as a bride.  220

## 221-65  *Peleus and Thetis*

For ancient Proteus had said to Thetis, "Goddess of the wave,
conceive: you will be the mother of a youth who shall in his sturdy years
excel the deeds of his father and be called greater than he."
For this reason, lest the world acknowledge anything greater than Jove,
despite the not merely tepid fires he had felt within his breast,                   225
had Jupiter from marriage with watery Thetis fled
and ordered his grandson, Aeacus' son, to woo her in his stead
and enter into the embrace of the maiden of the sea.
There is a bay of Haemonia[34] shaped like a sickle into a curved bow
with arms that extend forward: had its waters been deeper, it would              230
have been a port; the water just skims the top of the sand;
it has a solid beach that does not preserve the tracks of feet
or slow one's pace; and seaweed does not cover its slope.
A grove of myrtle lies near, with bicolored berries thick.

---

33 Nereus, father of Thetis.
34 The inner part of the Gulf of Malia beneath Thessaly (Haemonia).

A cave is in the middle, whether created by nature or art                    235
it is not clear, yet probably more by art: often to this place,
upon your harnessed dolphin seated nude, Thetis, you would come.
And Peleus caught you there as you lay in the bonds of sleep,
and since you, when importuned, refused to respond to his appeals,
he turned to force and wrapped both his arms about your neck;                240
if you had not proceeded through your frequently changing shapes
to use your accustomed arts, he would have succeeded in his bold attempt;
when next you were a bird, he held on to that bird;
when next you were a heavy tree, Peleus clung to that tree;
your third form was that of a spotted tigress: by her                       245
was Peleus terrified and released his arms.
Then, pouring wine upon the waters and offering entrails of sheep
and smoky incense, he worshiped the gods of the sea
until the Carpathian prophet[35] from the midst of the deep
proclaimed, "Son of Aeacus, you will gain the marriage you seek,            250
but when she lies deep in slumber in the rocky cave,
be sure to bind her unsuspecting with ropes and tight chains;
and do not let her deceive you when she feigns a hundred forms,
but hold her down, whatever she is, until she returns to her previous form."
When Proteus has spoken, he hid his face in the sea,                        255
releasing his final words into the waves.
     The Titan[36] was bending low, his sinking chariot now
above the Hesperian[37] sea, when the lovely Nereid[38] left
her sea and advanced to her wonted bed of rest;
no sooner had Peleus set upon her virgin limbs                              260
than she transformed her shapes, until she felt her limbs
held fast and her arms in opposite directions spread.
Then did she groan at last, and says, "Not without divine will do you win,"
and made herself manifest as Thetis: the hero embraces her when she confessed
and gains what he wished and with mighty Achilles makes her full.           265

### 266-409   *Peleus, Guest of Ceyx*

     Now Peleus was happy in his son, happy in his wife,
and, if you except the crime of strangled Phocus,[39] was blest
in all things: found guilty, however, of a brother's blood
and exiled from his father's home,[40] by Trachis'[41] land was he

---

35 Proteus, associated with the sea of that name around the island of Carpathus between Rhodes and Crete.
36 Phoebus Apollo, the Sun.
37 I. e., western.
38 Thetis, as daughter of Nereus.
39 Peleus and his brother Telamon slew Phocus, their half-brother, son of Aeacus and the Nereid Psamathe (see 7. 268).
40 The island of Aegina.
41 City of Thessaly near Mt. Oeta.

*Peleus and Thetis, Baur*

received. A kingdom here without force, without the shedding of blood,       270
was ruled by Lucifer's[42] son, Ceyx,[43] who bore upon his face
his father's splendid grace. At that time he was in a state of grief
and mourning, bereft of the brother[44] so unlike himself.
When hither Aeacus' son, weary with care and travel, had come
and entered the city with only a small band and had left                     275
the flocks of sheep and cattle which he had brought
within a sheltered vale not far from the city walls,
as soon as he found a chance to come before the tyrant's face
and offer with suppliant hand the branches wound with fillets of wool,
he gives his name and the name of his sire, but conceals his crime.          280
He falsifies the reason for his flight and pleads to sustain himself
in either field or city. The Trachinian responded with peaceful mien
in words like these: "Our humble folk's resources, Peleus, to you,
lie open, nor is this kingdom to strangers unkind;
you add to this attitude persuasive force, a famous name                     285
and Jove as your grandfather; waste no time with pleas!
Whatever you seek you shall receive and call your own a share
of all that you see! Would that better were what you see!"
And then he wept: the cause that moved such grief
both Peleus and his companions ask; his response was this:                   290

---

42 The morning star. See 2. 722-25.
43 The Greek name means "Sea-gull."
44 Daedalion, whose story Ceyx will tell.

### 291-345   Daedalion and Chione

"Perhaps you might think this bird, which lives by rapine
and frightens all birds, had feathers from the beginning of time:
in fact he was a man (and—for so unchanging is his spirit—even then
was that man headstrong and in war both ferocious and ready to fight);
his name was Daedalion. Of that father[45] were we born                  295
who rouses Aurora and is last to leave the sky;
while I forever practised peace, and peace and spouse
were my concern, my brother's pleasure was in savage war.
The valor that vanquished nations and kings
is now transformed and harries Thisbe's[46] doves.                        300
A daughter Chione was born to him, with great beauty endowed,
who had a thousand suitors and with twice seven years was ready to be wed.
Returning by chance one day, Phoebus and Maia's son,
the former to his Delphi, the latter to Cyllene's[47] peak,
catch sight of her at the same time and at the same time blushed.         305
Apollo postponed his hope for love to the hours of night;
the other could bear no delay, and with a wave of the wand
that brings on sleep he touched the virgin's face: she lay beneath
that powerful touch and suffered the god's force. Night had filled the sky
with stars as Phoebus, disguised as an old woman, took those pleasures,
        already enjoyed.                                                  310
As soon as her ripened belly had completed its appointed time,
a child is born from the crafty clan of the wing-footed god,
Autolycus,[48] most ingenious at every kind of deceit,
who had the power to change things black to white,
and white to black, not unworthy of his father's skill;[49]              315
from Phoebus is born (for she brought forth twin sons)
Philammon, famous for lyre and tuneful song.
But having borne two sons and having pleased two gods
and being the daughter of a brave sire and shining grandsire,
what good is that? For many is glory not the cause of woe?                320
For her it was, most certainly! She dared to set herself
above Diana and faulted the beauty of that goddess, who, stirred
with terrible wrath, exclaims, "We shall find favor with our deeds!"
Without delay she bent the bow and thrust an arrow into
the string and pierced that deserving tongue with her shaft.             325
The tongue is silenced, and neither voice nor the words she sought
came forth, and her life and blood left her as she struggled to speak.
How wretched I was, embracing her then, as I felt in my heart

---

45 Lucifer, the Greek Phosphoros "Bringer of Light" or Eosphoros "Bringer of Dawn."
46 Town of Boeotia, noted for its doves (see Hom. *Il.* 2. 502).
47 The mountain birthplace of Mercury (Hermes) in Arcadia.
48 Father of Anticleia, mother of Ulysses (Odysseus). See on 8. 738
49 Mercury's trickery.

*Diana and Chione, Baur*

her father's grief and to my loyal brother spoke comforting words;
the father receives them not otherwise than a crag receives                    330
the murmur of the sea as he mourns the daughter he has lost;
indeed, in seeing her on the pyre, four times he made a rush
to enter the midst of the flames, four times was he restrained;
at last he commits his stricken limbs to flight and like
a bullock whose neck bears the stings of wasps                                 335
he rushes off where there is no path. Then I thought he ran
more quickly than a man, and you might think he had taken wing.
He therefore flees us all and quickly, in his desire to die, gains
Parnassus' peak; but Apollo took pity when
Daedalion cast himself from the lofty rock,                                     340
and made him a bird and lifted him up with sudden wings
and gave him a curved beak, gave him curved hooks for claws,
retaining his earlier valor, even greater than bodily strength;
and now he is a hawk, to none sufficiently just; against
all birds he rages and in grieving becomes the cause of grief."                345

### 346-409   Peleus Continued

While Lucifer's son is telling the wonders about
his brother, Phocian Onetor,[50] the guardian of the flock,
comes running, gasping for breath from his haste
and says, "Peleus, Peleus, I come as herald of great calamity
to you." Peleus commands him to reveal whatever he has                         350

---

50 Meaning "Helper," the name suits his role as Peleus' herdsman.

to say, and the Trachinian[51] himself was anxious, his face filled with fear.
Onetor replies, "I had driven the weary bullocks to
the crescent shore, when the Sun at his highest in mid-course
looked back upon as much as he could see in front of him;
some bulls had bent their knees upon the yellow sand                    355
and lay on their sides, looking out upon the water's wide expanse,
while others were wandering lazily here and there;
still others are swimming and rising above the water's plain only with
their necks. A temple was near the sea, bright with neither marble nor gold,
but made of thickly set beams in the shadow of an ancient grove:        360
the Nereids and Nereus possess it (a sailor told me, as he dried
his nets upon the shore, that they were gods of the sea);
a marsh lies near it, filled with dense willow trees,
which tide-water from the sea had turned into a swamp:
from there a huge beast of a wolf, creating a crashing din, terrifies    365
the area nearby and emerges from the marshy underbrush
besmeared with foam, his flashing jaws drenched
with blood, his eyes suffused with ruddy flame.
Although he rages with madness and hunger at once,
his madness is more severe: he thinks not to end his fast               370
and awful hunger with the slaughter of bulls but instead
inflicts harm upon the whole herd and like a foe levels it all.
And some of us as well, wounded by his deadly jaws,
as we defend ourselves, are given to death: the breakers on
the shore are red, the marshes, too, that echoed with the bellowing herd.  375
Delay, however, is ruinous, no hesitation is allowed:
while some of us are left, let's all come together with arms,
or take up arms and wield our weapons as one."
        So spoke the rustic: Peleus was by the disaster left unmoved,
but, mindful of his wrong, surmises that the bereft Nereid[52]          380
was sending destruction as a sacrifice to dead Phocus in the underworld.
The order of the Oetaean[53] king is for the men to arm themselves
and take up savage spears; he was himself preparing to go
with them, but Alcyone his wife was awakened by the row
and rushed forth, her hair not fully arranged,                         385
her tresses hanging loose, and fell upon her husband's neck,
imploring him with words and tears to send aid but not
himself and to save two lives with one stroke.
The son of Aeacus replies, "Dispense with your fears,
both pious and seemly! I am full of gratitude for your promise of aid.    390
I do not want arms taken up against this strange monster on my behalf;

---

51 Ceyx.
52 Psamathe, daughter of the sea-god Nereus, whose son Phocus Peleus had killed.
53 Ceyx is king of Trachis, near Mt. Oeta.

I must appeal to the divinity of the sea!" There was a high tower,
a lighthouse at the top of the citadel, well known and loved by weary ships:
They reach its height and with a groan behold the bulls
laid low upon the shore, and the ravager ferocious with                    395
his bloody mouth, his shaggy coat stained with gore.
Then, stretching his hands towards the shore of the open sea,
to cerule Psamathe Peleus prays that she end her wrath
and bring her aid; and by the pleas of Aeacus' son
she is not moved, but Thetis as suppliant for her spouse                   400
obtained her forgiveness. Yet the wolf, though summoned from
his eager slaughter, persists, made savage by the sweetness of blood,
until the goddess changed him as he clung to a wounded heifer's neck
to marble: except for its color the body is preserved in every detail,
for only the color of the stone revealed that it                          405
was not a wolf and need not be feared.
But still the fates do not allow banished Peleus to settle in
this land; as a wandering exile he goes to Magnesia and there
received from Haemonian[54] Acastus[55] purification for spilling blood.

### 410-748   *Ceyx and Alcyone*

Disturbed and anxious of heart was Ceyx, meanwhile, by                     410
the marvels of his brother and those that followed his brother's fate;
in order to consult the sacred responses—that comfort of mankind,
he plans to go to the Clarian[56] god, for impious Phorbas and his
Phlegyans[57] were making the journey to Delphi's temple unsafe.
Before he left, however, he informed you of his intent,                    415
most faithful Alcyone; at once her inmost bones received
a chill, a pallor quite like boxwood covered her face,
and tears in profusion moistened her face.
She thrice attempted to speak and three times drenched her face
with tears and, with sobs breaking into her pious complaints,              420
exclaimed, "What fault of mine, my dearest, has changed your mind?
Where now is that concern for me you were wont to show before?
Can you so casually now depart with Alcyone left behind?
Does now a lengthy journey appeal? Am I when absent dearer to you?
But since, I suppose you'll say, the journey's by land, I'll only have      425
to grieve, not really fear, and my concerns will be lacking in fright.
The oceans, however, terrify me, and the picture of the angry sea:
and recently I saw shattered planks upon the shore,
and often I have read the names on empty tombs.

---

54 Haemonia is an archaic name for Thessaly.
55 King of Thessaly, son of Pelias.
56 In order to reach Claros, a city in Ionia and its temple of Apollo, Ceyx must travel by sea.
57 Phorbas was leader of the Phlegyans, Minyans from Boeotia, who plundered the temple of Apollo at Delphi. A Phorbas and Phlegyas are mentioned as followers of Phineus in 5. 74 and 87.

Do not let false confidence touch your mind                                    430
in having Hippotades as your father-in-law, who contains
the powerful winds[58] within his prison and calms the sea at will.
When once the winds have been released and possess the sea,
to them is nothing forbidden: abandoned to them is all the earth
and all the deep; they also vex the clouds of the sky                          435
and hurl forth from their wild collisions red fires.
The more I know them (for I do know them and often as a child
within my father's home I saw them), the more I deem them to be feared.
But if you cannot be turned from your intent by any pleas of mine,
dear husband, and on going you are all too bent,                               440
then take me with you as well! Then surely we shall together be dashed,
and I shall only fear what I shall suffer, and together we shall endure
whatever shall come to pass, together over the wide sea shall we be borne."
      The starry[59] husband of Aeolus' daughter is moved by words
and tears like these, for the fire of love he felt no less than she,           445
but is not willing to set aside his plans to cross sea,
nor in the peril to allow Alcyone to have any part,
and answers with many words that comforted her heart.
Yet even then she does not approve of his plan; he adds therefore
another assurance, which alone brought his lover's consent:                    450
"However long we be delayed, by my father's fires I swear
to you that, if the fates grant my return,
I shall return before the moon has twice filled her orb."
When by these promises hope of return is raised,
he orders at once the ship-builders to launch a pine ship                      455
into the sea and to fit it out with all its gear.
In seeing it Alcyone, as though foreseeing the future, was filled
again with terror and let go her welling tears
and wrapped her arms about him; when, with sorrowful face
and filled with woe, she said "Farewell," she completely collapsed.            460
The young men, however, despite Ceyx' attempt at delay,
draw back the oars in twinned rows to their stout-hearted breasts
and split the sea with even strokes: she lifts
her tear-moistened eyes and sees as he stands upon
the crescent[60] prow her husband waving first to her with his hand,           465
and she waves back her familiar hands; when the land recedes
still further and their faces can no longer be discerned by their eyes,
she follows while she can the pine ship as it vanishes from sight;
and even when it was so far removed as scarcely visible,

---

58 This patronymic refers to Aeolus, ruler of the winds, the son of Hippotes. In Homer, *Od.* 10. 1-79,
   Aeolus is human, in Vergil, a god. Alcyone is the daughter of Aeolus.
59 As son of Lucifer.
60 Translating *recurva puppe*, instead of *relicta* (nominative) "left behind."

she still gazes at the sail floating at the top of the mast; 470
and when she no longer sees the sails, in anguish she sees her empty bed
and lays herself upon the couch: both bedchamber and couch renew
Alcyone's tears and remind her of her now absent part.
They left the harbor and the breeze moved the ropes:
the captain turns the hanging oars to the ship's side 475
and raises to the top of the pole the yard-arms and from all the mast
spreads out the sails and catches the facing winds.
The prow was plying either less or certainly no more
than mid-sea, and the opposing shores were equally far apart,
when in the depth of night the sea begins with swelling waves 480
to whiten and the headwind of Eurus[61] to blow with greater force.
"Reduce at once the yard-arms," the helmsman shouts,
"and make fast the whole sail to the yards."
He gives the order but the opposing gusts impede his commands,
nor does the roar of the sea permit any voice to be heard: 485
while others on their own, however, hasten to draw in the oars,
still others shore up the sides and others deny the sails to the winds;
one sailor bails out the flood and pours the sea back into the sea;
another takes hold of the yards; while this is happening in disarray,
the storm's severity increases, and the ferocious winds 490
wage war from every direction and stir to fury the flood.
The helmsman himself is afraid, admitting that he himself
knows not the condition of the ship, nor what to order or forbid:
the greater the mass of woe, the mightier its power over skill.
Indeed the men create a din with shouting, with whistling the ropes, 495
the heavy water with the fall of waves, with thunder the sky.
The ocean rises high with its waves and seems
to reach the sky and touch the covering clouds;
and now, when it roils up from the bottom the yellow sands,
it takes on their color, and the next moment the wave is blacker than the Styx, 500
and sometimes it is brought low and grows white with hissing foam.
The Trachinian ship itself is driven by these variable winds,
now lifted high as though from a mountain top
appearing to gaze down into the valley and even to Acheron below,
and now, when the arching sea surrounds it riding low, 505
appearing to gaze up at heaven's height from the pit of hell.
It frequently makes a great creaking sound when its sides are struck,
and, pounded, resounds no more lightly than when the iron battering ram
or catapult sometimes strikes the shattered citadels,
and when fierce lions, gathering strength within their breasts, 510
are wont to oppose the hunters' weapons and threatening spears,

---

61 Eurus is the East Wind.

and thus, when the wave had taken in the force of the rising winds,
it rose against the ship's walls and stood higher than they;
and now the pegs are weakening, and, deprived of their coating of wax,
the chinks are gaping and offer access to the lethal waves.                    515
Behold, the heavy rains are falling from the opening clouds:
you might have thought the whole sky had descended into the sea
and that the swollen sea had ascended into the expanse of the sky.
The sails are soaked by the rain and with the celestial waves
are mixed the ocean's waters; the ethereal sky lacks its lights,             520
and gloomy night is oppressed by the storm's darkness and its own.
But yet the flashing lightning splits them open, providing light:
and even the rains are ablaze with the lightning's fires.
The flood makes a leap into the curved fitted hull of the ship;
and like a soldier who stands out above all the rest                          525
and, having repeatedly leapt against the defending city's walls,
at last, inflamed with love of praise, gains his hope
and one alone among a thousand fellows seizes the wall,
just so, when nine times the waves have dashed the lofty sides,
the force of the tenth rising wave rushes more destructively                  530
and does not cease assaulting the weary ship until
it leaps, as it were, within the walls of the captive ship.
While part of the sea was trying to invade the bark,
a part of it was already inside: all within were no less afraid
than when a city trembles as those outside are digging through               535
the wall and others inside have gained control of the wall.
All skill is useless, courage sinks, and deaths seem to come
in number equal to the waves and to break in and invade.
This man cannot hold back his tears, that one is dazed, that one calls
those blest who wait for burial, this one worships with his vows             540
divinity, raising his ineffectual arms to the sky he cannot see
and begging for help; to one his brother and father come to mind,
his house and children to another and all that had been left behind.
Alcyone moves Ceyx, Ceyx' mouth speaks of nothing but
Alcyone, and though he wishes for her alone,                                  545
that she is absent makes him glad; he would also wish to look again
upon the shores of his native land and turn his final gaze upon his home,
but knows not where he is. With huge whirling pools the sea
is so aboil, and a shadow emerging from the pitch-black clouds
conceals the whole sky, and doubled is the face of night.                    550
The mast is shattered by the watery cyclone's attack,
the rudder is shattered, too, and one surmounting wave,
exulting like a victor in the spoils, rolls in, looking down upon
the other waves; no lighter than if someone had torn from their roots

*Alcyone, Juno and Iris, Solis*

both Athos[62] and Pindus[63] and cast them into the open sea                        555
does that plunging wave fall and at the same time with its weight
and force send that ship to the bottom of the sea; and with it
the greater part of the crew is overwhelmed by the heavy flood
and unreturned to the air meets its doom; the others cling to bits
and pieces of the hull; Ceyx himself with the hand that used                          560
to hold the scepter clings to fragments of the ship and invokes,
alas, his father-in-law and father! And most of all, yet vainly, is
Alcyone his wife upon the swimmer's lips: he thinks of her and calls
her name and prays that the waves bring his body before
her very eyes that in death he be buried by loving hands.                             565
Whenever the flood allows him as he swims to gasp for breath,
he cries out the name of absent Alcyone and murmurs it into the waves
themselves. Behold, above the midst of the flood a black arch
of water is breaking, and, once the wave breaks, it sinks and hides his head.
Obscure was Lucifer, nor could you recognize anyone in such                           570
a light, and since he could not leave the sky,
he covered his face with dense clouds.
        The daughter of Aeolus, meanwhile, unaware of this great woe,
is counting the nights; already she hastens to prepare raiment
for him to put on and for herself as well to wear for the day                         575

---

62 Mountain in Macedonia.
63 Mountain in Thessaly.

when he would come and is looking forward to his return in vain.
To all the gods above was she offering pious incense in truth,
yet more than those of the others she tended Juno's shrine,
approaching that altar for her husband, who was no more,
and praying that her husband would safely return                                    580
and love no woman more than her. This last alone
of all she asked was it possible for her to obtain.

    The goddess, however, no longer endures being implored
on behalf of one already dead and, to keep her altar untouched
by hands of mourning, said, "Iris,[64] faithful messenger of my voice,            585
go quickly and visit the hall of soporific Sleep[65]
and order him to send dreams to Alcyone in the form
of Ceyx, already dead, that will tell his true fate."
The goddess had spoken: Iris dons her thousand-colored cloak
and, marking the sky with the curve of a bow, seeks out                            590
the cloud-concealed home of the requested king.

    There is a cave near the Cimmerians[66] in a deep recess,
a hollow mountain, the house and inner courts of indolent Sleep,
where Phoebus neither rising nor setting nor at his height
can ever enter with his rays: clouds filled with gloomy mist                       595
rise out of the ground along with the wavering light of dusk.
No vigilant bird in that place with the songs of its crested head
evokes Aurora, nor do the voices of watchful dogs break
the silence, nor those of geese, even more intelligent than dogs;
no beasts of the wild, no flocks, no branches moved by the breeze                  600
produce a sound, no clamor of human tongues.

    Mute silence inhabits the place; but, rising from the stony floor,
the stream of Lethe's[67] water glides, its wave making murmur with
the clattering rustle of pebbles and inviting sleep.
Before the entrance of the cavern poppies in profusion bloom                       605
and countless herbs, from whose juices damp Night
collects her slumber and spreads it over the darkened earth.
In all the house there is no door, in case the hinge should creak
when turned; upon the threshold there is no guard;
but in the midst of the cave there is a lofty couch of ebony,                      610
made soft with down, dark-colored, bedecked with a coverlet of drab,
upon which the god himself lies asleep, his limbs relaxed.
Around him lie scattered empty Dreams imitating vain
and varied forms, as many in number as the harvest grains,
as many as the forest's leaves, the sands tossed upon the shore.                   615

---

64 Goddess of the rainbow and messenger of Juno.
65 Somnus.
66 A mythical people thought to live in a dark, cold region beyond the north shore of the Black Sea.
67 Lethe means "Forgetfulness" in Greek.

   As soon as the maiden entered and dispelled with her hands
the Dreams that opposed her way, her holy raiment filled the house
with splendor, and the god, who scarcely raised his eyes, weighed down
and sluggish, again and again falling back asleep
and striking the top of his chest with his nodding chin,                           620
at last raised himself upon his elbow and got free of himself
and asks why she (whom he recognized) had come. And she:
"O sleep, repose of all things, Sleep, serenest of gods,
and peace of mind, you, shunned by care, you, who soothe
all bodies made weary with service and restore them for toil,                      625
command the Dreams, which match in imitation true forms,
to go to Alcyone in Herculean Trachis in the likeness of
the king and fashion the image of the wrecked ship's remains.
This order is from Juno." Iris, after delivering the commands,
departs: for she could no longer endure the force                                  630
of slumber and felt sleep moving slowly over her limbs
and flees and retraces the bow by which she had just now come.
   The father, however, arouses Morpheus from the multitude of
his thousand sons, that creator and simulator of shape,
than whom no other expresses more cleverly the walk                                635
and face and sound of one who speaks;
he puts on the garb and words customary to each.
He imitates, however, only human beings, for another son
becomes a wild beast, becomes a bird, becomes a long-bodied snake:
the gods call him Icelos,[68] but the mortal host name him Phobetor;               640
there is a third as well with a different skill,
called Phantasos, who changes all things deceptively into soil
and stone and water and tree-trunk and everything lacking life.
Of these some reveal their faces to kings and chiefs by night,
while others wander through the masses and common folk.                            645
Old Sleep passes over these sons and chooses but one of all
the brothers, Morpheus, to carry out what Thaumas'[69] daughter decreed.
This done, again is Sleep overcome with gentle weariness:
he lay down his head and hid himself within the lofty couch.
   His wings making no sound, Morpheus flies through                               650
the shadows and with but brief delay reaches the town
of Haemonia and, freeing his body of its wings,
assumes the appearance of Ceyx, and in this ghastly form,
resembling the dead man, of raiment completely bare,
he stood before the couch of his wretched wife; the husband's beard               655
looks soaked, and from his dripping hair the water seems to flow.

---

68 The Greek names in this list of Somnus' sons are meaningful: Icelos "Resembling," Phobetor
    "Causing Terror," Phantasos "Imager," and Morpheus "Shape."
69 Thaumas "Marvel," father of Iris.

Then leaning over the bed, his face streaming with tears,
he says this: "Do you recognize Ceyx, most sorrowful wife,
or has my face been changed by death? Look carefully, you will know
and find in place of your spouse your spouse's shade!                          660
Your prayers, Alcyone, have brought us no help,
for we have died! Cease promising me to yourself in vain!
A cloud-filled Auster[70] caught my ship at sea
and tossed and wrecked it with the intensity of its blast
and, as I cried out your name to no avail, my mouth                            665
was filled by the flood. —No ambiguous inventor announces this
to you, nor are you hearing this through rumors of uncertain source:
in person do I myself, the victim of shipwreck, reveal my doom.
Arise, get up, pour forth your tears, put on robes of grief,
do not allow me to go to unsubstantial Tartarus unbewailed!"                   670
And Morpheus applies to these words the voice that the wife
would think her husband's (and seemed to weep genuine tears
as well), and used the gestures of Ceyx's hands.
Alcyone groans amid her tears, and still sleeping moves
her limbs and, seeking his body, merely embraces the air                       675
and cries aloud, "Wait, where are you rushing off to? Let's go
together!" Disturbed by her own voice and the vision of the man
she shakes off sleep, and first looks about to see if he is there
whom she had just now seen (for servants, alerted by her cries,
had brought in light). After finding no one anywhere,                          680
she strikes her face with her hand and tears her robe from her breast
and beats the breasts themselves nor bothers to let down her hair:
she cuts it and, to the nurse who asks the reason for her grief,
exclaims, "Alcyone is no more, is no more. She has died along
with her beloved Ceyx. Away with all consoling words!                          685
He died a victim of shipwreck: I have seen and recognized
him as I stretched forth my hands, seeking to hold him back as he left.
Although he was a shade, yet the shade was clear and in truth
my husband's. He did not have, in case you're wondering,
his usual expression nor the radiant[71] mien he had before:                   690
but pale and naked and with his hair still soaking wet
did I, alas for me, behold him. He stood in this very place,
the wretched man." And then she checks to see if any footprints remain.
"This very thing it was, the very thing I feared with my prophetic mind
in begging you not to abandon me and follow the winds.                         695
But surely it would have been my wish that since you were leaving to die
that you had taken me along: it would have been very useful to me
if I had gone with you, for then I should not have spent

---

70 South Wind.
71 As son of Lucifer.

*Ceyx/Morpheus Appears to Alcyone, Baur*

a part of my life without you, nor death have come to us separately.
But now I perish apart from you, and apart I am also tossed by the waves,    700
and even without me the sea possesses me. More cruel than the sea
itself would be my mind if I should struggle to extend my life
yet further and fight to survive a sorrow so great!
Yet neither shall I fight nor shall I abandon you, wretched man,
and now at least I shall come as your companion, and in one tomb    705
if not one urn the written epitaph shall unite us: if not
your bones with my bones, yet shall I touch your name with my name."
Her sorrow restrains her from saying more, all speech is replaced
by lamentation, and groans are drawn from her stricken heart.
    The morning had come: she goes from her dwelling to the shore    710
and finds again in sorrow that place from which she had seen him depart,
and as she tarries awhile and as she says, "Here he untied the ropes,
upon this shore he kissed me as he left," and as she recalls
his memorable actions in this place and looks out
to sea, she catches sight at some distance among the waves    715
a body-like something, uncertain what it was
at first; but after being pushed closer by the wave,
it clearly appeared to be a body, even if not yet near.
She knew not who it was, but since it was a shipwrecked man
the omen moved her, and, as if to shed a tear for one unknown,    720
she says, "Ah, wretched man, whoever you are, and if you have a wife!"
The waves have brought the body closer: the more she looks at it
the less and still less is she in control of her mind. Ah woe!
She sees it now brought close enough to the shore to recognize:

it was her husband! "It's he!" she exclaims, and at once                    725
she tears her face, her hair, her raiment, and, stretching out her trembling hands
to Ceyx, says, "Is this the way, O dearest husband, is this
the way, O pitiful man, you return to me?" In these waters there is
a mole made by human hands, that breaks the sea's
initial wrath and weakens in advance the onrush of the waves.               730
She takes a leap (a marvel that it was possible!) and flew,
and, beating the thin air with her new born wings,
she skimmed along the tops of the waves as a wretched bird,
and, as she flew, her mouth emitted a sound like one
in grief, complaining shrilly with its slender beak.                        735
However, when she lit upon the silent and bloodless corpse,
embracing the beloved limbs with her recent wings,
she gave him frigid kisses with her hardened beak.
Did Ceyx feel this, or did he seem to lift his face in the motion of
the waves? The people were unsure, but he had indeed                        740
perceived the kisses: and finally, with the gods taking pity, both
are changed to birds. Though subject to the same fate,
their love remained even then, nor was the conjugal bond
dissolved in their winged form: they become parents and mate
and in the season of winter for seven placid days                           745
Alcyone sits brooding in her nest suspended on the water's plain.
The wave of the sea lies becalmed: for Aeolus checks and keeps
the winds from escaping and surrenders to his progeny the sea.

### 749-95   Aesacus and Hesperia

A certain old fellow observes them flying side by side
above the wide sea and praises their love, preserved even to the end:       750
the man next to him, or perhaps the same one, said, "This one, too,
you see skimming the sea with his close-fitting legs"
(he pointed at a diver endowed with its long neck)
"has royal descent, and if you wish to trace in full
his line down to him, this is the origin of his line: Ilus first            755
and Assaracus and Ganymede, stolen by Jove,
then old Laomedon and Priam, allotted in her final years
to Troy; the brother of Hector was he, and had
he not met his death in the prime of youth,
perhaps he would have a name not less well-known                            760
than Hector. Although Dymas' daughter[72] gave Hector birth,
it's said that Alexiroë, two-horned Granicus'[73] child
bore Aesacus in secret at shady Ida's[74] foot.

---

72 Hecuba.
73 A river of Mysia in Asia Minor.
74 A mountain near Troy.

*Aesacus and Hesperia, Solis*

He hated cities, and far from his shining court
inhabited secluded mountains and humble fields                              765
and went but rarely to the throngs of Ilium.
Possessing no rustic heart, however, nor one invincible by love,
he often caught sight of Hesperia in all the woods
and watched the daughter of Cebren,[75] when she dried in the sun
the locks that fell over her shoulders as she sat upon her father's bank.    770
Once noticed, the nymph takes flight, just as the frightened doe
runs from the tawny wolf and the river duck, espied from afar,
abandons her pond and flees the hawk. The Trojan hero pursues
the girl, made swift now by fear, himself made swift by love.
Behold, a serpent hiding in the grass with curving fangs                     775
just grazed the foot of the fleeing girl and left its venom in her form;
her flight is ended with her life: he madly takes her in his arms
now lifeless and shouts, 'Wrong was I, wrong was I to follow you!
But this I did not fear, nor did I wish to win at such a price.
We both have destroyed you, wretched girl: the wound was given by            780
the snake, the cause by me! I am more accursed than it,
unless by my death I provide you some comfort in death.'
He spoke and from the cliff which the roaring wave had eaten away
he cast himself into the ocean. Tethys,[76] taking pity as he fell,

---

75 A river of the Troad.
76 The Titan sea-goddess.

received him gently and covered him with feathers as he swam 785
and did not grant him access to the death he sought.
The lover is indignant that he is forced, unwilling, to live
and that his soul is hindered when it wants to leave
its wretched home, and since he had taken on new wings, 790
he soars aloft and once again casts his body down upon the sea.
His pinions lighten his fall: Aesacus rages and dives headlong into
the deep, and tries endlessly to find the path of death.
His love made him thin: long were the legs between his joints,
his neck remains long, from his body his head is far away;
he loves the sea and has his name[77] because he dives in it." 795

---

77 He is called Mergus "Diver."

# BOOK 12

| | |
|---|---|
| 1-38 | The Greeks at Aulis |
| 39-63 | Fama (Rumor) |
| 64-145 | Cycnus and Achilles |
| 146-209 | Caeneus |
| 210-535 | Nestor Narrates the Battle of the Lapiths and Centaurs |
| 393-428 | Hylonome and Cyllarus |
| 536-79 | Periclymenus |
| 580-628 | The Death of Achilles |

## 1-38  *The Greeks at Aulis*

Since father Priam was unaware that Aesacus had taken wing
and lived, he was in mourning; Hector had also offered empty funeral rites
along with his brothers and inscribed a name upon a tomb.
The presence of Paris at the sad ceremony was missed,
who with his stolen bride soon brought a lengthy war                                    5
into his native land: conspiring together, there came in pursuit
a thousand ships and the Pelasgian nation's whole community;
nor would her vindication have been delayed if the savage winds
had not made passage impossible, and the Boeotian land
had not held back the ships ready to sail at Aulis that teems with fish.          10
Just as the Danaans[1] were preparing here to make the ancestral sacrifice to Jove,
and as the kindled flames made the ancient altar glow bright,
they saw a blue-green serpent creeping up
a plane tree standing near the sacrifices then underway.
A nest of twice four birds was at the top of the tree:                                   15
as soon as the serpent snatched them up with the mother flitting about
her loss and hid them in its greedy maw,
they all stood amazed, except that augur of the truth,
the son[2] of Thestor, who says, "We shall be victorious! Pelasgians, rejoice!
For Troy will fall, although the delay of our toil will be long,"                      20
explaining the nine birds as nine years of war.
But meanwhile the serpent, as it coiled itself about the tree's green limbs

---

1 The Greeks or Argives, as descendants of Danaus.
2 Calchas.

becomes a stone, and that rock preserves the image of a snake.[3]

While Nereus[4] remained violent in the Aonian[5] waves
and did not transport the war, causing some to believe                              25
that Neptune was sparing Troy because he had built the city's walls,
the son of Thestor did not agree: for he is neither unaware nor silent about
the need for virgin blood to placate the virgin-goddess'[6] wrath.
When once the public need had conquered piety
and kingly office the father, and Iphigenia, preparing to give                      30
her innocent blood, stood before the altar even as the attendants wept,
the goddess was overcome and cast a cloud over their eyes; and in
the exercise and intensity of the rite and the cries of those who prayed
they say that she exchanged a doe as substitute for the Mycenaean girl.
When therefore, as was fitting, Diana had by the sacrifice been assuaged,          35
and both the wrath of Phoebe and of the sea had passed,
the thousands ships receive the winds at their back
and after many adventures gain the Phrygian[7] beach.

### 39-63   *Fama (Rumor)*

There is a place in the middle of the globe twixt land and sea
and heavenly expanse, the confines of the three-fold world,                        40
from which all that ever was, though removed from these spheres,
is seen, and every word penetrates empty ears.
Here Rumor dwells and makes her home at the top of the citadel,
and gives her mansion unnumbered entrances and a thousand passages
and blocks entrance to her thresholds with not a single door.                      45
By night and by day that house lies open: made entirely of sounding bronze,
the whole house moans and issues voices and repeats what it hears;
there is no stillness within and no silence anywhere,
and yet there is no clamor, instead, the murmuring of a little voice,
like waves of the sea, if heard from afar,                                         50
or like the sound of the lingering rumble of a thunderclap
when Jupiter has made the black clouds resound.
Confusion fills the courts: the fickle mobs come and go
and spread at random their fabrications mixed with truth
and thousands of rumors and jumbled stories fly about;                             55
from these some fill with talk their empty ears,
some bring the stories to others, and the extent of the lies
increases, and each new author adds something to what was heard.
Credulity is there, there, too is Error, reckless in thought,
vain Ornament and frantic Fears                                                    60

---

3 See Hom. *Il.* 2. 318.
4 God of the Sea. Housman emended to *Boreas*, North Wind.
5 Aulis was in Boeotia, also called Aeonia.
6 Diana.
7 Phrygia was the region of Asia Minor containing Troy.

*Iphigenia Saved, Solis*

and sudden Sedition and Whispers of dubious origin:
whatever is done in sky or sea or earth
she sees and pries for information throughout the world.

### 64-145  *Cycnus and Achilles*

Since she had announced the approach of the Greek ships
and strong army, not unexpected does the armed enemy                    65
arrive: the Trojans ward off their landing and protect
their shore, and first to fall in death by Hector's spear
are you, Protesilaüs,[8] and for the pitched battles the Danaan host
pays dearly, and in the slaughter Hector gains renown for bravery
of soul. And the Phrygians[9] felt with no little letting of blood      70
the power of the Achaean[10] right hand. Already the Sigean[11] shore
was growing red, already Cycnus, Neptune's son, had sent
to death a thousand men, already was Achilles in his chariot pressing on
and laying low whole enemy lines with the blow of his Pelian[12] spear;
and as he sought either Cycnus or Hector among the ranks,              75
he met up with Cycnus (Hector to the tenth year had been
postponed) and urged on his steeds, their shining necks

8 Hom. *Il.* 2. 698-702.
9 Trojans.
10 Greek.
11 A promontory near Troy.
12 I.e., that had once been a tree on Mt. Pelion in Thessaly.

weighed down by the yoke, and aims his car against the host
and, brandishing with his arms the quivering spears,
exclaimed, "Whoever you are, O youth, take comfort for your death          80
in this, that Haemonian[13] Achilles cut your throat!"
Aeacides[14] said only this: the heavy spear followed his voice,
but even though there was no error in that certain spear,
he failed to accomplish anything with the hurled iron's sharp tip
that only made a thud against his chest as though with a dull blow.          85
"O son of a goddess, for by Rumor we have heard of you,"
says Cycnus, "why should you marvel that we are without wound?"
(Achilles did marvel.) "For neither this tawny helmet with its horse-hair crest,
you see, nor the hollow shield that weighs upon my left arm,
is helpful to me: mere decoration is their intent;          90
for even so does Mars arm himself! Remove their ability
to shield and I will walk away with merely a graze.
Some merit there is in not having been born a Nereid's son,
but rather his[15] who rules Nereus and his daughters and all the sea."
He spoke and cast a spear that would be fixed into the shield          95
of Aeacides, which pierced both the bronze and the nine
next layers of bull's hide, though slowed by the tenth.
The hero knocked it out of his shield and launched with his stout hand
a quivering spear: again the body was free
of any wound; nor does a third spear's cusp have any ability          100
to injure Cycnus, who made an open target of himself.
Not otherwise did Achilles rage than a bull in an open ring
that with its terrible horns rushes at the provocations of
the red-dyed cloak and sees it avoid his wounds;
Achilles checks to see if the spear had lost its iron tip:          105
it clung fast to the wood. "Has my hand then become weak,"
he asks, "and the strength I once had in this one instance failed?
For strong, indeed, it was, both when I was first to break down
Lyrnesus'[16] walls and when I filled Tenedos[17]
and Eetion's Thebes[18] with their own blood,          110
and when the Caicus[19] flowed red with the blood of its tribes
and Telephus[20] twice felt the work of my spear.

13 Thessalian.
14 Achilles, son of Peleus, son of Aeacus.
15 This Cycnus is the son of Neptune and not the son of Sthenelus (2.367 ff.) or the son of Apollo
(7.371). The story was part of the *Cypria,* a poem of the Epic Cycle, as excerpted by Proclus,
*Chrestomathy* 1 (see Cypria and Proclus in the Index/Glossary).
16 A town near Troy.
17 A small island off the Trojan shore. Cf. Verg. *Aen.* 2. 21.
18 The Thebes of Mysia, whose king was Eetion, father of Andromache, wife of Hector.
19 A river in Mysia.
20 This king of Mysia, son of Hercules and Auge, was wounded by Achilles' spear at Troy and, following
an oracle's advice, was healed when Achilles later rubbed the spear upon the wound. Euripides'
*Telephus* treated the story of Telephus as suppliant, clad in rags.

Here, too, there are piles of slaughtered men along the beach
that I have made and see, and my right hand had the strength to do it and
still does." He spoke and, as if he gave little credence to his earlier deeds,    115
against Menoetes of the Lycian folk he cast a spear
and pierced at once both his cuirass and the breast beneath.
The head of the dying man struck the hard ground,
and from the warm wound Achilles pulls out that spear and says,
"With this hand, with this the spear have we been victorious just now,    120
the same that I shall use against this man, and, I pray, with the same result!"
With this declaration he aims again at Cycnus, nor does the ashen spear go
astray as it resounds upon his left shoulder, not escaped,
from which it is repelled as if from a wall or solid crag;
yet at the site of the blow Achilles had seen a sign    125
of blood on Cycnus and had rejoiced in vain:
there was no wound, to Menoetes belonged that blood!
Then truly enraged, from the lofty chariot he leapt
headlong and in trying to fight his untroubled foe
with shining sword hand to hand, he sees that though the shield    130
and helmet were cut through, the hard flesh had dented his sword.
Achilles took no more of this and, since his enemy's shield
had been dislodged, he bashed the hilt of his sword into his face
and hollow temples three or four times, and in pursuit confounds
and rushes the astonished man, denying him any rest: fear seizes him    135
and darkness swim before his eyes, and as he steps back
a stone trips him up in the middle of the field.
As Cycnus' body falls backwards upon the stone,
Achilles, with great force, upturns and flings him to the ground.
Then pressing his shield and hard knees into his chest,    140
he pulls the straps of his helmet, which press beneath his chin
and choke his throat and stifle his means of breath and the path
of air. Achilles prepares to strip the spoils from the conquered man:
he sees instead abandoned weapons; the god of the sea has changed
the body into a white bird, whose name[21] he had owned till now.    145

### 146-209  *Caeneus*

This labor, this battle, brought a respite of many days
and both sides laid their arms aside for a rest.
While watchful guards protected the Phrygian walls
and watchful guards protected the trenches of the Argives as well,
a festal day was at hand, in which Achilles for Cycnus' defeat    150
was placating the goddess Pallas[22] with a slaughtered heifer's blood;

---

21 The swan, *cycnus*, in Latin.
22 Athena or Minerva.

and when he had placed upon the flaming altars the sacrificial parts,[23]
their fumes, perceived by the gods, reached heaven on high;
the holy ones had their share, and on the tables the rest was laid.
The chieftains reclined on their couches and with roasted flesh                     155
made full their bodies and with wine relieved both care and thirst.
These men not in the lyre, these men not in the voices of song
or in the long pipe of many holes find their delight,
but draw out the night instead with talk, with tales
of manly courage: they tell of battles, their enemies' and their own,               160
and each in turn takes pleasure in recalling dangers met
and survived; for what would Achilles talk about,
or what would they in the presence of great Achilles talk about instead?
The most immediate talk was especially about Cycnus' defeat
and Achilles' victory: it seemed miraculous to them all                             165
that this youth's body should be impervious to any spear
and not subject to wounding and yet make an iron sword dull.
Aeacides himself was marveling at this, and the Achaeans were, too,
when Nestor speaks up: "In your generation there was only one
who scorned the sword and impenetrable by any blow,                                 170
this Cycnus. But I myself once saw as he endured a thousand blows
Perrhaebian[24] Caeneus, with his body unharmed,
ah yes, Caeneus of Perrhaebia, renowned for his deeds,
who dwelt on Othrys,[25] and the more marvelous thing about him
was being born a woman." The strangeness of this miracle moves                      175
them each and all, and they beg him to tell the tale: among
their number Achilles: "Come now, tell us, for we all desire to hear,
O eloquent old man, for you are the font of wisdom in our age,
who was this Caeneus, why was he changed to the opposite sex,
in what warfare, in the contest of what strife was he known                         180
to you, by whom was he defeated, if defeated by any at all?"
The old man replies: "Though sluggish old age may stand in my way,
and many things I saw many years ago may escape me now,
yet many things I do recall, and there is nothing so imprinted within
my heart amidst so many deeds in war and at home as this,                           185
and if lengthy old age was able to make anyone
a witness of many deeds, it was I who have lived
two hundred years and now am living in my third.[26]
      "The offspring of Elatus,[27] Caenis,[28] was for beauty famed,
the loveliest of Thessalian maidens, and among both cities nearby                   190

23 The entrails.
24 Perrhaebia was a mountainous region of northern Thessaly.
25 A mountain range in southern Thessaly.
26 Ovid misunderstands Homer's "two generations of men," *Il.* 1. 250, as "two centuries."
27 One of the Lapiths, a people of Thessaly.
28 The ending of the name Caenis, like that of Iphis in Book 9, is ambiguous in gender. The name will
    be changed to Caeneus, clearly masculine.

*Caenis and Poseidon, Solis*

and yours, Achilles (for she was a compatriot of yours)
the eager offers of many suitors sought her in vain.
Perhaps even Peleus would have tried to win her bed:
but either his marriage with your mother had already occurred
or had been promised. And Caenis had committed herself                     195
in marriage to none and, strolling one day on a secluded shore,
was taken by force by the water's god (so goes the tale),
and Neptune, having found pleasure in this new love,
declared, 'Your wishes will not be refused,
choose now, what you desire!' (This, too, is Rumor's tale).                200
Replying, Caenis says, 'This wrongful act has created the great
desire of being able not to suffer such a thing again; grant me not
to be a woman and you will have granted all!' Her final words she spoke
with deeper voice and might have seemed to come from a man's voice,
which was the case; for already had the god of the deep sea assented to   205
the wish and granted besides that he have the power to remain
unwounded by any blow and not succumb to any sword.
Atracides[29] departed, content in the gift, and spent his life
in manly arts as he roamed the Peneian[30] fields.

---

29 Caeneus, descendant of Atrax, founder of the town of Atrax in Thessaly.
30 Thessalian, since the river Peneus runs through Thessaly.

### 210-535    Nestor Narrates the Battle of the Lapiths and Centaurs.

"The son[31] of bold Ixion[32] had brought Hippodame[33] home                 210
to be his bride and bid the wild cloud-born clan[34] to recline at his tables set
in order within a secluded recess protected by trees.
Haemonian chieftains were there, and we were there ourselves.
The royal palace rang with the disorderly crowd.
Behold, they're singing hymns to Hymen, the courts are smoky with fires,   215
the maiden is present, surrounded by a band of older and younger wives,
outstanding for her beauty; we declared Pirithoüs happy in
that bride and almost confounded the wedding omens by doing so,
because, Eurytus, the wildest of all the wild Centaur clan,
your breast burns as much with wine as for the maid you see              220
and drunkenness doubled by lust has sway over you.
The tables are upturned and the celebration set headlong in disarray,
the newly married bride is seized by the hair and stolen away.
Eurytus steals Hippodame, the others whichever one they desired
or could, and the image is that of a city taken in war.                  225
The house rings with the shouting of women: at once we all
spring up, and Theseus first says, 'What is driving you mad,
Eurytus? And why do you provoke Pirithoüs while I'm alive
and foolishly thus do violence to the two of us at once?'
[Or lest that great-souled man have said this in vain, he routs          230
the Centaur crowd and rescues the stolen bride from their mad grasp.][35]
The other said nothing (for he could not possibly defend
his deeds with words), but attacks the avenger's face
with wanton hands and pummels that noble breast.
By chance there was at hand an ancient mixing bowl                       235
with markings in high-relief; the huge object did Aegeus' son,
more huge himself, lift high and hurl at his opponent's face:
who, vomiting clots of blood with brains and unmixed wine
from both the wound and his mouth, fell back upon the soggy sand
and kicked in convulsive death. His bi-formed brothers grow hot          240
in seeing his death and all eagerly speak with one voice, 'To arms, to arms!'
The wine gave them courage and at the onset of battle the cups
are hurled and flying about, and rounded caldrons and fragile jugs,
intended once for the banquet, are now applied to killing and war.

"Amycus, Ophion's son, was first to despoil without fear                 245
the courts of their gifts and first tore loose from the house
a chandelier containing many glittering lamps;

---

31 Pirithoüs, king of the Lapiths.
32 For attempting to rape Juno, Ixion is made to ride a perpetual wheel in the Underworld, 4. 461. Cf.
       9. 124 and 10. 42.
33 Also known as Hippodamia.
34 Having intercourse with a cloud made to resemble Juno, Ixion became the father of the Centaurs.
35 These bracketed lines are omitted in principal manuscripts and are probably not genuine.

he lifted it high, like one who strives to break
with sacrificial axe the shining neck of a bull,
and smashes it against the brow of the Lapith Celadon                    250
and left unrecognizably disfigured the bones in his face.
His eyes popped out, and his nose was driven back
into the broken bones of his face and fixed within his throat.
Pelates of Pella, having twisted off a leg of the maple table, knocked
him to the ground with his chin fallen upon his chest                    255
and with a second blow sends him spitting out teeth
commingled with dark blood to the shades of Tartarus.
        "Grynaeus next, as he stood gazing with terrible mien
upon the smoky altar, says, 'Why don't we use this?'
and lifted up the enormous altar, fires and all,                         260
and hurled it directly at the Lapith host
and weighed down two, Broteas and Orios. Mycale was
Orios' mother, who had often drawn down with her spells,
as all agreed, the horns of the reluctant moon.[36]
'You'll not escape unpunished, if only I get my hands on a spear!'       265
Exadius had said, and finds a spear in form of the horns of a stag
that had been hung as a votive offering[37] on a lofty pine.
Two branches of it are thrust into Grynaeus' lights
and gouge out his eyes, one of which sticks to the horns,
the other oozes into his beard and hangs clotted with blood.            270
        "Look there, Rhoetus snatches up from the altar a torch
of plum-wood and from the right smashes clean through
Charaxus' temples, covered with yellow locks.
His hair, set ablaze like dry grain by the rapid flame,
was burned, and the blood, seared within the wound,                      275
gave off a terrible crackling sound, like that of iron made red
by fire when with the curved tongs the smith has drawn
it out and dipped it into the tank: but then
it hisses and crackles, submerged in the tepid wave.[38]
Despite his wound he brushes the greedy fire out of his thick hair       280
and raises upon his shoulders the threshold from the ground,
as heavy as a wagon. Its very weight prevented the throw
from reaching his foe: its rocky mass, however, did crush
an ally, Cometes, standing closer. Rhoetus did not
suppress his joy and says, 'I pray that your camp's                      285
remaining forces be just as brave!' He sought again
the wound and renewed the flame with the half-burnt torch

---

36 Thessalian women were notorious for witchcraft.
37 Probably to Diana, goddess of the hunt.
38 Translating *tepida*. With *trepida*: "in the agitated wave" (the water being afraid of the hot iron or set
   in motion by it); with *intrepida*: "in the fearless wave" (the water being unafraid of the hot iron).
   The MSS vary.

and, striking three or four times a heavy blow against his crown,
broke through the skull so that the bones settled into the oozing brains.
  "The victor moves on to Euagrus, Corythus, and Dryas[39] next;  290
When one of these, his cheeks clothed with first down,
had fallen, Corythus by name, Euagrus says, 'What glory do
you gain in killing a boy?' But Rhoetus allows him to say
no more and fiercely buries in the mouth of the man as he spoke
his ruddy flames, and on through his mouth into his chest.  295
He makes for you as well, savage Dryas, whirling the torch about
his head, but against you the result was not the same:
for as he boasted of his uninterrupted series of slayings, you stab
him with a fire-sharpened stake where his shoulder joins his neck.
He groaned and with effort pulled out the stake from solid bone,  300
and then Rhoetus, drenched in his own blood, took flight.
And Orneus fled, and Lycabas, and, his right shoulder dealt
a wound, Medon, and with Pisenor Thaumas, too,
and Mermeros, who in running had lately excelled them all,
but now moved more slowly from the wound he had received.  305
And Pholus and Melaneus and Abas, hunter of boars
and Asbolus, who had failed to dissuade his comrades from war,
an augur: he said to Nessus, fearing wounds,
'Don't bother to flee! You'll be kept safe for Hercules' bow!'
Eurynomus, though, and Lycidas, and Areos and Imbreus did not  310
escape their deaths; Dryas' right hand overwhelmed all
these foes. You also were wounded in the front,
Crenaeus, even though you had turned to flee:
for as you looked back, you were pierced by iron between
your eyes where the nose is joined to the lower brow.  315
  "In all the commotion, overcome by endless sleep
in all his veins, Aphidas[40] lay unwakened and clasping in
his languid hand a drinking cup of mixed wine,
stretched out upon an Ossaean[41] she-bear's shaggy pelt;
when Phorbas saw from afar that he wielded no arms—to no avail,  320
he fitted his fingers into the thong and said, 'You will drink
your wine mixed with the Styx!' Without further delay
he hurled the javelin against the youth, and the iron-tipped ash
was driven through his neck as he lay by chance upon his back.
Death came unfelt to him, and from his choking throat  325
black blood flowed onto the couch and into the drinking-cup itself.
  "Petraeus I myself saw trying to heave up from the earth
an acorn-bearing oak; as he grasps it in his embrace

---

39 Three Lapiths.
40 A Centaur.
41 Pertaining to Mount Ossa.

and shakes it this way and that and tosses about the weakened tree,
Pirithoüs' lance was aimed at Petraeus' ribs     330
and fastened his heaving breast to the hardness of the oak.
They said that by Pirithoüs' virtue Lycus fell,
by Pirithoüs' virtue Chromis, but neither gave the victor
such fame as Dictys and Helops gave,
for Helops was pierced by a javelin that transfixed     335
his temples, and, cast from the right, bored through the left ear,
and Dictys, slipping on the uneven edge of a cliff
while fleeing in terror as the son of Ixion pursued,
fell headlong and crashed down with the weight of his body upon
a huge mountain ash and impaled his groin upon its broken limbs.     340
    "Aphareus the avenger is present and tries to hurl
a stone wrenched from the mountain and, as he tries, Aegeus' son
attacks him with an oaken club and breaks his elbow's great bone,
and having neither time nor desire to give to death
his useless body, he leaps upon tall Bienor's back,     345
unused to carrying anyone but himself,
and pressed his knee against his ribs, his left hand
grabbing and pulling back his curly mane, and smashed
his face and threatening mouth and hardened temples with
an oaken club. And with this club he lays Nedymnus low     350
and Lycopes, the thrower of spears, and Hippasos, too,
whose chest was covered by his overgrown beard, and Ripheus, taller than
the highest trees, and Thereus, who on the Haemonian heights
caught bears and brought them home alive and against their will.
Demoleon scarce could bear any longer Theseus' success     355
in battle: he tries with enormous force to uproot
an ancient pine along with its great trunk;
because he could not do it, he broke it off and cast it at
the enemy, but Theseus retreated far from the incoming spear
when Pallas[42] warned him (or so he himself wanted it to be believed).     360
The tree, however, did not fall to no effect; for it hacked away
tall Crantor's chest and left shoulder from his neck:
that man, Achilles, had been the bearer of your father's arms;
Amyntor,[43] the ruler of the Dolopians, when vanquished in war,
had given him to Aeacus' son[44] as a faithful pledge of peace.     365
As Peleus from afar saw him laid low by this foul wound,
he says, 'Crantor, most pleasing of youths, at least receive
this offering to the dead' and with his sturdy arm hurled against
Demoleon with all his might an ashen spear,

---

42 Minerva.
43 Father of Phoenix, the tutor of Achilles and king of the Dolopians, a tribe in southwest Thessaly.
44 Peleus.

which broke the cage of his ribs and quivered as it stuck 370
within his bones. With his hand Demoleon pulls out the wooden shaft
without the point (the shaft was hard enough to retrieve): the point
was fixed in his lungs. Pain itself gave his spirit strength:
he rears up fiercely against his foe and kicks the man with his equine feet.
The other takes the resounding blows on his helmet and shield, 375
protects his shoulders and holds his weapons on guard
and with one blow through the shoulder pierces that twofold breast.[45]
Before this, however, he had given Phlegraeos and Hyles to death
by striking from afar, and in close combat Clanis and Iphinoüs;
to these is added Dorylas, who guarded his temples with 380
the pelt of a wolf and in place of a savage spear wore the curved
and splendid horns of bulls, reddened with copious gore.
    "To him I said (for courage supplied strength), 'Regard
how greatly your horns must yield to our sword,'
and bent my javelin: unable to avoid its blow, 385
he put his right hand to his brow at which it was aimed:
his hand is pinned to his brow; he raises an outcry, pinned
and overcome by the painful wound, but Peleus (who
stood closer) thrust his sword directly into his guts.
Dorylas dragged his entrails upon the ground where he darted ahead 390
and trampled on those he dragged and crushed those he trampled on,
and hobbled his legs within them and with empty belly collapsed.

### 393-428 *Hylonome and Cyllarus*

    "Cyllarus, neither did your beauty ransom you as you fought,
if truly we concede that beauty exists in that nature of yours.
The beard was beginning, a beard of gold, and golden hair 395
hung from his shoulders midway down his sides.
A pleasing vigor lay upon his face; his neck and shoulders and hands
and chest were very close to the lauded statues of the sculptors, and
wherever he was man; nor beneath that man was his guise
inferior as a horse; just give him a neck and head of a horse 400
and he will be worthy of Castor:[46] his back was so well-seated, his chest
so lofty and muscular. Though his torso throughout was as black as pitch,
his tail was shining white; the color of his legs was also white.
Though many girls from his clan had sought after him, only one
had won him, Hylonome, than whom no lovelier female among 405
these half-wild beings inhabited the high woods;
by blandishments and loving and confessions of love,
this girl alone holds Cyllarus, and also her grooming, as much

---

45 Where the Centaur's human and equine parts met.
46 Called by Homer the "breaker of horses."

as there could be grooming in such limbs: her hair was well-combed,
she decks herself now with rosemary, now with the violet or rose            410
or even sometimes wears lilies shining white,
and twice each day bathes her face in the falling springs at the top
of Pagasa's[47] forests, and dips her body twice into the stream,
nor does she stretch out the skins of any but
the choicest beasts upon her shoulders or left flank.                       415
Their love was equally shared: they roamed the hills,
together entered the caves; and together had they come into
the Lapith halls, together were they waging war:
a javelin (its owner unclear) came from the left
and pierced you, Cyllarus, just below where the neck                        420
is joined to the chest: the heart had suffered only a small wound,
but when the spear was pulled out, it and the whole body grew cold.
Immediately, Hylonome supports his dying limbs
and lays her soothing hand upon the wound and touches her mouth
to his and tries to block the path of his fleeing soul;                     425
but as she sees that he has died, she spoke words the clamor kept
from reaching my ears, and upon the spear she fell that
already pierced him and, as she died, held her husband in her embrace.
    "Before my eyes stands also the one who had bound
six lion skins together with firmly tied knots,                             430
Phaeocomes, protected both as man and horse;
he heaved a trunk, which two teams of oxen could barely move,
and smashed Tectaphus, Olenus' son, on the top of the head;
[the broad crown of his head thus broken, his soft brains
oozed down through mouth and hollow nostrils and eyes                       435
and ears like clotted milk through an oaken wicker work
or viscous fluid that under a weight trickles through
a wide-spaced sieve as it is expelled through the thickly packed holes.][48]
    "But I it was who, when he began to strip the fallen of his arms,
(your[49] father knows this) thrust a sword into the despoiler's guts.      440
And Chthonius, too, and Teleboas lie dead because
of our sword: the former had wielded a forked branch,
the latter a javelin; with the javelin he wounded me.
You see its marks! The old scar is visible even still.
I should have been sent in those days to capture Pergamum;                  445
in those days I could have delayed, if not overcome,
great Hector's arms with mine! But in those days, there was
no Hector, or maybe a boy, and now my life is running out.
Why tell you about Periphas' victory over Pyraethus of double form,

---

47 Pagasa was a town and district near Mount Pelion in Thessaly.
48 Bracketed because found only in late MS.
49 Nestor addresses Achilles.

of Ampyx, who thrust his cornel spear without                                    450
its shaft into four-footed Echeclus' opposing face?
Macareus drove a crowbar into the heart of Pelethronian[50] Erigdupus[51]
and laid him low; I recall as well the hunting spears sunk
into the groin of Cymelus[52] by Nessus' hands.
You must not believe that Mopsus, Ampycus' son, only told              455
the future: for by the cast of Mopsus' spear double-formed
Hodites fell and tried in vain to speak with his tongue
pinned fast to his chin and his chin to his throat.
      "To death had Caeneus sent five: Styphelus and Antimachus
and Bromus and Elymus and Pyracmus, armed with an axe.                 460
Their wounds I don't recall, but I have noted the number and names.
Beclad in the arms stripped from Emathian[53] Halesus, whom he had sent
to death, Latreus dashed forward, a man in body and limbs
of greatest size: his age was midway between old man and youth,
but youthful was his strength though his temples were spotted with gray.    465
Conspicuous in his shield and helmet and Macedonian pike[54]
and facing both the lines of battle, he banged his arms
and rode his equine limbs around in a circle and poured
forth boasting words in high spirits into the empty breeze:
'Shall I put up with you, Caeneus? For you will always be a woman to me,   470
to me you will be Caenis. Doesn't the origin of your birth
remind you, and don't you recall for what deed you gained
this boon and at what cost this feigned appearance of a man?
Consider what you were born or what you have endured,
and go, take up the distaff and basket of wool, with your thumb           475
unwind the yarn, leave war to men.' Amid such boasts, Caeneus
ripped open his side in full gallop with the cast of his spear,
at just that point where the man was merged with the horse.
Enraged with pain, he strikes the Phylleian[55] youth's bared face with his pike:
it bounces back, like hail upon the rooftop or if                          480
a pebble is thrown against a hollow drum.
He next attacks hand to hand and struggles to bury his sword
into his tough flank; the spot is impervious to the sword.
'No matter, you will not escape! I'll kill you with the blade of my sword
if somehow the point is dull,' he says, and angles his sword against        485
the flank and caught his loins within the grasp of his long right hand.
The blows resounds like a piece of marble when struck,
and from that tough smitten hide the shattered metal blade recoiled.

---

50 A region of Thessaly.
51 A Centaur.
52 A Lapith.
53 Emathia was a part of Macedonia. Halesus is a Lapith.
54 The *sarisa,* 14 to 16 feet long, used in the Macedonian phalanx.
55 Referring to the town of Phyllos in Thessaly.

*Caeneus and Centaurs, Baur*

When Caeneus had given him time to wonder at his unwounded limbs,
he says, 'Come now, let us try out upon your body our sword!'                    490
and into his shoulder thrust up to the hilt
his death-bringing sword and concealed it within his guts
and twisted his hand and inflicted a wound within the wound.
Behold, with a vast roar the mad and bi-membered ones rush forth
and all bear and cast their weapons against this one man.                        495
The weapons are blunted and fall: and amid all those blows
the son of Elatus, Caeneus, remains unbloodied and unpierced.
The strangeness of this thing left them stunned. 'What a huge disgrace!'
Monychus exclaims. 'We, a whole tribe, are being outdone by one,
and one scarcely a man; but he is a man, while we with our sluggish deeds   500
are what he was before. What use is there in our great limbs?
Or in our twofold strength or that in us were joined
by double nature the strongest living forces in the world?
Not born of a goddess mother, not sons of Ixion are we,
I think, of him who was so great as to hope to have his way                     505
with Juno on high: we are being outdone by a half-male foe!
Roll down upon him rocks and limbs and even whole hills
and dash out his lively soul with a barrage of trees!
Mere mass shall oppress his throat, and weight will serve as a blow.'
He spoke and picked up a beam that Auster's maddened force                      510
had felled and hurled it against his sturdy foe
and set an example, and in a short time Othrys was bare
of trees, and Pelion was lacking in shade.
Beneath the weight of a vast heap of trees Caeneus writhes
and bears upon his shoulder the piles of oaks                                   515

but once the weight increased upon his face
and head and gave him no air to breathe,
he sometimes weakens, but then tries to lift himself
in vain for air and roll away the forest hurled
upon him and sometimes moves it, as when we see,                                  520
imagine it, steep Ida shaken by the quaking of the earth.
The outcome remains unclear: some claim his body was pushed
to Tartarus' empty depths by the mass of the woods;
the son of Ampyx denies this and sees from the midst of the pile
a bird with tawny wings rise up into clear air,                                   525
and I saw it, too, for that first and final time.
When Mopsus spied it, ranging above its camp
in gentle flight and making a great clamor and stir,
and followed it with both his mind and eyes,
he said, 'O glory of the Lapith people, hail,                                     530
though once a very great man, Caeneus, now a bird unique in kind!'
Its author brought belief to the tale: but grief produced wrath,
we bore it ill that one had fallen at the hands of so many foes;
nor did we cease to exercise our grief with the sword
until some had been given to death, the rest removed by flight and night."    535

### 536-579  *Periclymenus*

The man from Pylos told this battle between
the Lapiths and Centaurs, but Tlepolemus[56] did not
keep silent his annoyance that Alcides[57] had been passed by
and said: "That praise of Hercules has been
forgotten by you amazes me, old man; for my father often told             540
me that the cloud-born creatures had been defeated by him."
The Pylian angrily replies: "Why do you compel me to recall
great woe and lay bare grief that years have hidden and
confess my hatred for your father and his wrongs?
In truth, by the gods, he did incredible things, and filled                       545
the world with his merits, which I should happily deny if I could;
but neither have we praised Deiphobus[58] or Polydamas[59]
nor Hector himself, for who will want to have praised a foe?
That father of yours once leveled Messenia's walls
and ruined the undeserving cities of Elis and Pylos and                           550
attacked my Penates with sword and flame,
and, not to mention others that he destroyed,
the sons, twice six, of Neleus were we, distinguished youths,

---

56 King of the Rhodians and a son of Hercules.
57 Hercules.
58 A valiant brother of Hector.
59 Son of Panthoüs and friend of Hector. See, e.g., Hom. *Il.* 15. 518-22.

twice six minus one who fell to Hercules' might;
that others could be vanquished must be borne:                          555
the death of Periclymenus[60] was a marvel, who had
the power of taking any form he wished and shedding it
again. He had the power from Neptune, author of Neleus' line.[61]
In vain having changed into all sorts of shapes,
he put on the appearance of that bird which is wont to carry in          560
his curving feet the thunderbolts most pleasing to the king of the gods;
the bird made use of his strength, his wings and hook-like beak
and barb-like claws, to tear at the face of the man.
The hero of Tiryns bends his all too certain bow at this bird
and, as it carried its members aloft and soared among the clouds,        565
he hit it exactly where its wing is joined to its side;
the wound is not grave, but its strength, broken by the wound,
is weakened and restrains its motion and ability to fly.
It falls to earth, unable to catch the breezes with its wings,
now weak, and where it had been fixed lightly into the wing,             570
the arrow is pressed down by the fallen body's weight
and driven from the left side of its neck though the top of its breast.
Now do you think I owe service as herald of your Hercules,
most handsome captain of the Rhodian fleet?
However, further vengeance for my brothers I do not seek, except to leave   575
in silence those heroic deeds: solid is the friendship twixt you and me."
      When Neleus' son had told all this with his sweet mouth,
they moved from the old man's tale to renew Bacchus' gift
and rose from their couches: the rest of the night was given to sleep.

### 580-628  *The Death of Achilles*

      That god, however, who tempers the watery waves with his spear      580
continued to grieve with a fatherly mind for the body of his son turned into
the bird of Phaethon;[62] despising savage Achilles thoroughly,
he plied more than civilly his unforgetting wrath.
The war had already dragged on for twice five years
when he addressed the unshorn Sminthean[63] with words like these:       585
"O dearest to me by far of all my brother's sons,
who helped me build the walls of Troy in vain,
do you not groan when you behold this citadel so near
to its collapse? Or do you not grieve at so many thousand deaths
of those defending the walls? Lest I refer to them all,                  590

---

60 One of the twelve sons of Neleus and the brother of Nestor.
61 See Hes., *Catalogue of Women* 10.
62 Ovid brings together here two heroes named Cycnus: Neptune's son and Sthenelus' son, who had in
   his grief for Phaethon been transformed into a swan. See 2. 367 ff.
63 An epithet of Apollo, either from the town of Sminthe in the Troad, or as protector against mice.
   *Smitheus* is a Mysian word meaning "mouse." See Hom. *Il.* 1. 39.

*Death of Achilles, Baur*

does not the shade of Hector come to mind, dragged around his Pergamum?[64]
And yet that wild man, more cruel than war itself,
lives on, Achilles, the destroyer of our handiwork.
Just let him give himself to me: let him feel what I
can do with my triple spear; but since I'm not allowed to fight hand to hand    595
the enemy, with an unseen arrow destroy him unawares!"
The Delian assented and, indulging both his own mind and
his uncle's, he comes concealed in a cloud to Ilium's lines
and midst the slaughter of men he catches sight
of Paris casting at undistinguished Achaeans an occasional dart.                600
Revealing himself as god, he says, "Why spend your shafts
upon the blood of commoners? If you have for your people any care,
divert yourself to Aeacides[65] and for your slaughtered brothers take revenge!"
He spoke and pointing out the son of Peleus as he was laying low
the bodies of Trojans with his sword, against him he turned his bow            605
and with his death-dealing right hand aimed the unerring dart.
That since the death of Hector aged Priam could rejoice,
this was the cause; Achilles, you the victor of so many men,
have been defeated by the timorous thief of a Greek bride!
But if you had to fall at the hand of a womanish Mars,                          610
you would have preferred to fall by a double axe of Thermodon.[66]

    That terror of the Phrygians, of the Pelasgian name
the glory and guardian, Aeacides, that head invincible in war,

---

64 The acropolis of Troy.
65 Achilles, as descendant of Aeacus, father of Peleus.
66 A river into the Black Sea in the territory of the Amazons. The allusion is to the Amazon princess
   Penthesilea, whom Achilles loved and slew.

was burned: the same god had armed[67] him who set him aflame;
but now he is ashes, and of great Achilles there only remains                615
some little something that not quite fills an urn;
but yet he lives as glory that fills all the world.
In this glory will lie the measure of that man, and in this
the son of Peleus is equal to himself and feels not the void of Tartarus.
His very shield, to assure that you can recognize whose it was,              620
still causes war and for his arms arms are borne.
Nor Tydeus' son[68] nor Oïlean[69] Ajax is so bold,
nor Atreus' lesser son[70] nor the greater[71] in age and war,
as to demand those arms, nor are any others: the sons alone
of Telamon and Laërtes expected to gain such praise.                         625
Tantalides[72] removed the burden of envy from himself
and bid the Argive chieftains sit down within the camp
and handed over the judgment of the dispute to them all.

---

67 Hephaestus (Vulcan) had forged the arms of Achilles. See Hom. *Il.* 18. 368-617.
68 Diomedes.
69 Oïleus was the father of this Ajax, to be distinguished from Telamonian Ajax.
70 Menelaus.
71 Agamemnon.
72 Agamemnon as descendant of Tantalus.

# BOOK 13

## 1-398 Debate for the Arms of Achilles

## 1-122 Ajax, Son of Telamon

The leaders sat down and, with the commons standing round about,
lord Ajax of the sevenfold shield stood up to face
them and, quick to anger as he was, looked grim-faced back
towards the Sigean shore and the fleet upon that shore
and, stretching forth his hands, declares "By Jupiter, we plead        5
our cause in front of the ships, and yet Ulysses is compared to me!
But he did not hesitate to yield to Hector's flames,
which I withstood, which I drove away from this fleet.
Contending with false words is safer, therefore,
than combat with hands, yet speaking is not easy for me              10
and deeds are not easy for him: I excel in fierce Mars
and in the battlefront as much as he excels in making a speech.
Yet I do not intend, Pelasgian men, to recall my deeds
to you: for you have seen them; let Ulysses tell of his,
those deeds without witness, which night alone has seen!              15

293

Admittedly a great reward is sought: but my rival detracts
from its esteem: to gain whatever Ulysses has sought
is not a source of pride to Ajax, however great the prize;
in fact he has already gained his reward in this attempt,
for after his defeat, it will be said that he contended with me.                20
        "And if my virtue were ever in doubt,
by noble birth alone would I prevail, as son of Telamon,
who took the walls of Troy with mighty Hercules
and reached the shores of Colchis in the Pagasaean ship;[1]
his father was Aeacus,[2] who there among the silent ones gives                25
his laws, where Sisyphus, son of Aeolus, urges on his heavy stone;
and highest Jupiter acknowledges and claims Aeacus as
his offspring, which makes Ajax third in line after Jove.
And yet let not even this lineage be of point in this case,
Achaean men, if with great Achilles there is no common link:                   30
he was my brother,[3] I claim a brother's rights! Why do you,
the child of Sisyphus' blood and so like him in thievery and fraud,
now graft yourself onto the names of Aeacus' alien clan?
        "Or is it because without an informer[4] I heeded the call to arms
that arms should be denied to me, and he should appear superior               35
in being the last to do so and, by feigning madness, put off
his service in arms until one more clever than he
(though less self-serving) unroofed the lies of his cowardly mind,
the son of Nauplius,[5] and dragged him off to the arms he had shirked.
Should he take up the best of arms because he refused to take up any at all,  40
and we be dishonored and deprived of our cousin's gifts
because we betook ourselves to the very first dangers of the fray?
        "Oh would that his madness had been real, or believed,
and he had never come as comrade to the Phrygian citadel,
that instigator of crimes! If so, you, the son[6] of Poeas, would not          45
be held by Lemnos when you were set ashore to our disgrace!
They say that you are now a recluse in a forest cave
and make the rocks shudder with your cries and imprecate Laërtiades[7]
with what he deserves, which, if there are gods, you will not pray for in vain.
And now that man,[8] having taken the same oath of arms as we                   50
(for shame!), and one of our leaders, whom the arrows of Hercules
now claim as heir, is broken with hunger and disease

---

1 The ship Argo was built in the Thessalian coastal town of Pagasa.
2 Aeacus, Rhadamanthus, and Minos were the three judges of the dead in the Underworld.
3 Telamon was the brother of Peleus and the father of Ajax, Achilles is only the cousin of Ajax, but in
    ancient kinship cousins are often viewed as siblings.
4 Palamedes, who exposed Ulysses' attempt to avoid the draft by pretending madness.
5 Nauplius was king of Euboea and father of Palamedes.
6 Philoctetes. Ovid draws upon the plot of Sophocles' *Philoctetes*.
7 Ajax now refers to Ulysses by the patronymic of Laërtes, but calls him the child of Sisyphus in 33.
8 Philoctetes, referred to now in the third person.

and clothed and fed by birds, and in hunting birds
employs the darts that are meant for Troy's fated doom.
At least he lives, by not being in Ulysses' company!                              55
Unhappy Palamedes as well would prefer to have been left behind
[and be alive or at least to have died without blame],
whom my opponent, never forgetting his madness exposed,[9]
incriminated falsely with treason against the Danaan cause and proved
the trumped-up charge by revealing the gold[10] he had buried before.            60
With either exile, then, or murder, he has sapped Achaean strength:
he fights this way, in this way is Ulysses to be feared!

"Although he may excel even faithful Nestor in eloquence,
he'll never convince me that his desertion of Nestor was not
a crime. For Nestor, slowed by the wound of his horse,                           65
exhausted with the years of old age, and appealing to Ulysses for help,
was left in the lurch by his ally; that I am not fabricating this crime
the son of Tydeus knows well, who rebuked him again and again
by name and reproached the flight of his timorous friend.[11]
With righteous eyes the gods above behold what mortals do!                       70
See now, in need of help is he who gave none, and just as he left Nestor behind
he ought to be left as well: a judgment that he rendered against himself.
He cries out[12] for help from his allies: I see him there now as he shakes
and pales with fear and trembles at the approach of death;
I offered the weight of my shield and protected the prostrate man                75
and saved his useless life (little praise in this!).
So if you persist in this debate, let's return to that site:
bring back your foe[13] and your wound and your wonted cowardice
and hide behind the breadth of my shield and beneath it contend with me!
But after I rescued him,[14] whose wounds had not given him the strength         80
to stand, he fled, unslowed by any wound at all.

"Now Hector is here and brings with him the gods into the fray,
and wherever he rushes, Ulysses, not only you are greatly terrified,
but even brave men are: so much terror does that man create.
But I, as he exulted in the success of bloody slaughter, laid                    85
him low from afar with a stone of great weight,[15]
and I, as he demanded someone with whom to contend,[16]

---

9 In the *Cypria* Odysseus attempted to avoid participating in the Trojan expedition by feigning madness.
   Palamedes exposed this pretense by having Odysseus' son Telemachus seized for punishment.
10 Ovid probably draws upon the lost *Palamedes* of Euripides. Cf. Apollodorus *Epitome* 3. 8: Ulysses
   forces a Trojan prisoner to forge a letter from Priam to Palamedes and bury gold in Palamedes'
   tent. Agamemnon finds the letter and gold and had Palamedes stoned as a traitor.
11 This story is found in Hom., *Il.* 8. 75-111: the Greeks all flee at the clap of thunder sent by Zeus.
   Diomedes chides Odysseus and rescues Nestor, whose horse had been wounded by Paris.
12 Ajax now tells how he (with Menelaus) came to the rescue when Odysseus, wounded by Socus,
   "thrice cried out as loud as the head of a man can shout," Hom., *Il.* 11. 462 ff.
13 Socus.
14 Ulysses.
15 At Hom., *Il.* 14. 409 ff. Ajax knocks Hector to the ground with a heavy stone.
16 The reference is to Hom., *Il.* 7. 45 ff., where Hector calls for a duel with the best of the Achaeans.

alone withstood him: Achaean men, you hoped that the lot
would fall to me, and your prayers were answered. If you ask
the outcome of this duel, I was not defeated by him.[17]                    90
Behold, the Trojans are bringing swords and flames and Jove
against the Danaan fleets: where is eloquent Ulysses now?
In fact with my breast I defended a thousand ships,
the hope of your return: in return for so many ships give me the arms.

    "But if you allow me to speak frankly, honor is sought            95
more eagerly by the arms than by me, and our glory is associated with theirs:
the arms are claiming Ajax, not Ajax the arms.
To my deeds let the Ithacan compare his Rhesus[18] and Dolon, weak
in war,[19] and Helenus,[20] Priam's son, taken captive with the stolen Palladium:[21]
nothing here was done in daylight, nothing if Diomedes is removed;           100
If ever you bestow these arms in return for such meager deeds,
divide them and let Diomedes have the greater share.

    "Yet how can you give them to the Ithacan at all, who always acts
in secret, and always unarmed, and takes his foe by stealth?
The very splendor of his helmet, gleaming with rays of gold,              105
betrays his snares and exposes him as he hides in ambush;
but neither will the Dulichian's[22] head beneath Achilles' casque
be able to bear such weight, nor the Pelian spear[23] not fail to be
a heavy burden for this weakling's arms,
nor will the shield embossed with the image of the world                 110
be suitable for his left hand, so timid and born for theft.
But why do you seek an honor that will only weaken you,
which, if the Achaean nations bestow it upon you by some mistake,
will furnish a reason for you to be despoiled instead of feared by the foe,
and slow that ability to flee in which you excel all other men,           115
you faint-hearted man, if you carry burdens as heavy as these?
And after all, your present shield, so rarely tried in he fray,
is quite intact, while ours, having endured a thousand blows,
is full of dents and needs a successor in its stead.

    "And finally (what need for speeches?) let us be judged by what we do!   120
Just send the arms of that brave man into the enemy's midst:
then order us to go after them and decorate the retriever with what's retrieved!"

---

17 The duel ended undecided, Hom., *Il.* 7. 175 ff.
18 An oracle said that if the horses of Rhesus, a Thracian king, drank from the river Xanthus, Troy could
    not be taken. Ulysses and Diomedes in a night ambush slew Rhesus and drove his horses back to
    the Greek camp. During this episode, Ulysses and Diomedes slay the Trojan spy Dolon, himself
    on a night exploratory mission. The tale is told in Hom., *Il* 10.
19 His stealth as a spy is equated with cowardice.
20 A Trojan prophet.
21 The wooden image of Pallas Athena (Minerva), said to have fallen from heaven, was stolen by
    Diomedes and Odysseus. Troy was said to be safe as long as the statue was kept safe.
22 An epithet of Ulysses from the small town of Dulichium on the island of Ithaca.
23 Its shaft made of wood from Mt. Pelion.

### 123-381   *Ulysses' Speech*

The son of Telamon had finished, and from the commons a roar
attended his final words, until Laërtes' heroic son
stood up and, holding his eyes to the ground for awhile,[24]                    125
raised up his eyes to the princes and opened his mouth
with its awaited words, nor is there lack of grace in his eloquent speech.
    "If your desires and mine had prevailed, O Pelasgian[25] men,
the heir of this great contest would not be in doubt,
and we would have you still, Achilles, and you, your arms,                    130
but since inequitable fate has denied him to me and to you"
(he wiped his weeping eyes at these words with his hand)
"who better should come into Achilles' estate
than he through whom Achilles came to the Greeks?
Just let it not be to Ajax' advantage that he seems dull-witted (and is),      135
nor let it be to my disadvantage, Achaeans, that my intelligence
has often been in your service; and let whatever skill in speech I have,
if any, which speaks now for its master[26] but often has spoken for you,
be not a cause for envy, and let no one deny his own worth.
    "For family and ancestors and what we have not done ourselves         140
I scarcely call our own, but now since Ajax has claimed
to be the great-grandson of Jove, our line's author is Jupiter as well,
and we are separated from him by the same number of steps:
Laërtes, you see, is my father, and Arcesius his,
and his was Jupiter, nor among them was any to exile condemned;[27]            145
Cyllenius[28] brings through my mother a second source
of noble birth: in both my parents a god is found.
But neither my being of better birth on my mother's side
nor that my father is innocent of shedding a brother's blood
would justify my claims to these arms: on merits judge the case,              150
but do not let the fact that Telamon and Peleus were brothers or
the lineage of his blood supply the proof of Ajax' deserts,
but rather let the honor of these spoils[29] be sought in valorous deeds!
Or if proximity of kinship and the first heir be sought,
Achilles' father is Peleus, Pyrrhus the son:                                  155
What claim does Ajax have? To Phthia[30] or to Scyrus[31] send the arms!

---

24 Ehwald cites Hom. *Il.* 3. 216 as the inspiration for this line.
25 Greek.
26 Ulysses himself.
27 An oblique reference to Telamon's exile for slaying his brother (see 11. 266 ff.).
28 Mercury. The father of Ulysses' mother Anticlea was Autolycus, the son of Mercury and Chione.
    Autolycus, noted for his trickery (see 11. 313), was the husband of Erysichthon's daughter
    (8. 738).
29 Achilles' arms.
30 Native city of Achilles in Thessaly.
31 The Aegean island where Thetis sent Achilles to avoid the Trojan War. The story is not Homeric.
    See Hyginus, *Fab.* 96.

No less a cousin of Achilles is Teucer[32] than he:
he's not seeking the arms, is he? He wouldn't win them, I think, if he did.
Since, then, the plain issue here is a matter of deeds,
though I have done more than I have the ability to recount                      160
in words, I shall review each of them in turn.
    "His Nereid mother,[33] foreseeing his coming death,
disguised her son in clothing, and all were deceived,
among them Ajax, by the ruse of the dress he assumed:
but I among his girlish playthings added arms to rouse                          165
his masculine mind, and the hero had not yet put off
his feminine garb when, as he held the shield and spear,
I say, 'O goddess-born, for destruction at your hands
is Pergamum[34] reserving herself! From overturning Troy why do shrink?'
I then laid my hand on him and sent the brave man off to brave deeds.           170
The works of that man are therefore mine: with my spear
I conquered Telephus[35] as he fought, and I healed him, a suppliant subdued:
that Thebes[36] was conquered is due to me; believe that I
took Lesbos, that I took Chryse and Cilla,[37] Apollo's towns,
and Scyrus as well; consider that by my right hand                             175
the battered walls of Lyrnesus[38] were leveled to the ground;
and, leaving others aside in silence, that it was I who really gave you the man
who had the power to bring down Hector: through me glorious Hector lies dead!
Because of those arms[39] through which Achilles was found out, I seek
these arms: I supplied arms to the living, I reclaim them after his death.      180
    "When one man's[40] anguish affected the Danaans all,
and at Euboean Aulis a thousand ships filled the shore,
the long awaited winds were either absent or opposed
the fleet, and Agamemnon was ordered by harsh oracles
to sacrifice to cruel Diana his daughter, an innocent child.                    185
Her father refuses and is angry at the gods themselves,
and in the king there is yet a father, but with my words
I turned the father's kind nature to meet the public good:
indeed, I had (I confess, and may Atrides[41] forgive what I say)
a difficult cause to make and before a biased judge.                           190
The people's best interest, a brother,[42] and the lofty scepter assigned

---

32 Teucer, son of Telamon and Hesione, is the cousin of Achilles and half-brother of Ajax.
33 Thetis, daughter of Nereus.
34 The citadel of Troy.
35 See 12. 112 and note.
36 Telephus was king of this city of Mysia.
37 Cities in the Troad.
38 A town in the Troad.
39 Achilles' first arms, supplied by Ulysses, were lent to Patroclus, who lost them to Hector. The present
    arms were fashioned by Hephaestus (Vulcan) at the request of Thetis (Hom., *Il.* 18).
40 Menelaus, brother of Agamemnon.
41 Agamemnon, son of Atreus.
42 Menelaus.

to him persuade him to weigh praise against blood;
I'm sent to the mother,[43] not to be commanded, but deceived
by cunning, to whom if had Telamon's son been dispatched,
the sails would even now be bereft of their winds.                              195
    "I'm also sent as a bold ambassador[44] to the citadel of Ilium,
and saw and entered the senate house of lofty Troy,
still filled with men; without fear I put forth
the common cause that Greece had commanded me to make,
accusing Paris and demanding that Helen and the booty be returned,            200
and I persuade Priam and Antenor,[45] who shares Priam's view.
But Paris and his brothers and those who joined his theft
just barely held back impious[46] hands (Menelaus, you know this) from me,
and that was the first day that our[47] peril was shared with you.[48]
    "A long delay would be needed to treat my usefulness                      205
in counsel and action throughout this drawn-out war.
The first pitched done, the enemy held themselves within
the city walls at length, and there was no opportunity for
the open work of Mars; in the tenth year we have fought at last:
in all this time what are you doing, Ajax, who know nothing but the fray?     210
Your purpose, what is it? But if you ask what I have done,
I've plotted against the foe, I've girded our fortifications with a trench,[49]
I've helped the allies bear the tedium of the lengthy war
with calmness of mind; I've taught us how to supply and arm
ourselves, I've been sent on missions when the situation required.            215
    "Behold, at Jove's behest, the king,[50] deceived by the image of sleep,
commands the end of the prosecution of the war under way.
He's able to defend his command by citing its source:[51]
Let Ajax refuse and demand that Pergamum be destroyed,
and let him fight, a thing he can do! But why is he not holding those back    220
who want to quit? Why doesn't he take up arms and give the fickle mob
a model to follow? This surely wasn't too much for one who only speaks
to boast. In fact, he fled himself! I saw it, and saw it with shame,
when you were turning your back and making ready your sails in disgrace.
Without delay, I said, 'What are you doing? What insanity                     225
has driven you, O allies, to abandon captive Troy,
and what are you bringing home after ten years except disgrace?'

---

43 Clytemnestra is made to believe that she is to bring Iphigenia to Aulis as a bride for Achilles.
44 For the embassy of Ulysses and Menelaus to Troy see Hom., *Il.* 3. 225 ff and 11. 139 ff.
45 For Trojan Antenor's desire to return Helen, see Hom. *Il.* 7. 347-53; for his hospitality to Odysseus
    and Menelaus, see *Il.* 3. 203-24.
46 Because ambassadors were sacrosanct.
47 The royal plural.
48 Menelaus.
49 Hom., *Il.* 7. 337 342, makes Nestor, not Ulysses, propose the trench.
50 Agamemnon (see Hom., *Il.* 2. 1-34).
51 Jove.

With arguments like these and others, in which distress itself had made
me eloquent, I brought them back from their fugitive fleet.
The son of Atreus convokes the allies who are trembling with fright:          230
and Telamon's son[52] dares not even now to open his mouth,
though even Thersites[53] makes bold to rail at the kings
with words of insolence not left unpunished by me!
I rose and exhort the fainted-hearted citizens to face the foe
and with my speech I restore the valor they had lost.                          235
And since that time, whatever brave deeds my opponent can seem to have done,
is my work, who turned him round when he turned his back.

    "Among the Danaans, finally, who praises you, or seeks you out?
Yet Tydides[54] discusses his deeds with me,
approves of me and always confides in Ulysses, his friend.                     240
There is some value in being, of all the soldiers of the Greeks,
the one sought out by Diomedes! The casting of lots did not demand
that I should go: yet spurning the danger from the night and the foe,
I slay[55] the one who dared the same, that Dolon of the Phrygian tribe,
but not before I have forced him to reveal what he knew                        245
and learned what Trojan perfidy was planning to do.
I found out everything and had no further reason to spy
and now could return for the promised praise.
But hardly satisfied with that, I head for Rhesus' tents
and slay the man himself and his comrades within his camp,                     250
and as a victor, my vows accomplished, I mount
my captive chariot as though in a joyful triumph hailed;
deny the arms to me of him[56] whose horses for that night's work
my enemy[57] had demanded as a reward, and let Ajax be more kind!
Why mention the lines Lycian Sarpedon[58] led,                                 255
wiped out with my sword? With great shedding of blood
I laid Coeranus low, the son of Iphitus, and Alastor and Chromius,
and Aleacer and Hailus, and Noëmon and Prytanis I gave
to death along with Chersidamas and Thoön
and Charops and Ennomus, driven by unkind destiny,                             260
and by our hand some less noted men fell
beneath the city's walls. And, citizens, I do have wounds,
made beautiful by their location; don't believe mere words,
just look, here they are," he says as he opens his cloak with his hand,

---

52 Ajax. See on 30.
53 An ungainly fellow who railed at his Greek leaders (Hom. *Il.* 2. 211-42).
54 Diomedes, son of Tydeus.
55 In Homer, it is Diomedes, not Odysseus, who slays Dolon (*Il.* 10. 454-56) and Rhesus (*Il.* 10. 482-83).
56 Achilles. Dolon had asked Hector for the horses of Achilles (*Il.* 10. 322-23). Ulysses is responding to Ajax's point at 101-02.
57 Dolon.
58 Son of Jupiter and Europa, and slain by Patroclus.

"and on this chest every time, in your service employed. 265
But Telamon's son has spent no blood through all the years
in service to the allies and keeps his body free of wounds![59]
   "What difference does it make, if he claims to have borne
his weapons for the Pelasgian fleet against the Trojans and Jove?
I grant that he did (for it is not my way to belittle with ill will 270
another's good deeds), but let him not take for himself alone what belongs
to all in common and let him grant some respect to you as well,
for Actor's son,[60] safe beneath Achilles' appearance repulsed
the Trojans when the ships, their defender,[61]and all were about to burn.
He thinks that he was alone in daring to compete with Hector's spears, 275
forgetting the king and other leaders and me,
although he was the ninth to offer his service and chosen for duty by
the lot.[62] But what, O bravest one, was the outcome of your fight?
With no wound at all, Hector walks away unhurt!
   "How sad I am when compelled to recall 280
the time when Achilles, that wall of the Greeks,
was felled! And neither my tears nor grief nor fear
deterred me from bringing back that humbled body, lifted high:
upon these shoulders, these shoulders, I say, I myself
bore Achilles' body, arms and all, which now again I'm striving to bear. 285
I have the strength required to bear such weight,
I certainly have the mind to perceive the honor you would bestow:
was it for this that his sea-blue mother for her son
was so ambitious, that these heavenly gifts,
the work of such great skill,[63] should clothe a crude 290
and dim-witted soldier? He doesn't even understand the shield's
reliefs, the ocean and lands and stars within the lofty sky
and Pleiades[64] and Hyades[65] and Arctos[66] untouched by the sea,
the unlike cities[67] and Orion's gleaming sword.
He's asking to receive arms that he doesn't comprehend! 295
   "And as to his assertion that I avoided the duties of harsh war
and to the toil underway came late, does he fail
to see that in such a charge he is slandering great-hearted Achilles, too?

---

59 Cf. Ajax' "with my breast" (93).
60 Patroclus.
61 Ajax.
62 At Hom., *Il.* 7. 161-312, from nine Greek leaders, Ajax is chosen by lot to meet Hector in a duel,
   the outcome of which is a draw. Ulysses, contrary to his assertion of acknowledging good deeds,
   distorts the Homeric passage to make it appear as if Ajax were the ninth to volunteer for the
   drawing of lots.
63 Hephaestus (Vulcan) made new armor for Achilles after the death of Patroclus.
64 The seven daughters of Atlas and Pleione.
65 Sisters of the Pleiades found in the head of Taurus (the Bull). Their waning marked the onset of rainy
   weather (*hyein* in Greek means "rain").
66 The Bear, comprising both Ursa Major and Ursa Minor.
67 The city of peace and the city of war inscribed upon Achilles' shield in Hom., *Il.* 18. 409 ff.

If having dissembled you call a crime, then dissembled have we both;
if hesitation is a fault, then I am prompter than he.[68]                          300
A pious wife detained me, a pious mother detained
Achilles; to them were our early years devoted, the remaining to you:
I scarcely fear a charge, even though against it I have no defense,
that so great a man has shared: but he was detected by
Ulysses' intelligence, by Ajax' intelligence Ulysses was not!            305
       "And lest we be amazed that he poured out against me
the accusations of his foolish tongue, he casts shameful blame
on you as well. Or for me to have accused Palamedes is
it base while noble for you to have convicted him?
But neither did the son[69] of Nauplius have the strength to refute      310
a crime so great and so apparent, nor did you merely hear
the charge against him: you saw the deed exposed in the bribe.[70]
       "Nor should I be blamed because Vulcan's Lemnos contains
the son of Poeas[71] (defend yourselves for the deed, for you
consented to it), nor shall I deny the fact that I urged                 315
that he withdraw from the toil of the journey and the war
and try to soften his terrible pains with rest,
to which he agreed—and is alive! Not only was my view
conveyed with honesty, it was fortunate, yet it were enough
that it was honest. Since now our seers demand him for Pergamum's       320
destruction, do not entrust that task to me! Telamon's son will better go
and with his eloquence soften that man raging with sickness and wrath
or shrewdly produce the man with some kind of ruse!
The Simois will reverse its course and Ida stand
bereft of leaves, and Achaea[72] promise Troy her aid,                   325
before my breast retire from service to you,
before the cunning of stupid Ajax serve the Danaans' cause.
Although you're hostile to the allies, to the king, and to me,
O bitter Philoctetes, although you execrate and never cease
to curse my head and long for me to be given by fate                     330
to you in your pain and to drink our blood,
and, just as I had power over you, that you have power over me:
yet I would go to you and strive to bring you back with me
and even gain control over your arrows (should Fortune smile)
the same way I gained control over the Dardanian seer,[73] my prisoner,  335
the same way I revealed the responses of the gods and Troy's fate,
the same way I stole the statue from Phrygian Minerva's inner shrine

---

68 Achilles.
69 Palamedes.
70 See on 60.
71 Philoctetes.
72 Greece.
73 See on 99.

*Ajax, Odysseus and Achilles' Armor, Solis*

right out of the midst of the foe. And would Ajax compare himself to me?
Indeed when the fates were keeping Troy from being taken without
that statue, where is Ajax, the brave? Where are the boastful words          340
of that mighty man? Why now are you afraid? Why does Ulysses dare
to pass among those on guard duty and entrust himself to the night
and pass through the hostile swords not only into the Trojan walls
but even into the highest citadel and from its temple steal away
the goddess and bring her back through the enemy lines?                      345
Had I not done these things, in vain would he of Telamon born
have wielded with his left hand the seven hides of bulls.[74]
The victory over Troy was gained by me in that night:
I conquered Pergamum at that moment when I made her conquerable.

      "Stop pointing out to us with muttering and scowling face              350
that Tydeus' son was with me: he has his share of praise in that deed!
For when you were shielding the allied fleet, you were not
alone: you had a host of comrades, among whom I was one.
If Diomedes didn't know that the warrior is weaker than the sage
and even to the indomitable right hand no rewards are owed,                  355
he would himself be seeking these arms; the lesser Ajax would seek
them, too, and fierce Eurypylus and famous Andraemon's son,[75]
no less than Idomeneus and he, of the same country[76] born,

---

74 Metonymy for "shield."
75 Thoas, son of the Aetolian king Andraemon (Hom. *Il.* 2. 638), not the Lemnian father of Hypsipyle
   (see on 400).
76 Crete.

Meriones, and seeking them would be the brother[77] of the greater Atreid:
though obviously strong of hand and not second to me in the work of Mars,  360
they yield to my counsel. Your right hand is useful to you in battle, but
your native intelligence it is that requires our own as a guide;
you exercise force without thought, my care is for what's to come;
you have the ability to fight, the time for fighting did Atreus' son
determine with my advice; you will serve with your body alone,  365
but we with our mind; the one who controls the helm excels
in service those at the oar, as much as the leader excels the soldier in the ranks,
and just as much am I greater than you. And in this body of ours
the heart is not weaker than the hand: all the force of life is there.

"But you, O chieftains, give to your guardian the prize,  370
and for the care and anxious service I've given over so many years
do grant this reward in return for our meritorious works:
my labors are now at an end; I've removed the opposing fates,
and having made Pergamum's capture possible, I captured her.
Now by our common hopes and the walls of Troy about to fall  375
and by the gods, I pray, the gods whom I lately stole from the foe,
by anything else that through wisdom must be done,
if some bold and dangerous venture must be sought,
if something yet, you suppose, remains to be done for Troy's doom,
remember me! Of if you do not give the arms to me,  380
then give them to this!" And he points to the image of Minerva, so dire.

### 381-98   *The Victory of Ulysses and Suicide of Ajax*

The gathering of chieftains was moved, and what eloquence can do,
was clear in the result, and the fluent speaker won the hero's arms.
That man, who so often stood alone against Hector, the sword and fires
and Jove, does not withstand one wave of furious wrath,  385
and anger vanquishes an invincible man: he seizes his sword
and says, "Surely this is mine, or does Ulysses claim this one as well?
It is to be used by me against myself, and what often was wet
with Phrygian gore will now grow wet with its master's blood
lest anyone be able to conquer Ajax but Ajax himself."  390
He spoke, and into his chest, at last having suffered a wound,
he sank the deadly sword[78] as far as the iron was exposed.
And hands had not the strength to draw out the weapon fixed therein:
the gore itself expelled it, and the earth made red by the blood
produced a purple flower upon the verdant turf,  395
which earlier had sprung from the Oebalian[79] wound.

---

77 Menelaus.
78 The sword once belonged to Hector, Hom., *Il.* 7. 303.
79 A general name for Spartan, from the Spartan king Oebalus; here referring to Hyacinthus (see 10. 217).

*Suicide of Ajax, Baur*

And letters common to both the boy and the man are inscribed
upon the center of the petals, these of a name,[80] those of woe.[81]

### 399-575   The Sorrows of Hecuba

The victor sets sail to Hypsipyle's and famous Thoas' land,
notorious for the slaughter of the men of long ago,[82]                    400
in order to bring back the Tirynthian[83] weapons and shafts.
When he, in the company of their master,[84] returned them to the Greeks,
the final hand is laid at last upon the drawn-out war.
Together Troy and Priam fall. The unhappy wife
of Priam after all of this lost her human form                             405
and terrified with strange barking the foreign air
where into the narrows the long Hellespont is enclosed.[85]
As Ilium burned, and its fires had not yet died down,
and after Jove's altar had drunk the little blood that Priam had left,
and as the priestess[86] of Phoebus, dragged by the hair,                  410
stretched forth her helpless hands to the ethereal sky,
Dardanian mothers, embracing while they could

---

80 AIAS, the Greek spelling of "Ajax."
81 AIAI, a cry of grief.
82 After the women of Lemnos neglected Aphrodite's rites, she gave them a foul odor that made them
   repugnant to their husbands. The women then killed all the Lemnian men except Thoas, who was
   hidden by his daughter Hypsipyle. Ovid alludes to Apollonius of Rhodes, *Argonautica* 1. 609 ff.
83 I. e., once belonging to Heracles of Tiryns and now in the possession of Philoctetes on the island
   of Lemnos.
84 Philoctetes. See Sophocles' *Philoctetes*.
85 404-07 appear to summarize the narrative of the sorrows of Hecuba that follow. The sources are
   Euripides' *Hecuba* and *Trojan Women* and ultimately the *Iliupersis*.
86 Cassandra, daughter of Hecuba and Priam.

the statues of their native gods and thronging the burning shrines,
are taken as envied prizes by the conquering Greeks.
Astyanax[87] is hurled from those towers from where                     415
he often used to see his father, as his mother pointed him out,
engaged in battle for him and defending his forefathers' realm.
When Boreas[88] calls for sailing, and with the supporting breeze
the moving sails resound, the captain gives the order to use the winds;
"Farewell, O Troy! We are being stolen away," the Trojan women cry,     420
and plant kisses upon the ground and leave behind their smoking homes.
The last to board the ship—a pitiful sight to see!—
was Hecuba, who had been found among her children's tombs,
embracing the graves and planting kisses upon the bones.
Dulichian[89] hands drag her off. Of one, however, she gathered up      425
the ashes, Hector's, into her bosom, and carried them away;
and on the grave of Hector she left a gray lock of hair from her head:
her offerings to the dead, her hair and tears.

### 429- 38  Polydorus

The land opposite Phrygia, where Troy once was,
Bistonian[90] men inhabit. Polymestor's rich and royal keep            430
was there, to whom, O Polydorus, your father had entrusted you
in secret to be cared for and fed, removed from Phrygian arms,
a sensible measure, except he had sent as well great wealth,
the prize for crime, the incentive for the greedy mind.
When Phrygia's fortune fell, the impious king of Thrace                435
took his sword and thrust it into the throat of his foster-child,
and, thinking the crime could be concealed with the corpse,
he cast the lifeless body from a cliff into the waves below.

### 439-575  Polyxena

The son of Atreus had moored the fleet to the Thracian shore
until the sea was calmed, until more favorable the wind:               440
but suddenly, as big as he was when he was still alive,
Achilles rose with menacing mien from a wide break in the ground,
his face recalling that time when fierce with wrath
he threatened unjust Agamemnon with his sword.
"Achaeans," he says, "are you leaving without thought                  445
of me? Is any gratitude for our valor to be buried with me?
Don't do it! And lest unhonored be my tomb,
appease Achilles' shade with Polyxena sacrificed!'"

---

87 Child of Hector and Andromache, slain as in Euripides' *Trojan Women.*
88 The North Wind.
89 I. e., belonging to Ulysses. Dulichium is a small island off Ithaca.
90 A people of Thrace at the mouth of the Hebrus River.

*Polymnestor kills Polydorus, Baur*

He spoke, and the allies obeyed the pitiless shade:
thus, snatched from her mother's bosom, to whom almost she alone          450
brought comfort, the brave and unhappy virgin, surpassing womankind,
is led to the grave and becomes a victim to the awful tomb.
The girl did not forget herself when she was conducted to
the cruel altar and saw that the barbarous rites were being readied for her,
and as she saw Neoptolemus standing by, his sword in hand,          455
and saw him fixing his eyes upon her face,
she said, "Spill at once this noble blood
without delay; and bury the sword in my throat or breast,"
and bared both her throat and her breast.
"Indeed, as Polyxena, I refuse to be anyone's slave.          460
By no means will you please any divinity with such a sacrifice!
My only wish is that my mother not be told that I'm to die:
my mother stands in the way and weakens my joy in death,
though she ought to shudder not at my death but at her life.
But you, lest I not as free-born woman approach the Stygian shades,          465
stand far from me, if my request is fair, and keep your male hands
away from my virgin skin! More acceptable to him,
whoever he is whom you wish to appease by killing me,
will be the blood of one free-born. If the final words of our lips
can move anyone (the daughter of King Priam asks this          470
of you, no captive), to my mother return my body unbought
and let her buy the sad right to a tomb not with gold,
but tears! Back then, when she could, she would have paid in gold."
When she had spoken, the tears that she held back

the people did not; the priest himself, unwilling and in tears,                    475
broke through the breast she offered with a thrust of the knife.
Although her knees grew weak as she slipped to the ground,
she kept her fearless expression to the final moment of death;
and even then she took care when she fell to veil those parts
that should be covered and to preserve the honor of her shamefast modesty.   480
        The Trojan women gather up her body and count up all the lamented sons
of Priam and how many deaths had been given by just one house,
and mourn for you, O maiden, and you, so recently called queen and wife
and royal mother, the very image of Asia in flower,
and even now unlucky as booty, whom victorious Ulysses would not              485
have wanted except that you had produced Hector in birth:
to find his mother a master Hector labored long and hard!
As she embraced the body now emptied of its so valiant soul,
those tears she had so often offered for country, sons, and spouse
she offers to this child again; she pours the tears into the wounds          490
and covers her lips with her mouth and beats her oft-beaten breast,
and as she tears her white hair thick with blood,
she uttered many things from her mangled breast, and also this:
"My child, the final grief of your mother—for is anything left?—
my child, you lie in death, and I see your wound, my wounds:                  495
behold, lest I lose any of my children without their being slain,
you, too, have a wound; I thought, however, that as a woman, you
were safe from the sword: you have fallen, even as a woman, by the sword,
and what destroyed so many of your brothers has destroyed you as well,
that ruination of Troy, Achilles, the agent of all our loss!                 500
But after he fell by Paris' and Phoebus' shafts,
now surely, said I, Achilles is no longer to be feared:
yet even now was I to fear him; the ashes from the tomb
still rage against our family, and even from the grave we have known this foe:
for Aeacus' descendant was I fruitful! Mighty Ilium lies flat,               505
and in that grievous event the public slaughter found its end;
at least it is over and done with; to me alone Pergamum remains:
my grief is still in progress. So recently reigning supreme,
so powerful in so many sons-in-law, and children, daughters-in-law and spouse,
I now am dragged away as an exile, helpless, torn from the graves of my own,  510
a gift to Penelope, who will, when I am spinning out my allotted tasks,
display me to the women of Ithaca and say, 'Of Hector is she
the famous mother; this is Priam's wife.'
Now you, after so many lost sons, you, who alone relieved
your mother's sorrows, have propitiated an enemy's pyre!                      515
I mothered funeral sacrifices for the foe! For what do I still live, with heart of iron?
For what do I tarry? For what do you preserve me, knotty old age?
For what, you cruel gods, unless I must behold even new deaths,

do you keep this ancient woman alive? Who would have thought
that Priam could be called happy after the fall of Pergamum?                    520
But happy is he in his death; for he doesn't behold you dead,
my child, and quit in one stroke both kingdom and life.
Your dowry, I suppose, will be a funeral, royal maiden, and
your body will be laid within an ancestral monument!
The fortune of our house forbids: your mother's funeral gifts                    525
to you will simply be her tears and a handful of foreign sand!
We've lost it all. But one reason does survive for me to live
a short while yet, an offspring to his mother most dear,
my only son now, for Polydorus, the youngest of our sons,
was brought to these shores and given to the Ismarian[91] king.[92]              530
But meanwhile, why do I delay to cleanse your cruel wounds
with water and your face bespattered with savage blood."
        She spoke and proceeded at an old woman's pace to the shore,
her whited hair in disarray. "Trojan women, give me an urn!"
the unhappy woman had said, in order to fetch pure water from the waves:   535
she sees Polydorus' corpse cast out upon the shore
and its enormous wounds created by the Thracian spears.
The Trojan women cry out, but Hecuba is struck dumb with grief,
for grief itself had devoured both her voice and the tears
that rose within her, and quite like an unyielding stone                         540
she stands unmoved, sometimes fixing her eyes upon the ground,
and sometimes raising her angry countenance to the ethereal sky,
now looking at the face of the body, now at the wounds of her son,
especially at the wounds, and arms and girds herself with wrath.
When once her anger blazed forth, although she remained a queen,                 545
she chose to take revenge, entirely intent on punishment,
and as a lioness, deprived of her nursling cub will rage
and, having found the footprints, pursues the foe she does not see,
so Hecuba, when once she had mixed her grief with wrath,
forgetting never her passion, forgetting entirely her many years,                550
seeks a parley with Polymestor, the perpetrator of the murderous crime:
she claims she wants to show him where hidden gold
was left behind that she would give him for her son.
Believing her, the Odrysian,[93] so familiar with the love of spoils,
approaches her privately: then the smooth-tongued, cunning man                   555
declared, "Hecuba, put all delay aside, give the gifts for your son!
Whatever you give and what you gave before will be his,
I swear by the gods above." In anger she watches him speaking there
and swearing falsely. She swells with boiling wrath

---

91 I.e., Thracian, from Mt. Ismarus in Thrace.
92 Polymestor (see 430).
93 I. e., Thracian.

and, having laid hold of him, summons a host         560
of captive mothers and buries her fingers into those treacherous eyes
and pushes the eyes out of his cheeks (her anger supplies the strength)
and plunges in her hands and, stained with that guilty blood,
drags out not only his eyes (which were gone) but the sockets of the eyes.
Incited by the slaughter of their king, the people of Thrace     565
begin to attack the Trojan women with a volley of spears
and stones, but Hecuba with a raucous sound chases and bites
the flying stones and with her jaws prepared for words
she barked when she tried to speak: the place is still there
and takes its name[94] from this event, as she, remembering long her ancient ills,   570
continued even then to howl with sorrow throughout the Sithonian[95] fields.
Her fortune had moved her Trojan women and the Pelasgian foe,
her fortune had moved all the gods as well,
had moved them all, so that even the wife and sister of Jove herself
denied that Hecuba had deserved an end like that.        575

### 576-622   Memnon

     Aurora, even though she had favored the same side in war,
does not have time to be moved by the death and fall of Troy and Hecuba.
The goddess is anguished by a closer sorrow and personal grief,
the loss of Memnon,[96] whom the saffron mother saw upon
the plains of Phrygia perishing by Achilles' spear;        580
she saw him, and that color by which the morning hours blush
had paled, and the ethereal sky hid within the clouds.
However, to behold the limbs laid upon the final fires
the mother could not endure, but just as she was, with her hair
in disarray, was not ashamed to cast herself at the knees     585
of mighty Jove and to add these words to her tears:
"Inferior to all the goddesses that the golden sky supports
am I (for I have the fewest temples in all the world),
but as a goddess, no less, have I come, not that you grant me shrines
and festal days of sacrifice and altars to grow hot with fires:    590
but if you consider what I, a woman, offer you
when with new light I confine the limits of the night,
I hope you think a reward is due; but neither is it the concern
nor purpose of Aurora now to request the honors due to her:
I come deprived of my Memnon, who bravely bore arms     595
in vain for his uncle and in his early years
by mighty Achilles (just as you planned) was slain.

---

94 The "Tomb of the Bitch" is a landmark on the Thracian Chersonese.
95 Thracian.
96 Her son by Tithonus, the brother of Priam. Memnon's day on the field of valor was told in the *Aithiopis.*

I pray that you grant him some honor, some solace for his death,
O highest ruler of the gods, and soften his mother's wounds!"
When Jupiter nodded his assent, the soaring pyre of Memnon collapsed          600
in lofty flames and the clouds of black smoke
discolored the day, as when the rivers exhale
their daughter mists that block the sunlight in its descent;
the blackened ashes fly about and, gathered into one form,
grow dense and acquire an appearance and assume both warmth          605
and spirit from the flames (whose lightness supplied the wings);
and first like a bird, but soon truly as a bird
it made a whirring sound with wings, and with it whirred
its countless sisters, whose natal origin was the same;
three times they circle the pyre, and the concordant beating of their wings          610
three times ascends into the air, but in the fourth flight the troop divides;
two tribes then from opposite sides wage furious war
and with their beaks and hooked claws ply their wrath
and weary their wings and opposing breasts,
and bodies kindred to the buried ashes fall as offerings to          615
the dead and remember that they were created from that brave man.
Their author gives the sudden birds a name: from him
they have the name Memnonides.[97] When the sun has passed through all
twelve signs, in the ancestral manner,[98] willing to die,[99] they fight anew.
To others, then, the barking of Dymas' daughter[100] seemed sad;          620
Aurora, though, was intent upon her grief and offers even now
her tears with which she sprinkles all the world with dew.

### 623-968   Aeneas

### 623-631   The Journey to Delos

The fates do not permit the hopes of Troy to be destroyed:
her sacred images, and what is also sacred, his father, a venerable[101] weight,
are carried upon the shoulders of Cytherea's[102] heroic son.          625
Of all his wealth the pious son chose that prize
and also his son Ascanius and is carried with his exiled fleet
across the sea from Antandros[103] to the thresholds of wicked Thrace;

---

97 Daughters of Memnon, changed to birds who return each year to Memnon's tomb and over it fight
   in their father's honor.
98 Translating the *parentali ... more* of many older MSS and read by Tarrant. The MSS vary: with *voce*,
   accepted by Ehwald, *"in the idiom of the Parentalia"* (see the next note); with *morte* (found in some
   later MSS), "for their father's death." Heinsius conjectures *Marte*, "in combat for ancestors."
99 Alluding to the Roman *Parentalia*, funeral for ancestors, often the occasion for gladiatorial combat,
   hence "willing to die," translating *moriturae*. Cf. the gladiatorial salute to the emperor: *morituri
   te salutamus*.
100 Hecuba.
101 A play on the name of Venus, who bore Aeneas to Anchises.
102 Venus, so called because she was born from the sea near the island of Cythera.
103 A port city of the Troad.

*Aeneas and Family Escape, Picart*

he quits that land still drenched in Polydorus' blood,
and with the help of the winds and a favorable tide                    630
he enters the city of Apollo in the company of his friends.

### 632-74  *The Daughters of Anius*

There Anius, whom mortals duly esteemed as king
and Phoebus as priest, received him in his temple and home
and showed him his city[104] and famous shrines[105] and those
two trees to which Latona clung in giving birth.                       635
When incense is applied to the flames and wine upon the incense poured
and entrails of slaughtered bulls are burned according to ancient rite,
they seek the royal palace, and, seated upon lofty couches covered with rugs,
partake of Ceres' gifts along with Bacchus' wine.
Then pious Anchises says, "O elected priest of Phoebus, am I           640
mistaken, or do I recall that when first I saw these walls
you had a son and twice two daughters as well?"
To him Anius nods his temples wreathed
with snow-white fillets and sadly replies: "O greatest hero, you
are not mistaken; you saw me as the father of five,                    645
whom now (so great the uncertainty of human affairs)
you see almost completely bereft. For what help to me is my absent son,

104 Delos.
105 Of Diana and Apollo.

whom Andros, that land[106] that takes its name from his,
now holds, who rules there in his father's stead?
The Delian[107] god gave him augury, Liber[108] bestowed other gifts        650
upon my female offspring, gifts passing prayer or belief:
for everything at my daughters touch
would turn to grain and the liquid of pure wine
or fair Minerva's oil, and there was wealth in using them.
When Atreus's son, the destroyer of Troy, learns of this        655
(in case you think that we in another region failed to feel
the storm you suffered), he resorts to force of arms
and takes them from their father's bosom against their will
and orders them to nourish the Argive fleet with their heaven-sent gift.
They get away, each as best she can: Euboea[109] is sought        660
by two, and their brother's Andros by the other two.
An army arrives and, if they're not handed over, threatens war:
his piety overcome by fear, he surrendered his kindred blood
to punishment; but you could forgive the brother's fear:
Aeneas was not here to act in Andros' defense,        665
nor Hector, because of whom you held out those ten years.
And even as the chains were being set about their limbs,
they raised their arms, still free, to the sky
and said, 'Father Bacchus, bring help!' and in fact
the author of their gift brought help, —if in some strange way        670
the loss of their form is rightly called bringing help,
without my being able to know how they lost it or to say how even now;
the ultimate result of this woe is known: they took on the plumes
of your own consort's[110] birds and departed as snow-white doves."

### 675-704  *The Daughters of Orion*

When they had finished the banquet with such stories as these        675
and others, the table was removed and they sought out sleep,
and rise with the day and go to Phoebus's oracle.
He[111] ordered them to seek their ancient mother and kindred shore.
The king attends them and gives them gifts as they prepare to go,
a scepter to Anchises, a mantle and quiver to his grandson, a mixing bowl        680
for wine to Aeneas, which long ago Ismenian[112] Therses, his guest,
transported to him from the Aonian[113] shores:

---

106 Andros is an island just southeast of Attica.
107 Apollo, from the island of Delos.
108 Bacchus, the "Liberator."
109 A long island northeast of Attica.
110 Venus. For her doves, see 14. 597 and 15. 386.
111 Anius, both oracle-priest and king.
112 Theban.
113 Boeotian.

the vase had been sent by Therses, but Hylean[114] Alcon it was
who made it and who carved upon it a lengthy tale.
There was a city, and you could point out all the seven gates          685
revealing its name[115] and showing what city it was.
Before the city are funerals and tombs and flames and pyres
and women with hair in disarray and mothers baring their breasts,
displaying their grief; the nymphs themselves appear to weep,
complaining that their springs were dry; the trees stood bare          690
of leaves, the she-goats gnaw at the arid rocks.
Behold, he sets the daughters[116] of Orion in the midst of Thebes,
with this one making a unwomanly wound to her naked throat,
with that one having thrust a sword into her valiant breast,
who, having died for their people, are being carried through the town  695
with funeral pomp and burned in an honored place.
And then from the virginal ashes twin youths emerge,
lest all their line should perish, whom tradition calls
Coronae,[117] and for their mothers' ashes they led the funeral march.
Upon the ancient bronze this much the gleaming signs revealed;         700
the top of the crater bristled with gilded acanthus[118] leaves.
The Trojans respond with gifts not unequal to these
and give a case in which to keep incense to the priest,
and give as well a saucer and crown, shining with jewels and gold.

### 705-29   *Departure from Andros; Crete; Strophades; Buthrotus;*
### *Arrival in Sicily*

From there, the Teucrians,[119] remembering their origin was derived    705
from Teucer's blood, went to Crete, where, unable to endure for long
the place and Jove's weather, they choose to leave
its hundred cities and head for Ausonia's[120] ports.
The storms of winter rage and vex the men, and when they reach
the Strophades'[121] treacherous ports, Aello[122] the harpy frightened them.   710
Already had they skirted the Dulichian ports
and Samos,[123] and Ithaca, the homes of Neritos[124] as well,

---

114 From Hyle, a town of Boeotia.
115 Thebes, famous for its seven gates.
116 Ovid's story, instead of changing the Coronides, the daughters of Orion, into stars as in Anton. Lib.
   4, makes twin youths arise from their ashes.
117 Ehwald and others read a masculine form of the name, *Coronos.*
118 A thorny plant whose large and jagged leaves often decorate Corinthian capitals.
119 Trojans.
120 Italy, so named for a mythical founder, Auson.
121 Two small islands in the Ionian Sea.
122 Verg., *Aen.* 3. 210 ff. gives the name Celaeno to the harpy who predicted that the Trojans would not
   find peace until they ate their tables. *Aello* means "Storm" in Greek.
123 The Ionian, not the Aegean, island.
124 A mountain on Ithaca and a small island nearby. The "homes" are those under the sway of
   Ulysses.

deceitful Ulysses' kingdom; Ambracia,[125] subject of strife
among the gods, they see (and the crag in the image of
the transformed judge), made famous by Apollo of Actium[126] now,          715
and Dodona's land, with her speaking oaks,[127]
and also Chaonia's[128] gulf, where King Molossus' sons
escaped on their added wings from impious fires.[129]
    They next seek the Phaeacians' fields,[130] set thick
with fertile fruit, and land at Buthrotos in Epirus,                        720
a simulated Troy that the Phrygian seer[131] ruled.
From there, informed of what would be because of all the son
of Priam, Helenus, had foretold in his friendly advice,
they come to Sicania:[132] it runs out into the sea in three tongues,
from which Pachynus[133] faces the rainy south,                            725
the gentle Zephyrs[134] meet Lilybaeum,[135] while
Pelorus[136] looks to Boreas and the Bear that knows not the sea.
The Teucrians come to Sicily, and with oars and favoring tide
by nightfall the fleet gains Zancle's[137] sandy shore.

### 730-748    *Scylla*

    Infesting the right side is Scylla, restless Charybdis the left;        730
the latter seizes and sucks down the ships and vomits them up again,
the former is girt about her gloomy loins with ferocious dogs,
but has the face of a maiden, and, if not entirely false
the stories bards have told, she was in former days a girl,
whom many suitors wooed. Having rejected them all,                         735
she used to go to the nymphs of the sea, nymphs to whom she was most dear,
and told them of the disappointed loves of the youths.
As Galatea allows her to comb her hair,
with frequent sighs the maiden[138] speaks to her these words:
"Dear maid, by no means rude has been the sort of youths who seek          740
your hand, and it has been possible for you to refuse them without harm;

---

125 A city of Epirus for whose possession Hercules competed with Apollo and Diana. The arbiter of the
    strife, Cragaleus, decided for Hercules and was turned into stone by Apollo (Anton. Liberalis, 4,
    citing Nicander, *Heterooumena*, 1). See Index/Glossary.
126 Octavian attributed to Apollo his victory on Sept. 2, 31 B. C. over Antony and Cleopatra off the
    Ambracian promontory of Actium.
127 The ancient oracle of Zeus at Dodona in Epirus spoke through its rustling oaks.
128 The northwest coastal region of Epirus.
129 Jupiter changed them to birds when Molossus' palace was set aflame by attacking robbers (see
    Anton. Liberalis, 14).
130 The island Corcyra. See Hom., *Od.* 6 and 7.
131 Helenus.
132 An old name for Sicily.
133 Town at the southeast corner of Sicily.
134 West winds.
135 A promontory at the southwest corner of Sicily, near Marsala.
136 A promontory at the northeast corner of Sicily, near Messena (modern Messina).
137 An older name for Messena.
138 Galatea.

for me, however, whose father is Nereus and whom dark-blue Doris bore,
who have a throng of sisters to keep me safe, it was
not granted to refuse the love of the Cyclops[139] without coming to grief."
And tears impeded her voice as she spoke.                                    745
The maiden,[140] wiping away her tears with her marble-like thumb,
consoled the goddess and said, "Recount the story, dearest one,
and do not conceal (for I am your friend) the reason for your grief!"

### 749-897   *Acis and Galatea*

The Nereid in turn replied to Cretaeis'[141] child:
"Of Faunus and the nymph Symaethis[142] was Acis born,                       750
to both his father and mother the source of great joy,
but still greater to us; for he had bound himself to me alone.
So handsome he was, and his second eight years had come
and marked his tender cheeks with but a hint of down.
I yearned for him without cease, the Cyclops for me.                         755
And if you should ask whether my hatred for Cyclops or love
for Acis were stronger, I should have to say
that love and hatred were matched. O my, how great the power of
your reign, O gracious Venus! Indeed that creature is so uncouth
he makes the woods themselves bristle in horror; no guest                    760
has ever seen him without being harmed by this despiser of Olympus and
its gods! He suffers the feelings of love, seized by powerful desire,
and burns with passion, forgetting his flocks and his caves.
Your beauty, your ability to please is now your concern,
and now, Polyphemus, you comb your stiff tresses with a rake,                765
and now you like to trim your shaggy beard with a pruning-hook
and in the water to gaze at and set in order your savage countenance.
Your love of slaughter, your savagery and enormous thirst for blood
give way, and ships now come and go unharmed.
To Sicul[143] Aetna, meanwhile had Telemus[144] been brought,               770
Eurymus' son Telemus, whom no bird had ever deceived;
approaching awful Polyphemus, he said, 'The single eye
you wear in the midst of your brow will Ulysses steal from you.'
The Cyclops laughed and said, 'O most foolish of prophets, you're wrong,
another, a woman, has already stolen it!' He scorned the one who warned      775
the truth in vain and either treads heavily with enormous steps
upon the shore or wearily returns to his shady cave.
Projecting out into the sea with a long point, there was

---

139 For this tale see Theocritus 6 and 11.
140 Scylla.
141 Mother of Scylla.
142 Daughter of the god and river Symaethus (modern Simeto), near Catania.
143 The Siculi and Sicani were ancient tribes of Sicily.
144 See Hom., *Od.* 9. 510.

a wedge-shaped hill with breakers of the sea on either side.
The savage Cyclops went up the hill and sat down on its peak;     780
his wooly sheep, without a guide, followed after him.
Then, laying at his feet the pine he used for a staff,
quite suitable for a sail-bearing mast,
he reached for a pipe composed of a hundred reeds,
and all the mountain range heard the shepherd's sibilant song,     785
the waves heard it, too; hidden beneath a cliff and reclining in
my Acis' arms, from afar I took in with my ears
these words and learned what I heard by heart.
    " 'O Galatea,[145] whiter than the snowy privet's leaf,
more blooming than the meadows, taller than the lofty alder tree,     790
more gleaming than glass, more playful than the tender kid,
more smooth than the shell worn by the constant sea,
more pleasing than winter suns and summer shade,
more nimble than the doe, more sightly than the soaring plain,
translucenter than ice, sweeter than grape when ripe,     795
more soft than feathers of the swan and curdled milk,
and fairer than a well-watered garden, if you do not flee.
    " 'Yet fiercer this same Galatea than a heifer untamed,
more rugged than the ancient oak, more deceitful than the waves,
than willow branches and white brambles harder to break,     800
more rigid than these cliffs, more violent than a torrent's stream,
more haughty than the lauded peacock, keener than fire,
more prickly than thistles, quicker to anger than the nursing bear,
more heedless than the sea, more cruel than the serpent under foot,
and, what I especially wish I could deprive you of,     805
not only than the stag driven by the brightly baying hounds
but also than the winds and the passing breeze more fleet!
    "But if you knew me well, you would regret that you fled,
condemn your delays and strive to keep me yourself!
I own a cave, a part of a mountain, hanging with living rock,     810
in which the sun is not felt in midsummer heat,
nor felt is the winter chill; I own fruit that weighs the branches down,
own grapes that look like gold upon the long rows of vines,
own purple grapes as well: we are saving both kinds for you.[146]
And you yourself with your own hands will pick soft strawberries grown     815
beneath the forest shade, you yourself the cornel cherries in fall
and plums not only purple with dark juice,
but also the noble kind that imitates fresh wax.
And as my wife you will not want for chestnuts, nor want

---

145 The name means "Milky."
146 In Euripides' *Cyclops* Polyphemus is unfamiliar with the grape. But see Theocritus, 11. 21 and 45-48.

for arbutus fruit: at your service every tree will be.                         820
     " 'The whole of this flock is mine: while many roam within the vales,
the forest hides many as well, and many are stabled in the cave,
and, even if you asked me, I could not tell you how many there are:
the poor man counts his flock; you won't believe me when
I praise them, but if you were there, you could see for yourself          825
their udders so swollen they can scarcely get round them their legs.
And lambs there are, the younger brood, within the warm pens,
and goats as well, in age the same but in other folds contained.
I always have plenty of snow-white milk: from which a part is kept
for drinking, and part the liquid rennet congeals.                             830
     " 'And yours will be no simple pets
and ordinary gifts, but does and hares and a goat,
a pair of doves or a nest removed from a peak:
I found a set of twins that could play with you,
so like each other, you can scarcely tell them apart,                          835
the cubs of a shaggy bear taken from a mountain top:
I found them and said, "For our mistress these we'll keep."
     " 'But now raise your glistening head from the deep-blue sea,
come forth now, Galatea, and do not spurn our gifts!
For surely I know myself and saw myself within                                 840
the clear water's image, and I liked the form I saw.
Just look how big I am: Jupiter above is no greater than
this body (for you people are always talking about
some Jove who rules); a good head of hair overhangs
my awesome face and shades my shoulders like a grove;                     845
and do not think my body unseemly because it is very thick
with bristling hair; unseemly is a tree without leaves,
unseemly the horse, unless a mane enfolds its tawny neck;
the birds are covered with plumage, their wool adorns the sheep:
the beard and bristling body-hair befit grown men.                            850
I have one eye in the middle of my forehead, but its form
is like a giant shield. So what? Doesn't the Sun behold
this world of ours from the sky? Yet singular is the orb of the Sun!
     " 'Moreover, within that sea of yours my father[147] reigns:
I offer you this father-in-law; only take pity and hear                        855
the prayers of a suppliant! For to you alone do we humble ourselves,
and though I scoff at Jove and heaven and his piercing thunderbolt,
I fear you, O daughter of Nereus, for greater than lightning is your wrath.
And I would endure being scorned like this,
if you refused all others; but why with Cyclops put to scorn                860
do you love Acis and prefer Acis to my arms' embrace?

---

147 Neptune.

*Acis and Polyphemus, Baur*

Yet let him please himself and let him please you, too,
although I wish he didn't please you, Galatea. Just let me have
the chance to make him feel the might of a body so great!
I'll tear out his living bowels and rip apart his limbs     865
and scatter them over the fields and over your waves (let him mate with you then!).
I'm burning, and, wounded now, my fiery passion burns hotter still.
I think I carry Aetna transferred with all its might
within my breast, but, Galatea, that makes no difference to you.'
    "With such complaints as these (for I saw it all),     870
he rises and, like the bull enraged that the cow has been removed,
he can't stand still and roams about through woods and familiar glens,
when, catching sight of me and Acis unawares nor fearing such a thing,
the savage beast exclaims, 'I see you, and I'll make sure
this union of your Venus will be the last.'     875
His voice was just as big as an angered Cyclops ought
to have, so big that Aetna shook from the sound of it.
In terror I plunged into the neighboring sea;
to flee, the Symathian[148] hero had turned his back
and cried, 'O Galatea, help me, I pray, and parents, lend     880
your aid and, now that I must die, admit me into your realm!'
The Cyclops pursues, and hurls a part of the mountain he'd torn
away, and although only an extreme corner of the rock
reached Acis, it completely overwhelmed and buried him,
but we did only what the fates allowed     885

---

148 See note on 750.

and brought it about that Acis assumed his ancestral[149] might.
From under the mass purple blood began to seep
and soon its redness begins to fade
and takes on the color of a stream roiled after the first rain,
and gradually clears; then the mass that had been hurled                   890
gapes open and through the fissure rises a tall and living reed;
the hollow mouth of the rock resounds with exulting waves,
and suddenly, what a marvel, there rose waist high
a youth girt round with new horns[150] made from twisted reeds,
who was, if not something greater, with a face entirely blue,              895
still Acis, yes even now he was Acis, transformed
into a river, and its streams kept their former name."[151]

## 898-968   *Scylla and Glaucus*

When Galatea's tale and their meeting had come to an end,
the Nereids part and swim away on peaceful waves.
But Scylla returns, for she dares not entrust herself to the open sea      900
and either wanders about unclothed upon the thirsty strand
or, when she wearies, finds a secluded recess of a bay
and in its sheltered waters refreshes her limbs.
But, skimming the sea, a new denizen of the deep,
his body in Euboean Anthedon[152] lately transformed,                      905
behold, Glaucus is here. The sight of the maid fills him with
desire, and thinking he might detain her from flight, he speaks
to her. She flees no less and, made swift by fear,
arrives at the top of mountain next to the shore.
It looms enormous over the ocean flood, formed into one peak,              910
its forested pinnacle sloping towards the spreading sea:
she stops, secure in this place, not knowing what he is,
a monster or a god, and marvels at his complexion and
the curly locks that covered his shoulders and the back beneath,
and that the form of a twisted fish ended at his groin.                    915
He saw her and, leaning upon a neighboring cliff,
he says, "O maiden, neither a monster nor savage beast am I,
but rather a god of the sea: no greater power over the sea
have Proteus and Triton and Palaemon, son of Athamas.[153]
However, once I was a mortal, but as if I were destined for                920
the seas, that is where I always worked even then,
for sometimes I would haul in the nets with their haul of fish,

---

149 His mother was a water-nymph.
150 Symbol of a river-god.
151 The name is preserved in several Sicilian towns, including Acireale.
152 A town of Boeotia on the Euboean Gulf.
153 For the metamorphosis of Palaemon, see 4. 416–542.

and sometimes sitting on a pier I would wield a cane pole and line.
A shore lies next to a verdant meadow, one side of which
is bound by the waves, the other by grasses that                              925
no horn-bearing heifers have injured with their bite,
nor have you peaceful ewes or shaggy nannies browsed on them.
No busy bee has taken and gathered the flowers from there,
no bridal wreaths from there were given for the brow,
nor ever have scythe-bearing hands mowed therein; I was the first             930
to sit upon this turf, while I dried my sodden lines,
and so to count in order my catch of fish
I spread out those that fortune had driven to the nets
and those whose credulity had lured them to the hooks.
It sounds like a lie, but what good does it do for me to lie?                 935
In contact with the grass my catch begins to move
and flop about and move on the ground as in the sea.
And as I pause in wonder, the whole haul escapes
into their waves and leaves their new master and the shore.
I stood dumbfounded, completely at a loss, and seek the cause:               940
'Was this the work of a god? Was this done by the juice of the grass?
What force then can grass have,' I say, and with my hand
I pluck the meadow and bit with my teeth what I plucked.
My throat had scarcely finished drinking down the unknown juice
when suddenly I felt my insides begin to tremble and                         945
my breast overwhelmed with yearning for a nature of another kind;
I could not long resist and said, 'O earth, never to be visited again,
farewell!' and sank my body into the sea.
The gods of the sea deign to receive me within their honored ranks
and ask that Oceanus and Tethys strip me of all                              950
mortality I possess. I am examined by them,
and, after a ninefold song is sung to purge me of my wickedness,
they order me to submerge my body in a hundred streams;
without delay, the rivers springing from diverse parts
direct all their watery courses upon our head—                               955
this far I can tell you what I can recall,
this much I remember, but after this my mind went blank.
But when my senses returned, I received a new self,
a body completely different than before and different mind as well.
Then first did I see this beard green with mold,                             960
my curly locks, with which I sweep the spreading seas,
and these huge shoulders and these sea-blue arms
and legs that are curved to a point like a finny fish.
Why then this shape, why have I pleased the gods of the sea,
what use is there in being a god, if you are not touched by these things?"    965

As he was saying this and about to say more, Scylla left
the god; incited to rage at this repulse,
he seeks out the ominous halls of Circe, the Titan's[154] child.

---

154 The Sun.

# BOOK 14

## 1-74  *Glaucus, Circe and Scylla*

And Aetna now, imposed upon the Giant's[1] jaws,
and also the fields of the Cyclopes, not knowing the rake or use of the plow
nor owing anything at all to the yoking of bulls,
are left behind by the Euboean tiller[2] of the swollen waves,
and left behind are Zancle and Rhegium's[3] walls that opposite lie,                    5
and also the shipwrecking narrows, pressed between twin shores,
that mark the boundaries of the Ausonian[4] and Sicul[5] lands.
From there then, Glaucus, swimming with mighty strokes
across the Tyrrhenian[6] Sea, approaches the herb-growing hills and halls
of Circe, daughter of Sol, that were teeming with various beasts.              10
As soon as he saw her, when greetings had been given and received,
he said, "O goddess, take pity on a god, I pray! For you alone,
if only you think me worthy, can relieve this love of mine.

---

1 Typhon.
2 Glaucus, born in Euboea (see 13. 909).
3 Rhegium (modern Reggio di Calabria) is on the Italian shore of the straits of Messena (Messina).
4 Italian.
5 Sicilian; the *Siculi* and *Sicani* were peoples of Sicily.
6 Etruscan.

O daughter of Titan, the power of herbs is better known
to no one than to me, who have been transformed by them.                    15
In case the cause of my mad passion is unknown to you,
it was upon the Italic shore, opposite Messena's walls,
that I saw Scylla. I'm embarrassed to tell my promises and prayers,
my flattering compliments and rejected words;
but if songs have any power, then from your holy mouth                       20
produce a song, or if herbs are more effectual,
then use the tested strength of those effective herbs.
Nor do I ask that you cure me or heal these wounds;
I seek not an end of my passion, but only that she share its heat."
But Circe (for no woman had a character more suited to                       25
such flames, whether the cause lay in herself
or Venus made her so because of her father's offense[7]),
replies with these words: "Better would it be for you to pursue
a person who wanted and sought the same, one caught by the same
desire. You deserved to be wooed for your own sake (and certainly could),    30
and if you offer any hope, believe me, for your own sake you will be wooed.
But lest you have doubts and lack confidence in the beauty of your form,
look here, though I am a goddess, though I am the daughter of the Sun,
and though my power of song is great, and great the power of my herbs,
let me be yours, I pray. Spurn the one who spurns, respond in kind           35
to her who yearns for you, and in one act both women requite.
To her temptations Glaucus replies, "Leaves will grow in the sea
and seaweed on the mountain tops before our love will change
while Scylla lives." The goddess is indignant, and since
she could not do him harm (nor did she wish to, being in love),             40
she turns her wrath against the one who is preferred to her;
offended by the refusal of love, she quickly grinds up herbs
notorious for their fearful juices and to her mixture adds
the charms of Hecate and dons a dark-blue cloak
and through the host of fawning beasts                                       45
proceeds from the middle of her court
and, heading for Rhegium opposite Zancle's cliffs,
she walks upon the waves that boil with the tides,
in which she sets her paces as though upon dry land
and skims with feet still dry the surface of the sea.                        50
There was a little pool, a bay in the form of a bow,
a pleasant place for Scylla to rest: there she retired from the heat
of both the sea and sky when the sun was strongest in
the middle of the firmament and created the least shade from its height.
The goddess corrupts and pollutes the place with wonder-working drugs;       55

---

7 See 4. 167 ff., the story of the Sun and Leucothoë.

*Scylla Changed to Monster, Baur*

she sprinkles it with potions pressed from noxious roots,
and murmurs with her magical voice a thrice-ninefold repeated song,
obscured by a confusing maze of strange words.
When Scylla arrives and had entered the waters up to her waist,
she sees barking monsters disfiguring her loins;                                    60
believing at first that to her own body those parts did not belong,
she tries to flee and to chase them away and is frightened by
the impudent snouts of dogs, but drags them along as she flees,
and when she reaches for a body formed of thighs and legs and feet,
she finds in place of those parts Cerberean[8] jaws:                                65
she stands on raging dogs and contains the backs of
furious beasts between her belly and mutilated loins.
        Her lover, Glaucus, wept and fled from Circe's embrace,
who had too cruelly applied the strength of her herbs.
But Scylla remained in that place and as soon as she had the chance,              70
fulfilled her hate for Circe by despoiling Ulysses of his friends;[9]
she soon would have sunk the Teucrian[10] ships
except that she had already been transformed into a cliff,
a rocky eminence even today, a cliff the sailors abhor.

8 Belonging to Cerberus, the watchdog of Hades.
9 Hom., *Od.* 12. 245 ff.
10 Trojan.

### 75-608 The Wanderings[11] of Aeneas Continued
### 75-100 Scylla, Charybdis, Dido, Sicily, Islands of Aeolus, Palinurus, Inarime, Prochyte, and Pithecusae

The Trojan vessels had overcome Scylla with their oars                    75
and also Charybdis; they were already nearing the Ausonian coast
when winds divert them towards the Libyan shores.
With heart and home the Sidonian woman[12] received
Aeneas there, and would not gladly bear separation from
her Phrygian husband; and on a pyre, constructed under the guise         80
of sacrifice, she fell on a sword and, disappointed herself, disappointed all.
Once more[13] in flight from the new walls of this sandy land,
Aeneas goes again to the abodes of Eryx[14] and Acestes, his loyal friend,
and honors his father's tomb with sacrifice.
The ships that Junonian Iris had almost burned                           85
he loosens from their moorings and leaves behind Hippotades' realm[15]
and lands, smoking with glowing sulphur, and the rocky shores
of Acheloüs' daughters, the Sirens, and the pine-made ship, of its helmsman[16]
bereft, skirts by Inarime[17] and Prochyte[18] and Pithecusae, located on
a barren hill, so called from its inhabitants' name.[19]                  90
Indeed the father of the gods, detesting the Cercopes'[20] ancient fraud
and the deceits and wrongdoing of that trickster tribe,
deformed the men into a disfigured animal,
dissimilar to humankind and able to seem similar as well;
he shrunk their limbs and flattened the turned-up nose beneath           95
their brow and with aging wrinkles furrowed their face
and covered all their body with yellow tufts of hair
and sent them to this place, but did not fail to take away the use
of words and the harmful perjury of their native tongue;
he only left them the ability to complain in a raucous screech.          100

---

11 Ovid's narrative draws upon events treated by Vergil's *Aeneid*.
12 Dido, of Tyre and Sidon, the founder of Carthage.
13 The first time was the failed attempt to overcome the winds that had diverted him from Italy to Libya (see 76).
14 The son of Venus, brother of Aeneas, and eponymous hero of the mountain and city of Western Sicily. See Verg., *Aen.* 5. 23-24.
15 The Aeolian or Liparian Islands (modern Isole Eolie or Lipari) belonging to the god of the winds, Aeolus, son of Hippotes.
16 Palinurus.
17 Modern Ischia, an island off the northern promontory of the Bay of Naples.
18 Modern Procida, a smaller island between Ischia and the Cape of Misenus (Miseno) on the mainland.
19 *Pithecusae* means "Apes" in Greek.
20 Tradition made them a deceitful people of Lydia.

## 101-153   *The Sibyl*

When he has passed by these and left behind on the right
the walls of Parthenope,[21] he approaches on the left the tomb
of Aeolus' tuneful son[22] and a place that teemed with swampy sedge,
the shores of Cumae and the long-lived Sibyl's cave,
and pleads to go by way of Avernus to his father's shades.                     105
But she, holding long her gaze upon the ground
and finally maddened by the reception of the god,
declared, "Great is what you seek, O man most mighty in deeds,
whose right hand has been tested by the sword, whose piety, by fire.
But lay aside all fear, O man of Troy: you will gain your desire;             110
with me as your guide you will find the homes of Elysium and the world's
last realm and your father's beloved shade.
No path is impassable to valor." She spoke and revealed
the branch that gleamed with gold in Avernal Juno's[23] wood
and ordered him to tear it away from its trunk.                               115
Aeneas obeyed and sees terrible Orcus'[24] wealth
and his own forefathers and the ancient shade
of great-hearted Anchises; he learns the laws of that place,
and perils that must be faced in wars to come.
From there he bore his weary steps on the upward path[25]                     120
and lightened the labor by talking with his Cumaean guide.
And as he made his way on the frightening journey through the twilight gloom,
he said, "Whether goddess incarnate or most pleasing to the gods,
a beacon of divinity will you be for me; I will proclaim
my debt to you for allowing me to approach the land of death                  125
and then to escape the land of death, once seen.
When with your service I have come to the airy breezes above,
I'll dedicate a temple to you, I'll offer incense to you."
The prophet looks back at him and, breathing many a sigh,
declared, "Neither goddess am I, nor do I deem this human head                 130
deserving of the gift of holy incense, but lest you wander uninformed,
eternal light and life without end were being offered to me,
if only my virginity had agreed to submit to Phoebus' love.
However, while he still has hope, while he seeks to weaken me
with gifts, he says, 'Select, O Cumaean maid, whatever you desire:            135
what you desire, you will gain.' I pointed to a heaped-up pile
of dust, and made the foolish request to have

---

21 Another name for Naples, "Virgin-face," named for a Siren according to Pliny, *Nat. Hist.* 3. 62.
22 Misenus, whose tomb forms the hill of Cape Misenus (Capo Miseno).
23 The Juno of Avernus, the entrance to the Underworld, is Proserpina. For the "golden bough" see
   Verg. *Aen.* 6. 136-211.
24 World of the dead.
25 Verg., *Aen.* 6, describes the Underworld in the *katabasis*, the journey down; Ovid concentrates on
   the *anabasis*, the journey up.

as many birthdays as the pile had grains of dust,
forgetting to ask that those years remain forever young.
He offered those years, however, and eternal youth as well                          140
if I submitted to Venus: having rejected Phoebus' gift,
I do remain unwed: but now the happier time of life
has turned its back, and feeble age has come with tremulous foot
and must be long endured. Seven centuries have I consumed
already, and yet before I equal the grains of dust,                                145
three hundred harvests, three hundred vintages remain to be seen.
The time will come when the length of days will make small
this body of mine, and my limbs, consumed with age,
will be reduced to the lightest weight: and I shall seem unloved
and not to have pleased the god, and Phoebus perhaps himself                        150
will either not recognize me or deny that he loved me once.
So changed will I become that I will be visible to none,
yet by my voice will I be known; the fates will leave me my voice."[26]

### 154-222 *Macareus Meets Achaemenides*

As over the winding path the Sibyl tells her tale,
Aeneas of Troy emerges into the Euboean city[27] from                              155
the realm of Styx and, after the favorable sacrifices custom required,
approaches the shores that not yet had gained the name of his nurse.[28]
Here, too, had remained, wearied from his labors' lengthy toil,
Neritian[29] Macareus, of much tried Ulysses the companion and friend.
He recognizes Achaemenides,[30] left behind earlier on Aetna's crags;              160
amazed to find him, suddenly, still alive,
he asks, "Achaemenides, what fate or god has kept
you safe and why are you, a Greek, carried by
a foreign prow? What land is sought by your ship?"
Replying to his query, but now no longer shabbily clad,                            165
his clothing no longer sewn together with thorns, Achaemenides
declares, "May I again behold Polyphemus and
those jaws that ran with human blood,
if ever my home and Ithaca are more important to me than this ship,
if ever I honor Aeneas less than my father; were I                                 170
to offer all to him, I could never give proper thanks.
As long as I speak and breathe and gaze upon the sky
and stars of the sun, how could I ever be ungrateful or forget?
Aeneas kept my life from entering the Cyclops' mouth,

---

26 The voice of the Sibyl was thought to be emitted from the caves at Cumae.
27 Cumae, founded by Greeks from Euboea.
28 Caieta, eponym for modern Gaeta on the coast of Campania, (see 441-44).
29 Neritos, son of Nereus, is also the name of a small island off and a mountain of Ithaca.
30 For Aeneas' rescue of Achaemenides, left behind inadvertently by Ulysses, from the Cyclops, see
   Verg., *Aen.* 3. 588ff.

assuring when once I leave the light of life,                                     175
that I'll be buried either in a tomb or at least not in that paunch.
What was my state of mind (assuming that fear had not taken away
my mind and senses altogether) when I was left behind and saw
you making for the open sea? I wanted to cry out, but feared to expose
myself to the enemy; Ulysses' outcry had almost harmed your ship        180
as well.[31] I watched as he tore from the mountain a huge crag
and cast it far out into the midst of the waves;
I watched again as he hurled with his Giant-like arms,
a catapult of strength, those enormous rocks,
and, having forgotten now that I was not on board, I was terribly afraid  185
the sea and wind in the wake of the stones would overwhelm the ship.
When flight, however, had brought you back from certain death,
the Cyclops roams about all of Aetna, groaning as he goes
and feels his way through the forests, bereft of his sight,
colliding with the cliffs and reaching out towards the sea                 190
his arms smeared with putrid gore, and cursing the Achaean race,
exclaiming, 'If any good fortune brings Ulysses back to me,
or any comrade of his, I'll vent my rage on him,
I'll eat his entrails, my right hand will tear apart
his living flesh, his blood will flood my throat, and all                    195
his limbs will be shattered and tremble beneath my teeth.
How little or nothing the loss of my eye would be compared to that!'
The savage said this and more. A sickening fear envelops me when
I see his face still soaked with slaughter even then
and his cruel hands and the empty socket of his eye,                        200
his limbs and his beard stiff with human blood.
Before my eyes stood death, but that seemed the least of my woes,
as I imagined now myself in his clutches, now my entrails about
to sink into his; and the memory was fixed in my mind
of when I saw my companions' bodies, two at a time,                        205
dashed down upon the ground three times and a fourth,
while he, lying upon them the way a shaggy lion would,
was packing away into his greedy belly the entrails and flesh
and white-marrowed bones and half-living limbs.
A trembling assailed me; I stood there despondent and drained of blood,   210
beholding as his mouth chewed and spit out the bloody feast
and vomited the pieces combined with unmixed wine,
and thought of the doom being prepared for me;
for many days I lay in hiding and shuddered at every sound,
in terror of death and yet wanting to die.                                  215
While staving off hunger with acorns and grass mixed with leaves,

---

31 When Ulysses shouted out his true name from his ship (Hom., *Od*. 9. 475 ff.).

alone and helpless and without hope, abandoned to death and pain,
I spied in the distance a ship after a long time had passed
and prayed for escape by waving my hand and ran to the shore
and moved the men to pity: a Trojan ship takes on a Greek!                    220
Now you, O dearest of companions, unfold the tale of your fate and that
of both your leader and the company entrusted with you to the sea."

### 223-440  *Macareus' Story*

Macareus tells of Aeolus, who rules over the Tuscan deep,
the Aeolus who is Hippotes' son,[32] confining in his prison the winds;
when they were contained in a bull's hide, a memorable gift,                  225
the leader from Dulichium[33] took them and with their favoring breeze
in nine days had come in sight of his long-sought land;
but when on the ninth Aurora next roused herself,
Ulysses' friends were overcome with envy and desire for loot;
suspecting gold was hid within, they undid the bindings of the winds,         230
by which the ship returned to the waves just traversed,
and came again to the harbor of the Aeolian king.
"From there we came to Laestrygonian[34] Lamus' ancient town,"[35]
he says, "within the land that Antiphates ruled as king.
Dispatched to him I was, with two others in our group,                        235
and only barely did one companion and I escape alive;
our third companion stained with his blood
the impious mouths of the Laestrygonians. Antiphates pursues
and rouses up an army against us as we flee; they come
together and hurl rocks and timbers and sink our men and sink the ships.      240
One ship, however, that carried us and Ulysses himself,
escapes. Lamenting that part of our friends have been lost
and grieving bitterly, we finally put in at those lands
you see way off there (believe me, may I only behold from afar
that island!), and you, goddess-born Aeneas, of Trojans most just,            245
(for now that the war is over, you aren't to be called
an enemy), I warn you, flee from Circe's shores!
We, also, when our pine ship had tied up at Circe's shores,
remembering Antiphates and that savage Cyclops, too,
refused to go ashore, but we were selected by lot                             250
to enter that unfamiliar habitation: the lot sent faithful Polites and me
together with Eurylochus and Elpenor, who was too full of wine,
and twice nine other companions to visit Circe's walls.
As soon as we reach them and stand at the threshold of the house,

---

32 Not Aeolus of Thessaly, father of Sisyphus.
33 Ulysses. See 13. 107.
34 For the Laestrygonian cannibals see Hom., *Od.* 10. 116 ff.
35 Formiae (modern Formia, on the coast just below Gaeta), founded by Lamus.

a thousand wolves and lionesses and she-bears, among the wolves,                    255
came running and frightened us, but none was to be feared
and none intended to do our bodies any harm;
in fact they even wag their friendly tails in the air,
and follow our steps with fawning until
the servants take them away and through the marble halls                            260
conduct us to their mistress: she is seated in a lovely recess
upon a solemn throne, and arrayed in a shining cloak,
and covered above by a golden veil. With her
are Nereids and nymphs, who card no gathered wool
with running fingers nor lay thread upon successive thread:                          265
instead they organize the grasses and the flowers strewn about,
and place the herbs of various colors into separate wicker bins;
directing all they do herself, she understands how to use
each leaf and the harmony produced when they are mixed,
and pays close attention as she weighs and examines the herbs.                       270
As soon as she saw us and greetings had been exchanged,
she put on a friendly face and offered signs favorable to our desires.
Without delay she orders barley cakes of roasted grain to be prepared,
and honey and powerful wine and milk that rennet had congealed,
and stealthily adds juices, which beneath this sweetness remain                      275
concealed. We accept the cups from that dire and divine right hand.
No sooner had our parched and thirsty throats drunk them down,
and she, the awful goddess, had touched the tops of our heads with her wand,
than I begin (I'm ashamed to tell it) to grow rough with bristles, and,
unable to speak any longer, to emit noisy grunts instead                            280
of words, and, bowed low, to face completely the ground.
I feel my mouth growing hard with a spreading snout,
my neck swelling with muscles, and with those hands,
which only now had received the cups, I've now made tracks,
and with the others who had suffered the same (so great the power of drugs!)  285
I'm shut within a sty; we see that Eurylochus alone lacks
the shape of a pig: for he alone refused the proffered cups,
and, if he had not avoided them, I should even now remain
a part of that bristly herd and, not having been informed of that
disaster, Ulysses would never have come as avenger to Circe's home.              290
Cyllenius,[36] bringer of peace, had given a white flower to him;
the gods call it moly; upon a black root it stands.
Made safe by it and also by the heavenly advice,
he enters Circe's home and, invited to those treacherous cups,
he thrust her away as she tries to stroke his hair with her wand                    295
and held her at bay in terror of his brandished sword.

---

36 Mercury, born on Mt. Cyllene in Arcadia.

When pledges and right hands are exchanged, and he is received into
her wedding chamber, he demands as dowry the bodies of his friends.
We're sprinkled with better juices of an unknown herb
and smitten on the head by a blow from the opposite end of the wand,          300
and words are uttered contravening the words she had spoken before.
The more she sings, the more we stand erect, lifted from
the ground below, and the bristles fall away, and the cleft
abandons our cloven feet, our shoulders return and forearms join
our upper arms: in tears we embrace him, also in tears,          305
and cling to our leader's neck nor uttered any words
before those attesting to our gratitude.
A year's delay held us there, and in such a span of time
I personally saw many things, took in many things with my ears,
and this is one story among all reported in secret to me          310
by one of the four attendants assigned to such awesome rites.
For when with my leader Circe was dallying alone,
that handmaid showed a statue of snow-white marble to me;
it represented a young man wearing a woodpecker on his head;
remarkable in its shrine because of its many wreaths.          315
Who was the man and why was he venerated in the shrine
and why he carried the bird, all this I asked and wanted to know;
replying, she says, 'Macareus, hear and learn from this how great
the power of my mistress is; and apply your mind to my words!'
    " 'Once Picus, the son of Saturn, in Ausonian lands          320
was king and was fond of horses, useful in war.
The man's appearance was as you see; you may yourself
behold and approve his actual beauty from the sculpted form.
His spirit was equal to his beauty; he had not yet over the years
observed the quinquennial contest in Greek Elis[37] four times.          325
The man had turned the attention of the dryads[38] born
in Latium's mountains to his appearance, and the goddesses of the springs,
the Naiads, were pursuing him, whom Albula,[39] and the waters of Numicius,[40]
and those of Anio[41] and those of Almo,[42] shortest in its course,
or those the rushing Nar[43] held, and the Farfar[44] in its dark shade,          330
and those that attend Scythian[45] Diana's wooded pool
and neighboring lakes. But having rejected them all,

37 A region of northwest Greece, the site of the Olympic games.
38 Nymphs of oak trees.
39 Old name of the Tiber.
40 Small river of Latium.
41 River of Latium.
42 Small tributary of the Tiber.
43 The modern Nera, a tributary in Umbria into the left bank of the Tiber.
44 Small tributary of the Tiber in Sabine territory.
45 Referring to Artemis of the Taurian (Crimean) Peninsula, to whom Diana's cult at Aricia near Lake
    Nemi is compared here and at 15. 489. Euripides' *Iphigenia among the Taurians* treats her demand
    for human sacrifice.

he cherishes one nymph alone, whom once upon the Palatine hill
Venilia[46] had born to Ionian[47] Janus of double face.
As soon as she was ripe in age for her marrying years,                    335
the nymph was given to Laurentian[48] Picus, who was preferred to all the rest;
the beauty of her face was rare indeed, but rarer her skill in song,
the reason her name was Canens:[49] she used to move the woods and rocks
and calm wild beasts and hold back the rivers' long streams
and check with her voice the birds in their aimless flight.                340
As she was singing a song with her female voice,
Laurentian Picus had come forth from his house into the fields
to shoot the native boars and was riding the back of an eager horse
and carrying in his left hands a pair of spears
and clad in a purple mantle fastened with tawny gold.                      345
The daughter[50] of Sol had come to the same woods
to gather new herbs on the fruitful hills
and left the Circean lands called by her name.
While hidden in the brush, she saw the young man
and stood at once amazed: from her hand fell the gathered herbs,           350
and into the depths of her marrow a flame seemed to roam.
In passion's grip, she collected her thoughts as soon as she could
and was about to say what she desired: but the running horse
and surrounding band of companions blocked her approach to him.
"You'll not escape," she says, "not even if you're snatched away by the wind,  355
if truly I know myself, if not all the force of my herbs
has vanished, and my tuneful charms fail me not."
She spoke and created a false effigy, lacking body, of a boar
and ordered it to run in front of the eyes of the king
and seem to enter a grove that was dense with trees,                       360
just where the forest was thickest and impassable by horse.
Without hesitation, Picus in his ignorance goes after that shadow of
a prey and quickly dismounts from his frothy steed.
Pursuing his empty hope, he wanders through the deep woods on foot.
But Circe concocts prayers and utters magic words                          365
and prays to unknown gods with an unknown song,
with which she often darkens Luna's[51] snow-white face
and covers her father's head with a web of misty clouds.
Again the song she sang made the sky grow dark

---

46 Vergil, *Aen.* 7. 171, makes her also the mother of Turnus.
47 Why Ovid makes Janus, an ancient Italic deity, of Ionian (Greek) origin remains unclear, but perhaps,
    as Ehwald suggests, it is because of the word play in *Ionio ... Iano.*
48 Pertaining to Laurentium, the city of Latium, later ruled by Latinus. Ovid (449) and Vergil, *Aen.* 7.
    45-49, make Faunus, son of Picus, the father of Latinus by the nymph Marica. Elsewhere Latinus
    is the son of Hercules and Fauna or the Bona Dea.
49 Ovid here derives the name from *cano* "sing," not from *caneo* "be white or grey."
50 Circe.
51 The Moon or Diana, whose brother, Sun or Sol, is referred to in the next line.

and clouds of mist come from the ground so that within the gloomy trails  370
the king's companions go astray and leave him without his guard.
She found the right place and opportunity, and said, "O by those eyes
of yours that have captured my heart, and, most handsome fellow, by
your beauty that has made me, a goddess, your suppliant, look upon
our fiery passion with favor and receive as your father-in-law the Sun,  375
who sees all things, and do not look down upon Circe, the Titan's[52] child."
When she had spoken, he was furious and rejects both her and her appeals
and says, "Whoever you are, yours I am not; another has captured my heart
and holds me fast, and let her hold me for all time, I pray,
nor will I stain my promised engagement with an alien love,  380
so long as the fates preserve Janus-born Canens for me."
Titania[53] tried her prayers again and again in vain
and says, "You'll not go unpunished nor shall Canens be yours,
and what an insulted woman, what a woman in love can do, will you
find out; but Circe is also a woman and insulted and in love!"  385
She then turned twice to the west, twice to the east,
and touched the youth thrice with her wand, and uttered three songs.
He flees, but wonders himself why he runs
more swiftly than usual: upon his body he sees the plumes,
and, outraged that he was suddenly a strange bird in the Latin woods,  390
he pierces the scrubby oaks with his stubborn beak
and in his wrath upon the long branches leaves his wounds.
The plumes took on the purple color of his cloak;
the gold that once had been the clasp that pinned the robe
is changed to plumage and his neck is ringed with tawny gold,  395
and nothing of the former Picus is left except his name.[54]

    " 'And meanwhile, the companions, who had called in vain
throughout the fields to Picus and not found him anywhere,
discover Circe (for now she had cleared the air and allowed
the clouds to be dispersed by the winds and the sun)  400
and ply her with true accusations and demand the return of their king
and threaten force and prepare to attack with their angry spears:
she sprinkles them with juices of poison and a harmful drug
and summons Night and the gods of Night from Chaos and Erebus[55]
and prays to Hecate with drawn-out howls.  405
The woods leapt up from where they stood (a marvel to tell),
the ground moaned, the neighboring trees grew pale,
and, spattered with those bloody drops, the grass grew damp;

---

52 See note on 1. 10.
53 Circe, as daughter of the Sun (Titan). See on 1. 10.
54 *Picus* means "woodpecker."
55 Chaos is the empty mass out of which the world is formed in Book 1; Erebus is the god of Darkness;
    here both just mean the Underworld.

and stones seemed to emit bellowing moans
and dogs were barking and the ground was befouled                                410
by black things that crawled, and thin souls of the dead flitted about:
astonished by the omens, the company quakes with fear and as they quake
she touched their wondering faces with her poisoned wand,
and at its touch monstrous forms of savage beasts
come over the youths: not one kept his own shape intact.                         415
    " 'The setting Phoebus had spread his light upon the Tartessian[56] shores
and Canens' husband had been awaited with eyes and mind
in vain: the servants and people scurry through every wood
and carry torches out to meet him as they went.
It's not enough for the nymph to weep and tear her hair                          420
and beat her breast (though all this she does), she rushes out
and wanders frantically over the Latin fields.
Six nights and an equal number of the returning lights
of Sol beheld her lacking both sleep and food
and roaming over the ridges, through the vales, wherever chance                  425
would lead: Tiber was last to see her, by journey and grief
exhausted and resting her body upon his spreading bank.
And there she mourned with tears and poured forth words
with murmured voice that she tuned to match her very grief,
as sometimes the dying swan sings his funereal song.                             430
Thus in her final grief, her tender marrow liquefied,
she melted away and gradually vanished into thin air,
although the place is sealed by fame, which is named
correctly Canens by the Camenae,[57] those nymphs of old.'
    "Recounted to me and seen as well were many things                    435
like this. Sluggish and by lack of activity made slow
to take to the sea again, we do receive the order to sail again.
Titania had said that the way would be unsure,
the journey vast, and that perils of the cruel sea remained:
I was alarmed, I admit, and, having gained this shore, I stuck to it."           440

### 441-511  *Diomedes, Acmon*

    Macareus had finished, and Aeneas' nurse, at rest
within a marble urn, would have a brief song[58] upon her tomb
MY· NURSLING· OF· NOTED· PIETY· STOLE· ME· FROM· THE·
        ARGIVE· FIRE·
AND· HERE· WITH· FITTING· FLAMES· CONSUMED· HIS· CAIETA·

---

56 Of Tartessus, a Phoenician colony in Spain.
57 The native Italic Muses were the Camenae. Perhaps Ovid is suggesting some kind of folk etymology
    connecting *Camenae* to *cano* "sing" and *Canens*. There is no known place bearing the name of
    Canens.
58 HIC· ME· CAIETAM· NOTAE· PIETATIS· ALUMNUS·
    EREPTAM· ARGOLICO· QUO· DEBUIT· IGNE· CREMAVIT·

They loosed the rope that was tied to the grassy bank                                   445
and leave the treachery and home of the notorious goddess far
behind and head for the groves where, covered in shade,
the Tiber erupts with its yellow sand into the sea;
Aeneas gains the home and daughter of Latinus, Faunus' son,
but not without the work of Mars. With a strong-willed folk[59]          450
a war is waged, and Turnus rages because of a promised bride.[60]
The whole of Tyrrhenia[61] competes for Latium, and long
through clash of arms is arduous victory sought.
Each side increases its might with forces from abroad,
and many defend the Rutulians and many the Trojan camp,                  455
and not in vain had Aeneas gone to Evander's walls,[62]
but Venulus[63] had all in vain gone to the city[64] of exiled Diomedes: that man
had founded very great walls within Iapygian[65] Daunus' realm
and ruled over the fields brought by the dowry of his bride.
But after Venulus delivers the requests of Turnus                        460
and asks for aid, the Aetolian[66] hero says his resources are too weak:
he will not commit to battle the peoples of his father-in-law,
nor does he have men of his own nation whom he could arm,
"And lest you think this a fabrication, although
recalling them brings back anew the bitter grief,                        465
I shall recall them just the same. After lofty Ilium was burned
and Pergamum had fed the Danaan flames,
and after the Narycian hero[67] had from a maiden[68] stolen a maid,[69]
the punishment he alone deserved to pay he brought upon us all:
we Danaans are scattered and, ravished by the winds upon the hostile seas,   470
endure the wrath of sea and sky, the lightning, night,
and stormy rain and Caphereus,[70] the height of our woe,
but lest I detain you by citing our sad misfortunes in order, let
me say that Greece could seem lamentable even to Priam then.

---

59 The Rutulians, whose chief city was Ardea.
60 Lavinia, promised by her father Latinus first to Turnus, the king of the Rutulians, and then, changing
   his mind because of an oracle, to Aeneas (see Verg., *Aen.* 7. 37-106, 249-86, 341-72).
61 Etruria.
62 Pallanteum, on the Palatine Hill of Rome. Evander was a Greek settler from Arcadia (see Verg., *Aen.*
   8. 454-519).
63 Sent by Turnus on a fruitless mission to seek aid for the Rutulians from Diomedes. See Vergil, *Aen.*
   8 and 11. 225-30.
64 Arpi, in Apulia, where Diomedes had married the daughter of Daunus, in Vergil the father of Turnus.
   Verg., *Aen.* 11. 246, calls the city Argyripa (from *Argos*, Diomedes' native city, and *Euhippe*, his
   bride), which is then shortened to Arpi.
65 Apulia, called Iapygia after Iapyx, son of Daedalus or Lycaon. Daunus was the son of Danaë and
   Pilumnus, a male fertility god and founder of Ardea, or son of Lycaon (see 513).
66 Greek.
67 Ajax, son of Oïleus, of Naryx, a city of Ozolian Locris.
68 Minerva.
69 Cassandra.
70 A promontory of southeast Euboea where the Greek fleet was wrecked (see Verg., *Aen.* 11. 260 and
   1. 45).

The care of arms-bearing Minerva snatched and rescued me from                   475
the waves, but from my ancestral fields I am expelled again,
and nurturing Venus, still remembering, exacts payment for her wound
of long ago,[71] and I sustained so many labors upon
the high seas, so many labors in war on land
that often I called those happy whom                                            480
the common storms and Caphereus' savagery had sunk
into the waters, and wished I had been one of them.
       "My comrades, having now suffered the worst in war and on sea,
are weary and demand an end of wandering, but Acmon, a man
of passionate spirit, was indeed by our disasters sorely vexed,              485
'What is there, comrades, that your endurance will refuse
to bear,' he said, 'what more can Cytherea do to us,
supposing she means to? For when we fear worse things,
there is a reason for prayer, but when our lot is already the worst,
all fear lies scorned beneath our feet, the sum of woe no cause for concern.  490
So let her hear me, and let her hate, as truly she does,
all men who serve Diomedes, yet we will still despise her hate,
for in our eyes great power hardly counts for much.'
Annoying Venus with such words, Acmon, of Pleuron town,[72]
incites her to action and revives her former wrath.                             495
The words of Acmon please only a few, and most of my friends
and I reproach him; but when he tried to reply,
his voice and the path of his voice were reduced, and his hair
becomes feathers, his new neck is covered with plumes,
his chest and back as well; the feathers his arms take on                       500
are longer, and his elbows are bent into delicate wings;
his toes take up much space, his face becomes hard
with horn and comes to an end in a beak.
Nycteus looks at him in wonder, and Lycus, and Idas, and Rhexenor, too,
along with Abas, and as they wonder they all receive the same                   505
appearance, and the greater number of that band
take flight and fly about the oars with clapping winds.
If you should ask the form of these sudden birds,
it wasn't quite that of swans, but to white swans was very close.
Indeed, as son-in-law of Iapygian Daunus it is all I can do to retain           510
this homestead and thirsty land with but a remnant of my men."

---

71 Diomedes wounded her hand ( Hom., *Il.* 5. 336).
72 A city in Aetolia.

### 512-65  *Venulus, Aeneas' Ships*

When Oenides[73] had finished, Venulus left the Calydonian realm,
and Peucetian[74] gulf and the Messapian fields, in which
he spies a cave, overhung with a very dense wood
and hidden by pleasant reeds, the present haunt                                    515
of half-goaty Pan, but once the home of nymphs.
The shepherd Apulus frightened them from this place
and put them to flight, and filled them with fear at first, but soon,
regaining their composure, they looked upon their suitor with scorn
and formed choric dances with the rhythmic motion of their feet.              520
The shepherd mockingly imitates them with a rustic leap
and adds boorish raillery to his obscene words,
nor does his mouth grow silent until a tree conceals his throat:
for now he is a tree, whose nature can be known from its sap.
The wild-olive, in fact, exhibits the mark of his tongue                          525
upon its bitter berries: into them has passed the harshness of his words.
When from that journey the embassy returned with the news
that they had been refused Aetolian arms, the Rutulians continue the war
without those forces, and on either side much blood
is lost; but look, against the pine-wrought ships Turnus brings                 530
his greedy torches, and those the waves had spared are now in fear of flames.
Already Mulciber[75] was burning pitch and wax and other nutriment of fire
and spreading his flames over the lofty mast to the sails,
and smoking already were the rowing benches of the hollow ships,
when, mindful that these pines had been felled on Ida's crown,                 535
the holy mother[76] of the gods made the air resound
with beaten bronze and the murmur of boxwood, filled with breath,
and, carried by her conquered lions through the gentle breeze, declares,
"With sacrilegious right hand do you hurl these ineffectual fires,
O Turnus! I shall steal the ships away, nor shall I let the hungry fire        540
consume the limbs and members of my groves."
It thundered as the goddess spoke, and following in the thunder's wake
a heavy downpour of rain fell amidst the bouncing hail,
and air and swollen sea are suddenly made to collide
and thrown in confusion by the Astraean brothers,[77] and enter into war.      545
The fostering mother, employing the power of one of these,
first breaks the hempen hawsers of the Phrygian fleet
and pushes down their prows and submerges them within the main;

---

73 Diomedes, son of Tydeus and grandson of Oeneus, the king of Calydon (see 8. 486).
74 Peucetius, Iapyx, and Daunus were sons of Lycaon. Daunus ruled the north of Apulia, Peucetius ruled
    the gulf of Tarentum (modern Taranto), and the Messapians (the people of Calabria) ruled the part
    from Tarentum to the southeast tip of Italy (see Anton. Liber. 31).
75 Vulcan.
76 Cybele.
77 The Winds, the sons of Astraeus and Aurora (see Hes., *Theog. 378*).

*Aeneas' Fleet Changed to Sea-nymphs, Baur*

their sturdy wood made soft, their timbers into bodies transformed,
the curving poop-decks are altered into the appearance of heads,                550
the oars are changed to fingers and swimming legs,
and what before had been a side, is a side, and the keel
beneath in the middle of the ship assumes the work of a spine,
the linen sail becomes soft hair, the sail-yards become forearms,
cerulean, the color, as before, and within the wave they used                555
to fear, now with girlish dalliance the watery naiads play,
these creatures born upon the rugged mountain tops,
and, dwelling within the gentle waters, remain untouched by their origin;
yet not forgetting how many perils they often endured
upon the deep, they often placed their hands                560
beneath harried ships, unless Achaeans[78] were on board:
still mindful of the Phrygian disaster and hating still Pelasgians,[79]
with joyful faces they saw the shattered Neritian[80] ship,
with joyful faces saw Alcinoüs'[81] ship
grow rigid as it turned from wood to stone.                565

### 566-608   The Death of Aeneas

Now that the fleet had come alive as nymphs of the sea,
one hoped that the Rutulian, in reverent fear of the omen, could quit the war:
instead he perseveres, and each side has its gods and, what is like the gods,

---

78 Greeks.
79 Ancient name for Greeks.
80 Ithacan, referring to Ulysses.
81 King of the Phaeacians. Poseidon turned the Phaeacian ship to stone after it brought Odysseus to
   Ithaca (see Hom., *Od.* 13. 163).

has courage: not so much a dowered kingdom do the sons-in-law seek,
nor scepter nor, maiden Lavinia, even you,                                            570
but rather victory, and with all restraint and shame laid aside
wage war, and at length Venus beholds her son's
victorious arms, and Turnus falls: Ardea falls, as well,
a powerful city as long as Turnus lived; but after foreign fires
destroyed her and her homes in ashes lay hid,                                        575
there rises from the pile of rubble a bird not seen before,
that beats the ashes with its flapping wings.
Its sound and thinness and pallor and everything that befits
a captured city and even the name of the city itself
remain in it, and the heron[82] beats its breast with its wings.                      580
        The valor of Aeneas had already compelled all the gods
and even Juno herself to bring their ancient wrath to an end,
when, after the prosperity of growing Iulus had been secured,
the sky could in due season claim Cytherea's heroic son.
Already had Venus gone around amongst the gods,                                       585
and, falling on her father's neck, had said,
"O father, never harsh with me at any time, be kindest now, I pray,
and to my Aeneas, who from our blood made you
a grandfather, may you grant some divinity, however small,
O best of fathers, if only you grant him some! Once is enough                         590
upon the odious realm to have gazed, once to have gone to the Stygian streams."
The gods approved, and even the royal consort kept not her face
unmoved and with placated countenance nodded her assent;
the father then says, "Worthy of a heavenly gift are both you
who ask and he for whom you ask: receive, my daughter, what you desire!"  595
When he had spoken, she rejoices and to her father expresses her gratitude
and, carried through the gentle breezes by her span of doves,
approaches the Laurentian shore, where, concealed in reeds,
Numicius[83] glides with his river waters into the nearby sea.
She orders him to wash away from Aeneas whatever is subject to death                  600
and carry it away in his quiet stream to the sea;
the horn-bearing river god carries out Venus' commands
and with his waters purges and washes away in Aeneas all
his mortal part; his finest part remains unchanged.
His mother sprinkled and anointed the body with divine perfume                        605
and with a mixture of ambrosia and sweet nectar touched
his mouth and made him a god, whom Quirinus' multitude
invokes as Indiges[84] and with temple and altar reveres.

---

82 *Ardea* means heron.
83 The god of the river (see on 328).
84 The name of the deified Aeneas means "Native" and signifies the Italian origin of his line,
   reaching back to Dardanus. The sanctuary of Aeneas Indiges lay between Lavinium and the river
   Numicius.

*Pomona and Vertumnus, Solis*

### 609-851 Romulus

The Alban and Latin state came next under Ascanius' rule,
who had two names.[85] Silvius succeeded him. 610
The latter's son, Latinus, gained that name again[86]
along with the ancient scepter, and brilliant Alba took Latinus' place.
Epytus followed him, and Capetus and Capys after him,
but Capys was first; Tiberinus took the throne after them
and having drowned in the waves of the Tuscan stream 615
bestowed his name upon the waters; of him were born
both Remulus and Acrota. Remulus, the older in years,
the rival of thunder, was killed by a thunderbolt.[87]
More moderate than his brother, Acrota hands down
the scepter to valiant Aventinus, who lies buried on 620
the very hill where he had reigned, and gave his name to the hill.
And now Proca holds sway over the people of the Palatine.

### 623-771 Pomona and Vertumnus

Pomona lived under this king. No other among
the Latin wood-nymphs gave the gardens more care that she,
or paid more attention to the fruit of the trees; 625
she owes her name to this:[88] she loves neither woods

---

85 Three, according to Vergil, *Aen.* 1. 268, who says Ascanius was called Ilus (after the first king of
   Ilium, see 11. 755-56) while Troy still stood, but later Iulus.
86 The name of the original Latinus, father of Lavinia.
87 Ehwald compares the punishment of Salmoneus, Verg. *Aen.* 6. 585-91, who imitated Jove's lightning
   by the way he drove his chariot.
88 *Pomum* means "fruit" in Latin.

nor streams, but rather the tilled fields and branches full of fruit;
her right hand heavy not with the spear but with the pruning-hook,
with which she sometimes restrains excessive growth
and sometimes cuts back the spreading limbs, and sometimes inserts a twig    630
into the split bark and offers juices from a foreign foster-bough;
she never lets her plants feel thirst and keeps moist
the twisted fibers of the thirsty roots with flowing streams.
Her love, her interest was this; desire of Venus is there none;
yet fearing the violence of the rustics, she keeps her orchard closed,    635
and from the inside prohibits and refuses access to men.
What did the satyrs, those youths with the gift of dance,
not do, and the Pans with their horns wreathed in pine,
and also Silvanus,[89] always more youthful than his years,
and also the god who scares away thieves with his sickle or groin,[90]    640
to have their way with her? Vertumnus, though, surpassed
them all in loving, and he was no more successful than they.
Alas, how often in the garb of a sturdy reaper did he
bring baskets of grain, the very picture of a reaper he was!
By often wearing his temples wreathed with fresh-cut hay,    645
he could indeed appear to have just turned over the new-mown grass.
He used to carry an ox-goad in his roughened hand, and you
would swear he had just freed the weary bullocks from the yoke.
With pruning hook, he was a pruner and trimmer of the vine;
with ladder mounted on his back, you would think he were about to pick fruit;    650
with sword, he was a soldier, an angler, with cane-pole in hand;
in short, by means of his many shapes he often found for himself
a way inside and took much pleasure in gazing at her form.
Having bound his brow in a fancy headdress and placed grey hair
about his temples, he even assumed the guise of an old crone    655
and entered the well-kept garden, leaning on a cane.
The woman praised the fruit and says, "But even more marvelous are you!"
and gave the girl she had praised a few kisses, such as an old crone
would never have given, and, with crooked spine, sat down upon the sod,
while looking up to the branches bent low by autumn's weight.    660
A splendid elm stood opposite, hung with shining grapes:
When she had praised it along with its companion vine,
she says, "But if the tree stood unmarried to the vine,
no purpose would it have beyond its leaves;
this clinging vine supports itself upon the elm:    665
if it were not married, it would lie prostrate upon the ground;
but you will not be moved by the example of this tree
and flee from conjugal love and are not concerned to be wed.

---

89 Italic god of the woods and fields.
90 Priapus.

I do wish that you were! Helen would have been wooed
by no more suitors than you, nor she[91] who stirred the Lapiths' strife          670
nor even the wife of Ulysses, of him all too tardy to return.
And even now, although you shun and turn aside
your suitors, a thousand men desire you, and demigods and gods
and all the divinities that haunt the Alban hills.
But if you're sensible, and want a good marriage and to heed          675
an old woman's advice, who loves you, more than all the rest
and more than you believe: reject the proposals of the common herd
and choose Vertumnus as the companion of your couch! And take
this pledge from me: I know the man as well as myself;
he does not wander aimlessly over all the world,          680
but keeps only to this place; unlike most who woo,
he does not love the last girl he sees: you will be for him
his first and final flame and devote his years to you alone.
Consider also that he is young, that he has the gift
of natural good looks and will usefully assume every shape,          685
and on command will become anything at all you command.
Consider also that you both love the same things, the fruit you tend
he'll be first to have, and hold your gifts in his gladdened hand!
But neither does he desire the fruit gathered from your trees
nor herbs with their gentle juices that your garden feeds,          690
nor anything else but you: have pity on his passion and believe
that he who seeks your hand were present, his entreaty in my words.
Respect the avenging gods with fear and the Idalian[92] goddess who hates
the hard of heart and the goddess of Rhamnus[93] and her unforgetting wrath!
And that your fear be even greater, (because my great age          695
has taught me much) I'll tell a story all Cyprus knows very well
that should allow you to be easily persuaded and tamed.

### 698-764  *Vertumnus' Tale of Iphis and Anaxarete*

"Anaxarete, nobly born of ancient Teucer's[94] line
was seen by Iphis, a man born of humble stock.
As soon as he saw her, he conceived a passion in all his bones.          700
He fought against it long, but when with reason he could
not vanquish it, he came as a suppliant to her doors
and soon told her nurse of his wretched love
and begged her by her hopes for her foster-child not to be harsh with him,
and soon had flattered, of her many servants, each and every one,          705

---

91 Hippodame, wife of Pirithoüs. See 12. 210 ff. for the battle of the Lapiths and Centaurs.
92 Venus, so-called because of her association with Mt. Idalium in Cyprus.
93 The goddess Nemesis "Destruction" had a cult at Rhamnus in Attica.
94 Son of Telamon and Hesione, who was cursed by his father and fled to Cyprus, where he founded
   the city of Salamis.

and sought to gain their favor with anxious words;
he sometimes put his words on seductive tablets to be sent to her,
and meanwhile hung garlands moist with the dew of his tears
upon the doorposts, and upon the stubborn threshold he laid
his tender body and complained of its hostile bolts. 710
More cruel than the surging sea in the season of the falling Kids,[95]
and harder than iron forged by Noric fire[96]
and living rock that clings even still to its roots,
she spurns and mocks him and adds to her heartless acts
conceited words of cruel intent and robs the lover of even hope. 715
Unable to endure the torments of his enormous grief,
before the doors Iphis spoke these final words:
'Anaxarete, you win. At last no more annoyance will you have
to bear because of me: joyful triumph now prepare,
sing hymns to Paean,[97] and bind shining laurel round your head! 720
For you have won, and gladly do I die: iron maiden, come, rejoice!
Since you will be forced to praise one thing in my love
that pleases you, and acknowledge our good deed:
remember that my care for you had not come to an end
before my life, and that I had to lose both of my lights[98] at once. 725
No rumor will come to announce my death to you:
I shall be present in person and visible to you, have no doubt,
so that you may feast your cruel eyes upon my lifeless form.
But if, O gods above, you have any regard for mortal affairs,
remember me (my tongue has not the strength to pray 730
for more), and let our story be told through the length of time,
and all the years you took from my life bestow upon my fame!'
He spoke and as to the doorposts often adorned by his wreaths
he lifted up his weeping eyes and failing arms,
he tied the bonds of a noose to the lintel of the doors 735
and said, 'May these garlands please you, cruel and shameless one!'
and put his head within the noose, but even then turned his face towards her,
and with his neck now broken, hung there, an unhappy weight.
The door, struck by the motion of his quivering feet, appeared
to utter the sound of being knocked for entrance. When opened, it 740
revealed the deed; the servants cry out, having lifted him down
in vain, and (since his father was dead) brought him to his mother's house.
She took him to her bosom and enfolded the frigid limbs of her son

---

95 The *Haedi*, two stars in the constellation Wagoner (*Auriga*), set in mid-December, signifying the onset of the winter storms.
96 Celtic Noricum, noted for its smelting of iron, was bounded on the north by the Danube, on the south by the Carnian Alps, Rhaetia on the west, and Pannonia on the east. Its capital was near the Magdalensberg in Carinthia. It became a Roman province under Tiberius.
97 Apollo, god of healing and victory.
98 His life and the object of his love.

*Iphis and Anaxarete, Solis*

within her arms, and, after she had uttered the words
of grieving parents and completed a grieving mother's deeds, 745
she led in tears the funeral procession through the city's midst
and carried out the ghastly limbs to be burned upon their bier.
By chance her house was near the street whereon the sad procession passed,
and sounds of lamentation reached the ears of harsh
Anaxarete, already harried by an avenging god. 750
But moved, she says, 'Let's observe this pitiful funeral,'
and went to the wide-spread windows at the top of the house;
as soon as she saw Iphis laid out duly upon the bier,
her eyes froze in fear , and from her body the warm blood fled
and left her pale, and when she tried to move back her steps, 755
she stood there fixed, and when she tried to avert her face,
this too she could not do, and gradually her limbs are seized
by stone, as hard as her heart had been before.
And lest you think this merely a tale, even now Salamis[99] preserves
a statue of that lady's form and has a temple named 760
for Venus Belvedere.[100] —Mindful of these things, my darling nymph,
I pray you, lay aside your stubborn disdain and to your lover be joined:
and in return, may the frost of spring not nip your fruit
in bud nor swirling winds break it off in bloom!"

---

99 The city on Cyprus.
100 *Venus Prospiciens.*

When all in vain the god,[101] disguised in decrepit form,                    765
had told the tale, he returned to his youthful form and removed
the apparatus of age and appeared to her as when
the image of the sun most brilliantly dispels
the clouds and shines with nothing in the way,
and offers force: but for force there is no need, and by the figure of        770
the god the nymph was captured and felt love's mutual wound.

### 772-804   Amulius, Titus Tatius

The armed force of unjust Amulius[102] was next to rule
the riches of Ausonia,[103] and old Numitor with his grandson's[104] aid
takes back the kingdom he had lost, and on the day of the Palilian[105] feast
the city's walls are founded. Tatius[106] and the Sabine fathers go            775
to war,[107] and, when the hidden way to the citadel is revealed,
Tarpeia[108] worthily pays with her life, beneath the heap of arms.[109]
And then the sons of Cures[110] in the manner of silent wolves
repress their speech and attack the bodies overcome by sleep
and seek the gates that the son of Ilia[111] had made fast                     780
with solid bars; but Saturnia[112] herself had opened one
of these and made no noise as she it turned upon the hinge;
though Venus alone heard that the bars of the gate had dropped
and wanted to lock the gate again, the gods are never allowed
to cancel the deeds of gods. Ausonian naiads possessed                         785
the place adjoining Janus' temple, sprinkled by the cold spring's mist:
the goddess seeks their help, nor did the nymphs refuse
her just request and evoked the fountain's veins
and streams; not yet, however, were Janus' open mouths
barred shut, nor had the waters yet blocked the way:                           790
the nymphs put sallow sulfur beneath the fertile spring

---

101 Vertumnus, Italic god of the changing seasons.
102 Amulius had taken control of the kingdom from his brother Numitor.
103 Whereas Ausonia usually refers to Italy, here it refers to the area around the future city of Rome.
104 Romulus (with Remus).
105 Pales was a shepherd divinity, honored on April 21 in the Parilia or Palilia, the feast of the founding
    of Rome (see Ovid, *Fasti* 4. 721 ff.). The ceremony included lustration of the herds and bonfires
    through which participants jumped three times. Vergil, *Georgics* 3. 1, and most authors refer to
    Pales as feminine, but Servius' note on the passage says that Varro treated Pales as masculine. Pales
    is masculine also in Arnobius (3rd A. D) and Martianus Capella (5th A. D.).
106 King of the Sabines.
107 In retribution for the rape of the Sabine women at games celebrating the recent foundation of
    Rome.
108 Daughter of the Prefect in charge of the citadel on the Capitoline Hill.
109 In return for her betrayal, Tarpeia was promised whatever the left hands of the Sabines wore.
    Instead of the gold bracelets she expected, the Sabines gave her their shields, beneath which she
    was crushed.
110 Chief city of the Sabines.
111 Translating the metronymic *Iliades*, but as a patronymic it would mean "Trojan." See on 798 for the
    parentage of Romulus and Remus.
112 Juno, daughter of Saturn.

and light with smoky pitch the hollow veins.
With these and other forces a steamy vapor penetrates
the depths of the spring, and you waters, that dared to vie
but now with Alpine cold, cede place not even to fire itself!                795
Twin doorposts now are smoking from the flame-bearing spray,
and, promised in vain to the sturdy Sabines, that gate
is blocked by this new fountain, until the soldiers of Mars[113]
could arm themselves. When Romulus took the lead
and sallied forth, the Roman soil was strewn                                 800
with Sabine bodies and with its own, and the impious sword
commingled the gore of sons-in-law[114] with the blood of fathers-in-law.[115]
The decision, however, is to conclude the war in peace and not
to strive to the end with the sword and to let Tatius join the reign.

### 805-51   *Quirinus, Hersilia*

At Tatius' death, Romulus, you were dispensing laws                          805
now equal to both peoples: Mars, his helmet laid aside,
addresses the father of men and gods in words like these:
"The time is at hand, father, since the Roman state stands strong upon
a firm foundation and does not depend upon the protection of one,
to pay the reward you promised to your worthy grandson and                   810
to me and to carry him from the earth and place him in the sky.
You once declared to me in the council of the approving gods
(with mindful heart I noted your pious words and recall them now)
'There will be one whom you will lift to the blue of the sky,'
you said: now let the full intent of your words be confirmed!"               815
After nodding his assent, the all-powerful one hid the air
in darkened clouds and with thunder and lightning frightened the globe.
Gradivus[116] sensed that the signs had ratified promised rapine,
and, leaning on his spear, he fearlessly mounted the span of steeds
subdued by the bloody tongue, rebuked them with the snap of his whip,        820
and, after gliding headlong down through the air,
atop the hill of woody Palatine he halted and took away
the son of Ilia even as he was rendering royal justice to his
Quirites:[117] The mortal body into the thin air
dissolved just as when by a broad sling a leaden shot                        825
is cast and disappears in the midst of the sky;

---

113 Romulus and the Romans. Romulus was the son of Mars and Ilia.
114 Romans, who had stolen the Sabine women.
115 Sabines.
116 Epithet of Mars.
117 Translating *suo non regia iura Quiriti* (Ehwald, Tarrant); with *suo iam* (or *nunc*) *regia iura Quiriti*,
    "already rendering royal justice to his Quirites." *The ius Quiritium* contained the civil rights of
    Roman citizens, who were called Quirites (another spelling of Cures, see on 778) after the union
    with the Sabines.

his face assumed a beauty more worthy of the divine feasts
above, and his form is that of Quirinus in robes of state.[118]
    His wife Hersilia was weeping for her loss
when royal Juno commands her Iris to descend on her curving path        830
and carry to the bereft woman the following commands:
"O woman, of both the Latin and Sabine folk
the special splendor, and most worthy to have been
the wife of him who was earlier a man, and of Quirinus now,
desist from your weeping, and, if you wish to see        835
your husband, follow me and seek out a grove on Quirinus' hill,[119]
which shades with green the temple of the Roman king."
Obeying, Iris glides down to earth through her colorful bow
and hails Hersilia with the commanded words.
With reverent mien she barely raises her eyes and says,        840
"O goddess (for though I cannot not say which one you are,
you clearly are a goddess), lead on, lead on and bring to me
my husband's face; if only the fates allow me to behold
it once, I shall claim to have won heaven itself!"
Without delay, she goes with the daughter[120] of Thaumas to the hill        845
of Romulus: a star had fallen there from the ethereal sky
to earth; her hair having caught fire from its light,
Hersilia vanishes into air with the star:
the founder of the Roman city receives her with
familiar hands and changes her body and her former name        850
and calls her Hora,[121] united as a goddess with Quirinus now.

---

118 Perhaps referring to a statue of the deified Romulus dressed in the *trabea*, a white mantle with horizontal purple stripes.

119 The Quirinal Hill, containing a temple dedicated to Quirinus (see *Fasti*. 2. 511).

120 Iris (see 4. 480).

121 The name means "Hour." The Greek *Horae* were fertility goddesses. Hora was in particular a goddess of youth, like the Greek Hebe.

# BOOK 15

| | |
|---|---|
| 1-59 | Numa and Myscelus |
| 60-478 | Pythagoras |
| 479-546 | Egeria and Hippolytus Virbius |
| 547-621 | Cipus |
| 622-744 | Aesculapius |
| 745-870 | Julius Caesar and Augustus |
| 871-79 | The Poet's Epilogue |

## 1-59  Numa and Myscelus

In the meantime there was a search for one to bear the weight
of so great burden and with the ability to succeed so great a king:
for supreme power, she who heralds the truth, Fama[1] marks
the brilliant Numa; for that man, merely to know the rites
of the Sabine people is not enough: with his capacious mind           5
he conceives of greater works and searches into the nature of things.
For love of this pursuit he left his native Cures[2] behind
and went all the way to the city[3] that had been host to Hercules.
When he inquired who first had established Greek walls
upon Italian shores, of the native elders one made this              10
reply, a man not ignorant of the early days:
"A wealthy man, the son of Jove, with his Iberian[4] cattle, they say,
set foot during his fortunate course upon the Lacinian[5] shore,
and, while his herd grazed upon the tender grass,
had entered great Croton's[6] welcoming home and roof               15
and eased at leisure his lengthy toil
and, as he left, had said, 'in my descendants' time
this place will be a city,' and his promises were true.
For there was a certain man, of Argive Alemon born,
Myscelus, to the gods the most esteemed man of his day.             20

1 Latin *Fama* has here the positive sense of Glory or Fame or Public Opinion rather than Rumor.
2 Capitol city of the Sabines.
3 Crotona, in the toe of Italy, a Greek colony founded ca. 712 B.C., famous for its cult of Hercules, the modern Crotone.
4 I.e., Spanish.
5 Lacinium was a promontory just south of Crotona.
6 Croton in this tale will become the eponymous hero of the city of Croton.

Above him, as he lay weighed down by heavy sleep,
the club-bearer[7] bent and spoke: 'Arise, abandon your ancestral home
and seek the distant Aesar's[8] rocky waves!'
And lest he disobey, he warned him of many fearful things.
When once both sleep and god have left,                                    25
Alemon's son gets up and silently reviews in his mind
what he has seen, and wrestles long with his thoughts:
the deity commands him to leave, the laws forbid him to leave,
and death is the penalty for changing at will one's fatherland.
In Ocean bright Sun had hid his shining head                               30
and thickest Night had lifted her starry head:
the same god[9] seemed to be present and to give the same advice
and, lest he disobey, to threaten more and graver things.
Despite his fear, he prepared to transfer his ancestral home
to a new site: in the city muttering is heard,                             35
and he is accused of having scorned the laws, and with
the trial already done and the charge revealed and without witness confirmed,
the wretched defendant, raising his face and hands to the gods above,
declares, 'O you upon whom the law of heaven twice six labors lay,
I pray you, give me your aid, for you are the author of my crime.'         40
The ancient custom was to use little stones, white and black,
the latter to convict defendants, the former to absolve them of guilt;
on that occasion, too, the stern verdict was rendered, and all
the pebbles cast into the pitiless urn were black:
but when the up-ended urn emptied its pebbles for the count,               45
the color of all had been changed from black to white;
the radiant verdict, accomplished through the power of Hercules,
had freed the son of Alemon. He gives his sponsor thanks,
the son of Amphitryon, and, sailing with favoring winds
the Ionian Sea, skirted by Neretum[10] of the Sallentines[11]             50
and Sybaris and Tarentum of the Lacedaemonians
and Thurii's[12] bay and Crimisa[13] and the Iapygian land.[14]
And no sooner had he passed the lands that face these shores
than he discovered the destined mouth of Aesar's stream
and not far from there a tomb, where the soil concealed                    55

---

7 Hercules.
8 A river of southern Italy.
9 Hercules, after his apotheosis.
10 A town in the heel of Italy, modern Nardò.
11 A tribe inhabiting the heel of Italy, ancient Calabria.
12 Translating *Thurinosque sinus*; Thurii was a Greek colony founded in 444/3 B.C. on the site of
    Sybaris; with Ehwald's *Sirinos*, "Siris' bay," referring to a town and river in Lucania on the Gulf
    of Tarentum.
13 A town and promontory in the toe of Italy, north of Croton. Tarrant prints *Nemesen* Nemese, a town
    in Bruttium.
14 Iapygia, named for Iapyx, a son of Daedalus or Lycaon, is here the region around the promontory
    south of Croton on the Ionian Sea.

the sacred bones of Croton; and there in the bidden land
he founded walls and named the city from the one buried there."
Tradition leaves no doubt that this was the origin of both
the place and the city established in the land of Italy.

### 60-478 *Pythagoras*

There was a man of Samian origin, but he had fled      60
both Samos and his masters, and, despising tyranny,
had made himself an exile. Despite their remoteness in celestial space,
he neared the gods with his mind and what nature denied
to human sight he drank in with the eyes of his heart,
and with his mind and watchful care observed everything,      65
disclosing what was to be learned and teaching the throngs
that wondered in silence at his words the beginnings of the vast universe
and the causes of things and what their nature was,
what deity was, whence the snows, what the origin of lightning was,
did Jupiter cause thunder, or the winds from a shattered cloud,      70
what shook the earth, how the stars in their courses move,
and whatever lies hidden; he first forbade animals to be placed
upon tables, and with words like these was he the first
to open his mouth, learnèd, but not believed:
"Desist, O mortals, from desecrating with sacrilegious food      75
your bodies! There is grain, there is fruit bending down
the branches with its weight, and grapes swollen upon the vines,
sweet herbs there are and those that flame
can soften and make tender; and flowing milk is not
denied to you, nor honey, scented with flowering thyme:      80
extravagant earth lavishes wealth and gentle nourishment
and offers feastings without slaughter and blood.
The beasts of the wild settle their hunger with flesh, but yet not all,
for horses and flocks and herds of cattle live on grass;
but they whose nature is untamed and wild,      85
Armenian tigers and lions, full of wrath,
and wolves and bears find pleasure in meals of blood.
Oh, what a crime it is to store bowels inside bowels
and make the greedy body with ingested body fat
and for one that breathes to live by the death of another that breathes!      90
Or is it so that in such rich blessings produced by earth,
the best of mothers, you find no pleasure if you cannot chew
with cruel teeth the cruel wounds and repeat the Cyclopes' ways,
and, if you cannot destroy another, you cannot satiate
your voracious and savage stomach's needs!      95
"But that earlier time we called the golden age,
with fruit from the trees and herbs from the ground,

was happy, nor did it pollute mouths with blood.
In those days birds moved their wings in safety through the air,
and in the open fields the hare roamed without fear,                                    100
nor did its own credulity suspend the fish upon the hook:
no creature lay in wait to attack or feared any guile
and all were filled with peace. But a useless inventor then,
whoever he was, begrudged the lions[15] their feast
and buried within his greedy belly a meal of flesh,                                     105
and laid the path to crime; and from killing savage beasts
the sword may have first grown warm, stained with blood
(the killing would have sufficed), and we admit
that creatures seeking our death can be killed with piety intact,
although, when slain, they should not be eaten as well.                                 110
        "From that beginning this wickedness spread, and the sow is thought
to have deserved to die as the first victim, because she uprooted the seeds
with her spreading snout and cut short the hope of the year.
The goat that nibbles the vine is said to have been slain upon
the altar of vengeful Bacchus: their own faults brought harm to both!                   115
But why have you deserved ill, you sheep and peaceful flock,
created to nurture humanity, you that bring nectar with udders full,
who furnish us for soft raiment your wool
and help us more with your life than with your death?
Why have the oxen deserved ill, animals without offense or deceit,                      120
not harmful, simple, born to endure work?
Unfeeling is he in the end, and unworthy of the gift of grain,
who, once the weight of the curved plow was removed,
could slaughter the tiller of his fields, who struck with the axe
that neck worn down with toil, with which he had renewed                                125
so often the hard ground and produced so many crops.
It's not enough that such wrong is committed: with that
same crime they have branded the gods and believe
that heavenly powers rejoice in the slaughter of hard-working bulls!
The victim, lacking fault and most splendid in form                                     130
(for to have pleased brings it harm) and marked with headbands and gold,
before the altar stands and, not understanding, hears the one who prays
and sees being poured between the horns of his brow
the grain that it produced and, stricken, stains with blood
the knives he has perhaps already seen in the limpid pool.                              135
At once they rip the entrails from the living breast
and pore over them and probe the mind of the gods in them;

---

15 Translating Bothe's *leonum*. With Burman's *ferorum*, "begrudging the wild beasts of their feasts;"
   with Heinsius' *priorum*, "dissatisfied with their former feasts;" with the MSS' *deorum* (daggered
   by Tarrant), "begrudging the feasts of the gods", but would Ovid want to make Pythagoras imply
   that gods had received animal sacrifice before animals were eaten by humans? Bothe's emendation
   seems best.

and next (for so great is human hunger for forbidden food)
you dare to eat them, O mortal race! I beg you, do
not do this and to our warnings turn your minds!                                    140
For when to your palate you give the slaughtered oxen's limbs,
be sure to see that those are your farmers you consume.
    "And since a god moves my mouth, I will duly obey
the god that moves my mouth, unlock my Delphi and heaven itself,
and open to view the oracles of that lofty mind:                                    145
magnificent things never investigated by those who have gone before,
and long concealed, will I sing. I will delight to walk aloft
amid the stars, delight to leave the idle habitat of earth behind,
to soar upon a cloud and on the shoulders of mighty Atlas to stand
and down upon humanity as it wanders thoughtlessly hither and yon                   150
to gaze from afar, and, as they tremble in fear of death,
to give encouragement and unravel the order of fate!
    "O race dumbfounded by the dread of chill death,
why do you fear the Styx, why the shades and empty names,
the stuff of prophets, the silly terrors of a spurious world?                       155
Think not that bodies can suffer any ill, it makes
no difference whether the flame of the pyre or the decay
of age takes them away! But souls are free from death and when
they leave their earlier habitats, live on and reside in new homes:
for I myself (remembering it well) in the time of the Trojan war                    160
was Panthoüs' son Euphorbus,[16] into whose opposing breast
the heavy spear of the younger Atreid once was fixed;[17]
I recognized the shield, the burden of our left hand,
just recently in Juno's temple in Abas'[18] Argive town!
All things are changing, nothing perishes: the spirit roams from there,             165
comes here, from here to there, and occupies whatever limbs
it chooses, and from wild beasts passes into human forms
and ours into the forms of beasts, and never does it die;
and just as a tablet of wax with new letters is marked
and does not remain as it was or keep the same shape                                170
yet is the same, so, according to my teaching, the soul,
though migrating into various forms, is ever the same.
Therefore, lest piety be overwhelmed by the belly's desire,
desist, I warn you, from disturbing kindred souls
with wicked slaughter, and do not let blood be fed by blood.                        175
    "And since I am carried upon the vast sea and to the winds
have given full sail: there is nothing that lasts in all the world.
All things are in flux,[19] and every shape is formed to change;

---

16 The name, meaning "Well-fed," appears to relate to Pythagoras's dietary laws.
17 Menelaus.
18 Father of Acrisius and King of Argos.
19 Plato, *Cratylus*, 402a, attributes this sentiment to Heraclitus of Ephesus (fl. 500 B.C.).

the ages themselves with constant motion wane,
no different than a river; for neither the river nor                              180
the fickle hour can stop: but as wave is impelled by wave
and pressed by the one preceding and presses the one ahead,
just so the times flee and follow alike in turn
and always are new, for that which was before has been left behind
and what had not yet been is coming to pass and all motion is renewed.    185
    "You also observe how the measured nights proceed to the light,
and how this shining sun gives way to the black of night:
the color of the sky is not the same when the weary world
reclines in quiet rest and when brilliant Lucifer comes forth
upon his shining horse; the color changes again when, heralding the day,    190
Pallantias[20] stains the celestial globe for Phoebus to receive.
The shield itself of the god, when raised from beneath the earth,
is red in the morning, red when hidden beneath the earth,
but white at midday, because the nature of the aether there
is better and has escaped the contagion of the earth far below.              195
Nor is nocturnal Diana's form able to be alike or the same
at any time and forever, and always today's moon,
in waxing, is smaller than the morrow's, greater, if on the wane.
    "What's more, don't you see that the year proceeds
in four appearances that complete an imitation of our life?                  200
For tender and full of sap and quite like the age of a child
it is when spring is new: then the grass, greening and lacking strength,
begins to swell and, not yet fully formed, delights the farmers with hope.
Then all is in flower, and with flowery colors the nurturing field
makes sport, nor is there yet manly vigor within the leaves.                 205
A stronger year passes on to summer after spring,
becoming a sturdy youth: for there is no stronger time,
nor more abundant, nor one that more fiercely burns.
Next comes the autumn, youthful fervor laid aside,
both ripe and mellow, and between the young man and the old,                 210
it stands midway in time, its brow also sprinkled with grey.
Then shivering old winter comes with tremulous steps,
deprived of his hair, or, with what he has, now white.
    "Our own bodies always and without rest
are also changing, nor what we were or are                                   215
will we tomorrow be; that day is gone when as mere seeds
and as the hope of humankind we dwelt[21] within our first mother's womb:
then nature applied her skillful hands and refused
to let our bodies be buried within our swollen mother's flesh

---

20 Aurora, the Dawn, as daughter of the Titan Pallas.
21 Translating the MSS' *habitavimus;* with Riese's emendation (printed by Tarrant) *latitavimus,*
    translate "we hid."

and sent us forth from our home into the open air.                                      220
Brought forth into the light, the infant lay without strength,
soon moved his limbs in the four-footed manner of wild beasts,
and little by little, wobbling on knees not yet firm,
stood up, its sinews aided by some support.
Once strong and swift, he passes through                                                225
the period of youth, and, when the years of middle age are done,
he slides down the sloping path of declining old age
that weakens and demolishes the strength
of former years: and old man Milon[22] weeps when he beholds
those limbs now hanging limp that with the mass                                          230
of solid muscle were once like those of Hercules.
Tyndareus' daughter[23] weeps as well when in the mirror she sees
those aging wrinkles and wonders why she must be stolen twice!
O Time, devourer of all, and you, envious Old Age,
you ruin all and gradually consume all things,                                          235
corrupted by the teeth of aging with sluggish death.
    "Nor do these things forever last that we call the elements.
What changes they achieve (apply your minds), I will teach.
The everlasting world contains generative bodies, in number four;
of these, two are heavy and by their own weight                                         240
are carried downwards, water and earth,
and just as many lack weight and with nothing to press them down
seek out the heights, air and fire, even finer than air.
Although these stand apart in space, yet all things arise
from them and decay into them: the earth is released                                    245
and rarefied into the clear waters, the liquid is refined
and vanishes into the breezes and air, and, its weight removed,
the very thin air flashes forth into the highest fires;
from there they return and the order is retraced again.
For fire condensed passes into the dense air,                                           250
the air into the waters, and earth is formed from the compacted wave.
    "The shape of nothing abides, and she who renews
all things, Nature, remakes new forms from other forms:[24]
and nothing in the world, believe me, completely dies,
but rather changes and renews its appearance. Being born                                255
is called the beginning of something other than what was before,
and dying, ceasing to be the same. Although some things perhaps
are transferred here and others there, the whole remains the same.
    "Indeed that nothing long endures with the same shape

---

22 Milon of Croton, later 6th c. B. C., often victor at the Olympic and Pythian games (Pausanias, 6.
    14. 2), carried a bull down the racetrack, killed it with one blow, and ate it in one day (Athenaeus,
    10. 412).
23 Helen.
24 See note on 1. 2.

is what I think: as from the golden you came to the iron age,                260
so, too, with the ages, the fortune of places is changed.
I saw, myself, what once had been the firmest ground
become an ocean strait; I saw land produced from the sea;
and far from the ocean seashells have lain,
and on the mountain heights an ancient anchor was found;                265
and what was a field a waterfall has made into
a vale, and by erosion a mountain has been brought to the sea;
from marshy land the ground suffers thirst with dry sand
and ground that brought thirst grows wet with marshy pools.
In some places nature set free new springs, in others, though,        270
obstructed them, and, stirred up by the deep tremors of the globe,
the rivers spring forth, or, having dried up, subside.
Just so, when the Lycus[25] is swallowed by the gaping earth,
it rises again far away and is born from another source;
just so is great Erasinus,[26] now swallowed up, now gliding in        275
a hidden stream, returned to the Argive fields,
and Mysus regretted his former source and banks
and now flows along as the Caicus,[27] people say;
the Amenanus,[28] rolling along its Sicanian[29] sands,
is flowing now, though when its sources fail, at times is dry.        280
Though potable once, now you wouldn't touch
those waters the Anigrus[30] pours forth, since the time, unless
all trust is to be denied to bards, the two-formed ones[31] bathed
therein the wounds which the bow of club-bearing Hercules had made.
What's more, isn't the Hypanis,[32] from the mountains of Scythia born,        285
which once was sweet, polluted now by bitter brine?
      "Antissa[33] and Pharos[34] were surrounded by streams
and also Phoenician Tyre: of these none is an island now.
Old-timers among the farmers say that Leucas[35] was on the mainland once:
the seas now surround it. Zancle,[36] too, is said to have been joined        290
to Italy, until their common borders were stolen away by the sea
and intervening waves thrust back the land.

---

25 Herodotus, 7.30, reports that the Lycus river of Asia Minor disappears under ground only to emerge about a half a mile away, where it is joined to the Maeander.
26 Herodotus, 6.76, says that this stream flowed from Lake Stymphalus underground, emerging in Argos.
27 A river in Mysia, in Asia Minor.
28 A river in Sicily.
29 The Sicani were a people of Sicily.
30 A river of Elis in the Peloponnesus.
31 The Centaurs.
32 The Bug, flowing into the Black Sea.
33 A town of Lesbos.
34 The lighthouse island near Alexandria in Egypt.
35 An island off the coast of Western Greece.
36 Older name for the city of Messana (Messina) in Sicily.

If you should ask about Helice and Buris, Achaean towns,[37]
beneath the waters you will find them, and even now sailors
are wont to point out the tilting cities along with their walls.                    295
A hill lies near Pittheus' town of Troezen,[38] steep
and bare of trees, at one time the flattest area of the plain,
but now a hill; for (a frightful thing to relate)
the savage force of the winds, confined within dark caves,
desiring to exhale somewhere and having struggled in vain                          300
to gain use of a freer sky, when in their prison they could find
no crack, no outlet for their blasts,
made swell the ground, just as the breath of one's mouth
is wont to make a bladder swell or the hide stripped from
a two-horned goat; the swelling of that place continued and has                    305
the look of a lofty hill and has endured through the length of time.
        "Though many things we have heard and known come to mind,
I'll mention only a few more. What about this: does water not give
and take on new shapes? Horn-bearing Ammon, midway in the day
your waves are cool and at dawn and dusk grow warm;                                310
the Athamanians[39] by applying water set wood on fire,
it's said, when the moon has attained her smallest phase.
Ciconians[40] have a river that when drunk turns entrails to stone,
transforming to marble everything it has touched;
the Crathis and the Sybaris[41] next to it, in our own clime,                      315
make hair look like electrum[42] and gold;
what's more, the waters are wonderful that have
the strength to alter not only bodies but even minds:
for of Salmacis' impure waters[43] who has not heard,
and Ethiopia's lakes? The person whose gullet drinks these in                      320
will either go mad or endure a sleep of wondrous weight;
and anyone who slakes his thirst from the Clitorian[44] spring
avoids wine and in pure waters takes abstemious delight.
Perhaps there is a force in water opposed to the warmth of wine,
or, as the natives say, perhaps the son[45] of Amythaon,                           325
who after he had freed from madness the daughters of Proetus
with magic songs and herbs, cast into those waters drugs
that purified the mind and left in the waters an aversion to wine.

---

37 Strabo, 1. 3. 18. p. 59, reports their disappearance (in 373 B. C.), Buris in a chasm, Helice in a tidal
    wave.
38 Pittheus, son of Pelops and grandfather of Theseus, was king of Troezen, on the northeast coast of
    the Peloponnesus.
39 Athamania is a district of southern Epirus.
40 A people of southern Thrace.
41 The Sybaris flows into the Crathis, which empties into the Gulf of Tarentum.
42 Either amber or an alloy of gold and silver.
43 Cf. 4. 271.
44 Pertaining to the town of Clitor in Arcadia.
45 The celebrated soothsayer and healer Melampus.

The Lyncestian[46] river flows with a different effect,
and anyone who drinks with even temperate throat the slightest bit          330
grows tipsy no less than if he had drunk pure wine.
There is a place in Arcadia, the ancients called it Pheneos,
suspected for its ambiguous waters, which you should fear by night:
at night they render harm when drunk, no harm by day.
Thus lakes and rivers all contain powers peculiar to themselves.          335
There was a time when Ortygia[47] floated in the waves,
yet now she's fixed in place; the Symplegades,
sprayed by the stricken waves, the Argo once feared:
they now stand unmoved and resist the winds.
And Etna, hot with sulphurous furnaces, will not          340
be always on fire, nor in fact was it always on fire.
For if the earth is an animal that lives and has
in many places vents for exhaling flame, she has
the power to change the channels of her breath and, when
she moves, to close these caverns and open others up;          345
or if the nimble winds are confined in the deep-set caves
and dash rocks against rocks and strike matter that contains
the seeds of flame, from those blows that matter catches fire,
yet when the winds settle down, the caves will be left cold;
or if bituminous matter catches fire,          350
or yellow sulphur burns with little smoke,
be sure that when the earth ceases to give rich food
and fuel to flame and its force is depleted in the length of time,
devouring nature will have lost its nourishment,
and will not endure hunger and, deserted, desert those fires.          355
The story is that in Hyperborean Pallene[48] there are men
whose custom is to cover with light plumage their limbs
by immersing themselves nine times in the Tritonian[49] lake.
Indeed, I scarcely believe it: the women of Scythia are said
to practise the same arts by sprinkling their bodies with magic herbs.          360
        "Yet if to things that have been tested be given faith,
do you not see that bodies, putrid with time
or melting heat, are changed into tiny animals?
Just sacrifice choice bulls and bury them in a pit:
experience proves that from the rotted innards everywhere          365
are born the flower-culling bees, which, following their parents' ways,
inhabit the field, support the work and bring hope with their toil.[50]

---

46 The Lyncestae were a people of western Macedonia.
47 Earlier name for the island of Delos.
48 Perhaps referring to the most western peninsula of Chalcidice in the northern Aegean Sea, but then
    *"Hyperborean"* would be mere hyperbole for "northern."
49 Since Lake Tritonis in North Africa was sacred to Minerva, she is called Tritonia.
50 For this strange phenomenon, the *bugonia*, see Vergil, *Georgics* 4. 261-314.

The hornet's origin is the warhorse, buried in the ground,
and if you remove the curved claws of the crab on the shore
and place the rest of it in the earth, from the buried part                    370
the scorpion emerges and will threaten with his hook-like tail,
and caterpillars of the countryside are wont to make webs around the leaves
with threads of white (a thing the farmers have observed)
and change their shape to that of the funereal[51] butterfly.
    "The mud has seeds that produce green frogs,                    375
creating them deprived of feet, but soon supplying the limbs
adapted for swimming and adapted for making long leaps,
the hind-legs surpassing the length of the front.
The cub to which the she-bear has just given birth
is nothing but flesh, barely alive, but the mother's licking forms              380
its limbs and draws it into a shape proportionate to her own.
Have you not seen the young of the honey-bearing bees,
enclosed in the hexagonal wax, being born as bodies without limbs
and later gaining feet and later their wings?
And that the bird of Juno, wearing the stars within its tail,                   385
and Jove's arms-bearer, and Cytherea's[52] doves,
and all the tribe of birds are from an egg's inner parts
who would believe, except we know that it is so?
Some people believe that when the spine has rotted, enclosed
within the tomb, the human marrow changes into a snake.                        390
    "Though these derive from others the origin of their birth,
there is one bird that restores and reproduces itself:
Assyrians call it the phoenix; it lives not on grain or grass,
but on the juice of amomum[53] and the sap of frankincense.
When it has finished five centuries of its life,                               395
at once upon the branches and peak of a quaking palm
it builds itself a nest with its claws and pristine mouth.
As soon as it spreads within the nest both cassia and spikes
of tender nard and broken cinnamon with tawny myrrh,
it places itself therein and ends its life upon these scents.                   400
And then, they say, to live an equal number of years,
the little phoenix from its father's body is born again.
When time has given it strength and it can carry weight,
it lifts the burden of the nest from the branches of the lofty tree
and with devotion bears its cradle (and its father's tomb)                     405
across the gentle breezes until it gains the city of Hyperion[54]
and lays it down before the sacred doors of Hyperion's shrine.

---

51 Because the butterfly symbolized the departed soul.
52 Venus.
53 An eastern spice-plant.
54 The Sun.

"In all of this if there are things both marvelous and strange,
let's marvel at the hyena's alternating forms, who at one time
as female endures a male upon her back, at another, is a male;                410
and also at that animal,[55] nourished by air and the wind,
that quickly imitates the colors it has touched.
To Bacchus, adorned with clusters of grapes, vanquished India gave
the lynxes, from which, they say, whatever their bladders emit
is turned into stones and congeals at the touch of the air.                   415
Thus coral hardens as soon as it comes in contact with the air;
but earlier it was the sweet grass beneath the waves.
    "The day will end and Phoebus will dip his heaving steed
into the depths of the sea before I have finished with my tale
of all the things assuming new forms: thus we observe that the times       420
themselves are being changed, that some peoples gain strength
while others fall; thus, Troy, once great with wealth and men
and able for ten years to give so much of her blood,
is humbled now with nothing but ancient ruins to show
and, in the place of riches, her ancestors' tombs.                           425
Once famous was Sparta, great Mycenae was strong,
the citadels of Cecrops and of Amphion as well.
Mere dirt is Sparta now, lofty Mycenae has collapsed,
and what but a name is Oedipodean Thebes?
Pandion's Athens, what remains of her but a name?                            430
Tradition has it, too, that Dardanian Rome is now on the rise,
which next to Apennine-born Tiber's waves
beneath her great mass is laying the foundations of the world:
she changes her shape by growing and one of these days
will be the head of the boundless globe! So people say the fates            435
and fate-revealing oracles declare, and as far as I recall,
to weeping Aeneas, with his survival in doubt,
the son of Priam, Helenus, declared, when Trojan affairs
were teetering, 'Goddess-born, if you fully understand what
our mind foretells, all Troy will not fall so long as you survive!          440
Both flame and iron will grant you passage: you will go
and seize and carry Pergamum[56] away with you until you reach
a foreign field, friendlier to you and to Troy than your fatherland.
And there I perceive that to your Phrygian descendants a city is owed,
whose size is not, nor will be, nor has been seen in ages past.             445
While through the centuries other leaders will make it great,
one born of the blood of Iulus will make it mistress of the world.
When earth has used him, the celestial realm will delight
in him, and his ultimate end will be the sky.'

---

55 The chameleon.
56 Troy.

These words that Helenus to Penates-bearing Aeneas sang                    450
I well remember and recite by heart and rejoice that those kindred walls
are rising and that the Pelasgians'[57] victory has served the Phrygians[58] well.
    "But lest, with our horses forgetting to head for the goal,
we stray too far from the track, the sky and everything under it
change shape, and the earth and everything it contains.                    455
We, too, are a part of the world, since we are not bodies alone
but also winged souls and can reside in wild beasts
and be concealed within the breasts of stock,        -
and should allow those bodies that may have held our ancestors' souls
or those of our brothers or of those joined to us by marriage bond,        460
of humans in any case, to be safe and have respect
and not fill our bellies with Thyestean feasts!
How evil the habit of him who impiously readies himself
for human blood and cuts the throat of the calf
with iron and to its bellowing offers unmoved his ears,                    465
or able to slaughter a kid uttering cries like a child's,
like those of children, or to feed upon a bird
that he himself has given food! How far is that
from outright crime? After this what step is next?
Allow the ox to plow and blame his death upon his many years,              470
against freezing Boreas[59] let the sheep supply a defense,
let ewes offer to hands their swollen udders to be milked!
Be rid of nets and traps and snares and arts of deceit!
And use not twigs smeared with sticky lime to catch the birds
or frightening feathers to corral the stags                                475
and do not conceal bent hooks within deceptive food.
Kill any that cause harm, but only kill even these:
let mouths be free of blood and partake of kindly nourishment!'"

### 479-546   *Egeria and Hippolytus Virbius*

    By such and other sayings his breast informed,
they say that Numa returned to his native land,                            480
and freely chosen, took the reins of the people of Latium.
Delighting in a nymph for a wife,[60] and the Camenae[61] as his guides,
he taught sacrificial rites and converted a nation trained
in cruel war to the arts of peace.
When he had completed his reign and life, quite old,                       485
the Latin matrons and people and fathers wept

---

57 Greeks.
58 Trojans.
59 The North Wind.
60 Egeria. See 15. 547 for her name.
61 The Roman Muses.

at Numa's death; for leaving the city, his wife
lies hidden away in the dense woods of the Arician[62] vale
and by her moans and complaints impedes the rites
of Orestean[63] Diana. Ah, how often the nymphs of the grove and lake          490
did warn her to cease and spoke to her with words
of consoling! How often the Thesean hero[64] said to her as
she wept, "Desist now, for yours is not the only lot
to be lamented; of others consider similar fates:
more easily will you bear your own, and would that my own                      495
examples were not the ones to bring you relief! But they can.
      "If, as I think, word of a certain Hippolytus has reached
your ears, how by his father's credulity and wicked stepmother's deceit
he died, you'll be amazed, and it will be hard for me to prove,
but I am he. Pasiphaë's daughter[65] one day feigned,                          500
in vain having tempted me to violate my father's couch,
that I had wanted the thing she wanted, and, turning the charge around
(in fear of being exposed or rather offended by the rebuff?),
pronounced me guilty, and though I was completely innocent,
my father banished me from the city and upon my head lay a curse              505
with hostile imprecation as I left. In my exile's chariot I sought
Troezen, the city of Pittheus and was already plying the shore
of Corinth's waters, when the sea rose, and a huge watery wave
as large as a mountain was seen to billow and to grow
and to bellow and to split at its highest crest,                               510
from which a horn-bearing bull is cast from the broken waves
and, rising into the gentle breezes as far as his breast,
spewed forth from his nostrils and gaping mouth a part of the sea.
The hearts of my companions are afraid, my mind remained unterrified,
concerned with its exile, when my fierce steeds turned their necks            515
to the sea and, shuddering with ears erect,
in fear of the monster they run amok and dash
the chariot upon the steep crags. I struggle in vain
to hold the reins now white with foam
and, leaning back, pull against the sturdy lines.                              520
The horses' panic would still not have overcome my strength,
except a wheel, where it spins unceasing about its hub,
collided with a projecting branch, broke, and was torn away.
I'm hurled from the chariot, and, with the reins holding my limbs, you could
have seen my living bowels torn out, my sinews left upon the branch,          525
my members partly dragged along, partly seized and left behind,

---

62 Aricia (modern Arricia) is a town in Latium south of Rome.
63 Because Orestes brought the image of Diana (Artemis) from the Tauric peninsula to Aricia.
64 Hippolytus, son of Theseus.
65 Phaedra, daughter of Minos and Pasiphaë.

my broken bones emitting awful sounds, my weary soul
exhaling its last, and nothing in my body left
that you could recognize: one wound was all that remained.
To our disaster, O nymph, you couldn't compare your own,                    530
or dare to, could you? I also saw the realms that have no light
and warmed my wounded body in the waves of Phlegethon,[66]
nor but for the strong medications of Apollo's son
would life have been restored to me. When with powerful drugs
and Paean's[67] aid I did regain it, against the will of Dis,[68]            535
then Cynthia[69] cast dense clouds around me—
lest by my presence I be the author of envy of this gift—
to keep me safe and unharmed when seen,
and made me older nor left my face to be recognized
and hesitated whether to give me Crete for my home                          540
or Delos: rejecting both Delos and Crete, she placed
me here and at the same time ordered me to put off my name,[70]
which could recall my horses, and said, 'You who were
Hippolytus shall be Virbius now!'[71]
Since then, I have dwelt in this grove and as one of the minor gods         545
I hide beneath the deity of my mistress and tend to her."

### 547-621   Cipus

Another's sorrows, however, were unable to ease
Egeria's mourning; lying prostrate at the bottom of a hill,
she melts into tears until, moved by the woman's grief,
the sister of Phoebus made of her body an icy spring                        550
and lengthened her limbs into eternal waves.
This strange event touched the nymphs. The son of the Amazon[72]
was no less amazed than when the Tyrrhenian at his plow
observed the fateful clod in the middle of his fields
when first, with no one stirring it, it moved by itself,                    555
and soon took on human form and lost the form of earth
and opened its new mouth to reveal the fates to come:
the natives called him Tages, who first taught
Etruscan folk to reveal things to come;
or than when Romulus saw the shaft of his spear, that once                  560
had clung to the Palatine Hill, suddenly grow green,
because of fresh roots, not standing with its driven point fixed

---

66 "Blazing," one of the rivers of the Underworld.
67 Paean or Paeon "Healer" was an epithet of Apollo.
68 Pluto.
69 Diana.
70 Hippolytus means "Loosened by Horses."
71 Virbius was worshiped at Aricia with Diana.
72 Antiope, the Amazon mother of Hippolytus.

and not as a missile, but as a tree of pliant branch,
affording unexpected shade to those who stood amazed;
or when within the river waves Cipus saw                                   565
his horns (he saw them indeed!) and, thinking that to trust
the image was wrong and moving his fingers often to his brow,
felt what he saw, and, no longer blaming his eyes,
paused during his return as victor over the conquered foe,
and, raising toward heaven his eyes and his hands,                         570
declared, "Whatever, O gods, this sign portends,
if fortunate, let it be fortunate for Quirinus' folk and my fatherland,
if threatening, then let it threaten me." An altar made of green turf
he supplicates with sweet-smelling fires
and offers bowls of wine and consults the slaughtered goats               575
to learn what the quivering entrails portend for him.
As soon as the seer of the Tyrrhenian people upon them gazed,
he saw within them things of great moment for the world,
yet not quite clear; but when he raised his sharp eye from
the entrails of the sheep to the horns of Cipus, he says,                 580
"All hail, O king! for you, Cipus, you and your horns
this place and the citadels of Latium will obey.
Just break off your delay and enter with haste
the open gates! The fates demand it so; for once received
within the city you will be king and safely win eternal sway."            585
But he drew back and turning his grim face from the city walls
replied, "Far, oh far away may the gods drive all this!
More justly by far should I as an exile spend my life
than let the Capitol behold me as its king."
He spoke and called together the people and solemn Senate at once,        590
but first conceals with peaceful laurel his horns
and stands upon the ramparts the brave soldiers made
and after praying to the ancient gods in the accustomed way,
exclaims, "there is one here, who, unless you drive him away,
will be your king: who he is I will declare not with a name but a sign:    595
there are horns upon his brow! The augur says to you
that if he enters Rome, he will establish a slavish rule.
Indeed he could have burst through your open gates,
but I have blocked his way, though none is closer to him
than I: you Quirites[73] from your city keep this man,                     600
or if he deserves it, bind him in heavy chains
or end your fear with the fated tyrant's death!"
A murmur like that in the thick foliage of the pines
whenever cruel Eurus whistles or like that the ocean's waves
create if someone listens from afar,                                       605

---

73 Originally the Sabines, but after the union of the latter with Rome, Quirites stands for Romans.

arises from the people; but over the confused words of
the murmuring crowd one sound stood out: "Who is this one?"
And while they examine their brows and look for the touted horns,
again Cipus says to them, "You have the one you seek,"
and took the crown from his head, against the people's will, 610
and showed his temples marked with twin horns.
They all lowered their eyes and gave forth a groan
and looked (could anyone believe it?) unwillingly upon
that head distinguished with service: then refusing to let
it lack in honor, they laid upon it a festal crown. 615
The nobles, however, because you could not enter the walls,
bestowed on you, Cipus, the honor of as much land
as with a plow attached to a team of oxen you
could circle from dawn to the end of the day.
They also carved the horns, displaying their wondrous form, 620
upon the bronze gates to remain there for all the length of time.
　　Reveal now, Muses, you attendant spirits of bards,
(for knowledge is yours, and you have not forgotten ages past),
from where the island about which the deep Tiber flows
contributed Coronis' son[74] to the city's sacred shrines. 625

### 622-744  *Aesculapius*

　　A dreadful plague had once polluted the air of Latium,
and bodies, pallid with bloodless sickness, lay in sorry state.
Exhausted by their dead, when once they clearly see
that mortal attempts are vain, vain the healer's skills,
they seek the aid of heaven, and go to Delphi, in 630
the middle of the globe, where Phoebus' oracles reside,
beseeching that he willingly help them in their wretched state
and with healing fortune end so great a city's distress.
The site and the laurel and the quiver he wore
resounded together, and from the depths of the inner shrine 635
the cauldron[75] gave back this word and moved their fearful hearts:
"You seek here, Roman, what you should have sought from a nearer place,
and even now should seek from a nearer place: nor do you need
Apollo to lessen your grief, but rather Apollo's son.
With favorable auspices go and summon my child." 640
The Senate, after wisely accepting the commands of the god,
inquires as to the city in which Phoebus' youthful son dwelt,
dispatching an embassy to sail with the winds to the Epidaurian shores.
As soon as they touched those shores with their crescent prow,
they went to the assembly of Greek elders, imploring them 645

---

74 Aesculapius (Asclepius), son of Coronis and Apollo.
75 The cauldron that rested on the tripod of the oracle.

to hand over the god that with his powerful presence he end
the deadly plague of the Ausonian[76] people; for this the oracle clearly said.
Contentious and varied are the views. Some think
that aid is not to be denied, many urge delay,
opposed to offering help and handing over their god:                           650
they hesitated till dusk had driven out the late evening light,
and darkness had drawn its shadows over the orb of the earth,
when in your sleep, O Roman, the healing god appeared
to stand before your couch and just as he is wont to be
within his own temple, holding in his left hand his rustic staff             655
and stroking with his right the hoariness of his long beard
and uttering words like these from his peaceful breast:
"Away with fear! I shall come and abandon my form.
Examine now this snake whose coils encircle this staff,
and mark it continually with your eyes that you know it well!               660
I will be changed into this: but larger will I be and seem as great
as heavenly bodies should when they're transformed."
At once the god and his voice depart, and sleep with voice and god,
and nourishing light followed the flight of sleep.
As morning came and Aurora had routed the fiery stars,                      665
uncertain what to do, the leaders came to the well-wrought temple of
the god they sought and pray that he himself make clear
with heavenly signs in what home he wishes to reside.
Their wish was barely expressed when, shining like gold
with lofty crests, the god in serpent form hissed his will                  670
and with his approach moved the statue, altar, temple doors,
the marble floor and the roof-tops of gold,
and in the midst of the shrine, with his breast raised aloft,
he stood and cast about his eyes that flashed with fire:
the frightened throng is terrified, but the priest,                         675
his sacred locks in gleaming fillet wreathed, recognized divinity
and said, "Behold the god, it is the god! Guard your tongues
and minds, all you who are present! O most glorious one, may you
appear with profit and help those who revere your holy rites."
The heralded god is worshiped by one and all who were there,               680
and all repeat the words of the priest, and in mind
and voice the sons of Aeneas offer their pious thanks.
To them the god gives his nod and, shaking his crests, confirmed
three times with the hiss of his darting tongue the favor they sought.
At this, he glides down the shining steps and, turning his face,            685
looks back upon his ancient altar he is now to leave
and bids farewell his familiar home and temple shrine.

---

76 Italy, so named from Auson, son of Ulysses and Calypso.

*Aesculapius, Solis*

Upon the ground covered with scattered flowers, he crept
from there with his huge form and, bending his coils, headed for
the city's center and the port defended by its mounded banks.　　690
And here he halted his course and, appearing to dismiss
with placid mien the service of the attending company, placed
his body upon the Ausonian bark: that hull perceived
the burden of deity and sagged beneath the weight of the god.
Aeneas' descendants rejoice, sacrifice a bull upon the shore,　　695
festoon the ship and set its twisted moorings free.
A gentle breeze drove the bark along: the god towered high
and, resting heavily his neck upon the crescent prow,
surveyed the sky-blue waters, and over the Ionian plain,
made calm by the breezes[77] at Pallas' daughter's[78] sixth rise,　　700
reached Italy, is borne along the Lacinian shore
ennobled by the temple of the goddess,[79] the Scylacean shore as well;[80]
he passes Iapygia[81] and on the left oars' side avoids
Amphrisia's rocks,[82] and on the right side the Cocinthian crags.[83]

---

77 Translating *Zephyris* here generically as "winds," instead of literally as "West Winds," because the
　ship is sailing *westward*.
78 Here referring to Aurora, not as the daughter of Hyperion (Ovid, *Fasti*. 5. 159), but of Hyperion's
　brother Titan, Pallas.
79 The temple of Juno. See 15. 13.
80 Scylacium, modern Squillace, was a city on the east coast of Bruttium, the toe of Italy.
81 See on 52.
82 Their location unknown, these rocks seem to be named for Apollo who tended the flocks of Admetus
　along the Amphrysos, a river in Thessaly.
83 Cocinthus is a promontory in Bruttium.

He skirts Romethium[84] and Caulon[85] and Narycia,[86]                    705
surmounts the Sicilian sea and Pelorus'[87] straits
and King Hippotades' home[88] and Temesa's mines,[89]
and points towards Leucosia[90] and Paestum's[91] rosy beds.
From there it skirts Capreae and Minerva's cape[92]
and Surrentum's[93] hills rich in vines                                    710
and Hercules' city[94] and Stabiae and, born for leisure,
Parthenope,[95] and from there to the Cumaean[96] Sibyl's shrine.
And then the warm springs[97] and gum-bearing Liternum[98] come
and, dragging with its current a multitude of sand,
Volturnus and Sinuessa,[99] teeming with snowy doves,                      715
and grievous Minturnae[100] and she whom her foster son entombed,[101]
and also the home of Antiphates[102] and Trachas,[103] surrounded by swamps,
and Circe's land and the hard-packed beach of Antium.[104]
When thither the sailors bent the sail-bearing prow
(for now the sea was rough), the god unfolded his orbs                     720
and, sliding his teeming coils and swollen form,
he enters his father's shrine that touched the tawny shore.
The sea now calmed, the Epidaurian left
his father's altar and, having enjoyed the hospitality of his kindred god,
plows through the sandy beach with the train of his rustling scales        725
and, leaning on the helm of the ship, laid his head
upon the lofty stern until to Castrum[105] he arrived
and to the sacred seat of Lavinium[106] and to Tiber's mouth.
From every direction masses of people rushed to meet
him there, matrons and fathers and those who guard                         730

---

84 Location unknown.
85 City on the east coast of Bruttium.
86 Naricium (Naryx), on the Malean Gulf, founded the colony of Locri Epizephyrii in Bruttium.
87 The most northeastern promontory of Sicily (modern Punta del Faro), at the mouth of the straits of
    Messina.
88 The Aeolian Islands, named after Aeolus, king of the winds and son of Hippotes.
89 Copper mines of Temesa, a town in Bruttium.
90 A small island near Paestum.
91 Originally founded by Sybaris, Paestum or Posidonia, a city of Lucania, was noted for its rose
    gardens.
92 The southern cape of the Bay of Naples.
93 Modern Sorrento.
94 Herculaneum.
95 I.e., Naples.
96 Sanctuary of Apollo on the coast north of the Bay of Naples.
97 At Baiae.
98 Town on the coast of Campania.
99 Town of southern Latium near the border of Campania. Volturnus is a river in Campania.
100 A town of southern Latium on the Appian Way, "grievous" because of its malaria-ridden marshes.
101 Caieta, on the coast of Latium, named for the nurse of Aeneas whom he buried there (Verg., *Aen.*
    7. 1-2). See 14. 443-41.
102 A king of the Laestrygonians (see 14. 249 and Homer, *Od.* 10. 199).
103 Terracina, on the coast south of Rome.
104 Modern Anzio.
105 A coastal town near Ardea.
106 A coastal town in Latium founded by Aeneas and named for Lavinia.

*Aesculapius changed to a serpent, Baur*

your fires, Trojan Vesta,[107] and with joyous shouting greet the god.
And where against the opposing stream the ship is quickly drawn,
and incense burning upon the line of altars erected upon the banks
gives off its sound from both sides and perfumes the air with smoke,
the victim is struck and warms the cutting knives of sacrifice.                    735
Already had he entered the head of the world, the city of Rome:
the serpent, rising high moves his neck about as it leans against
the top of the mast and looks about for a fitting home for himself.
The river, as it flows around, divides into two parts
(its name is the Island) and on either side                                        740
it stretches limbs of equal length with land in between:
the serpent of Phoebus, leaving the Latin bark, went there
and, with his celestial form regained, imposed
an end to sorrow and came to the city as a bringer of health.

### 745-870   *Julius Caesar and Augustus*

Though as a foreigner that one to our shrines had come,                            745
yet Caesar[108] in his own city is a god; distinguished in the work of Mars
and toga,[109] not more did the wars completed in triumph and
the deeds done at home and the ensuing fame of those deeds
transform him into a new star and heavenly light with flowing hair
than did his very offspring; for among Caesar's acts                               750

---

107 Aeneas brought the fires of Vesta, goddess of the hearth, out of Troy (see Verg., *Aen*. 2. 296-97).
108 Gaius Julius Caesar (100 - 44 B.C.), who adopted his nephew Gaius Octavius (63 B.C. - 14 A.D.),
   who upon adoption became Gaius Julius Caesar Octavianus. He gained the title "Augustus" in
   27 B. C.
109 Metonymy for domestic deeds.

there was no greater work than to be known as the father of this man:
unless it be greater to have subdued Britain's folk by waters bound
and through the seven-flowing streams of papyrus-bearing Nile
victorious rafts to have driven and given the rebels of Numidia[110] and
Cinyphian Juba[111] and Pontus, puffed up with the names                    755
of Mithridates,[112] as gifts to Quirinus'[113] folk,
and to have earned many a triumph and celebrated some,
than to have brought forth so great a man, with whom as head of the world,
how gracious, O gods, have you been to human kind!
Lest he be born then of mortal seed,                                         760
the father had to become a god. As Aeneas' golden mother saw
both this and that a bitter death was being prepared
against the pontifex[114] and conspiring weapons aimed,
she paled, and to any and every god she met
would say, "Behold with what might the snares                                765
are being laid for me, what deceit is aimed at that head,
the only thing of Dardanian[115] Iulus[116] that I have left.
Shall I alone be ever harried by just concerns,
and I alone wounded by the Calydonian spear of Tydeus' son,[117]
and now confounded by the walls of poorly defended Troy,                     770
behold my son being forced to wander long
and vexed upon the sea and entering the homes of the silent dead
and waging war with Turnus, or, if we admit the truth,
with Juno more? Why now do I recall the former wrongs
my family endured? To remember the past my present fear                      775
forbids; look there, you see those accursed swords being honed!
I pray you, stop them, prevent the crime, nor let the flames
of Vesta be stilled by the slaughter of her priest.[118]
Such words does Venus anxiously spread in vain
through all of heaven and moves the gods, who though                         780
they cannot break the ancient sisters'[119] ironclad decrees,
the signs they give, no less, of the coming grief are not unclear:

---

110 A country of nomads, southwest of Carthage, under Juba I, defeated at Thapsus in 46 B. C.
111 Son of Juba I and King of Mauritania in Northwest Africa, led in triumph by Caesar in 46 B.C.
   A cultivated ruler who sought to introduce Greek and Roman culture to his land, which was
   bequeathed to Octavian in 33 B.C., but handed over by the latter to Juba to rule in 25 B.C. The
   Cinyps is a river of Libya, used generally for "Africa."
112 Six rulers named Mithridates had ruled Pontus in Asia Minor, the last defeated in 63 B.C.
113 Quirinus was the deified Romulus.
114 Caesar was a *pontifex* (priest) since 73 and *pontifex maximus* (chief priest) since 63.
115 I.e., Trojan, because Dardanus, born in Cortona, had founded Troy.
116 The son of Aeneas, from whom the Julian clan, to which Julius Caesar belonged, was descended.
   Originally called Ilus after an early king of Ilium (see 11. 756), his name was changed to Iulus.
   He was also called Ascanius.
117 Tydeus, father of Diomedes, was the son of Oeneus, king of Calydon. Diomedes wounded
   Aphrodite's hand in Hom. *Il.* 5. 330-40.
118 Julius Caesar.
119 The Fates.

they say that in the black clouds there was clashing of arms,
alarming tubas and trumpets were heard in the sky
that warned of wicked acts; and the image of an angry sun                    785
exposed to the troubled lands its lurid light;
below the stars torches were often seen to blaze,
among the clouds bloody drops often fell;
the face of a cobalt Lucifer[120] with a murky rust
was strewn, the lunar chariot with blood was strewn;                         790
the Stygian owl in a thousand places gave sad omens forth,
in a thousand places ivory wept tears, and they say that songs
and threatening words in sacred places were heard.
No victim offers favorable omens, and that great tumults are at hand
the lobe of the liver warns, and the crown in the entrails is found to be cut,  795
and in the forum and about the homes and temples of the gods
they say that nocturnal dogs howled, and the shades of the silent dead
were roaming, and with tremors the city shook.
But even so the treachery and coming doom could not
be conquered by the warnings of the gods, and swords profane                 800
the temples: for in the city no other place
would suit this crime and baneful slaughter except the Curia.[121]
Indeed, Cytherea[122] then struck with both her hands
her breast and strove to hide Aeneas' descendant[123] within the cloud
in which once Paris was stolen from his Atreid foe,[124]                     805
and from the sword of Diomedes Aeneas had fled.[125]
Her father addressed her thus, "Do you alone, my child
propose to move invincible destiny? Enter yourself
the homes of the sisters three, and there you will behold
within a vast edifice of bronze and solid iron the records of things,        810
that, fearing neither heaven's might nor my lightning's wrath
nor any destructive force, remain forever secure.
Therein you will find incised in everlasting adamant
your family's fates: I myself have read and inscribed them in my mind
and shall relate them, lest even now of your future you be uninformed.       815
The one for whom you toil, Cytherea, has fulfilled
his time and completed the years he owed to earth.
That as a god he enter the sky and in temples be revered,
will be your work, and his son, the heir of his name,
will bear alone the burden imposed and, of his father slain                  820

---

120 Lucifer, the Morning Star, was the son of Aurora and Cephalus (implied perhaps by Aurora's
     abduction of Cephalus at 7. 700-04).
121 The meeting place of the Roman Senate.
122 So called because Venus was born on the island of Cythera.
123 Julius Caesar.
124 Menelaus, son of Atreus, in Homer, *Iliad* 3. 380-82.
125 Hom., *Il.* 5. 314.

as an avenger most valiant, have us on his side for his wars.
Beneath his auspices besieged Mutina's[126] conquered walls
will sue for peace, Pharsalia[127] will feel his might,
and Emathian[128] Philippi[129] will again be soaked with gore,
and in Sicilian waters a great name[130] overwhelmed,                    825
and of a Roman general the Egyptian wife[131] will fall,
who trusted wrongly the marriage torch, and threatened
in vain that our Capitol would of her Canopus[132] be the slave!
But why recount to you the barbarous nations and those who dwell
beside both oceans? Whatever region the earth preserves               830
for human life will belong to him: the sea will serve him as well!
      "With peace bestowed upon the lands, he will turn his mind
to rights of citizens and be the fairest author of laws
and by his own example set the rules of human conduct, and, looking ahead
to future ages and coming generations,                                835
command that from his blameless wife[133] a scion be born
to bear his name together with his cares;
nor till, advanced in age, he has matched his merits with
his years will he touch the ethereal realms and kindred stars.
But meanwhile, this soul, from the murdered body taken, make          840
a heavenly light[134] that upon our forum and Capitol
divine Julius may ever gaze from his dwelling on high!"
No sooner had he spoken than in the Senate's midst
did nurturing Venus take her stand, to be seen by none,
and from her Caesar's limbs stole away the yet living soul, and did   845
not let it be scattered into the air, and brought it to the heavenly stars
and, as she bore it, saw it grow bright and catch fire,
and from her bosom let it go free: higher than the moon it flies,
and, drawing its flame-bearing hair in its spacious train,
the star shines bright and, beholding his son's good works, admits    850
that they are greater than his own, rejoices in fact to be outstripped by him.
Although he[135] forbids that his own be set ahead of his father's deeds,
yet fame is free and, bound to no commands,
gives precedence to the son against his will and in this alone disobeys:
just so did great Atreus to Agamemnon honors cede,                    855

---

126 Octavian defeated Antony in the battle of Mutina (modern Modena) in 43 B.C.
127 In Thessaly, where Julius Caesar was victor over Pompey in the decisive battle of the civil war.
128 Macedonian.
129 By poetic exaggeration as though Philippi and Pharsalus were in the same place.
130 Sextus Pompey, the pirate son of Pompey the Great, who also called himself the "Great," defeated
      by Agrippa in 36 B.C.
131 Antony and Cleopatra, defeated at the battle of Actium in 31 B.C.
132 A town on one of the western mouths of the Nile.
133 Livia Drusilla (58 B.C.- 29 A.D.), married to Augustus in 39 B.C., was first married to Tiberius
      Claudius Nero by whom she had a son, Tiberius. Augustus adopted Tiberius as his heir in 4 A.D.
134 See 15. 749.
135 Augustus.

*Deification of Julius Caesar, Solis*

just so was Aegeus by Theseus, just so was Peleus by Achilles excelled.
And finally, if I may use examples the match of those,
just so is Saturn less than Jove: Jupiter controls
the citadel of ether and realms of the threefold[136] world,
the earth is subject to Augustus, father and ruler are both.                    860
I pray, O gods, companions of Aeneas, to whom both sword and fire
have yielded, and you, O gods Indigetes,[137] and you, Quirinus, the author of
our city, and you, Gradivus,[138] of unconquered Quirinus the sire,
and Vesta, hallowed amidst Caesar's household gods,
and with Caesarian Vesta, you, Phoebus, protector of our homes,               865
and lofty Jupiter, you who keep the Tarpeian citadel,
and all others it is meet and right for the bard to invoke:
may that day be slow to come , and after our own life is past,
on which the Augustan head, with the world that he rules left behind,
should enter heaven and absent heed our prayers!                              870

---

136 Jupiter controls the sky, sea, and underworld.
137 The deified Aeneas became the god Indiges "The Native" at 14. 608; according to Livy 1. 2. 6,
    Aeneas' full divine title was *Iovis Indiges*; the plural *Indigetes* comprises all the local gods.
138 A title of Mars, father of Romulus.

### 871-879 The Poet's Epilogue

And now I have finished my work, which neither Jove's wrath
nor fire, nor sword nor devouring age will be able to destroy.
May that day that has no power except over this body of mine
complete when it will the span of my uncertain years:
yet with my better part will I be borne eternally above                    875
the lofty stars, and indelible will be our name;
and where Roman culture reigns upon the conquered earth,
upon the lips of people will I be read, and in glory through every age,
if prophecies of bards have ought of truth, will I live.

# REFERENCES AND BRIEF BIBLIOGRAPHY

## Editions and Commentaries

Anderson W. S., *P. Ovidii Nasonis Metamorphoses.* 6th ed. (1993 Stuttgart: Teubner edition) = Anderson.

_____, *Ovid's Metamorphoses, Books 1-5, Edited with Introduction and Commentary* (Norman and London, 1997)

_____, *Ovid's Metamorphoses, Books 6-10, Edited with Introduction and Commentary* (Norman and London, 1972).

Bömer, F. *P. Ovidius Naso Metamorphosen.* 7 vols. (Heidelberg, 1969-86).

Haupt, M., Müller, H. J. *Die Metamorphosen des P. Ovidius Naso* I (*B.* I-VII), 9th ed., O. Korn, II (*B.* VIII-XV), 4th ed., revised by R. Ehwald (1915/1916 Berlin); corrected with bibliographical supplement by M. von Albrecht (Zürich 1966) = Ehwald.

Hill, D. E. *Ovid, Metamorphoses I-IV, V-VIII, IX-XII, XIII-XV, Edited, with translation. and commentary* (Warminster, 1985, 1992, 1999, 2000) = Hill.

Hollis, A. S., *Ovid Metamorphoses Book VIII: Edited with an Introduction and Commentary* (Oxford 1970).

Hopkinson, N. *Ovid Metamorphoses, Book XIII* (Cambridge, 2000).

Lee, A. G., *Ovid, Metamorphoses Book I* (Cambridge, 1953).

Miller, F. J. *Ovid. Metamorphoses.* (1916) 2 vols., 3rd ed. revised by G. P. Goold (Cambridge, Mass. and London, 1977 and 1984: Loeb edition) = Loeb.

Moore-Blunt, J. J. *A Commentary on Ovid Metamorphoses II,* (Uithoorn, 1977)

Tarrant, R. J. *P. Ovidi Nasonis Metamorphoses,* recognovit brevique adnotatione critica instruxit (Oxford, 2004: Oxford Classical Text) = Tarrant

*375*

**Books and Articles**

Albrecht, M. von and Zinn, E. *Ovid; Wege der Forschung* 92 (Darmstadt, 1968)

Boyd, B. W. ed., *Brill's Companion to Ovid* (Leiden, Boston, Köln, 2002).

Fränkel, H. *Ovid: A Poet Between Two Worlds* (Berkeley and Los Angeles, 1945).

Galinsky, G. K. *Ovid's Metamorphoses. An Introduction to the Basic Aspects* (Berkeley and Los Angeles, 1975).

Keith, A. "Sources and Genres in Ovid's *Metamorphoses* 1-5," *Brill's Companion to Ovid*, 235-69.

Kenny, E. J. "Ovidius Prooemians," *Proceedings of the Cambridge Philological Society*, n.s. 22 (1976), 46-53.

Otis, B. *Ovid as an Epic Poet* (Cambridge, 1966).

Rand, E. K. *Ovid and his Influence* (New York, 1963).

Solodow, J. B. *The World of Ovid's Metamorphoses* (Chapel Hill and London, 1988).

Tarrant, R. J. "Editing Ovid's *Metamorphoses*: Problems and Possibilities," *Classical Philology* 77 (1982) 257-86.

**For the life of Ovid see the Perseus website:**

http://www.perseus.tufts.edu/cgi-bin/ptext?doc=Perseus: text:1999.02.0069

**Illustrations:**

Buechler, J. *Publius Ovidius Naso Sulmonensis: An Exhibit of his Works at the Bailey/Howe Library and the Robert Hull Fleming Museum at the University of Vermont April-May 1985.* This catalogue, printed by the fine Stinehour Press of Lunenburg, Vermont, describes the collection of illustrated editions of the *Metamorphoses* at the University of Vermont. It is from this collection that the illustrations for this translation have been taken.

Anonymous Woodcuts for an edition of Raphael Regius (Venice ca. 1513) = Venice ca. 1513.

Vergilius Solis (1514-1562): for the edition of Johann Postius von Gemersheim (Frankfurt, 1563) = Solis.

Johann Wilhelm Baur (1600-1641): 150 copperplate engravings with original verses in Latin and German (Nuremberg 1639).

Anonymous artists, Martin Bouche (1640-93), Peter Paul Bouche (b. 1646), Frederick Bouttats (d. 1676), and Peeter Clouwet (1629-1670): 124

copperplate engravings for the Dutch translation of J. V. Vondel and commentary of Pieter Du Ryer (two different editions: Brussels, 1687 and Amsterdam, 1703) = Amsterdam 1703.

Bernard Picart (1673-1733) and other able masters: Engravings for an English translation from the French of Abbot Banier (Amsterdam, 1732) = Picart.

# INDEX AND GLOSSARY

References are to the book and line (5. 137 = Book 5, line 37) of the translated text (usually the same as or close to the original text) or to a footnote within a book (5n. 9 = Book 5, footnote 9). Adjectival forms, if not glossed, will be explained by the related noun (for "Achaean" refer to "Achaea").

Albula (another name for the river Tiber) 14. 328
Alceus (father of Amphitryon; grandfather of Hercules) 9n. 3
Alcathoë (another name for Megara) 7. 443
Alcathoüs (son of Pelops; founder of Megara) 7n. 63, 8. 8
Alce (hound of Actaeon) 3. 217
Alcidamas (father of Ctesylla) 7. 369, 7n. 39
Alcides (descendant of Alceus; Hercules) 9. 13, 50, 109, 216, 11. 213, 12. 538
Alcimedon (Tyrrhenian sailor) 3. 618
Alcinoüs (king of the Phaeacians) 14. 564
Alcithoë (daughter of Minyas) 4. 1, 274
Alcmaeon (son of Eriphyle and Amphiaräus) 2n. 54, 9. 407, 415, 9n. 30, 32, 33, 34, 35, 37
Alcmena (daughter of Electryon; mother of Hercules) 8. 544, 9. 23, 276, 281, 313, 324, 395, 798, 9n. 11, 20
Alcmene (= Alcmena) 6n. 21
Alcon (Boeotian vase engraver) 13. 683
Alcyone (daughter of Sciron) 7n. 55
Alcyone (daughter of Aeolus, god of the winds; wife of Ceyx) 11. 384, 416, 423, 447, 457, 473, 544, 545, 563, 567, 587, 627, 661, 674, 684, 746, 11n. 58
Aleacer (slain by Ulysses) 13. 258
Alemon (father of Myscelos, founder of Crotona) 15. 19, 26, 48
Alexandria (city of Egypt) 9n. 74, 15n. 34
Alexiroë (nymph mother of Aesacus) 11. 762
Allecto (Fury) 10n. 41
Alma Tellus (Mother Earth) 2n. 78
Almo (small tributary of the Tiber) 14. 329
Aloeus (wife of Iphimedia) 6n. 27
Aloidae (giants Otus and Ephialtes, born of Iphimedia and Neptune, named for Aloeus) 6. 117
Alphean (referring to Arethusa, pursued by the river Alpheus) 5. 487
Alphenor (son of Niobe and Amphion) 6. 248
Alpheos (river of Elis) 2. 250
Alphesiboea (daughter of Phegeus; wife of Alcmaeon; = Arsinoë) 2n. 54, 9n. 34
Alpheus (= Alpheos) 5. 599, 5n. 64
Alpine 14. 795
Alps 2. 226
Althaea (mother of Meleager) 8. 446, 8n. 29, 49
Amathus (city in Cyprus) 10. 220, 531
Amathusian (of Amathus) 10. 227
Amazon 12n. 66, 15. 552, 15n. 72
Amazons (tribe of warrior women) 12n. 66
Ambracia (city of Epirus) 13. 713, 13n. 126

Anio (river in Latium) 14. 329

Anius (priest of Apollo and king on Delos) 13. 632, 643, 13n. 111

Antaeus (Libyan giant subdued by Hercules) 9. 183

Antandros (port in the Troad) 13. 628

Antenor (Trojan leader) 13. 201, 13n. 45

Anthedon or (town in Boeotia) 7. 232, 7n. 22, 13. 905

Anticleia (mother of Ulysses) 8n. 65, 11n. 48, 13n. 28

Antigone (daughter of Laomedon; changed to a stork) 6. 93

Antimachus (Centaur) 12. 459

Antioch (Syrian city on the Orontes river) 2n. 64

Antiope (daughter of Nyctaeus; mother of Amphion and Zethus) 6. 111, 6n. 20, 39, 15n. 72

Antiphates (king of the Laestrygonians) 14. 234, 238, 249, 15. 717

Antissa (town of Lesbos) 15. 287

Antium (town in Latium) 15. 718

Antoninus Liberalis (wrote, probably in 2nd century A.D., a mythography of metamorphoses, based upon the *Heteroeumena* of Nicander of Colophon, fl. 130 B.C.) 6n. 14, 7n. 39, 42, 51, 54, 13n. 116, 125, 129, 14n. 74

Antony (Marcus Antonius, 83-30 B.C., supporter of Julius Caesar; with Cleopatra defeated by Octavian at Actium in 31 B.C.) 15n. 126, 131

Anubis (dog-headed god of Egypt) 9. 690

Anzio (modern Antium) 15n. 104

Aonia (Boeotia) 1n. 49, 5. 333, 6n. 2, 9n. 7

Aonian 1. 313, 3. 339, 7. 763, 9n. 7, 12. 24, 13. 682

Aonids (Muses of Mt. Helicon in Boeotia) 6. 2

Aoos (river in Thessaly) 1n. 88

Apennine 15. 432

Apennines (mountain range in Italy) 2. 226

Aphareus (king of the Messenians) 8. 304, 12. 341

Aphidas (Centaur) 12. 317

Aphrodite (goddess of love = Venus) 4n. 23, 66, 13n. 82, 15n. 117

Apidanus (river in Thessaly) 7. 228, 7n. 20

Apis (Egyptian bull-god) 1n. 114, 9. 691

Apollo (= Phoebus, Sol, Sun, Helios, Titan, Hyperion) 1. 473, 1n. 6, 7, 67, 69, 72, 73, 74, 81, 2. 543, 632, 876, 2n. 7, 33, 35, 38, 107, 109, 127, 139, 3. 421, 4n. 27, 28, 29, 5. 329, 5n. 39, 6. 50, 6n. 51, 7. 389, 7n. 2, 30, 51, 54, 9. 332, 455, 9n. 56, 10. 167, 209, 10n. 17, 24, 11. 155, 306, 339, 413, 11n. 36, 56, 57, 12n. 15, 63, 13. 174, 631, 715, 13n. 105, 107, 125, 126, 14n. 97, 15. 533, 639, 15n. 67, 74, 82, 96

Apollodorus (mythgrapher of 2nd century A.D.) 2n. 152, 13n. 10, 4n. 77, 88, 6n. 50, 52, 64, 7n. 8, 34, 8n. 24, 11. 8

Apollonius of Rhodes (Alexandrian poet of the 3rd century B.C., author of the epic *Argonautica*) 2n. 152, 13n. 82

Apollo's horses 2. 153, 154

Appian Way (major road in Roman Italy) 15n. 100

Apples of the Hesperides (golden apples given by Earth as a wedding present to Juno and guarded by the nymph "Daughters of Evening" in a garden beyond the Atlas mountains; to retrieve them was one of the labors of Hercules) 9. 190, 9n. 15

Apulia (region of SE Italy) 14n. 64, 65, 74

Apulus (shepherd) 14. 517

Aquilo (North or Northeast Wind) 1. 262, 328, 2. 132, 5. 285, 7. 3, 10. 77

Arabia 5n. 13, 10. 478, 10n. 39, 44

Arabs 1n. 11

Arachne (daughter of Idmon of Maeonia changed to a spider) 6. 5, 34, 133, 150

Arcadia (region of north central Peloponnesus) 1. 218, 689, 1n. 29, 36, 37, 38, 91, 102, 106, 108, 2n. 55, 91, 97, 141, 5n. 14, 64, 7n. 47, 8n. 36, 40, 41, 14n. 36, 62, 15n. 44

Arcadian 2n. 54, 93, 8. 391

Arcadians 3. 210

Arcady (= Arcadia) 9. 192

Arcas (son of Lycaon's daughter and Jupiter) 2. 468, 497, 500

Arcesius (son of Jupiter; father of Laërtes, the father of Ulysses) 13. 144

Arctophylax (Boötes) 2n. 24

Arctos (Big and Little Bears) 2. 132, 4. 625, 13. 293

Arcturus (Boötes) 2n. 24

Ardea (city of Turnus) 14. 573, 14n. 59, 66, 82, 15n. 105

Areopagus (hill in Athens) 6n. 11

Areos (Centaur) 12. 310

Arestor (father of Argus) 1. 624

Arethusa (nymph of Elis) 5. 409, 487, 496, 573, 599, 625, 642, 5n. 64

Arges (Cyclops) 1n. 42

Argive (of Argos) 1. 726, 2. 524, 3. 560. 8. 267, 9. 313, 9n. 30, 12. 627, 13. 659 14. 443, 15. 19, 164, 276

Argives (people of Argos = Greeks) 12. 149, 629, 12n. 1

Argo (Jason's ship) 13n. 1, 15. 338

Argolid (region around Argos) 1n. 91, 7n. 46, 9n. 5, 20

Argos (city of the NE Peloponnesus) 1. 601, Argos 2. 240, 2n. 46, 3n. 30, 4. 609, 4n. 70, 5n. 20, 6. 414, 14n. 64, 15n. 18, 26

Argus (hundred-eyed monster) 1. 624, 625, 635, 636, 664, 670, 680, 720, 1n. 100, 2. 533

Argyripa (Vergil's name for Arpi) 14n. 64

Ariadne (daughter of Minos) 8. 172, 8n. 15

Aricia (town in Latium) 14n. 45, 15n. 62, 63, 71

Arician (of Aricia) 15. 488

Aries (constellation Ram) 10. 165

Caieta (nurse of Aeneas and city named for her on the coast of Latium) 14. 444, 14n. 28, 15n. 101

Calabria (in antiquity a region of SE Italy) 14n. 74, 15n. 11

Calais (winged son of Orithyia and Boreas; brother of Zetes) 6. 716, 7n. 2

Calchas (prophet son of Thestor) 12. 19, 27, 12n. 2

Calliope (Muse; mother of Orpheus) 5. 338, 10. 148, 10n. 17

Callirhoë (daughter of Acheloüs; second wife of Alcmaeon) 4n. 90, 9. 413, 431, 9n. 32

Callisto (daughter of Arcadian Lycaon; mother of Arcas) 2. 460, 2n. 97

Calydon (region of Aetolia; kingdom of Oeneus) 6. 415, 8. 270, 495, 526, 528, 8n. 50, 9. 112, 147, 798, 9n. 6, 14n. 73, 15n. 117

Calydonian 8. 324, 727, 9. 2, 14. 512, 15. 769

Calymne (Aegean island) 8. 222

Calypso (daughter of Atlas; held Ulysses on Ogygie for seven years) 15n. 76

Camenae (Roman Muses) 14n. 57, 15. 482

Camicus (Sicilian kingdom ruled by Cocalus) 8n. 24

Campania (region of western Italy south of Latium) 14n. 28, 15n. 98, 99

Canace (daughter of Aeolos; loved by Neptune in the form of a bull) 6n. 25

Canache (hound of Actaeon) 3. 217

Canens (daughter of Venilia and Janus; wife of Picus) 14. 338, 381, 383, 417, 434, 14n. 57

Canopus (town on a western mouth of the Nile) 15. 828

Capaneus (one of the Argive seven against Thebes, struck by Jupiter's thunderbolt) 9. 404

Capetus (an Alban king) 14. 613

Caphereus (rocky cape on Euboea) 14. 472, 481

Capitol (hill of Rome sacred to Jupiter) 15. 589, 828, 841, 880, 15n. 2

Capitoline (hill of Rome, = Capitol) 1. 561, 2. 539, 14n. 108

Capreae (island in the Bay of Naples, modern Capri) 15. 709

Capys (an Alban king) 14. 613, 614

Caria (region of SW Asia Minor) 4. 297, 9. 645, 9n. 47, 50, 10n. 48

Carian 8. 674, 9n. 51

Carinthia (province of southern Austria) 14n. 96

Carnian Alps (range between Austria and Italy) 14n. 96

Carpathian (of Carpathus) 11. 249

Carpathus (Aegean island) 11n. 35

Carthaea (town on island of Ceos) 7n. 38, 10. 109, 740, 10n. 16, 14n. 12, 15n. 110

Cartheian 7. 368

Cassandra (daughter of Hecuba and Priam) 13n. 86, 14n. 69

Cassiopea (wife of Cepheus; mother of Andromeda) 4. 736, 4n. 77, 5. 153

Castalian (of a spring on Mt. Parnassus) 3. 14

Deo (= Ceres) 6. 114, 8n. 67

Deoian (pertaining to Deo) 8. 758

Dercetis (Syrian goddess; mother of Semiramis) 4. 44, 5n. 41

Deucalion (son of Prometheus; husband of Pyrrha) 1. 318, 350, 390, 6n. 29, 7. 356

Dia (another name for the island Naxos) 3. 690, 8. 175

Diana (daughter of Latona and Jupiter; brother of Apollo; = Artemis; Luna; Moon) 1. 487, 695, 697, 1n. 7, 70, 103, 2. 208, 425, 451, 465, 2n. 26, 38, 92, 94, 96, 98, 3. 156, 173, 181, 185, 252, 4. 304, 5. 375, 619, 5n. 31, 75, 6. 415, 6n. 43, 7. 746, 8. 272, 353, 395, 579, 9. 90, 9n. 23, 10. 536, 10n. 45, 11. 322, 12. 28, 35, 629, 12n. 6, 37, 13. 185, 13n. 105, 125, 14n. 45, 51, 15. 196, 490, 15n. 63, 69, 71

Dictaean 3. 2, 8. 43, 9. 717

Dictaeos (hound of Actaeon) 3. 223

Dicte (mountain of Crete) 3n. 1, 8n. 4, 9n. 67

Dictynna (Cretan Diana) 2. 441

Dictys (Tyrrhenian sailor) 3. 615, (Centaur) 12. 334, 337

Dido (Queen of Carthage) 4n. 32, 14n. 12

Didyme (Aegean island) 7. 469

Dindyma (mountain of Phrygia, sacred to Cybele) 2. 223

Diodorus (= Diodorus Siculus, ca. 30 B.C. completed a universal history down to the year 60 B.C.) 8n. 24

Diomedes (son of Tydeus; Greek warrior at Troy; emigrated to Apulia) 12. 622, 12n. 68, 13. 68, 100, 102, 242, 354, 13n. 11, 18, 21, 54, 55, 14. 457, 478, 492, 14n. 63, 64, 71, 73, 15. 769, 806. 15n. 117

Diomedes of Thrace (king with man-eating horses, fed to his own horses by Hercules) 9. 194

Dione (daughter of Atlas; mother of Niobe) 6. 174, 6n. 38

Dionysus (son of Semele and Zeus; Greek god of wine; = Bacchus) 4n. 5, 7, 6n. 24, 32, 11n. 13

Dirae (Roman name for the Furies; = Erinyes) 4n. 53

Dirce (wife of king Lycus of Thebes; changed into a spring) 2. 239

Dis (Pluto) 4. 438, 511, 5. 384, 395, 569, 15. 535

Dodona (oracle of Jupiter in Epirus) 7. 623, 7n. 80, 13. 716, 13n. 127

Dog-Star (Maera transformed) 6n. 32

Dolon (Trojan spy) 13. 98, 244, 13n. 18, 55, 56, 57

Dolopians (a people of Thessaly) 12. 364, 12n. 43

Don (modern name for the river Tanais) 2n. 49

Dorceus (hound of Actaeon) 3. 210

Doris (daughter of Tethys and Oceanus, wife of Nereus and mother of the Nereids) 2. 11, 269, 2n. 77, (mother of Galatea) 13. 742

Dorylas (ally of Perseus) 5. 129, 130, (Centaur) 12. 380, 390

dramatic festivals 4n. 7

Dreams 11. 613, 617, 626

golden bough (Aeneas plucked a golden bough as a token of his right to enter the Underworld) 14. 114, 14n. 23

golden fleece (quest of Jason) 7n. 6

Gorge (daughter of Oeneus; sister of Meleager) 8. 544

Gorgon (Medusa) 4. 618, 699, 778, 4n. 71, 81, 5. 180, 196, 202, 209, 5n. 16

Gorgonian 4. 800

Gorgons (daughters of Phorcys: Euryale, Sthenno, and Medusa) 4n. 80, 88, 5n. 18

Gortynian (pertaining to Gortyn, city of central Crete) 7. 778

Graces (= Charites; usually three, Hesiod names them Aglaea, Euphrosyne and Thalia.) 6. 429

Gradivus (epithet of Mars) 6. 427, 14. 818, 15. 863

Graeae (daughters of Phorcys and Ceto, grey-haired from birth, sharing one eye) 4n. 87, 88, 5n. 18

Granicus (river of the Troad and father of Alexiroë) 11. 762

Greece 1n. 68, 4. 16, 5n. 74, 14. 474, 14n. 37, 15n. 35, 13. 199, 13n. 72

Greek 1n. 7, 10, 23, 29, 40, 45, 53, 77, 101, 110, 114, 12. 64, 609, 629, 12n. 10, 14. 163, 220, 325, 852, 14n. 19, 47, 62, 67, 71, 121, 15. 9, 645, 880, 15n. 3, 12, 111

Greeks 1n. 6, 17, 88, 113; 13. 134, 241, 281, 402, 414, 13n. 11, 14n. 27, 78, 79, 15n. 57

Grynaeus (Centaur) 12. 258, 268

Gulf of Malia (gulf south of Thessaly) 1n. 85

Gulf of Pagasa (gulf off Pagasa, the port of Iolchos and Pherae, = modern Gulf of Volos) 1n. 89

Gyaros or Gyarus (Cycladic island) 5. 252, 7. 470

Hades (Pluto) 5n. 69, (Underworld) 9n. 8, 14n. 8

Haedi (two stars in Auriga) 14n. 95

Haemon (eponymous hero of Haemonia; father of Thessalus) 1n. 82

Haemonia (Thessaly) 1. 568, 2. 543, 7. 159, 8. 813, 11. 229, 652, 11n. 34, 54

Haemonian (Thessalian) 2. 81, 599, 5. 306, 7. 132, 264, 314, 11. 409, 12. 81, 213, 353

Haemus (mountain in Thrace) 2. 219, 6. 87, 10. 77

Hailus (slain by Ulysses at Troy) 13. 258

Halcyoneus (ally of Phineus) 5. 135, 138

Halesus (Lapith) 12. 462

Hamadryads (wood nymphs) 1. 690

Hantaean (Boeotian) 8. 310

Harmonia (daughter of Mars and Venus, wife of Cadmus) 3. 133, 3n. 12, 4. 583, 4n. 64, 70, 9n. 30

Harpalos (hound of Actaeon) 3. 222

Harpies ("Snatchers, " birds with faces of women) 7. 4, 7n. 2, 4

Harpocrates (Horus as infant; Egyptian god of silence) 9n. 63

Harpyia (hound of Actaeon) 3. 215

Hebe (daughter of Juno, goddess of youth; wife of the deified Hercules) 9. 400, 416, 9n. 36, 37, 14n. 121

Hebrus (river in Thrace) 2. 257, 11. 50, 796, 11n. 7, 13n. 90

Hecate (daughter of Perses and Asterie, goddess of witchcraft; as Trivia, associated with Diana) 2. 416, 2n. 94, 6. 139, 7. 74, 174, 194, 241, 7n. 8, 9, 14. 44, 405

Hector (son of Hecuba and Priam; husband of Andromache; chief warrior of the Trojans) 11. 758, 761, 12. 2, 67, 69, 75, 76, 447, 448, 548, 591, 607, 629, 12n. 18, 58, 59, 13. 7, 82, 178, 275, 279, 384, 426, 427, 486, 487, 512, 666, 13n. 15, 16, 39, 56, 62, 78, 87

Hecuba (daughter of Dymas; wife of Priam) 11n. 72, 13. 404, 423, 538, 549, 556, 567, 575, 577, 13n. 85, 86, 100

Hekatombaion (first month of the Athenian year) 2n. 140

Helen (daughter of Leda and Tyndareus; wife of Menelaus) 7n. 33, 12. 5, 609, 13. 200, 13n. 45, 14. 669, 15. 232, 15n. 23

Helenus (son of Priam; Trojan prophet) 13. 99, 335, 723, 13n. 131, 15. 438, 450

Heliades (daughters of Sun = Helios and Clymene; sisters of Phaethon) 2. 340, 2n. 84, 10. 91, 263, 10n. 13, 35

Helice (Great Bear) 15. 293, 15n. 37

Helices (ally of Phineus) 5. 87

Helicon (mountain home of the Muses in Boeotia) 1n. 49, 2. 219, 5. 254, 664, 5n. 23, 32, 43, 6n. 2, 8. 534

Helios (Sun-god) 1n. 6, 2n. 83, 4n. 26, 7. 398, 7n. 10, 19, 53, 10n. 13, 35, 13. 968

Helle (daughter of Nephele and Athamas; sister of Phrixus; eponymous heroine of the Hellespont) 11. 195, 796, 11n. 25

Hellespont (strait from the Aegean into the Propontis) 11n. 25, 27, 13. 407

Helops (Centaur) 12. 334, 335

Helper (Apollo) 1. 522

Henna (city in Sicily) 5. 385, 5n. 56

Hephaestus (god of fire = Vulcan) 2n. 111, 4n. 20, 12n. 67, 13n. 39, 63

Hera (wife and sister of Zeus; = Juno) 4n. 56, 6n. 13, 14, 9n. 37, 11n. 18

Heracles (son of Zeus and Alcmena; = Hercules) 6n. 21, 7n. 42, 11n. 18, 13n. 83

Heraclid (descendant of Heracles) 5n. 57

Heraclitus (Greek philosopher of Ephesus, fl. ca. 500 B.C.) 15n. 19

Herculaneum (coastal city destroyed by the eruption of Vesuvius in 79 A.D.) 15n. 94

Herculean 11. 627

Hercules (son of Alcmena and Jupiter) 1n. 50, 7. 364, 7n. 34, 8n. 17, 9. 23, 135, 162, 257, 263, 278, 285, 798, 9n. 3, 5, 7, 9, 11, 15, 21, 37, 10n. 6, 11n. 30, 12. 309, 539, 554, 564, 573, 629, 12n. 20, 56, 57, 13. 23, 51, 13n. 125, 14n. 48, 15. 8, 22, 47, 231, 284, 711, 880, 15n. 3, 7, 9

Herdsman (Boötes) 8n. 19

Hermaphroditus (son of Venus and Mercury) 4n. 40, 43

Hermes (Greek name for Mercury) 1n. 37, 98, 2n. 127, 147, 4n. 22, 43, 5n. 42, 8n. 65

Hermochares (seduced Ctesylla, daughter of Alcidamas) 7n. 39.

Herodotus (5th century B.C., author of a history of the Persian Wars) 8n. 24, 9n. 62, 15n. 25, 26

Herse (daughter of Cecrops, king of Athens; sister of Pandrosos and Aglauros) 2. 559, 724, 739, 747, 809

Hersilia (wife of Romulus) 14. 829, 839, 848

Hesiod (early Greek epic poet, author of *Theogony* and *Works and Days*) 1n. 42, 2n. 124, 4n. 23, 60, 90, 5n. 24, 7n. 8, 12n. 61

Hesione (daughter of Laomedon; wife of Telamon; mother of Teucer) 11. 217, 11n. 29, 13n. 32, 14n. 94

Hesperia (daughter of the river-god Cebren; pursued by Aesacus; killed by a serpent) 2. 325, 4n. 72, 11. 768

Hesperian (western or pertaining to evening) 2. 143, 4. 214, 628, 11. 258

Hesperides (nymphs of the west who guarded the golden apples given by Earth to Juno as a wedding gift) 9n. 15, 11. 114, 796, 11n. 18

Hesperus (Evening Star) 5. 441

Hippasos (Centaur) 12. 351

Hippasus (son of Eurytus; hunter at Calydon) 8. 313, 371, 8n. 45

Hippe ("Mare, " the transformed Ocyrhoë) 2n. 125

Hippocoön (king of Amyclae; father of Enaesimus and other hunters at Calydon) 8. 314, 362

Hippocrene (fountain of the Muses, created by Pegasus) 5n. 26

Hippodamas (father of Perimele) 8. 593, 8n. 57

Hippodame (bride of Pirithoüs) 12. 210, 224, 14n. 91

Hippodamia (= Hippodame) 12n. 33

Hippolytus (son of Antiope and Theseus) 2n. 122, 15. 497, 544, 15n. 64, 70, 72

Hippomenes (son of Megareus and pursuer of Atalanta; changed by Cybele into a lion) 10. 575, 586, 608, 632, 639, 650, 658, 668, 689, 10n. 54

Hippotades (Aeolus) 4. 663, 11. 431, 14. 86, 15. 707

Hippotes (father of Aeolus, god of the winds) 11n. 58, 14. 224, 852, 14n. 15, 15n. 88

Hippothoüs (hunter at Calydon) 8. 307

Hister (Lower Danube) 2. 249

Hodites (Centaur) 12. 457

Hodites (Ethiopian) 5. 97

Holder of the Snake (constellation Ophiuchus) 8. 182

Homer (early Greek epic poet, traditional author of the *Iliad* and *Odyssey*) 2n. 58, 152, 4n. 20, 22, 7n, 73, 8n. 65, 12n. 26, 46, 13n. 55

Homeric 1n. 28

Hora (deified Hersilia) 14.. 851, 14n.. 121
Horae (Hours, fertility goddesses) 2. 118
Horus (falcon-shaped god of Egypt, identified with Apollo) 5n. 39, 9n. 63
Hours (= Horae) 2n. 13
Hyacinth (= Hyacinthus) 10. 185, 196, 217, 10n. 27
Hyacinthia (Spartan festival in honor of Hyacinthus) 10. 219
Hyacinthus (son of Spartan king Amyclus; beloved of Apollo) 10n. 20, 13n. 79,
Hyades (daughters of Atlas, sisters of the Pleiades, constellation) 3. 595, 13. 293
Hyale (nymph of Diana) 3. 171
Hyantean (Boeotian) 3. 146, 5. 312
Hyantes (ancient tribe of Boeotia) 3n. 14.
Hydra (polypod of Lerna, overcome by Hercules) 1n. 90, 4n. 62, 9. 69, 158, 192
Hyginus (author of a Latin handbook of mythology, probably 2nd century A. D.) 6n. 52, 7n. 48, 13n. 31
Hylactor (hound of Actaeon) 3. 224
Hylaeus (hound of Actaeon) 3. 213
Hyle (town of Boeotia) 13n. 114
Hylean (of Hyle) 13. 683
Hyles (Centaur) 12. 378
Hyleus (hunter at Calydon) 8. 312
Hyllus (son of Deianira and Hercules) 9. 278
Hylonome (female Centaur) 12. 405, 423
Hymen (god of marriage) 1. 480, 4n. 82, 9. 762, 765, 796, 10. 1, 12. 215
Hymenaeus (= Hymen) 2n. 130, 6. 429
Hymettus (mountain in Attica) 7. 702, 10. 285, 10n. 36
Hypaepa (small town of Lydia) 6. 13, 11. 152
Hypanis (river of Sarmatia, flowing into the Black Sea; = modern Bug) 15. 285
Hyperborean (of the far north) 15. 356, 15n. 48
Hyperion (Titan father of Sun, or the Sun himself) 1n. 6, 4. 192, 241, 4n. 24, 8. 565, 15. 406, 407, 15n. 78
Hypseus (ally of Phineus) 5. 98, 99
Hypsipyle (daughter of Thoas, king of Lemnos) 13. 399, 13n. 75, 82
Hyrie (lake and town of Boeotia) 7. 371, 380
Iacchus (name of Bacchus) 4. 15
Ialysus (city of Rhodes) 7. 365, 7n. 35
Ianthe (daughter of Telestes; bride of Iphis) 9. 715, 722, 744, 760, 766, 797
Iapetos 1n. 17
Iapetus (= Iapetos, Titan son of Cronos or Saturn; father of Prometheus) 1. 82, 1n. 63
Iapygia (region of SE Italy) 14n. 65, 15. 703, 880, 15n. 14

Mercury (son of Maia and Jupiter) 1. 682, 1. 713, 1n. 37, 98, 99, 105, 108, 2. 685, 691, 740, 2n. 127, 132, 135, 137, 141, 146, 4. 288, 754, 4n. 22, 43, 81, 5n. 14, 7n. 47, 8. 627, 8n. 60, 65, 11. 303, 11n. 47, 49, 13n. 28, 14n. 36

Mergus (a diving bird, the transformed Aesacus) 11n. 77

Meriones (Cretan companion of Idomeneus at Troy) 13. 359

Mermeros (Centaur) 12. 304

Merops (king of Ethiopia; husband of Clymene; supposed father of Phaethon) 1. 763, 1n. 116, 2. 184

Messana or Messena (city of Sicily; Zancle) 13n. 136, 137, 14. 17, 852, 14n. 3, 15n. 36

Messapian 14. 513

Messapians (people of Calabria in southern Italy) 14n. 74

Messenia (region of SW Peloponnesus) 2n. 129, 12. 549

Messenian 2. 679

Messina (modern name for Messena) 13n. 136, 15n. 36, 87

Mestra (traditional name of Erysichthon's daughter) 8n. 71

Methymna (city of Lesbos) 11. 55

Metion (father of Phorbas) 5. 74

Midas (king of Phrygia) 11. 17, 24, 92, 94, 102, 105, 146, 162, 174, 796

Miletus (son of Deione and Phoebus; father of Byblis and Caunus; founder of the city of the same name) 9. 443, 447, 635, 9n. 42, 46, 56

Milon (athlete of Croton) 15. 229, 15n. 22

Mimas (mountain range in Ionia) 2. 222

Minerva (daughter of Jupiter; goddess of wisdom; patron of Athens, = Pallas, Athena) 2. 563, 588, 710, 749, 752, 765, 788, 2n. 110, 116, 144, 3n. 11, 4. 33, 38, 755, 797, 4n. 81, 91, 5. 46, 250, 263, 265, 270, 296, 336, 375, 645 5n. 21, 6n. 1, 50, 8. 250, 265, 275, 664, 8n. 54, 62, 12n. 22, 13. 337, 381, 654, 13n. 21, 14. 475, 14n. 68, 15. 709, 15n. 49

Minos (son of Europa and Jupiter; king of Crete) 7. 456, 472, 7n. 72, 8. 6, 24, 42, 45, 64, 95, 152, 157, 169, 174, 187, 884, 8n. 8, 14, 15, 24, 9. 437, 441, 445, 13n. 2, 15n. 65

Minotaur (monster son of Pasiphaë) 8. 133, 156, 169, 8n. 8, 14, 9n. 68

Minturnae (city of Latium) 15. 716

Minyan 4. 389

Minyans (tribe of people in Boeotia and Thessaly; Argonauts) 6. 720, 7. 1, 8, 115, 120, 11n. 57

Minyas (king of Orchomenos in Boeotia) 4. 1, 32, 425

Miseno (modern name for the northern cape of the Bay of Naples) 14n. 18, 22

Misenus (son of Aeolus; companion of Aeneas; musician; cape named for him = Miseno) 14n. 18, 22

Mithridates (= Mithradates, name of several kings of Pontus) 15. 756, 15n. 112

Mnemonides (daughters of Mnemosyne and Jupiter; Muses) 5. 267, 280

naiad 1. 690, 4. 49, 329, 356

naiads (water nymphs) 1. 642, 2. 325, 3. 505, 4. 289, 304, 6. 329, 453, 8. 580, 9. 87, 657, 11. 48, 14. 328, 556, 785

Nape (hound of Actaeon) 3. 214

Naples (Greek city in Italy) 5n. 72, 10n. 4. 14n. 17, 21, 15n. 92, 95, 96

Nar (river of Umbria; tributary of the Tiber; modern Nera) 14. 330

Narcissus (son of the naiad Liriope and the river Cephisus; changed into a flower) 3. 346, 370

Nardò (modern name for Neretum, town in southern Italy) 15n. 10

Naricium (Naryx) 15n. 86

Narycia (region around Naryx) 15. 705

Narycian (epithet of Ajax, son Oïleus) 14. 468

Narycian (of Naryx) 8. 312, (epithet of Ajax, son Oïleus) 14. 468

Naryx (city of Locris) 8n. 34, 14n. 68, 15n. 86

Nasamonia (region SW of Cyrenaica in North Africa) 5n. 6

Nasamonian 5. 129

Nature 15. 253

Nauplius (king of Euboea; father of Palamedes) 13. 39, 310, 969, 13n. 5

Naxos (Cycladic island; = Dia) 3. 636, 640, 649, 8n. 16

Nebrophonos (hound of Actaeon) 3. 211

Nedymnus (Centaur) 12. 350

Nelean 6. 418

Neleus (king of Pylos in Messenia; son of Tyro and Neptune; twin of Pelias; father of 12 sons, all but Nestor slain by Hercules) 2. 689, 12. 553, 558, 577, 12n. 60

Nemea (town in the Argolid) 9. 197

Nemean (pertaining to the lion of Nemea, slain by Hercules) 9. 235

Nemesis (Greek goddess of retribution with a sanctuary at Rhamnus in Attica) 3. 406, 14n. 93

Neoptolemus (son of Achilles; = Pyrrhus) 13. 455

Nephele (hound of Actaeon) 3. 171

Nephele ("Cloud, " first wife of Athamas and mother of Helle and Phrixus) 7n. 6, 11. 195, 11n. 25.

Neptune (son of Saturn; god of the sea; = Poseidon) 1. 275, 1n. 47, 2. 270, 574, 876, 2n. 3, 4, 134, 152, 4. 533, 539, 4n. 70, 5. 24, 5n. 50, 6. 75, 115, 6n. 28, 7. 367, 7n. 36, 8. 595, 602, 851, 853, 8n. 57, 9. 1, 798, 9n. 1, 10. 606, 639, 665, 12. 26, 72, 198, 558, 629, 12n. 15, 62, 13. 854, 13n. 147

Nera (tributary of the Tiber river in Umbria) 14n. 43

Nereian (referring to Phocus, son of the Nereid Psamathe) 7. 685

Nereid 11n. 39, 12. 93, 13. 162, 749

Nereids (the fifty daughters of Nereus, a sea-god) 1. 302, 2. 269, 2n. 6, 77, 5. 17, 11. 361, 13. 899, 14. 264

Neretum (town in the heel of Italy, modern Nardò) 15. 50

Nereus (god of the sea; husband of Doris) 1. 187, 1n. 48, 2. 268, 7n. 87, 11. 219, 361, 11n. 33, 38, 52, 12. 24, 94, 13. 742, 858, 13n. 33, 14n. 29

Neritian (pertaining to Neritos) 14. 159, 563

Neritos (mountain on Ithaca) 13. 712, 14n. 29

Nessus (Centaur; attempted to rape Deianira) 9. 101, 108, 111, 113, 119, 121, 131, 153, 798, 9n. 8, 12. 308, 454

Nestor (son of Neleus, king of Pylos) 2n. 131, 134, 8. 313, 365, 8n. 44, 12. 169, 536, 12n. 49, 60, 13. 63, 64, 65, 71, 13n. 11, 49

Nicander (of Colophon, fl. 130 B.C., wrote the *Heteroeumena "Metamorphoses,"* used by Ovid and Antoninus Liberalis) 7n. 28, 39, 42, 13n. 125

Night 4. 452, 7. 192, 11. 606, 14. 404, 15. 31

Nile 1. 422, 728, 1n. 114, 2. 254, 5. 188, 324, 5n. 2, 9. 774, 15. 753, 15n. 132

Nileus (ally of Phoenix) 5. 187

Nineveh (capital of Assyria) 4n. 17

Ninus (founder and king of Assyrian Nineveh; husband of Semiramis) 4. 88

Niobe (daughter of Tantalus; wife of Amphion; mother of 14 children slain by Apollo and Diana) 1n. 64, 6. 148, 155, 165, 273, 287, 301, 6n. 39, 44, 53

Nisus (father of Bacchus by Thyone, according to Cicero) 4n. 5

Nisus (king of Megara; father of Scylla) 8. 8, 17, 35, 90, 126, 145

Nixi (Latin goddesses of childbirth) 9. 294

Noah (Biblical patriarch) 1n. 17

Noëmon (Lycian slain by Ulysses) 13. 258

Nonacrian 8. 427

Nonacris (mountain and city in Arcadia) 1. 690, 1n. 102

Noric (pertaining to Noricum) 14. 712

Noricum (Celtic region in Austria, became a Roman province under Tiberius) 14n. 96

North Wind 1n. 14, 6n. 65, 10n. 11, 15n. 59

Northeast Wind 2n. 15

North-northeast Wind 7n. 3

Notus (South Wind) 1. 264

Numa (Pompilius Numa, second king of Rome, successor to Romulus; husband of Egeria) 15. 4, 480, 487

Numicius (river of Latium) 14. 328, 599, 14n. 84

Numidia (region of North Africa conquered by Caesar in 46 B.C.) 2n. 144, 15. 754

Numitor (restored to the throne of Alba by his grandsons, Romulus and Remus) 14. 773, 14n. 102

Nyctaeus (son of Chthonius; king of Boeotia; father of Antiope, and in some sources of Nyctemene) 2n. 117, 6. 111, 6n. 20, 39

Nyctelius (a name of Bacchus) 4. 15

Nyctimene (daughter of Epopeus or Nyctaeus or Proteus, changed to an owl) 2. 590, 592, 2n. 114, 117, 6n. 20

Pamphaos (hound of Actaeon) 3. 210

Pan (woodland and pastoral deity) 1. 699, 705, 1n. 38, 104, 11. 147, 153, 161, 171, 14. 516

Panathenaic Games (celebrated at Athens) 2n, 140, 7n. 66

Panchaia (island east of Arabia) 10. 307, 478

Pandion (king of Athens; father of Procne and Philomela) 6. 427, 436, 495, 521, 634, 666, 676, 7n. 76, 15. 430

Pandrosos (daughter of Cecrops; sister of Aglauros and Herse) 2. 559, 738

Pannonia (Roman province south and west of the Danube) 14n. 96

Panomphaean 11. 199

Panomphaeus (epithet of Zeus as author of divination) 11n. 28

Panope (city of Phocis) 3. 19

Panopeus (hunter at Calydon) 8. 312

Pans (woodland and pastoral deities) 14. 638

Panthoüs (father of Euphorbus) 12n. 59, 15. 161

Papa-Silenus (fat old tutor of Bacchus and the satyrs) 4. 26, 4n. 12

Paphian (epithet of Cyprus) 10n. 37

Paphlagonia (region of northern Asia Minor between Bithynia and Pontus) 4n. 41, 6n. 33

Paphos (city of SW Cyprus) 10. 290, 297, 530, 10n. 37

Paraetonium (port town of North Africa) 9. 773

Parcae (Roman Fates) 2n. 124, 5. 532

*Parentalia* (Roman funeral festival for ancestors) 13n. 98, 99

Parian (of Paros) 3. 419

Parilia (= Palilia) 14n. 105

Paris (son of Priam) 2n. 32, 7n. 33, 12. 4, 600, 13. 200, 202, 501, 13n. 11, 15. 805

Parnassian 11. 165

Parnassus (mountain of Phocis, sacred to Apollo and the Muses) 1. 317, 467, 1. 320, 1n. 52, 2. 221, 4. 643, 5. 278, 5n. 29

Paros (large Cycladic island noted for its marble) 7. 465, 8. 221

Parrhasia (town of Arcadia) 2n. 97

Parrhasian 2. 460, 2n. 97, 8. 315

Parthaon (king of Calydon; father of Oeneus) 8. 542

Parthenope (another name for Naples) 14. 102, 15. 712

Pasiphaë (daughter of the Sun; wife of Minos; mother of the Minotaur, Ariadne and Phaedra) 8. 122, 136, 884, 8n. 8, 15, 9. 736, 9n. 68, 15. 500, 15n. 65

Patara (city of Lydia) 1. 516

Patrae (city of Achaea) 6. 417

Patroclus (descendant of Actor; son of Menoetius; friend of Achilles) 13. 273, 13n. 39, 58, 60, 63

Pharos (lighthouse island off the coast from Alexandria in Egypt) 9. 774, 15. 287

Pharsalia (region around Pharsalus) 15. 823

Pharsalus (city of Thessaly) 15n. 129

Phasian (pertaining to the Phasis; epithet of Medea) 7. 297

Phasis (river flowing into the Black Sea near Colchis) 2. 249, 7. 6, 7n. 26

Phegeian (belonging to Phegeus) 9. 412

Phegeus (king of Psophis in Arcadia) 2n. 54, 9n. 33, 34

Phegian (belonging to Phegeus) 2. 244

Phene (wife of Periphas) 7. 399, 7n. 54

Pheneos (place in Arcadia with a miraculous spring) 15. 332

Pheres (king of Pherae in Thessaly; father of Admetus) 8. 310

Phiale (nymph of Diana) 3. 171

Philammon (son of Apollo and Chione; lyre-player and singer) 11. 317

Philemon (husband of Baucis) 8. 631, 682, 706, 714, 715

Philippi (city of Macedonia, site of the defeat of Brutus by Octavian and Antony in 42 B.C.) 15. 824, 15n. 129

Philoctetes (son of Poeas; lit the funeral pyre of Hercules) 9. 231, 9n. 16, 13. 45, 314, 329, 969, 13n. 6, 8, 71, 83, 84

Philomela (daughter of Pandion, king of Athens; sister of Procne) 6. 451, 475, 503, 511, 553, 572, 601, 643, 658

Philyra (daughter of Oceanus; mother by Saturn of Chiron) 2. 676, 2n. 126, 7. 352, 7n. 27

Phineus (brother of Cepheus) 5. 8, 12, 30, 36, 89, 92, 109, 157, 210, 225, 231. 5n. 17, 11n. 57

Phineus (blind Thracian prophet) 7. 2, 7n. 2

Phlegethon (river in the Underworld) 5. 544, 15. 532

Phlegon (horse of Apollo) 2. 154

Phlegra (region of Macedonia) 10n. 18

Phlegraeos (Centaur) 12. 378

Phlegyans (band of robbers in Thessaly) 11. 414, 11n. 57

Phlegyas (of Larissa; daughter of Coronis) 2n. 107

Phlegyas (ally of Phineus) 5. 87, 11n. 57

Phobetor (son of Somnus) 11. 640, 11n. 68

Phocaea (city in Ionia) 6n. 5

Phocaean (of Phocaea) 2. 569, 6. 9

Phocian (of Phocis) 11. 347

Phocis (region between Locris and Boeotia) 1. 313, 1n. 60,  5. 277, 5n. 29, 7n. 49

Phocus (son of Aeacus and Psamathe) 7. 477, 668, 670, 674, 732, 795, 796, 7n. 87, 11. 267, 381, 11n. 39, 52

Phoebe (Diana, Moon) 1. 11, 476, 1n. 7, 2. 415, 723, 6. 216, 6n. 49, 12. 36

Phoebean (pertaining to Phoebus) 9. 663

Phoebus (Apollo) 1. 338, 451, 452, 463, 490, 495, 553, 752, 1n. 7, 56, 70, 2. 23, 36, 110, 398, 544, 608, 628, 876, 2n. 7, 3. 9, 10, 18, 130, 151, 4. 349, 715, 5. 330, 389. 6. 122, 215, 486, 7. 324, 365, 8. 31, 350, 9. 444, 10. 133, 162, 178, 197, 214, 11. 58, 164, 165, 303, 310, 316, 594, 11n. 36, 13. 410, 501, 633, 640, 677, 14. 133, 141, 150, 416, 15. 191, 418, 550, 631, 642, 742, 865

Phoenician 4n. 32, 67, 14n. 56, 15. 288

Phoenicians 2n. 119, 3. 46

Phoenix (son of Amyntor) 8. 307, 12n. 43

Phoenix (son of Agenor) 2n. 152

Pholus (Centaur) 12. 306

Phorbas (ally of Phineus) 5. 74, 78

Phorbas (Phlegyean leader) 11. 413. 11n. 57

Phorbas (Lapith) 12. 320

Phorcynid 4. 743

Phorcys (father of the Gorgons and the Graeae) 4. 774, 4n. 80, 5. 230, 5n. 18

Phoroneus (son of Inachus; brother of Io) 1n. 97, 2n. 103

Phoronid (referring to Io) 1. 668

Phoronis (Io) 2. 524

Phosphoros (Lucifer) 11n. 45

Phrixus (son of Nephele and Athamas; brother of Helle; escaped from Ino on the golden-fleeced ram) 7. 7, 7n. 6, 11n. 25

Phrygia (region of NW Asia Minor, associated with Troy) 2n. 32, 42, 59, 6. 400, 6n. 8, 46, 8. 621, 11. 203, 12n. 7, 13. 429, 435, 580

Phrygian 4n. 36, 6. 146, 166, 177, 8. 162, 11. 91, 10. 155, 740, 10n. 15, 12. 38, 148, 13. 44, 244, 337, 389, 432, 721, 14. 80, 547, 562, 15. 444

Phrygians 12. 70, 612, 15. 452

Phthia (city of Thessaly; birthplace of Achilles) 13. 156

Phyleus (hunter at Calydon) 8. 308

Phylius (lover of Cycnus) 7. 372, 7n. 42

Phylleian (of Phyllos; epithet of Caeneus) 12. 479

Phyllos (town of Thessaly) 12n. 55

Picus (son of Saturn; husband of Canens; changed by Circe into a woodpecker) 14. 320, 336, 342, 362, 396, 398, 14n. 48, 54

Pierus (king of Emathia, in Macedonia; father of nine daughters who competed with the Muses in song) 5. 302

Piety (loyalty to gods, country, and family) 10. 321, 323

Pilumnus (fertility god; founder of Ardea; father of Daunus) 14n. 66

Pindar (Boeotian lyric poet, ca. 518-ca. 446 B.C.) 4n. 26

Pindus (mountain in Thessaly) 1. 570, 2. 225, 7. 225, 11. 555

Piraean (pertaining to Piraeus) 6. 446

Piraeus (a port of Athens) 2n. 138, 6n. 57

Pirene (spring created by Pegasus at Corinth, sacred to the Muses) 2n. 48, 7n. 52

Timolus (mountain and god of the mountain in Lydia; = Tmolus) 6. 15, 11. 87

Tiresias (Theban seer; father of Manto) 3. 323, 6. 157

Tiryns (city of the Argolid) 6n. 21, 7. 410, 9. 66, 798, 9n. 5, 20, 12. 564

Tirynthian (of Tiryns) 6. 112, 9. 268, 13. 401

Tisiphone (a Fury) 4, 473, 481, 4n. 61, 10n. 41

Titan (child of Earth and Uranos)
   (Sun) 1. 10, 395, 1n. 6, 2. 116, 6. 438, 7. 398, 7n. 53, 10. 78, 174, 10n. 24, 11. 257, 13. 968, 14. 14, 376, 14n. 53
   (Iapetos ) 1n. 17, 63
   (Tethys) 2n. 101, 9n. 44, 11n. 76
   (Atlas) 4n. 87, 8n. 60
   (Latona) 6. 185
   (Oceanus) 7n. 8
   (Pallas) 9n. 38, 15. 20

Titania (Diana) 3. 173

Titania (Latona) 6. 346

Titania (Circe) 14. 382, 438

Titans (Coeus) 6n. 40,

Titans (Coeus and Phoebe) 49

Tithonus (son of Laomedon; husband of Aurora) 9. 421, 9n. 38, 13n. 96

Tityos (giant punished in the Underworld for trying to rape Latona) 4. 457, 10. 43

Tlepolemus (son of Hercules and king of the Rhodians) 12. 537

Tmolus (mountain and god of the mountain in Lydia; = Timolus) 11. 138, 150, 156, 163, 164, 170, 194, 796, 11n. 11, 23

Toxeus (son of Thestius; sister of Althaea; slain by Meleager) 8. 441

Trachas (= Tarracina, modern Terracina, town on the west coast of Italy) 15. 717

*Trachiniae* (*Women of Trachis,* tragedy of Sophocles) 9n. 9

Trachinian (Ceyx, king of Trachis) 11. 282, 351

Trachinian (of Trachis) 11. 502

Trachis (or Trachin, city of Thessaly at the base of Mt. Oeta) 11. 269, 627, 11n. 53

Trinacria (Sicily) 5. 476

Trinacrian 5. 346

Triones ("Plowers, " stars in the constellation Big Dipper) 2. 171

Triopas (a king of Thessaly; father of Erysichthon) 8. 751, 8n. 71

Triopeid (daughter of Erysichthon, son of Triopas; Mestra) 8. 872

Triptolemus (son of Celeus of Eleusis; Athenian youth commissioned by Ceres to teach the growing of grain; killed by Lyncus) 5. 645, 650, 653

Triton (sea-god, half man, half fish; son of Neptune) 1. 333, 2. 8, 2n. 3, 13. 919

Triton or Tritonis (lake in NW Africa) 2n. 144